A DIFFERENT KIND OF LOVE

Also by Sheelagh Kelly

THE KILMASTER SAGA
A Sense of Duty
Family of the Empire

THE FEENEY FAMILY SAGA
A Long Way from Heaven
For My Brother's Sins
Erin's Child
Dickie

My Father, My Son
Jorvik
Shoddy Prince
Complicated Woman

SHEELAGH KELLY

A Different Kind of Love

HarperCollins*Publishers*

HarperCollins*Publishers*
77–85 Fulham Palace Road,
Hammersmith, London W6 8JB

www.fireandwater.com

Published by HarperCollins*Publishers* 2003
1 3 5 7 9 8 6 4 2

A catalogue record for this book
is available from the British Library

ISBN 0 00 225741 6

Typeset in Postscript Linotype Sabon
by Palimpsest Book Production Limited,
Polmont, Stirlingshire

Printed and bound in Great Britain by
Clays Ltd, St Ives plc

AUTHOR'S NOTE

The first section of this book follows the exact movements of a real regiment, the 9th Battalion York and Lancasters, taken from the official war diaries. Certain officers and men who died have been accorded their real names – my apologies for any confusion over the two who bore an identical surname – and particular events recorded as they actually occurred. However, for the purposes of the story I have added a number of fictitious characters and incidents that are in no way intended to reflect the actions of those who actually took part, my real purpose to pay tribute to their bravery.

My thanks for the use of articles on the period too numerous to mention; *Kitchener's Army* by Peter Simkins; for the memoirs of E. Buffey, late Y&L Regiment, and in particular for the awesome works of Lyn Macdonald.

To my dear daughter,
Vanessa

PART ONE

ONE

January 1915

Nerves were stretched almost beyond endurance. They had been waiting hours for the enemy to show, eyes striving against the night to detect any hint of movement, ears pricked for the slightest crackle of undergrowth, forcing themselves to take shallow inhalations lest the white clouds of breath or even a rumbling gut might betray their position. Yet all that was to be heard was the desolate pitter-pat of rain.

Throughout their training no one had told them that the waiting would be the worst part. So keyed up had some of them become that they were seriously contemplating a dash to safety. Even those whose mettle held true were not immune to the cold. The daytime temperature had been mild for January but with nightfall it had plummeted and they lay here at its mercy, wet and aching, spread-eagled beneath the dripping bushes, unable to relax one muscle, for the honour of the company depended on the swiftness of their reactions.

A sudden noise jerked everyone back to full alertness. Morale instantly renewed, the warriors tensed, ready to fulfil that which was demanded of them. A dark outline appeared through the veil of drizzle and after a moment's hesitation began to creep towards their position, closely followed by others. Flattening themselves into the wet undergrowth, those intent on ambush remained hidden, blinking the raindrops from their lashes, squinting down gun barrels, taking aim at the threatening silhouettes, fingers tightening on triggers . . . but they had been given the order to hold fire until the enemy was almost on top of them and wait they would, tension throbbing inside each breast.

Across the dark expanse the leading silhouette inched nearer. *Wait for it, wait for it* – then all at once he appeared to trip and those in his wake capsized like dominoes, landing in a heap on top of him. There was a loud expletive, then helpless laughter and whilst the enemy was thus involved an order rent the night air – 'Fire!' – and a volley of shots erupted, closely followed by the command 'Attack!' – and the soldiers charged, hurling themselves at the hapless tangle of bodies, pulverizing these and any others who came afterwards, pounding all mercilessly until their leader cried for mercy.

But mercy did not come – 'You frigging bastards, we've been waiting hours for you!' – and another flurry of blows was inflicted. Meanwhile a collection of obsolete rifles ejaculated more harmless bullets, aimed at one victim after another: 'Bang! You're dead! And you and you! Bang! You're all dogmeat!'

Only when the rifles were employed more brutally as clubs was the enemy provoked into fighting back and a vicious free-for-all ensued.

It was on to this bloody scene that RSM Kilmaster charged; just arrived to observe a military exercise he found instead an exhibition more befitting a saloon brawl, and quickly screeched a halt.

'A bladdy fiasco!' After segregating the two companies, he demanded to know of the officer in charge of the 'enemy' what had gone wrong.

'I'm most terribly sorry, sir!' The young trainee officer, battered from the mêlée, did not find it so hilarious now, especially at the confrontation with the RSM. 'My compass-reading's none too hot, I'm afraid. I funked it and we went a little astray.'

'Astray?' Probyn Kilmaster's face was the colour of raw meat. 'You've lost half your force! I'm sure Major Lewis would be highly impressed to learn you've taken his lectures so seriously – and correct me if I'm wrong but wasn't Mr Postgate meant to be leading the attack?'

Deeply intimidated by this monster, the handsome brown-eyed youth could not look him in the eye and flicked nervously at his muddy uniform. With his plump, pink hairless cheeks and cupid's-bow lips he appeared no more than twelve. 'Postgate sends his regrets, sir, he has a dinner party to attend.'

'A –!' Too angry to complete his outburst, Probyn fumed for three seconds before his eyes sought out another, addressing him tersely. 'Are you aware of your brother's whereabouts, Mr Postgate?'

4

Guy Postgate, a more adult-looking figure in command of the opposing force, shook his head in apologetic manner. 'I have absolutely no idea, sir.'

Wearing a look of disdain, Probyn turned back to the original informant, his Yorkshire accent camouflaged by a manufactured version of those in higher command. 'Might you be enlightened as to where this dinner party is taking place, Mr Gaylard?' At the affirmative response he added, 'Then would you kindly go there now and convey to Mr Postgate that we require the pleasure of his company at once? Tell him that RSM Kilmaster anticipates no delay.'

Young Robert Gaylard fled immediately.

Meanwhile there was a prolonged wait in the cold whilst an NCO was sent to look for the lost recruits who were eventually brought in, drenched and fed up, to receive a severe admonishment from their RSM.

The initiator of this débâcle hurried up shortly afterwards with his friend Gaylard, still wearing his dinner suit plus a look of repentance. His brother Guy immediately set upon him for letting the side down and the two had come to blows before they could be separated. But Louis Postgate was less concerned about the filial violence than that promised by the RSM's face; after only a few weeks in this tyrant's company he knew it was foolhardy to antagonize him. That the Yorkshireman stood only five foot seven and his hands were dainty and tapered was but a smoke-screen. This was a man to be feared.

Beef. That was what one saw when viewing Mr Kilmaster: a big thick neck supporting the bullish head with its immaculately trimmed hair and waxed moustache, fourteen stones of beef with bulging arms and thighs that strained to rip free of the khaki. With this bearing down on him Louis imagined what a matador must feel like as he prepared to confront *el toro*. Yet, despite its weighty trunk the visage was not that of a slovenly man but an intelligent, noble face with blue-grey eyes that were mesmerizing in their lustre, a resolute jaw and well-defined features.

Louis had not previously found him susceptible to charm but, with this his only option, he applied a compunctious smile, doffing his top hat as he spoke. 'I'm most frightfully sorry, sir. I do hope you will accept my deepest apologies.'

Such contrition was lost on Probyn, who fixed him with an intimidating glare. That Louis and his elder brother, Guy, were the sons of a viscount cut no ice with him. 'You might be an Honourable at home, Mr Postgate, but here you have shown a conspicuous lack of honour towards your comrades! These unfortunate men whose fate it is to depend on you for leadership have been floundering around in the mud all evening awaiting your command. A command that was sadly absent.'

'Truly, sir, the last thing on my mind was to cause inconvenience. That is why I gave prior warning of my engagement!'

The RSM proceeded as if the other had not spoken. 'A command you shirked, indicating not only a total disregard for their welfare, but even worse, a gross misuse of resources!'

A rapid series of contrite nods from the dark head. 'Thoroughly reprehensible. I really cannot express sufficient regret. Yet I had no idea my presence would be missed. Gaylard's abilities are on a par with my ow –'

'Oh, I would agree there! Your abilities are equally nil!' Appearing to calm a little, Probyn cocked his head at the night sky. 'So, Mr Postgate, let me get this absolutely right. You are in France and about to lead your squad on a reconnaissance into enemy territory, when an invitation to a dinner party arrives –'

'Forgive me, sir!' A boyish chuckle intervened, its owner attempting to lighten the atmosphere. 'It isn't quite the same. We're not in France but Hampshire.'

'Ah!' It was almost a caress. 'So if the Boche suddenly descend on Aldershot we should tell them, hold on until Mr Postgate has finished his dinner?'

'But the Germans won't –'

'Who is to say?' Probyn spread his hands, his rebuke at first having a quite reasonable tone, though it was soon to increase in power, every word emerging like canon-shot to punch the night air with clouds of vapour. 'This is a war, Mr Postgate, not a game! It might seem like one big lark to you whilst we're on English soil but, believe me, once you're in France it won't stay that way and it will certainly be a lot more horrible if officers don't take their responsibilities seriously!'

'But I do, sir!' It was a heartfelt plea.

'Really?' Menacingly calm again, Probyn seized a lantern and directed its beam at one of the tired and bloodied soldiers whose dark figures moved about the rain-swept park, erecting makeshift shelters from branches. 'Tell me the name of that man over there.'

'That's, er . . . I'm afraid I can't remember,' said Louis, then added defensively, 'There are rather a lot of them.'

'That is Private Skeeton! He joined the battalion on the fifteenth of September last year.' The beam of his lantern moved to another

6

wretched figure. 'Perhaps you can recall the name of that man to Private Skeeton's left?'

'I think that's . . .' Louis's answer petered out on a shake of head.

'You don't *know*, Mr Postgate?' Probyn leaned forward as if unable to credit what he had heard.

'As I said, sir, there are a lot of them.'

The RSM was looking him directly in the eyes again; in the glow of the lantern his demeanour most terrifying. 'There are many hundreds more in the battalion, Mr Postgate, and I can tell you the names of every one of them.' It was an exaggeration but served a vital purpose. 'It is beyond credibility that you will ever reach the heights of company commander, but should you be allowed one day to take charge of a platoon – assuming that some miracle occurs to prevent you being kicked out of the army altogether – you will find yourself responsible for sixty men. You will be expected to know not only every one of their names but their characters and abilities too, to feed and clothe them, to find them billets, be accountable for their efficiency and the good order of their arms and equipment, and also to lead them in warfare . . . that is to say, when you are not attending your *dinner parties*.'

Louis Postgate's dark head sagged lower and lower as the minotaur poured contempt on him. He felt more like nine than nineteen.

'Well, I trust you enjoyed your little soiree whilst your men were wet and cold and too exhausted even to defend themselves!'

Louis dared to lift his remorseful blue eyes, his promise genuine this time. 'It won't happen again, sir.'

'No, it will not, Mr Postgate! Because every man in your company is dead. Yes, that is right! Due to the lack of proper command they were ambushed by the other side, who were ready and waiting and who slaughtered them without mercy!'

The rain trickling down his face, Louis's posture became more and more dejected.

'It is therefore just as well that this was only an exercise and they can be resurrected – *this* time.' Probyn continued to glare at his victim for several seconds until content that he had driven home the seriousness of the crime. 'I hope you remembered to bring your greatcoat with you? No? Ah, that *is* a shame. It's a very cold night.'

Reduced to a mere infant now, Louis gripped the rim of his silk topper, showing an eagerness to please. 'You mean you'd like me to stay, sir?'

7

'We should very much like you to join us, yes, Mr Postgate, if it wouldn't be too much of an imposition.' Probyn's manner was transformed to one of cheerful respect, though all knew it for a sham. 'Could I coax you into inspecting that nice little piece of ground over there for your bivouac? I'm afraid I cannot promise you a ground sheet. Perhaps if you'd arrived a teeny bit earlier . . . Never mind, you'll find those branches keep the rain off quite adequately. I bid you a good night, Mr Postgate, and trust that you'll enjoy it as much as the rest of your evening!' Reverted to his normal stern pose, he waited until the subaltern, all confidence drained, had tramped away to assemble his bivouac before marching off himself. However, he was to be quickly drawn back as the row resumed between the two brothers, Guy, slightly taller, two years older and more suitably clad, rebuking Louis for shirking his duty.

'I didn't shirk anything!' argued Louis. 'I merely delegated the role to anoth –'

'Rot!' The face was squarer and harder, the eyes a pale grey. 'You found something better to do – you *always* have something better to do – so you found a mug who'd shoulder the onerous task for you.'

'What the devil does it matter to you who was leading the force?' demanded Louis.

'Because it made me appear a fool in front of the RSM when I couldn't say where you were – or, even worse, a liar! And I'm sure it would matter to the men whom you're supposed to be leading if it had been a genuine operation. You just will not take responsibility for your actions, will you?'

Louis could take any amount of rebuke from a superior but was not about to be so lectured by one with equal inexperience. 'Oh, stop being so damned pompous! It wasn't genuine, it was just play-acting!'

'That's exactly the lack of judgement that made you put Gaylard in charge! He couldn't find his own backside unless it had the Union Jack sticking out of it.'

'It was just bad luck, that's all.'

Guy threw down his hat in aggravation, displaying hair that was wavier and a much lighter shade of brown than his brother's. For a second he gritted his teeth, before swapping his anger for sarcasm. 'Yes, I suppose it is rather bad luck to have one's troops massacred. Just like all the other bouts of bad luck you seem to encounter when it comes to competition.' Close as the siblings were, he, the more ambitious, was never happier than when getting one over on his brother.

'You've got a remarkably short memory!' came the younger man's dark retort. 'My section beat yours only two days ago.'

'In the cleanliness contest!' Guy issued a derisive leer. 'I'm sure that should earn you a Military Cross in the trenches. Oh, clear off to bed, nancy!' In dismissive manner, he had half turned his back when Louis, goaded beyond his limit, finally launched himself at the offender and grappled with him.

'*Cut it out!*' Upon gaining their attention, Probyn fixed them with his penetrating gaze for long seconds before adding, 'Whilst rivalry within the context of training is to be commended, gentlemen, I would remind you that we are supposed to be on the same side. I do trust you will have dispensed with this petty squabbling by the time we're in France.'

Wrenching themselves apart, the Postgate brothers issued a last glare at each other, apologized to Mr Kilmaster and went their separate ways, allowing the exasperated RSM to do the same.

Under temporary cover of a large fir tree, whilst the bedraggled soldiers bedded down for a long night, Probyn spoke for a time with a company sergeant-major, an old regular like himself and long past retirement age, both agreeing what a shambles the exercise had been, the other demanding to know how they were going to win a war with these officers barely out of public school.

'I hear there are more of the Honourable Postgates at home,' came the sour utterance from beneath a grey walrus moustache. 'Thank the Lord they only sent us two.'

Probyn's anger was quick to evaporate – had in truth been only a display to educate those in his care rather than serious aggression, and now they were no longer here to witness it he spoke in a more equitable tone. 'Don't despair, Bert, we'll lick them into shape. They're good lads at heart.' Even cold and saturated as he was, RSM Kilmaster would raise no private grumble, for this was where he belonged. Oh, he loved his wife and children deeply, but here amongst the regiment was where Probyn was truly in his element. That he had a war to thank for delivering the supreme rank that had eluded him during his term with the colours was a sobering thought, but then he would see little combat. Too old now for hand-to-hand fighting maybe, but he derived almost as much pleasure from grooming these young men for victory.

Admittedly, there had been much work to do. None of those in his charge was a regular soldier but part of the New Army, the ranks formed mostly of miners. That in itself was a miracle – colliers and soldiers were normally found on opposite sides, he himself had been sent in to break their strikes and knew how vicious the opposition could be. But the national emergency had overridden traditional enmities. The only current source of trouble was an occasional bout of drunkenness . . . and sibling rivalry between the Postgates.

Whilst there had been a patriotic rush of enlistment by ordinary ranks to form the new 9th Battalion, York and Lancaster Regiment, the officers were still arriving in dribs and drabs, some from Officer Training College, cocksure and insular, others totally unqualified with nothing in their favour save enthusiasm, and Probyn was expected to turn them all into warriors. But it was not so hopeless as it seemed: the basic material was good, the intention noble, and he dubbed tonight's episode as a mere aberration. Within hours of their arrival he had marked Guy and Louis Postgate as decent human beings and worth the effort that would be expended on them. They would make good officers eventually.

Eventually was a significant word, thought Probyn, accepting a cigarette from CSM Dungworth. The war that the newspapers had decreed would be over by Christmas was in stalemate. This was no revelation to old sweats like the RSM and his companion. The same disparaging remarks now directed at the Germans had once been uttered over the Boers and that so-called tea-party had lasted three years. Yet however much he tried to convey this to the young gallants in his charge they remained frantic that it would all be over before they arrived, just like the last lot had been. His thoughts strayed to the decimated ranks of the original BEF across the Channel, valiantly holding the line and waiting in the mud and cold for reinforcements. He knew all too well what that was like. Yet war could produce all sorts of bizarre situations; only last month he had been billeted in the manor of a millionaire. Just wait till he told Grace!

Finishing the cigarette, Probyn took his leave of CSM Dungworth and made for a warmer place to spend the night, which was one of the privileges of rank. First, though, he made a brief diversion.

Huddled beneath his improvised shelter of branches, rain dripping off the leaves, Louis Postgate had managed to procure sympathy from a fellow trainee, who had rustled up a ground sheet, a coat and two blankets into which Louis had now wrapped himself, though with only a dinner suit beneath, his teeth still chattered. Sequestered in misery, he rolled into a ball and tried to sleep, but angry thoughts prevented it: a pox on Guy for his sanctimony and on the heartless RSM.

It was upon such a picture of woe that RSM Kilmaster intruded, his unsmiling face peering into the welter of branches. 'Ah, I'm glad to see someone has taken pity on you, Mr Postgate!'

Teeth still juddering, the fledgeling officer uncurled from his cold tight ball and tried to sound cheerful. 'Yes, thank you for your concern, sir! I shall be fine.'

The reply was frigid. 'Oh, do not attribute my observation to kindness, Mr Postgate, it is merely expediency. It'll save me an explanation to the colonel as to why one of his officers has frozen to death through his own stupidity.' Probyn gave a contemptuous nod and marched away. Yet once his back was turned he allowed a smile to play at his lips and, taking horse-drawn transport, he went off to his billet.

His current landlady, an elderly widow, was there to welcome him the second he arrived, her bony hands helping him off with his greatcoat and directing him towards a fire that turned the parlour into a furnace and his nose into a waterspout. 'Your slippers are waiting on the hearth, Mr Kilmaster!'

The stentorian bark was displaced by soft Yorkshire vowels. 'Eh, you pamper me, Mrs Shepherd.' Laying his prized new officer's hat on a heavily carved ebony sideboard, Probyn sank into the fireside chair and unwound his puttees, exchanged his wet boots for the slippers that this motherly soul had bought especially for him, then was in turn provided with a bowl of hot water, soap and warm towels and a delicious beef stew.

'You look tired, dear,' crooned the old lady, enjoying watching him eat his meal. 'Have those naughty boys been acting up again?'

Only now in this homely presence could Probyn allow himself to relax and smile at tonight's farce, and for answer he threw up his eyes in mock despair. It did not come naturally to play the bully. As a young recruit he had made a name for himself as defender of the weak, but his current position required him to be terrible and terrible he would be. These youngsters were going to war and he must ensure they were fully prepared. If they hated him for it, so be it.

The days crept by and still the call to war did not come. It was just as well, thought Probyn, out for a brisk walk that frosty Sabbath and catching sight of Robert Gaylard totally lost and confused despite being in possession of a map and compass. Yet this was no great cause for despair; a lad who was keen enough to be out so early was bound to succeed in the end. Moreover, upon return to the vastly swollen barracks at Aldershot, Probyn was to witness

11

other young subalterns poring over textbooks, yet more pushing matches about a table in representation of troops – all in their free time – and most refreshing of all, the beasting he had given Louis Postgate seemed to have taken effect, for since that night the lad had diligently refrained from accepting invitations to dinner, instead staying up late to prepare his work for the following day. Would that enthusiasm could win a war, for these young gentlemen possessed it in abundance.

Yet Probyn's work was never done, for just as these youngsters started to resemble officers another bunch of novices arrived, and inevitably there were those amongst them who thought they already knew it all.

Aided by years of experience to recognize a weak link the moment he laid eyes on one, Probyn watched his latest candidate strut around in pathetic imitation of an officer, lording it over his peers when it was obvious he was no more versed in military matters than they, and he relished the thought of demolishing this poseur. For now, though, he bided his time, content to observe Major Harry Lewis trying to instruct the newest intake in company drill: required to command a bunch of equally raw recruits, their efforts were chaotic.

Looking at the pasty-faced collection, some of them more used to weighing out bags of tea and currants, Probyn experienced a momentary flash of despair. The original mongrel-mix of scarlet tunics, civilian overcoats and flat caps might have been replaced by emergency blue uniforms but by no stretch of the imagination could this be termed a fighting force. However, most of them were keen to learn and he was equally determined to transform them, itching now to take over from the major, a man in his fifties, whose patience had obviously become tested to the limit for, with a gesture of hopelessness, he called to the RSM, 'Mr Kilmaster, would you mind standing in whilst I go and commit suicide.'

Gladly, Probyn stepped forth, his tone adopting an upper-class inflection. 'Now, gentlemen, we can't have you upsetting the major like this. You're going to have to buck your ideas up.' Bringing the recruits back into line, he invited one of the subalterns to try again.

But, even under the experienced guidance of the RSM the youngsters were to perform no better. The weakest link, instead of observing was apparently away in some far-off land, his expression bored, his posture slouched and his cane idly tapping.

'Mr Faljambe!' The culprit was startled from his reverie by the RSM's bark. 'Are we boring you?'

The well-fed, rather arrogant-looking youth with the blond moustache began, 'Well, I have already seen this done several –'

'Ah! Then you'll know exactly what to do. In that case kindly do not keep slapping your thigh with your cane, we are not auditioning for the part of Dandini in a pantomime!' Having gained his full attention, Probyn instructed, 'Take charge of your company, please.'

Faljambe did so. The performance was abominable, as reflected in the RSM's pithy comment.

'Why, Mr Faljambe, I was given to understand that you knew all there is to know about soldiering!'

Faljambe caught the smirk that flickered between his companions. 'I beg your pardon, RSM,' his large jaw and the set of his mouth gave him a rather superior air, 'I might perform better were I –'

'You will call me *sir*, Mr Faljambe!' A smouldering volcano, Probyn glared at him. 'I may occasionally call you sir, the only difference is that you will mean it!' After Faljambe's insincere apology, he added, 'You were about to explain your abysmal performance.'

'Well, I was just about to say that I might function a little better were I given real soldiers who knew what they were doing.'

Probyn held the speaker with glittering eyes. 'You want *real* soldiers, Mr Faljambe? I wonder, would you recognize a real soldier if it jumped up and ran you through with a bayonet?'

Faljambe looked shocked and offended. 'I'm sorry, it was just a suggest –'

'No, no!' Probyn assumed an air of reason. 'Far be it from me to stunt an officer's development. I can see you are far too highly skilled for the awkward squad. If Mr Faljambe wants real soldiers he shall have them.' He wheeled to instruct one of the new recruits. 'Private Willett, go across to Sergeant Glew and ask if these officers may borrow his men. At the double now!'

Private Willett dashed off across the overcrowded square to where other, slightly more experienced troops were being put through their drill. These were marched up at double time.

After thanking Sergeant Glew, Probyn announced, 'Now, Mr Faljambe will give us the benefit of his experience.' Turning to address the more qualified squad, he added, 'This officer is now going to put you through your drill. Carry on, Mr Faljambe.' He made a sweeping gesture of invitation and took a step back to remove himself, thereby initiating a period of humiliation for the overconfident youth.

Regretting his braggadocio now, and somewhat anxious at having antagonized his tutor, a blushing Faljambe reluctantly stepped from the cluster of fellow trainees who shared his apprehension. 'I shall try my best, sir.'

'I am sure you will, Mr Faljambe.' The beefy face displayed quiet confidence.

Poising before the ranks of strangers, Hugh Faljambe tapped his cane on his gloved palm for a few moments, before remembering the earlier admonishment and tucking it under his arm. 'What exactly would you like me to do with them, sir?'

'I leave it entirely in your hands, Mr Faljambe.' Momentarily distracted by the jingle of harness, Probyn saw that the colonel, sauntering by on his grey polo pony, had stopped to watch. Ergo, he prompted the young man. 'Mr Faljambe?'

After further hesitation, Faljambe became more decisive. 'Right!' But when some of the men stamped a right turn he called to them hastily, 'No, hang on! I didn't mean for you to turn –'

'Oh, you mustn't issue an instruction unless you mean it, Mr Faljambe.' A shake of head accompanied Probyn's quiet admonishment. 'These men are primed to follow your every command.'

Faljambe hardly dared to open his mouth now. The CO's horse clip-clopped away, a look of faint disgust on its rider's face.

'Perhaps you'd like to march them around the square?' submitted Probyn when no movement was forthcoming.

Faljambe brightened. This seemed easy enough. 'Very well, you chaps, on my command, by the left, quick march!' Having launched the squad into action he began to march briskly alongside with the RSM following and his fellow subalterns hurrying in their wake.

'They're spreading out, Mr Faljambe!' Probyn called a warning. 'Would you like me to whistle up a sheepdog to assist you?'

Somehow, Faljambe brought the files back into order and seemed to be coping quite well until they reached the corner of the parade ground. But there, instead of turning, the men continued down a path that led to the kitchens, and when in his panic he failed to call a halt they proceeded to march straight into a wall, instead of marking time the files at the rear marching into those in front and the whole display collapsing into levity.

Throwing up his hands, Faljambe turned to the RSM for explanation.

'You omitted the order to left wheel, Mr Faljambe,' reproved Probyn.

Faljambe's blond moustache was skewed by disdain. 'Oh, but one would think they could do that without being told!'

'These are *soldiers*, Mr Faljambe,' Probyn explained as if to a toddler. 'The only thing they are able to do without being given a command is to breathe – Mr Reynard, hands out of pockets, if you please!'

Standing some distance away the podgy offender almost jumped out of his skin as the sharp command was bellowed at him. 'I'm sorry, sir, it's just so dreadfully cold, isn't it? My fingers have gone numb –'

'In keeping with your brain then!'

Upon the RSM's contemptuous interjection Reynard dropped his gaze to the floor, finishing his sentence on a lame note: '– due to a circulatory problem.'

'You are not alone. Mr Faljambe appears to have a circulatory problem too,' Probyn turned back to his former target, 'for he cannot manage the simple task of marching his troops around the square! Now bring them to order and start again, and stop wafting that cane about as if you were conducting a blasted orchestra!'

Annoyed at being ridiculed in front of his peers – not to mention the lower ranks – Faljambe assembled the men as best he could and set them off marching again in the direction of the parade ground. Unfortunately, an obstacle blocked their passage. Lacking any instruction to go around it, the men seemed to take great delight in kicking their way through the line of dustbins, setting them rolling with a dreadful clamour and scattering rubbish everywhere.

Hands over his ears, a dismayed Faljambe told the RSM, 'This is quite ridiculous. I shall just have to admit defeat.'

Probyn narrowed his eyes at the rankers, who to his mind were extracting far too much glee from this, but for now he let the matter lie, concentrating on the young officer's efforts. 'Defeat is not a word we even *think*, Mr Faljambe. *Sharp, tight, smart* – those are the words I would have tattooed upon your brain! You are all far too slovenly for my liking.' At this, he ran his penetrating eyes over the entire gathering. 'Henceforth, I expect every move you make to be as sharp as Jack Frost's –'

'Prick,' muttered a ranker out of earshot.

'– tongue!' Detailing two of the worst offenders to clear up the rubbish with a lance corporal to supervise, Probyn assisted the trainee officer in bringing the men once more into straight lines, their ranks now including the newer recruits too.

Again and again the humiliated Faljambe was called to repeat the instructed movements until he began to get a grasp of matters, and until Probyn was quite sure he would not repeat his mistake. Even then, he and his fellows were made to re-enact the exercise over the next few hours until they finally gained competency.

At first the men under their command had seen this as the opportunity for a lark, but the monotonous repetition had now begun to grate.

'Is he going to keep this up all fooking day?' The grumble was delivered with a South Yorkshire accent. 'We could've marched to fooking France at this rate.'

'Halt!' Probyn took command. 'Very well, gentlemen, that will suffice for now.'

The relieved subalterns were about to retire when Hugh Faljambe was called to a private aside from the RSM.

'And the moral of this morning's exercise, Mr Faljambe: do not pretend you know what to do when you quite obviously do not. The bullets in France are all too real.'

Unusually subdued, Hugh Faljambe slunk from the parade ground.

But the RSM had not finished with the rankers. 'That man there, six paces forward!'

In unpolished fashion, the man who had sworn, a newcomer, did as he was ordered, though judging from his expression he remained unimpressed by authority. The frame might be impoverished but the attitude was tough. It was an unlikeable face, a face old beyond its years, the cheekbones jutting like shelves of slate, the jade eyes equally uncompromising.

Recognizing a persistent defaulter in the making, Probyn decided to nip this tendency in the bud and stalked up to him. 'You seem to be having trouble getting the grasp of marching, Private Unthank!'

'Not if I'm given the proper order . . . sir.'

'Don't you slaver at me! If I say you have trouble in marching then you have trouble!' His nose only inches away from Unthank's, Probyn glared at him, daring the other to meet his eye.

Unthank glared back insolently. Feared as a rough character in his own mining community, he tried hard to maintain his resistance, but eventually the force of that personality was just too strong. His green eyes wavered and he was compelled to break his gaze.

'Sergeant Glew!' Still, Probyn did not remove his piercing eyes from Unthank's face. 'I thank you for the loan of your men. The rest of them are once more at your disposal, Private Unthank will remain here to receive extra discipline. Hand me that pace stick, if you will.

'Now,' he told the defaulter when there was just the two of them. 'Let's put you through your paces!'

Unthank resisted. 'I've done all you've asked. This is victimization. I'm not doing it.'

Rarely had Probyn been confronted by such an obstinate man. Normally the sheer strength of his personality would frighten offenders into submission. It would have been easier just to sling him in the guard house. Instead of bawling, however, he again focused his hypnotic gaze on Unthank. 'Tell me, Private, for I'm finding it very hard to comprehend, why did you join the army?'

Unthank hesitated. It could be a trick question, an invitation to fatigues. 'To kill Germans,' he said eventually.

The beefy face showed incredulity. 'You think that's all there is to it?'

Unthank's waxen brow furrowed. 'What else is an army for but to win wars?'

'Ultimately, yes, but there are other benefits.' Probyn voiced individual beliefs. 'One would hope that such association might help instil pride in yourself, pride in your regiment.'

Unthank scoffed. 'I dig coal for a living. That's what I'll be going back to once we've given the Boche an 'ammering.'

It was only one intransigent voice, yet it was akin to encountering the piece of gristle that ruins the entire meal. An ex-miner himself, Probyn might bear the same blue coal scars as did Unthank, but the two were cast from very different moulds. Against his better judgement Probyn had yearned to make something of this New Army whom all the old regulars derided, hoped that along with the patriotism they obviously felt for their country these men might also learn to share his love of soldiering. But now he had to concede that one could not force them to share his regimental devotion, could only equip them for the fight.

'Very well,' he responded grimly, still holding the other's eyes. 'If that's all you're here for then so be it. But you *are* here and you are under my command, and if you want to get out of the war alive you'd better heed what I tell you because you won't last five minutes otherwise.'

'And all this drilling rubbish is going to save me, is it?' came the impudent enquiry.

'Not from a German bullet, maybe, but it will certainly save you from a spell on prison rations, because, Private Unthank, if you continue to refuse an order that is where you will find yourself – *so get your useless carcass moving now*!' His vocal crescendo and his sheer presence having finally jolted Unthank into obedience, the formidable RSM proceeded to harry him around the square, screaming at him constantly – *''Eft-'ight-'eft-'ight-'eft-'ight-keep moving!'* – going through all the drill in the book, putting Unthank through sweating torment for half an hour up and down the parade ground, making him start right from the beginning if he got one foot wrong – *'And again!'* – until the man's legs began to buckle and he was finally released.

Yet, though his eyes swam with exhaustion there was, too, a flash of defiance for his tormentor as a crimson-faced Unthank finally staggered from the parade ground.

Having felt pleased with himself for taking the wind out of Faljambe's sails, Probyn was surprised to hear the sound of his distinctive foghorn laughter coming from the lecture room only a few hours later. Creeping noiselessly along the corridor, he paused outside the open door to listen. Assembled in the lecture room, the young subalterns had found themselves without a tutor and, to stave off tedium whilst they waited for Major Lewis to arrive, were having an impromptu concert – at their superior's expense. However, it was not Faljambe who was the star. Guy Postgate held the stage, a moustache of black paper glued to his upper lip – obviously not with anything stronger than saliva, for it kept falling off, much to the audience's amusement – and a pointer in his hand which he directed at the blackboard in imitation of Major Lewis, his instructions bordering on the ridiculous. Remaining hidden, Probyn enjoyed the fun for a moment, then craned to look at Louis Postgate, who was huddled in a far corner with his back to the audience, appearing to be in the act of shoving items down his clothing.

The laughter was just dying down over Guy's impersonation, when suddenly Louis burst onto the stage, evoking immediate roars of mirth. Adopting a theatrically ramrod stance, a cushion shoved up his tunic, various items up his sleeves and down the legs of his trousers to give the impression of bulging muscles, Louis Postgate strode up to face his audience, a cane tucked smartly under his arm and his cheeks puffed out like balloons. 'Settle down, gentlemen!' The voice was an absurd mix of Yorkshire and upper class. 'Mr Faljambe, is that a smirk I see upon your face? Well, take it off before I rip it off! I will not 'ave it! You are not 'ere to enjoy yourself, you are 'ere to learn. Now, pay attention!' He spun intricately on his heel and proceeded to swagger up and down, his false stomach jutting ahead of him, whilst the others howled with laughter.

Probyn bristled as he recognized the grossly overblown impression of himself. The impudent little . . .

Gritting his teeth he continued to spy.

'You've forgotten the pair of horns, Louis!' called someone, prompting another to make bellowing noises.

Spurred by the applause, Louis was in full flow, cavorting about the stage and permeating his speech with bull-like snorting. 'What was that you said, Mr Reynard? Moo? I will not hear such defeatist talk! *Snort*, *roar* and *bellow*, those are the only words in my vocabulary!'

Faljambe fell off his chair, his infectious braying sending the others into near hysterics.

At this, the fake RSM bawled in horror, 'Major Lewis, sah, these gentlemen har historical, what ham I to do with them?'

'Gentlemen?' Still in his role of major, Guy cocked his ear. 'Did I hear you call these slapdash oafs gentlemen, RSM?'

All set to burst in and deliver a grilling to his detractors, Probyn turned quickly at the arrival of the genuine major.

'What are they up to, Mr Kilmaster?'

Probyn moved aside, murmuring, 'See for yourself, sir.'

Upon recognizing Louis's impersonation, Major Lewis recoiled. 'The dashed impudence – but who is Postgate senior meant to be?'

Probyn tweaked his moustache, a slight twinkle in his eye. 'Well, it's a bad portrayal but I think it's meant to be you, sir.'

'Hmm.' The major looked only slightly amused. 'Would you like the pleasure, or shall I, Mr Kilmaster?'

'Oh, be my guest, sir.' A calm Probyn remained where he was.

The brothers were too involved in their repartee to notice the imminent danger.

'Sorry, sah, I did not mean to call them gentlemen!' To rising hysteria, Louis's deportment became increasingly preposterous. 'Miserable buffoons like –'

'Buffoon is certainly the word, Mr Postgate!' Heads shot round at Major Lewis's interjection, the laughter immediately displaced by a deathly hush as he stalked up to those involved in parody. 'Take off that ridiculous moustache!' Guy was told.

'Sir, I –'

His attempted apology was curtailed. 'This is the sort of infantile behaviour one might expect from schoolboys, not officers of the

19

British Army!' Major Lewis glared at both subdued faces, then at everyone in the room, all of whom looked equally abashed.

'I beg your pardon, sir,' Guy finally managed to insert.

The major's face remained severe. 'It is not that I object to being the butt of your puerile humour, gentlemen – though I should refrain from the use of that term, for your behaviour towards the RSM was far from being gentlemanly!'

Louis tendered his own apology. 'We meant no harm, sir, it's just that laughter is our only form of revenge.'

'Revenge?' Major Lewis looked astounded. 'Mr Kilmaster is not the enemy!'

'No, sir . . . but it sometimes feels as though he is.'

Still outside listening, Probyn gave an inward sigh as another added his voice in support of Postgate. 'The RSM has been rather hard on all of us this week, sir.'

Major Lewis uttered a laughing gasp, then shook his head. 'Hard? Are you complete and utter idiots? You don't know the meaning of the word! It will be a damned sight harder when you get to the front.'

He paused for effect, glaring at each boyish face in turn. 'Let me tell you about the man you chose to ridicule. RSM Kilmaster joined the army in eighteen ninety, earned his first Good Conduct Medal before some of you were even born, took part in quashing the Matabele revolt, served obediently in Africa and any other part of the British Empire to which the army chose to send him in his twenty-one-year career, and contributed most illustriously to the Relief of Ladysmith. There is nothing Mr Kilmaster does not know about the army; from the cookhouse to the musketry range to the orderly room, the scope and skill of his organization are phenomenal and are to be admired not mocked, *do* I make myself clear?'

'Yes, sir,' came the humble chorus.

'Good! For without men like RSM Kilmaster there would *be* no army!' The major concluded with a decree, clenching his fist to emphasize. '*Listen* to him, learn all he is willing to impart, take any rebuke on the chin for you can be sure that it is not issued for the good of his health but the good of yours. In short, *gentlemen*, it is Mr Kilmaster's expertise that may avert your own premature demise.'

TWO

Snow had fallen and at noon was four inches deep but by the time they had tramped miles to the Revue ground it had been converted to slush by a heavy downpour. The men had now been poised here for almost two hours waiting for General Kitchener and the French Minister of War to inspect them, officers with swords drawn, water streaming down the bright blades, ears turning from red to blue to purple, boots full of water, uniforms weighed down by icy spears of January rain, the ground a morass of mud.

It would all be good practice for them, thought their equally drenched RSM, and though he himself was suffering the torment of rheumatism, one would not have guessed it from his proud bearing. Under his glittering gaze, the battalion stood firm as the deluge soaked all to the skin. Amongst the massive gathering of troops men of other brigades were performing all sorts to keep warm – even playing leapfrog – but Probyn would allow no such antics. To keep his own mind occupied he began a tally of those who fainted and had to be carried off, proud that his own men held the most splendid discipline.

Shivering, waiting. It was all part of army life but it was one thing Probyn detested and he turned his mind to sunnier thoughts, at the same time keeping his eyes honed to spot a frozen hand creeping into a pocket. The major's words were still fresh enough in his mind to cause his breast to swell. *The scope and skill of his organization are phenomenal*. A tremor of delight went through him, making up for all the discomfort and ridicule by the callow officers – though he had forgiven them now, could even laugh about their tomfoolery. They were only youngsters after all.

21

His musings were permeated by the faint sounds of a motorcar splashing through puddles, and a familiar Yorkshire voice muttered, 'At fooking last,' as General Kitchener's vehicle came into view. Or rather, Probyn could only surmise it was the general's car, for it did not stop but drove straight past the sodden ranks of men, the whirr of its engine evaporating into the distance.

Not a salute nor even a wave – after two hours! Frozen to the core, Probyn glanced bleakly at the adjutant. The adjutant in turn looked to the colonel who stared back at him through the rain for an outraged second, before the order was issued from tight lips for the battalion to prepare to march home.

Probyn snapped into action, bawling orders, and rank by rank the drenched men squelched an orderly, if grim-faced, return to Barossa Barracks.

There it was a different story, much cursing and insurrection to be heard as Probyn toured the overcrowded building, its rooms filling with steam as the scramble began to find a place to hang each waterlogged uniform.

In the trainee officers' quarters Reynard was driving his roommates to distraction with his constant whimpering, wringing his bloodless hands in an attempt to restore the circulation and monopolizing the stove. 'I shall have to see the MO, I'm sure I've contracted frostbite.'

'For heaven's sake, Foxy, you weren't the only one out on parade,' spat a shivering Gaylard out of mottled red cheeks.

There was immediate objection from the robust-looking Reynard, whose nickname was a poor choice for he was unlike a fox in every way, his hair black, his nose more like that of a turtle and his eyes projecting not cunning but inertia. 'Yes, but I doubt any of you almost died from pneumonia before you were a year old! I was a very delicate child. Mother only allowed me to join on the condition that I'd look after myself.'

'What are you, a soldier or a sop?' Faljambe's arrogant jaw came jutting towards the stove. 'Quit moaning and stop hogging the fire.' And Reynard was elbowed aside.

Louis Postgate was complaining to his brother Guy with whom he was on friendlier terms again. 'What a damned liberty! Keeps us waiting all that time without even a second glance, the miserable arse.'

'Mr Postgate, I trust it is not your general of whom you speak?' Almost by, Probyn took an exaggerated backwards step and looked through the doorway to reprove the youngster.

'Most certainly not, sir!' came the falsely cheerful reply, the culprit trying to avoid that penetrating glare.

Guy followed through, issuing suavely, 'My brother was just remarking what a miserable afternoon it is, sir.'

Probyn directed a shrewd eye at the brothers, allowing them to see that he did not believe them for one minute. Turning his attention to Foxy Reynard's pained countenance, he was even less forgiving. 'Mr Reynard, what is the condition of your men?'

Reynard looked confused. 'I should think they are rather wet and cold as I am, sir.'

'I should think they are. We all are. But might it not be time to stop putting yourself first and tend to the needs of those who rely on you?' He glared at the other occupants of the room. 'And that applies to every one of you, gentlemen.'

He thought he heard a muttered oath as he moved on, but it was mild in comparison to the ripe language amongst the rank and file.

'Much more of this crap and I'm pissing off home,' declared Tom Unthank. 'I volunteered to fight a war not stand around getting fooking pneumonia.'

And though Probyn screeched an end to it he could not disagree with the sentiment. General Buller would never have kept the men waiting like this. Kitchener might be a great commander but he was possessed of an inability to recognize the fleshly weakness of lesser mortals. Yet who was to say which was the better general? He who put the comfort of his men above all or he who had the greater military skill? It was not for Probyn to judge. Lord Kitchener was renowned as a master of organization – on a far vaster scale than he himself could ever hope to achieve – and was said to be a man who never spared himself, so how could one expect him to spare others?

Nevertheless, as Hugh Faljambe had pointed out, these were not *real* soldiers and some of them were too fond of quoting their rights. At the thought of mutiny Probyn was forced to address the issue with the colonel, to whose office he strode now.

'It's going to be a massive job to get everyone dried, sir. There's not enough space to hang things. The place looks like a Chinese laundry. What a pig of a day.'

Handing his sodden leather gloves to his batman, Lieutenant-Colonel Addison shared his concern. 'We'll have to give them something to take their minds off their discomfort.' He turned to the adjutant. 'Max, a quick change, then go into Aldershot and buy some rum.'

Despite his bedraggled state the thin-faced captain showed no aversion. 'Yes, sir, how much?'

'Enough for the whole battalion. Don't worry, I'll arrange to have it deducted from battalion funds rather than your imprest. I can't have a repeat of October.' During that month, under canvas in bad weather, large numbers had fallen victim to influenza. As the adjutant left to fulfil his request, the colonel turned his concerned eyes on his regimental sergeant-major, who, like himself, remained drenched, one spike of his waxed moustache carrying a twinkling droplet of rain. 'Get out of those wet clothes and warm up, RSM. I'll see you later when we're both recovered.'

'Sah!' In the beginning, Probyn had not really liked the idea of serving under an officer from a different regiment but had soon come to admire Colonel Addison, who never shirked his leadership and seemed to enjoy being dragged out of retirement as much as he himself did.

He retreated, though only after making certain that those in his care were halfway warm and dry did he tend to his own needs. By the time the rum had arrived, putting the men in better mood, he was sitting by a stove, wrapped in a blanket, rubbing his painful calves, wet clothes steaming from an overhead rail.

'Tip a drop of rum into that, Arrowsmith,' he instructed his batman, who had placed a cup of tea before him. 'And take some for yourself.'

'Very good of you, sir.' A tailor in civilian life, Ralph Arrowsmith had been selected for his well-spoken, reserved manner and impeccable tidiness. 'Will you have your last bit of pork pie now?'

Probyn took a grateful sip of hot tea. 'I'd better before it crawls off on its own, it's turning decidedly grey.' The pie had arrived in his last parcel from his wife, donated by Mr Kaiser, the German butcher from his home village. He enjoyed a tinge of irony as he bit into it, at the same time ripping open his mail.

More irony was to come. His eldest sister, Ethel, was writing to announce that she was getting married at last – and to a Catholic! She was the second of his five sisters to change her Wesleyan religion, and this after they had not contacted him for years in protest at his marriage to the Catholic Grace. Not a birthday card nor a letter had he received from them until now. Ethel had probably had to ask Aunt Kit for his address. Well, at least she had the decency to tell me herself, thought Probyn with affection, not like Wyn, who had still not informed him personally. He was about to take another bite of pork pie when it occurred to him that he was eating meat on a Friday. The momentary guilt at what Grace would say soon vanished and he finished the pie without qualm. As a latecomer to Catholicism, and only then so that he could marry Grace, he had often found it impracticable to maintain its rules when away from home. Later, whilst coughing over a Woodbine, he was to scribble a brief but friendly reply to let Ethel know she was forgiven. He declined the invitation to her wedding – not just because there was a war on but because all his sisters, especially the eldest, made him feel like a little boy. It would not do for a man in his position, especially one whose *scope and skill of organization were phenomenal.*

Grinning to himself, he shifted his aching legs, took a glance out of the window to see that it was still raining and moved nearer the fire. God grant them some better weather before they went to France.

Thankfully the weather was a trifle more clement on the day of the route march. Even so, many were to fall out even before the halfway mark, an elderly NCO bawling at each dawdler – 'Stop dragging your arse! You're acting like a bunch of pensioners. I was doing twenty miles a day at your age!'

'And he was probably weaned on iron-filings,' grumbled a sweating Reynard, pausing to heft the leaden pack that was carving a raw groove into his shoulders, before plodding on. 'Oh God, my poor old barking dogs can't go another step.'

'Buck up, Foxy!' panted an equally lathered Louis Postgate. None of the young officers had been spared the ordeal, most of them tramping doggedly alongside the men they would one day lead in battle. 'Where's the old house spirit? We're supposed to teach by example.' This in mind, he called words of encouragement to the stragglers, having made it his business to learn all their names since the RSM's admonishment – 'Keep it up, Rawmarsh, nearly there!' – and he reached out to catch hold of the other's sleeve, hauling the exhausted man onwards, though feeling close to collapse himself. 'I don't want to have to take any names!' So far none of his platoon had dropped out, though along with his own obsolete rifle Louis had been forced to shoulder two others if their jaded owners were to have any chance of continuing. 'Well done, everyone, not far to go now!'

What joy and relief was to be heard upon the appearance of a horse-drawn Lyons delivery van, which marked the halfway point, awaiting them with sandwiches and tea. Here, a great clatter arose as rifles and packs were cast aside, their owners falling gratefully to the verge where they were to lounge for an all-too-brief period of rest before it was up and onwards again.

Stoically shouldering his heavy pack and equipment, young Postgate shouted orders for his men to move, his words of encouragement rousing them to further heights, though before very long he was to find himself the possessor of three extra rifles as their owners again began to flag and had to be physically supported.

There was no need of such assistance for Unthank who, through sheer obstinacy, strode on, though under the weight of his kit his grim face was like a tomato and his nose dripped sweat.

Miles were pounded.

Amongst the steaming, struggling pack, Rawmarsh tripped and fell. Immediately a corporal was upon him yelling at him to get up, taunting him. 'I thought you miners were supposed to be hard? You're nothing but a bunch of fucking wasters, the lot of you!'

Taking exception to this, Unthank broke away from the bunch, an expression of dark intent upon his face. Recognizing that there was going to be violence, for Unthank was fast making a name for himself in this area, Louis Postgate yelled at him, 'Give me a hand here, Unthank!' and bent swiftly to issue words of motivation to Rawmarsh, trying to pull him to his feet.

Diverted, Unthank went to the officer's aid, tucking a hand beneath the straggler's left armpit, and between the two of them they managed to get Rawmarsh up and moving again.

Thenceforth, Unthank urged his exhausted sidekick onwards under a tide of expletives, motivated not by comradeship but by the knowledge that one man's failure would prevent everyone else from going to the front. 'Come on, you weak twat, I'm not having him saying that about us colliers. If I get shown up because of thee I'll rip your fooking throat out.'

Somewhat shocked, Louis felt that, as leader, he should remonstrate with Unthank despite the intimidation the man induced in him. 'I say, there's no call for such language.'

His arm ostensibly still supporting the other, Unthank panted a grim reply. 'Nay, he knows I don't mean it seriously, dunt thee, lad?'

An exhausted Rawmarsh was none too sure of this; he did not like Unthank, but under the other's threateningly tight grip he was forced to summon a good-natured response.

Louis smiled too, though in a somewhat confused manner. Whatever its intention the remark seemed to have given Rawmarsh new energy, enabling him to move under his own steam and allowing the officer to direct his own more courteous brand of encouragement at others who were floundering. 'Well done! Keep it up. Nearly there.'

Up ahead, his sibling Guy was issuing similar valiant command, though his urging of the men was born more from a desire to reach the finishing post before his brother than out of a genuine regard for their wellbeing.

An equally competitive Faljambe remained consistently at the front of the pack, whilst Reynard was now miles in the rear, though trying gamely to keep up, too out of breath to pant encouragement to those in his charge, many of whom were dropping further and further behind.

In fact, hours later, when the battalion reached an exhausted terminus and re-formed on the parade ground it was much under strength.

Though not taking part in the route march, from the vantage point of a commandeered wagon Probyn had tried to keep a steely eye on everyone who had, but one officer seemed to have evaded him. 'Has anyone seen Mr Gaylard?'

'Over here, sir!' An exhausted hand performed a limp but cheerful wave.

Probyn looked and sounded impressed. 'My, my! Your navigational skills are improving a treat, Mr Gaylard! I was anticipating having to come and collect you from Basingstoke – congratulations.'

Overlooking the gibe, the recipient smiled his gratitude. 'Thank you, sir!'

Those who had stayed the distance were to receive similar praise, whilst those who trudged in late received little except a lecture and the promise of being driven harder next time.

With all finally accounted for, the officers and men were dismissed, first to attend their throbbing feet, then to lay upon their beds, wriggling their toes, enjoying copious amounts of tea and filled with pride at having completed their most strenuous test to date.

For Probyn there was to be discussion of the performance with his CSMs, jotting down certain names for promotion. In particular, Unthank had been singled out for the way he had rallied those around him, albeit in crude manner. There was the risk that, armed with a stripe, Unthank could become a bully but Probyn hoped a sense of responsibility would prevail. Such a ruse had worked before.

However, he turned to a waiting sergeant shortly afterwards to be informed that Unthank had turned down the offer.

'Blow me! Even when I try to do him a favour I can't win. Bring him here.' Probyn made ready to apply pressure.

'I'm told you've refused promotion, Unthank.' There was a mixture of disbelief and threat in the RSM's tone.

Spent from his ordeal, Unthank took a while to come to attention and tiredly reiterated the statement he had made to his platoon sergeant. 'What's the point? It'd only be for a few months. The war'll probably be over before they send for us.'

'I think you're wrong there and I'd like you to reconsider.'

'No, sir.'

Probyn remained calm. 'Nobody's forcing you, but I'd urge you not to be too hasty in throwing away the chance of helping your comrades. Unless, of course, you're afraid of responsibility?'

It was the wrong sort of bait. 'I'm not freetened. I'd just rather stay as I am.'

'You're intent on refusal?'

Unthank remained aloof. 'It's my right to do so, sir.'

God preserve us from union men, thought Probyn, casting his mind back to his own youthful eagerness to attain his first stripe and feeling a deep sense of insult over this bogus soldier's rejection. Knowing that no amount of cajolery would shift the man, he let the matter lie with a, 'So be it,' silently damning Unthank for his intransigence, but not allowing the other to see that it annoyed him.

There was something else that had annoyed him too. His ire not confined to the lower ranks, he sought out Louis Postgate, initially to praise him. 'Congratulations for staying the course, Mr Postgate.'

Jumping from his cot, a spontaneous grin permeated Louis's tired expression. 'Why thank you, sir!'

'I couldn't help noticing, however, that on more than one occasion Private Unthank omitted to pay you the courtesy of a title.'

Weary but proud of his achievement, Louis shrugged this off with a diffident smile. 'Oh, I don't think it was intentional, he just forgot.'

Probyn lowered his voice but spoke firmly. 'You must not allow him to forget, Mr Postgate, nor must you make excuses. You are an officer. A man such as Unthank is liable to take advantage if he thinks he can get away with it.' Upon this advice, he strode away, unmoved by Louis's deflated expression, for it would do this well-bred youth no favours to be soft on offenders.

Yet in the main, Probyn had noted that some form of camaraderie had sprung up between officers and men during that torturous march, and for that he must be heartened.

That route march was not to be their last, superseded by even longer ones and interspersed with competitions in entrenchment, barrack-room cleanliness and battalion drill. February saw them tramping yet again the well-trod path to the Long Valley, across low sand holes covered in heather, to spend the day on a barren plain undergoing bayonet training. Observing the two lines of men – nay, boys, thought Probyn – descend on each other to practise their moves, some of them grinning cheerfully as they jabbed and thrust in mock combat, treating it as a jolly jape, their RSM imagined the scene when they were required to stick the blade into a real human being, vividly recalling his feeling of horror at his own first kill before quickly banishing it from his mind.

A trail of sand marked the battalion's return to barracks, trickling from pockets and seams to be ground into the floorboards by milling boots. Yet today's fatigue was soon to be displaced by great exultation, for there were khaki uniforms awaiting all, inspiring boyish excitement in the young officers' quarters as the Postgate brothers and their ilk transformed themselves to authentic soldiers, some rashly regarding the provision of khaki as a sign that they were a step closer to the war.

Probyn quashed the assumption, eyeing them up and down. 'Very dapper, gentlemen, but before you go haring off, you might find you need more than uniforms.'

Guy Postgate was quick to grasp the RSM's meaning. 'Ah yes, a rifle apiece would come in slightly handy.' There being not enough weapons to go round, thus far, companies had been forced to do musketry in shifts. Moreover, with virtually no ammunition it was impossible to complete the course, and the men had learned little more than the theory of how to handle their arms.

'When do you think we're likely to get them, sir?' came an eager enquiry.

Probyn maintained the air of a schoolmaster towards his pupils. 'I do not know, Mr Sillar, I am not equipped with a crystal ball, but I think it rather unwise to go to the front until suitably armed so you'll just have to hold your wisht like the rest of us.'

Not as adept as their RSM at being patient, the would-be warriors were dismayed to find that the following weeks held only more training. Yet the fact that the route marches were growing longer did show promise, and when at the end of February such a gruelling hike took them to the Folkestone area, which was near the coast, Probyn was hard-pressed to dispel the excited rumours. Alas for the battalion, housed in workhouse, school and private dwelling, it was still drill and yet more drill, musketry, manoeuvres and field days, battalion training in the park, another inspection by another general. Notwithstanding the amount of concerts and entertainment provided, this was not the type of theatre for which their hearts yearned.

At least the weather was gradually improving, May bursting into bud under glorious sunshine, the soldiers finding nightpost operations no longer a chore but a joy to be out under the stars. More young officers joined, were lectured and drilled by Major Lewis, teased by those who had been here for months now and who considered themselves seasoned leaders, until the new batch too became versed in map-reading and signalling, and as eager as their fellows to get to France.

Despite all the RSM's efforts to contain the notion that a move to the front was imminent, the men's optimism continued to burgeon, for now came mass inoculation – surely a sign that foreign lands beckoned – and the same rush to avoid it that Probyn had been forced to dissuade over his long career. Moreover, each week the battalion, as part of the 70th Brigade, now combined with the whole 23rd Division for manoeuvres and field days. Hence, the words of hope gained new veracity with every utterance: *surely*, the time was close.

Eventually, Battalion Orders informed them that a move was indeed afoot, though they were none too pleased to discover that it was only to Maidstone, where the troops would gain experience in digging. Thenceforth, working parties entrained every day for Otford, where they were to labour on the defences of London under civilian supervision.

Unthank and his skilled fellow miners took great umbrage at being taught to suck eggs. Yet this was nothing compared to the rage they felt upon their defence being afterwards inspected by Lord Kitchener and informed by the said gentleman that, 'It would not keep out the Salvation Army!'

Having got to know the men inside out between the months of September and May, it came as no shock to Probyn when he heard that Tom Unthank was in serious trouble yet again.

He heaved a sigh, preparing to convey this news to the CO. 'What for this time?'

'For calling Lord Kitchener an ignorant fucking arsehole, sir,' replied the sergeant without the trace of a smirk.

Probyn bristled, but withheld comment, merely turning on his heel and heading for the CO's office where he delivered the news in couched terms.

Colonel Addison matched his RSM's displeasure. 'I sincerely hope that man's going to be as big a nuisance to the Germans as he is to us!'

'My sentiments exactly, sir,' agreed Probyn, and underwent a moment of empathy with the colonel who, formerly of the 2nd Irish Rifles, must find it equally difficult to feel any kinship with this hybrid crew. 'Perhaps once he's in France his attitude will improve.'

He was about to leave when the colonel spoke again. 'By the way, Mr Kilmaster, any news of an arrival yet?'

His mind focused on all things military, it took a second for Probyn to realize that his superior referred to the coming addition to the Kilmaster household. 'Oh, not yet, sir! Any day now, though.'

'It's most regrettable that we won't be able to spare you. I trust your wife understands that you're just too valuable to us – as you must be to her, of course, but . . .'

'Oh, that's quite all right, sir.' Even after two decades in the army Probyn could still be gratified by such a compliment, and by the thought of his own indispensability. 'Grace will cope admirably, she's had years of experience in being a soldier's wife.' But just for that instant he felt a twinge of homesickness and longed to see her dear little face, wondering what the rest of his loved ones were doing now.

THREE

In South Yorkshire, a hint of May had begun to creep through the dark thorny hedgerows, sunlight reflected in the celandines that lined the banks of the River Don. The dried tufts of brown between the limestone crags had yielded to a brilliant green. Yet despite the optimistic flush of verdancy, a collection of slag heaps and winding gear, a network of railway lines, the smoke that belched from countless chimneys, a powder works, a glass factory and rows of grimy cottages marked this as a place of monotonous industry.

Denaby Main would grace no artist's canvas. With neither a village green nor a duck pond its buildings meandered higgledy-piggledy along the main highway. When the mine had been sunk in the nineteenth century, ranks of terraced housing had been erected for the workforce. Over the years, to accommodate the growing population, churches of various denominations had been added, plus a few shops, pubs and a cinema. But the lifeblood of the village was transfused by the Denaby and Cadeby Colliery, whose black pulleys, towers and gantries dominated the valley, as its owners dominated the inhabitants. Almost everything and everyone in the village belonged to the Company.

Inside the miners' cottages it was possible to pretend one was elsewhere. If one looked from Grace Kilmaster's bedroom window one could see, framed within the dusty sash, grassy acres sprawling into the distance, thickets of oak and elm. At this moment, however, a heavily pregnant Grace was in the kitchen, preparing bread-and-butter as an accompaniment to the family's evening meal whilst trying to ignore the signs of imminent birth of her seventh child, who had chosen this inconvenient moment to make its entrance.

It was Friday. To good Catholics that meant no meat and the family was waiting at the tea table for Augusta to return from the fried-fish shop. Through the open window came the sound of a barrel organ; the youngest child swayed in his high chair in response to its gay tune. Normally Grace would be dancing too, but not this evening. Leaning against a work table, buttering bread and trying not to wince as each twinge of pain grew stronger, she hoped the baby would hold on until after its mother had eaten. Her knife flashed across a final slice of loaf. She swivelled her ripe body and extended the plate of bread-and-butter to her eldest son.

'Here, put this on the table, Clem.'

Retaining his seat, Clement reached out with fingers that were stained with ink from his clerical duties at the pit manager's office, but in taking acceptance he mishandled the plate and it fell to the floor, decorating the rug with grease. A quick-tempered youth, he uttered a gasp of frustration.

'Frog's sake!' exclaimed his two-year-old brother, and from his high chair looked down on the mess with a throaty chuckle.

Grace turned on her eldest son with indignation. 'You've been swearing in front of Baby again!'

'I never said a word!' Fourteen-year-old Clem jumped from his seat to pick up the bread. 'Anyway, he only said "frog's sake".'

'We both know the word he's trying to copy isn't frog!' retorted Grace, her anger exacerbated by the discomfort of labour. 'How many times have I warned you about your pit language in this house?'

Whilst the rest of his siblings hung their heads, hoping to keep out of this, flame-haired Clem did not even bother to maintain his innocence, reminding his mother as he set the plate of fluff-covered bread on the table, 'You swear.'

Unmasked as a hypocrite, Grace was even angrier. 'Not the kind of vile stuff as I've heard you spout when you think I'm not listening, and you wouldn't dare behave like this if Father were here!' With his father absent, Clem had slipped into the role of chief protector but was also apt to try to order his mother about. Normally a gentle soul, Grace was nobody's doormat. Now, furious at her son's insolence, she propelled her tormented bulk across the kitchen, grabbed him by the ear and hauled him into the scullery. 'Well, you might think you're a man but you're not too big for your mother to teach you a lesson.' And clamping her arm around his auburn head she rammed a cake of green naphtha soap into his mouth, leaving him gagging in disgust. 'Now get back to the table and show some respect!'

'Thou'll poison me!' His hawk-like face contorted, Clem tried to wash away the foul taste with a glass of water, spitting and retching over the sink. Then at a push from his mother he slouched back to the table, thoroughly humiliated at being treated like a juvenile.

Grace was about to lower her weight onto a chair when she uttered a groan and sucked in her breath, leaning on the table, one hand on her distended abdomen. This baby was not going to be the considerate type. 'Madeleine, go fetch Nurse.'

Six-year-old Madeleine gawped at her mother.

'Now!' urged Grace. 'And the rest of you go out and play until Gussie comes with the chips.' To still their objections she added, 'You can take some bread with you – and don't come back till you're bidden!' She chivvied them from the house, then went to the cupboard, grabbed an old sheet and took it upstairs to protect the mattress, calling anxiously over her shoulder, 'Ooh, don't be long, Maddie!'

Whilst Madeleine pelted along the terraced street to fetch the midwife, Clem slouched off in the opposite direction, lighting up a cigarette as he went, glad to be removed from the source of his embarrassment. The rest of his siblings, Joseph Fitzroy, seven, Beata Honoria, almost five, and the youngest, Marmaduke James, were left on the front doorstep to nibble at their pieces of bread.

Within seconds Madeleine was coming back along the sunlit street with midwife Fanny Gentle, a dark-haired, handsome woman, though bony, with a chest as flat as a board and a stance that warned she would take no nonsense. The knot of neighbours who gathered around the barrel organ nudged each other and smiled in recognition that there was to be another Kilmaster birth.

As the two arrived, Beata tried to get back into the house with them but was shoved none too gently away by her elder sister. 'You have to wait outside till Mother's got t'new baby.'

'And so do thee!' came the nurse's rude instruction as she shut the door in Madeleine's face.

Madeleine collapsed in a sulky heap on the doorstep to chew on the remnant of her crust. The others had already devoured theirs and now their eyes were fixed hypnotically on Marmaduke, like cat upon mouse, wondering how to coax him into parting with his. In the event they did not have to.

'No want it.' The infant threw his bread-and-butter down.

Instantly the others fought to peel it from the stone flag, Beata quickly being pushed out of the way by her elder siblings, Joe emerging the winner.

Disappointed, Beata stood beside her sister on the step, feeling its coolness invade the paper-thin soles of her footwear. 'Has Nurse fetched the baby in her bag?'

'Greedy pig!' Madeleine was still concentrating on the bread that was fast disappearing down her brother's throat. Then she gave Beata a shove. 'And you get your mucky booits off my step.' It had been her turn to donkey-stone it that morning.

Her question unanswered, Beata left the others to squabble and watched the people dancing to the tingalary man. But then the memory of being held in her father's arms jiggling about to this same music caused her eyes to stray wistfully along the street, hoping for a sight of him.

He had gone away to somewhere called The War. Born towards the end of Probyn's military career, unlike her elder siblings Beata could never remember a time when he was not there, and she yearned to see him now. Instead, she glimpsed a man in a black cassock weaving an unsteady passage across the end of the street and, hoping Father Flanagan might be on his way to the sweet shop, she set off at an excited gallop, little legs working like pistons, affecting not to notice the priest as she overtook him but continuing to race towards the main road.

The priest stalled as the little figure dashed past him, putting him off his stride and causing him to totter. Then, noting her identity he grinned to himself and redirected his shabby boots along their way, knowing what he would find when he got to his destination.

Sure enough, when he came within sight of the confectioner's there she was, nose pressed up against the window, acting for all the world as if she was unaware of his existence until he spoke to her.

'Hello to you, Beat!'

She beamed up at him, before turning back to the window and staring pointedly at that which had caught her attention.

Father Flanagan bent his tall thin figure and leaned on his knees to peer into the window alongside the little girl. Between the fine strands of white hair slicked back with grease were sections of pink scalp. 'What's that you're looking at?'

Beata willingly inhaled the fumes that emanated from beneath his long Irish upper lip. Father Flanagan had a lovely smell about him. The smell of Christmas she called it, because she had only ever experienced it in her own house when her mother mixed the Christmas pudding. A warm, fruity and intoxicating smell.

'A chocolate doll in a bed.' She pointed a grimy finger.

'What a marvellous creation to be sure.' Father Flanagan breathed more alcoholic fumes upon the child before coming upright and rolling up the sleeves of his darned cassock, a look of purpose on his face. 'Away in then, we shall have her!' And cupping his hand to Beata's wavy auburn bob he steered her into the shop.

When they emerged the priest carried a bag of mints, one of which was rattling around his false teeth, and the child clutched the tiny chocolate doll in its bed.

'Aren't ye going to eat it?' asked her benefactor, walking along-side.

Beata shook her head. It was much too precious to devour. However, by the time they had reached the street where she lived, her resolution to keep it intact had caved in and she began to nibble along the edge of its arm, though she still cradled it with reverence. Weaving an unsteady passage, Father Flanagan smiled down at her and the smile was reflected in her blue-grey eyes.

The hurdy-gurdy had moved on, though its faint strains could still be heard along with the trilling of canaries through the open windows.

'We're not allowed in,' the little girl informed the priest on arrival at her front door, the chocolate doll now decapitated. 'Mother's getting a new baby.'

'Indeed?' Father Flanagan paused for a second, then cocked his ear at the open bedroom window from where came the mew of a new-born. 'Sounds like it's arrived.' And with a tap at the door he opened it, calling, 'Are we right to come in?'

An aroma of fish and warm newspaper filled the kitchen. The family's meal temporarily installed in the oven to keep hot, Augusta was entertaining the smallest child by giving him horse rides on her back. Dislodging Marmaduke, she scrambled to her feet and granted immediate permission to the priest, a look of respect on her face.

'Yes, of course, Father! Can I get you a cup of tea?'

'Haven't you enough to do looking after this lot, Gussie?' Swaying, Father Flanagan grabbed a chair for support and observed the other more boisterous youngsters to whom he proffered the bag of mints.

'It's no trouble. Please, sit down.' Recognizing the smell of whisky beneath the whiff of mint, Augusta thought she had better invite him to sit before he fell down. In a fussy, adult manner she proceeded to serve the guest with tea from the pot that she had just brewed.

'My, you deserve a medal,' slurred the priest and, rummaging in his cassock, he brought forth a silver oval disc bearing the head of the Virgin Mary, which he handed to the eleven-year-old.

36

Radiating pleasure, Augusta thanked him and with lustrous gaze studied the religious medallion for a moment whilst the priest flopped onto a chair to drink his tea, but then the midwife came downstairs carrying a bundle, asking if the bath was ready.

Clutching the medal in her fist, Augusta indicated the zinc bath by the fire.

'And this would be the new arrival, would it?' Father Flanagan's glazed blue eyes peered at the newcomer's face. 'Is it a man or a woman?'

'A little lass, Father.' With great dexterity Fanny Gentle unwrapped the crumpled new-born and placed it in the water, proceeding to sluice away the detritus of birth.

The priest asked what she was going to be called. Augusta did not know.

'Your mother says Millicent Mary,' revealed the nurse.

Two-year-old Marmaduke tried to repeat the name. 'Mims.'

Father Flanagan guffawed along with the rest. 'Ah well, there you have it! Mims, it is.'

The other children soon lost interest in their new sister and asked, 'When are we going to get us teas?'

Fanny relayed a message to Augusta. 'Your mother says for you to feed these gannets, and you're to take her a plate up.' She herself dried and dressed the baby and took it back upstairs.

In her usual capable manner, Augusta had doled out the children's tea, had given the priest a chip sandwich and was taking a plate up to her mother when her elder brother poked his hawkish nose tentatively round the door.

'Hello there, young Clem,' said Father Flanagan, munching. 'Away in, 'tis safe now.'

Clem was subdued. 'Mebbe not for me, Father.' He turned to Augusta. 'Is Mother all right?'

'Yes, I'm just taking this up to her.'

'I'll save your legs.' Clem reached for the plate, sucking in his breath at the heat of it and using his shirt cuff as protection.

'Frog's sake,' laughed his two-year-old brother.

Clem cast a humorous eye at him, warning, 'Eh, don't start that again, me laddo.'

'What's that he said about frogs?' quizzed the priest, but received only titters.

'Me come.' Unrestricted, the toddler followed him upstairs, ignoring calls from their sister to return and eat his tea.

Using a knee to prevent the little one from worming past him,

Clem tapped at his parents' bedroom door and, given authorization, entered. 'Is it all right if Babby comes in, Mother?'

Cradling the new arrival in her arms, Grace's heart went out to the toddler, who had suddenly been displaced in her affections and whose alarm now caused him to try to scramble up onto her bed. 'He's not Baby any more, are you, dear? He'll have to learn his proper name now.' She passed her new-born to the midwife. 'But that doesn't stop us having a little cuddle before I eat my chips.' And leaning over she dragged him into her arms where he clung possessively, glaring at the one who had usurped him.

'I'll be off now and let thee get tha tea.' Fanny Gentle planted the baby in the top drawer that served as its crib. 'See you tomorrow, Grace.'

'Thank you, Nurse. Your money's in an envelope on the mantel.' Grace watched her go, then, after giving Marmaduke a last squeeze, told him he would have to get down. He didn't want to go but Clem grabbed a handful of the infant's red plaid dress and dragged him off the bed, holding him like a carpetbag whilst presenting Grace with her meal and a humble apology. 'Sorry about before, Mam.'

'I should think so!' For a second Grace's hooded blue eyes looked stern; but she couldn't maintain this for long and, in the flush of relief that followed her travail, was able to bestow her warm happy smile. 'Oh, I suppose I'll forgive you! I always do, don't I?' She reached out to cuff him gently. 'But you'll have to learn to curb that impetuous streak, Clem. It'll get you nowhere.'

Glad to be forgiven, Clem impishly stole a chip from her plate, then, laughing at her pretend outrage, he threw Marmaduke over his shoulder and went down to eat his own.

When the midwife came on Saturday she brought with her a bag of jam and coconut buns, which were happily devoured by the children, who sat round whilst Nurse Gentle bathed and dressed the baby by the fire. At the same time, out of the blue, came another visitor. Jam around their mouths, the children jumped up to greet Aunt Charlotte, all frantically happy to see her big square face with its tiny gleaming emerald eyes, each vying for her attention whilst their eldest sister fought to keep their sticky fingers away from the visitor's nice clothes. Whilst the house saw frequent visits from neighbours and local clergy, for their mother was very popular, it was rare for them to see an outsider, and the extent of their excitement testified to this. Charlotte was not a relative at all, but their mother's lifelong friend.

After paying court to the new addition, Charlotte removed the small feathered hat and primped her dark blonde curls, speaking to Fanny Gentle, her tone aghast. 'Have you seen the dreadful news?'

'That ship you mean?' Bony legs apart under the apron, the baby splayed on her lap, Fanny issued a grave nod. 'I don't know all the facts yet but the summary said it was torpedoed yesterday afternoon just before this little lass were born.'

Charlotte was eager to provide details, her face projecting horror. 'Nearly two thousand souls on board and most of them feared dead, little babies and all.'

The midwife's reply lacked emotion as she fitted a last article of clothing on the infant and bound it tightly in a shawl. 'Nay, it doesn't surprise me in the least. They can't beat our lads by fair fighting so they descend to this poisonous gas, so I wouldn't put anything past them, even drowning bairns.'

Charlotte gave a theatrical shudder.

Clem tapped the newspaper he had been reading before her arrival. 'There's a letter from a soldier who reckons the war's almost won. June by the latest.' There was no enthusiasm in his remark for he lamented the fact that he was too young to fight and only if this war were to persist for years would he have a chance of achieving his ambition.

'Let's pray he's right.' Charlotte studied her engagement ring for an anxious moment, thinking of her sweetheart, George, who was already in France, then made as if to go upstairs.

'Here, take this article with you if you're off up.' Fanny Gentle extended a bundle.

With a fond laugh Charlotte received the new baby and went upstairs where, after an initial hug, congratulations to Grace and compliments over Mims, the subject of the *Lusitania* was repeated, though there was little detail to go on.

'If this doesn't bring the Americans in, nothing will,' announced Grace. Then she became even angrier. 'Oh, and have you read the latest? You won't believe it! Some clot of a professor has suggested that we ought not to sing "Rule Britannia" for fear of upsetting the Germans. Have you ever heard owt so bloody daft? It's all right for them to kill bairns –' She broke off and hugged Mims protectively to her breast.

Moved by her friend's vulnerability, Charlotte sought to comfort. 'The reports might be exaggerated; it might not be so bad as it sounds.' Not wanting to believe that any nation could be so vile, the words were uttered as much to convince herself as Grace. 'Perhaps most of them have been saved.'

And, needing to share her faith, Grace nodded and quickly changed the subject, the pair going on to chat about happier topics.

On Sunday, though, an emergency war edition gave full report of the dastardly occurrence. The German torpedo had claimed fifteen hundred victims, many of them children.

In the days that followed, an inquest on the tragedy found the Kaiser guilty of murder.

'Kaiser?' blurted Grace whilst Fanny Gentle made the daily examination of her nether regions. 'They should change his name to Herod.'

Fanny patted Grace's bare buttock to signify that she should cover herself. 'Everything's healing nicely.' She went to sluice her hands in a chipped bowl. 'Aye, and I'll warrant the emperor's not the only one who should be changing his name. Did you hear they smashed up the German butcher's shop in Mexborough?'

Grace pulled her nightgown over her nakedness and adjusted the covers, deploring such violence. 'Mr Kaiser didn't fire the torpedo! He can't help his ancestry.'

The handsome woman showed scant sympathy. 'No, but he can help putting up his prices and taking advantage of the fact that there's a war on.'

Grace did not argue for fear of incurring accusations of favouritism. Mr Kaiser had been very good to the Kilmasters. Instead she pursued the relevant matter, her anger towards the enemy being as keen as any other patriot's as she grabbed the newspaper from the bedside table to read again. 'It says here that the King's going to strike him off the Roll of the Order of the Garter.' Grace read a last line before tossing the paper aside and taking possession of her baby, addressing herself more brightly to the infant. 'He'll have nothing to keep his socks up then, will he, cherub? And serve him right too!'

Waiting until the midwife had gone, for Fanny could be less than gentle with patients who did not do as they were told, Grace informed her eldest daughter of her intention to get up. She shouldn't be on her feet after only five days but felt guilty at poor Gussie missing school and having to run about after everyone. However, the excuse she voiced was, 'It's such a grand day and I'm sick of lying in bed. The registrar will be coming today –' he came two afternoons a week to Denaby Main – 'I might as well take advantage and give you children some fresh air at the same time.'

Later, the conspirators prepared to leave the house, Augusta carrying Marmaduke and first making sure the way was clear before hurriedly summoning her mother, Grace sneaking through the doorway, babe in arms, then all fleeing with Beata in tow.

'Hurry, before Nurse catches us!' Grace's pale cheeks were illuminated with the laughter of a naughty child as she and her offspring scuttled down the sunlit terrace.

Once around the corner, though, they relaxed somewhat and assumed a leisurely pace, exchanging an occasional hello with others and stopping for friends to admire the new baby. Grace could not help noting that one or two of the women to whom they spoke appeared a lot happier of late, and guessed that it was not due simply to the glorious sunshine, but was because their husbands were away at the front. It made her sad that it took a war for them to escape domestic violence – sad too because she missed her own husband dreadfully.

They proceeded to the registrar's office.

Leaving Gussie outside with the others Grace went in and, initially, things went smoothly, name, address and date of birth being written down without a problem.

'Father's rank or profession?' enquired the registrar, pen at the ready.

'Well, he's normally a weighman but he's gone to serve his country,' replied Grace, then seeing that the man had begun to write 'Private' said hastily, 'Hang on! He's a regimental sergeant-major.'

Testy at being corrected, the man made great play of looking the shabbily dressed woman up and down. 'I rather think you must be mistaken.'

Grace flushed both with embarrassment and anger. 'No, he's sergeant-major of the 9th Battalion York and Lancaster Regiment.'

'My good woman,' the tone was supercilious, 'that cannot possibly be so.' A quick dip into the inkwell and his nib resumed its action, completing the word 'Private'.

Grace was furious. She wanted to tell this man that she was proud of her husband, that Probyn had worked so valiantly to earn that title and she would not let him be robbed of it. But for that instant emotion forbade it. If she spoke again she felt she would cry. Taking a deep breath to calm her rage, she began to rock Mims, who had been woken by the altercation, and finally managed to blurt, 'He is *not* a private.'

'Well, I've written it now!' came the annoyed retort.

'Then you should have listened to what I said!' Don't cry, Grace warned herself, hugging and jiggling the baby.

Just then, someone else entered the office. Humiliated and angry, Grace was loath for anyone to witness her distress, yet remained at the desk to argue her point. 'I tell you he is a regimental sergeant-major!'

An exasperated sigh from the official. 'Ridiculous!' He stood and thrust the certificate at Grace, obviously expecting her to depart. Automatically she took the piece of paper but did not budge. Upon craning his neck to ascertain the identity of the person behind her, the man's attitude became only marginally civil. 'Mr Kaiser, what may I do for – Thank you, madam, good day!' He broke off to readdress Grace, his glare demanding obedience.

Mr Kaiser looked bemused. He had come to register the birth of his own child but seeing Grace in such distress he sought to aid her. 'Mrs Kilmaster, vat –'

'A simple mistake.' The registrar dismissed the matter with a flick of his hand. 'She's trying to tell me her husband's an RSM.' He rolled his eyes, then gave terse indication at the chair. 'Now, would you take a seat?'

The butcher demurred. 'I can assure you, my man, zat vot Mrs Kilmaster tells you is ze truth.'

The registrar did not appreciate being made to look stupid by an immigrant. With a quick-tempered sigh, he grabbed the certificate from Grace, amended it to give the authentic details, then thrust it back at her.

'Now! Do please sit, Mr –'

'Thank you, no!' Disgusted, Mr Kaiser began to steer Grace gently to the door. 'I shall make my registration some other time when you haf learned some manners.'

Both the humiliation and the butcher's kindness were too much for Grace and there was moisture in her eyes as she emerged into the sunshine. One arm cradling the baby, she used her other to grope for a handkerchief and dashed the tears away, hoping the children would not see them. 'I'm sorry, Mr Kaiser, I –'

'Do not mention it, my dear. Ze man is an oaf.'

Grace shoved her handkerchief away, but too late to avoid her elder daughter noting the brightness in her eyes. Augusta flew protectively to her mother's side, wondering what had caused the tears – not that it had to be anything life-threatening. Mother was easily upset these days, ever since THE DAY THE BROWN LADY CAME. She thought of that day in capital letters for it had been so momentous. Though not fully comprehending what had happened – and the great screaming rows had never been witnessed again, nor had the incident even been referred to – Augusta knew that that day had borne great significance and was responsible for her mother's ill health.

Bossily ushering the other children into movement, she linked arms with her mother as a quiet gesture of support and the little knot made its way home, Mr Kaiser's portly figure bumbling alongside.

Grace was more composed now and gave a little laugh of appreciation. 'A good job you were there, Mr Kaiser. I don't think my husband would appreciate the demotion.'

He sighed and shook his big Teutonic head. 'Good for you, Mrs Kilmaster, maybe, but not for me. I am only in Denaby because some hooligans smashed my Mexborough shop and I fear zere is more violence to come.'

Grace looked respectfully sombre. 'Ah yes, we heard about that. I am sorry. I hope the damage wasn't too bad.'

'Bad enough to close me down until repairs are done.' The butcher shook his head in despair. 'Do zey tink I like what my countrymen do?' He corrected himself. 'Besides, zey are not my countrymen, *zis* is my country now. Twenty years I haf chosen to live here, how long must it be before I am accepted?'

Grace privately marvelled that his accent remained so thick after two decades, but openly sympathized and asked about Mrs Kaiser and the latest baby.

'My wife has taken the children to stay with relatives. It is safer. I must stay to protect my business. Anyhow, it is not your problem.'

'Well, thank you for helping me.' Grace still harboured a trace of distress. 'I wish there was something I could do in return.'

The butcher had always felt sorry for this nice, pretty woman with the alluring blue eyes, having so many children to feed and looking so neglected herself, and told her now, 'Perhaps you might be able to do me a favour. I haf made some brawn just before my Mexborough shop was wrecked.' He pronounced it deep in his throat like a growl, *brrrawn*. 'A lot of the meat was plundered but they left zat behind. It is perfectly good to eat but I haf also a great deal at my Denaby shop, too much to be able to sell it all. Could you take it off my hands? Othervise I shall haf to throw it away.'

Grace knew it for a charitable lie but with such a large family she could not afford to be proud, and so went with him along the busy sunlit street to his shop. There were no customers, though three youths were viewing the contents of the window. They seemed to make Mr Kaiser uneasy and he gave them a suspicious glance as he shepherded Grace inside. Telling his assistant he would see to Mrs Kilmaster, the butcher first nipped a few slivers of ham from the bone and approached Grace's children. 'Here ve are, kiddivinkies!' And smiling at their enjoyment of the titbits he patted each on the head before going to don his striped apron. Thereafter he scooped a generous dollop of brawn onto a piece of paper, chatting to Grace as he wrapped it. During this, one of the youths who had been looking in the window finally entered.

'Are them German sausages?' It was issued with a challenging sneer.

In the act of handing over the package of brawn, Mr Kaiser tensed, his unease infecting Grace. 'They are perfectly goot *English* sausages.'

The youth was obviously intent on mischief. 'How can they be English when they're made by a Hun?'

'Oh, eh, not again!' wailed Mr Kaiser, clutching his big grey head. 'See here, I vill not be treated like zis!'

The scruffy tormentor drew back his lips in a snarl. 'Then get back where you belong!' And he swiped a tray of black puddings to the floor.

Grace felt she ought to say something in the kindly butcher's defence, but was too stunned. She gathered her children and made a move to go but her way was blocked as the assistant came from behind the counter and tried to expel the transgressor, grappling with him in the doorway whilst he and his friends continued to harangue the butcher for his German origins. 'Boche, baby-killer!'

Hearing the row, passers-by gathered outside, first to watch, then to join in, shoving their way into the shop, calling insults, setting carcasses swinging on their hooks, their actions becoming bolder as a demented Mr Kaiser tried in vain to eject them.

Unsure what to do, buffeted by larger bodies, Grace wheeled to face a corner, trying to shield the children with her frame, her back to the angry mob and her baby secreted at the centre of the huddle whilst behind her the jostling worsened. She should speak up for the one who had just helped her, she really should, but when a brick came smashing through the window, shattering the glass and propelling it all over the shop she thought only for the safety of her offspring and, acting on impulse, elbowed her way through a gap in the crowd, shoving the children ahead of her.

Not before time. Even as they fled from the shop a crowd of women and youths were converging upon it with sticks and stones and, ignoring Mr Kaiser's angry pleas – 'I haf served in ze Doncaster Yeomanry!' – proceeded to turn the contents upside down, joints of beef and lamb and pork rolling together in the sawdust whilst others disappeared under aprons and were spirited away. Word had spread, troublemakers were running from everywhere, goblin-like glee on their faces. Ignoring all, heart thumping, Grace did not stop but urged the frightened children onwards, her mind fixed on home.

At last they reached their haven. Breathing heavily, the grateful mother was about to usher her brood inside.

'Oy! Madam – bed!'

Grace almost jumped out of her skin as Fanny Gentle pounced. It was all she could do to emit sheepish apology. 'Sorry, Nurse, we've just bee –'

'Never mind where you've been!' Fanny was unmoved. 'You're as bad as Mrs Orange. I shall take one of you to bray the other. The times I tell you mothers about getting up early. Prolapse isn't funny, you know. Don't come crying to me when your child-bed's dangling between your knees like a football.'

'No, I'll apply to Doncaster Rovers,' muttered an irritated Grace under her breath as she turned to go in, but managing to cover it with a profuse apology as she shoved her children indoors.

'I shall post a guard!' came Fanny's warning before the door was slammed.

Inside the dimly lit kitchen, Augusta took charge and put the kettle on without being told whilst her harassed mother paced the room. The other children seemed to have recovered quickly from the fright. Catching sight of herself in the mirror, Grace was dealt a shock and began to understand how the registrar had made his mistake. You really don't do credit to an RSM's wife, she scolded herself and, laying the baby on the table, she took up a comb in an attempt to tidy her brown hair but found that her hands were trembling and had difficulty inserting the hairpins.

'Shall we have this soused lugs for tea?' In an attempt to divert her mother Augusta held up the parcel of brawn.

Grace experienced guilt. Not only had she failed to stand up for Mr Kaiser after he had defended her but had callously run away without acknowledgement of his gift. People who didn't try to stop the violence were as bad as those who committed it. There was her husband, prepared to risk his life to fight the German bullies, but when she herself was put to the test she was found wanting.

The thought was to keep her awake all night.

In the morning before her offspring departed for work and school, goaded by conscience, Grace went down to Mr Kaiser's shop, taking with her a dustpan and brush. The least she could do was to help him tidy up.

But on approaching it she faltered. There were a few dubious-looking characters loitering outside, mostly women, but some of the miners' wives could be rougher than their husbands. One of them in particular, Sadie Barnes, was known both for her lax morals and handing out white feathers to reluctant recruits. Moreover, she had a violent streak. Determined not to let herself down, Grace squared her shoulders and, at the risk of being dubbed unpatriotic, marched on, though her legs were somewhat weak. The assembly turned as one to examine her as she gave a polite but firm, 'Excuse me.' However, as they made way for her, she saw that the shop was completely boarded up and closed for business. To discourage further outrage Mr Kaiser had pinned a sign to the boarding. 'THIS IS NOT A GERMAN SHOP. GOD SAVE THE KING.'

Feeling foolish with her brush and dustpan in hand, Grace turned to go.

'Won't get your bit of German sausage this morning,' uttered Sadie, her lewd innuendo provoking laughter amongst the others.

Hating such coarse behaviour, Grace's instinct was to remove herself from its presence, but to do so without first offering rebuke would be the act of a coward. Looking directly into the hard face, she said more calmly than she felt, 'Mr Kaiser's done nothing to deserve this. He didn't start the war.'

The women gave a combined crow of outrage, Sadie articulating it. 'What're you defending him for when your husband could be killed by one of his countrymen?'

'That still doesn't make it right,' countered Grace, braver now that no violence had been offered. 'How would you like it if someone came round and smashed your house up for no other reason than you had a foreign name?'

'Well, I haven't! I've got a good English name, me. And old Kaiser'd better get himself one and all if he knows what's good for him.'

Knowing it was futile to try to reason with such bigots, Grace shook her head and moved on, though feeling rather pleased with herself for tackling them, albeit belatedly.

'Let's see if you hold the same opinion when your old man cops a German bullet!'

To all intents and purposes Grace ignored the riposte. During her sixteen years of being an army wife she had learned to cope with this worry and, besides, Probyn had told her he would not be engaged in the fighting.

However, the unpleasant incident had resurrected another concern that she had been trying desperately to suppress. Out there were hundreds of zealous Sadie Barneses, all willing to throw themselves at the departing soldiers. To Grace, these were much more of a threat than any German sniper.

FOUR

Throughout that week the local vigilantism was to burgeon into an anti-German protest across the globe. Racked by shame for deserting her benefactor in his moment of need, Grace made a trip to Confession. Though this might be of little use to poor Mr Kaiser, whose shop in Denaby Main was to remain closed, Grace's guilt was absolved by the penance of having to walk much further to buy her meat.

Attributing the throb in her calf to the latter fact, it was not until she woke one morning and swung her legs out of bed to find that one of them was too painful even to put to the floor that she realized it was more serious. Wincing, she lifted her nightgown to explore the offending limb. What had merely been swollen last night was now a labyrinth of angry red lines, her hand encountering hard knots that made her cry out even under tentative pressure.

'Ooh, Gus, will you go fetch Nurse?'

In the next room Augusta was already up and dressing the younger ones but now flew to her mother's command. Clem, too, popped his head in to investigate.

At the urgent tone of voice, Beata turned enquiring eyes on Madeleine. 'Is Mother having another baby?'

Overhearing, Grace chuckled despite her pain. 'Nay, don't wish that on me! It's just a poorly leg.'

When Fanny Gentle came she pressed her hand to Grace's brow to gauge her temperature and confirmed what the other had already guessed. 'White-leg. Back into bed, my dear, right now – and you'll stay there this time.'

Whilst the ever-efficient Augusta gave her siblings breakfast,

48

packed Clem up for work and bundled most of the others off to school, Fanny went to fetch laudanum and, on return, sprinkled it on a hot-water cloth in which the leg was gently enfolded.

Holding Marmaduke, Augusta watched with interest as a mackintosh was wrapped around the limb. 'Would it help if I rubbed it the way I do Father's?' She often provided this method of relief for the soldier's aching calves.

'Nay, you'll kill her!' Deciding her response had been too harsh, Fanny gave softer explanation to the child. 'It's right dangerous. You might dislodge a clot that would go to your mother's heart.'

Shocked almost to tears, Augusta could give no reply.

Fanny was kinder now. 'Just make sure she has constant rest. She mustn't get out of bed at all.' A stern addition for the patient. 'And I mean that, missus!'

In fact Grace was unable even to contemplate leaving her bed, for, during the next ten days, in addition to the agonizing pain, she became extremely ill, both her pulse and temperature soaring, and would not even have been lucid enough to recognize her children had it not been for the administration of quinine. Neighbours rallied to help, Father Flanagan and Canon McLafferty taking turns to hold regular vigils.

Even when the agony and tension in her leg had subsided it was still greatly swollen and had to be wrapped in cotton wool, forbidding her to leave the house. Therefore, each day, Fanny Gentle would pop in to check that her orders were being obeyed. She was not pleased to find that Augusta was back at school and Grace had eschewed the assistance of neighbours to cope with the little ones alone, but Grace replied that it was unfair that her eldest daughter should be expected to play surrogate mother, *she* was their mother and would cope as best she could.

Fanny was astonished by such a viewpoint – what else was a daughter for except to help around the house? Grace could not bring herself to reveal the deep guilt she harboured, wanting desperately to forget the time when grief over her husband's infidelity had caused her to neglect her precious children for almost a fortnight until she had come to her senses, ever since when she had been trying to make amends for the dereliction of her motherly duties, knowing that she could never forgive herself.

But to her interrogator she responded blithely, 'I've got Beat into school. Mims is lying asleep in the top drawer all day – I can just reach out to her when she wants feeding.'

'And what about Ally Sloper?' A sceptical Fanny indicated the more adventurous Marmaduke.

Grace countered by showing her a rope. 'I'll fix this round his middle and tie him to my chair leg so I can just reel him in if he's trouble. Honestly, Nurse, I won't move an eyelash.'

Whilst not fully content with this, Fanny would have been even less pleased had she witnessed the scene in her absence, during which Grace ignored her own discomfort to provide a wholesome dinner for her offspring at midday, using the rest of the afternoon to stand baking and cooking and ironing, whilst ensuring that by late afternoon, when the children came home, she was seated calmly in her fireside chair, so that Gussie could truthfully report to Nurse that Mother was doing as she was told.

Nevertheless it was an exhausting and worrying time, and devoted though she was to her brood it was hard not to dismiss some of their needs as trivial.

'Mother!' Madeleine had obviously run all the way home from school for she was first in and panting, a request forming as she rushed straight to Grace's chair. 'Can I be called something different?'

'Hello to you too, Maddie!' All the standing had caused Grace's leg to swell up again, the pain making her unusually brusque as she ploughed her way through a stack of mending.

The child was contrite. 'Sorry – hello, Mother.'

'That's better.' Grace was less stern now, laying aside the bodkin and half-darned sock to shove her daughter's red fringe from her eyes. 'And why, pray tell, do you want to change your moniker?'

'They call me Mad-Ellen, or Loony.'

'Who do?'

'The kids at school.' Madeleine wrung her hands.

The mother's reply was blasé. 'They're just daft. Think how much more upsetting it would be if you really were mad. You know you're not or you'd be locked up. It's a lovely name and you're keeping it. Heaven knows, there are more important things to think about.' Grace's eyes strayed to the newspaper. Stuck indoors she had had much time to ponder on the reports from the front. According to these, the war was nearing crisis and there was fighting all along the line from Arras to the sea, more terrible and costly than ever. Instead of the one or two names that had originally appeared there were now whole pages of casualties. Yet perversely this served to ignite a flicker of hope in Grace's heart, for the sheer savagery of it might mean that the war would be won before Probyn could be sent overseas.

'What things?' whined Madeleine.

Jerked from her thoughts, Grace looked at the innocent little face and resisted infecting the child with her own anxiety. 'Like new Whitsuntide wear!' she said brightly, at the same time reaching into her sewing basket for a tape measure. 'We want you all looking posh for when your father comes home.'

'Is Father coming home?' The others had just arrived, a collection of grubby knees, creased pinafores and loose hair ribbons, tumbling through the door en masse.

'Soon,' replied Grace as she measured her daughter, and hoped very much that it might prove true.

The months of training in open countryside had had a splendid effect on the troops. Pale-faced miners now boasted the rosy glow of farm boys, the good food, the constant route marching and digging had built muscle and stamina, but most of all, aside from the abominable Unthank who seemed to want no part in it, an *esprit de corps* had been forged between the ranks, each officer taking a personal pride in his squad and striving to make it the best in the battalion. If Probyn had a complaint now it was that some of them had become rather too close. Guy and Louis Postgate, the viscount's sons, had been brought up to be tolerant of the shortcomings of the lower classes and to treat them fairly; but whilst Guy did not let this interfere with his role of leadership, Louis was still far too sentimental with defaulters. He might feign harshness when in the presence of his RSM but Probyn knew his true nature and, having had to overcome a trait of sentimentality himself, feared for Louis's sanity on the battlefield.

There was now little doubt amongst the troops that the eve of departure was nigh, for, at the end of June a move had been made to Quebec Barracks at Bordon, where they were finally equipped with long-range rifles and every other item required for warfare. Another agonizing month of night operations and musketry courses on Longmoor Ranges, then, a vital clue: they were issued with a small amount of precious ammunition and told this would be their final visit to the range.

'Does this mean we're going, Sarg?' an excited Private Hamm demanded of his NCO.

Probyn overheard. 'You won't be going anywhere unless you hit those bulls – and do not let me hear you use that corruptive term again – it is Serg*eant*!'

Once upon the range he was to make wider announcement. 'Poor performance from one soldier will result in the entire battalion being held back. So you had better make it good!'

There was an affiliated murmur of dismay, all eyes turning to those renowned as bad shots, issuing silent warning that there would be no forgiveness from their comrades should they cause postponement.

Firing commenced. The RSM paced the line, eyes alert for anyone missing the target; this certainly did not apply to Unthank, whose shooting was most impressive, his bullets landing so close together they almost formed one hole. Giving praise where it was due, Probyn was annoyed to receive only a grunt in return and soon moved on.

Stopping behind one inferior participant, he called out, 'Sergeant-Major Dungworth, this man's rifle appears to be faulty. Have a look at it, please!' Marching onwards, he drew immense satisfaction at not having to stop again until coming almost to the end of the line where a substantial amount of ammunition had been expended without actually having made much impact. Not usually one to tolerate incompetence, he found himself empathizing here, recalling the way he himself had yearned to be crackshot in the regiment. Bagshaw, formerly a puny youth, had built himself up through sheer effort, striving throughout the course to do his best. Though the results might not be spectacular there was nothing Probyn liked more than a trier, and in Bagshaw's desperate attempts to avoid failure he recognized a true soldier.

'Stop firing, Private Bagshaw! I think we may have another faulty rifle here. Let me have a look at it.' Affecting to rearrange the sights, he muttered, 'I'll just try it out,' and proceeded to do so, thus hitting the required number of bulls to raise Bagshaw's score, before handing it back. 'Just needed a little adjustment.'

'Thank you, sir.' A somewhat amazed Bagshaw acknowledged the favour.

Nodding curtly, Probyn glanced heavenwards as he walked away, enjoying a secret grin, imagining his friend Greatrix up there laughing at the thought of Kilmaster hitting bull's-eyes for someone else, when it had taken him years to learn how to hit anything smaller than the side of a barn.

Ecstatic that all of them had completed the musketry course, the troops were to find this only one of many bonuses, for almost immediately came the announcement that each was to receive seven days' leave, a cast-iron indication that they were about to go overseas.

Everyone was in great spirits, especially the local photographers whose bank balances were swelled by demands from the military. Probyn had already appeared in group photographs with the colonel and his warrant officers, but today he was undergoing individual portraiture, the result of which would be sent home to take centre place on the family sideboard.

Many others were assembled for this same reason, amongst them the Honourable Postgates and a group of their fellow officers. All were fully kitted out now in their second lieutenants' regalia, except for Guy, whose exceptional skills had already earned him a captaincy.

Spotting the RSM, a great deal of nudging went on, and Probyn overheard whispered exhortations – 'You go! No, I'm jolly well not risking it!' – until as a bunch they finally approached him, Louis at their head.

Politely cheerful as always, he began, 'Forgive the intrusion, Mr Kilmaster; it appears I've been appointed spokesman. My friends and I were wondering whether you'd object were we to order a copy of the photograph you've just had taken?'

It was the last thing Probyn could have expected. Seeking duplicity, he held Louis's blue eyes for a second; there was the glint of laughter in them, but then again this was a natural attribute of the young subaltern, and impish rather than malicious. Even so he remained dubious and studied each face carefully before responding.

'Dear me, gentlemen, I am quite taken aback. Had it been one of the other ranks voicing this request, I'd harbour the suspicion that he wanted it merely to throw darts at, but I know, of course, that an officer is above such barroom pursuits.'

The skin around Louis's eyes crinkled. 'I assure you we would never contemplate such an act of gross disrespect, would we, Guy?'

His brother gave rigorous confirmation, and this in turn was endorsed by the others. All seemed totally genuine.

Guy explained, 'It's simply that we'd like to show our families the man responsible for knocking us into shape. We've told them so much about you, Mr Kilmaster.'

'Oh, I'm sure you have, Captain Postgate!'

There were self-conscious grins all round but Louis was to echo his brother. 'I assure you that every word was complimentary. Truly, we owe you a great deal.' After months of adverse comment over the RSM's sadistic demands, those with any intuition had come to recognize that underneath all that browbeating was a true professional who had their best interests at heart.

Probyn experienced a swell of gratification, but as yet did not sanction their request for his photograph.

Gaylard's cupid-bow lips added his contribution. 'And may we take this opportunity of thanking you for your patience, Mr Kilmaster. We must have proved a great trial.'

'I wouldn't refute that, sir.' The RSM's mouth did not smile, but the shimmer of mischief in his eyes gave the game away and the remark provoked laughter. Undergoing a moment's contemplation, Probyn hid the fact that he was deeply touched, before voicing a dignified addendum: 'If you wish to waste your money I shall not object to you purchasing my portrait. Thank you, gentlemen.'

Encouraged, Louis went one further. 'Thank you so much, Mr Kilmaster – erm, it would be an even greater honour if you'd allow us to be photographed alongside you.'

'Now this really is a jape!' A hint of steel returned to Probyn's eye, but reassured by their vociferous denials he agreed to return with them to the photographer. However, his critical eyes had detected a flaw. 'Very well, but before accommodating you I can't bite my tongue any longer. Mr Reynard, sir, please remove that strand of lint from your uniform.'

Hurriedly casting his eyes downwards, Reynard had to hunt for some moments before spotting the offending fragment and, annoyed with himself, nipped it from his breast, his pimply face turning pink at being singled out, especially as the others all passed the RSM's muster.

'Very good. Lead the way, gentlemen!'

The normally ebullient Faljambe lagged behind to issue a confidential adjunct. 'Mr Kilmaster, might I just add my personal thanks for all your decency in the face of such thickheadedness.'

'Why, Lieutenant Faljambe, you cannot be referring to yourself?'

'Oh, I am.' Faljambe was oblivious to the sardonic edge to Probyn's voice. 'It must have seemed to you at times that I was very obtuse but I do appreciate what you were trying to drum into us. My only explanation is that it all seems so unreal. I won't feel as if I'm a genuine soldier until I come to grips with a real German on a real battlefield. I only hope I perform a little better then.' Having exposed himself to further criticism, a twitch of embarrassment played around his sandy-lashed eye.

But there was no opprobrium this time. 'We were all new soldiers once, sir. We none of us could see the point behind the constant repetition and play-acting. I'd like to be able to assure you that it will stand you in good stead when you come to face the real thing, but in truth no one can know how he'll react in the presence of danger. We can but give you the training so that when the moment arrives you won't let your comrades down. The honour of the British Army is dependent upon you.'

'I shall strive to uphold it,' came the youthful pledge.

This was getting far too intimate for the RSM's liking. 'Well, for now, Mr Faljambe, you must only strive to keep still. A tall order for you, I know, but if you'd like to choose your position . . .' Taking his own place in the midst of the group, a Postgate brother on either side of him, Lieutenants Faljambe, Gaylard, Reynard, Sillar, Geake and Stroud round about, Probyn stood magnificently erect whilst the photographer took aim.

Once the shot had been captured for posterity the group broke up, Probyn returning to his usual blunt manner. 'Well, I haven't the time to stand around here all day, gentlemen, and neither have you. I shall look forward to seeing you all again in August – assuming Mr Gaylard is able to find his way back.'

Gaylard took the joke in good part, riposting, 'You are optimistic, Mr Kilmaster. I must first find my way home.'

Whilst the others chortled, Probyn cast a cynical eye at him, then finally made to withdraw. 'Well, make the most of your time amongst your families, gentlemen. It might be the last you have for some while.'

The comment induced a bleak, inevitable jolt in his breast as he left the group chatting in gay abandon in his wake. For a few of them this might be the last leave they ever had. Having no wish to speculate on the identity of those unfortunate few amongst men he had grown to like, he banished it from his mind, looking forward instead to his own spell at home.

Even after two months' encasement in cotton wool and bandages Grace's leg had not returned to its normal size and the slightest exertion caused her discomfort. So painful was it today that she had been forced to keep Beata from school in order that the child might take Clem's dinner to the pit office. Rather this than have Augusta miss another day's education for, with so much time off, she would be ill-equipped to pass her coming scholarship exam. Thank goodness it would soon be the summer holiday.

Shortly before noon the five-year-old set off with a pudding bowl wrapped in a tea towel and headed for the pit. At this same time the children began to trickle out of school for dinner and, spotting one of her brothers, Beata called to him.

Joe came running over and, after asking where she was going, said, 'I'd better come and look after you.'

Severe thunderstorms had flattened the long grass that grew by the main road, but the weather was glorious today. Along the sunny route he pointed out the train wagons full of bombs and shells from the powder works, bound for the front. 'Boom! The Germans'll soon be blown to smithereens!' He performed a madcap cartwheel.

Clinging onto her pudding bowl, Beata grinned at his antics. 'Then will the war be over?' She hardly knew what the war was.

'Aye! Anyroad, it's almost over now. There's been thrilling dispatches from Sir John French, you know.'

Confused by this technical term, Beata padded on in silence, her brother strutting like a warrior.

In the noisy colliery yard women had taken over many of the jobs normally undertaken by men who had gone to war, their skirts sooty with coal, brawny arms grappling with tubs and harness. Joe crunched a passage through the industrious scene, Beata following, a layer of coal dust settling unnoticed upon her black boots and socks. Even before they reached the pit manager's office they could hear Clem's angry voice through the open window and glanced at each other apprehensively before proceeding. With Beata's little hands clamped to the pudding bowl, Joe whipped off his cap and opened the door for her. She had barely gone inside when an inkwell came hurtling through the air towards the man with whom Clem had been arguing and hit him smack in the chest, and the vee of white shirt above his waistcoat turned navy blue.

There was a moment's horrified silence whilst the man dashed a handkerchief over his furious, ink-spattered expression, then he snapped at Clem, 'Right, that's it, get out and don't come back – and expect to receive a bill for the damage!'

Red cheeks clashing with his auburn hair and starched white collar, Clem grabbed his jacket and strode for the door. 'Go whistle for it!'

In his angry path, Beata took a few backwards steps and, encumbered by the bowl, would have tottered had not Joe righted her. Then with nary a backwards glance the pair scampered after Clem, their boots sending up explosions of coal dust.

The younger ones, in awe of their brother's volatile temper, both hung back whilst a grim-faced Clem marched ahead. It was only when they were preparing to cross the main highway that he remembered his obligation towards them and grabbed their hands to escort them across.

'Look, there's Father!' On spotting the military figure ahead Joe pointed excitedly.

'Oh, shite!' groaned Clem, and just in time grabbed Joe's collar preventing him from dashing after Probyn. 'Hang on! You're to say nowt about me getting the sack.'

'What's the sack?' Beata squinted up at him.

Clem dropped to his hunkers and clamped her cheeks between his palms to issue explanation, looking deep into her eyes to make sure Beata knew the seriousness of this. 'I've lost me job and Father'll be mad, so you mustn't breathe a word of it or I'll get sherracked. Is that my dinner you've brought for me?' He took quick possession of her bowl and also grabbed the spoon that jutted from her pocket. 'Right, I'm off up on t'Crags to eat it. Wait till I've gone before you shout him – and don't say owt to him or Mother, either of you. Promise.'

His brother and sister vouched loyalty and waited until Clem made his getaway before pelting after their father.

Hearing their excited yells, the smiling soldier paused to wait as his children ran up the slope to meet him. There was no disappointment that he did not hug them, for the Kilmasters were not given to overt exhibitions of affection, but his love was sufficiently displayed by a warm pat of each auburn head. After telling Joe how much he had grown, Probyn surveyed Beata and merely gave a fond chuckle. With her bobbed hair, stocky limbs and eyes that appeared to have seen everything before, she resembled a little old woman.

'And what have you been up to then?' he finally asked.

'I've just taken Clem's dinner,' announced Beata. 'Mother's got a poorly leg.'

Probyn's attitude changed. With a concerned murmur he took hold of her hand and, Joe lolloping off in front, the three went home.

Grace had not been informed that her husband was coming and was overwhelmed to see him, so much so that she momentarily forgot her swollen leg and leaped from her chair, emitting a whoop both of excitement and pain. Voicing disquiet, Probyn clasped his rather untidy wife in a quick embrace, she returning his loving gaze before he deposited her back into the chair and lifted her skirt to examine the offending limb.

'Eh, what does your father think he's doing lifting ladies' petticoats?' joked Grace to her children, who giggled and tucked their chins into their chests. Pulling down her skirt she reassured him that with rest it would soon deflate. Then to distract his worried attention she said, 'I'll bet you hardly recognize this mob, do you?'

'I almost mistook Joe for Clem, he'd grown so big! And Beaty's right grown up too.' Probyn turned to greet the rest of his children. Hungry to lay eyes on them after so long, he studied each lovingly: practical and obliging Augusta with the face of an angel and a purity of spirit exuding from eyes like two tranquil lagoons; Madeleine a much plainer child but nevertheless endearing, like a studious little owl; then back to friendly, adventurous Joe, and Beata with her knowing gaze. They would all make fine people.

'Eh, and who's this big lad? It surely can't be our Duke?'

Marmaduke had been viewing the boisterous proceedings with some apprehension, and now, as the strange man loomed over him, seemingly ready to pounce, he let out a shriek, burst into tears and hoicked his plaid dress to cover his face.

Everybody laughed, Probyn too, and he beat a hasty retreat to spend the next few moments straightening a picture that was hanging crookedly.

Grace dragged her youngest son onto her lap to comfort him. 'Mims is in the drawer. Go and meet her.'

'I don't know if I dare after that response!' But smiling, Probyn approached the latest addition, now three months old, and was rewarded by a happy beam. 'Oh, you must have finally stopped churning out copperknobs.' This one had inherited her mother's light brown hair, as had Marmaduke. 'Did you say Mims?'

Grace laughed at his expression. 'Her real name was too big a mouthful for Duke and it just stuck.'

'I like it.' Probyn turned to smile at Marmaduke, but this did not seem to pacify the little boy, for he burst into tears yet again – as indeed he was to do every time Probyn so much as looked at him.

In the end this grew so tiresome that Probyn said, 'I'd best ignore him till he gets used to me. Right, is that dinner I can smell? How've you managed that with your bad leg, Gobbie?'

'I just chucked a load of veg in a pot and left it to fend for itself so I don't know if it'll be up to much.' Grace tried to rise but winced.

'Bide there!' commanded her husband. An old hand in the kitchen, he took charge of the stewpot and delivered a plateful to Grace before ordering the children to the table where all were to enjoy a happy reunion meal until it was time to go back to school.

Even in their absence there was little chance of husband and wife becoming more intimate, for every time Probyn so much as leaned towards Grace young Marmaduke set up a terrified wail. And as if this were not irritating enough, there came a constant stream of visitors throughout the afternoon: Fanny Gentle, Mr Rushton the colliery policeman and his wife, and a host of others, amongst them Father Flanagan, who arrived just as the children returned from school.

''Tis only meself!'

Grace was first to respond. 'Sorry for not getting up, Father, but –'

'No need, Grace! The leg bothering you again? Get a wooden one, it'll be less trouble. Sit yourself there. I just came to see your man here. Probe, how are you?' He came forth to join in a brisk display of handshaking with the soldier. 'Heard you were back and came to pay my respects.'

'Eh, they don't waste any time broadcasting things round here!' joked Probyn, not so relaxed as his wife in the priest's company. 'I've only been back a couple of hours and we've had half the village in already.'

'Ah, you can't keep any secrets here 'tis true, especially when the subject is so illustrious. My, would you look at the cut of him, Grace! With such a man in charge the war will be won in no time at all.'

Grace invited Father Flanagan to partake of tea with them. 'We're just waiting for Clem,' she explained as the girls laid the table. 'He should be here any time.' And they chatted for a while, the children gathering round them to listen in respectful silence.

During a lull, with her father in so liberal a mood, Beata shuffled up to put the question she had been itching to ask for so long. 'Father, may I ask something?' Permission was granted. 'Why do you call Mother Gobbie?'

'Because she's got such a mouth on her.' Probyn chuckled and moved his head aside as Grace reached out to swipe him with a rolled-up newspaper.

It was left to Mother to explain. 'My initials before I married your father were GOB. I had them embroidered on my apron the first time we met and he's been calling me that ever since, the cheeky monkey.'

At this juncture, the missing constituent arrived, Clem glancing rather apprehensively at Joe and Beata before perceiving that his dismissal remained a secret for now.

Probyn stood to greet his eldest son, who, apart from the auburn hair, was totally unlike him in appearance, the hooded blue eyes inherited from his mother, the wiry build, narrow chest and long face with its eagle's beak from heaven knew where. But the differences were superficial – there was great affection between the pair and they joined in a loving handshake, before everyone assembled round the table for tea.

The priest stayed for two hours, joining the audience whilst Clem, as was his habit, read aloud from the daily newspaper of British glory at Ypres, singling out chronicles headed 'Yorkshire Bravery at the Front', a common banner in this local gazette. Tonight his recital had the bonus of postponing the moment of confession.

There was talk too about the proposed conscription. 'What's your view on it, Probe?' enquired Father Flanagan, accepting a Woodbine and inserting it under his sharp nose.

'It's sure to come, but I hate the thought of press-ganging.' The military man leaned towards God's servant with a lighted match. 'If a man has to be dragged there he's no good to me.'

'I'd go if they let me,' volunteered Clem.

Though proud of such a son, Probyn gave warning as he put flame to his own cigarette. 'Just so long as you don't try and enlist until you're old enough.' As a boy he himself had run away from home to such a purpose.

Had Clem known this he perhaps would not have nodded so compliantly.

'I'm joining too when I'm old enough,' announced Joe, and wondered why this made them laugh when they hadn't ridiculed Clem.

Flanagan's long upper lip clamped on the cigarette as he took a long drag. 'Grace tells me your skills are used only for training others these days, Probe. Bet you're glad not to be in the thick of it.'

'Well, I shall be going with the lads to France, but I'll be well away from the fighting.' This untruth was for Grace's benefit.

'That's good.' Father Flanagan nodded. 'You earned your medals in that shenanigans with the Boers. We want you back in one piece.'

This led them on to a discussion of General Botha's great military achievement in capturing Windhoek, which practically meant the complete possession of German South West Africa. The Kaiser's dream of extending his power over that part of the world had been well and truly quashed. 'Yes, it's forced me to eat my words,' admitted Probyn, taking a narrow-eyed drag. 'I never for the life of me expected such loyalty from the Boers – never once doubted their bravery mindst, they were a tough opponent for us – but not in a hundred years did I expect them to rally to the British throne. I feel odd even saying it, but good old Botha and Smuts have done a magnificent job.' Behind the sentiment lay an even greater sense of relief that, despite the efforts of a handful of Nationalists, the Empire he knew and cherished had not fallen apart as he had feared when the Boers had been granted self-government.

Grace remarked that all over the globe others were rallying to Mother Empire's defence. 'It said in the paper that some Australians walked three hundred miles to enlist! They're almost ready to take the enemy position in the Dardan –'

'And there's them Indian fellas with the bandaged heads an' all!' piped up an excited Joe, then shrank as his father's stern eye castigated him for interrupting his mother, whilst Grace merely exclaimed, 'Oh yes! And the Canadians and New Zealanders. And who would've thought the Russians would be fighting on our side? It doesn't seem five minutes ago they were sinking English trawlers. They're doing a splendid job in Poland, by all accounts.'

Probyn was not so gullible as to depend on newspaper stories, for he knew what they could disguise, but he was gratified by the total co-operation of their allies and paid them quiet tribute. 'Yes, everyone's doing admirably.'

'Pity the same can't be said for the Americans,' interjected Father Flanagan. 'All they do is whine about our blockade interfering with their business. You would think they'd see the policy is totally justified after all the German outrages, especially after the *Lusitania* with so many of their own people on board.'

Considering that liberal attitudes were being applied tonight, her siblings having been allowed their say, Augusta added her view. 'I think it's awful that the poor Belgians are starving and the Germans are refusing to feed them.'

'Well, what else do you expect from the murdering Hun?' muttered Clem, annoyed not at his sister but at the enemy's lack of compassion.

'I think these children have been indulged enough, Mother!' decided Probyn abruptly, and in a muttered aside to Grace he added, 'Best not let them read too many newspapers, it's not healthy.'

'Well, it's away home for me!' With stick-like arms, Father Flanagan pushed himself upwards, his host rising with him.

Grace spoke from her chair. 'Have another cup of tea before you go, Father.'

Feeling the urge for something stronger and knowing he would not get it in this household, the priest demurred.

Probyn's back was turned as he went to open the door. With a quick rummage in her pocket, Grace reached out to the priest, affecting to shake his hand, but in reality pressing threepence into his grip, her face instructing him not to thank her. Tapping his nose in confidential manner, he smiled and mouthed, 'God love ye,' before dropping the coin in his pocket.

'Oh, we'd better arrange Mims' christening now that Probyn's home,' remembered Grace.

'If you're sure you can get to church?' With Grace's assurance that she would be fine enough by Sunday Father Flanagan said he would expect them, calling as he left, 'God bless all!'

With Augusta and Maddie attending to the washing-up, Probyn relaxed into his chair with a deep sigh of pleasure. As eager as her husband for the two of them to be alone, Grace told the younger ones to get ready for bed whilst she herself fed the baby and settled her into the makeshift crib. But barely had the children changed into their nightgowns and said their prayers at Mother's knee when another knock came at the door.

Just about to unlace his boots, Probyn let out a groan. 'Oh, who is it now come to disturb us? We'll have the blinkin' colliery band trooping through the kitchen next.'

He opened the door to reveal the pit manager.

The man's lower jaw fell at the sight of his former weighman. 'Probyn! I hadn't heard you were home.'

'You must be the only one who hasn't. Come in, Mr Shaw, sir.'

The smartly dressed man did so, removing his bowler. 'I really came to see Mrs Kilmaster. I knew she'd be worrying and I just came to say the maid managed to get the ink out of the shirt so there's no need . . .'

Probyn had stopped listening. Catching the look of guilt that was fast spreading over Clem's face, his attitude was now one of suspicion. 'I'm sorry, Mr Shaw, I think I'm lacking some information here.'

The pit manager noted a subdued Clem. 'Yes, I can see your boy hasn't told you.' He came straight to the point, his brief account of the incident drawing gasps of horror from the parents. 'I'm afraid I had no option but to dismiss him. Apart from being extremely disrespectful he could have inflicted serious injury with that inkwell. I warned him to expect a bill for the damage but, as I just said, the girl managed to get the ink out of my shirt and, knowing how Mrs Kilmaster would be worrying about the added expense, I thought I'd just come and put her mind at rest.'

'That's very considerate of you, Mr Shaw,' replied a deeply humiliated Grace. 'I'm so sorry you've been put to such inconvenience, not to mention *rudeness*.' She glared at her son, who hung his fiery head in shame.

Clem was then made to voice repentance.

With further profuse apology from the youth's parents, the manager appeared mollified. Indeed, the embarrassment of these courteous people seemed to infect him too and after unnecessary inspection of his gold pocket watch he replaced it in his waistcoat and turned briskly to go. 'Apology accepted – of course that doesn't mean I'll take him back.'

'I wouldn't expect you to,' replied Probyn with dignity. 'Don't you worry, sir, he'll be dealt with.' On this ominous note he closed the door.

Grace had already started ordering the children up to bed.

His face dark with intent, Probyn confronted his son. 'In the yard!'

Following the direction of the pointed finger, Clem slunk past his father into the evening sunshine.

The onslaught began. 'If this is your idea of how to be man of the house whilst I'm away then you can bally-well think again! Well? What have you to say for yourself?'

There was no excuse, just a nervous murmur. 'Sorry, Father.'

'Sorry? Sorry doesn't butter any bread! How's your poor mother to manage without your wage? You're hardly likely to get a decent job without a reference! And before you get any more big ideas you can forget all about joining the army. They want disciplined men, not silly little boys with a vile temper such as you've got! What set it off this time?'

Clem felt sick. 'He passed –'

'*He?*' boomed Probyn. 'Who's he?'

'Mr Shaw passed a rude remark on my handwriting and he said I had to work overtime to write it all out again. He's been going on at me over one thing or another for months now and I'd just had enough.'

'Had *enough*?' came the astounded roar. 'You don't know you're born! Do you see me throwing tantrums because I haven't had a day at home since last year? Do you?'

'No, Father.' It was rare for Clem to hear such a raised voice, his father normally a placid man.

'No! And I'd have every justification because I've fought damned hard to achieve the rank I hold now – unlike you, who are a

63

mere lackey! You hear that? A lackey, the lowest of the low until you've earned the right to be anything else. So if I *ever* hear so much as a peep that you've shown disrespect to your superiors – whether you regard them as such is immaterial, they *are* your superiors – then, by God, your feet won't touch the ground! Is that understood?'

'Yes, Father.' A rapid nod.

'Good! Now, until the time when you're able to earn your keep once again we must consider you a child and you'll be treated like one. Get up them stairs with the others now!'

Grace bit her lip as her son hurried aloft to the bedroom he shared with his brothers and sisters.

Probyn let out a noisy sigh, angry and upset at being so let down. 'What a homecoming!'

His wife limped over to him and rubbed his arm in a gesture of support.

After a moment of head-shaking and sighing, he became pensive. 'You don't think I was too hard on him?'

She let out a negating chuckle.

'No, I mean it.' Anxiety paid an infrequent visit to his strong features. 'The look on his face when I called him a lackey . . .' He would hate his son to regard him in the manner of one of his recruits, a mixture of fear and loathing.

Smiling, Grace reassured him. 'No! He wants teaching. He's been getting too big for his boots while you've been away.'

'I don't know who he gets it off.' He heaved another sigh. 'Ah dear, I suppose this means I'll be trailing round all day tomorrow looking for somebody to take him on – Oy, what are you doing standing up? You're meant to be resting that leg!' Enveloping her in a beefy embrace he lowered her back into the chair.

'Eh, anyone'd think I was an invalid!' complained his much younger wife – she was only thirty-four. But as he bent over her, Grace trapped his big bristly head between her palms and kissed his whiskered lips.

He returned her kiss with ardour, before asking, 'Shall I make us some cocoa?'

Grace cocked her head. 'You've been away for the best part of a year and you're asking me if I want cocoa?'

He laughed and, under that seductive blue gaze, became even more fervent. 'But what about your leg?'

'Bugger that.' She gave an affectionate snicker at his look of admonishment for the swear word, then glanced at the clock.

'Still, it is only half-past seven. Best give the children time to get to sleep first.'

Calling her a spoilsport he made do with a mug of cocoa. But it was not long before his eyes were moving to the staircase again and at his latest gesture she laughingly acquiesced.

Sandwiched in a narrow iron bedstead alongside two smaller bodies, Clem lay awake listening as his parents creaked their way up the staircase. All went quiet for a while, the only sound to be heard his little brothers' peaceful breathing and that of his sisters in the bed on the other side of the draped clothes-horse, which divided the room. Then his ears pricked as a rhythmic sawing of bed springs heralded marital reunion and, slightly embarrassed, he turned over, pressing his head into the pillow, covering his other ear with a palm. Ashamed and sorry for causing such upset on his father's homecoming, he questioned his inability to control his temper. And determined as he was to try and curb it in future, he feared it would rear its ugly head over and again.

The next day after breakfast, leaving the little girls to squeal over the beetles that had been hiding under their damp wash flannels in the scullery, Probyn accompanied his son into Mexborough to help him find work.

When they returned Grace was pleased to note that the tension between husband and son had lifted. Clem even mustered a smile as he told his mother that he would be starting a new job on Monday. It was nothing special – the position of junior clerk in an office – but was more than he deserved.

'I was considering visiting Mr Kaiser to ask if he had any work for the lad,' said Probyn, 'but I noticed his shop was closed. Clem told me about the trouble.'

'He did reopen but when that Zepp killed all those people in Hull they had another go at him – just an excuse for violence if you ask me. Anyway, he's decided to stay closed for now. Poor man, I do feel sorry for him. He went to court to try and claim compensation for the damage, and apparently he needed to provide his naturalization certificate. He didn't have one so they fined him five pounds.'

Probyn threw up his eyes. 'I suppose that's the end of my favourite pork pies then.'

'You're so altruistic,' teased Grace. 'Oh, by the way, I got Maddie to post the letters to my sisters and Charlotte about the christening.'

'You're sure you'll be able to make it to church by then?'

'Look!' Grace lifted her skirt to reveal a leg much reduced, the strap of her shoe once more meeting the buckle. 'It's gone right down overnight.' Her hooded blue eyes twinkled.

Enjoying the memory of last night too, Probyn did not of course make reference to it with their son in the room. 'Best keep resting it as much as you can. Did you send Aunt Kit an invitation?'

'Yes, though I don't suppose any of them will come.'

She was to be right in the main about this; apart from Charlotte, only sister Millie and her husband were to witness Mims' baptism, turning up mainly in honour of the namesake, for it was a fair distance to travel from York.

Though still encumbered by a limp, Grace looked quite elegant that Sunday in a long flared skirt and white yoked blouse with a gold crucifix, her brown hair pinned up in glossy coils. Starved of female affection for the last nine months Probyn found it hard to keep impure thoughts from obscuring the holiness of the occasion and tried instead to focus on Mims, who looked most comically cute in a boy's cap with a veil that had been brought out of tissue paper at various intervals since Clem had worn it fifteen years ago.

Joyous days amongst his family were to follow. The children now off school for the summer, they went for the occasional outing, Grace's leg permitting, and their evenings were dedicated to games of housey and patriotic songs around the piano that Father had bought Mother before the war. It was a lovely, lovely time . . . and yet, the newspaper forbade complacency, its pages warning of a fresh crisis in Poland. The Russians still held Warsaw but the Hun was getting perilously close to smashing a way through. Were their sacrifices of the last year to be in vain?

'Good heavens, a year ago today it started,' murmured Probyn, perusing the gazette whilst his children washed and dressed on what was his last morning of leave.

'What did, dear?' Folding her husband's shirts ready for packing, Grace sounded distracted.

'The war! Where have you been, missus?'

With a mound of household chores still to be done and seven children to look after, it was sometimes easy to forget. 'Sorry, I've been trying not to think about it.' The week had seemed to fly past as it always did when her husband was on leave. He would soon be getting on a train and Grace did not know when she would see him again.

Probyn gave what he hoped was a reassuring smile.

Joe emerged from the scullery, his face pink and clean, russet hair neatly slicked down with water. 'The Australians have taken the Turks' position at Gapil – Gallipoli.'

'Oh yes, Mr War Correspondent, and how do you know that?' asked his father, casting an amused look at his wife.

'It's in big writing in the paper – Why have you chopped the ends off your tash, Father?'

Disconcerted, Probyn fingered the moustache that he had trimmed right back, knowing from experience that there was no way he could keep it neatly waxed on the battlefront. 'Your mother complained it was tickling her.'

This appeared to satisfy Joe and he went about his business.

Beata came in. 'I had six blackclocks hiding under my flannel. I killed two but t'others ran away.'

Probyn merely chuckled. Catching his wife's gaze, he locked eyes with her for a wistful moment, before returning to his newspaper, Grace to her folding. But no amount of occupation could take their minds off the coming farewell. It was perhaps worse for having to be done in stages; he had been forced to issue a separate goodbye to Clem before the boy went off to work this morning. Weighing his words, Probyn had tried to make amends for his belittlement over Clem's sacking; lackey was not a tag to hang on one's son and Clem had behaved impeccably during the last week. Nevertheless, a degree of warning laced his parting sentiment: he knew Clem would not let him down and he expected to hear only good things about him in his mother's letters.

The moment all had been dreading finally arrived. With his valise packed, Probyn gave last-minute instructions to the children. 'You'll notice I've put up new Battalion Orders.' This was a list of household chores he had devised years ago, each child making daily contribution. It had been revised, he explained, to include Beata who, due to her recent birthday, was old enough now to take her turn.

'But she can't read,' protested Maddie.

'Then you'll have to relay the information.' Probyn patted her head. 'Think you can manage to wash the windowsills, Beat?' Her eager nod gained praise. 'Good girl. That'll be your job for today when you get back from seeing me off. Right, fall in!'

At his father's brusque tone, Marmaduke started to cry as he had done throughout Probyn's stay. The latter was unable to suppress a groan.

'Have you put him on Battalion Orders, Father?' teased Joe,

peering from beneath the neb of his man's cap, which was far too large.

Probyn gave a mischievous tug of his son's hat, pulling it down over his nose. 'No, I think we'll just send Mameluke down the salt mines and have done with it.' With the rest mustered for inspection, his keen blue-grey eyes perused the row of little figures, most in white pinafores and black stockings. Looking at their uplifted innocent faces, he could have wept.

Then, with a swift 'Carry on!' they were away.

Owing to Grace's impediment, it took longer to reach the small station and the train was already straining to go when they arrived, its glossy black engine working up a cloud of steam. Planting quick kisses, Probyn got immediately on board, then leaned out of the open window to maintain his link with home. Other soldiers were catching the train too, their families handing over last-minute gifts of cigarettes and chocolate.

Leaning on a walking stick, Grace put a hand to her lips. 'Oh no, I didn't get you anything . . .'

He replied warmly, 'Doesn't matter, I've plenty of fags.' Funny, the things that jumped into your mind, thought Probyn, picturing another departure many years ago when his awkward, undemonstrative father, unable to show his love, had instead shoved a box of his favourite sweets into his haversack. *God, I hate all this waiting.*

His prayers for the train to depart were answered by a shrill whistle.

'There it is. We're off! Take care! Write to me! I will! Byebye! 'Bye!'

Amid a great sobbing and chugging and belching of smoke the train eased its way from the station, Grace and the children moving alongside Probyn's carriage until it became impossible to keep up, whence they stood amidst the crowd and set up a frantic waving. Craning his neck from the carriage window, Probyn looked back at the sea of fluttering hands, trying to focus on his own straining throng until they became indistinguishable from the rest.

The train receded into the distance and a silence fell. Left with but a whiff of acrid smoke, the mass of women and children on the platform became all at once forlorn. Trying to remain cheerful for the children's sake, Grace said they would buy some sweets on the way home. It took every ounce of willpower not to cry.

FIVE

Probyn had been gone only a couple of days when the chilling report came that Warsaw had fallen and an urgent appeal for more recruits was sent out. Hence, Bank Holiday Monday was spent in an abnormal state of tension, no one save the very young in the mood to be gay, particularly as hostile airships chose that time to revisit the east coast. There would be no building of sandcastles this year.

The valiant recapture of trenches at Hooge was but a temporary remission. This war was definitely far from over.

If members of the public were not encouraged by these tidings, others were, and none so glad as the young officers and men of Probyn's battalion, for it meant that they were sure to have a good old bash at the Hun before things fizzled out.

But when? They were almost halfway through August now and still only play-fighting – though not infrequently an air of reality was lent to the combat as the boiling hot weather and an impatience to be off caused tempers to erupt.

Then, at last, came the long-awaited announcement: the battalion had a week's notice to prepare itself for embarkation. The atmosphere in the barracks was electric, its occupants being even more thrilled on hearing that there was to be precursory inspection by the Sovereign. No one objected to spit and polish now! No grumbles to be heard over cleaning a hundred items of equipment that they would probably never use, each beavering to make himself a glittering example in honour of His Majesty.

Those in command were suitably proud too. 'Well, this is it, RSM.' Prior to the review Colonel Addison shook Probyn's hand warmly.

'You've given us a battalion of which to be proud. The adjutant and I are deeply indebted to you.'

The adjutant underwent a similar gesture. 'Most definitely, and may I convey my own admiration on a superb feat, Mr Kilmaster.'

Though such accolade was manna to one who thrived on adulation, Probyn was obliged to display modesty. 'Thank you very much, sir, but I didn't do it alone.'

'Yes, and we are most beholden to our NCOs too,' came the gracious addition from his commanding officer. 'Please extend our warmest thanks and congratulations. Although I shall, of course, be addressing everyone later, I just wanted to take this opportunity to convey my personal gratitude to you for your own most substantial part.'

'It's very much appreciated, Colonel, sir. May I say it's been a privilege to train such willing young men, truly wonderful.' It was no lie. Living with them through their struggles, Probyn had become enormously fond of the volunteers. 'I've trained a few in my time but a finer bunch of soldiers doesn't exist.'

'Yes, let the critics of the New Army eat their words,' announced the adjutant.

'Hear hear,' breezed the colonel. 'But our work is yet ahead.' Smiling, he gathered his reins and prepared to mount his grey. 'Come, gentlemen, let us go display the results of our endeavours before His Majesty. Then on to the real job!'

Such laudation giving briskness to his step, Probyn went directly to convey the officers' praise to his CSMs and sergeants, adding his own heartfelt acknowledgement. 'They said it couldn't be done but we've managed it, lads, we've turned a sow's ear into a silk purse. Look at them,' he ran his eyes over the troops assembled in full regalia, 'drink in that sight and give yourself a pat on the back. You've done a grand job. Well done.'

Given little time to savour the praise, the recipients were soon off and marching alongside the battalion they had helped to create, sweat beginning to flow almost immediately under the blazing August sun.

Having finally assembled them amongst the vast columns of the 23rd Division, waiting for the King to arrive, Probyn strode up and down the ranks, his eyes keener than ever for a pinprick of rust upon a weapon, a speck of mud or a tarnished button, occasionally tugging a man's hat to comply with regulations, yet finding nothing overtly slapdash. They had certainly pulled out all the stops today. Even Unthank seemed eager to pay his respects to the Monarch.

Gratified, Probyn issued one last reminder. 'Keep wriggling your toes, lads, it'll help to pump the blood.'

He marched off to take up his own position, snatched a quick inspection of the overall view – a stupendous array of weaponry, horses and warriors – before settling down to wait. But his eyes never rested, constantly flitting over the ranks, ready to quell the slightest hint that boredom had set in.

The sun rose higher over the vast acres of men; thousand upon thousand of blushing faces, turning ever more pink as the minutes ticked by, those who had been here longest a dangerous shade of red. Beads of sweat oozed from each forehead, meandering in a steady, stinging trickle around the eye sockets and along the side of the nose to drip, drip, drip from each chin.

Probyn shared their suffering, his own vision blurred by a curtain of brine. One could smell the heat. Whilst others began to topple like skittles, he fought to stay erect, concentrating on his men, some of whom were beginning to sway in ominous manner, willing them with his piercing gaze to remain stalwart. The air became almost too thick to breathe. Too hot to sing, the birds had taken refuge in the leafy shade. Naught was to be heard save the creak of leather as an officer shifted sweaty buttocks in his saddle, the jingling of harness from wilting horses, the thud of another man hitting the ground. The sky bore down on all, an electric blue, the only clouds being those of troublesome flies who buzzed around the twitching rumps of chestnut and grey, pathetic docked tails flicking in vain to remove them.

Probyn saw it about to happen but could not move quickly enough to stop it. Staring vividly from a face the shade of magenta, Captain Guy Postgate's pale grey eyes suddenly turned from a state of desperation to one of unconsciousness as they rolled up into his skull and he fell back, landing on the bayonet of the man at ease behind him. At the spurt of crimson from his neck there followed a murmur of panic amongst his fellows, some jumping away.

'Steady! Steady,' came the gruff warning from their RSM, who had deftly stepped in to minimize the calamity and immediately they moved back into place.

But their eyes kept darting to the gash in the young captain's neck, reacting with mute horror to the runnels of blood fast congealing under the hot sun, as if suddenly made aware how inauspiciously could their own lives ebb away. With unobtrusive authority Probyn summoned two RAMC men, conveniently parading nearby with their equipment, to remove the unconscious officer from the field, and in no time at all he had the battalion to attention as if nothing had occurred, which was extremely fortunate, for the King and Queen Mary chose that moment to arrive.

The appearance of the royal pair instantly revived flagging spirits, poor Captain Postgate temporarily forgotten. Probyn's loyal heart throbbed with devotion as, disdainful of the blazing sun, the Monarch rode patiently around each unit of the entire Division taking a keen interest in every one. God bless him, he was always there when his subjects needed him.

Following the parade, one of RSM Kilmaster's first acts was to enquire as to the seriousness of Captain Postgate's injury and, upon being informed that despite the sunstroke and loss of blood Guy was in no danger of expiry, he was much relieved.

But with the additional information that the young officer would not recover in time to travel to France, and imagining his bitter disappointment, Probyn felt obligated to visit the hospital and offer his condolences.

The sight of Louis Postgate at his brother's bedside temporarily stalled Probyn's approach, though when Guy noticed his entry to the ward and made an anaemic but welcoming signal, he proceeded forth.

Advancing upon the bed, he overheard Louis's murmured sincerity. 'I feel wretched for you, Guy. You know that if there was any way I could make them send you in my stead I would.'

Fighting his depression, the bandaged invalid nodded in appreciation of his brother's words. 'Oh, it's just such dashed bad luck.'

They clasped hands, then Louis made to leave. 'I'll return later.'

Probyn was quick to deter him. 'Don't go on my account, Lieutenant Postgate. I'm merely here to enquire after the captain's health. I shall intrude but a few moments.'

'Please don't consider it an intrusion, Mr Kilmaster.' Louis's baby-blue gaze held esteem. 'And, thank you, I will stay if you don't object. Guy is rather low at being unable to accompany us.'

Probyn interpreted the flicker of annoyance on the young captain's face at this reminder from his brother: considering himself the superior soldier, Guy was absolutely livid that he had been the one to faint. 'Keep your chin up, sir. They're sending batches over every week; you're sure to be amongst one of them. May I ask what's the prognosis for your injury?'

The pale grey eyes were despondent. 'Apparently it'll take a good few months to get the muscle back into working order. With the luck I'm having it could all be over by then.'

Probyn was momentarily grim. 'I doubt that very much, sir.' Then he brightened. 'And once you're out of this hospital bed and exercising your way back to fitness the days will fly past. Before you know it I'll be back here putting you through more paces.'

Guy made a weak joke. 'Ah well, that is something to look forward to.'

'I knew you'd appreciate that, sir.' His face creased in a rare smile, Probyn reached for the limp hand upon the bed sheet and grasped it, trying to restore sanguinity to those tragic features. 'Never fear, Captain Postgate, you'll be back amongst us in no time, and until then you'll be with us in spirit. Well, goodbye, sir, all the best.' With a quick adieu to the brother, Probyn marched away, too quickly to overhear Louis's softly uttered sentiment.

'What a compliment him coming to see you. He really is a splendid old chap, isn't he?'

From the wan face on the pillow came half-hearted agreement. 'It's absolute hell not to be going, but at least I feel secure knowing he'll be there to look after my little brother.'

Hurt by this slur on his manhood, Louis fought the inclination to retaliate, deciding that it was punishment enough for one so ambitious to be excluded from the adventure. To cover his annoyance, he dipped into his tunic and withdrew the photograph of Probyn, which many fellow officers had acquired. 'I don't suppose you've got yours to hand so I shall leave this here and the RSM can watch over you whilst I'm away.' Ignoring Guy's objections he propped it against a jug of water. 'There you are, a guardian angel.'

Though the mouth smiled the reply was far from gracious. 'It's you who needs the guardian angel. Just remember to keep your mind on your responsibilities. You're there to fight, not to quaff wine with the mademoiselles – and do take that blessed photo; it'll only get wet next to the water jug. Besides, I thought you intended to carry it as a talisman?'

'Don't need it when I'll have the real thing.' Louis censured himself for being unable to resist the barb, though as he left the ward a grin of one-upmanship played around his lips.

Two days after the King's inspection, news came that the British transport ship *Royal Edward* had been torpedoed by an enemy submarine with the loss of a thousand lives. Such dastardly deeds were occurring quite regularly now: their vessel grounded in Danish waters, the helpless crew of the E13 were mercilessly picked off like ducks, a White Star Liner, *Arabic*, torpedoed and sunk with more loss of life. Yet even pushed so far the Americans still offered no more than angry words, leaving any retaliation to the Allies; and retaliate they surely did, an angry swarm of British aeroplanes descending on German positions to inflict huge losses and extend a new British line on the Western Front.

In English streets such valour was re-enacted by a million small boys. Bereft of an aircraft, Joe Kilmaster performed the next best thing: arms outstretched he ran zooming round his mother as she chatted to Fanny Gentle and Mrs Rushton in the evening sunshine, interspersing his engine noises with sporadic gunfire, dipping and weaving about imaginary skies.

A bomb exploded. Grace broke off the conversation to chastise her son. 'Joseph, we're trying to speak! Go play down there with the other hooligans.' The boy roared off along the terrace, leaving the three women to their gossip.

There was much to discuss, for the weekend had witnessed new developments. Not only had Italy declared war on the Turks, but there had come the decision of Britain and France to place cotton in the category of absolute contraband, so upsetting the United States. 'I can't see why they're chuntering,' objected Grace. 'It's nothing compared to what the Germans have done to them. Well, all right they might have a genuine grievance – but for heaven's sake we've waited a year before putting this embargo on. How can you have an effective blockade if you've got to let certain people through? Maybe now they won't waste any more time in idle chitchat with the enemy and help us get this damned war over with.'

They spoke disparagingly about the recent food riots in Germany for a while, until Grace glanced down the street and saw her daughter coming along it with a newspaper bundle. 'Oh, here's our Gussie and I haven't even warmed the plates.'

Augusta arrived. 'I didn't have enough money so I could only afford four fish, but I've made it up with extra chips.'

Grace frowned. 'But I gave you a florin.'

'Cod's gone up to fourpence.'

'My God! It'll be classed as a luxury import soon,' exclaimed Grace with an outraged look at her neighbours. Steering Augusta inside, she instructed, 'Divide it between the rest of you, I'll just have chips. I'm not really hungry.'

Fanny shared her disgust. 'What were we just saying about food riots in Germany? They'll be having them here if they aren't careful!'

Grace roundly condemned the Hun for robbing them of their tea. 'They sit there lurking in their blasted submarines, too cowardly to come out and face our navy but instead firing at trawlers and anything else that comes into their sights . . .'

All at once remembering that very soon her husband would be venturing into those dangerous waters, Grace felt the sun eclipsed by an awful chill of fear and she crossed herself swiftly, before saying goodbye to her friends and heading indoors.

The recurrent sinkings also provided sober thought amongst those about to embark themselves. Knowing that Grace would be frantic about his own imminent voyage, Probyn snatched a moment to pencil a brief joky letter to her, before being dragged back to the business of coping with soldiers chafing to be off.

Towards the end of August, on another boiling hot summer's day, the 9th York and Lancasters finally departed Quebec Barracks, marching in files along a road clogged with dust, bound for Liphook. With nary a drop consumed, the mood was extremely merry. Louis Postgate, sympathetic as he might feel towards his brother, was totally intoxicated by the thought that after a nine-month slog they were deemed to be proper soldiers and were finally embarking on their great adventure. Foxy Reynard and Hugh Faljambe, Gaylard, Sillar, Geake – even the dour troublemaker Unthank singing his heart out with the rest – warriors all.

The sun was still shining by the time the battalion reached the station, though its glare was much tempered. A crowd of friends had gathered to shower everyone with sweets, packets of tea, coffee and cigarettes. Someone grabbed Probyn's hand and shook it ardently. Unfazed by such demonstration from a complete stranger, he smiled politely, his jaw beginning to ache as the hand was replaced by another and another and many more, until a loud hailer ordered everyone to their carriages.

In civilian life an unhurried soul, Probyn would have derived much pleasure from watching the bevy of female figures in circulation. Today as supreme organizer, he concentrated only on getting the men aboard, demanding excellence. Averse to the stuffy, sun-warmed moquette of the interior, the squaddies hung out of the windows, looking for pretty girls to engage in conversation. Hearts were pledged, promises were made to write, words that would normally never have passed a soldier's lips were issued freely by those going off to battle.

Alerted by an ear-splitting whistle, the crowd moved as one in a last-minute surge to the windows to grasp hands and wish the Tommies luck. Then, to deafening cheers and waving of Union Jacks, the train steamed out of the station.

On arrival at Folkestone they embarked immediately. Giving the order for everyone to put on lifebelts, Probyn donned his own, then took out his watch and underwent a few moments' reverie in the balmy evening. It was nine thirty. The children would be in bed. Grace too would be almost ready to go up, perhaps sipping the last of her cocoa and thinking of him.

A more romantic summer's night one could not ask for, the few lamps that were ignited on the coast playing like stars upon the inky rippling waters. Probyn watched them shrink to pinpricks as the ship steamed further out to sea, soon to be engulfed in a cloak of midnight blue.

'Truly magnificent!' Lieutenants Faljambe and Postgate had come to share the view with Probyn. 'All it requires is a cigarette and I'd be in heaven.' Owing to the rumoured presence of German submarines, the crossing was to be undertaken in darkness, even the glow of a match forbidden.

Gasping for a smoke, the RSM gave a murmur of empathy, though added wise advice. 'I understand your excitement, Lieutenant Faljambe, but it might pay to keep that foghorn down.'

'Oh, was I shouting?'

'You were, sir. Noise carries a long way upon water.'

Peeved to be toppled from his pedestal of fully fledged warrior, Faljambe gave stiff apology and, lest this killjoy dampen any more of their enthusiasm, he and Louis excused themselves and moved away.

Escorted by two black silhouettes that sliced their way through the murky current, the ship reached Boulogne just after eleven, anchoring amongst several other vessels outside the harbour. Whipped to higher excitement by the fleets of French and English destroyers shifting around them all the time, the men were barely containable by the time the pilot led them in.

Upon disembarkation they were ordered to march, but only for a mile and a half to a large shed where they were joined by masses of others. The whole world seemed comprised of khaki.

Breakfasting at Ostrohove rest camp, they were to remain there throughout that day, acclimatizing themselves to French soil. Evening saw them once more putting their boot leather to the test, at the end of their hike entraining for Audruicq in the late afternoon, their mode of travel provoking much disgust.

'We come to save their skins,' ejaculated Private Rawmarsh to vociferous agreement from his comrades, 'and they stick us in trucks meant for bloody animals!'

But, eager to get to the front, well drilled by their sergeants and watched over by RSM Kilmaster's steely eyes, the troops complied with alacrity, the whole battalion transferred from platform to train in record time.

At the other end of the track, the machine-gunners branched off for Wizemes; the rest were to spank the roads again.

'Now I appreciate the reason for all that route marching at home,' announced Louis to his peers, though it was not issued as a complaint for after so much excellent training their bodies were honed to withstand any test.

Nevertheless, Lieutenant Reynard managed to look hard done by, wincing under the burden of his equipment. To drown his moans, Louis formed his lips into a whistle, the men soon joining in as they tramped jauntily along the pavé.

'Look at these old buggers, Pork!' An amused Private Hamm indicated the column of men who were plodding towards them, covered from head to toe in dust, their expressions quietly reflective.

'No wonder they need us here,' opined his friend, whose name was actually Porks but since they were almost inseparable and had become known as Pork and Hamm, no one ever remembered to add the S. 'They must be off to draw their pensions!'

Overhearing, a sergeant commanded them to cease the derogatory remarks as the two columns marched past each other. Probyn, who had heard it all before, remained silent. It was no use trying to explain to these carefree boys that in a few months on the battlefront they would look similarly worn out. Instead, he merely shared a look of understanding with the commander of the other unit, before proceeding with his own buoyant troops on the road to Nordausques.

Whilst no surprise to Probyn, it came as anti-climax to his

whistling, singing band that on arrival here they were not to join in any real battle but were to undergo a further two weeks of training. However, once the groans had died away they were alerted to the sound of gunfire in the distance, and suddenly their play-acting was given a sense of purpose.

Their RSM began to note a change in their attitude, an air of apprehension, the cocky ones unusually reticent. Though Probyn did all he could to bolster them, his words of encouragement were overshadowed by the horrors of war that had begun to creep upon the scene: bloated corpses of black-and-white cows burst open like overripe pods, emitting a stench that made some physically sick; the bomb-ravaged homes; the queue of wounded outside a dressing station; crimson seeping through hastily applied bandages; but much worse, the mangled remains of a human being awaiting interment – English, German or French, it hardly mattered – what had once been living flesh and muscle and bone rent apart as easily as a doll by some truculent child, its only purpose now to host a buzzing swarm of flies.

Probyn watched the young men's expressions change as they glimpsed the true awfulness of war for the first time, knew what was going through their minds, saw the realization dawn – how pathetically fragile was the human form – but he offered them no words of solace for, in the end, it was up to each man to cope in his own way.

Unable to equip his young officers with bravery, he could and did, however, warn them of the underhand tactics the enemy would employ; it was a lesson even the company commanders must learn, for most of whom it was their first experience of war.

Visiting them in the deserted *estaminet* that acted as their billet, he advised: 'Before you go into the line, gentlemen, it might be as well to warn your troops that if they hear the order to cease fire they should ensure that it comes from their own side. The Boers wreaked havoc on our lines before we realized they'd learned our bugle calls – our lads would heed the call to retire and be sitting ducks. The Boche will no doubt try something similar; they're cut from the same cloth.'

'How very unsporting,' objected Faljambe, sifting through his collection of gramophone records and placing one on the turntable, the crumbling room dotted with other such home comforts.

Louis agreed, but made a wistful digression. 'I must confess I feel rather unsporting myself, going through the men's private letters.' Censoring had lately come into force.

78

'It's got to be done, sir. If they should fall into enemy hands –'

'Oh, I understand that, Mr Kilmaster, and I'm certain their families don't wish to hear some of the lurid accounts I've had to delete today. You should have seen the stuff Unthank wrote to his parents.'

'Unthank has parents?' Winding the gramophone, Faljambe sounded amazed. 'It was my understanding he'd been spawned by the devil.'

Whilst others showed mirth, including the RSM, Louis gave a reproving smile. 'You might be further surprised that some of it was quite eloquent.' He pondered for a while, almost blushing at the memory of Rawmarsh's lustful pencillings to his sweetheart. 'But reading the men's intimate thoughts . . . I feel so intrusive.' Then he laughed. 'Poor Skeeton, he hasn't really grasped the concept of all this secrecy business yet. After I'd finished with his letter there was more crossed out than there was written.' Still smiling, he rose to carry out his role of orderly officer. 'Well, I'd better make my rounds and leave the rest of you to your beauty sleep.'

'Sleep?' Reynard inserted a toffee into his worried, pimply face. 'With that row going on?' He could not get used to the constant bombardment, however distant.

'You're such a happy carefree soul, Foxy,' Louis teased him, then took his leave, giving parting address to the RSM. 'Thank you for that useful piece of information, Mr Kilmaster, I shall pass it on.'

Probyn moved alongside him, lowering his voice so as not to ridicule the lieutenant in front of his peers. 'Revolver, sir.'

Thus reminded, Louis gave a wince at his own slackness and as casually as he could, went back to pick up his revolver, checking first to see that it was loaded before strapping it on, with a murmur of thanks. 'My brother said I should need a guardian angel.'

With a wry glance at each other, the old soldier and the new went out into the rumbling night, their eyes and ears alert for spies.

It was hard for such a formidable personality to melt into the background, but as much as he could Probyn tried to remain anonymous, to watch and to listen without interference as those in his care struggled to mould themselves into an effective fighting machine. For most, having learned to work well together even before leaving England, the dangerous environment only helped to cement these ties. Yet, despite all the months of practice, there remained some who had yet to accept the rules.

Towards the end of the fortnight's training, before leaving

Nordausques, the order came for the battalion to turn out for a special parade, a request that did not suit Private Unthank.

'Parade?' he exploded. 'I hoped I'd left all that crap behind in England.'

'It's to honour Brigadier-General Kinloch,' the corporal informed him. 'He's leaving the brigade.'

Unthank scoffed, 'Another bloody general? There's more generals than there are men. I wish they'd all bugger off and leave us to get on with the job.' However, he dragged himself out to parade, albeit with bad humour.

All were assembled in arrow-like precision, focused on the brigadier-general, who expressed sorrow that he would not be there to lead them into action and thanked them for their loyal support through the long and arduous period of training, when suddenly a hare came bounding through the ranks. Probyn tensed. His eyes immediately fell on Unthank, who had broken the neat formation. Feeling those eyes boring into him, Unthank met the other's gaze and reluctantly stepped back into line, though his expression showed that he itched to give chase. As if acting in mischief, the hare chose to sit right in front of him and proceeded to clean its whiskers with a paw, whilst a glowering Unthank and the RSM duelled with their eyes, the latter daring Unthank to move a muscle. Finally, totally ignored, the hare bounded from the scene as quickly as it had appeared, leaving behind only a taste of sweetness in Probyn's mouth. Such steadiness augured well for the trials yet to come.

Departing Nordausques the battalion set out on a long trying march over the pavé. It was too hot to sing now, or even to speak. Each weighed down by sixty pounds of equipment, they were to suffer greatly, many stops having to be made along the way in order to gulp from the water wagons. Even then there was no comfort to be found in shade, for the ancient hedgerows of home were absent here, the fields coming right up to the road and leaving the soldiers exposed to the full attack of the sun.

If younger men endured discomfort, the manifold sufferings of their regimental sergeant-major would have been pitiful to behold had he confessed to them. Overweight, plagued by aching joints, his heart pounding in his bullish chest and his face crimson, Probyn had never endured such a trial, felt as if he might drop dead any minute, was driven only by sheer willpower, for he could allow no one to glimpse his frailty.

Any respite was all too brief. After billeting for the night at Compagne, they were to march again through the furnace, a similar feat being expected on the third day, at the end of which the mass desire was simply to flop down and drift into unconsciousness. Responding to this urge, Unthank, Rawmarsh and others sought refuge in a barn and had just begun to doze when the order came to turn out for parade.

Whilst Rawmarsh duly obliged with the rest of his platoon, Unthank showed incredulity that they could be in for yet another inspection. 'In the middle of a bloody battleground? We've just tramped miles! What the hell is it in aid of this time?'

Sergeant Holroyd, a shop manager in civilian life, tried to be firm. 'It doesn't have to be in aid of anything! You're a soldier and you'll do as you're told.'

Unthank called the other's bluff. 'Go bugger yourself. I'm fagged and I'm not budging.'

Competent at organization but unschooled in dealing with such a ruffian, Sergeant Holroyd was apprehensive at tackling him and stalked off to relay the news to his platoon commander.

Interrupted whilst trying to make himself presentable in this wretched heat and dust, Louis's heart sank at being told that Unthank was causing trouble yet again. Bracing himself, he went with the sergeant to handle the matter, employing his firmest tone.

'Unthank, on parade at once!'

Eyes closed, Unthank ignored him.

'I don't want to have to put you on a charge!' Up to now Louis had ensured that it had been others who had done this for him.

There was still no response, only the steady tramp of boots from beyond the barn walls and the rumble of cannon.

Acting from a sense of chivalry, Sergeant Holroyd moved outside so as not to embarrass the lieutenant but in so doing attracted the attention of his CSM, who was on his way to parade with a mass of others, chivvying slackers into action. 'Jildi! Jildi!'

Caught dithering, Sergeant Holroyd was forced to admit the reason.

'What do you mean he won't get up?' Walrus moustache bristling, the elderly CSM Dungworth poured scorn upon this new breed of NCO that the war had inflicted on him. 'Just give him a kick up the arse and don't go bothering your superiors with trivia! Call yourself a sergeant . . .' Nevertheless, he poked his head into the barn to check on the situation.

Realizing that he was under observation, Louis felt inept and, not knowing what else to do, he tried to appeal to Unthank's better nature. 'Man, you're letting your comrades down!'

Unthank was unmoved, mumbling into his bed of straw, 'I don't mind getting up at dawn to meet the enemy and I'll fight 'em as 'ard as you like, sir, but I'm buggered if I'll be dragged out of bed for some general to check if me bloody hat's on straight.'

Frustrated, Louis took a step away, demanding with false jocularity of the CSM, 'What answer can one give to that? He's right. It is idiotic.'

Whilst fully capable of having Unthank moving in seconds, CSM Dungworth was reluctant to denigrate this popular young lieutenant, and so took him aside, speaking in avuncular manner. 'We can't have one man acting on his own rules, sir. We've got to have regimentation or the whole thing will fall apart.'

'What do you suggest?'

'If that wasn't just a rhetorical question, sir, I'd suggest that Unthank be given detention.'

Louis was dubious. 'That's a bit harsh, isn't it?'

'We are on active service, sir. He could by rights be shot.'

'It's not as if he's refusing to fight – in fact he's the keenest of the bunch. I've no wish to demoralize him. Let him stay there for the moment, I'm sure when he's mulled over the implications he'll comply.'

'With respect, sir –' began CSM Dungworth.

But Louis felt a big enough fool as it was. 'Thank you, sergeant-major, carry on.'

Indicating that the discussion was over, he waited until the CSM had exited, then turned back to the recalcitrant and addressed him firmly. 'You've been given an order, Unthank. I shall expect to see you on parade in five minutes, otherwise it'll be the captain's office.' In as businesslike a manner as he could, he beat a retreat, inwardly cringing at his own inefficiency.

'I'm not having this,' muttered CSM Dungworth to no one in particular as he himself strode away. 'If he gets away with it they'll all be at it.'

Going directly to the RSM, he informed him bluntly, 'Unthank's refusing to parade, sir.'

Still exhausted from the march, Probyn was irked. 'You're not telling me you can't control him, Bert?'

A grunt of disapproval. 'I could, if I were permitted to.'

Probyn got the other's drift. As bold and enthusiastic as Louis Postgate might be, he still lacked the ability to discipline those under him. 'What does your officer have to say?'

'Lieutenant Postgate was disinclined to accept my suggestion, sir.'

As much as Probyn liked the young officer, there was nothing that exasperated him more than those who had to be nannied and in this Louis had finally used up all his patience. Incensed, but managing to keep his temper under control, he strode off to investigate.

Seeing the beefy individual's approach, Louis tried to avoid him but failed.

'Ah, Lieutenant Postgate!' Not caring that others were present to witness this, Probyn pulled no punches. 'I'm told Unthank is threatening mutiny.'

Louis blushed with alarm. 'Oh, I wouldn't use so emotive a term, Mr Kilmaster. He's just dug his heels in – quite understandably, in my view.'

'And, with respect, in my view, sir, it is classed as indiscipline. Where is he?' Upon being told, without further ado he summoned a sergeant and two men, and marched to the barn, a look of grim intent upon his florid face.

'Unthank, on your feet!' Without giving the offender time to obey he drew back his foot and dealt Unthank a hefty kick in the back, sending him tumbling.

'I'm informed that you're refusing to obey the order of a superior officer!'

The man was upright now but no less co-operative. Receiving only a shrug, Probyn wasted no further time. 'Then let's see what your attitude is after a week's detention! Sergeant, remove him!'

Under close arrest, a seemingly unrepentant Unthank was marched to a crumbling outhouse that acted as the guardroom, and in its dark stuffy interior was compelled to remain whilst his comrades lined up for parade.

Blissfully ignorant of this internal crisis, the inspecting general expressed himself so very pleased by the men's appearance and by the way they handled their arms, telling them that from what he had heard of the battalion he was quite sure that when the time came all ranks would acquit themselves well. These words imbuing him with a sense of failure over the handling of Unthank's obduracy, Louis glanced at RSM Kilmaster, who briefly met his eyes, both sharing the grim hope that Unthank would soon be directing all that vitriol at the enemy rather than his own superiors.

After a night in bivouac at Erquinghem the battalion tramped into the line at Armentières. Still under close arrest, Unthank was released only in order to go on the move and at every halt found himself back in whatever bomb-damaged hovel passed for a guardroom.

In time of peace it would have been a delight to be in this pretty countryside with its whitewashed farms and red-bricked cottages, roofs of tile and thatch. The air was fresh, the day bright and, though the twittering of birds was punctuated by the sound of gunfire this did not appear to deter the French peasants, who continued to toil in their fields even with artillery shells bursting in the near distance. A stoical grandmother, her ample figure bound in rough skirt and checked blouse, a headscarf to guard against the sun; the daughter with braided hair coiled around a pretty, apple-shaped head; infants romping between rows of cabbages; flowers in the sunlit meadows that were pitted with craters; the smell of smoking ruins; the coils of barbed wire; the fly-blown corpses of man and beast; a surreal blend of heaven and hell.

Ensconced in Battalion HQ in a farmhouse near Armentières, over cigarettes and rum, Probyn, the adjutant, the colonel and his company commanders were given intelligence by the outgoing officer, who first unrolled a series of maps that conveyed the position. The Germans, foiled in their initial rush to Paris, had retreated and settled down into a long dug-in line of defence reaching from the Swiss Mountains to the sea. This line had varied little over the past year. An attempt last spring to break through at Neuve Chapelle had been thwarted and, consequently, a desolate air of stagnation had settled over the area. The present incumbent's relief at escaping this was evident. Despite being worse for wear due to lack of washing facilities, he was quite chirpy as, rolling up the maps, he invited the newcomers on a tour. 'I'm afraid Fritz has got the upper hand when it comes to observation, so be advised to keep your heads down.'

Invited to come along, a procession of eager young subalterns followed.

The moment Probyn set foot in the defences it was clearly evident that this was to be a war like no other. In South Africa the word trench had signified a twelve-inch gutter that had taken hours to scoop from ground baked hard as cement; these splendid excavations were much more sophisticated, deep enough to contain a tall man, and shored up with wood and sandbags. With their shovels and picks the Tommies had carved a town in miniature, with high streets and side streets and back alleys, all named, complete with earthen dwellings. Moreover, the surrounding hedgerows and orchards bristled with weaponry, the barrels of machine guns protruding between brick stacks and ruined houses.

Aside from a reconnaissance of the area, the outgoing officer was also to provide them with snippets of useful information.

'We've found that if poison gas is creeping towards us on a night the birds raise a frightful clamour and soar high in the air. It's a really effective alarm as it gives one time to put on respirators without a mad panic.'

Ear cocked attentively, Hugh Faljambe stored this away.

Going along the shallower communication trench they reached a sap where Faljambe, eager to impress, paused to ask the sentries a question. The CO put a finger to his lips and was in the act of summoning the newcomers away when an object plopped in beside them. In a moment of alarm the officers and sentries were about to hurl themselves to the ground when they saw that it was only a piece of paper wrapped round a stone – obviously launched by catapult. Unfolding it, the CO swiftly revealed the message: it was a note of welcome for the new battalion.

'My word, they're that close?' breathed Colonel Addison, ducking like the others as they were ushered back down the communication trench.

His counterpart gave a wry nod. 'We're lucky it wasn't a mortar; it usually is.'

Their discourse was interrupted by a burst of enemy machine-gun fire, like the cackling of magpies except more deep-throated and ten times more vicious. Moving at a crouching dash, they made for the comparative safety of the farmhouse.

Thrilled to be here, at first the men responded keenly to the early morning order to stand to, poised alertly on the fire-step with bayonets fixed to ward off attack, their excitement burgeoning as darkness lifted, and exchanged vigorous rifle fire with those in the opposing trench, then retired for breakfast feeling exhilarated. Even the filling of sandbags and digging of latrines assumed an air of importance out here in the thick of conflict.

But within days the routine grew very tedious – indeed proved to be something of a sham. To young minds the act of going to battle had envisioned valiant charges against the enemy, hand-to-hand struggles, perhaps a medal. But thus far no one could actually claim to have made any impact on the Germans, apart from damaging their trenches. Between random pot shots and the occasional burst of machine-gun fire in retaliation, most of the day was passed in repairing the damaged breastworks, which the enemy proceeded to do their best to wreck again.

Annoying and dangerous though this was, it did have compensations, the latest being a cache of buried wine. The finders, Pork and Hamm, were sneaking along the trench, intending to stash this away for themselves when Lieutenant Faljambe emerged from his dugout.

'Hello, what have we here?' Upon lifting a soil-encrusted bottle from the crate, he gave an exclamation of delight before reverting to his stern manner. 'I trust you were bringing this to me, Hamm.'

'Naturally, sir.' The dark expression on Hamm's face made him less than convincing.

'I'm pleased to hear it. This requires a more discerning palate than either of you fellows possess.' So saying, the blond officer relieved them of the crate, told them to return to their working party, and was about to duck into his burrow when Major Lewis and RSM Kilmaster came along the line.

Unable to hide his booty, Faljambe was obliged to hold up the crate of wine as if only just making the discovery himself. 'Look what I've found, sir!'

'Why, how very kind, Hugh!' Major Lewis seized a bottle in either hand, examining them with pleasure. 'You won't mind if I take one for the colonel? And I'm sure our regimental sergeant-major would appreciate a glass with his supper, wouldn't you, Mr Kilmaster?'

Though wine did not usually feature in Probyn's menu, no luxury was turned down in a war. 'Thank you very much, sir. This will go down a treat with those potatoes Private Arrowsmith unearthed.'

'You're very welcome, I'm sure.' Hugh Faljambe spirited his remaining bottles into the dugout before anyone else could make away with them.

Grinning at each other, the RSM and the major went on their way, Probyn continuing alone as Major Lewis branched off on separate business. It was a very pleasant morning and comparatively quiet. With no hostility from either side the men were repairing breastworks damaged in the last bout of hate. It promised to be another sweltering day, yet down here the sun's fierceness was deflected by the cool piles of turned earth.

Appreciating this same coolness after the suffocating heat of his prison, Tom Unthank was coming along the warren of trenches from another direction. Completing his sentence this morning, he had been given back his rifle and was determined to use it. There was little action at the moment though: men squatted smoking or writing letters home. In fact it was so quiet he could hear faint banter wafting through the long parched grass of no-man's-land. Reaching his own sector he hopped onto the fire-step and peered cautiously over the mound of bleached sandbags.

Almost fully exposed to enemy fire, a group of men were erecting new stakes and rolls of wire where the section had been destroyed by artillery shells. So narrow was the distance between his own trench and the enemy's that on this bright day Unthank was able to recognize men from his own platoon. Showing not the slightest caution, Skeeton was sitting upright, working away with his pliers on the wire, chatting as he might on a street corner. Outlined against the blue sky, he made the perfect target. Damning him for a bloody idiot, Unthank hoisted his rifle to his shoulder and pretended to take aim. But no sooner had he fixed Skeeton in his sights when a pickelhaube crept into his field of vision and hurled something at the group of friends. Without a moment's hesitation Unthank fired at the wearer. The German fell, there was a cry of shock and a collection of stunned faces wheeled round to see where the shot had come from, before there was a mad scramble for cover.

But Skeeton was transfixed by the agonized death throes of the German to whom he had only a moment ago been chatting. Lying flat on his back in no-man's-land, the man's fingers clutched at the hole in his throat, his eyes wide and staring, pleading with Skeeton to do something as the blood poured into his lungs.

'Skeets! Come on!' In anticipation of the enemy's wrath, his companions had hurled themselves into the nearest sap, abandoning the rolls of wire. They called to him frantically again and again.

But Skeeton remained motionless, hypnotized by the worm-like writhing of the wounded man, until, braving the retaliatory whip-crack of rifle fire, his friend Rawmarsh performed a mad, crouching dash and forcibly dragged him to safety.

At the far end of the main trench, Probyn heard the disturbance and turned about, but as yet remained where he stood.

Behind the wall of sandbags Unthank rushed up to claim his glory. Expecting thanks, he was taken off guard when a mortified Skeeton turned on him, his eyes bright with tears. 'You dirty bloody dog!'

There came an incredulous laugh. 'Sorry, I thought that was what we were here for, to kill Germans. He was creeping up on you, for Christ's sake!'

The other's hand brandished an artefact, his tone almost hysterical. 'He was just returning the mallet I lent him!'

'Well, you got it back, didn't you?' scoffed Unthank, before turning away with a derisive snort.

The Germans had set up a ferocious volley of rifle fire, but the bullets smacked harmlessly into the pile of sandbags. Skeeton did not even hear them as, deafened by the thunderous roar of blood in his skull, he launched himself at the retreating figure, flattening Unthank beneath his full weight and by this element of surprise managing to inflict a frenzied series of blows with the mallet. 'You murdering bloody swine, we had a truce!'

But so inflamed was he that most of the blows fell wild and Unthank soon had the upper hand, bucking Skeeton off, spinning him round and delivering a few more accurate punches of his own before the two were wrenched apart by their comrades.

Unfortunately the matter could not be contained within the ranks and they were still struggling as Louis Postgate barged his way through.

'I've come here to kill fooking Germans!' Unthank railed at Skeeton. 'If you don't want to do it you can go sit in a bloody shed for a week like I've been doing!'

Louis berated him. 'Unthank, if you don't cease this disgraceful behaviour you'll find yourself back in there!'

There was a marked lack of deference. 'What, for killing the enemy?' Above the jutting shelves of slate the jade eyes were sardonic.

'For brawling!' Chagrined at the other's constant trespass against his good nature, the young officer projected uncharacteristic fury. 'I'm damn well sick of you, Unthank, and if you don't stop this insubordination it'll be Field Punishment number one!'

Unthank's first instinct was to be unimpressed. Younger, less worldly than himself, the lieutenant had always been an easy touch, but looking closer he detected a truly murderous glint in the normally smiling blue eyes. So furious was Louis that his uncontrolled lips pitched a rain of spittle along with his words. This in itself caused Unthank to stop and think. There were few things more dangerous than a placid man losing control. But more importantly, he had just caught sight of the RSM watching from a distance and who now began to walk in this direction. The seven days of excruciating boredom were still fresh in his mind, he was determined not to repeat the experience. Hence, his attitude towards the lieutenant underwent a swift metamorphosis. 'Sorry, sir. It's just that being cooped up so long I've been dying to have a pop at Fritz.'

Louis's angry expression was tempered by surprise at this unexpected apology. He glared for a good few seconds into the soulless green eyes, trying to make out if he was still being taken for a fool, before coming to the conclusion that Unthank meant what he said and finally allowing, 'Well . . . that's quite understandable.' But he was still frowning as he turned his eyes on Skeeton. 'So, what was the blessed argument all about?'

The frenzied pumping of blood in Skeeton's brain was gradually returning to its normal rate. Faced with Unthank's declaration and the amount of missiles now coming from the enemy trench it sounded ludicrous to condemn him for murdering Germans. 'Nothing really, sir.' Out in no-man's-land the horrible gurgling had stopped, though Skeeton's stomach continued to churn with disgust.

'You risked detention over nothing?' Still concentrated angrily on the transgressors, Louis was unaware of the imposing figure approaching from behind.

But Skeeton was, and he mumbled accordingly. 'It was just a misunderstanding, sir. He didn't know we had a truce.'

'What truce?'

'It was just a private arrangement, sir. We had a word with Fritz and, well . . .' The RSM almost upon them, Skeeton's voice petered out and his eyes darted a warning.

'One can't have private truces!' sputtered Louis.

'Everything in order, sir?'

Though startled by the RSM's voice Louis revolved with an automatic beam on his face. 'Perfectly, Mr Kilmaster! I was just informing Unthank of my decision to make him a sniper, put his talents to good use.' Stern of face again, he directed Unthank to go about his business, receiving a curt nod from the other that acknowledged him as a saviour from more detention. Dispersing everyone else in similarly efficient fashion, Louis turned again to the RSM, wondering how much Mr Kilmaster had witnessed.

But Probyn made no reference to what he had overheard. Reading the faces of those involved, he interpreted with some satisfaction that, despite the cock-and-bull story, Louis had at last found a way to deal with his *bête noire*. 'A very good idea that, sir.'

The trench was under mortar fire now, the increasing ferocity of the explosions compelling both to move on, but in doing so Probyn looked back and made reference to the bottles under his arm. 'Oh, by the way! You might be interested to know, sir, that Lieutenant Faljambe has come into possession of some very fine wine.'

At Louis's grin of thanks, he headed back for HQ to the accompaniment of a noisy exchange of mortars. Casting one last look over his shoulder, he saw Louis approach Private Skeeton and startle him from his morose paralysis with a cheery pat on the shoulder.

Prodded into action, Skeeton took up his position on the fire-step. Though before doing anything else he withdrew from his pocket the portion of German sausage that he had been given in barter for the loan of the mallet and flung it as far as he could into no-man's-land. He would never be able to eat it.

SIX

In general, Probyn had found that one's daily existence in war was little different from that of ordinary life, a matter of just getting on with things, coping with one's lot and managing quite well until some bombshell exploded and ruined everything. Except that in war the bombshells were not metaphorical.

Having enjoyed a passable dinner, made excellent by Faljambe's wine, the occupants of HQ had gone to bed merry, only to be woken this morning by the scream of one such bombshell homing in on them.

Fully dressed, Probyn hurled himself out of the wire-netting hammock and in the same protective movement dragged his flea-bag over him just as the shell landed, exploding in the garden with a tremendous, ear-splitting roar and throwing up great columns of earth. It was followed by several others, all of which shook the walls and sent shards of plaster tumbling from the ceiling, peppering everyone and everything, burying desks, maps and paperwork under a layer of dust.

Fearing that he was going to be buried too, when the explosions appeared to have stopped Probyn came from under his mattress and called out to check if others had been hurt. Reassured by their answers, he joined the exodus. In the aftermath of the incendiary shells several buildings were ablaze and the area resembled a dog sprinkled with flea powder, its inhabitants scurrying around in alarm, officers' grooms trying to calm horses that screamed in panic, that bucked and wrenched at their tethers, their flanks punctured and bleeding from shrapnel. Along with the colonel, adjutant, clerks and orderlies, Probyn staggered through the choking pall of smoke to emerge covered in dust.

A cheer arose from the trenches.

Slightly dazed, bashing the bits of ceiling from his hat and blinking rapidly to rid his eyelashes of debris, the colonel wondered aloud, 'Are they cheering for us or the bomb?'

'I wouldn't care to hazard a guess, sir.' Wearing a wry expression, Probyn coughed twice and, crunching grit between his teeth, spat distastefully through a powdery moustache.

Along the line, squinting through the weak early morning sunlight, Hugh Faljambe had been observing through field glasses. Relieved to see all unhurt, he joked to his companions, 'That'll teach the blighters to thieve our wine.'

Convinced that all were safe, Louis chuckled at the black humour.

However, back at the scene the mood had turned grim upon discovery that the battalion had accrued its first casualties. Added to the stench of gunpowder and hot metal was that of blood, seeping amongst the broken bricks. Small crowds had gathered around each of the two injured men, projecting anxiety and fascinated horror. There were excited demands for medical aid, no one seeming sure how to help the victims but wanting to feel that they were doing something by making wild gesticulations for assistance.

Calmly, despite his close shave, Probyn stepped forth to carve a way for the stretcher bearers, ordering the onlookers to get about their business and so they did, but still they could not tear their eyes away from the sight of human skin shredded to rag, milk-white bones protruding through rent flesh, and the pitiful cries of their comrades.

After such an experience it was good to be back in billets. For Probyn, besides being a welcome relief from the trenches there was to be pleasure in conversation too, for a draft from the 3rd York and Lancasters were also billeted here, and amongst them he met old comrades who had fought alongside him in South Africa.

Days of glorious weather were to follow, each devoured with the zest of those who teetered on the brink of death, misty morns dedicated to fishing in the Lys, evenings to the pursuit of feminine company and champagne.

Clad in shorts, their knees and cheeks as brown as conkers, the young officers seemed to Probyn's eye more like boy scouts than soldiers as he watched them on this sunny afternoon. During a rest from training, Faljambe had brought his gramophone outside and, in the lack of more suitable partners, men waltzed together.

Louis had draped a white silk scarf over his head to resemble female hair and was partnering Bob Gaylard. Sashaying provocatively, he called to the portly figure seated on a chair in the shade of a bomb-damaged wall. 'This is a gentlemen's excuse me if you'd care to interrupt, Mr Kilmaster!'

Pulling on a cigarette, Probyn smilingly declined. Though he might act the clown at home it was beneath an RSM's dignity to do so here.

But a fellow lieutenant obliged, rushing up to come between Gaylard and his partner.

'Ah, *monsieur*, would like to dance with me?' Louis puckered his lips at Sillar and prepared to be embraced but Sillar brushed him aside roughly. 'Not likely – this one is far younger and prettier!' And he hugged Gaylard to his chest before launching him into a waltz, leaving Louis to stalk off in a pretend huff and grab another partner.

The frivolity was interrupted by the tack-tack-tack of fighter planes. Abandoning their dancing, the youths grouped excitedly to tilt their faces heavenwards, shielding their eyes against the glare of the sun. Probyn looked up too, but, fascinating though the aerial duel undoubtedly was, after a while he lowered his gaze and instead began to watch the rapt expressions of the young officers, glowing with exhilaration, each obviously yearning to be up there.

A sudden cheer arose – the Hun was hit – and Probyn quickly turned his eyes skywards again. How flimsy the enemy aircraft seemed now, disintegrating like a moth that had come too close to the flame. The British aeroplane soared triumphantly above its victim, looping the loop whilst the other broke into three pieces, the men below cheering even louder. Then came a slight falter as they watched the German pilot make frantic attempts to escape the cockpit before it fell, but fail and plummet with it to earth.

Probyn looked again at his young warriors, noted the varied expressions; even now some continued to cheer the death of their enemy, but others, possessed of a deeper sense of humanity, went quiet and turned away, as if to pretend it had not occurred.

Slowed almost to a stop, the gramophone emitted a distorted groan. Rushing to it, Louis wound it vigorously and gave the tune life, summoning others back to the dance floor.

Towards the end of a sweltering month to the accompaniment of intense bombardment by their own artillery, the battalion moved to

Brigade Reserve HQ at Grispot, accumulating two more casualties along the way.

That evening it began to rain heavily, the day's gunfire eclipsed by a violent thunderstorm. By morning it had slowed to drizzle, though a pewter sky forewarned more to come. Save for a brief respite when a rainbow arched over the German lines, it continued to rain throughout the next day, each fresh downpour washing away Probyn's former admiration of the trenchwork. Whilst in the duckboarded sections there was no more than six inches of mud, an unfloored zone was like a quagmire, becoming knee-deep in parts. Trenches filled up as soon as they were dug, in the flat landscape impossible to drain.

He had marched through mud before but had rarely been forced to dwell in it. Remaining still for more than five seconds he found himself imprisoned by the ankles. His thighs ached from the constant effort of having to negotiate such a morass. It was like living with some foul subterranean beast that would suck at his boots, dragging them into its loathsome mouth and hampering each step, the air filled with a constant squelching as he and others fought their way through it, churning the mire to even greater slime.

Still dogged by bad weather, caked in mud from head to toe, the battalion moved forward in anticipation of the attack on the German-held town of Loos. Though still in reserve there was in every heart the hope that they might be called upon to join the action. Most were already awake when, after a night of heavy rain, they were roused before four and told to cotton wool their ears in preparation of the bombardment. The sky was clear and starry but such tranquillity was destined not to last, and within half an hour the barrage had opened, its indescribable proportions shattering their senses as never before, the flimsy barrier of fluff in their ears of little effect against such an inferno of noise, its reverberations felt in the very earth beneath their feet.

In response to the British bombardment, German shells came whooshing from their batteries, whistling and screaming with devilish intent. Even a mile behind the front lines Probyn and his men came in for a considerable battering, cowering in their waterlogged trenches, listening to the cries of those being hit, full of admiration for the valiant medical officer who risked his life to tend them, whilst, all around, houses and farms were exploded off the map, along with their animals.

Then, about noon, during a lull in the barrage, a message was received along with the handing out of extra ammunition: 'Stand to, ready to move!' Whilst some knew only raw excitement, it suddenly became clear to those with any imagination that they could die today, and Probyn dispersed his old regulars amongst the virgin troops with orders to keep them cheerful. He himself visited his young officers, by his calm presence hoping to instil confidence. One of lesser experience might have assumed from their stalwart demeanour that they had no need of this, but Probyn knew the weaknesses of everyone around him.

'Everything all right, sir?' He struggled to make himself heard above the guns.

Young Postgate's eyes were bright. 'Yes, everyone is most enthusiastic!'

'Enthusiasm is all very well, sir, but they have to know what to do when they get to their destination. They're all primed, I trust?'

Louis gave an eager nod. But then his exuberance made way for sober admittance. 'Well . . . there are a few doubts over the use of the bayonet.'

Inserting a sentence between bangs, Probyn spoke with confidence. 'I wouldn't let that concern you too much, sir. Once their blood is up they'll take it in their stride.'

'But will I?' murmured Louis. The constant battering from high explosive had made him dizzy and numb, the reek of lyddite doing naught for his bilious stomach. All the noble thoughts about rescuing oppressed nations were gone, his thoughts concentrated on self-preservation.

'What was that, sir?' bawled Probyn, cupping his ear.

Louis shook his dark head, thinking what a terrible responsibility it was to have so many souls under one's protection.

Guessing from the sick expression, Probyn mouthed, 'I'm certain you'll be fine, sir.'

Louis threw the RSM a grin for this vote of faith – but then a man in his platoon was hit by shrapnel and in a trice he was running to give aid.

The man was crying out in panic and holding his chest. 'I'm going to die! Help me!'

Louis was doing the best he could for the victim but needed assistance and his sergeant-major quickly gave it, employing a calm but firm tone as he squatted to instruct the casualty. 'Spit on your hands, Watson. Come on, do as I say.'

His eyes still dilated with fear, the man beheld him dumbly at first, then complied.

Probyn dealt him a nod of satisfaction. 'Oh, you're going to be all right. See?' He took Watson's wrist and held the man's palm to his face. 'The spittle's clear. If you'd been hit anywhere vital that would have blood in it.'

This reasoned tone from a man so respected had the desired effect, the victim calming sufficiently to be stretchered away.

Still under fire, the RSM at his side, Louis went back to his position with a sigh. 'I think that I shall never know as much as you, Mr Kilmaster.'

Probyn was self-effacing. 'Me? I don't know a jot about anything medical, sir, but it helped to calm him down, didn't it?' Giving Louis a reassuring nudge, he further explained, 'I've seen men die of little more than a scratch just because they got all worked up and terrified. Say anything you can to keep them calm, even if it's a lie. It'll help them one way or another.' With a supportive wink, he moved on to lend his strength to others.

Lieutenant Reynard seemed grateful too for the company of this old professional. He smiled but it was a nervous little effort and he constantly fidgeted with a blemish on his chin. 'Thank God that ghastly row has finished. I've heard of people being sent mad by noise, now I know why.'

Probyn voiced understanding.

'It's almost as bad as the waiting.' Reynard slumped back into the thoughts that had possessed him before the RSM had arrived, his fingers moving from his chin to his neck. 'I've heard reports that a number of men have been shot for cowardi –'

'Not in this regiment, sir,' Probyn cut in proudly.

'Even so, it makes one think.'

'Doesn't pay to think like that, sir.' Probyn displayed no empathy here. 'Don't spare any pity for them. They let their comrades down.'

Reynard admitted, 'That's the thing I'm most afraid of.'

'You won't let anybody down, sir.'

Sweat poured down the spotty face as bullets hissed around them. 'Gosh, I could drink Lake Windermere dry.'

Probyn noticed that the young man's hand continually explored his neck. 'Something wrong with your throat, sir?'

'I'm not sure. There appears to be a lump. I might take a trip to the MO once this is over.'

Probyn spoke kindly. 'I think you'll find that once it's over the lump will have vanished, sir. It's not real, it's just nerves.'

Reynard was only half-relieved. 'Truly?'

A firm, reassuring nod. 'I'm sure most of the men here are

experiencing the same thing. I myself am well acquainted with it.'

A sceptical smile, for, even under this terrible barrage the RSM barely flinched. 'I find that hard to credit from your demeanour, Mr Kilmaster. But, tell me, what should I do to stop myself being afraid?'

'Only a fool isn't afraid, sir. Just bear it in mind that the Germans are more afraid than you are. Don't worry, you won't let anyone down.' Having succeeded in bolstering Foxy, the old hand moved on to work his magic elsewhere.

But all the soul-searching and reassurance turned out to be for nothing. The order to move was never received.

Told to stand down, there came bitter complaint from Hugh Faljambe. 'Always the bridesmaid, never the blasted bride!'

'Don't be so eager to die, sir,' Probyn sought to caution him.

'Believe me I'm not, but we're still as likely to die by just sitting still! I'd much rather take my chances out there.'

Alas, despite complaints, this was the way things were to proceed for the 9th York and Lancasters, being bogged down in one place or another, constantly waiting to take part, yet never called upon to do so, but under equal threat of death as those who were.

Thankfully there was very little shelling during the week that followed, the battalion moving back and forth between various sectors, as usual in the chaos of war sometimes being fed, sometimes not, the last few days of the month finding them in Brigade Advanced Reserve.

An armful of orderly books under his arm, Probyn entered the colonel's office on the last Tuesday in September, saluted, then laid the collection on his desk.

The imposing moustachioed face looked up. 'Thank you, RSM. It's hard to believe that we've almost completed our first month overseas, is it not?'

'Yes, sir. We've been remarkably fortunate having so few losses.'

'Most certainly. I've just been totting them up and there's less than a dozen – and no one killed. Isn't that gratifying?'

Probyn agreed that they were very lucky. 'I wonder how many the Germans have lost.'

'There's one thing for sure, Unthank will be responsible for most of them. He's a marvellous shot, if nothing else.'

'Maybe we should all go home and leave him to it, sir.' Smiling, Probyn left the office.

But barely had the congratulatory words over the lack of deaths been uttered than Private James Gilligan earned himself the unenviable distinction of being the first man in the battalion to be killed.

Probyn watched the young men rush to tend him, saw their shocked faces gradually withdraw at the realization that Gilligan was not just unconscious. His death too swift to register, his eyes were still open, though the lustre had gone from them. Reluctant to meet death's gaze, Louis was the one who kneeled and passed a reverent hand over the departed's eyelids. But as he took his palm away, the shutters reopened. Deeply affected, Louis quickly pressed the lids again, rewarded this time by a wink from the corpse. No matter how many times he tried, those eyes kept flickering open. Not until Gilligan was wrapped in a sheet for burial, could Louis escape them.

There was to be much worse.

Gilligan had scarcely been committed to earth when a projectile came whistling towards the support line and everyone dived for cover, but luckily the shell overreached its target and exploded with a roar some twenty yards behind. Crouched against the blast, Faljambe yelped and put his hand to his cheek. Feeling what he assumed was a splinter of metal, he was unable to extricate it yet for the earth that had been thrown skywards in a huge column was now raining down on them again, peppering their backs with smouldering debris. Only after the shower of earth and metal had stopped did the occupants of the trench unfurl from their defensive positions to examine the damage.

Gingerly, Faljambe nipped the sliver of shell from his cheek, looked at his bloodstained fingers, then frowned, seeing not a piece of metal but a glittering fragment of bone. Aghast, he looked at those around him, checking their identities; everyone appeared to be unhurt, yet each of them wore a similar grisly memento, pieces of flesh and white shards of cartilage, yellow globules of fat adhering like sago pudding to the khaki, all of which made them recoil in horror and a hurried wiping of clothing ensued. In the confused hiatus, it took a moment to identify the donor. But then Faljambe's eyes fell on the spot where a moment ago he had seen his friend Lieutenant Sillar and where now was just a smoking crater. Rushing forth, he and his group of fellow subalterns converged on the hole but could only gape at the sight. There was little hope of identification here, though there was no doubt that this remnant of tangled tissue had once been the nineteen-year-old Sillar, for he was nowhere else to be found. Realizing that he still held the thorny piece of bone between his forefinger and thumb, Faljambe stared at it in revulsion but did not know what to do with it, it seemed so callous to throw it away. With some reverence, he stooped and dropped the fragment gently beside the rest of Sillar's remains.

He was still looking extremely upset when, some time later, the RSM came amongst them to find everyone standing about motionless.

Barking smartly at the men for their inaction, Probyn turned his attention to the wan-faced subalterns. 'Has the war finished then, sirs?'

'You obviously haven't heard, Mr Kilmaster,' a doleful Hugh Faljambe informed him. 'We've just lost Tom Sillar.'

'Yes I am aware, sir,' came the grim reply, 'but that's no reason for everyone to be standing around doing nothing.' Probyn moved away temporarily to chivvy others.

Faljambe spoke angrily to his companions, Louis and Gaylard. 'Did you hear that? It's as if poor Sillar had caused him some personal inconvenience by being blown to smithereens!'

Louis was forced to agree. 'One minute you think he's a decent fellow then the next he seems positively heartless. How can he not react to this beastly carnage? I don't think I'll –'

'My God!' As was his habit, Faljambe spoke over the other. 'I don't know how I'll ever get over seeing Sillar like that, it was absolutely ghastly, yet the RSM didn't spare him a thought! Makes one wonder what reaction, if any, oneself would inspire were one to –' Too late he noticed from their looks of constipated panic that his friends were trying to warn him that Mr Kilmaster was coming back.

Caught out, the young man felt obliged to apologize, but though his arrogant jaw turned pink his demeanour was not wholly contrite.

'Contrary to your opinion, sirs,' Probyn encompassed all three in his hypnotic gaze, his voice gruff, 'you might be interested to learn that I am as much devastated by Lieutenant Sillar's death as are yourselves. I considered him to be a fine and valiant officer and a credit to the regiment.'

Gaylard immediately allowed a look of remorse to break through, as did Louis who spoke for them both. 'We're sorry, Mr Kilmaster, we obviously misunderstood and spoke without thinking. It's just that we're so desperately upset over poor Sillar.'

Probyn's gaze was now fixed on Faljambe, who showed little sign of contrition for his words. However, under that imperious gaze he wilted somewhat. 'Well, if I have maligned you, Mr Kilmaster, then I apologize. It's just that Sillar was a particular friend and I was rather annoyed to hear of him referred to in such a –'

'Lieutenant Sillar will be sorely missed, by myself as much as anyone,' the eyes were hard and glittering, 'but if I were to go around moping over the death of one soldier I should not be of very much value to the rest of the battalion, should I, sir?'

Apologizing again, Louis and Gaylard melted away.

Unmoving, Faljambe ran a hand over his mouth and pondered the RSM's words, beginning to see that there was wisdom in such lack of emotion. 'You're saying I'll be no good to the men if I don't pull myself together.'

'Something like that, sir. One just has to get on with the job in hand. But don't presume to imagine that just because I don't cry, I don't feel.'

Faljambe shook his head emotionally, looking all at sea. 'Then, for pity's sake, can you let me in on your secret?'

'Secret, sir?' Probyn held the youngster with a candid eye. 'I don't know that there is any secret. I can only put it like this: remember during training how the straps on your heavy pack used to cut into your shoulders, the raw wounds they gouged into your flesh, wounds so tender you thought they'd never heal? How you finally became numb to the pain and in the end a callus formed? It's the same as that, sir, only a callus of the soul.'

His mind still throwing up the horror of his friend's death over and over again, Faljambe's tone was hollow as he voiced doubt that he would ever be able to form such a layer.

'It's for your own preservation, sir, believe me,' said Probyn, before walking away.

Summer had finally gone, October's grey cloak settling upon the area and doing naught to alleviate the feeling of stagnation. River, ditch and brook, swollen by incessant rain, burst their banks and ran together, transforming the flat plain into a gigantic lake. Between moving back and forth from billets to trenches, training and more training was all Louis and his fellows ever seemed to do. Training for what?

Conjointly some had grown morbid, their discourse hinging on when and how they might die.

'I never knew blood had a smell,' Probyn overheard Gaylard's musing after breakfast one morning – another idle day stretching ahead. 'It's vile, isn't it? Especially when it's warm.'

'Oh, do put a sock in it!' Desperate for action and to escape the gloom, Louis ripped himself away from the group and accosted his company commander, who was talking to the RSM. 'Forgive me for butting in, sir, but couldn't we at least be allowed to raid?' His tone was begging. 'The men are awfully keen.'

Captain Cox looked at Probyn, his expression dubious. 'I shall relay your request to the CO but don't get too excited, I'm sure he'll say no.'

Carrying this appeal to HQ, Probyn was asked for his opinion, duly replying, 'It wouldn't hurt to put them to the test, sir.'

Colonel Addison shared his view, recognizing that he must do something to bolster his young officers who, by never being allowed to take an active role in battle, were in danger of becoming stale. 'I'll speak to the OC Artillery and arrange something.'

Subsequently, whilst in Reserve billets, the excited young officers were drawn together and lectured on the plan of attack.

Moving back into the line, they could hardly wait to put the lecture into practice. It was a very long day indeed, waiting for darkness to fall. However, there was a flurry of excitement to precede this.

Paying a midday visit to the trenches the RSM was almost bowled over as two privates sloshed through the quagmire in a state of excitement. 'Lieutenant Gaylard's captured a German spy, sir!'

Sure enough, a dirty, frightened-looking man in field grey, his hands upraised, was coming along the trench, occasionally losing his footing in the slime, coaxed by a pistol from behind.

'Well done, sir!' congratulated Probyn. 'Where did you find him?'

'Skulking near our line! I'm taking him to HQ.' Applauded by the men of his platoon a highly excited Gaylard gesticulated with his pistol, brown eyes shining. 'Sergeant, bring two men and come with me!'

Saying he would see Gaylard at tonight's raid, Probyn went on his way too.

After splashing across waterlogged fields for over an hour, Lieutenant Gaylard began to suspect that he had taken a wrong turn. Totally lost, he was unwilling to appear a fool in front of his men by asking the sergeant for help and so, after quick consultation of his map, set off again with fake confidence in his step.

An hour later, though, presented with a network of footpaths, some of which disappeared under water, he was forced to stop again in order to contemplate which of them to take.

Interpreting the problem, the German timidly intervened. 'Excuse please, my English is not goot.'

'I speak German, if you'd prefer,' replied Gaylard, casting a vague eye over the bleak landscape.

Brightening, the prisoner continued in his own language. 'May I ask where you are taking me, sir?'

'You should know, you're a spy.' Gaylard opened his map again.

A negating smile. 'I am no spy, I merely got lost in the darkness whilst out on patrol.'

Lifting his face from the map, Gaylard examined the other's expression. The man looked completely harmless. 'Well, if you must know we were heading for HQ but I'm afraid . . .' His voice tailed away in vacillation.

The German politely enquired. 'Would that be your Divisional HQ?'

Gaylard studied him. 'Er . . . no, Regimental.'

'Ah! Then, may I?' In a friendly manner the captive reached for the map.

A scowling Gaylard objected, snatching it out of reach. 'I think not!'

The sergeant levelled his rifle, the others following suit.

Alarmed by the click of bolts, the prisoner quickly raised his hands and explained to his main captor, 'You are not giving away any secrets! We are quite aware of all your positions. I just wish to save us all trailing round in circles. You have already come five miles out of your way.'

Gaylard flushed, hoping that none of his men were as fluent in German as he. A sly peek at their expressions made him none the wiser. Ordering them to lower their rifles, he explained that the German did not present a threat. 'We're just having a chat. I've managed to coax him into giving us details of their positions.' If they disbelieved him it did not show on their faces.

'If you will allow me to show you?' wheedled the prisoner.

Feeling extremely foolish in requiring such help, Gaylard kept tight hold of the map whilst allowing the other to indicate the right track, mumbling rather sheepishly, 'That's very decent of you.'

Making no apologies to the sergeant and men for making them walk further than was necessary, he began to head for the correct HQ, glad that others remained ignorant of his blunder.

Having already returned to the deserted *estaminet* that was HQ, Probyn was taking advantage of one of its bright fires, warming the backs of his aching, middle-aged calves whilst addressing the adjutant. 'A fine capture by Lieutenant Gaylard, sir.'

Crouched over a desk perusing some correspondence, Captain Max Lewis barely glanced up, his voice uninterested. 'Really? What was that?'

Probyn looked askance, remaining so for a couple of seconds. 'But you must have seen the prisoner by now, sir.'

The adjutant raised his eyes. 'I've seen neither prisoner nor our friend Gaylard.'

Probyn frowned, and quickly outlined the capture of the spy. 'Then I wonder where the lieutenant's got to.'

Both were left to wonder for some while. Even several hours later, when darkness was falling and Probyn revisited the adjutant's office, Gaylard had still not shown up.

'He's meant to be taking part in this blessed raid,' stormed Captain Lewis, in the glow of candlelight examining his watch for the umpteenth time. 'What am I to tell the colonel?'

'About what?' His superior came in, the draught from his entry rippling the frayed squares of hessian that cloaked each shattered window.

Probyn took the liberty of explaining.

The colonel groaned, then dismissed the matter for the time being. 'Well, whilst we're waiting have a look at this, Max.' He laid an enlarged aeroplane photograph on the adjutant's desk and held a candle over it.

'I say, what a novelty,' remarked Captain Lewis, his thin face brightening.

'What do you make of it, RSM?' The colonel signalled for Probyn to move nearer.

Having been respectfully standing by, Probyn came to stoop over the aerial photograph, his tone incredulous. 'Isn't it marvellous what they can do these days, sir?'

'It certainly is.' Colonel Addison turned his head swiftly as the flame of his candle guttered under a draught and someone else joined them; seeing that it was Gaylard his voice adopting a waspish barb, 'Although no amount of technology would be of assistance to some of us!'

'Where the devil have you been, Bob?' demanded the adjutant. 'We were about to send out a patrol.'

Lower limbs caked in mud, Gaylard directed his bashful answer at the olonel. 'I'm afraid I lost my bearings, sir.'

'For pity's sake, how can you get lost? It's only two miles!'

Gaylard appeared even more shamefaced. 'I can't quite get used to this new sector – the water and all that. I headed for Divisional HQ by mistake.' At the shared look of despair that passed between the RSM and his superior officers he added hurriedly, 'But it turned out all right in the end! The prisoner was decent enough to put us on the right track.'

'Oh well, that's all right then.' Captain Lewis's closely set eyes dealt him a withering look, then shook his head at the RSM.

'You haven't forgotten you're part of the black hand gang?' said the colonel.

'No, sir, I'm just about to go and prime my men.' An embarrassed Gaylard hurried away, followed by a sarcastic retort from the colonel.

'Sure you can find your way back?'

Exchanging an amused smile with his CO, Probyn asked, 'Mind if I go with him, sir?'

'No, you go ahead, RSM. I'll join you later.'

Probyn hurried to catch up with Gaylard.

The despondent subaltern begged him not to tell anyone.

'I won't, of course, sir, but you know what awful gossips soldiers are.'

The cupid face grimaced. 'I can't believe my own stupidity. I really thought I'd mastered it.'

'You have, sir. It was just a small digression.' Feeling sorry for the youngster, Probyn was led to reveal, 'I myself once got lost in Ireland. In a right scrape, nearly got murdered by Fenians.'

Gaylard drew no comfort in this. 'Yes, but one doesn't expect such incompetence from an officer.'

Overlooking the remark as a callow utterance, Probyn did not take the insult to heart, though his reply was delivered in cryptic tone. 'I hope Lieutenant Faljambe didn't charge you for those lessons in diplomacy, sir?'

'What? Oh, I beg your pardon, I had no intention of being rude. I'm just so angry with myself.'

'We've all messed up, sir – even officers.'

Leaving the candlelit HQ, they emerged into darkness and hurried down a bomb-damaged road towards the communication trench, an occasional bullet hissing overhead. Under threat from the enemy's fixed rifle battery, entry to the trench was made at a dash. Thudding across muddy duckboards, they hurried onwards over a bridge, across a stream and through a farmyard. A Very light went up, illuminating a heap of ruins, a broken ploughshare, a wasteland of gaunt stripped trees, rats scuttling amongst the sandbags and wire, then darkness enclosed them again.

Upon being reunited with his company, Gaylard found that, despite his efforts to conceal it, news of his débâcle had circulated around the entire battalion, and he was the butt of cruel teasing until, at RSM Kilmaster's suggestion, his tormentors directed their energies towards the more important issue of the raid.

Gradually, the noise of the day was dying down. By the time the CO came to meet them it was moderately peaceful. Gathering his officers and the party of volunteers, the colonel was able to address them in normal volume, giving last instructions in the minutes before the artillery was due to start up. Before the latter could drown out his voice, however, a great twittering commotion arose from birds, who should have long since been at roost.

Admiring his own quick thinking, Lieutenant Faljambe shouted, 'Gas!' And with a mass movement approaching panic, everyone struggled to don their respirators, fingers scrabbling to help less nimble comrades, hearts thudding in apprehension whilst an authoritative Faljambe strode amongst them, making sure they had done everything right.

Clad in their own masks, the CO and his RSM were striding masterfully along the line to ensure that all were prepared.

'Lieutenant Postgate!' The RSM's muffled bark emerged as if through a drainpipe and was incomprehensible, but the angry gaze which almost shattered the mica eyepiece was sufficient.

Following his pointing finger, Louis saw to his alarm that Unthank was seated calmly on the fire-step, smoking a cigarette. Immediately he yelled through his own mask, 'Unthank, get that helmet on!'

'There's no gas,' came the unruffled reply, Unthank taking another calm drag of his cigarette.

'What did he say?' Too far away, an agitated Louis demanded interpretation from others. But the fact that Unthank appeared to be breathing quite normally was indication in itself. One by one, in the darkness, those around him were beginning to untie their balaclava-style helmets.

'Dozy bastards,' growled Unthank to his neighbour Rawmarsh, the glow of a Very light illuminating the smirk on his face. 'It's a fooking owl.'

'What?' Frowning, Louis strode up, closely followed by the CO and Probyn, who also ripped off their hoods. The birds were still making a terrible din but there was not a whiff of gas.

Unthank was only slightly more polite in the officers' presence, dropping his cigarette before pointing at a dark silhouette atop a ruined house. All eyes on him, the owl spread his wings and glided silently into the night. Whilst the rest of the observers squinted without comprehension, it soon dawned on Probyn, who was a keen bird-watcher, and with a soft chuckle, he explained to the colonel at his side what all the din had been about. 'They can't stand owls, sir. Listen, they're settling down now.' Sure enough, the disharmonious chirping was fading away.

The CO was unamused. 'What fool shouted "Gas" in the first place?'

Having acted in the hope of commendation, an extremely defensive Hugh Faljambe owned up. 'I did, sir. But I was only acting on information given by the previous –'

'Well, thanks to you and cock robin,' the CO cut in tartly, 'there's little point in going ahead with the raid now. Captain Cox, I think it safer to wait until they've had a little more practice.' He winced impatiently as the artillery boomed into voice, drowning out the rest of his words. Mouthing a terse, 'Good night, gentlemen,' he stalked away.

Forming a small O with his mouth, Probyn teasingly regarded them as a bunch of naughty boys before following the colonel.

'Clown!' Louis dealt the embarrassed Faljambe a playful slap round the head as, to groans, the raid was postponed indefinitely.

After a great deal of persuasion of their company commander, Gaylard and Faljambe were given the opportunity to redeem themselves the following night and allowed to take their platoons out on patrol. Spotting a column of Germans, Faljambe took command and told Gaylard to run back to report the suspected attack whilst he and his men laid low to fend off the enemy should the situation become dangerous. Encountering no problem this time, Gaylard rushed directly to inform Captain Cox, so managing to foil the assault, Faljambe's platoon creeping up on the enemy's flank and killing many of them at the small expense of one of his own, the whole performance earning praise from the CO.

Others too began to show improvement. Living amongst the relentless squalor, Lieutenant Reynard had managed to overcome his natural tendency to think only of himself, and Probyn was often to see him going from man to man, enquiring as to their wellbeing, even if he could not help an expression of self-pity from permeating his concern, his face a vision of misery as he murmured, 'It's just so cold, isn't it? So jolly cold.'

Pork and Hamm distinguished themselves by repairing telephone wires under shell fire, earning themselves the Military Medal.

And Unthank, tucked away from everyone else in his sniper's hidey-hole, was proving to be much less of a nuisance, so long as there were Germans to kill. He had taken to carving a notch on the wooden butt of his rifle for each hit. There being already a considerable number of these indents, Probyn opined to Louis that at this rate the butt would be reduced to fretwork by the end of the war, but fought the urge to remonstrate with Unthank for defacing army property. If taken up for every misdemeanour, the man would be permanently in the guardroom. As far as Unthank was concerned they were here to kill Germans and no one could accuse him of failing in this. Far better to use his dubious skills and to keep him happy.

But it was in general a miserable period for everyone, the battalion sloshing from one waterlogged position to another, existing much of the time on biscuits and tinned stuff, men succumbing to frozen feet and influenza rather than bullets.

The end of October found them in the Cordonnerie Sector, still bailing and digging. Out in no-man's-land was a crater large enough to put a house in, and the amount of water that had accumulated in the bottom could have drowned an entire regiment. In fact, at times that appeared to be the case, for quite regularly bodies would float to the surface, the constant churning and pounding of the mud fetching up the putrefying corpses of Germans buried a year ago. The smell was sickening.

'My God, it's like something from an Hieronymus Bosch canvas,' Probyn heard a disgusted Faljambe mutter to his companions as yet another supplicating arm protruded through the slime to invade their living quarters.

To Unthank it was just 'a fooking shitheap'.

It was remarks like this that sapped their RSM's spirits as much as anything. Despite using the odd oath in anger Probyn had never contributed to the base vernacular of the lower ranks and as much as he knew it was not indicative of a man's nature nor of his bravery, he could not help but find it morally repugnant and he hoped they would not be in this position too long.

The relentless downpour was to continue into November, weakening the parapet and causing it to disintegrate in parts, so exposing the battalion to regular casualties. Trenches were knee-deep in water and the dugouts in an appalling state. With the frost setting in at night the suffering was intense. Frostbite was one thing their RSM had never experienced but, well aware that once it took hold a man was done for, Probyn did everything in his power to make life a little more comfortable for those in his care. Yet in truth their only comfort was that the Germans were in the same boat and an attack was impossible, allowing them to huddle into their funk-holes and keep warm as best they could, the rats snuggling under the blankets beside them.

Frustrated by his own lack of achievement and by the unforgiving environment, Louis gave voice to his boredom as he stamped his feet and looked out over icy lagoons, a sight to chill the heart. 'It'll be Guy Fawkes Night soon. For all the good I'm doing here I'd rather be at home organizing the fireworks display.'

Exercising their frozen limbs, his companions were equally miserable. 'We always have a lovely bonfire,' said Reynard wistfully, wringing his gloved hands and shivering, his dispirited gaze fixed on a wisp of smoke that curled from the German trench. 'With roast potatoes, toffee apples . . .'

Overhearing, the equally frozen RSM paused to offer a crumb of encouragement. 'I can't promise toffee apples, sir, but perhaps I can persuade the colonel that we should have some fireworks.'

Hunched into their greatcoats, the dishevelled young officers beheld him with muted interest. 'A raid, you mean?' sulked Louis. 'Mr Kilmaster, if you can arrange that you're even more of a magician than I thought. The CO thinks we're a pack of dolts.' Since the aborted raid he and Faljambe had constantly begged to be allowed to do another but had always been refused.

Saying he would do what he could, Probyn directed his aching legs back to HQ, where he put his idea to the colonel.

'Perhaps now's the time, sir. Fritz won't be expecting us in this foul weather. It'd raise spirits no end.' And mine too, he thought.

Having been entertaining the idea himself, the colonel was amenable and, the date of November the fifth appealing to his sense of humour, said he would arrange for the artillery to send over a few rockets.

Louis and his fellow subalterns were overjoyed upon receiving the go-ahead and were to shower effusive thanks upon the RSM for his part in persuading the colonel that they were up to the task.

How sad, then, that it had to be Probyn who was to disappoint them. Visiting the trenches some hours prior to the attack, their RSM chatted for a moment with the exuberant young officers, inwardly smiling at their repeated prayers for darkness to fall, then took a casual glance through a periscope.

More intuitive than his companions, Louis immediately noticed the alteration in the RSM's stance. 'What have you seen, Mr Kilmaster?'

Probyn rotated his gaze from the periscope, his expression grimly apologetic. 'I'm sorry to be the one to put the kibosh on it, sir, but we'll have to postpone your raid for another night.'

'Not likely!' The young officers shared vociferous denial.

Stepping back, Probyn invited, 'Have a look.'

Frowning, Louis put his eyes to the periscope whilst an impatient Faljambe risked a bullet by raising his head over the pile of sandbags and employing field glasses. Beyond the tangle of frost-coated barbed wire a board had been erected on the German line. The words that had been daubed upon it in paint were misspelled but the message was clear. 'FIREWORKS DISPLAY ON GUY FOX NIGHT. TOMMIES TO RECEIVE A WARM WELCOME.' And just as an added taunt, the Germans shot down the periscope through which Louis was peering.

'The swine, they must have ears like elephants!' Wearing a bad-tempered expression, Faljambe jumped down from the fire-step.

'They probably heard you blabbing about it!' accused Louis, equally crushed.

Able only to offer a sympathetic shrug, Probyn felt the young men's keen disappointment as yet another opportunity evaporated on the frosty air, along with Reynard's doom-laden mutterings, 'So cold, so blessed cold.'

Such tribulation could not endure for ever and towards the end of November the battalion was withdrawn from the line. Though not overjoyed at incurring more punishment to their tingling feet, Probyn's men set forth uncomplainingly on their two-day march to Steenbecque, to his great admiration not one of them falling out.

It was a pleasant village, quite untouched by war, only the rumble of guns and distant reflections of Very lights reminding one of its proximity, and with excellent billets to be had. They were to remain here for several weeks, under constant progressive training.

'Maybe one day it might come in useful,' quipped Louis to the RSM.

As a pre-Christmas treat everyone was allowed to throw a live grenade. It proved to be not such a treat for Skeeton, who managed to blow off his hands.

Whilst he went home, never to return, others had recovered from their minor wounds and bouts of influenza and now rejoined the battalion, along with a draft from England. Amongst the latter, to his brother's joy, was Captain Guy Postgate.

Watching their fraternal reunion, Probyn was quick to note the difference in the two. It was Louis who now appeared the elder, on the surface still a whirlwind of enthusiasm, yet inwardly matured by the horrors he had witnessed. Yet to be blooded, Guy remained as before, full of ambition and keen to be involved. However, his first ordeal was to run the gauntlet of the scruffy, lice-ridden bunch of fellow officers who ribbed him for his pristine apparel, a teasing he did not take kindly to; after his enforced stay in England he had expected sympathy. Attached to the same company as his brother in replacement for an officer who had gone sick, he wasted no time in compensating for this joshing by running down Louis's achievements.

'Still in bally training, eh? So I haven't really missed anything after all.'

Instead of listing all he had been through, Louis just formed a self-denigrating smile. 'No, just good champagne.'

'I thought as much.' Guy smiled back, though with just a hint of superiority, before casting his eyes around the peaceful area that was veiled with incessant rain. 'So you've got off lightly up to now, apart from this dreadful weather.'

If Louis was willing to let his brother get away with this the other listeners were not, Faljambe butting in, 'And apart from poor Sillar being killed.'

'Ah yes, I heard.' Guy hung his head for a moment, looking pensive. 'How did that happen?'

Faljambe was unusually reticent, merely announcing, 'A shell got him.'

'You're fortunate not to have witnessed it,' Louis told his brother quietly, the horror showing in his eyes.

But Guy took this as an insult. 'I have seen bodies, you know. Probably more than you. I came through some rough fighting on the way here.'

110

Louis despaired that his brother had to turn everything into a competition, but, having nothing to prove himself he merely nodded. 'Have they given you a decent bed?'

Guy looked impressed. 'Yes, I must say it's somewhat cushier than I imagined.'

Sharing a wry smile, Louis and his companions offered to show Guy round the training area, to which he was amenable though he strode out in front as if he already knew where he was going. Unfortunately, he was not as conversant with the lay of the land as he purported to be. Skidding on an uneven patch of ground, his feet went from under him and he slithered down a muddy slope, landed in a flooded hole and was drenched from head to foot.

There was a stunned hiatus, before the rest exploded into guffaws, bending double as Guy emerged like some slimy creature from the underworld. Having the grace to see the joke, the victim burst out laughing too and extended his hands for his comrades to haul him from the bog, even allowing himself to be paraded before the men as Christmas entertainment before going off to clean himself up.

In addition to this joyful pantomime, a mass of parcels arrived from home. Whilst this was no novelty to the pampered Reynard, who received a food hamper every month, there was an excited rush from other beneficiaries. Delighting over his own hamper, Louis put aside the tinned commodities for 'a rainy day' whilst dividing the rest fairly so that every man in his platoon might receive a treat. Faljambe thought him mad, but when Louis pointed out that if the perishables weren't consumed immediately the rats would only get them, he saw the logic.

Few of the men were without a gift of food from home; still they accepted their lieutenant's offering with gratitude – for some a quail's egg, others a skein of orange, others a sliver of mince pie – all except Unthank. Watching the scene, Probyn could have kicked the man for his surly refusal, and his heart went out to Louis who, desperate to connect, made numerous attempts to get beneath the layer of permafrost that was Unthank's skin, before finally giving up with a sad smile.

But the rest seemed glad to accept the lieutenant's little gift, for a few of their parcels had shrunk when opened, being padded out with newspapers – although these were something of a gift in themselves, the men reading out extracts to one another, laughing over the discrepancies between the reports and the reality.

'Listen to this!' said Rawmarsh. 'There's a chap here writing in to say he's never been so well fed as in the trenches – he must have come from the bloody workhouse then!'

'We're not so badly off today, though,' chirped Axup, holding up a quail's egg before shoving it in his mouth. 'Blimey, aren't we posh?'

'What did you get?' Though not liking him, Rawmarsh tried to include Unthank who, as always, sat aloof.

'Me mam sent a bit of Christmas cake and some socks,' came the guttural murmur.

Rawmarsh shook his head. 'No, from the lieutenant.'

'I don't need his fooking handouts.'

'Ungrateful get,' muttered Axup who, along with everyone else, really liked the platoon commander. Then in louder voice, asked, 'Did you send your mother anything in return, Unthank?'

'Aye, a Mills bomb wrapped in fancy paper,' joked another, only to receive a vicious kick in the back from the humourless Unthank.

Returning to his paper, Rawmarsh read aloud the newsprint that told that the deadlocked situation at Suvla Bay in the Dardanelles had been turned around by a wonderful military achievement: the whole force of Anzacs had been withdrawn without the Turks knowing a thing about it. 'Eh, I wonder if they could do the same here, then we can all go home for Christmas.'

But with training in full swing, few were lucky enough to receive a leave warrant, the rainy days up to Christmas taken up by divisional manoeuvres.

One of the fortunate recipients, mainly because he was required at home to train more troops, Probyn took leave of his young gentlemen, telling them how sorely he felt that they must remain here.

They gathered round to shake the RSM's hand and thank him for all he had done for them.

'Home to Yorkshire then, is it?' said Louis. 'You must call in at Postgate Park. I'm sure my parents would be delighted to make your acquaintance. They've turned the place into a military hospital, you know.'

Wondering whether it was said out of politeness or mere naivety, Probyn thanked the Viscount's son anyway. 'That's very kind of you, sir. I shall if I get the opportunity.' Though he would never take up the offer.

'So we shall have to rely on God above to keep us safe until you get back, Mr Kilmaster.' Faljambe was the last to shake his hand.

Probyn thought it rather blasphemous that the young man compared him to the Deity, his answer slightly reproving. 'We're all at the Lord's mercy, sir.'

Whilst the Division marched for Wardrecques and he towards home, this sobering thought was to be prominent in Probyn's mind, and, on his way to the railhead he was seized by a moment of vulnerability, dreading that one of the many pieces of shrapnel that hissed through the air had his name on it, or that a shell might flatten the train before he could be reunited with his beloved wife.

Even on a ship to Blighty there was no slackening of tension, wondering what lurked beneath the dark icy waters. Only when his beefy thighs strode upon home ground was he finally able to relax.

SEVEN

Oh, what simple pleasure it was to be rid of the mud, to walk along a dry street and gaze into shop windows, even if the displays were much reduced. It was Christmas but one would not have known it from the lack of illumination. Normally one would have to fight through the crowds at this time of year but this evening his passage home was easy, the only hazard caused by the prohibition of headlights.

A racking cough greeted his arrival in Tickhill Street, the kitchen cluttered with jugs of lemon and honey, a concoction of liquorice and herbs bubbling away in a brown glazed pot on the range. A martyr to bronchitis most years, Clem had obviously fallen victim yet again. This was a worry: time off work meant no pay. However, money was not Probyn's first concern as he ducked under a festive paper chain and came amongst his family, his initial act being to clasp his delighted wife in a bear hug. Barking and retching, almost to the point of vomiting, an exhausted-looking Clem threw his tab-end on the fire and rose to shake hands with his father, the children too gathering excitedly round him.

'Give me those fags!' Releasing Grace, Probyn good-naturedly divested his son of the cigarette packet. 'I'm not listening to the sound of that beffing while I'm on leave.' He lit one himself whilst accepting the offer of a cup of tea from his wife, considerately directing the smoke up the chimney. 'No peeking in that bag!' he teased the children, who were nosing round it.

Telling her siblings to allow their father room to breathe, a happy Augusta went back to feeding Mims. Beata watched the seven-month-old baby eating her milky rusks, eyes fixed on the

114

spoon as it was lowered and raised, willing her sister to leave some for she liked them too. In the transfer from spoon to mouth, a dollop fell onto the child's bib. Quick as a flash, Beata whipped it off with a finger and inserted it into her own mouth.

Witnessing this, her father scowled, then grinned to show he was only pulling her leg. Whilst his eyes were on the children, Grace winked at Clem and with a swift movement knocked a picture askew, before going back to stirring the pot on the range. 'How long have we got you for, dear?'

'Seven days at home, but I'll be staying in Blighty for three months, getting more men into shape so I might be able to nip home again before I go back to France.'

Noting how tired and drawn he looked, she turned anxious. 'But you're not involved in any fighting, are you?'

'No, no.' He gave a pacific smile. 'I'm only training those who are.'

Grace expressed gladness, 'But what a time they chose to send you home. I'd have saved you some tea if I'd known. Let me see what I've got in the pantry.'

'I can go down to t'chip 'oile,' volunteered Joe, hoping for some chips himself.

Probyn said this was unnecessary as he had already eaten, at the same time he noticed the crooked picture and automatically went to straighten it. Hearing clandestine laughter, he whirled on Clem and Grace. 'Eh, I haven't been in five minutes before your mother's having me on!'

Everyone laughed, Joe taking advantage by asking if Father would organize a game of housey.

'It's almost bedtime,' said Mother, to moans of dismay, before conceding, 'All right, you can stay up a while, but let's at least get you into your nightclothes.'

A smiling Probyn bent to pat Mims on the head. 'This one'll be going to bobies, though.'

Grace was quick to disabuse him of this supposition. 'Oh, she won't go to sleep before the others.'

'Won't go?' said an amazed RSM, hands on hips.

'No! She's got a will of iron, has that one.'

He responded with derision. 'Will of iron – she's not a year old! Just put her down and let her get on with it.'

'Don't say I didn't warn you!' The bright reply from Grace bore a note of challenge, and she laid the child down. Immediately Mims began to wail and fought to sit up.

'It'll stop in a minute.' Probyn sounded confident.

'I'm sure you're right, dear.' Grace smiled sweetly.

He sensed mockery. 'Just leave her!'

But in the end, with his eardrums so under assault and Mims's bad-tempered screams threatening to wake the whole village, Probyn was forced to give in. 'Good grief, I thought I'd come home for a bit of peace, but what with Clem's cough and this one it's noisier than being in France. All right then – but just for five minutes!'

'That's what you think.' Laughing, Grace went to pick up the sobbing Mims and, cradling her in a rocking embrace, began to lull her towards sleep. 'Go to sleep, my baby, close your pretty eyes . . .'

Gradually, everyone fell silent, similarly calmed by their mother's gentle singing. Even Mims finally succumbed, her eyelids growing heavier with each rendition and eventually closing altogether.

Probyn too appeared drowsy, having to jerk himself awake and smiling at his dear wife. No matter what horror and degradation lay outside that door, in here Grace's loving spirit could always make everything right.

Her voice becoming softer, fading to a hum, Grace fell silent and moved with stealth towards the cot – at which Mims was suddenly alert and wailing again.

Immediately, to her husband's groans and children's laughter, Grace broke into fresh verse, continuing to sing and hum until, finally, the rebellious babe drifted off to sleep.

Banning the proposed game of housey as too noisy lest it wake Mims, Probyn merely indulged the rest of his offspring in desultory chat for a while until it was their bedtime. Seating herself at his feet, Gussie unwrapped her father's puttees and began to massage one of his sturdy legs as she had done since being very young. Watching, Beata asked if she might rub the other leg and was allowed to do so before all were dispatched to bed.

Then, at last he and Grace were alone, sitting in the gentle hiss of gaslight.

But the final treat of the night was yet to come. After enjoying first a bath, Probyn groaned in ecstasy as he lowered himself into a bed that had been moulded over many years to his own form. 'Oh, sumptuous! Oh, I can't tell you how good this is! Oh, heaven!'

'Better keep it down, dear, the neighbours will wonder what we're up to.' His wife cuddled him. 'You stay in bed tomorrow. I'll light a fire so it's nice and cosy for when you get up and I'll bring your breakfast up when I come back from Mass.'

Giving an appreciative murmur of her bodyheat, he declined. 'I can't lie in bed while you're in church. I'll come with you. I'll need my suit, though; my uniform's lousy.'

Grace felt a surge of panic. Surprised by his unexpected homecoming she had completely forgotten that his suit was in pawn. As a result of lending a neighbour money, she had run short herself; Probe would go mad if he found out. 'Don't forget it's Midnight Mass tomorrow. There's no need for you to go twice in one day.'

He did not need much persuading, snuggling up to the one he had thought about so often whilst away, his desire quite evident.

Relieved, a smiling Grace reached out to turn down the gas flame, then fitted her body into his, making a mental note to redeem his suit first thing in the morning.

Having inherited her mother's devotion, Augusta often accompanied Grace to morning Mass. Hence, it was Maddie who was left to get the others out of bed and to give them breakfast. She was also given a coin and the pawn ticket and told to redeem her father's suit, with the instruction that it must be done with discretion.

'Hang it in your father's wardrobe as quietly as you can. I don't want you waking him.' Grace and Augusta left for church.

Regarding the laying-out of breakfast as enough to contend with, Maddie went upstairs to rouse Beata telling her, 'You're to go to the pawn shop and get Father's suit.'

It was most unfortunate that she omitted the rest of the instruction. Beata had no idea as she strained to hang up the garment, rattling hangers and sending them clattering to the floor, that she was meant to observe secrecy.

Woken by the noise, Probyn jerked upright, ready to jump out of bed in the face of attack. Then remembering he was at home he spoke grumpily to the person responsible. 'Beat, what are you rummaging about at in my wardrobe?'

'Sorry, Father. I was just trying to hang your suit up.' With anxious face, the old-fashioned little creature with the bobbed auburn hair strained on tiptoe to hook the hanger over the rail.

His beefy visage creased from sleep, he frowned and worked his lips to rid them of a wayward whisker of moustache. 'How come it fell down in the first place?'

'It was at the shop. I just bought it.'

'Bought . . . ?' Drowsy or no, it took only a few seconds for Probyn to realize that the suit had been in pawn.

117

Sighing and flopping back on his pillow, he told Beata to leave it over the chair and go downstairs. He lay there for a few moments longer, rubbing his eyes and wondering what his comrades were doing in France, until Clem's coughing drove him out of bed. There was a fire dancing merrily in the hearth; Grace must have crept in and lit it whilst he was deep in slumber. Donning his clothes that had been warming on the tiles, he went downstairs.

After a quick cup of tea he went out to surprise his wife, saying he would have breakfast when he got back.

Already on their way home from church, Grace and Augusta were chatting about how good it was to have Father home for Christmas. Up ahead of them was a limping man who accosted passers-by along the way, occasionally receiving alms, at other times refused. Walking briskly, Grace and her daughter soon began to catch up with him. Hearing their approach he turned; Grace prepared to be accosted.

First, though, she was surprised by a ragged, elderly man who stepped as if from nowhere. 'I don't suppose you've got any jobs you need doing, missus?'

Faltering, a sympathetic Grace recognized him as the village lamplighter; due to the blackout he would doubtless be redundant now. He certainly looked as if he were on his uppers. But she was forced to tell him, 'No . . . I haven't I'm afraid.'

He touched his cap politely and moved on.

Even more hard up than usual, Grace looked at her daughter and anguished for a second – if she refused a destitute man she would never forgive herself – then taking a much-needed penny from her purse she called him back and pressed it into his hand.

Cutting through the allotment gardens at that precise moment, her husband saw what had transpired but was too far away to stop it. He marched on grimly.

No sooner had the lamplighter bestowed her with sincere thanks than Grace was presented with the eager outstretched hand of the limping man. 'Spare a penny for a wounded soldier, missus?'

Grace set her mouth, pointed to her eye and announced in firm tone, 'Do I look green?' And maintaining her stern expression she walked on, hooking her arm through Augusta's.

Noting her daughter's surprise, she explained. 'I might be a soft touch but I'm not completely gaga. Didn't you see he kept limping on different legs? Wounded soldier, my Aunt Fanny!'

Augusta gave a respectful laugh for her mother's astuteness, then exclaimed as she spotted her father.

Upon reaching his wife, Probyn scolded her. 'I hope you weren't giving him money?'

'Of course not! He was a crook.'

'I saw you give the other one something, though!'

Grace felt foolish. 'Oh, but he was needy, Probe.'

'Aye, and so must we be if you had to resort to pawning my suit!'

Grace winced at being found out. 'Sorry, it was just that Mrs Wilson's having such a hard time and –'

'And of course you feel responsible for the whole world. Eh dear!' Probyn shook his head in loving reproach and planted a firm hand upon her shoulder, saying jokingly to Augusta, 'Let's get your mother home before she starts giving away the family silver.'

But for all he affected to rant about his wife's lack of control on the purse strings, he would not have Grace any other way than the generous, warm-hearted, compassionate woman she was, and he could not fault the wonderful Christmas she laid on for her loved ones. Ensconced in the bosom of his family during that comforting time at home, Probyn knew that the children shared his adoration of her. From the look on their faces one would have thought she had given them the world instead of the penny, apple and orange and handful of nuts that she had somehow afforded to put in their stockings. Watching them all gathered around Mother at the piano, rapt faces concentrated on her as she sang for them, for a split second he was on the outside looking in and had an overwhelming sense of envy, as if he did not belong. But, then Grace caught his eye, winked and bestowed him with that seductive loving smile that drew him immediately back into the circle.

Much as he enjoyed the company of his children, most of all he looked forward to the time when every night they went off to bed, leaving him and Grace at liberty to cuddle on the sofa and talk, much of their discourse centred on those at the front who comprised his other family, his warmest words being reserved for the young officers straight out of school who struggled to cope with their heavy responsibility.

On his last evening at home, Grace was seated beside him but seemed more intent on her knitting. 'I'll only be a few minutes, then you can have my whole attention,' she said to his accusation that she was neglecting him. 'I'm just racing to finish this before you leave. Only another inch or so to do.'

'What is it?' Probyn lit a cigarette.

'A balaclava.'

'Grand, it'll keep me little lugs warm.'

Hands working like pistons, Grace chuckled. 'Gussie's knit you one too but she casts on so tightly that I doubt you'll get it over your head. Still, you must say it's lovely when she gives you it.'

Row after row, the balaclava was finally completed and, after being tried on, was tucked into his kit bag. 'I've put two tins of cocoa in here as well,' Grace told him. 'One for you, one for the boys.' Having come to know many of their names, pictured them in their terrible plight, Grace felt as strongly for them as did her husband.

He donated a smile for her goodness. 'I shall save it till I'm back in France – now will you stop ferreting in that bag and come and sit down and talk to me?'

Scooping a handful of nuts from the bowl on the table, Grace returned to her warm seat on the sofa and they were soon involved in conversation, even if it was mainly about the conflict.

'They're proving as stubborn to shift as the Boers, aren't they?' Her head on his shoulder, she held the collection of nuts in her lap, handing one after another to her husband who wielded the crackers.

Shattering a hazelnut, the kernel of which he gave to her, Probyn nodded. 'It's only because they've got better machinery, though, that we haven't beaten them yet. Nobody's to blame, you can only make calculations on what's gone before. I don't think any of us expected it to get this big.' Nothing in his past had equipped him to cope with a war of this gargantuan scale. Loath to move away from Grace's soft warmth, he made a half-hearted effort to throw the bits of nutshell into the fire but they fell onto the hearth to join others that were scattered there. 'Still, look on the bright side, we might not have had the expected success but, even with all their weaponry, neither have they. Now that this Coalition Government's taken charge of munitions we should see an improvement.'

Chewing, Grace handed him another nut. 'Listen to us, talking about the blessed war and you only having a few hours left at home. Oh, I wish you could be here to see the New Year in with us. Still, it's been lovely to have you for Christmas. I shouldn't grumble.'

He grimaced over a tough shell, finally succeeding in cracking it and handing her the contents in fragments. 'No, we've been lucky not to have more Christmases apart. That first one was a bit rough wasn't it?'

Grace smiled at the memory, for it was when she had been expecting their first child. 'Eh, it seems only yesterday, I can't believe our Clem'll be sixteen this next year.' Then her gaze drifted to the photograph of Probyn's young officers, seeing it through a mother's eyes; many of them still had the baby fat on their cheeks. She was momentarily sombre. 'I hope to God this war finishes before he's old enough to join up.'

'It will.' Probyn gripped her knee supportively. 'Next year belongs to us, you'll see.'

EIGHT

March opened, as stiff and uninviting as a frozen sheet on a washing line.

Back at the front with another batch of troops that he had spent the last three months training, Probyn found it very cold and quiet, neither side showing interest in the war, although it was immediately obvious that during his absence there had been a great deal of activity from aeroplanes and artillery, for the landscape was radically altered. Battalion Headquarters had been all but demolished, the adjoining houses reduced to charcoal stumps. However, his alarm was quickly expunged on finding its occupants unharmed and now sleeping in dugouts across the road.

'After three direct hits we decided it would be safer here,' explained Colonel Addison smilingly upon their reunion. 'Welcome back, RSM.'

Following the exchange of a few genuine pleasantries with his CO, Probyn's first query was about the strength of the battalion. Gladly, no more of his young officers had been killed in his absence, though Lieutenant Riddell had been wounded, along with seventeen others. Informed of the four rankers who had died, he registered momentary sadness over their loss, before storing their names away at the back of his mind along with the dozens of others from previous conflicts. Thenceforth, his immediate impulse was to re-establish contact with those who had become his particular favourites.

First, however, he deposited the rest of his kit in a similar excavation to the colonel's, and with the help of his batman put Grace's tins of cocoa to good use, boiling up two large containers of the beverage. It did not matter that on freezing nights to come there would be none for himself; these lads had been stuck here for three months, he hadn't. 'Shame there's not enough for everybody,' he told Arrowsmith, 'but at least it'll warm a few cockles. I suppose it's too much to hope that we've got any fresh milk to put in it? I hate this condensed stuff.'

'Let me just go and have a word with Violet, sir.' Wearing a canny expression, Ralph Arrowsmith excused himself.

The French had been very generous with their dairy produce, but Probyn was surprised by the amount of milk in the bucket that Arrowsmith brought back. 'I hope your friend Violet hasn't left herself short on our account.'

'You can ask her yourself, sir, she's only in the next dugout.' Arrowsmith laughingly explained that the battalion now had its own cow. 'I found her wandering loose. Well, I couldn't leave her to fend for herself, could I?'

Probyn was most admiring of his batman's resourcefulness. 'By, is there nothing you can't lay your hands on, Ralph? You'd have made a good regular.'

But the tailor was quick to dispel this. 'Ooh no, sir, it's all a trifle too windy for my liking. If I'd known how bad it would be I'd never have volunteered.'

'At least you're honest. Here, have a cup yourself.' Wearing his new steel helmet and carrying a dixie in each hand, Probyn went out along the frozen line, picking his way amongst the shellholes and the bits of man and horse that dangled from the barbed wire, distributing cocoa along his way and instructing the recipients to, 'Warm yourselves up, boys.'

Leaving a ripple of appreciation in his wake, and with just enough cocoa left, he went to seek out his young officers, finding five of them in Louis Postgate's dugout, four sitting round a table, the fifth pacing uncomfortably before a charcoal brazier that gave out dreadful fumes.

Grown tired of Foxy Reynard's complaints about the cold, Louis seemed immensely pleased to see the regimental sergeant-major and jumped up from his battered chair, his exclamation forming a cloud on the freezing atmosphere. 'Why, Mr Kilmaster, welcome back!'

'Good to be back, sir.' Of course it wasn't, what fool would gain pleasure from this? But there was partial truth in that he had missed the company of these brave young men. 'Got your mugs handy?' When these were hurriedly produced, plus an extra one for him, a smiling Probyn shared the last of the cocoa between them, receiving more expressions of gratitude. Steam began to drift around the earthen hovel.

Now as dishevelled as his brother, his eyes holding that same haunted look, Guy Postgate wrapped filthy hands around his tin mug, the others doing likewise. 'Whilst this is gratefully acknowledged, Mr Kilmaster, I sincerely hope it's not all you've got with you?'

Probyn returned his smile and took a sip from his mug, wiping his eyes that had begun to water from the pungent fumes of the brazier. 'No, I've brought your reinforcements, sir, although they're very green, as you might expect.'

Louis grinned at his fellow troglodytes. 'Does this mean we may now consider ourselves veterans?'

'You certainly may, sir.' It had been a gap of only three months since he had laid eyes on them, but long enough for those left behind in the trenches to have developed a layer of world-weariness. Saddened for their lost youth, Probyn turned his attention to the array of saucy postcards that were pinned to the sandbagged walls above Louis's hammock and made tutting sounds of disapproval that he knew would amuse the young men.

At least most of them. A look of discomfort on his pimply face, after a few sips Reynard had left his mug on the table and started pacing again, stamping his feet and beating himself with his arms, moaning about how numbingly cold it was.

As was customary, everyone ignored him, demanding to hear from the RSM what was going on at home.

Before Probyn could relate this Faljambe interjected with a snarl of condemnation, 'For the last time, Foxy, will you stop blocking the fire!'

Mumbling apology, a pain-faced Reynard sat down and, whilst Probyn relayed his news, began to remove the mud-caked boots.

Gaylard presented his schoolboyish face with its old man's eyes, eager to know. 'Can you give us any inkling of how much longer we might be here, Mr Kilmaster?' Rumours abounded of impending pushes, but still they were kept motionless in the cold.

Speaking truthfully, Probyn said he did not know but doubted that they would be going far in this atrocious weather.

'I *told* you I had bad circulation!' A triumphant Reynard held up one of his socks, to which adhered two blackened appendages that had once been his toes.

Whilst others beheld the spectacle with disgust, Probyn stepped forward with calm advice: 'Better hop down to the aid post, sir. Come, let me give you a hand.'

Reynard's expression of triumph had quickly turned to one of dismay as he gazed upon his frost-bitten foot. Disregarding the RSM's offer of assistance, he looked up with a stunned expression on his face. 'Does this mean I'll be going home?'

'It does, sir.' Probyn saw the briefest flicker of relief take over Reynard's face before being replaced by manufactured woe.

'Oh, but I feel such a fraud! I did so want to make a contribution.'

'And you have, sir.' Probyn spoke genuinely and took one of Reynard's arms, Louis hurrying to take the other, Faljambe and his companions gathering round to voice concern.

'Bad luck, Foxy.' His face sincere, Guy delivered a sympathetic pat to the victim's shoulder. 'We'll be sorry to lose you.'

Showing disbelief that his valiant career had been cut short after just six months and still holding the sock with its putrefied attachments, Reynard uttered a forlorn goodbye that totally concealed his gladness to be going from this shambles, before allowing himself to be supported to the aid post.

There was no time to dwell on his departure for the scream of shells heralded an attack, sending everyone diving for cover. It was too dangerous to move, so Probyn stayed put, his ears and nerves tortured by the constant bombardment as his own howitzers set up retaliatory fire. When he finally returned to HQ after darkness he found that the cow had been hit by a splinter of shell and had bled to death.

Lieutenant Reynard was not the only one to suffer from the freezing mud of winter. Coming out of the line and removing their louse-ridden garb, many more were to discover they had become unwitting victims of frostbite. Private Porks barely had time to observe that one of his toes had turned black before it subsequently dropped off.

Trying to hide his distress at being parted from his close friend, a cheerful Hamm piggy-backed him to the ambulance and, along with other comrades, waved him off to Blighty, telling him how lucky he was.

Hugh Faljambe looked particularly despondent as the ambulance pulled away.

'Don't take it to heart, Hugh,' said Louis.

'What?' The tone was confused.

'I know you were fond of Pork but –'

'Oh, it's not that!' Rather haughtily, Faljambe set his friend straight. 'No, I'm just put out that I appear to be losing my charm.' His arrogance blinding him to the others' shared mirth, he told them, 'I was snooping around the village and came across this old landaulet which would be absolutely ideal for jaunts into Estaires. Unfortunately the wretched woman wouldn't let it go. It's sitting there covered in cobwebs – what use is it to her? I threatened to commandeer it but she refused to budge. Got quite rude, in fact.'

'I can't imagine why,' murmured Louis, sharing a sly smile with the RSM before addressing Gaylard. 'Go find some petrol, Bob – er, don't get lost – we'll show him how it's done.'

'You're very certain of yourself,' scoffed Faljambe as Gaylard went off.

'Not at all, but I have two friends who are certain to sway Madame's opinion.' Ducking into his lair Louis rifled through the Fortnum and Mason hamper bequeathed by Reynard and emerged, hands laden with luxuries.

'Would you care for some pâté, Mr Kilmaster?'

Gratefully accepting the offering, Probyn smiled as he watched the young men embark on their sortie, Faljambe in the lead, Gaylard lugging a can of petrol and Louis advising Faljambe that he should keep out of the woman's way once they arrived and to let him do the talking.

Probyn was not to see the results of their foray until some days later. Making an impromptu decision to spend his final night of rest enjoying a night out in Estaires, he was walking the three miles into the town when, at the insistent honking to his rear, he turned to see a motorcar pull alongside him. Polished and painted with the battalion sign, the landaulet was a very superior vehicle to the one he had imagined.

A merry invitation pierced the rumbling of war in the background. 'Can we offer you a lift on the Postgate Express, Mr Kilmaster?'

Before the surprised RSM could respond another voice leaped in, sounding rather indignant. 'Er, why not Faljambe's Flyer? I was the one who found it.'

'But I was the one who *won* it,' insisted a grinning Louis, and explained to Probyn how the vehicle had been transformed from its previous cobwebby state. 'Madame even helped us find some paint. Jump in, Mr Kilmaster!'

Susceptible to Louis's laughing blue eyes himself, Probyn could well imagine how the owner of the car had fallen to his charms. Accepting the invitation, he squeezed in beside the gay young officers and, though contributing few words, he smiled in quiet appreciation of their youthful repartee during the journey that remained.

Upon reaching Estaires he thanked them for the lift and, refusing Louis's invitation to join them, said he had a prior engagement and saw them on their way, chuckling at Faljambe's murmur of relief. 'Thank God, I thought he was going to ruin my night.'

Taking the opposite direction, the RSM went off to a concert, alone.

Some of the turns were excellent, others atrocious, consisting of bad jokes, monotonous monologues and caterwauling fiddles. Deciding to leave if the next act did not show more talent, he was jerked back into his seat by the announcement of a name that was most familiar to him. Smiling broadly, he sat back to enjoy the dulcet tones of Michael Melody.

It was a sentimental ballad, of course; what else could one expect from Mick? But he enjoyed it as much as the rest of the audience and there were many shouts of 'Encore!' before, to rapturous applause, the Irishman was allowed to leave the stage.

Pleased with himself, Mick was going along a corridor when a disembodied voice called, 'Halt! Who goes there?'

He stiffened at first, then a hint of recognition came into his stance. ''Tis meself,' he answered, a cautious smile playing at his lips.

'Advance yourself and be recognized!' The owner of the voice emerged from his hiding place.

'Pa, you old sod!' Mick beheld him with obvious pleasure, his manner still that of a friendly young animal, though he must be over forty now. 'Didn't I know it was you! In God's name, will ye ever look at him – wasn't I always saying you'd make RSM!' Grinning widely, he enjoined in a strenuous shaking of hands with Probyn, looking the bullish figure up and down in amazement.

Despite joining the army at the same time and sleeping side by side until Mick had been transferred, they had little in common and had never been close, Probyn regarding the Irishman as a wastrel for not using his many talents to improve his status. Even so, he was an immensely likeable sort and Probyn was happy to see this chummy face, not much altered, despite the hint of grey around the temples and widow's peak, and the ribbing he gave was not malicious. 'I see you've still managed to avoid a stripe, Mick.' The other's khaki sleeve bore only the insignia of the RAMC.

'I have indeed, though they tried their very best to force me into it! Well, fancy that, among all these millions of soldiers we manage to bump into each other!'

'Oh, never underestimate such coincidence,' smiled Probyn, still engaged in the other's grip. 'Only last week I found myself next to Grace's brother.' Amidst thousands, passing on the road, he and Fred had exchanged news and cigarettes before marching their separate ways.

Mick could not rid himself of the incredulous expression. 'How are ye? Oh, 'tis great to see ye! How long has it been?'

'His Majesty's Coronation, I think!'

'Aye, it must be!' Another vigorous shaking of hands.

Amid much smiling and incredulity, it transpired that Mick was billeted in Estaires for the moment. Flouting regulations, the regimental sergeant-major immediately accepted the hospital orderly's invitation to have a drink with him, and off they went together to the Ping-Pong Café.

Upon entering there was a welcome draught of warm air from the stove, and the not so welcome sight of Private Tom Unthank, who was obviously the worse for drink, for he was slumped low over the table and his face was even more morose than usual as he lectured his drinking partner, stabbing his finger to make his point. Probyn almost turned round and went out, but then Unthank was quiet compared to Hugh Faljambe's braying laughter that now assaulted him.

At the centre of the room, in a soft pool of light provided by oil lamps, the group of young officers was having a whale of a time, Louis apparently in his element surrounded by daughters of the owner Agnes, Estelle, Berthe and Pauline, the champagne flowing freely.

'Don't go, Mr Kilmaster! There's plenty of room.'

Quietly acknowledging Louis's greeting, but declining the offer to join his table, Probyn deftly steered Mick to one cast in shadow and less obtrusive. The last thing he wanted was attention from the drunken Unthank.

Madame approached with a jug of beer from which Mick accepted a glass, his companion choosing coffee.

Then, between bursts of loud laughter from the officers' table, the friends' questions began. 'Still living in York, Mick?'

'I am! And you?'

128

'No, Denaby Main.' Probyn explained that after his military term was over he had gone back to mining. 'And how's Mrs Mick these days?'

'Ah, she's a wonderful woman!' The other's ruddy face projected ecstasy. 'Wasn't too pleased at me coming here, I can tell ye, but a man has to do his bit, doesn't he?'

'He does indeed.' Probyn took a sip of his coffee. 'You were expecting your first bairn the last time I saw yo –'

'Ah yes! Mary's four years old now, God love her.' Mick looked fond. 'Then there's Brendan, he's three, and another on the way. Yourself?'

Probyn gave a sheepish laugh. 'Seven.'

'God love us! And you accusing the Catholics of taking over the world.'

A wry smile. 'You're forgetting I'm one of your lot now.'

'Ah, that's right. There's nothing like a convert for taking the teachings so literally.'

'Well, I suppose I've an excuse. I did have a head start on you.' Probyn had been married seventeen years to Mick's five.

'Aye, fair play to ye – and how is the lovely Grace?'

Thus the conversation went on, the old pals reminiscing of former comrades and their early days in the army, to every one of Probyn's sentences Mick rattling off ten. Someone began to play a mouth organ, its sentimental songs of home reducing the Irishman's volume, his face becoming dreamy.

'So what d'ye think of France? 'Tis beautiful light here, don't ye think? When the bombs are not dropping, I mean.'

Lacking Mick's artistic eye, Probyn had not noticed until having this pointed out to him. 'Yes, I suppose it is – Oh deary me, that's not such a beautiful sight, though.' The door had suddenly opened and the convivial atmosphere changed dramatically, all heads turning to the military policeman framed within its jambs. From beneath the slashed peak of his cap a suspicious glare encompassed those in the room, seeking out offenders and coming to rest on the regimental sergeant-major. Though apprehensive, Probyn met the gaze squarely, hoping the redcap might use his discretion and overlook the lower rank of his drinking partner. But one glance at those eyes and his heart sank, intuition telling him even before the other opened his mouth that here was a stickler for the rules. Out came a notebook and the MP began to stalk across to him, pencil at the ready to take his name and number. Uttering an inward groan, Probyn mentally cursed Michael Melody as a jinx. What infernal stroke of fate had caused their paths to cross? He prepared himself for arrest and trial for the breaking of Divisional Orders, to be demoted from the rank he had coveted so long.

But then, the MP's eye was distracted by another pair of transgressors at a table and he made a sudden diversion.

'You know the rules about drinking with lower ranks!' The MP addressed Unthank's drinking companion, the unfortunate Corporal Bebby, who had been corralled by Unthank and dragged in here against his will; rather than pulling rank he had decided to take the easy way, or so he had assumed; he was not so sure now.

Before he could answer the charge however, a belligerent Unthank got to his feet and pushed back his chair. 'He can drink with who he likes.'

'Right, I'll have your –' Pencil at the ready, the MP dropped like a stone under a blow from Unthank.

Whereupon, Madame was to lose her entire clientele, everyone crowding for the exit as if someone had shouted 'Fire!' Probyn and Mick too put the diversion to good use, striding over the recumbent form of the MP. But whilst others seemed keen to leave, Unthank remained to take vicious pleasure in kicking his victim and would have gone on to kill him had he not been dragged off and bundled outside.

Apologizing for his part in the matter, little Corporal Bebby promised his officers and the RSM that he would get Unthank safely back to billets, and hence rushed the troublemaker away before the MP regained consciousness.

Everyone else too made to depart the scene, Probyn laying accusations at Mick's door: 'I always get involved in something when I'm with you!'

Mick roared with laughter. 'Sure, 'tis almost like old times! Go on then, I can see you're haring to be off.'

'I want to be well away before yon fella wakes up,' grinned Probyn.

This same thing in mind, the young officers were moving again towards their landaulet, Louis hailing the RSM. 'Are you heading back to Fleurbaix, Mr Kilmaster?'

Calling back that he was, Probyn took hurried leave of the Irishman, telling Mick he hoped they would meet again soon. 'It was good to see you, chum.'

'Oh, and you too, old marrow!' Mick shook Probyn's hand, calling after him as the space between them widened, 'All the best to ye, Pa!'

Regarding the young officers as too drunk to drive, Probyn took it upon himself to navigate the car through the darkness whilst they draped themselves happily across the leather upholstery, singing their heads off.

Bumping along the cratered road, he came across Unthank and Corporal Bebby, arm in arm, and made to steer around them.

'Let's stop!' cried Louis, and made as if to invite the pair into the car.

But Probyn said firmly, 'I think Corporal Bebby can cope, sir.' And he drove on.

'Back to fairyland,' slurred Gaylard, observing the line of Very lights soaring, hovering, falling upon the glowing orange horizon whilst the rumble of distant thunder punctuated his speech.

'Pa?'

Probyn stiffened at Hugh Faljambe's address from the back seat.

'Why did that fellow call you Pa, Mr Kilmaster?'

Concentrating on the steering wheel, the driver's answer was thrown over his shoulder. 'An old nickname, Mr Faljambe, short for Padre because of my tender, fatherly nature.'

There came a honk and stifled sniggering from behind him. Inwardly smiling, Probyn allowed it to pass, saying only, 'Though I should be obliged if you didn't use it.'

'Oh, we wouldn't dream of it, Mr Kilmaster!' came Louis's merry reply, but for him there was a grain of truth in the nickname and, swamped as he was in champagne, he put voice to it. 'Though I consider it most fitting – a blessed marvel that you're able to look after hundreds of men when I have a hard enough time just keeping my platoon safe.'

'You do well enough, sir,' Probyn told him.

'That's most gracious of you, most gracious,' yawned Louis, then despite the jolting passage, fell asleep with his head on Gaylard's shoulder.

Back amongst the ruins of Fleurbaix, Probyn steered the car outside the door of the officers' billets and alighted to assist the merry group who came tumbling out.

Faljambe narrowed his eyes and pointed to a group of soldiers. 'Am I seeing things?' Without caution, he headed straight across the road, the rest of the group following him, Probyn trying to keep them from harm.

'Pork, what the deuce are you doing back here?' Faljambe's grubby blond moustache was awry with incredulity, giving a brief glimpse of yellow teeth. 'Weren't you a Blighty case?'

A rueful Pork explained. 'Well, when I got to the ship, sir, the order was no more stretcher cases so I thought we were expected to get up and walk on board. The OC said, "If your feet can carry you up the gangway they can carry you back to your regiment." So here I am.'

There were sounds of disgust from the officers, Faljambe making all sorts of threats against the ignorant offender. 'How dare he send one of my men back?'

Probyn asked with genuine concern, 'Are you able to carry on, lad?'

There was not a trace of bitterness in Pork's reply. 'Yes, sir, I'd rather be here with my pals than at home, anyway.' Receiving commendation, he limped away.

'What an absolutely disgraceful way to treat a man,' objected Louis to Probyn.

But Faljambe already seemed to have forgotten him, turning away and calling over his shoulder. 'Good night, Pa!'

'Thank you, Michael Melody,' growled Probyn under his breath. 'Just wait till I see you again.'

But he was not to see Mick again, nor were there to be any more jaunts to Estaires. Someone from Divisional Staff had noticed the spruced-up landaulet and after a bunch of correspondence was exchanged it was requisitioned. Not that it mattered to those back in the line and under bombardment. Besides which towards the end of the month a heavy snowfall was to make the roads impassable.

Ironically, at this same time the order came to prepare to move. After derisive laughter came excitement.

'Does this mean we're heading for the show down south?' a shivering Louis asked Probyn.

'That's what it looks like, sir.'

'Let's hope it's a bit warmer down there,' opined Lieutenant Geake.

'Oh, I think I can promise you that, sir,' smiled their RSM. 'At least you won't feel the cold, what with all that training I've got lined up for you.'

Parading at one thirty in the freezing cold morning, the battalion marched to the station at Merville and boarded a southbound locomotive, detraining at three in the afternoon to be swallowed up in the massive ocean of khaki that was gathering on the Somme.

Marching to billets at Vignacourt, they were to halt in Amiens, and such were its attractions that many wanted to extend their stay. Presided over by a Gothic cathedral, the city boasted smart cafés, bars and restaurants, the stench of war momentarily obliterated by the aromatic draughts that wafted from perfumiers, delicious scents at every turn. Virtually untouched by hostilities, it was nevertheless a city under military rule, a city of refugees, of impoverished locals with sorrowful expressions, of red-hatted staff officers and journalists.

During the halt, tantalized by the smell of eau-de-Cologne, Probyn thought of his wife and, suddenly remembering that Grace's birthday was coming up, he bought a card decorated with lace and embroidery and scribbled an affectionate note in it before dispatching it along with a postal order.

It was good that he had done so for there was little on offer in the village where they were billeted, apart from real beds for the lucky few – besides which, they were to move again within days, merging with the vast masses of troops that converged on the Somme valley.

The sun had come out, there were catkins dangling in the breeze, crimson anemones beneath the trees – some of the latter had even begun to blossom. All at once winter had turned to spring, but it was a mixed blessing to those compelled to march. The frozen fields had reverted to bogs, further churned by heavy-calibre weapons. What had once been a village street was now an obstacle course of watery holes around which they must weave a path whilst trying to avoid the flying debris that came whistling overhead. The air alive with devils, the ground throbbing and bouncing them around like peas on a drumskin, the soldiers spent more time throwing themselves flat than walking. It took four and a half hours to cover ten miles and all along the way there were men being shot or blown to bits, those who accrued only a layer of filth considering themselves to be the fortunate ones.

Though snuggled in a valley and protected by a ridge from the battlefront, Albert was almost completely wrecked. Thus it was nigh impossible to find a billet where the bitter wind did not howl through shattered windows and doors. Yet standing poignantly defiant amongst the wreckage was a golden statue of the Virgin, balanced precariously upon a half-demolished column and holding her Child in outstretched arms.

Parading before the church at seven o'clock on that last day of March, Probyn looked up at the Holy Babe and thought of his own children, pictured his wife at Mass as she would be at this hour, perhaps lighting candles for her husband and his men. Would that a candle was all it took to save them. This month had seen the grim toll doubled, with seven killed and twenty-one wounded, most of them within the last few days. Finding little time for God in the trenches, Probyn nevertheless offered a silent invocation to the statue now, praying not for himself but for his young officers upon whom had been heaped such great responsibility. Over months of eavesdropping on their intimate conversations, watching them twitch in their nightmarish sleep, he knew each of them almost as well as his own sons. And he prayed for the young Postgates now, for Faljambe and Gaylard and the rest, asking that they be imbued with even more courage and ability than they already possessed, so that they might protect their men from harm during what he sincerely hoped would be the final push.

'Have you heard?' An excited Hamm broke the news to his chums the following morning. 'We're all going home!'

So convincing was his joy, that they leaped eagerly to the bait. 'When?'

'When hell freezes over – April Fool!'

'You bastard!' Each dealt out personal punishment, wrestling the offender to the ground, but ending up laughing despite their terrible disappointment.

'Bet you can't pull one on Pa,' Pork challenged him.

Omnipresent, their RSM stiffened at the sound of his old nickname that had rapidly been disseminated throughout the battalion. Half flattered at the celebrity, half annoyed at their lack of respect, he burst amongst the men, transforming the light mood. 'Enjoy a little April Fool joke, do you, Pork? Well, here's one for you: we're going to the circus.' He pointed to the line of observation balloons strung along the horizon.

Hence, on that first day of April, amongst considerable risk of shrapnel and rifle grenade, the battalion took over its first Somme trenches in front of Albert, the defences stretching downwards from the Tara Ridge and giving a clear view right across the enemy position, lending plenty of opportunity to observe and to the snipers. Finding himself a comfortable little nook, well apart from the rest, Unthank was in his element as he picked off Germans like crows.

After forty-eight hours of being shelled and strafed by enemy machine guns, and rifle grenades fired at them even at night, the third day was quiet, though there was much aerial activity, squadrons of aeroplanes passing over, escorted by large observation craft, the fighter planes occasionally looping the loop as if cocking a snook at those on the ground. 'Ruddy show-offs,' Faljambe called them.

And so the month was to proceed, one day uneventful with no one hurt, the next erupting in mayhem with shrapnel and whizz-bangs injuring half a dozen. Some days saw no hostility from either side, men grabbing the opportunity for a mass washing and shaving operation, otherwise darning socks, forming working parties, mending the wire, digging trenches or shooting rats.

Today being such a day, Probyn held a pair of field glasses to his grubby face, watching the considerable movement along the Ovillers – La Boisselle road, the drone of aeroplanes overhead. The sky was lifeless; neither grey nor blue it just stretched for miles like a dirty, limp rag.

Protected by a wall of sandbags, Colonel Addison moved beside him to take up a similar position. 'Seen anything of interest?'

His RSM continued to inspect the enemy lines, the glint of German field glasses directed back at him bringing a smile to his lips. 'Not really, sir, just them watching us watching them watching us.' He lowered his binoculars.

'I have.' Colonel Addison held out his hand, upon which was a tiny frog.

Probyn chuckled at the minuscule creature, he and the colonel spending some moments in contemplation, each remembering boyhood summers, until the frog sprang away into the mud.

Probyn became serious again. 'I'd like to try and do something about those machine guns, sir.' Whilst the shelling was bad enough, it was these that were most lethal, the Germans using them to devilish effect.

'Quite.' Colonel Addison brushed his palms. 'However, I'm afraid any remedy will have to wait until we return. We're being pulled back to Divisional Reserve.'

Thus, after a march to Hennencourt Wood camp, commenced another bout of training in the wet and the mud.

Back at Albert, towards the end of the month there was heavy shelling in the afternoon but by evening things had quietened down and Padre Farrington thought it safe to prepare the special dinner that he had originally planned to celebrate St George's Day. With asparagus and potatoes dug from a garden by the resourceful

135

Arrowsmith, plus a chicken that had been foolish enough to wander from its home, the officers and their RSM were looking forward to it immensely. But at seven thirty, as they were sitting down to eat, sharp heavy enemy gunfire started along the whole front. Whilst this might have been ignored, the use of tear gas could not.

The first warning came from the birds that started twittering and flying high into the air. From every dark corner rats and mice came scurrying in their hundreds, holding their heads aloft in a frantic effort to breathe fresh air, the occupants of HQ quickly joining this endeavour, pulling on their gas helmets, grabbing their weapons and rushing out to repel the enemy attack.

For three hours they battled, returning the German fire with equal ferocity, many acts of gallantry being performed before the belligerency eventually ceased. Cold, worn out and ravenous, Probyn wandered back to the table, only to find it a seething colony of rats.

On the first of May the battalion took over from the 8th York and Lancasters at a spot known as the Glory Hole, where the lines were some sixty yards apart with nine large craters between them and the enemy, the whole terrain honeycombed with mining operations. Under continual assault from missiles they had nicknamed oil cans, each weighing forty pounds and packed with high explosive, it was to be a very demoralizing period, the overwhelming ambience one of blood. Blood of every hue: bright pillar-box red that gushed in life-sapping fountains to spatter the unwitting bystander; crimson as the Lancaster rose, worn by Yorkshiremen alike; black like tar and rife with maggots. Neither the artillery nor the aircraft, hampered by thick cloud, had made any effect on the spot from where the oil cans were observed to emerge, and the frightfulness continued unabated.

Furthermore, at lunchtime that day, a direct hit was scored on Battalion HQ.

Probyn had just settled down with a bowl of soup when, to the accompanying moan of a German trench mortar, the roof fell in and everything went black. Seeing the dugout caved in and its occupants completely buried, an alarmed Louis and several others dashed to help, scrabbling at the earth and pulling at the arms and legs that protruded. In the agitated scramble it was hard to gauge to whom the limbs belonged, the colonel receiving less respectful treatment from his underlings than he was wont to expect. But it did not appear to matter, for upon ridding his eyes of soil and straightening his metal helmet he dealt them cheerful thanks and joined the rescue.

One after the other, most of the occupants were pulled out unharmed, if dazed and more than a little filthy, the worst casualty being Ralph Arrowsmith, who suffered a broken leg. But Louis remained anxious at the non-appearance of the RSM. 'Mr Kilmaster's still under there somewhere!' And he began to scrabble again.

Despite his own agony, the loyal Arrowsmith refused to be stretchered away and waited anxiously to see what fate had befallen Pa. Guy spoke encouragingly to him – 'He'll be all right, everyone else is' – but he was none too optimistic as he laboured beside his brother to move the debris.

'He's here!' A foot was spotted jutting from under a leaning sheet of corrugated iron.

Everyone converged on it, praying that the foot was attached to a man, vigorously hurling aside the sandbags that held the sheet in place and finally dragging it aside.

His broad back coated with earth, the RSM was doubled over, his face between his knees, no one was sure if he was dead or alive. Then, slowly, to their great relief, he began to come gingerly upright and they saw that his eyes glittered with life, saw also to their amazement that a bowl of soup was balanced upon his wide thighs. In no rush to move, the face below the tin hat showing utter distaste, Probyn used finger and thumb to remove a lump of soil from his soup, telling the onlookers calmly, 'I don't mind fighting for France but I'd rather not eat it.'

Having made everyone laugh both with relief and for his audacity, he called for water with which to rinse his mouth, hoping none would guess that behind his cool exterior he was trembling at such a close call. With no time to move before the explosion he had simply hunched over his precious dinner and hoped for the best.

Only now did Arrowsmith allow himself to be taken away. Probyn hurried to wish the casualty a speedy recovery. 'Good luck, Ralph, and enjoy your little rest in Blighty.'

'I will, sir,' grunted Arrowsmith, lifting his contorted face for a last glimpse as he was stretchered along the trench. 'And you keep yourself safe.'

'I'll try.'

'Do try a little harder, Mr Kilmaster.' Louis camouflaged his own huge relief by a quip. 'We thought that minnie had your name on it.'

'Where did it come from?' Colonel Addison enquired of witnesses.

'Wye Sap, I think, sir,' offered Louis.

'That damned place again! Well, that's the final insult,' announced the colonel, a glint of resolution in his eye. 'I'm not sitting here putting up with this. Louis, you've been dragging at the bit to do a raid, well, now's your chance.'

'Me too, sir?' Faljambe and Guy spoke eagerly in unison.

'The whole bally lot of you, if you choose. I want that sap out of action.'

An hour after midnight, under cover of heavy artillery fire, the participating squads waited tensely for the signal to leave their trench. Taking part along with Louis were Guy and Hugh Faljambe, plus two officers from another company, with their faces blackened, only their voices betraying their identity.

As usual, the waiting was the worst part.

'I'm bloody freezing.' Hugging himself, Louis grumbled to the person at his side.

Probyn murmured a gentle tease: 'You sounded just like Lieutenant Reynard, sir.'

A laughing groan. 'God forbid!'

'Besides, you're not permitted to be cold before October. Army regulations.'

'Right, over you go!' Directing the operation, Captain Cox gave the order and everyone crept enthusiastically into action.

Watching the raid from the fire-step, Probyn felt the draught of the field gun's shells on his neck as they *whooshed* overhead, his hair bristling at the thrill of it, wishing he could be amongst those young men who disappeared behind the wall of thick smoke, his heart leaping over the parapet with them and on towards the enemy sap. But he must perforce remain here, enveloped in the choking miasma, nostrils tingling at the reek of high explosive, his eyes those of a worried father, deafened by the scream of shells and the deadly stuttering of machine guns, wondering if any of those vicious tongues of flame that licked the night had found a human target.

Cries of alarm interspersed the gun fire; it was impossible to tell whether they came from his own men. The wait for them to return seemed endless.

Captain Cox spoke. 'They should be here by now. I'll give them some light.'

Unleashed hissing into the darkness, the cartridge sizzled and shimmered into life, momentarily illuminating the desolate landscape with its ravaged buildings and splintered trees. Through the mist loomed several figures heading stealthily towards his own front trench. Squinting through the drifting veil of smoke and dust, Probyn saw them duck against the unwanted limelight, flattening themselves into the mud.

'No more light!' called a voice he recognized as Hugh Faljambe's and as the glare died he turned to address the captain but not in time to stop another launching.

This time other figures were to be seen, hopping, hobbling, scurrying towards him, crouching under the onslaught of machine-gun bullets, mortars bursting all around them. They did not try to hide from the spotlight now but came hurrying onwards, flinging themselves the last few yards and into the trench.

Probyn was delighted to see Lieutenant Faljambe in one piece and also everyone under his command. Another anxious wait ensued whilst, one after another, the rest of the raiders hurled themselves into the trench – Lieutenant Buxton, Captain Postgate, all their men intact, Lieutenant Postgate's squad commanded by a sergeant – but where was Louis himself? Clambering back onto the fire-step, Probyn squinted worriedly through the thick haze. Damn the boy, where was he?

After another half an hour, the firing petered out, the night eventually becoming quiet. Yet, however much Probyn strained his eyes across no-man's-land, no human could be seen.

Still pumped with excitement, Guy had only just been notified that his brother was missing and, sharing the RSM's anxiety, announced, 'I'm going out to find him!'

'Very good, sir.' Knowing how Louis would detest being rescued by his rival, Probyn delayed the young captain. 'Though it might be best just to give it a few minutes.' But a bubble of nausea had begun to swell in his throat as he wondered over Louis's fate.

He had almost given up hope and was preparing to watch Guy go over the top again when two more figures came stumbling through the haze, carrying a third.

'Hold your fire!' The cry went up and several tense seconds followed, during which Probyn strained to make out the incomers' identities but not until they heaved themselves and their wounded comrade into the trench and the glint of baby-blue eyes penetrated the smoke did he ascertain that Louis was safe and the heart-warming announcement was made: 'They're all back.'

With an inward sigh of relief, Probyn assumed his normal air of authority and supervised the removal of the injured man, who was suffering dreadfully.

'Thank goodness. I was just coming out to rescue you,' Guy told his brother.

Fizzing with exhilaration, Louis was deaf to the insult and, as the firing petered out and the night became quiet, he made his report.

'Wilson did a marvellous job! It's a devilish shame that he was hit on the way home.' Despite his genuine concern for the man his eyes were bright with invigoration. He did not even seem to notice that he had left part of his sleeve on the barbed wire along with a fragment of earlobe, the rest of it encrusted with dried blood. 'But we scuppered their listening post! Managed to get two of the occupants before the other bolted. Sorry about the delay in getting back but Corporal Bebby and I were forced to lay doggo in a hole with Wilson until it died down.'

Congratulating everyone on a good job, Probyn went off to bed, though it was to be a very brief sleep, broken by a shower of earth and stones as Fritz showed his displeasure by blowing a mine in the early hours.

There was to be further hate throughout that day, the Germans sending over everything they had but only managing to inflict one slight wound. Encouraged by the previous night's success, the members of the battalion were equally vigorous in their response. After such a demoralizing time it was an uplifting moment. Probyn hated to be the one to knock Louis from his dizzy heights.

On a morning visit, he chose to hold the good news until later, first announcing the bad. 'I regret that Private Wilson died of his wounds, sir.'

Louis screwed his eyes shut and hung his dark head. 'I was the only one who lost anybody.'

'Can't be helped, sir.'

'It could if I'd taken better care of him.' Louis's tone betrayed self-disgust.

'On a happier note, the CO asked me to convey his congratulations, sir. He's received a message from Brigade HQ complimenting you on your night's work.'

Louis nodded, still downcast. All at once the thrill of his exploit was lost.

After eleven consecutive days, the longest it had spent in the trenches, the tired and worn out battalion was relieved in the early morning.

Jaws that had been clamped so long in fear of death, now fell slack, giving their owners an idiotic appearance, but Probyn held them in the greatest esteem as he marched his beleaguered force back into Divisional Reserve at Hennencourt Wood.

They were to remain there for the rest of May, training, supplying working parties and digging trenches.

Here to make up the numbers of those who had fallen, the first draft of Derby Scheme men began to arrive, in their undefiled uniforms sticking out like sore thumbs. Many of the old hands were to grumble that this distinguished battalion must adopt such reluctant recruits and told them to their faces that they would never be able to fill the boots of brave men. Probyn treated all alike. To him they were here, that was all that mattered and he drove them as hard as the rest in preparation for the return to Albert.

For others, though, the mention of Derby had different connotations. 'Hold on,' said Colonel Addison, a spark of interest in his weary eye. 'I'd forgotten what day it is. The big race is coming up. We must have a sweep.' Seizing a mud-streaked newspaper, he produced a list of runners and requested his servant to cut up scraps of paper for the draw. 'We'll require a bookie. RSM, you're the most trustworthy of us!'

'I'm sorry, sir, I can't allow you to entice me into bad ways,' Probyn reproved him with a frown. 'I was raised in a non-gambling, teetotal household.'

'Oh, I do apologize . . .'

The frown turned instantly to a grin. 'Just teasing, sir. The army led me into bad ways years ago. I'm sorry, though, I can't be your bookmaker, I haven't the foggiest what it entails. I wouldn't object to a little flutter, though, if that's all right.'

The colonel assured him it was and a sweepstake was duly organized, though he was to be less than complimentary when his RSM turned out to be the one who won the large cash handout.

Sending his winnings home to his wife, Probyn enjoyed a quiet smile, wondering what comment his strait-laced father would have made on his gambling. Then a shell burst to distract him, sending the horses into a panic as several of their number were maimed, and the thrill of his windfall was to be overridden by a fleeting sense of parody as he imagined his winner bursting past the finishing post whilst these poor unfortunate brutes were blown to bits.

*   *   *

Gradually, the unrelenting quagmire succumbed to the persuasive caress of sunshine and a new layer of grass fought to take hold, soon to be adorned with cornflowers and poppies. Between the deadly blasts of noise, those birds that had so far managed to escape the German guns and the French pot were singing their hearts out.

It was hard for the soldiers to enjoy the lengthening days of summer, their lines continually strafed by machine-gun fire, pounded by shells, shrapnel and grenades, tormented by black clouds of bluebottles, but they managed to make the most of it, grasping at aught to stop themselves from going mad.

A pair of robins had nested amongst a pile of stones in one of the trenches last month and, though thought to be doomed, had managed to hatch three chicks, an amazing feat of endurance that Probyn was discussing with the CO and Major Lewis when Guy Postgate's servant appeared, handing each an envelope.

Colonel Addison read his aloud in a tone most appreciative. 'Captain Postgate asks if we will attend a convivial evening at his residence to celebrate his brother's twenty-first birthday – why, we should deem it an honour! Wouldn't we, Harry?'

Major Lewis gave cheery confirmation.

Probyn too inclined his beefy head in gracious acceptance. 'Please tell Captain Postgate I regard his invitation as uncommonly kind.'

'Thank you, sirs. The captain would also be obliged if you kept it under your hats. It's a surprise.'

It certainly was. Louis had just seen his batman die in agony after being disembowelled by a shell, but, desperate to blot out the image and touched by his brother's gesture, he threw himself wholeheartedly into the party that had been arranged for his coming-of-age. With the MO, the adjutant, Padre Farrington, Major Lewis, Captain Cox and the rest of the company officers on the guest list too, the dugout was cramped but the atmosphere immensely chummy, all rank dispensed with and the colonel telling a series of risqué jokes, giving rise to others. Slightly disapproving, Probyn nevertheless laughed out of politeness, thinking to himself what a remarkable thing was the human spirit as he watched those laughing mouths spouting endless humour whilst inside they must be almost insane from the awfulness that enveloped them.

Eaten from makeshift utensils, the contents of the birthday hamper were scrumptious, as was the wine, drunk from empty jars that had been preciously hoarded over the year.

'I considered serving drinks on the terrace but perhaps it's a trifle windy,' smiled Guy, then led the toast to his brother. 'To Louis!'

'To Louis!' Those gathered raised their variously shaped jars.

There was a brief hiatus, invaded only by the ever-present buzzing of flies. Urged to put a record on his gramophone, Hugh Faljambe selected a lively tune, causing feet to tap.

Major Lewis remarked, tongue in cheek, 'I'm rather surprised that you didn't invite Private Unthank. Surely no guest list is complete without him?'

Whilst others laughed and continued to beat time to the tinny refrain, Colonel Addison went on to shake his head in mock despair. 'In all my years in the army I have never known a man without one redeeming feature – not one. Even a civil question he takes as an insult.'

Guy made chuckling addition. 'You tell him to do something and he snarls at you – like this.' His accurate demonstration brought laughter from his audience.

From his brother too, though Louis entreated them, 'Oh, he's not that bad!'

'He is!' Captain Cox threw up his eyes. 'Normally I wouldn't stand for a tenth of the insubordination he presents but were I to take action he'd never be out of the blasted guard room. Any other commanding officer would have him shot, but all that would achieve is to deprive us of a damn good sniper. Better just to give him a wide berth and let him get on with it, I say.'

'I've got one just like him at home.' This was the RSM's first contribution and all looked at him expectantly. 'She's just over a year old. You should have heard the stink that bairn kicked up at bedtime! I tell you, we should employ her as a secret weapon. The Germans would soon give up.'

The officers found it hilarious that their iron-handed RSM could be so outdone by an infant.

'Still, I think it rather cruel of you to compare her with Unthank, Mr Kilmaster,' smiled the colonel, turning to Louis with a frown of incomprehension. 'Tell me, Louis, how can you possibly defend him? He is the most appalling fellow.'

Louis let forth his contagious laughter. 'Oh, I'm sorry, sir, but you sound just like . . .' another giggle, 'just like my old nanny! She used to say I brought home the most appalling boys.' Having succeeded in infecting everyone with his merriment, he finally simmered down and replied philosophically, 'Oh, under all that hostility I feel sure there must lie a noble streak. After all, Unthank and his fellow miners gave up a well-paid job to be here.'

Smiling into his jar, Probyn wondered whether to disabuse the optimist of this notion, but, remembering when he himself was young and idealistic, decided to remain silent.

But the colonel spoke his mind. 'I hate to shatter your illusion, Louis. Whilst the rest are undoubtedly spurred by patriotism I suspect it's not a motivating force for Unthank.'

'Why else would he exchange good wages for a soldier's pay?' demanded the young lieutenant.

'Because it's worth the drop in money to be allowed the legal right to murder!'

'Oh, surely –'

'Louis,' a hint of weariness in his tone, Colonel Addison spoke as if to a simpleton, 'the man's here because he wants to kill people and they won't allow him to do it at home.'

Major Lewis shared a laughing nod with the adjutant.

'Well, I beg to differ.' Louis turned to Probyn. 'What's your opinion, Mr Kilmaster.'

Probyn weighed his words. 'Unfortunately, I have to agree with the colonel –'

'*Unfortunately*, RSM?' Colonel Addison donned a look of mock reproach.

Probyn smiled before continuing: 'But I don't think anyone here can say he isn't a handy man to have around in a war.'

'There!' said a triumphant Louis.

'Well, it wasn't exactly a compliment, sir –'

Louis would not be swayed. 'He's risking his skin the same as the rest of us, and that's good enough for me.'

This induced a chorus of, 'For he's a jolly good fe-llow!' And afterwards: 'Speech! Speech!'

With Hugh's gramophone stilled, Louis was about to oblige when a soldier entered and saluted. 'Excuse the interruption, sir, but it's important.' He handed over a communiqué.

Puffing to remove the fly that invaded his nostril, Colonel Addison unfolded the piece of paper and a look of shock wiped the smile from his face. He bowed his head, allowing it to rest on his chest for a second, before raising grave eyes. 'I'm sorry to ruin your party, Louis, and I'm afraid it's going to cloud many birthdays to come, but as everyone's gathered . . .' Reciting from the message, he took a deep breath and announced: '"By His Majesty's Command. The King has learnt with profound regret of the disaster at sea by which the Secretary of State for War has lost his life" –'

The listeners shared a groan.

'– "while proceeding on a special mission to the Emperor of

Russia. Field Marshal Lord Kitchener gave forty years of his distinguished service to the State and it is largely due to his administrative genius that the Country has been able to create a place in the field the Armies which are today upholding the traditional glories of an Empire. Lord Kitchener will be mourned as a great soldier, who under conditions of unexampled difficulty rendered supreme and devoted service both to the Army and the State."'

Finishing his reading, the colonel folded the message and stared at the earthen floor. 'Now we really must make the attack count, as a memorial to the great man.'

To this purpose the following days of June were devoted to intensive rehearsal, Probyn driving the men perhaps harder than ever across the training area, not caring that he earned less flattering nicknames than before or that many cursed him as heartless, focused only upon the Great Advance and having the battalion totally prepared for it.

It was difficult to imagine how they could fail with such massive power at their disposal and the amount of times the strategy had been enacted. Despite not taking part in the real attack, he had attended the officers' lectures and knew every single stage of the plan, from Zero and the amount of water carried on each person to the clearing up details, felt a thrill of pride to be associated with such an enormous undertaking and in what was surely to be the turning point in the war.

It was to transpire that others besides Probyn would not be taking part in the attack. After another brief stint in the trenches the battalion was moving out of the line when a shell exploded at its centre, the smoke eventually clearing to reveal the usual carnage. The only creature still upright was a horse, the sight most unusual in that it was not galloping about in the crazed way that Probyn had witnessed a hundred times before, but remained completely motionless, its head hanging low and blood dripping from its lip, not even screaming, just making pathetic whickers of distress. Then it just keeled over and died.

At this same instant a scream arose from another source. Unthank was amongst those injured but it had taken him a moment to discover just how badly. Not only had the shell detached a chunk of his right leg but along with it had taken his masculinity. Deranged by pain he was screaming at those around him to put an end to his misery. Instead, they merely stared at the appalling damage and yelled for a medic to tend his blood-sodden lower half.

'Shoot me!' gasped Unthank in agony. 'For pity's sake, shoot me!'

'I can't do that, Unthank!' Swiftly, Guy kneeled and applied field dressings to the victim's hip and groin area, more of an attempt to cover up the emasculation than genuine assistance.

'Shoot me, you cunt!' Unthank's face was contorted with hatred and suffering.

Probyn was about to stride forth but was preceded by a blur of movement. He saw Guy shoved aside as his brother rushed up, levelled his revolver and shot Unthank through the heart.

Amongst the onlookers, and for the perpetrator too, there was a moment of suspense at the enormity of what Louis had done. Then, he turned to his brother, his eyes, as no one had seen them before, holding a look that dared Guy or anyone else to make accusation. Rising from where he had been so rudely deposited, Guy merely laid a hand on Louis's back, then quickly shrugged off his daze, reverted to his usual competent self and organized the removal of Unthank's body along with the rest, and the battalion marched on its way.

At their destination, brushing off his company commander's attempts to tranquillize, Louis said that he would like to assume the unenviable task of writing to Unthank's family. 'Considering that it was I who killed him.' So saying he excused himself and rushed away.

Witnessing this, Probyn quietly followed Louis to his tent, standing for a moment to watch the stooped and traumatized figure before murmuring quietly, 'And what are you going to tell them, sir?'

Louis glanced up at the intrusion to his quiet corner, his face a picture of anguish as he made the dull enquiry, 'How do you tell a mother that you've murdered her son?'

'You didn't murder him, sir. You did the only kind thing.'

'Shot him like the poor inhuman brute that everyone held him to be.' Louis shook his head in utter despair, his fingers raking through dark locks. A youth who wanted to be a friend to all – it had become a sad obsession that he had never managed to charm Unthank. 'I never did succeed in getting him to like me.'

Watching those tortured eyes, Probyn guessed what lay behind them, recalled the moment long ago when he himself had discovered the brute within, had done things he could never have contemplated.

Louis did not speak for a while, fingering the piece of paper on which he was supposed to be composing a letter. 'I suppose it sounds crass after what I've just done, but I regard this as the worst thing about the whole blessed job, knowing what to say to a man's mother.' From past experience he knew she would want to know that her son had died instantaneously.

But it took the RSM to confirm it. 'Tell her what she wants to hear, sir,' came the quiet advice.

With a shuddering breath, Louis nodded and directed his pencil at the sheet, his voice impassioned. 'This war, this bloody, fucking wretched war. Will it never be over?'

Dealing him a look of empathy, the RSM drifted away and went to organize yet another rehearsal for the coming attack.

The constant practice did indeed make perfect, but proud as he was at the achievement of his troops it was all becoming a heavy burden for one of such mature years.

Taking a welcome rest from the intensive training, Probyn spread his mackintosh in a grassy field and sat down to light a cigarette. Whilst towns and villages along the front were gradually being reduced to ruins, beyond the bloody mayhem haymaking was in progress, the sweet fresh smell of newly mown grass reaching him even through the appalling stench of war, and immediately transporting him to happier times on Aunt Kit's farm.

Bees hummed. Whilst he smoked and immersed himself in thoughts of family, others around him played musical chairs, their instruments a comb wrapped with tissue paper, a couple of human bones which the player clickety-clicked using his knees as a percussion board. Relieved that the dreaded training was almost over and expectant of a good result in the real thing, the men were very cheerful, much of this stemming from an eagerness to revenge the many friends who had been killed or wounded during their time at Albert. The order was to kill as many Germans as they could. From his own experience Probyn knew that most would need no prompting.

A Whitsuntide parade came by. Led towards their battered church by a priest with golden crucifix aloft, the children were dressed in white for confirmation. Just like at home. Probyn imagined the coal carts that had been scrubbed and decorated with ribbons for the day, taking the village boys and girls around the houses, singing hymns. Soon he would be there, God willing. If he did not end as Lord Kitchener, at the bottom of the sea.

His own departure from France was preceded by the haunting tones of Last Post, the bugler's rendition not for him but to punctuate the memorial service for the Secretary of State.

CSM Dungworth was going home shortly too. Having previously discovered that Bert lived in the village next to his, Probyn arranged to meet him for a pint, then went to say goodbye to his young officers and to wish them luck in that for which they had striven so long.

'Well, this is what you've been waiting for, gentlemen.' He shook hands with every one of them. 'I wish with all my heart I could be part of it.'

'And we too,' was Louis's sincere reply. 'I'm sure my brother would prefer that you were here to take care of me.' He smiled at Guy.

'You're quite able to look after yourselves, sir.' Probyn assured him. 'I envisage great success.'

'Mr Gaylard, Mr Faljambe, Mr Geake, good luck, sirs.' Injecting them with a firm look of confidence, he backed away. 'Well, I'd better go and train a new lot so we can keep up this momentum. Once we've got Fritz running we want to make sure he doesn't stop.'

After taking leave of the rest, his final parting was reserved for Colonel Addison. 'All the best, sir. Good luck for the Show and I'll see you anon.'

NINE

Following an overnight crossing and motor vehicle transport from the coast, Probyn finally arrived in London. The metropolis, though hugely impressive, had always slightly unnerved him, the sheer volume of people on the streets, everyone a stranger, rushing past as if they had not a minute to spare, infecting him with their haste and causing him to increase his own gait. Crossing the wide thoroughfares was almost as big a risk as stepping into no-man's-land, horses almost totally replaced by motor vehicles that honked and pipped in irritation of him.

On entering Victoria Station, he stood for a moment to recoup his breath and get his bearings, as always a man apart. His eyes fell on a young attractive woman and followed her as she marched up to a man in civilian clothes. Her mouth set in a bitter line, she thrust a white feather under his nose. Embarrassed, the man tried to turn away but she grabbed his arm and hissed at him. 'Conchie!' Others heard and joined the condemnation as their quarry hurried to get away. His face impassive Probyn watched him being harangued for a moment, feeling no sympathy for one party nor the other: with no obvious disablement the man was more than likely a coward, his attackers totally ignorant of what it was like in France.

Between the milling travellers a notice caught his eye – 'French money exchanged here for officers and soldiers in uniform' – and he wove his way through the dead-eyed London crowd and an obstacle course of suitcases and portmanteaux towards the small booth where he swapped his remaining foreign notes for pounds, shillings and pence before seeking out the entrance to the underground.

Caught up in a torrent of bodies and not entirely sure if he was heading for the right platform, he had no option but to let the current bear him along, propelling him into an already packed carriage, hopefully the desired one, others shoving through the doors after him, all jostling for a place. Thenceforth he was trapped.

Not prone to claustrophobia, it was nevertheless a horrible feeling for one accustomed to living in open fields.

En route for King's Cross with the feathers of a woman's hat in his face and someone's elbow in his ribs, he asked himself testily, were these the people whose lives he had fought to protect at the risk of his own? No one offered to give up their seat, no one said well done or thank you, no one so much as looked at him. Indeed, when a vacancy occurred at the next station and instead of jumping into the seat he offered it to the woman whose hat had been such an annoyance, she edged past him as if he had the plague. Bored with their flag-waving, they now seemed inured to khaki-clad exploits. After twenty years a soldier he was hardly dumbfounded, though he doubted he would ever get used to such fickle treatment.

Eventually, feeling as if he had already travelled thousands of miles, he found himself on a train to the north, and at last felt able to relax.

After a delightful week amongst his family he returned south to resume training. With most of the men being here under compulsion and therefore not the eager recruits of old, his mind was not wholly on the task this bright Saturday morning, the faces of these raw conscripts transposed with those across the Channel whom he had nurtured and who would this day be battling for possession of the Somme.

In fact he had been thinking of them ever since he opened his eyes this morning, going through the plan of attack whilst to all intents and purposes shaving. At Zero minus three minutes the artillery would have barraged the front German lines, flushing out game for the snipers. Unthank's skills would be sorely missed now. At Zero, the two front waves of the assaulting battalions would have advanced to the attack . . . now the third and fourth waves commence to move out in succession into no-man's-land. He looked at his watch. At this moment his own battalion would be moving into the position of readiness; he saw them led out by their platoon commanders through the sallyports and into the front-line trenches, saw them individually, with their own quirky way of doing things, saw Bob Gaylard's fresh face making a worried last-minute inspection of the German trench map, Louis Postgate checking his revolver and his men's rifles, all of them swallowing nerves – so close had they become that he even felt nervous for them – wanting to drink but not allowed to do so whilst still in their own trenches. But now there would be no time to be windy, for as they watched the fourth wave evacuate the German front-line trenches the first wave of his own boys was up and over the parapet and moving across no-man's-land, the second file observing as their comrades stormed the German trenches, bombing and shooting and stabbing, carrying out to the letter the instruction to kill as many of the enemy as possible. Then they too would rise over the parapet and proceed to clean up those Huns who had slipped the net. He saw them as in practice, advancing in rushes, hauling their Lewis guns after them, wave after valiant wave, advancing to glory . . .

Spotting a wayward marcher, he came out of his fantasy to bark an acid command and, marching alongside, forced himself to concentrate on the matter in hand.

But it was difficult to focus with so much at stake in France, and again he checked his watch, noting with satisfaction that an hour had passed since last he had looked. If the attack had gone according to plan it would all be over now, the Germans routed, their lines captured, his boys back in their trenches and preparing to march back to billets, exhausted but victorious. He performed a mental roll call, this time thinking not of individuals but wondering how many might have fallen.

Never could he have imagined the reality . . .

In France, after a night of heavy bombardment, the dawn had broken fine but misty. Amongst the 25 officers and 736 men of the 9th Battalion York and Lancaster Regiment, Louis gathered his own around him, ensuring that each had a perfect vision of the plan. He set about checking that they had every requirement, like a mother whose infants were about to attend their first day at school. In addition to his haversack filled with iron rations and other necessities, each man carried four sandbags attached to his equipment bracing. Some had shovels, some had picks strung across their backs with which to hack steps into the captured parados. Besides their usual ammunition each was armed with two extra bandoleers, plus two Mills bombs.

'Remember, you're not to throw these indiscriminately, they're hard to replace.'

Fortified by a tot of rum, Private Axup quipped, 'If we don't use them on Gerry, sir, can we use them for fishing when we get back?'

'Certainly, Bill, so long as you don't expect me to eat what you catch,' retorted Louis, whose own experiments in this field had seen the kind of disgusting things stirred up by a bomb thrown into a river.

'We'll let you treat us to smoked salmon tonight then, sir,' grinned Rawmarsh.

'You may certainly dream about it, Rawbones,' Louis threw back, to laughter.

In Hugh Faljambe's platoon there was less warm-hearted joshing between men and commander, though with his reckless streak curbed by the things he had seen they trusted Foggy not to expose them to unnecessary risk. Nevertheless, all were apprehensive as the blond-haired lieutenant ordered, 'Fix bayonets!'

Each tried to combat nerves in his own way, some retreating into themselves, some, like Pork and Hamm, taking long drags of a shared cigarette and mentally praying it would not be their last, others engaged in idiotic banter, some even managing to laugh and causing others to laugh with them. But then fresh bombardment opened with tremendous violence and it was useless trying to speak, their only recourse to wait with dry mouths whilst the guns disgorged their load and the earth shuddered and heaved and groaned all around as if Hell opened its doors to suck them down.

At seven thirty all fell quiet, save for the ringing in their ears and the screams of injured beasts. Emerging from their crouch to an illusory snowstorm, the filthy wide-eyed men became even more nervous, waiting for the curtain of smoke of lift. Waiting, waiting . . .

And then to a shrill medley of whistles the first wave of infantry rose over the parapet and out into no-man's-land. Greatly encouraged to find that the German wire was completely cut, they strode resolutely on and within a few minutes of Zero the German first line was captured along the whole brigade front. Eager to consolidate this victory the first wave stormed onwards to the second line, capturing this too and, their blood up, some of the assaulting troops even reached the German third line.

The 9th York and Lancasters prepared to move up in support. Private Hamm shook hands with Private Porks, their eyes awash with misgiving. 'Look after yourself, chum.' But out in the field there was a moment of confusion. The centre brigade of the 23rd Division had now retired and the right battalion of the 70th Brigade, imagining it was also meant to withdraw, fell back to their parapet, taking some other troops over with it. Guy Postgate, Hugh Faljambe and Bob Gaylard suddenly found themselves presented with these extra troops and for a second there was indecision at how to distribute them. Moreover, the enemy was now putting down an intense barrage, high explosive hurtling towards them in every form. Raising his worried pale grey eyes to the sky, Guy was at the ladder preparing to lead his men over the top when he heard the shell scream upon them, but heard no more as it exploded him to pieces, obliterating Bob Gaylard too and every man around him, assaulting those on the outer edges with lumps of steaming flesh.

The air sucked from his lungs by the blast, Louis fought for breath, staggered to his feet and, spattered by his brother's blood and that of half the company, cried out – his shriek drowned by Colonel Addison's whistle as the rest of the battalion rose over the top. What else was he to do but follow suit?

But even as he made to clamber out, others toppled back into the trench, Pork and Hamm, one on top of the other, both dead. Yelling encouragement to those in his own platoon a wild-eyed Louis drove himself upwards and over the pile of sandbags.

The scene ahead was unimaginable, a detritus of mutilated men stretched out across no-man's-land, becoming ever thicker as one after another was cut down by the vicious sweep of machine-gun bullets that came tumbling in all directions from the German lines, whizzing through the grass like bees, men capsizing all around him, Axup, Rawmarsh, little Corporal Bebby, Sergeant Holroyd, his entire platoon soon lay dead or wounded.

Instead of the well-practised route there was now only chaos, men of other battalions mixed together, men he had never seen before. With no one left to lead, he cast his wild blue gaze about him, his face speckled with dried blood, searching for a friend. Then, he saw ahead of him Hugh Faljambe's blond hair curling from under his helmet and fixed his sights on this, taking Hugh's example, striding determinedly forth through the bloody brain-spattered mire, firing his revolver at an enemy he could barely see – until suddenly Hugh went down as well. Stooping on one knee beside his fallen comrade, his aspect distraught, Louis saw that there was naught to be done. Overwhelmed by a terrible feeling of loneliness, demented by grief and by the unearthly moaning and groaning and shrieking of wounded men begging for his help, spurred only by months of training and a sense of loyalty, he lurched onwards, calling

153

encouragement to terrified strangers, firing wildly with his revolver towards the German line – and then, thank God, oh, thank God, he caught sight of Colonel Addison waving him on and, rushing faithfully to his leader, he jumped into the German trench and started shooting, giving no quarter to those he found there, his only intention to kill . . .

It had been meant to be over in an hour. Instead, for the observers there was only confusion. By ten o'clock all communication with the troops of the 70th Brigade in the German lines had been completely cut off, runners were unable to cross no-man's-land and every telephone line was severed.

At midday General Gordon reported to Divisional HQ that until the enemy machine guns had been put out of action he could neither communicate with the German front line nor withdraw troops.

Not until nightfall was it safe for the exhausted remnants of the attacking force to limp in. Twenty-five officers and 736 men of the 9th Battalion York and Lancaster Regiment had gone out. Three officers staggered back. At roll, only 180 men were to call out their names.

In England, no proper news had come for days but there were unconfirmed rumours that Colonel Addison was missing, reported wounded, and Probyn had the gnawing sense that all had not gone well. He was on the parade ground, bathed in sunshine, when a corporal interrupted his training schedule to tell him that the colonel of the depot wished to speak to him.

There was a sombre atmosphere in the office and the CO found it difficult to meet Probyn's eye, even more difficult to know how to break the news. 'Grave tidings, I'm afraid, RSM.' His thumbs rubbed agitatedly at the document he was holding.

Probyn spared him, asking in quiet tone, 'Is it Colonel Addison, sir?'

A grave shake of head. 'Still missing. I'm afraid it's somewhat more serious than we imagined.' Slowly, his eyes devoid of spark, the colonel pushed the leaf of paper across the desk. 'Those are confirmed dead.'

With growing horror, Probyn read the names on the list: Major H. Lewis, Captain G. Postgate, Lieutenants H. Faljambe, R. Gaylard, B. Geake . . . L. Postgate . . .

Something leaped inside him, not a leap of love but a leap of horror. He was consumed by ice as one after another, dozen after dozen, those familiar names and faces sprang from the page. It was as if some malevolent claw had reached inside him and ripped out his heart. He had thought himself inured to death after seeing so much carnage, but one did not have to witness it to be affected. A vortex of reflections whirled around his mind: they had trusted him, under his tuition thought themselves invincible so long as they listened to what he told them. He had taught them how to advance, warned them of the sly tricks the enemy might play, taught them everything he knew, but he had forgotten one thing for never could he have visualized such an abominable outcome: he had omitted to tell them what to do in case of failure. They had been transported to the front in livestock wagons and that was how they had died, like beasts in a charnel house. *His poor, brave gentlemen.*

The colonel watched his face, knowing what he suffered. 'You haven't heard the worst of it, I'm afraid.'

Worse, how could it be worse? The battalion he had so lovingly nurtured had been annihilated. *His poor boys, so much ahead of them.*

'Altogether,' the colonel sighed, 'we accrued almost sixty thousand casualties.'

Overwhelmed by despair Probyn closed his eyes but remained stock-still. *Sixty thousand – on a single day.*

'I know, it's impossible to take in.' Faced with his RSM's acute shock, the colonel seemed eager to talk now, desperate to fill that painful hiatus. 'I can't stop thinking what this will mean. Of course it must be much worse for you who knew them all, but on a less personal scale it couldn't be more disastrous. Anyhow, Mr Kilmaster, I'm instructed to tell you that we shall be keeping you on home ground from now on.' He tried to inject a note of kindness, wringing his hands. 'You'll be very glad of that, I suppose.'

Probyn barely had the capacity to nod. How could he be glad of anything? *Sixty thousand.* My God . . . my God. His heart went out to those wretched survivors forced yet to dwell in that necropolis.

The colonel kept talking, trying to appear brisk. 'We need you here to drum up those replacements as quickly as possible. It's the devil's own job, I'm afraid . . .'

Probyn barely heard the rest, such was the daze he was in. When the CO had finished, he saluted and left the office.

Standing in the corridor, he fought to compose himself, to calm his anguished heart, wanting to lean against that cool wall for support but refusing to allow his mask to drop lest others witness this. What rubbish had he spouted to Hugh Faljambe – a callus of the soul?

155

There was no such thing. How could he go back out there and look into those faces, knowing what awaited them? Fortifying himself with a deep breath, he prepared to return to his instruction, but in that moment a decision was made: he could no longer allow himself to know them nor to like them; not when he was sending them to *that*.

When the RSM returned to the parade ground, to the men under his command, his demeanour was barely changed. Under his vicious treatment they damned him for a heartless tyrant. No one could have guessed that inside he was sobbing for his poor dear boys.

PART TWO

TEN

'"He pulled her petticoats up to her knees, tra, la, la-la-la-la-la!
Made the old woman shiver and sneeze, tra, la, la-la-la-la-la!"'
Deeply relieved to have her husband permanently back on home
soil, Grace was in fine voice that Saturday morning as she went
about the house with her offspring, each undertaking their own
task. Accustomed to using Mother's moods as a barometer, the
children were always delighted to hear her sing, for it meant that
everything in the world was well and Father was safe. Nothing could
hurt them if Mother was trilling.

Warbling like a linnet, Grace did not immediately hear Beata's
call. When the little girl rushed up and tugged at her skirt she
looked startled. 'Beat, I almost trod on you! Have you got those
sills nice and clean?'

'Aunt Charlotte's coming!' At Beata's information the rest of the
children poured out of the house with expressions of joy. Grace gave
fond exclamation too and went out into the sunshine to meet her
friend, wiping her hands on her apron.

But, as Charlotte neared, the puffy eyes and half-hearted greeting
told immediately that her visit was not a cause for celebration.
Quickly excusing the children from their unfinished chores, Grace
evacuated them from the premises. 'Go and pick your aunt some
flowers!' Employing a tone that brooked no objections, she closed
the door on them.

Pre-empting Charlotte's announcement in the hope of lessening
her friend's pain, she whispered in trepidation, 'It's George, isn't
it?'

Nodding, Charlotte heaved a deep breath to steady herself. 'He's

159

been wounded.' Then she burst into tears, hiding her big square face in a handkerchief. Upon recovery she was able to give snivelling explanation. 'He's in a French hospital. I might never see him again!'

Grace embraced her friend. 'Oh, you must go to him, dear! You don't need a passport, you know.'

Damp handkerchief bunched in a fist, Charlotte sniffed and hung her head. 'I know . . . but I've just spent all my wages on a new dress.'

Grace was astonished; extravagance was not in her friend's character.

'He wrote to tell me he'd soon be coming home on leave and I wanted to look nice for him. I tried to explain to the shop but they wouldn't take it back.'

This was no deterrent to Grace. 'I've read the authorities will pay in needy cases.'

'Yes, but only for one relative per soldier,' wept Charlotte. 'His sisters wanted to go too but we decided his mother must be the one.'

Grace did not falter, reaching for a tin on the mantel. 'Here!'

'Don't be silly!' A tearful Charlotte pushed away the offering. 'You've got seven children to feed. I couldn't let them go without in the face of my stupidity.'

'You think I'd let them go without? Take it!' Grace's cool fingers pressed it firmly into her friend's hand.

'Probe'll be cross with you . . .' Desperate to take the cash, which was her main reason for being here, Charlotte knew how much Grace's impulsive generosity enraged her husband.

'He'd never begrudge *you*, Lottie! He'd say the same if he were here. And I'm just so happy to have him home for good. Oh, I didn't tell you, he's not going overseas any more, I just feel so, *so* lucky when there's you here worried out of your wits about George.'

After playing down the danger whilst away in France, since the butchering of his regiment Probyn had finally confessed how terrible it had been, the loss of all those friends having shaken him to the core.

'Please take it. Pay me back whenever you can, but for heaven's sake, take it, stop wasting your time here and go to him.'

Blessing the other's kindness, Charlotte tarried only long enough to take succour in a cup of tea and to receive the children's flowers, then embarked straight away on her mission.

*   *   *

160

All that week Grace waited to hear the outcome. When the letter came she was initially delighted to read that Charlotte had met the challenge and had managed to visit her fiancé in the French hospital. Charlotte was now back in York and was writing to reiterate her gratitude and to set Grace's mind at ease over the loan. 'My dear, dear friend, I will repay the money as soon as possible, yet I shall never be able to repay your generosity of spirit in giving me the chance to see my beloved George before he passed away . . .'

Her excitement cruelly terminated, Grace uttered a little moan. The children watched her face as tears bulged over her lower lids and trickled down her cheeks as she conveyed the terrible news.

One or two of the girls shed tears of sympathy and came to lay their arms around Mother.

'Where's he buried?' Joe wanted to know.

Dabbing at her eyes, Grace consulted the letter. 'France, I think.'

'Will they dig him up after the war?'

'No!' Grace sought to warn her son, 'And I don't want any silly talk like that when Aunt Charlotte comes.'

Later, when alone, she reread the letter, horrified by Charlotte's description of the hospital and its occupants. 'It was *awful*, truly horrendous, Grace. You see the lists of wounded in the newspapers but you can't really imagine the reality until you go amongst them.' Grace skipped the grisly catalogue of injuries that followed; reading them once had been enough. Instead, her eyes focused on Charlotte's closing words. 'I know I have no need to tell you how lucky you are to have Probyn safe at home. Were I capable of feeling any happiness I would rejoice in your good fortune. I hasten to add that there is no bitterness over my own loss, I am truly glad for you, my dear friends. God bless you both and keep you safe. I shall come to visit when I feel able. I don't know when that will be, I have been awfully muddled lately. I am certain only of one thing: I shall never marry . . .'

Charlotte's tragedy was the precursor to a string of bad luck in her friends' household. Falling victim to scarlet fever, that same month Joe, Maddie and Beata were packed off to hospital at Conisbrough. Whilst the two elder siblings were quick to recover, poor Beata was to be detained with complications. It was a lonely and bewildering time for the little girl who, isolated from her family, waited day after day for them to come, beginning to fear she had been abandoned.

Working nearer to home, though not quite close enough to be

able to live amongst his family, Probyn was kept informed by letter. The fact that Beata had scarlet fever was bad enough, but when he received news that, whilst in the hospital, she had also developed typhus, his emotions took over and he applied to take immediate leave. During the frantic train journey to her side came the memory of his dead sister Beata. Had it been ill-omened to have named his daughter after her?

Nor was this mood to be relieved upon visiting the hospital, but rather exacerbated, for, due to the highly contagious nature of the disease, he and Grace were forced to view their daughter from afar through glass, to watch her shaven head with its dusky face roll deliriously from side to side, her little figure performing sporadic jerks beneath the sheet. They tried to be cheerful whilst in Beata's view, even if she was unaware of their presence, but upon their exit all stoicism collapsed, Probyn depicting an even more fraught example than his wife, wringing his hands at his own ineffectualness.

'I just feel so useless . . . and I know it's daft and superstitious but I can't help thinking it was tempting providence to name her after my sister. She was always a sickly lass.' Having been only small at the time of his eldest sibling's death, he had no real memory of Beata himself, but a legacy of warmly uttered remembrances from his other sisters made it seem as if he had. 'She was just a lovely person, you know, that's why I called Beata as I did . . .'

Her brow furrowed by concern, Grace linked arms with him, rubbing him briskly as if trying to draw strength from the beefier limb. She wanted to tell him it wasn't his fault, but felt that if she started crying she would never stop.

The forty-eight-hour leave showed no sign of improvement in Beata's health, and, his presence of no value to his daughter, the RSM was soon compelled by duty to return to barracks, though he insisted on daily letters from Grace and was to make periodic visits to Conisbrough over the fraught weeks to come.

It was therefore miraculous, upon his latest arrival with Grace, to see his little girl no longer in the isolation ward, but propped up, reading a book, still wan and terribly thin, but nevertheless snatched from death's door.

Probyn's huge relief at Beata's total recovery was manifested in an extravagance hitherto unknown in the Kilmaster family. 'She must have aught she wants, Grace! What would you like, Beaty? A dolly's pram?'

Gazing at her father's tanned, beaming face, Beata wanted to say that she would like a book. Whilst most of the nurses had been far too busy to tend anything other than medical requirements, Beata had endeared herself to one in particular, who had brought her an illustrated volume to alleviate the boredom. There was no library at home and Beata would have loved to acquire such an item. Yet, because it would make her father happy, she answered that a doll's pram would be lovely.

'Then a dolly's pram you shall have, me lass!' And exalting that his child had been spared, he bent to deliver a rare kiss to the top of her stubbly little head.

A source of much envy, the brand-new perambulator complete with occupant was trundled around the streets of Denaby by its proud owner, who, also excused daily chores for the time being, was to become rather unpopular with her siblings until Grace, realizing that such favouritism was doing Beata no favours at all, returned her name to Battalion Orders and life resumed its normal course – as normal as life could be with a war still decimating the nation's manhood.

Following the scare over Beata's health, Grace resolved to be extra generous with the child's diet in an effort to build her up, though it was difficult with the scarcity of food, and if she succeeded in restoring her daughter's wellbeing it was only at the expense of her own.

This was quite evident to her husband when next he came home on leave several weeks later.

'You've lost weight!' Probyn eyed her malnourished frame accusingly. 'I hope you haven't been skimping on food?' In times of strife, Grace had shown a tendency to neglect herself in favour of the children.

She tried to laugh it off. 'Well, what do you expect with all the shortages?'

'I know you!' He wagged a finger.

'I can't think what you mean!'

'Look at you. You've hardly any colour.' The physical change in her alarmed him.

'Oh, stop worriting!' And she put paid to any speculation by laying on a fine tea and heartily partaking of it herself.

But if Probyn had noticed a change in his wife then Grace was to undergo similar experience. He seemed distant and unhappy and, under his accusations that she was neglecting herself, she began to worry that he no longer found her attractive, her fear of losing him swiftly blowing this fear out of all proportion.

Finding her sobbing quietly in the scullery after the children had gone to bed, Probyn was astounded to discover that he was the cause of her distress.

'Nay I didn't mean anything!' He took her in his arms. 'I just don't want to see you fading away to a shadow through your generosity to others!'

'But is that all?' Still tearful, her blue eyes searched his face. 'You've hardly said a word other than to pick at me, Probe, and you seem miles away. There isn't anyone else is there?'

His jaw dropped. 'You daft clot, of course not!' He hugged her tightly and shook his head in exasperation. 'Eh, if I'd known what was going through your head . . . I'm sorry if I've been quiet – and picky.' He gave a little smile and dealt her a peck on the nose before turning sombre. 'We've just had word that they've found Colonel Addison's body.'

Grace exclaimed over her own selfishness. 'Oh, dearest, I'm so sorry!'

He shook his head and held onto her, saying nothing more.

Drawing perverse comfort from her husband's bad tidings, Grace rested her chin on his shoulder and gazed at the white-painted wall behind him, scolding herself for not immediately guessing the reason for his abstractedness – of course it would have to be something to do with the army! Was not the army his life? As if it were yesterday, she remembered how, as a young bride, those words had broken her heart. Now, of course, she had matured enough to know that love came in many forms; just because he adored the company of men did not mean he loved his wife any the less.

When he next spoke his announcement surprised her. 'I'm going to write to Aunt Kit and ask if we can spend a few days with her. The children aren't learning much at school, what with all the disruption. They need a break as much as us and the fresh air will do you a power of good – not that I'm being picky again!'

There was no argument from Grace. She had not enjoyed a trip since the year before Beata was born. Coincidentally, it had been to Aunt Kit's they had gone then too. It had not been a happy time but Grace was determined not to let bad memories get in the way and she gave her blessing to the proposal now.

'And I'm sorry I thought the worst,' she told him. 'I just love you.'

Squeezing her to show he felt the same, Probyn turned off the lights and led her up to bed.

*   *   *

164

Following Kit's reply that came by return of post the day after he had written, Probyn's family was on a train bound for York – all save Clem, who, forced to work, was to be looked after by a neighbour in their absence.

Far from being incommoded by the arrival of such a large tribe Kit was thrilled to see them and came wobbling down the path to greet her favourite nephew. Both he and Grace got quite a shock at how much fatter Kit had grown since last they had met, her hips almost brushing the door frame, but at heart she was still the same, enfolding him, then his wife and then each of their children in her fleshy embrace.

Not having seen this elderly lady very often the little ones were shy and especially self-conscious under her open-hearted hugs. They were also overawed by her enormous girth. Standing almost six foot tall, her corpulent body topped by large dramatic features, she presented rather a daunting figure. Yet, after only minutes in her company, laughing at her mimicry and jokes, they came to overlook the obesity, seeing Great-Aunt Kit for what she was, a natural entertainer and a good, kind woman.

Food played no small part in their affection for her, too, and though Kit apologized for the poor state of her table her guests were agog at the spread she had managed to conjure up with such shortages as there were. 'Well, I suppose it's a bit easier for us that have our own livestock,' she told them. 'You must take some chucky eggs with you when you go – not that I'm trying to get rid of you already!' She laughed, the rolls of fat under her chin wobbling. 'Oh, I can't tell you how lovely it is to have you all here!' And so warmly was it issued that everyone could tell that she meant it.

Despite Worthy's even taller bulk his was a quieter presence than his wife's. But then Worthy did not have to say anything to make one notice he was there. To the children, their father might give the impression of largeness, with his torose features and broad chest, but next to Worthy he was a midget.

The following hours were spent catching up with family news, Probyn's main enquiry being about cousin Toby, who was away at the battle front. Withdrawing a bundle of letters from the sideboard, a proud Kit told him that her son had earned himself a medal for tending a wounded officer whilst under fire.

Probyn voiced quiet acclaim. 'You must be right proud of him, Aunt.'

'We are.' It was a rather sad smile from Kit. 'I just pray the Lord'll send him home safe to us.'

Probyn gave words of comfort, thinking of his own lost boys. 'If he came through that lot on the Somme I think you can justly expect it.'

After spending the first day of their holiday merely enjoying their hostess's company, the next morning Probyn took his family on an outing, mainly in order to let Worthy get on with the smooth running of the smallholding, but also to give Grace as much fresh air as possible.

'Take our Toby's fishing rod with you,' instructed Worthy. 'We've got a net here somewhere for the young uns.' He rummaged about in an understairs cupboard for a while, before calling to his wife, 'Katherine, where's yon fishing net got to?'

'Why do you call Aunt Kit Katherine?' Small nose jutting from under his peaked cap, Joe looked up at the giant of a man.

From his lofty heights, Worthy replied in deadpan manner, ''Cause she doesn't like being called Bert.'

'Eh, you and your questions!' Probyn reproved Joe and along with the rest of the children, shooed him out into the countryside, the youngsters walking ahead of their parents so that Father could keep an eye on them.

Equipped with plenty to eat and drink, they were to spend the entire day walking and fishing, playing and lounging, as far removed from the war as one could possibly be. The autumn sun was hot. Upon their return, sunkissed and happy, Probyn seemed almost as youthful as his children as he related the afternoon's events to Kit and Worthy. 'We caught a fish this big! Didn't we, kids? Thought it was kinder to let him go, though.'

There was much laughter as they sat down to tea.

Afterwards, whilst chatting happily to her visitors, Kit brought out a skein of wool, ordering her husband, 'Hold out your hands, dear.'

Worthy sighed but presented his hands over which Kit hooked the skein of wool whilst she settled back to wind it into a ball, hardly drawing breath between words.

Fifteen minutes of desultory chatter elapsed in this fashion, Worthy sitting patiently, his outstretched arms occupied by the skein whilst Kit wound her wool, until eventually he was permitted to insert a question of his own. 'So, did you have any hand in catching that fish, Grace – by the way, how big did you say it was?'

'Oh, about that . . .' Grace held her hands apart and immediately found them encumbered by the skein of wool. She gave a burst of outraged laughter at Worthy's deft move.

'Eh, the crafty weasel!' scolded Kit, but laughed with Probyn and the others. 'Fancy doing that to a guest.'

The big man looked pleased with himself. 'Guests have to earn their keep in this house.' Still sporting a grin, he rose to stretch his tree-trunk legs, then faltered and stooped to peer through the window. The fowl were making a din; it might herald a fox. But no, there was a figure approaching through the dying sun. 'Eh, I think . . . Katherine, it's our Toby!' And he rushed to fling open the door, lumbering down the path with Kit in hot pursuit to greet their son.

Grace shared a look of happiness with her husband and children, then bent to retrieve the ball of wool that Kit had dropped in her excitement, and began to rewind it.

After thrilled, loving embraces the tall, well-built young man was escorted to the threshold by his proud parents, whereupon he halted. 'I can't go in, Mam, I'm lousy.'

'Nay, we don't mind a few bugs, lad!'

Toby was stubborn. 'It's more than a few. There's a whole legion running round in me pants. And if I come into your kitchen you won't get rid of the stink in days, honestly. Let me just have a sluice down under t'pump.'

'I can't allow that after you've been serving your country! Just give me a minute and I'll fill the bath. Come see who's here!' Mopping tears of gladness, Kit chivvied a protesting Toby into the porch.

His big features lit up at the sight of the visitors. Yet, Probyn noted, the torment of war was writ large upon that young face and no amount of exuberant words could disguise it.

Joe wrinkled his nose. 'Pooh, he stinks!'

His father cuffed him.

But Toby guffawed from the doorway, steadfastly refusing to go further. 'I'll look forward to talking to you, Probe, when I've got rid of me muck.'

His much older cousin called back, 'I look forward to it too! How long have you got, Toby?'

'Seven days!' came the answer.

'Well, it's right grand to see you. I know you must have been expecting to come home to a bit of peace and quiet and you

167

won't get that with us here so we'll make a move first thing in the morning.'

'Nay, I didn't think I stunk that bad,' joked Toby.

Kit dismissed her nephew's suggestion. 'Nobody's leaving.'

'You don't want us here spoiling your lad's homecoming.' Probyn hated such intrusions himself.

Grace held the half-wound ball and skein of wool on her lap. 'And we planned to leave the day after tomorrow anywa –'

'Then another day won't make any difference, will it?' replied Aunt Kit firmly.

'Don't be trying to get out of winding that wool, Grace,' Worthy wagged a teasing finger. 'You're staying put.'

Kit was too busy thinking to laugh. 'Now, let me see, I shall have to move the children out of Toby's bed . . .'

'That little stinker hasn't been sleeping in my bed, has he?' quipped Toby, pulling a face at Joe and making him laugh.

'. . . they can go in the loft above the byre – it's a warm night and the cows won't mind.'

With sleeping arrangements organized, Kit steered the guests into the parlour, then filled a zinc bath in the kitchen. Toby peeled off his lousy garments and dropped them outside before padding naked into the kitchen and straight into the bath, whereupon he groaned in ecstasy.

And for the remainder of the holiday, try as they might not to intrude on family intimacy, Probyn, Grace and their children found themselves embraced in all Kit's plans. It was the most wonderful interlude, serving not just as a respite from the war, but to bring back fond memories of the family get-togethers of Probyn's boyhood. If only these moments could last for ever.

ELEVEN

The battle of the Somme was to rage for another two months, its butchery regarded as the sacrifice that must certainly mark an end to the war. So, 1917 opened on an air of optimism, an emotion that especially prevailed in the Kilmaster household. With Charlotte's debt repaid, Grace had been able to afford a proper festive dinner and even some fruit and nuts to go in the children's Christmas stockings. Even presented with the news that Probyn had been posted to the Durham Light Infantry, Grace did not, as she might have done long ago, complain that he was taking her away from her friends and family, but was simply grateful that her husband was not being sent further afield. It would, of course, mean getting to know one's way around a new town, making new friends, but Grace was well used to this, and with her sisters residing in York she saw very little of them anyway.

The saddest thing to bear was that it would mean an end to Charlotte's already infrequent visits, especially with her friend still grieving over her tragic bereavement. Grace swore to keep in touch by letter.

Emotions were stirred too by all the farewell cups of tea amongst neighbours, in particular Nurse Gentle and Mrs Rushton. The parting with Father Flanagan and Canon McLafferty had also been sad. A good few tears were shed before it was time to pack.

'Bless me, I never knew I'd been sitting on this!' Having been sorting through the sheets of music in her piano stool, a red-eyed Grace paused to hold at arm's length a piece by a German composer as if it were contaminated. 'Here, Gus, put it with the old newspapers. It'll do to make a firelighter.'

'We could put it in the privy,' grinned Joe.

'No need for vulgarity,' replied his mother sternly. 'And what's all that rubbish you're shoving in the packing case?'

Joe put his hand on his hip. 'It's not rubbish! It's pictures of heroes.' Before the newspapers were disposed of, he had made it his job to cut out the photographs of soldiers who had been killed. He had amassed a thick pile now.

'There's no room for those, dear!'

'But it's not right to burn them,' defended Joe.

Grace capitulated with a sigh, reminding herself to remove them after Joe had gone to bed.

Then, all that was to be done was to lay down her own head and pray that this new beginning would go well.

There was quite a thrill upon arrival to find that West Hartlepool was on the coast, the tang of salt and the yelp of gulls conjuring visions of picnics on the sands. This was just as well, for the streets of this shipbuilding port were as grimy as the ones they had left, and further uglified by bomb damage, nor were there any green fields in which to romp. But at least the rented accommodation was not so cramped as they were used to, the garrison was situated nearby, meaning that Father could live at home, and the convent school that the children were to attend was just at the end of the street so they would be unlikely to get lost in this place of unfamiliar accents.

With a sovereign much reduced in value these days it was a relief that Clem found clerical work almost immediately. There was to be money from another source too. Augusta reasoned that there was no point in starting a new school; she would be of more use to her mother in earning a living. Whilst not disagreeing, it saddened Grace that such an intelligent girl was compelled to do menial work and her heart went out when first she saw the twelve-year-old trundling up the street with her milk churns.

Madeleine, Joe and Beata were dispatched to their place of education on Monday, any apprehensions they might have soon dispersed, for the other pupils were very friendly. Unfortunately this did not apply to the rest of the population and they were ambushed on the way home by a group of Protestant children whose name-calling extended to violence. Threatened by the bigger number, the Kilmasters ran, Beata's short legs taking her only yards before she received a thump in the back that sent her tumbling. They were on her then, slapping and pulling her hair.

Still running, Joe and Maddie took a moment to realize that their sister was not with them. No longer the quarry, they retraced their steps and peered around the corner to investigate.

On her feet now, a weeping Beata came towards them, taunted by her enemies.

'You'll have to learn to run faster,' advised an unsympathetic Madeleine, Joe offering no better help.

But just then a saviour came along in the person of their father and all fear vanished. Taking their oppressors to task, Probyn dabbed Beata's tears and shepherded his youngsters home.

When he opened the door there was no sign of his wife, just Mims sitting on her own, drumming happily on a pan with a wooden spoon. Then a movement caught his eye and he saw Grace crawl from the kitchen on her knees and elbows and disappear behind the sofa, trying to hold a jug of water upright.

'What's this, a commando raid?'

Her head bobbed up and a little sound of frustration emerged. 'Oh, Probe, you're early! I was just trying to get this over with before you came home. Can one of you just keep Baby occupied while I finish getting things ready for w-a-s-h-i-n-g her h-a-i-r.'

'Hair-washing at this time of day?'

'Oh, you've said it!' accused Grace as a loud bawl emerged from Mims. 'Now look what you've done.'

Probyn uttered a laughing gasp. 'How was I to know?'

'You've heard what a fuss she kicks up when she has her whatsit washed! I was just trying to lessen it. Well, that's it! All that crawling about wasted.' Wearing a look of disgust, she clambered to her feet and took the jug of water back to the scullery, calling over her shoulder to Mims, 'No, no, stop crying, there's no hair-washing today!'

Still, Mims' yelling raised the roof for a good few minutes.

'It's a ruddy madhouse,' muttered Probyn to himself.

Madeleine looked disapproving of the term but dared not correct her father.

Noting Beata's tear-stained face, Grace bent down to ask what was amiss.

'Some kids brayed her,' explained Probyn, ruffling his daughter's hair to lessen her hurt.

'I don't like living here,' sniffed Beata. 'I want to go home.'

But, though her mother gave her a comforting cuddle, the response was delivered with a laugh. 'This is home now, Beat. You'll just have to get on with it, I'm afraid.'

There was to be further unpleasantness for the rest of the week and Beata was glad when Easter provided a break from school. With Marmaduke's fourth birthday occurring in this period, it was decided that it was time for him to be breeched, thus lending an excuse for celebration, and even though food shortages were to prevent any extravagance, Mother still managed to lay on some kind of party.

Wanting to contribute, Beata asked for paper with which to make her brother a card and, this provided, settled at the table with a box of crayons.

Clad in white knitted trousers and jumper, shorn of his light-brown curls, a reluctant Marmaduke was shoved before his father for inspection: this was brief. Since the child seemed to cry every time a paternal eye was so much as cast in his direction, Probyn rarely wasted time on him. Today however, there was reward both laudatory and financial.

'Why, Mother, those breeches have worked a treat. He hasn't even cried one tear! Here you are, my big boy, that's all for you.' And with a broad smile Probyn extended a new sixpence. 'Put that in your pocket, sonny.'

Whilst Duke enjoyed this unaccustomed praise, Beata was to come in for chastisement as her father turned his attention to her artwork.

'Eh, what have you been taught about holding your pencil in the wrong hand?' An admonishing finger was directed at her. 'Don't let me catch you again or you'll be off to the Marmalade Home.'

Vilified by teachers for this sin, the six-year-old was now made to feel like an outcast at home. Dutifully, she swapped her pencil from left to right before continuing her task, even though it felt as if she were using someone else's hand and the writing it formed was atrocious. And though she bravely held back her tears and still handed over the finished card to Marmaduke, its presentation was robbed of all lustre.

Whilst the children might have had a difficult time of settling in, their mother had always been quick to make friends and within weeks had formed acquaintance with most of her neighbours, not a day going by without one or another of them visiting her kitchen for a cup of tea. Always a gregarious soul, Grace found their sisterhood even more welcome in the months to come, for, despite their army's valiant struggles, it had begun to look as if the Hun might win.

Fear had been ever-present, of course – fear that their husbands, sons and brothers might be killed. But never, *never* had anyone even contemplated that the British could be beaten. Today, the faces around the Kilmasters' table were drawn with worry as Grace and her neighbours discussed the unthinkable.

'The minute I hear they're across that Channel,' said one, 'I'll take a knife to me kids then kill meself. I've heard what they've done to the Belgian nuns, I'm not letting that happen to me or mine.'

Grace privately marvelled at the blithe way this statement was issued. Be that as it may, they were facing a very real threat and the question had to be asked. What would she herself do if the Channel was breached? She cast a tormented eye at little Mims, who played innocently on the rug, knowing she would never be able to stick a knife in her, even to prevent a worse fate.

It didn't do to dwell and she changed the subject, which was just as well, for the children began to trickle in from school.

Remarking on the time, the women rose to leave, but with so much to be discussed some were still tarrying on the doorstep when Probyn came home. Flinging him a quick greeting, the stragglers hurried away, but not before he had spotted a package in one of their hands.

'Cleared us out, have they?' Generous by nature, his wife had become even more so in these exacting times, swift to share some vital commodity with a person in need.

'Behave! They share things with us when they have them.'

'Aye – *when*! Nine times out of ten it's you who's doing the sharing.' Even as Probyn objected he knew it was useless. 'I'm all for comradeship, Grace, but nobody expects you to feed the entire nation.'

'Stop exaggerating!' She gave him a fond shove, directing him indoors where she deflected attention from herself by saying, 'It's good about the King, isn't it?' An announcement had been made that the sovereign had changed his name to Windsor. Hearing noises of approval from her parents, Madeleine took this as an opportunity to put her own appeal. 'If His Majesty can change his, why can't I change mine, Mother?'

'Because I say so,' answered Grace bluntly. 'Now, let me get started on tea.'

A knock came at the door.

Probyn groaned. 'Here's another of your cronies come to take the food out of our mouths.'

Delivering a quick clip as she passed, a smiling Grace went to answer the door.

It was a woman from further along the street, of whom she had yet to make acquaintance. She spoke with the native accent, much the same as that of Yorkshire but with a melodic little kick to certain vowels.

'Hello, my name's Crump, I live up the top end there.' The dark-haired buxom woman used her head to indicate a house further along the street, her arms occupied by a large, black-and-white cat.

Grace thought she detected an impending complaint. There was a gleam in the woman's dark eye that hovered between friendliness and friction, its outcome dependent on the reaction she received. Wanting to curry the former, Grace donned a winsome smile and gave her name. 'And what can I do for you, Mrs Crump?'

'Do you see anything odd about my cat, Mrs Kilmaster?'

Though thinking it a strange question, Grace examined the placid-looking feline. There was something not quite right about it. 'I can't see –'

'Have a closer look,' suggested the neighbour.

Grace made a sound of realization. 'Oh, it hasn't got any –'

'No, it hasn't! It did have when it went out this morning, until your little boy cut them off.'

Overhearing the bizarre exchange, Probyn came to attend, momentarily drawing Mrs Crump's attention. Meeting his hypnotic blue-grey eyes, her own dark orbs flickered with interest, then rambled all about him in the manner of a farmer weighing up the local fatstock, before moving back to Grace, who was in the process of apologizing.

'Eh, the little tinker! Probe, our Duke's cut this poor creature's whiskers off.'

'Mrs Simpson caught your youngest son in the act,' said Eliza Crump. 'He's as daft as a brush, our Blackie. He'd sit and let him do it.'

Using his RSM voice, Probyn bellowed, 'Marmaduke! Come out here.'

Beata peeped round an inner door. 'He's not here, Father.'

'Where is he?'

'On the cobbler's doorstep.'

'What the devil is he doing there?'

'I don't know – he always sits there.' Beata saw nothing strange in it. Told to go and fetch her brother she ran directly to the cobbler's and dragged home the four-year-old to face three angry adults.

'What did you think you were doing to this poor cat?' demanded his father.

Unaware of his crime, Duke spoke innocently. 'His moustache was too long so I cut a bit off like you do with yours, Father.'

Probyn joined eyes with Grace, then both looked away so that their son would not think their amusement endorsed his bad behaviour.

'Well, it was very naughty!' Probyn bent to chastise the little boy. 'Say you're sorry to the lady.'

Twisting one leg of his white woollen trousers between grubby little hands, a frightened Duke apologized, though he had no idea what for.

Luckily, the cat's owner saw the funny side too, her black eyes sparkling and her mouth forming a lopsided grin. 'Oh well, I suppose it'll save Blackie a trip to the barber's.'

Thanking her for being so understanding, Grace and Probyn took their wayward son indoors, his father warning him, 'You must never do anything like that again. How did you get hold of the scissors anyway?'

Duke took the question literally and gave demonstration. 'I just held them like that.'

Whilst Grace covered her mouth, Probyn fought not to laugh. 'I meant where did you get them from?'

'Oh, Mother left them on the chair.'

'That didn't mean they were there for the taking,' scolded his father. 'In future, don't touch what doesn't belong to you – and that includes cats' whiskers.'

When Probyn had gone from the room, a tearful Duke felt safe enough to grumble to his mother, 'The cat let me do it.'

Later, when the little boy had gone to bed, his parents were able to express their mirth, such precious incidents as these lending succour in the months of adversity that were to ensue.

Winter came, bringing a recurrence of Clem's bronchitis and made several times worse by the shortage of food and fuel. Accustomed to having a ready supply of coal through Father's peacetime work at the colliery, the Kilmasters had become blasé in its use. Now with this commodity rationed, every nugget was treasured, yesterday's cinders having to be reused the next morning. These barren lumps almost impossible to ignite, the simple act of lighting a fire had become yet another test of reserve, and with matches tuppence a box instead of tuppence per dozen boxes, Grace had suffered many a burned finger rather than waste one.

Even goods as staple as potatoes were often impossible to come by now, and though swedes were at first an adequate replacement it was not long before demand outstripped stocks. The only recourse was to fill up on bread, but with unprecedented action by U-boats, grain ships being sunk as effortlessly as a boy stoning toy boats in a pond, a campaign was launched to eat less.

To spare her family's suffering, Grace as usual took the burden upon herself. In consequence, her health began to deteriorate. Old maladies recurred and, added to a hacking cough, gave rise to bed rest. As ever, at the first sign of crisis, Probyn took charge, deeming it most fortunate to be living at home and thus able to keep an eye on her. The possessor of a master cook's certificate, it was no inconvenience for him to rustle up the Sunday meal, nor to wash and iron, a lifetime of looking after himself in the army having yielded competence in most fields. The demands of his military career were for once regarded as subordinate and with Gussie to help he ensured that his wife was spared any undue strain. Under such tender ministrations, Grace was soon on her feet again.

But Probyn himself was jaded. As feared, the conscripts were proving less than a joy to train, most lacking the enthusiasm of the recruits of those first heady days. He found precious little gladness in his role now, knowing to what wholesale carnage these boys were headed. To his last breath he would strive against the Hun, adamant that his friends' ultimate sacrifice would not have been in vain, yet he could not prevent others dying. They died every day in their hundreds.

Even today, as he leaned into the cold winter wind, tramping despondently along his street, he saw a telegram boy prop his cycle against the kerb and knock at a door. His heart plummeted even further, not because it was his door but because he knew what the telegram meant for another family. Missing or killed? What would it be? Trying not to stare he could not help but notice the sultry dark-haired woman who took possession of the telegram, watched her face crumple almost to the verge of tears, admired her fortitude as she managed to stave off the emotion and merely handed the telegram boy a coin before closing the door. Just before she blocked out the world however, she turned her head and locked eyes with him. Probyn felt a jolt deep in his belly as he recognized the owner of the mutilated cat, who had so boldly stared at him some weeks before. Then she was gone.

Entering his own house, he called a greeting to his wife before announcing gravely, 'Mrs Whatsername's just had a telegram. You know, the one with the cat.'

'Poor soul,' Grace bit her lip, though with other thoughts to occupy her, nothing more was said on the matter.

Probyn too had forgotten all about it when, weeks later, he was heading to the barracks early one morning. He waved to Augusta as she trundled her empty milk churns across the bottom of the street, back to the dairy. She waved in response.

'Excuse me, Mr Kilmaster!'

He glanced over his shoulder expectantly.

'Could you lend a hand? I've been trying to move a wardrobe and I've got it jammed in the doorway.' The speaker issued a foolish laugh.

Momentarily forgetting her name, he turned and came back up the street towards her, replying, 'I'll gladly do what I can, madam.'

Observed by the woman's young daughter and two sons, Probyn entered.

'You three get yourselves dressed!' instructed their mother in brusque tone. On their dispersal she headed up a staircase, inviting Probyn to follow.

With the minimum of effort he managed to unblock the doorway and, after asking her where she wanted it, shuffled the wardrobe into position.

Eliza looked impressed. 'My, you made it look as if you were shifting a feather! Thank you, it's really kind.'

Both embarrassed and flattered at the gushing compliment, Probyn tugged his tunic straight. 'It's my pleasure. Mrs Crump, isn't it?'

'You remembered!' Unconsciously, Eliza mirrored his action by smoothing her white pinafore. She seemed unable to take her eyes off him.

'How could I forget after what my son did to your cat?' He smiled, the woman chuckling with him. 'How is it, by the way?'

She folded her arms under her breasts, this having the effect of shoving them upwards and drawing attention to them. 'I don't know, we haven't seen him for months. Must've got sick of being the laughing stock. My Edwin used to say he looked like the Kaiser with his spiky little moustache.'

Still smiling, Probyn suddenly became conscious that he was standing in the woman's bedroom and made for the landing. 'Well, if you've nothing else that wants moving . . .'

'No, thank you for all your help. I shouldn't have tried to shift it on me own but, well, I've no choice now my man's gone.'

He lingered before descending. 'Yes, I saw the telegram boy. My condolences.'

Whilst he had paused she had moved up intimately close behind him. 'Thanks. I do miss him – though I should be used to being on my own, what with him being a regular soldier.'

'Oh, a regular, was he?' Probyn showed cheery approval, though he was made to feel ill at ease by her proximity, and began to go down the staircase.

Eliza followed. 'But still, it's a shock and there's things a woman can't do . . .'

'Well, if you need anything else I'm not far away.'

'Your wife won't mind?'

'No, she's always keen to help, is Grace.'

'Yes, she seems a nice woman.'

Upon reaching the foot of the stairs he turned and smiled. 'Yes, yes she is.'

'She looks a bit pale, though.' Eliza tilted her dark head. 'Is she ill? Tell me to mind my own business if you like –'

'No, no, that's all right. She has been ill, yes.'

She nodded as if in thought, allowing her molasses-coloured gaze to pour over him quite brazenly, alighting on his crotch. Albeit briefly, it had a powerful physical effect and Probyn found himself wearing a blush he had not sported since youth. Eliza's reply was loaded with meaning. 'Well, if there's anything I can do for you in return . . .'

He could not believe his ears – she was propositioning him, with her husband dead only weeks and his wife just yards away!

Making a hasty exit into the cold air, he assured her they could manage.

'You know where I am!' called Eliza.

Disturbed by his reaction to Mrs Crump's overture, Probyn determined to avoid her in future and sought to make greater fuss of his wife.

'Right, get on your best bib and tucker, Gobbie!' His announcement came out of the blue that Saturday afternoon.

'Why, where are we going?' Her back to him, Grace sounded vague as she cut up herbs and added them to a concoction on the stove.

'We're off to have our photos took!'

Slightly disappointed, his wife uttered a little moan. 'Oh, it's a lot of trouble to get all dressed up just to come straight home agai –'

'Who said anything about coming straight home?' Probyn spread his hands. 'Once we've impressed the photographer we're off to the theatre. I might even buy you fish and chips on the way home.'

'You'll need to take out a bank loan then,' joked Grace. Still unable to summon the energy to meet his proposal, she gave the excuse, 'Anyway, it's too cold, and I'm in the middle of making this.'

'Then turn it off! I'm sure Gussie can warm it up for tea.'

'I'm sure she can't – it's ointment.' Grace chuckled.

'Come on, lass! I haven't seen you dressed up for years.'

It was the note of entreaty in his voice that made her turn. Holding her husband's gaze and really plumbing those blue-grey depths, Grace saw eyes that were haunted by the atrocities of war, a deep-seated exhaustion combined with worry that, normally, he was so good at hiding. Treating him to a deeply affectionate smile, she reached behind her to untie her apron strings and went upstairs to change.

For the children, who rarely saw their mother in anything else but a shabby all-enveloping overall or lying in bed ill, it was thrilling to see the trim figure who emerged in a cream satin blouse with lace at its collar, her shiny brown hair expertly puffed and padded out and fastened with a tortoiseshell comb.

'You look like Mary Pickford!' gasped Joe.

Father too looked capital, his threadbare, lice-ravaged uniform replaced by a brand-new one, two sizes smaller than its predecessor. Beata heaved a wondrous sigh: what a handsome couple her parents made for sure.

The photographer was to share this opinion, the results of his handiwork consequently displayed on the sideboard some weeks later. Frame in hand, Probyn smiled fondly at the woman beside him in the photograph – Grace as he had not seen her for years, hooded blue eyes sparkling with that seductive gleam that had first lured him – and was glad that he had coerced this transformation. Eliza Crump could not hold a candle to his dear wife.

*   *   *

179

Apparently Eliza did not share this view, her self-esteem quite evident from the way she deported herself before him whenever he had the misfortune to encounter her in the street. The total antonym of a grieving widow, it was blatantly obvious that she had set her sights on Probyn and seemed to regard it as only a matter of time before he weakened.

Having done so much to avoid Eliza's clutches, he was dismayed one afternoon to hear her call out to him just as he was about to achieve sanctuary. Maintaining his grip on the doorknob, he turned to face the buxom figure who was hurrying up the terrace towards him, a basket of shopping in one hand.

'Sorry to bother you again!' Bosom rising and falling, Eliza put a hand to her side and took a few moments to catch her breath. 'Eh, I'm all out of puff trying to catch up with you. You can't half move! I just caught sight of you as I was coming out of the shop and thought I'd beg another favour. I need to borrow your strong arms again if that's all right.' She detected a look of hesitation. 'You did say . . .'

'Oh, certainly! I'll just . . . I'll just let Grace know I'm home, then I'll be with you in two shakes!'

'Good, I'll go take this shopping home and get the kettle on.' Beaming, Eliza hurried onwards up the street.

'Oh, there's no need. I'll be having my tea soon!' Ducking into his house, Probyn said as casually as he could to Grace, 'Hello, dear. Mrs Crump has asked me to shift something. Why don't you come and have a chat with her while I do it?'

Though bemused, Grace was a friendly soul and, removing her apron, picked up Mims from the floor. Feeling much safer in his wife and daughter's company, Probyn went along the street to do Eliza's bidding.

If Eliza was put out that the wife had come too she did not show it and was friendliness personified to Grace, indicating for her to sit down. 'Can I get you a cup of tea, Mrs Kilmaster?'

'That would be lovely.' Grace took the indicated chair and perched respectfully with Mims on her lap.

'I've got a nice bit of cake too.'

Grace raised her eyebrows. 'Cake? That's a luxury.' Sugar was almost impossible to get hold of these days, as was margarine.

'Ah, well I've got my contacts.' With a conspiratorial wink, Eliza disappeared for a moment, though after rattling a few cups and saucers in the scullery she crept into the cellar where Probyn was moving the boxes and in the darkness glided up behind him.

Feeling a hand snake between his legs, Probyn came upright with the shock of it and banged his head on a stone lintel. Eliza laughed softly and, whilst he was still dazed, took his head between her hands and kissed him full on the lips. 'You can't hide for ever, you know!' Shocked but excited at the same time, Probyn did nothing for the moment, just stood there in the dank cellar, his pulse racing, trying to make out her dark eyes but seeing only a devilish glitter.

When she made to kiss him again he jerked his head away.

But Eliza simply uttered a soft laugh. 'Anytime you want, pet!' With a lingering caress, she was gone.

Waiting for her tea, trying to keep a wriggling Mims entertained, Grace wondered why she felt uneasy. Eliza was very friendly and generous-natured, but it was the way her eyes had run all over Probyn that unsettled his wife. There was a hint of the cat on heat about her, in the way she preened and sashayed, as if flicking her tail at him – why she might just as well have shoved her backside in his face, thought Grace. Concerned about her husband, she was glad when he reappeared from the cellar, though he looked very flushed.

'I hope you haven't been overdoing it,' whispered Grace. 'You're all red.'

Probyn turned even redder, especially when Eliza came in bearing a tray laden with cake and tea and said, 'That's because he's a red-blooded male, Mrs Kilmaster, a real man. He's lifted all that heavy stuff as easily as if it were tissue paper. Eh, you're so lucky to have him.'

'I know.' Grace was at once alert, her smile becoming frozen.

Offered a plate of cake, she politely declined, though allowed Mims to sample it, she herself taking swift little sips of tea, eager to empty the cup and get out of here.

But Eliza seemed keen to chat, asking all sorts of impertinent questions.

Annoyed at being manipulated by this woman and even angrier that she was trying to hoodwink Grace, Probyn did not finish his tea; this was one time when politeness was uncalled for. 'I'm afraid we shall have to go now.' He stood, indicating for his wife to do likewise.

Grace required no prompting and made a beeline for the door, carrying Mims with her.

Eliza's voice held disappointment. 'Oh well, I hope you'll call again, the both of you.'

They were noncommittal.

Eliza showed them into the street. 'Thank you for moving all that junk for me, Mr Kilmaster, and I hope you'll allow me to return the favour one day.'

Ignoring the innuendo, Probyn took his wife's arm and steered her home.

'What the hell is she up to?' Grace hissed at him when they were safe inside. 'Don't tell me, I know!'

'You don't know the half of it, love.' Having learned the hard way many years ago that it was a mistake to keep secrets, Probyn revealed all.

'The slut!' cried Grace, her face depicting horror.

'Not in front of the baby, dear.'

'Sod the baby, I'll bloody kill her, the bitch!' Pressing a hand over her mouth, Grace flopped into a chair, eventually calming down, though she remained utterly aghast that anyone could stoop so low.

'Gobbie –'

'Don't Gobbie me!'

'Eh! You don't think I encouraged her, do you?'

After an angry moment, Grace closed her eyes and shook her head. Probyn hated that type of woman as much as she did. She sagged in her chair, watching Mims playing on the rug but not really seeing her. 'As if it isn't bad enough there are Germans almost at our door I have to put up with a harridan lusting after my husband!'

He came to perch on the arm of her chair, reassuring her with a squeeze. 'She can lust all she likes but it won't do her any good. As if I'd look at an old trout like her when I've got a wife so much younger and prettier. You trust me, don't you?'

Eventually, Grace gave him an affectionate bump with her head. 'Of course I do. It's not you I'm mad with. God, I still can't believe the audacity of her!'

They shared the embrace for a few moments longer, before the children came in looking to be fed.

But even whilst organizing tea, it was obvious that Grace could not push the matter from her mind. Seeing her preoccupation, Probyn tried to jollify the atmosphere.

'Well, children, only a couple of days to go until Christmas! I think we shall have to get the paper chains up after tea.'

'Does Father Christmas know we've moved house?' Beata whispered to her mother.

On her way to the table with a stack of plates, Grace smiled sympathetically. 'Yes, but don't expect him to bring too much this year.' Oranges had become far too expensive for Christmas stockings. 'What with those horrible Germans, he's having as difficult a time as the rest of us finding stuff to put on his sleigh. There's hardly anything at all in the shops.' Absent now were the gorgeous window displays of peacetime yuletides. Perhaps it was as well, for few could afford to be extravagant in these lean times, even at this festive period. Moreover, with the carnage in Europe set to bleed into yet another year, it seemed indecent to celebrate. 'We must just be grateful that we still have each other.' Laying down the plates, she glanced across the table and locked eyes with her husband, both knowing that she did not merely refer to the risk from a foreign enemy.

Probyn maintained his level gaze and tried to convey, through the warmth of his smile, that he would never allow anyone or anything to destroy their marriage.

TWELVE

Whilst the Kilmasters' marriage stood firm, other alliances began to crumble, the year coming to an end on the dreadful news that the Bolsheviks, who had overthrown the Russian throne, were now entering peace talks with Germany. The feeling of disgust and betrayal that swept the country was compounded by the knowledge that these former allies were probably on their way to reinforce German troops on the Western Front. Every sign was that this was to be the worst year yet.

'Nineteen eighteen,' marvelled Grace, taking down the last paper chain and storing it away in the cupboard. 'Who could have predicted a war would last this long?'

Behind the evening newspaper her husband was deeply meditative, his eyes touring the columns of dead. 'This is a war like no other, Gobbie.'

Knowing him so well, his wife read the pain beneath that remark but his children did not, regarding this as an opening to ask questions, Madeleine being first to sidle respectfully to his chair. 'Tell us what the war's *really* like, Father.'

'Noisy,' came the simple reply.

'Oh, please tell us, Father!' Joe, the would-be soldier, was quick to add his voice. 'How many Germans did you kill? Did you see anybody get shot?'

Beata too was keen to hear, though Duke hung back.

Lowering the newspaper, Probyn surveyed the row of expectant little faces, then crooked his finger summoning all to gather round him, which they did eagerly as he bent his head to confide some very important announcement. 'When you're old enough . . . I'll tell you how many beans make five.'

There was a collective 'Aw!' and the disappointed children fell away in accompaniment to their eldest brother's laughter.

'Leave your father alone now,' Grace bade them. 'And get ready for bed.'

Joe risked a final question. 'Will the war be over this year?'

'We'd all like the answer to that,' murmured his father, whilst Mother offered more encouraging response.

'If you pray extra hard I'm sure Our Lord will take pity on us,' she told her children.

Joe followed his siblings to the stairs. 'I'll do me best but I can't promise owt.'

Probyn suppressed a chuckle. 'Well, if you can't persuade the Lord to end the war could you just ask Him for some better weather? My rheumatism's giving me gyp.'

On his way out to the lavatory, Clem added his own jocular requirement. 'And ask Him for a couple of slices of that pink stuff that comes off pigs. Sorry I can't remember the name of it, it's been so long since I had any.'

'You're not supposed to ask for things for yourself,' Joe reproved his big brother before disappearing.

Clem grinned and, with a chesty cough, went out into the yard.

'Then I suppose it's a waste of time asking Him to make the Merry Widow vanish in a puff of smoke,' muttered Grace with all her offspring out of earshot. Undaunted by the cool reception, Eliza had wheedled and connived to make friends with her and to infiltrate the Kilmaster household along with other neighbours, but, aware that she was only out to ensnare Probyn, this was one person towards whom Grace refused to be charitable.

'I'm doing my utmost to evade capture.' That was certainly true. It had become most comical to watch Probyn's avoidance of Mrs Crump. Before leaving the house he would peer cautiously around the jamb to check if she was in the street. If she was, he would wait a while until she had finished scrubbing her doorstep or sweeping the pavement or whatever she was affecting to be doing whilst lying in ambush for him. He had even varied his times of departure just to outfox her. 'She'll get fed up in the end.'

Soon, though, there came much more to worry about than the predatory Eliza Crump. Three months into the new year, using reinforcements acquired from Russia, von Ludendorff launched a

185

massive offensive that threatened to smash through the Allied line. Thousands more casualties came flocking home to swell the already overcrowded military hospitals. Furthermore, out of the night sky came a noise that they had not heard for years.

Unable to get to sleep despite his exhaustion, Probyn was immediately alert at the faint whirring of an engine, and, within seconds of his hearing this the whole world erupted into a barrage of hate.

'It's a blasted airship!' He jumped out of bed, having no need to rouse Grace, for she was already rushing to the landing where they encountered Clem.

Hearing a wail from the children's room, Probyn spoke calmly, ordering his eldest son, 'Go back in and sit with them, Clem.'

An anxious, indecisive Grace pinched her chin. 'Shouldn't we get everyone out?'

'They're safer in bed.' Probyn remained calm. 'It's not overhead yet. If it comes any nearer we'll get them down then.' He led the way to the yard.

The dark sky was a network of searchlights, but the enemy was obviously flying at immense height, for he remained invisible as he committed his dastardly work.

Woken by the din, though not knowing what it was, the girls lifted their heads from the pillow as Clem entered their bedroom.

'It's all right.' Speaking softly, comfortingly, their brother hurried to the bedside and tugged the covers up under the row of chins. 'It's only thunder and lightning. Shut your eyes and it'll all be over by morning.'

Reassured and still muzzy from sleep, the girls allowed their heads to drop, and, with their big brother standing guard, soon drifted back to oblivion.

Pacifying the younger boys with the same excuse, Clem remained at hand, making periodic checks on all his siblings lest they should wake and be afraid.

Grace and Probyn too remained watchful until the noise decreased to a threatening rumble and finally faded away, though they did not sleep for the rest of the night.

Deceived into believing the cacophony had been an electric storm, the children were to discover the truth in the morning through a schoolfriend. Hence, when the rumbling came again on a second night, they were not so easily duped, and though daylight was to reveal little damage to the town and none at all to the Kilmaster house, it was still frightening to hear that nine people had been killed. The Zeppelins did not come again, but the fear was to remain.

On the Western Front the situation was becoming dire. By midsummer the enemy had forced the Allies back across the Marne and was once again threatening Paris. The demand for troops became all encompassing to those responsible for providing them, and Probyn was almost dead on his feet from trying to fulfil the urgent appeal. The strain of having constantly to ensure that his high standards were upheld was an extra drain on an already exhausted system. Certainly he was too worn out to care about Eliza Crump's sexual overtures. This being so, he hardly noticed when she gave up.

Grace noticed, though, and enjoyed a little smile of triumph. But there was no time to gloat with all that was going on, for the beleaguered nation had been assailed by yet another foe: an outbreak of influenza so virulent that the obituaries of those who had lost their lives in the trenches were in danger of being equalled by those who died at home.

The deaths were swift and cruel, victims drowning in their own blood within hours, and the disease so contagious that all places of entertainment were out of bounds to soldiers, the latter obviously responsible for conveying it from the trenches where it had been in evidence for weeks. Too poor to rely on any outside source for their entertainment, the closures did not greatly concern the Kilmasters. None the less, Grace worried for her brood, assiduously going through their handkerchief pockets to apply disinfectant, mixing up solutions that everyone was made to sniff before leaving the house.

Despite all this, throughout the duration of the epidemic, she was to remain worried, and when the normally stoical Probyn confessed to feeling unwell one morning, she was on him in a trice, dosing and disinfecting.

Cupping a puddle of Condy's Fluid in his palm, Probyn held it to his somewhat grey face and dutifully inhaled – but within seconds his knees had folded under him and he had collapsed upon the floor, apparently unconscious. Grace squeaked, pressed a hand to her mouth, then ran to him.

'Fetch the doctor, one of you!'

Normally Gussie would be first to respond but she was out on her milk round. Beata jumped into action; the doctor being a regular visitor to her mother, she knew where to find him.

Along with the distraught Grace, Clem attended his father, who was now coming round, the pair of them hauling him into a sitting position and dragging up a chair to use as a prop.

However, to everyone's great relief, the physician had only been in the house seconds before dispelling initial fears, his stethoscope applied to Probyn's broad chest as his patient slowly came to. 'I can tell you right away it's not influenza. Hello, Mr Kilmaster, are you with us?'

Still groggy, Probyn looked from one to the other, totally bemused. 'I just went all dizzy . . .'

Clem went immediately to open the window, shooing the children outside. 'Let's give Father some air.'

The doctor asked if there was any brandy and Grace hurried to fetch it, curling her arm around Probyn's broad shoulders whilst holding the glass to his lips. Having almost wept with gratitude to find it was not the deadly plague, she remained concerned. 'What do you think caused it, doctor?'

'Impossible to say without making deeper examination.' The physician replaced his stethoscope in his bag, addressing himself gravely to Probyn. 'Though it's quite obvious you're suffering from exhaustion.'

'Isn't everyone?' Probyn was a dreadful colour.

'Quite so.' The doctor too wore a look of deep fatigue. 'But I strongly recommend you have a thorough check from your own medical officer.'

After giving further advice he left, his grave comportment lending no reason for optimism, though Probyn continued to dismiss his wife's fears. 'Nay, it's summat nor nowt, Gobbie.'

Grace showed annoyance. 'Do you want me to speak to your MO myself?'

There was no arguing with her when she had that look on her face. Besides, Probyn felt too ill to put up a fight. 'All right, I'll go see him,' he muttered.

And, however unwillingly, he did submit himself for examination.

The diagnosis was to devastate him. That he was suffering from exhaustion came as no surprise, but this camouflaged a much more sinister malady, one that could spell the end of his career in the army. Barely was he able to convey the words to Grace when, upon his homecoming, she demanded an explanation for his tormented visage.

'They say I've got heart trouble, Gobbie.' Looking into her eyes, he was obviously shattered.

Grace was equally affected. 'Good grief! Oh, Probe . . .'

'Arteriosclerosis as well.'

Her horror grew. 'What's that?'

'Hardening of the arteries. They're arranging for me to go into hospital.'

'Oh, love!' She flew to him and hugged him. It was fortunate that the children were not around to hear this. 'When do you have to go?'

'Right away.' His own disbelief at hearing the news was still upon his face. 'They've only let me come home to tell you.' He held his barrel chest as if afraid that his vital organ would suddenly give out.

Grace's own heart had begun to throb. Her eyes filled with tears.

He tried to be brave and covered her hand with his, though the gesture lacked its normal strength. 'Nay, don't have me dead yet. I'll be all right after a few weeks' rest.' There came limp instruction. 'Be a good lass and pack my things for me.'

Fighting to stay calm, Grace delivered a last supportive grip of his hand before going to gather his requisites, and, after this was done, she accompanied him back to the barracks where they were to take their leave of each other for many days.

During the head of the family's stay in hospital, as if this were not bad enough, more disaster was to strike the Kilmasters. Examining the letter that had arrived as he was on his way to work, Clem murmured to his mother, 'It's from York.'

Shown the envelope, Grace recognized the handwriting as Kit's and, as she was up to her elbows in flour, said, 'You open it, Clem, the rest of you get out in the fresh air while you can. Beat, look after Mims.'

'Aw, we can't play properly with her hanging on!'

Clem warned Joe. 'You heard what your mother said.'

There was a mass exodus, Beata reluctantly dragging the three-year-old by the hand

On unfolding the letter, Clem groaned and allowed his chin to drop to his chest, his eyes closed in despair. 'Oh, Mam . . . Uncle Worthy's died.'

There was an intake of breath. Dismayed, Grace stopped working, floury hands clamped to her cheeks. 'Oh, poor Kit. Was it the flu?'

Her son nodded dismally. 'Father'll be upset, won't he?'

'I shan't tell him yet.' Blinking rapidly, Grace shook her head, then used the back of her hand to dislodge specks of flour from her cheeks. 'He'll be discharging himself from hospital to go to the funeral and I'm not having that. He doesn't need anything else on his plate.'

'We'll be going, though, won't we?'

Her reply was plaintive. 'We haven't the money, dear.'

'But Aunt Kit'll be on her own and one of us should go to represent the family – I don't mind walking.' There was an emotional edge to Clem's voice: he had been fond of his uncle.

'It's hundreds of miles! Besides, you couldn't take time off work. We need every penny. In fact you'd better get yourself off now or you'll be late.' Ridding herself of flour, Grace came to lay supportive hands on her son's shoulders, sharing his quandary. 'I feel terrible about it, but Aunt Kit knows our situation, she won't expect us to go. I'll write, of course, to explain that your father's in hospital and to check that she's all right herself. I wish there was more I could do, but I can't.' She gave a compassionate murmur, knowing how devastating the loss of a husband must be. '*Poor* Kit.'

Not until Probyn was discharged from hospital looking much recovered did Grace feel able to break the news to him. He was sorrowful, naturally, but had to agree that there was no way any of them could have travelled to the funeral.

With the rest of the family out at Sunday Mass, Grace admitted that, with no response to her letter of condolence nor to the further enquiries as to Kit's own health, she feared that either Kit, too, had fallen victim to influenza or else had taken deep offence over their nonappearance at Worthy's funeral.

But within minutes of this admission a letter dropped through the letterbox, the short missive absolving them of guilt and stating the hope that all was now well with Kit's favourite nephew. The funeral had been a quiet affair, wrote Kit. With Worthy disinherited by his own family who had abhorred his choice of wife, only local friends and villagers had been present. This made Probyn and Grace feel even worse, but Kit added that it was quite understandable that people found it impossible to travel in these trying times.

'Trying times indeed.' Guessing what agony lay between those sensible lines, Probyn heaved a sigh and folded the letter, remaining quietly thoughtful.

'There's something you're not telling me.'

He glanced up to find Grace studying him shrewdly. Looking her in the eye, he admitted, 'Aye, there is, but it's nothing for you to get worried about. In fact, I think you might be rather pleased. I've been classed as unfit for further service.'

She gasped in concern. 'Aw, love – but you look so much better!'

'Oh, I'm told I'll be fine if I take things easy, live a quiet life. So, no more soldiering for me.' He gave a tight smile.

'Aw, Probe, I'm that sorry!' exclaimed Grace, her face contorted by genuine sympathy. But something puzzled her and she scrutinized him for a while longer before making tentative addition. 'I thought . . . well, you don't look too devastated.'

'I am, and then again I'm not.' His words were delivered in monotone, his cropped sandy head lolling to one side as if too heavy for his neck to support. 'I'd have preferred to go out under more cheerful circumstances when we've won the war, but . . . I'm *weary*, Grace.' It showed, both in his expression and his voice. 'I'm just so damned weary.'

Rarely had Grace heard him so depressed. She came to sit on the arm of his chair, enfolded him in a loving embrace and kissed the top of his head. Neither of them uttered a word for some time, the crux of this matter remaining implicit. The army had been his life; what was he to do now? Unlike her husband, Grace had never entertained the grand dream. Oh, she would not have turned down the offer of a country cottage with furniture that smelled of lavender polish and lupins in the garden, but in the main any ambitions she did harbour were for her children. But that did not bar her from putting herself momentarily in his shoes. 'Well, at least you can say you've achieved the pinnacle you set for yourself. It's more than most can claim.'

'Aye, it's been a good, rewarding job.' Grateful for her words, he rubbed the feminine knee beneath the apron. 'Anyway, here's something that might cheer you. They've given me a desk job at the Infantry Record Office in York.'

Grace's impulse was to exclaim her delight – she would see her sisters and Charlotte again – but, feeling selfish, she swallowed the urge. Nevertheless he read it on her face and spoke of his gladness for her that she was to be reunited with her kin. His wife pointed out that he would benefit too. 'You'll be able to see more of Aunt Kit!'

'Aye, she'll be in need of family with Worthy gone. She must be scared for her lad too. The Lord willing, with the Americans on our side now it won't be too long before she has her Toby back safe.'

Grace made a fuss of him. 'Well, if it gets you out of the Merry Widow's clutches I'm all for it! I can't wait to see her face when she sees us moving out.'

He gave a feeble laugh and reached for a cigarette. 'Nay, she's not interested in a broken-down old thing like me any more.'

'Aw! Well, here's one who is.' She leaned over to plant a kiss.

He looked offended. 'You're meant to say, "You're not a broken-down old thing."'

Grace delivered an oblique smile. 'Sorry. So, when are we off?'

'Whenever we like. I don't have to hang on the colonel's permission now. I'm not a soldier any more.' The thought was bleak, but not unbearable.

And so the Kilmasters were once again uprooted, home now being a flat above a fish-and-chip shop on the corner of Blue Bridge Lane, so near to the headquarters of Northern Command, yet so far. The fact that it was cramped for nine of them meant nothing, for they were used to living like sardines, and the joy of regular meetings with the lovely Charlotte, still as sweet despite her own tragic loss, overrode any discomfort. Besides, Father said they were only to be here a few weeks until a permanent residence could be found.

Grace wasted no time in taking her children to visit the many aunts and uncles they had previously seen only once a year.

Concerned about his own aunt, one of Probyn's first acts upon settling in was to visit Kit. Owing to the summer closure, the children would not be starting their new school yet and so were able to enjoy this treat too, though their father felt it expedient to leave them romping in the fields whilst he and Grace had an intimate talk with the widow. However, though obviously sad, Kit seemed to be coping amazingly well and the fact that she had good neighbours who helped with the farm work reassured Probyn that she did not need him. Telling her she was welcome to visit them any time, he and Grace left feeling a lot happier.

'Well, that was a relief,' Grace echoed his thoughts on their way home. 'The last thing you need is another burden.'

'Aye – not that I think of Aunt Kit as a burden,' came Probyn's hurried addition, 'but I know what you mean. She's always been resilient, thank the Lord – she's needed to be.'

Upon taking up his sedentary job, Probyn's own wellbeing began to show gradual improvement, for which Grace was to give thanks at Mass. As in every other place she had lived, her immediate action upon arriving in York had been to seek out the local priest, only this time it was much easier, Father Murphy being an old acquaintance and keen to enfold her in his parish again. Surrounded by friends and family, Grace had not felt so happy in a long time.

Even so, life in general was to grow increasingly spartan for everyone during that fifth year of the war. It hardly mattered that there was less money to spend, for some foods had become unobtainable and to get the most basic ingredients one had to queue for hours outside the shops. Ice cream was a luxury of the past, there were few sweets, no icing on cakes, it was even against the law to sell a warm loaf. Ration cards were introduced, which helped to cut the queues but did little to improve supplies and in some cases made things worse; no meat except offal could be purchased without a coupon, hence, chitterlings were to become a staple constituent of the Kilmasters' diet. Never one to complain, upon being presented with such lowly offering yet again at lunchtime, Probyn tucked in stoically, trying not to inhale the tantalizing aroma of fried fish that permeated from the shop beneath and taking his mind off this by chatting to Charlotte, who was there that day to see her friend.

When the conversation petered out he turned to his eldest son. 'Anything interesting on the work front this morning, Clem?' Probyn asked this same question day after day.

Clem sounded despondent as he inserted another forkful of offal. 'No, nothing doing.'

'Oh well, don't get too downhearted.'

The seventeen-year-old donned a brave smile. 'No, I won't. Anyway, doesn't really matter if I find a job, I'll be old enough to join up in a few wee –'

'Clem! Promise you won't.' Grace dropped her knife and fork in alarm. 'Probe tell him not to.'

After wincing at the clatter of metal on china, her husband was uncooperative. 'Nay, once the lad's old enough he can make up his own mind.'

Grace wanted to yell that her son could be killed and didn't her husband care? But she knew that it would be pointless as well as cruel. Of course Probyn cared, he just did not view things the same way as a mother. Even so, she was not about to give up. 'How can you even think of joining up after what happened to Aunt Charlotte's fiancé?' Meal abandoned, she turned to her friend for moral support, begging, 'Make him see sense, Lottie.'

Annoyed with Probyn, though not showing it, Charlotte sided with his wife. 'Your mother's right, Clem.' Her tiny emerald eyes glanced up only briefly from her meal but the pain of her loss was still evident even after two years. 'Don't go till they send for you.'

Clem turned to his father for consent but Probyn refused to meet his gaze. With female opinion against him, the lad gave half-hearted assurance not to join up.

Feeling partly to blame for her son's gloom, after Probyn had gone back to the office Grace lifted the lid of her piano. 'Right, let's have a hooley! Cheer ourselves up.'

Charlotte fought sad memories and, donning a smile, grabbed Clem's hands. 'Well, I've got my dancing partner, I don't know about anyone else.'

Augusta paired up with Maddie, the younger ones happy just to watch as a great deal of joyful stamping and thudding began.

This shenanigans went on for a good half-hour before a knock came at the door.

The others too breathless and otherwise engaged, Beata scampered to open it. It was the woman from the chip shop beneath. 'Can you ask your mother to exercise her livestock somewhere else, please? You know, that herd of elephants she's been training.'

Grace uttered a guilty laugh and closed the piano lid. 'Sorry, Cissy, I didn't realize it was so loud. We'll shut up now.'

Cissy chuckled too. 'Nay, I'm only kidding, I've really come to ask if one of your bairns can give me a hand and peel some spuds for the tea-time fry-up. Three ha'pence per tub.'

Augusta was only too keen to offer her services. 'I'll do it!'

Grace welcomed any extra cash. 'Gussie's a good little worker.'

'Is she now? Then we might find something permanent for her,' said the woman as she left with Augusta, then paused briefly to give permission to the rest. 'Carry on!'

'No, I think we've had enough for the time being.' A smiling Grace left the piano, ignoring her children's moans. 'No, no, you've had enough fun with Aunt Lottie. I want to talk to her now.'

'Yes, I want to talk to you too,' announced Charlotte, her expression somewhat accusing. 'You're looking awfully pale and thin. Are you feeling all right?'

'Yes!' Grace skimmed over this blithely. 'I'm fit as a lop. Come on now, children, out to play.'

'Aye, I should be looking for work anyway,' proclaimed Clem and, in a happier mood after his dancing session, duly left. The younger ones lingered to whine about there being nothing to do.

Charlotte dipped into her purse and conveyed a handful of coppers to Madeleine. 'Here, you can get a tram right outside the door. Go to Knavesmire and watch the aeroplanes.'

'Aw, do we have to take her?' complained Joe, a disdainful eye on three-year-old Mims, who always cramped their fun.

'Yes, you do,' said his mother firmly. 'Wretched boy, be gone!'

Catching the tram as instructed, the siblings clambered up the staircase to perch on the top deck. But when the conductress had not come upstairs for their fares by the time they got to the terminus, they decided to stay on board and snatch a quick view of the biplanes from up here. Were they to remain quiet enough, they might even get the round trip for free and be able to spend the money on sweets.

If the conductress noticed them slip away without paying then she turned a blind eye as they dashed off the tram. Finding the six-month ban on ice cream had been lifted, they eagerly purchased some.

Passing through the chip shop on their way up to the flat much later that afternoon they found Augusta assisting in the serving of the tea-time fry-up, and proudly told her of their acquisition.

The chastisement they received was totally unexpected. 'You selfish little monkeys! You should have brought the money back to Mother instead of wasting it on rubbish. You know she can hardly make ends meet.'

Apart from Duke and Mims, who did not understand the extent of their sin, the children were mortified, the conscientious Beata most of all, for she idolized her eldest sister. On the brink of tears, she promised never to behave so again.

Augusta was immediately forgiving. 'Well, now you know, I'm sure you'll be a bit more thoughtful in future.'

With Clem still unable to find suitable work, Augusta herself seemed to have more than her fair share of job opportunities, her days spent behind the counter of a Co-operative Store, her evenings in the fish shop, both becoming sources of free nourishment for her family if the manager was out of the way.

After a few weeks of living cheek by jowl, larger accommodation was obtained and a lorry trundled the family possessions across the city. The house in Layerthorpe might be in a dank, run-down area of narrow lanes, tanneries and soup kitchens, the sour-smelling River Foss and the Derwent Valley Railway, but it was certainly a lot roomier, which was heaven for those who had previously lived so closely packed. The soot-coated terrace was sectioned into pairs, each pair sharing a passage that led into two back yards and each house having its own gate, though there was no lane at the rear, the properties backing on to other yards. There were four bedrooms, one of which was claimed by the parents, another by the boys, the third shared by Augusta, Madeleine and Mims. Beata was given a tiny one to herself and found it unsettling at first to sleep alone, and quite eerie on windy nights when the metal sign that hung outside squeaked back and forth. But on such nights she would pretend that her bed was a ship and by this means transport herself to the far-off sunny places of which Father had spoken and which she longed to visit.

In contrast, for once in his life Probyn wanted to be no place but here and, living near to his office in Colliergate meant that he could be home in minutes. After being away from his family for much of his married life, especially in these last four years of carnage, he was grateful now for the act of fate that had placed him behind a desk and given him the opportunity to spend more time with his loved ones.

They were a well-behaved brood and a joy to be with, apart perhaps from Duke, with whom he could not seem to get on, try as he might. It was as if the child's tears upon being reunited with his father so long ago had set the scene for the rest of their days together.

The lad seemed to take pleasure in rubbing him up the wrong way – at least that was how it appeared to Probyn. Grace always defended him, swearing that there was no malice in his acts, just a curious nature getting the better of him. Well, perhaps that might be so, and his antics were often amusing, but there was a wilful streak in Duke.

There had been just such an incident recently. Hearing a noise from the front room that should have been empty, Probyn had gone to investigate. 'What are you up to, Duke? You were told to go outside.'

Duke rotated guiltily, an open tin in his hand. 'What's this, Father?'

Probyn looked upon the white unattractive, misshapen slab inside the tin. 'It's chocolate sent to me by Her Majesty when I was fighting the Boers.'

'Can we eat it?'

'No, it's a souvenir. Besides, it wouldn't be very nice, it melted in the hot sun. Put it back now.' Stern of feature, Probyn made sure that his son replaced the tin in the sideboard before sending him back out to play. But later he was to venture into the sideboard for something and the tin was nowhere to be found.

Duke swore he had not touched it, but his father knew he was lying, and when the tin and its half-eaten contents were later discovered under the boys' bed he knew it was not one of the other occupants who had stashed it there.

Since the good hiding, the gulf between them had widened. Sad though it was, Probyn had come to accept that the boy would always be his mother's son.

Joe, on the other hand, was constantly eager for his father's attention, pestering to hear accounts of his soldiering days. During the hiatus between teatime and bed, when the children would occasionally be allowed to join in the parental conversation if it were not too serious, Joe's question would invariably be the same. 'Father, am I old enough yet to know how many beans make five?'

Then Probyn would break into a smile and draw his son to his knee and tell him of the olden days when, as a young recruit the RSM caught him sending his socks home to be darned and had frightened him so much that he had always mended his own socks ever since. And by this method he instilled in Joe and his other children the need to look after one's self, taught them how to cook and darn and wash and iron as he himself had learned to do.

But this was not what Joe had wanted to hear. He hated it that his queries were always treated as a joke, for if he was to be a soldier then he needed to be furnished with real exploits.

Yet Father constantly refused to speak about his fighting days, saying firmly if the matter was pressed, 'That's for another day,' a signal that the indulgence was over. Detecting the sadness in his eyes, Beata wondered what was going on in Father's head and what he felt inside him.

One night, eager to know more, she lay awake until Clem had got into bed, then sneaked down to perch in darkness at the foot of the stairs, trying to discern what her parents were saying.

Faced with the daily struggle of having to make ends meet and the awful fear that the Germans might win, Mother was questioning the wisdom of ever getting into this war in the first place. After all, it had not been their country under attack.

Then came Father's voice, gently reproving. 'It's our duty as members of a great Empire to help smaller nations, Grace. If we'd allowed the Hun to bully Belgium they would have seen our lack of action as weakness and tried to invade Britain. Thank God we never got round to building that stupid tunnel under the Channel. The Hun would have been up it like a rat up a sewer and we wouldn't have stood a chance.'

Mother acquiesced. 'You're right, of course. It's just getting me down a bit, that's all. I'm sorry, dear.'

Warm words: 'That's all right, lass. It's getting us all down.'

A short silence, then a plaintive appeal. 'We will win, won't we, Probe?'

There was the slightest hesitation. Then with a deep breath he dismissed the unthinkable. 'We have to. There's been too much suffering, too much sacrifice. All those poor brave men . . .' His voice caught with emotion, and, not for the first time, he began to purge himself of the horrors he had seen, unburdening himself to the keeper of his heart, unaware that an innocent little soul was eavesdropping.

Assailed by the reality of war, Beata sat transfixed and trembling, until she could bear it no longer and crept back upstairs to pull the covers over her head. She would never listen again.

Miraculously, after a month in which it seemed that the exhausted and demoralized British troops might be forced right back across the Channel, their fortunes took a remarkable turn. Bolstered by thousands of vigorous US reinforcements, tanks and planes by the hundred, the Allies managed to gain a foothold. Soon, not only were they holding the Germans at bay, but were actually pushing them backwards.

The seriousness of recent events being kept from them, the children had only their mother's mood as a barometer of the situation. For weeks she had been tense, but lately she had begun to sing again, removing any worry they might have had about the war.

This was all well and good, but fortunes on the home front remained mixed. Clem was still unable to find work, whilst Augusta had secured a job at Rowntrees, which provided a higher wage than her two existing jobs put together. Though the family could no longer enjoy their generous fish suppers, there were different treats to be had from the chocolate rejects which found their way into Gussie's overall pockets.

Not everyone seemed pleased about this state of affairs. Just returned from another fruitless venture to the labour exchange, Clem was positively rude when his mother offered him a chocolate as consolation.

'Oh, I'm sure that'll help!' Whipping off his cap to reveal an angry scowl, he brushed past her and headed into the yard.

'Just because you didn't get a job don't take it out on me, my boy!' called a furious Grace.

There was a brief pregnant interlude, then Clem strode back into the kitchen. 'Sorry, Mother. I'm just so blood – blinking disappointed!'

Not wholly pacified, Grace folded her arms under her breast and awaited an explanation. From the way he seemed reluctant to look at her, the depth of his anger, she sensed there was more to this than met the eye.

Finally he confessed. 'You might as well know, I haven't been to the labour exchange. I went to join u –'

'My God!' Grace threw her hands in the air, before taking him to task. 'You sly little – You never said a word when you went out this morning! Well, you can just get down there and unjoin!'

'I don't have t –'

'You bloody well do!'

'I don't because they wouldn't bloody take me!' Still unable to hold his mother's eye for long, Clem was suffused with frustration.

'Well, thank God for that!' she sputtered.

'Why?' Joe had been standing in the doorway with a bucket of coal, listening.

Red of face, Clem whirled on him. 'Speak when you're spoken to!'

Recognizing the depth of her eldest son's rejection, Grace took the coal bucket from Joe. 'Thank you very much for helping me, darling. You can go out and play now.'

Joe closed the door behind him, and Clem at last felt able to explain to his mother why he had broken his word. His face was tormented. 'I know I promised, but I just felt as if I were a sponger not being able to –'

'Aw!' Grace broke in, touching him comfortingly. 'It doesn't matter. Gussie brings a good wage in.'

'That makes me feel ten times worse, knowing my sister is worth more than I am!'

'It's not as if you haven't tried, love! I'd rather have you safe at home than out there risking your life.'

Clem sighed heavily. 'That's just as well, because you're stuck with me, I'm afraid, Mam. The army wouldn't have me because of my bad chest.' He looked and felt emasculated, could not bring himself to voice what was in his head: there was his father with a breastful of medals, the mightiest man in the regiment, and he himself was judged too puny even to slip into a pair of army boots.

He did not have to say it; his mother understood and her heart bled for him. 'Love, I'm sorry you've been disappointed, but I'm so, so glad to hear you're staying at home. Really I am.'

On the other side of the door, his ear to the wood, eleven-year-old Joe was glad too. Everyone had always taken it for granted that it would be Clem who followed in Father's footsteps, had always treated Joe's enthusiasm for the army as a joke. Now it would be he who carried the baton.

'You'll get a job soon, Clem, a clever lad like you. I'll vouch for it,' concluded Grace.

But he won't be a soldier, thought Joe with a satisfied grin.

As if his mother's opinion had been an edict, Clem was to acquire a job two days later, tallying the books for a local store. Yet, even in receipt of parental praise, he could not fully enjoy the achievement, for he knew that however far he rose he would always be eclipsed by his father's illustrious career.

Unaware of others' personal crises, whilst their elder brother and sister went off to work on a morning, the younger children enjoyed what remained of the school holidays, exploring the streets of York, occasionally watching the latest war news and film footage on the large screen above a chemist's shop in Parliament Street.

'It's a black day for the Germans.' Displaying wrinkled shirt-sleeves, thumbs hooked into his waistcoat, Joe looked up at the screen with an expression of pride. 'Our lads've nearly pushed them right back to the Hindenburg line.'

A passing man hawked and spat on the pavement. Admiring this skill, Duke tried to emulate, but his first attempt produced only a dribble down his chin. Summoning up more saliva, he threw back his head and expectorated as far as he could.

'Stop that!' A woman who had been rattling a collection tin nearby rebuked him. 'Do you think I want to waste my time standing here while you perpetuate those filthy habits?'

Embarrassed, the children moved on, but not before Beata's attention had been drawn to the placard around the woman's neck. 'Fight the white scourge – what's the white scourge, Maddie?'

'Consumption,' answered her sister and in the same breath asked, 'Shall we go for a picnic?'

They had always spent much of the summer holidays enjoying such outings and even a war could not prevent this.

Joe said he would have to use his pocket money on wool for

darning. Madeleine asked who did not have any essential item to obtain and upon hearing that Beata still had her tuppence, suggested that one of these pennies would buy enough carrots for four of them. 'Mims can share yours,' she told Beata generously. 'If we pool the rest we'll have enough to get the tram home.'

Calling in at a greengrocer's to make their purchase, then rubbing the carrots against a wall to remove the skins as they went along, they made their way out of the city to Knavesmire.

After a long period of racing about and cartwheeling on the vast green sward, they fell breathless upon the grass to gnaw on their carrots whilst watching all the military activity and the aeroplanes taking off. Finding that she did not have a carrot of her own but was expected to subsist on Beata's offering, three-year-old Mims burst into tears and worked herself into a state of near hysteria.

'Give her it, Beat,' advised Madeleine, calmly chewing on her own vegetable.

But even when the youngest had what she craved her whining did not diminish and the outing was thoroughly spoiled.

Joe had had enough, jumping up with the announcement, 'Bugger this, I'm off home!' And he set off running across the green. There was a flurry of bare brown legs as others followed suit, all laughingly ignoring Mims' wails for them to wait, making it a race as to who could be first to the tram stop. With a tram already waiting, they clambered onto the top deck, giggling all the way home at having played such a trick on their nuisance of a sister.

Once back in their own street, though, they argued as to who was to return and fetch the infant. 'Well, somebody's got to get her,' said Maddie. 'Mother'll want to know where she is.'

'She might not notice,' opined Beata.

'You started it,' Maddie accused Joe, who flung the accusation back.

The argument went on for so long that in the end it was decided that they must all go. This time with no tram fare, they were forced to walk the two and a half miles. But halfway there a lorry passed them, on the back of which was loaded a dead cow, and perched astride the corpse was a little figure in a green bonnet with astrakhan trimming, who waved merrily as she sailed past, heading for Layerthorpe.

Though using every ounce of stamina to chase the haulier, they failed to intercept Mims before she could relay their trickery to Mother. Berated for their meanness, they were banned from going on any more picnics for the rest of the holiday.

*   *   *

As it turned out this was not too great a punishment for the weather became showery.

It being too wet to play in the street, the children simply went calling, and there was never a shortage of people to visit, for, apart from aunts and uncles, their mother had countless friends. For Beata, however, these ports of call were not merely in order to escape the rain but entailed small acts of charity on her part. Whilst the others went elsewhere, Beata would think of Rose, a neighbour's child who was confined to a bath-chair, her useless limbs contorted into grotesque angles, unable even to turn a page for herself, and would choose to spend the afternoon reading to her. Even when the sun came out there was no eager dash to escape, or at least not without pushing Rose out for some sunshine too.

At other times Beata would go and read to Mrs Jordan, the landlady of The Spread Eagle, who was a diabetic. Seated on a wooden, cushionless settle beside the fire, or perhaps in Mrs Jordan's bedroom if the elderly woman was laid low, she would while away the hours reading to her. Occasionally, if she had just received her pocket money, Beata would use one of the pennies on a bunch of wallflowers.

Thanking her warmly, the recipient opined, 'Eh, you'll never be rich, Beat.'

But Beata smiled and said she did not care.

Often, Nurse Falconer would be there in her grey dress and big white cuffs, attending Mrs Jordan's ulcerated foot, then the calm and capable Beata would be invited to help put on a bandage. And admiring the little girl's efforts, both women would concur that here was a nurse in the making.

Beata refuted this firmly. 'I'm going to be an explorer.'

But the women simply shared a knowing smile and said, 'You wait and see.'

On other days Beata would take pity on Aunt Maude, a pathetic woman with large teeth and the cares of the world upon her shoulders, assisting in her shop on Walmgate by making up penny pokes of tea and quarter-pounds of sugar.

In fact hardly a day went by when Beata concentrated solely on herself. Rapidly becoming a favourite amongst her relatives for her lack of boisterousness and air of maturity, it was Beata they sent for when in time of need. And there always seemed to be one after another of them needing her, the latest being Aunt Nell, whose confinement meant that someone else would be required to look after the house.

'You're a right capable lass,' Uncle Charlie told Beata warmly as he put her on the train back to York after her week's stay in Bolton Percy. 'Tell your mother, I don't know what we'd have done without you.'

Thinking it might be considered boastful, Beata did not relay this, though was eager to tell her family all about the new arrival when she got home.

After paying close attention to all her daughter told her about the baby, Grace terminated the exchange with a sigh. 'Eh, I don't know, as one comes in another goes out.' And she burst into tears.

Father explained to Beata and her siblings, who were just as much in the dark as was she. 'Your Uncle Fred's gone to his Maker.'

Joe could not recall meeting anyone of this name. 'Who's Uncle Fred?'

'You haven't met him. He's been in hospital a long time, got poorly in the war.'

Joe studied Grace, whose face was buried in a handkerchief. 'Mother didn't cry when Uncle Worthy died.'

'Uncle Worthy wasn't my brother!' retorted a tearful Grace.

Joe frowned. He had never thought of adults as having brothers or sisters.

'Fred was your mother's only surviving brother,' explained his father patiently. 'Just think how upset you'd be if both your brothers died. Now, stop all your daft questions and get washed. We're going to pay our respects.'

Joe had only a moment to ponder on the demise of Clem or Duke, before being whisked off to don his Sunday best, and henceforth to the dingy shop in Walmgate where his uncle's open coffin was balanced on the counter.

One by one the smaller ones were lifted up to view his corpse, Beata particularly stricken by the contrast between that cold cadaverous cheek and the rosebud warmth of the new babe she had kissed only this morning.

A few days later they were to return, though it was not so bad this time, for the coffin lid was screwed down and Uncle Fred was borne away to the sound of a regimental band. In fact it was all a very exciting affair, for their uncle had been well-respected in the army and volleys were fired over his grave. Beata noticed, however, that not everyone's attention was on the ceremony, Mother attracting as many concerned whispers as the widow.

Probyn noticed this too and, during the funeral tea, whilst he and Grace were temporarily separated, he was to hear the reason from one of his sisters-in-law. 'We're all really worried about our Grace. Why, she must have lost a stone since we last met. That dress is hanging on her.'

Being at home all the time Probyn was not so conscious of such a drastic change, but had to agree that Grace looked unwell. 'What are we going to do with her? No matter what I say she puts our needs first.'

'What are you two plotting?' Grace reappeared bearing a cup of tea. 'I saw you, whispering away, looking in my direction.'

Her husband pulled no punches. 'We're on about you, tin-ribs. Your Millie's just saying how thin you've got.'

'So have you!' she retorted to her sister, then indicated Probyn. 'And you.'

'I can do to lose a few pounds,' he answered, patting his stomach, 'you can't.'

Grace dismissed this with a smiling shake of head. 'Have a look around, Probe. Everybody's thin, there's no food.'

'Even so –'

'Eh, apart from old Aunt Mary!' Deflecting attention from herself she gestured at her ancient relative by the fire. 'The shortages don't seem to have affected her, do they? I've never seen such bonny pink cheeks. I always said she'd outlive us all.'

'And if you don't take more care of yourself you'll be right.' Millie was not to be diverted, looking her sister up and down with a warning expression.

'Oh, behave! If you want to feel sorry for anybody what about poor Maude?'

Both Millie and Probyn acquiesced, the latter adding, 'Still, she won't be too hard up, what with having the shop.'

At this, Grace donned a look of thoughtful interest but did not elaborate until they were on the way home.

After speaking fondly of her dead brother for a while, her heart still heavy with the loss of him, she disclosed an idea. 'You know, it might benefit us to open a little shop like Maude and Fred's in our front room.' Her children liked the sound of this and asked if Mother would sell sweets but she said no, 'Just beer, lemonade, stout . . .'

'There are already two off-licensed premises in the street,' pointed out her husband.

'Look how many there are down Walmgate! And Maude makes a nice living out of hers.'

Probyn was quick to ratify her suggestion. 'You go ahead, dear, if you want to. I won't veto anything that brings more money in – as long as you spend it on yourself.'

Grace promised she would, so, as soon as was decent after her brother's funeral, she set about converting her front room literally overnight into a shop with the simple addition of a counter and a few barrels of ale.

But the children were not around to see how well it worked for, with the school holiday over, they were compelled to resume their education. Beata and the rest of her siblings were envious of Mims, who remained at home, the little one rather smug at having Mother all to herself as she waved the others off.

'And remember!' Grace called after them. 'You're not to go down Paver Lane, the gypsies will get you!' Once they had turned the corner, she turned to the child in her arms and jiggled her affectionately. 'Now let's you and I go make the beds.' Set on her feet, an eager Mims scampered up the stairs with Mother behind her, the pair of them going from bed to bed, chanting, 'Make the beds, shake the beds, turn the blankets o-over!'

Those on their way to school disobeyed their mother, risking capture by gypsies for the simple pleasure of tormenting Mad Billy, rapping like woodpeckers on his window, which they knew from past experience would drive him into hysterics and make him start ripping his pictures from the wall and smashing them. It was such fun. Today, however, even more demented by their cruelty, the poor creature hurled a wooden frame at the window, shattering the pane and sending them running and screaming in laughter.

Seeing Billy start to cry, Madeleine felt a rush of shame for her part in it. Condemning her fleeing siblings – 'You mean devils!' – she came back and stooped to gather the broken picture, placing it gently on the man's windowsill before going sheepishly on her way.

At their places of education, the brothers and sisters were seg-regated, the girls' school being at the end of Chapel Row and surrounded by a wall and a big iron gate. Banned from contact, the Kilmaster girls were totally ignorant of what went on in Joe's school, other than he was taught by the Christian Brothers. They themselves were to be instructed by the Sisters of Charity, who wore blue habits with a white collar, a large winged wimple and a black apron. The building had only one room but had been sectioned into four classes by a folding room divider.

Besides the nuns, there were lay teachers in charge of classes, and it was in one such class that Beata found herself on that first day.

Happily for a child eager to travel, after morning prayers the first lesson was geography and her interest was quickly secured, so much so that by the time the teacher asked the pupils to write down all that she had told them, Beata was the first to grab her pen.

'You, new girl, come out here!' Miss Ambler pointed a finger at the ground before her chair.

Beata raised a startled face from her exercise book. Guessing that the tone spelled trouble, she did not immediately realize what she had done but nevertheless answered the summons.

'Did I see you writing with your left hand?'

Beata blushed. 'Sorry, mi –' Barely had she issued her apology when the school mistress lashed out and struck her across the face.

'Now! You won't do it again, will you?'

'No, miss.' Her vision fractured by tears, Beata returned to her bench.

The imprints of Miss Ambler's fingers were still upon her cheek when she went home at lunchtime. Aghast, her mother demanded an explanation.

In Father's presence, Beata hardly dared confess. 'Teacher caught me writing with my left hand.'

'What have I told you?' Probyn wagged a stern finger, his words making Beata feel stupid, especially when her mother agreed.

'But look, Probe, it must have been a hefty clout to leave such a mark!' Grace showed matronly indignance. 'We can't have that.'

Stern but fair, Probyn had to agree that the teacher had been overzealous. 'You're in charge, Mother.'

'Right! I'll go and have a word after dinner.'

Beata dreaded the outcome.

But Grace was neither aggressive nor discourteous, addressing Miss Ambler in the gentle manner that had won her many friends. 'I realize that Beata was in the wrong – her father and myself have insisted that she holds her pen in the correct hand. But look,' she indicated Beata's cheek. 'It's still red two hours later – in fact it's turning to a bruise. I'd rather you didn't do it again.'

That Miss Ambler took heed of this came as a huge surprise to Beata, and for the next few weeks at least others were to be the recipients of the schoolmistress's foul temper.

But gradually Mother's warning seemed to fade from Miss Ambler's mind and her vicious nature once more took precedence. This coinciding with one of Mother's bouts of ill health, Beata chose not to add to her worries. Mother was a brave person who never moaned about her discomfort. Taking this as her example, Beata was to bear future punishments in silence.

Yet, despite Miss Ambler's violent nature she too had recognized Beata's natural propensity for tending those less fortunate, and whenever any of the pupils were taken ill at school, which was quite often in such a deprived locale, it was always Beata who was called upon to attend them. This morning she was appointed chaperone to a girl who required stitches in her arm.

Meeting her sister in the schoolyard, Beata said she didn't have time to chat. 'I have to get Mabel to Nurse Falconer's.'

On an errand herself, Maddie replied that she could not stop either, but had time enough to examine the bloodstained rag that bound the other child's arm. 'What's happened to her?'

Respecting her charge's feelings, Beata murmured confidentially in her sister's ear, 'Her mother slashed her with a knife. I think she must be loony.'

Before she knew it she was reeling from a shove. Without another word her sister stalked off, leaving a perplexed Beata to take an equally bemused Mabel on their way. With Nurse Falconer sewing up someone else and the wound too serious to wait, they went instead to the hospital. The stitching turned out to be quite an ordeal, for the victim at least, but Beata tried to comfort her as best she could, for which she was congratulated by the medical staff for her lack of squeamishness.

This praise, however, was no conciliation for a grumbling stomach. Delayed at the hospital until past midday and finding herself with no time to go home for lunch, it seemed that Beata would have to go hungry. In the playground was a group of lilac trees left over from a derelict garden and she sat despondently beneath them, hoping that one of the other girls who congregated here would share their chips with her. But just then one of her many relatives came shuffling by in her black dress and bonnet, and upon discovering the situation old Aunt Mary donated a penny bap which, filled with chips, provided a most delicious treat. And as she munched on it, Beata reflected on the kindness of her relatives and how wonderful it was to have so many of them.

Mother was to remark upon this too when Beata told her about it at teatime, reserving acid comment for Miss Ambler, whose fault it was that Beata had nearly gone without sustenance.

'I shall have to be having words with her again, I think,' she said sternly to her husband.

'Oh, it wasn't really her fault!' Beata did not want this, not out of concern for the teacher but so as not to upset her mother. Normally Mother's bouts of illness would last only a short time and she would be up and caring for her brood again. This time, though, even now that she was up and about she continued to look unwell. Moreover, the rasping little cough that had dogged her on and off for ages was refusing to go away, her eyes were sunken and she was even thinner and paler than before. 'It was Mabel's mother who's really to blame. I didn't mind taking the poor lass to hospital.'

Ready to dish out the tea, Grace looked dark. 'And you say she cut the child on purpose?'

'Somebody said she's loony – Ow!' Beata drew in her leg as it was kicked under the table and looked across to find Maddie scowling at her.

But, to escape accusation, Maddie quickly announced, 'I need to take a penny tomorrow, Mother. For the black babies.'

'Oh, right.' Serving spoon still in hand, expression vague, Grace moved as if to get her purse but was prevented.

'Mother, sit down!' Augusta grabbed the serving spoon from her hand.

'Oh, all right bossy-boots.' For once Grace did not resist, sinking onto a dining chair and allowing her eldest daughter to fill the plates.

'You look worn out.' Probyn was softly scolding.

'I shouldn't be,' said Grace. 'We've been sitting down all afternoon, haven't we?' She smiled fondly at Mims, whom she had cuddled on her lap, whilst singing songs and telling stories, too lethargic to do otherwise.

'If her ladyship's too much of a handful maybe you could send her to Baby Class.'

At a low ebb, Grace had been considering this herself, not because Mims was a nuisance but because she feared it was unhealthy to keep her shut up in this airless house all day. 'But she's so little, and if the teachers are all like Miss Ambler . . .'

'Sister Magdalene's lovely,' said Beata. 'They have sandpits to play in and little trestle beds to have an afternoon nap on.'

'Do you like the sound of that, Mims?' her mother turned to the youngest and asked.

Keen to be like her brothers and sisters, Mims nodded.

And so it was that the last of Grace's beloved children went off to school, bringing tears to her mother's eyes as she watched her toddle up the street the next morning. The task of looking after Mims fell to Beata, the others naturally according her this responsibility.

'She won't mind,' opined Maddie to the rest. 'Beat's good at looking after folk.'

It would not have mattered if Beata minded or not, for, thereafter, the taking of Mims to school assumed a regular routine in which she would drag her little sister along to Standard One for prayers throughout which Mims would fidget, before gratefully handing her to the care of Sister Magdalene whose kind nature was in total contrast to Miss Ambler's, the latter continuing to make her life a misery.

That autumn Beata took her First Communion. The white dress and veil worn by her sisters before her was brought out of storage, altered to fit, washed and starched. After breakfasting with the nuns at the convent in Fishergate she joined the procession to church where her family awaited. Father stood out from a congregation comprised mainly of women and grandfathers, the nation's manhood away at war. Notwithstanding this, it seemed the entire O'Brien clan had turned up to see her, plus all her mother's Catholic friends, many of them pressing copper or even silver threepenny pieces into her hand.

'Look!' The cupped hands she held out to Gussie almost over-flowed with coins. 'I didn't know so many people liked me.'

Her eldest sister was quick to discourage boastfulness. 'It's not because they like you. It's so you'll say a prayer to get them into heaven.'

Slightly disappointed, Beata was nevertheless pleased with her haul – maybe there was enough to buy a book! But then she remembered Gussie's chastisement over the ice cream and, prompted by the religious enrolment she had just received, she knew what must be done.

Presented with the entire amount, Grace's eyes filled with mois-ture. 'Oh, you're a good, kind girl, Beat!'

All feeling of sacrifice evaporated, for the look on her mother's face was reward in itself, as was the splendid dinner Mother was to cook when they got home, the first proper meal they had eaten in ages. And from that moment, Beata learned that the ultimate pleasure came not from acquiring wealth or luxuries but by giving to others, and that through such a channel the prize was handed back manifold.

'It's nice to have so many aunts and uncles, isn't it?' Beata smiled up at her mother.

The fragile face beheld her with devotion. 'It is, Beat.' Turning to her husband, Grace shared a sympathetic smile, for Probyn had been cut off from his sisters for many a year. 'It was kind of them all to come to see you today.'

'That big fat lady didn't come.' This observance was from five-year-old Duke as he carried his empty dinner plate into the scullery.

Realizing that he meant Aunt Kit, his eldest sister broke off the washing-up to cuff him. 'Don't let Father hear you call her that.'

'Father did hear,' Probyn called from the other room, 'and you're going to get a good hiding, my boy, if you're not careful. Aunt Kit isn't here because she's not a Catholic.' Even knowing there was little point, he and Grace had still sent her an invitation. He turned to his wife, feeling slightly guilty that he had not made time to go to see Kit. 'I wonder how she's managing these days.' With all their own hardships to endure there had been little thought for others lately. 'I should go and make sure she's all right. Aye, I'll go this weekend.'

But then the weekend came and all he wanted to do was to spend time with Grace and his family. Hence, his aunt was relegated to the list of things to be attended to in the future.

THIRTEEN

How long could this dreadful grief persist? If anything, time had made it worse, not better. It was like having a pain in one's stomach that no amount of bismuth could heal – a deep raw ulcer. Kit had watched other widows cope with their losses and wondered why she could not do likewise – but then surely they could not have felt the same intensity for their husbands as she had for her own beloved. Robbed of Worthy, alone and afraid, unable to sleep without his giant body beside her, she had become obsessed with the thought that she was going to lose her son too. Millions of mothers had lost their sons during those four terrible war years, why should she be spared? She prayed, oh how she prayed, but the others must have prayed too and it had not done them an ounce of good, and she had prayed for Worthy also, but the Lord had taken him just the same.

Kit had taken to sleeping downstairs, partly through difficulty of hauling her overweight person up the staircase, but mainly because she could not bear even to sit upon the bed she had shared with her beloved. With no beasts to care for now – the horses commandeered by the army, even the dairy cattle having to be slaughtered during those lean years – there seemed no reason to get up on a morning, except that the cockerel did not know this and hence woke her at the usual early hour. Only because it was worse just to lie there did she drag herself out of bed on yet another morning to feed the few chickens and geese that were left.

Afterwards, to try and comfort herself she made what would normally be termed a hearty breakfast though there was no heartiness in

211

its consumption and, unable to cram in any more, she just sat gazing into space, bogged deeper in despair.

'You're going to take root if you're not careful, missus!' It was the old white-bearded farm labourer, a man of eighty-five who had volunteered to work as a replacement when his youngest son, the normal helper, had gone off to battle. At that time there had still been cows and pigs to look after, and Kit and Worthy had accepted gladly. Now there was none, and with Worthy dead there were hardly any crops planted either, but Kit had not the heart to say she no longer needed the old chap.

Nodding sadly, she simply sighed.

'Tea's a bit stewed.' An earthy old hand tested the pot.

With what seemed like great effort Kit dragged her mourning-clad bulk from the chair and moved across the kitchen like an automaton to put the kettle on for a fresh brew.

'You're no good to anybody like this,' declared old William. 'Why don't you go and visit that family of yours? Stay for a while. I'll take care of things for you.'

'I've got to be here if Toby comes home.' With the kettle on, Kit flopped back into her chair, her rolls of fat quivering. Her girth had in no way been diminished by sadness, rather she had become even fatter from all the effort to comfort herself.

There was to be no sentimental twaddle from William. 'You won't keep him alive just by sitting there wishing it.'

She turned on him with annoyance, ready to upbraid him for this callous observation. But then, remembering that the old man had lost a son and two grandsons and still managed to function, her anger abated. 'I suppose I should make an effort . . .'

Yet it was to take a great deal of exertion on her part and a good deal more persuasion from William for her actually to go and pack a bag. As, one by one, she laid items in her case the thought occurred that it might be sensible to have a destination before she set off on her trip. Which of her family would she call on to make her feel better? Probyn, definitely, but such a trip would not require a suitcase for she could not expect a bed in his overcrowded abode. She had three sisters but two were in America. The third lived in England, but Gwen would only compound Kit's misery with one of her famously blunt remarks. That left her nieces, and a visit to them would mean various train journeys. But then why not? There was no one here to rely on her and nothing much for her to do in the way of farm work. It might help to pass the time until Toby came home . . . if he came home.

Whatever her final destination, with no railway station nearer it would mean having to pass through York in order to catch a train so she would visit her nephew at the same time. Acquiring a lift with another neighbour who was on his way to market, Kit reached Probyn's house at midday. Noting the flash of concern on Grace's face as she wondered how she was going to feed the visitor, Kit was swift to convey the basket of victuals she had thoughtfully brought along. By the look of her nephew's wife it was just as well she had done, for it seemed to Kit that Grace was on the point of starvation, her shoulder-blades jutting clearly through the back of her blouse, her face abnormally pale and her eyes sunken. But it was the dry, rasping cough that worried Kit most for she had heard that sound before.

The children were well-cared-for, though, and the younger ones were to provide delightful company during the afternoon.

Probyn was pleased to see his aunt when he came home from work. Yet it seemed abnormal for her to be dressed in black when she was usually so colourful, and though she tried hard to be her exuberant self he was shocked to detect melancholia under that superficial jollity. He had been foolish to presume that she was over Worthy's death. She wasn't over it at all – seemed totally lost without him – but he realized later when they had a chance to chat in private that this was not the only reason.

'She's near frantic that Toby isn't coming home,' he whispered to Grace in the privacy of the scullery as she prepared tea.

'I know. The poor soul's been sat twisting her handkerchief all afternoon, almost tore it to shreds.'

'I should have known she was only putting on a brave face when we last went to visit. I feel dreadful at neglecting her. We shall have to do something to cheer her up.' Probyn thrust his greying head back into the living room. 'You'll be staying a while, Aunt?'

This evinced a manufactured smile. 'No, no, I just called on my way to Merry's.'

'Nay, you'll stay the night at least.'

'Well, I wasn't planning to . . .'

'You'll never get to Huddersfield before the blackout!' Her nephew's face told Kit that the very suggestion was preposterous. 'The whole place will be in darkness by the time you arrive and you'll get lost. The old lass next door broke her ankle trying to find her way in the dark last wee –'

'Are you calling me an old lass?' teased his aunt in mock outrage.

Probyn laughed, but wagged his finger. 'I insist you stay, at least for one night.'

Kit looked at the children, affecting terror. 'Oh, well, if the RSM says I must stay I'd better not argue!'

Then, reverting to her serious mood she rose and drew him aside, murmuring confidentially, 'Grace doesn't look too well. Has she seen a doctor?'

Matching his aunt's secretive tone, Probyn replied that she had. 'It's not just the cough, she gets these awful night sweats. It's like sleeping with an oven. He says it's just her age, but she's only thirty-sev –'

'Aye-aye, what are you two cooking up?' A smiling Grace came in bearing a tray.

Briskly, Probyn relieved her of the burden. 'Aunt Kit was asking after your health. I was just telling her what the doctor told you.'

Grace blushed over the lie she had concocted for her husband, fully aware that Probyn knew she was lying over what the doctor had said. What he did not know was that she hadn't even consulted a doctor at all. As much as she might kid herself that it was lack of time that prevented this, at heart it was fear of what she would be told. 'What we females suffer, Kit, eh?' She wafted her face, affecting to be suffering from a hot flush. 'At least there won't be any more babies.' This was issued in a whisper, and punctuated with a little laugh.

Kit smiled back, but a glance at her nephew told her that Probyn was not convinced and neither was she, for she had caught Grace spitting discreetly into her handkerchief when she thought no one was looking, and there had been a trace of red.

But Grace changed the subject. 'Anyway, sit down and tuck in.'

Everyone did, no further mention made of Grace's illness. Grace herself made sure of that by nonstop conversation throughout the meal, even though it left her breathless. And afterwards, she supported her husband's decision that Kit must stay. 'You can have Beata's room. Beat, you can go in with your sisters.'

'I don't want to kick anybody out of their bed,' declared Kit. 'If Beaty doesn't mind sharing with me I don't mind either.'

With no option, it was good that Beata was a biddable child, and, squash though it definitely was in the single bed even positioned top to tail alongside Kit's legs, she secretly felt herself privileged to be the one to share with the visitor, especially as Kit delivered a kiss and cuddle before going to sleep.

*　　*　　*

In the morning, though, there was ribbing from Joe. 'Why, Beat, we expected to see you flat as a pancake!' Duke chortled at his brother's humour.

Beata defended her aunt. 'Don't be so mean. I like Aunt Kit.'

'So do I,' laughed Joe, 'but I wouldn't want to sleep with her.'

But despite the teasing all were genuinely sorry to see their aunt leave and, after breakfast, whilst Probyn, Clem and Augusta went off to work, the rest of the family accompanied Kit to the railway station.

Before embarking, Kit pressed a coin into Grace's hand, murmuring, 'Buy yourself something nice.'

Grace tried to refuse. 'Oh, Kit, you're too generous . . .' But in the end she was forced to pocket the money. 'Well, thank you, I'll get the children –'

'I said buy *yourself* something!'

Grace smiled and nodded, knowing she would not, already calculating what treats she was to purchase for her brood.

It was years since Kit had caught a train and upon trying to board she found that she was far too large to get into the carriage. Attempting to help, Grace applied her hands to Kit's back and shoved, the girls lending their assistance too, but no amount of pressure would squash that amount of flesh through the doorway. With the children's laughter becoming almost hysterical, what else could Kit do but treat it as a joke too?

'Can someone go and ask the porter for a jar of Vaseline?' After another vain attempt she gave up. 'Oh, there's nowt else for it, I shall have to ask if I can travel in the guard's van!' And with her giggling entourage in tow she wobbled valiantly down the platform to make enquiries.

But as Kit stepped through the wider door of the guard's van, Beata saw a flush of embarrassment percolate her great-aunt's smile and she urged her siblings to be quiet, though the boys still fell about laughing. Grace too, had noted the glint of tears in Kit's eye, and, in a rush of compassion for the woman, she slapped her boys and told them, 'That's enough!'

But it was too late, the damage was done. Despite Kit's merry wave as the door of the guard's van closed upon her, it was a very forlorn figure she presented.

It so plagued Grace that her children were, in part, liable for Kit's humiliation, that when Probyn's aunt made another brief

215

visit on her return journey, she did all in her power to make recompense. Noting that, under her smile, Kit was still experiencing worry over her son, Grace suggested that one of the girls should go and stay for a while at the smallholding to help around the place.

'I don't really need any help,' mused Kit whose spirits, having been lifted by the holiday, were now quickly plummeting at the thought of going home to an empty house, 'but I should be glad to have one of the lasses as company for a while – if the teacher won't object to their absence.'

'I'll come!' The first to volunteer, Beata's eager offer was accepted and Grace went to pack a few necessary items for her stay.

As usual there was no shortage of farm wagons on which to hitch a ride from York market, though Beata found it an uncomfortable journey on such a hard wooden seat, particularly as she had not visited the closet before leaving. Upon arrival at Aunt Kit's she was almost desperate but was first compelled to answer Kit's demand: 'Get the kettle on, Beat!'

Squeezing her thighs together, Beata did as required, hopping uncomfortably about the kitchen.

Kit noticed her fraught expression. 'Is owt wrong, lass?'

'No, Aunt, it's just . . . I'm busting to go to the farleymelow!'

Kit threw back her head and laughed, the kind, hearty laugh of old. 'By it's a long time since I've heard it called that!'

Crossing her legs for the moment, Beata, encouraged by her great-aunt's warmth, announced, 'That's what Father calls it but he won't tell me why. Is it rude?'

'Bless you, no!' And Kit explained that it was totally meaningless, just one of those silly words that had been passed down through the family. 'You know that song what goes, "Early one morning just as the sun was rising, I heard a maiden sing in the valley below"? Well, when our Wyn was a little lass when she came to the words "valley below" she sang "farleymelow" because that's what it sounded like when the teacher sang it to her! And she took it to be some kind of privy, so ever since then it has been, in this family, at least.'

Beata giggled.

Kit chuckled too at the way the child was contorting her lower body. 'So you'd better trot off there now. I don't want a puddle on me floor.'

In Beata's absence Kit made to unpack the child's bag of belongings. What a pathetic little bundle it was. The spare dress had obviously been handed down, for it was paper-thin. The drawers and stockings were also much darned. Compelled by a rush of emotion, Kit paused only a moment in thought before hurrying from the room.

When Beata returned Aunt Kit was nowhere to be seen, but her anxious call soon gained a reply and, following the sound, Beata thudded up a staircase to find her great-aunt rummaging through a chest. 'I've just remembered! I've got a lovely remnant in here somewhere, had it for years. It's far too small to make owt for me but I couldn't resist buying it and I knew it'd come in useful some day. It'll make a dress for you!'

Beata gasped. Never had she worn a dress that had not belonged to her elder sisters. There was an exclamation of triumph as Kit finally located the remnant under a pile of blankets and, with a flourish, spread it across the bed. 'There! Do you like it?'

Beata gazed upon the black-and-white material, her heart soaring with joy, the newness of its smell teasing her nostrils. She beamed at Kit, nodding rapidly.

'Good! We'll make a start right now . . . Oh, you might be hungry.'

'I'm not!' Beata was obviously as keen as Kit to have the dress started.

So they went downstairs where, after a few measurements from this expert seamstress, the pattern was soon mapped out and ready to sew. Throughout the afternoon Beata watched enraptured as her dress took shape, the large woman's surprisingly nimble fingers applying neat stitches. During a break for tea, the child inserted a digit into the silver thimble that Kit had put aside.

'Villa Garcia. Where's that, Aunt?'

'Oh, it's in Spain.' Not wanting to resurrect thoughts of her old lover, Kit fended off any more questions by saying, 'You shall have that thimble one day if you like it.'

Beata had never really been interested in sewing, but smiled her thanks as her aunt finished her cup of tea and continued on the dress which, by the evening, was ready to wear.

Throughout her short life Beata had never felt so special, inserting her hands into huge pockets that came right down to the hem, twirling happily and, at her aunt's instruction, moving to a full-length mirror to admire herself, an act not encouraged at home.

And standing behind the excited child, looking at the reflection in the glass, Kit saw her own face infected by the child's happiness, had

217

a momentary glimpse of her old self, and for that lovely interlude all the awful thoughts were exorcized.

Other devils were to be banished too. Rallied by one success after another, sweeping all before them, the Allies continued to maintain their glorious offensive, pushing the Germans ever backwards into autumn.

Even so, in those last lingering weeks of a war all but won there were times when Kit despaired that she would ever see her son again; feared that Toby would be killed before an armistice could be signed, or that she herself might be claimed when the dreaded influenza raised its ugly head for another attack, the sequential deaths exhuming painful memories of her husband.

'Oh, I'm glad I've got you, Beat,' she told her great-niece, who had become a regular visitor. 'I don't know how I'd ever get through it.'

Devoid of a suitable response, Beata could only grin. Yet this seemed enough for Aunt Kit, with whom she had forged a closer bond than any enjoyed by Probyn's other children; to them Kit remained just one of many aunts.

'Your mother must be proud of you.' Kit's smile turned pensive. 'We should invite her here for a holiday, you know. She needs feeding up and the fresh air would do her a power of good. When you go home, you must tell her.'

Beata promised that she would.

But, 'When would I have time for a holiday?' laughed Grace upon being told, even this simple action prompting a fit of coughing. 'Tell Aunt Kit it's very kind of her – maybe next year.'

'But I can still go, can't I?' Beata looked apprehensive.

'Why, of course!'

Brightening, the youngster rummaged in her pocket. 'Oh, I almost forgot!' She pulled out a stick of hard liquorice. 'I bought this for you, to make cough medicine.'

Tears sprang to Grace's eyes and she fought to hide them with an animated smile as she took acceptance. 'What a nice, thoughtful thing to do! I feel better already. Right, you go out and play until teatime and I'll set to work on this.' Clutching the stick of liquorice in her fist, she dealt Beata a friendly shove towards the door and closed it quickly behind her.

Once alone, she broke into quiet, heart-rending sobs, the stick of liquorice clutched to her frail bosom as she rocked back and forth in her chair, crying, coughing, spitting blood and swearing at the cruel hand of fate.

Winter had always resonated to the sound of Clem's bronchitic bark; now it had an ominous echo. Exacerbated by the lack of a proper diet, the seriousness of Grace's illness became all too apparent to her husband, especially upon discovery of the bloodstained handkerchiefs she had been so careful to hide.

'Right, I'm calling out the doctor! He must be half-witted to say this is due to your age.'

Alarmed, but too weak to argue, Grace allowed herself to be packed off to bed at the same hour as her younger children, making a joke with them over this as she was escorted upstairs.

Augusta was putting her coat on. 'You can't go,' wheezed her elder brother. 'It's too dark.' After a brief argument with his father over his own bad state of health, Clem insisted on being the one to fetch the doctor, and went out into the cold, damp night. Whilst she and her father waited, hearing her mother's painful cough from upstairs, a worried Augusta made constant trips to the front room shop, lifting the curtain to see if help was on its way.

She had just gone back into the living room when a brisk rapping came at the door and she hurried to admit the doctor. But it was only a warden.

The face under the tin hat was livid. 'Get that light off!'

Augusta realized that illumination from the back room was escaping into here and streaming out of the open doorway. Issuing apology, she rushed to close the inner door.

The warden was not satisfied. 'Somebody at this house keeps flashing!'

Augusta was instantly contrite. 'I'm sorry, that must have been me. We're waiting –'

'Waiting to direct the German bombers?'

'No! For the doctor.'

Overhearing the altercation, Probyn came striding to the door.

'Get that light off!' came the immediate yell.

Probyn slammed the door behind him, then came forth to behold the warden. 'Haven't you got anything better to do, you officious little twerp? We've got a sick woman in here!'

Deeply insulted, the other's face twisted in derision. 'And are you sick an' all? Too sick to wear a uniform?'

It took a lot to rouse this placid man, but that remark was just

219

too much. Probyn delivered a contemptuous shove with the flat of his palm. The warden stumbled and fell flat on his buttocks.

Hurrying along the dark street, coughing and wheezing, Clem was to witness all this and voiced apology to the doctor, who kept pace with him. 'I'm sorry, me father's a bit hot-headed.' Hiding a private smile behind his fist, he barked to clear his chest of the polluted air.

But there was no amusement later when the doctor was to announce his findings to the patient's husband, 'Of course, you know without being told what it is. She should have been admitted to hospital long before this.'

'Then why didn't you tell her that when she came to see you?' Probyn was incensed.

The doctor bristled in turn. 'Had she been to see me I should undoubtedly have done so!'

During the confused hiatus, one of the other two listeners demanded to know, 'What's up with Mother?'

Both the doctor and Probyn looked at Clem. 'It's tuberculosis,' the former told him less than gently. 'Of long duration, I suspect.'

Reaching out a comforting hand to his eldest daughter, who looked stricken, an equally upset Probyn sighed and apologized to the doctor. 'I'm sorry, my wife led me to believe she'd consulted you.'

'Well, I'm afraid she has not.' The overworked doctor still wore a look of affront, though it was starting to fade. 'Would you like me to arrange hospitalization?'

'Yes,' said Probyn firmly.

'No!'

Everyone turned to see Grace's nightgowned figure hanging onto the jamb for support. Hearing the raised voices, she guessed what had occurred. 'I'm not going into hospital.'

'Grace, why did you pretend you'd gone to the doctor's?' accused Probyn.

'Because I don't need to be told what's wrong with me. I'm not going into hospital and having the children coming home to an empty house.'

The doctor was brutally honest. 'It would surely be better than having them come home to no mother at all.'

'It would only be temporary. We'd cope!' Probyn begged her. 'Please, Grace, be –'

'No!'

Probyn beseeched the doctor, who was equally helpless to persuade Grace.

'Well, at least try to give yourself a better diet,' insisted the

220

physician. 'Eggs, butter, cream, cod-liver oil, plenty of fresh air – and complete rest.'

'I shall make sure she has all that, Doctor!' Probyn looked adamant as he threw his wife a warning. 'And you'd better stick to it, Grace, or I shall take you off to hospital myself, whether you like it or not.'

But as much as he tried to watch her like a hawk to make sure that she ate the proper foods, Probyn could not be with her all day, and despite all his efforts Grace's health showed little improvement. Adding their voices to his, her sisters tried to bully her into entering hospital, as did the priest, who called every Sunday, as did Charlotte, who came on her afternoon off every week, all to no effect. She refused to leave her children.

Charlotte came one afternoon and was relieved and pleased to see her friend laughing, though it was rather outraged amusement.

'Oh, Lottie, I wish you could have been here a minute ago! I managed to get hold of a bit of polony and I thought, I'll share it with the old lady next door, poor soul, she doesn't get out much, so I went in and gave it to her and she said, "Oh thanks, love, I'll just put it away," and she throws open this cupboard that's crammed full of tins of ham and salmon, biscuits, cake, oh, everything you could imagine! Then she puts my little bit of polony alongside it and closes the door – without offering me so much as a crumb! I suppose that teaches me!' Convulsed with laughter, she fell into a fit of coughing.

Charlotte was laughing heartily too until the barking grew so severe that Grace was almost sick into her handkerchief. Rushing to her friend she pulled the handkerchief away from Grace's mouth to examine it, seeing blood.

'Right, that's it!' Charlotte directed her big square face at the door. 'I'm fetching the doctor and you're going into hospital.'

'No, don't. I'll be all right in a minute!' Grace called after her friend, but her plea was ignored.

Returning with the doctor, Charlotte watched in consternation whilst he examined Grace, agreeing with all that he said. 'Mrs Kilmaster is ready to go into hospital – don't argue!' She pointed at Grace, tears of anger springing to her small emerald eyes. 'I won't stand by and watch my friend die through self-neglect!'

Grace knew when she was beaten. She would have sighed had it not made her cough. 'All right, but I'm not having the children come home from school and find me gone. I want to see them first.'

221

'I can go and collect them and explain,' pleaded Charlotte, afraid that, granted time, Grace would change her mind about going into hospital.

'No.'

Charlotte looked set to fly off the handle. 'I could strangle you!' Turning to the doctor, she asked him if he would arrange for the ambulance to come later that afternoon when the patient had seen her children.

Once he had gone, she sat beside Grace and took hold of her delicate hand, stroking it. 'I should nip down to Probe's office and let him know.'

Grace agreed that it was a good idea.

Giving her friend's hand a reassuring squeeze, Charlotte put on her hat and coat and went out into the November afternoon.

Though grateful that someone had managed to persuade his wife to go into hospital, Probyn knew the situation must be chronic for Grace to give in like this, and abandoning his work he raced home to be at her side.

However, he found that she required him to be of service elsewhere.

'Can you go and meet the children, Probe?' Her wan little face begged him. 'Break the news gently to them before they get home so it's not too much of a shock?'

With Probyn reluctant to leave his wife Charlotte said, 'I've told Grace, I'll go.'

'No, dear, if you don't mind, it's best their father goes.' Grace patted the sofa where she reclined. 'You sit here and keep me company.'

On her way to collect Mims from Baby Class, Beata was pleasantly surprised to find her father waiting there too and ran the last few steps to curl her arm around one of his sturdy thighs.

Successfully hiding his concern, Probyn smiled down at her, withholding the bad news for now. 'They very kindly gave me the afternoon off work so I've just been out for a stroll and thought I'd come by and walk home with my children.' He patted her. 'You run in and get Mims, I'll wait here for the others.'

When the two little girls came out of school their brothers and sister were gathered around Father, who had crossed the road and was talking to a man who stood at his door waiting for his own children. Beata vaguely knew the man's daughter, who was there with him. Mary Melody collected her sister from Baby Class at the same time as she collected Mims, but she had no other contact with the Melodys, who were in her opinion too clannish.

Noticing her and Mims, Probyn summoned them across the road, then went back to his conversation with Mick Melody. He was still trying to get over the shock of seeing his old friend. Though the widow's peak was still there, the crop of curls was much thinner and there was a lot of grey in it. Mick was no longer the youthful, animated soul he had been. But then, everyone who had served at the front had been robbed of their youth. When Beata and Mims arrived the men were talking about the German Empire and who would get what after the war, which was all but over, but now that all his children were here, Probyn finished the conversation, having more important things to discuss with them. 'Well, it's grand to see you, Mick! Sorry, I can't stop – we must get together one evening, though.'

Mick agreed, both men knowing they never would. They said it each time but it never amounted to anything. 'Great to see you too, Pa! God bless.' So saying, Mick ushered his children indoors.

Glad to have their father's company, the children vied for his attention on the way home, Joe trying to engage him man to man by resurrecting the previous topic about the German Empire. 'It isn't as big as ours, is it, Father?'

Wondering how to tell them about their mother, Probyn replied thoughtfully, 'Oh no, but the difference is much greater than size alone. The German Empire is based on oppression. We didn't have to force any of our Dominions to come and fight. They gave their blood freely for the Empire that's as much theirs as it is ours.'

'I built sandcastles.' Mims' bright little face looked up at him.

'Did you, deary? What a clever girl.'

The children still chattering beside him, Probyn led them along greasy pavements through town. With naphtha flares illegal the market folk were packing up early on this dingy afternoon, some carts already rumbling their way out of the city. Near to the office where he worked was a bench on which sat a pair of old soldiers whom he saw every day and he greeted them in passing. Old soldiers? They were in their twenties but looked ancient. The ground between their boots was flecked with blood and mucus, a result of the gassing they had suffered. Over the months he had seen their number whittled down from five. He wondered how much longer these poor decrepit chaps would last.

Steeling himself, Probyn finally managed to voice the reason why he had come for his children. 'By the way, erm, your mother's been taken ill . . . very ill. She's got to go into hospital.' Detesting the sight of their anxious faces he hurried on, 'She doesn't want to leave you! I had to force her to go and if she sees any tears she'll turn her hog out and stay at home, but she needs hospital treatment so I want you all to be very brave and not cry when you wave her off. Can you do that?'

'Yes, Father,' came the united murmur; though there was little conviction in its tone.

With everyone else fallen silent, and made suspicious by his mother's cough, Duke enquired, 'Has she got the white scourge?'

But his father didn't answer.

That evening, fighting the urge to cry, the children watched the ambulance come and take their mother away. Too young to remember her father's request, Mims allowed her tears to flow freely. It was all Probyn could do to stop Grace climbing off the stretcher.

'I'll get Lizzie to bring them to visit you,' he told her, holding her down gently as she was lifted into the ambulance. 'Don't worry, they'll be fine. We'll all be fine.'

True to his word, Grace's husband did arrange for visits to be made, her sisters taking it in turns to fetch her children to the hospital. But it was all too little, both to the mother and those who missed her.

Today was Beata's turn and she was looking forward to it eagerly, not merely to seeing Mother but to delivering her news, and came running down the ward to Grace's bed.

'The war's over, Mother!'

Grace pretended that this was the first she had heard, though the sounds of celebration from outside had told her hours ago. 'Isn't that wonderful?' She extended a thin arm to her daughter.

'We went to church to give thanks on our way.' Beata stood at her mother's bedside, holding Grace's hand and examining the ward, which rang to a medley of coughing. It was not like any hospital she had been in before, the ward a type of pavilion hut that had stable doors, the top one being open and emitting a cold blast, though her mother was well protected with a woollen bonnet and shawl in addition to thick blankets.

Having made every effort to eat and drink all the rich dairy food that had been put before her, Grace certainly looked a lot better.

'By, you look fitter than me, doesn't she, Beat?' remarked Lizzie.

'I don't suppose she needs this now. I might just sup it myself.' She tugged a bottle of stout from her bag.

Grace gave an expression of pleasure, then said, 'Keep it hidden a minute longer,' and she summoned a passing nurse to ask if she might have a glass of milk.

When it came, she pretended to drink it but once the nurse had gone she gave it to Beata with a smile. 'There, get that down you and I'll have my stout.'

'Eh, you could have ordered a cup of tea for me!' teased Lizzie, but poured the stout into a glass for her sister.

Smacking her lips, Grace asked how everyone was at home.

'Oh, they're all very well.' Lizzie nodded.

'Some men came in and squirted stuff all over,' provided Beata between sips. 'It really ponged.'

Quickly brushing over the fumigation, Lizzie said, 'Best to be safe.'

Beata withdrew her face from the glass, upper lip white with milk. 'Duke keeps running off.'

Quick to calm the mother's concern, Lizzie gave a light laugh, saying that he didn't run far. But Grace was not convinced, Lizzie could tell, and when later they departed she warned Beata not to say such things again. 'We don't want your mam running home before she's better, do we?'

Grace cried after Beata had gone, as she had done after all the previous visits from her children. Yet to see little Mims, she knew it would be an ordeal, and tried her best to stay cheerful when the youngest was finally brought. But, oh, it was hard not to cry, especially as the nurse had advised her against kissing, and when the time came for her baby to leave and Mims started protesting and screaming to be allowed to stay with her mother, Grace broke down and wept.

Fearing that such upset might jeopardize future visits, she soon dried her eyes and when the nurse came she was calm again, if deeply thoughtful.

The nurse stooped to pick an astrakhan bonnet from the floor. 'Does this belong to your little girl?'

Eyes still damp from crying, Grace's mouth formed an expression of woe. Taking the bonnet, she pressed it to her face, inhaling the scent of her youngest child's hair, breathing it in for a long decisive moment, fresh tears burning her eyes. It was no good. She couldn't desert them any longer; she must go home.

*   *   *

Probyn was annoyed that his wife had discharged herself after only a few weeks, but he had to concede that even this short spell of rest had done her good, and he was as glad as the children to have her home. With the wartime restrictions on food now being slackened they could at least maintain the diet she had enjoyed in hospital and hopefully get rid of that debilitating cough.

Horrified to learn that she was contemplating going back to running her shop, and knowing she would defy him if he did not provide some alternative, he said that Joe would be kept off school to do this. If she insisted on being at home she must sit still and rest.

Making her as comfortable as possible before going out to work on a morning, stoking up the fire as best he could with coal rationing still in force, wrapping her in warm clothes and blankets and propping her in a chair by the open window, he made her promise she would not move except to answer the call of nature. 'Gussie's got everything prepared for dinner. You don't need to do a thing. Just sit there and watch the dicky birds in the yard.'

Overjoyed to be back amongst loved ones, Grace swore she would not overdo things, though within a few weeks of being home, once her husband's back was turned she was up and dragging herself across town to meet the children from school and take them to see the magical Christmas grotto in Boyes's shop window.

Though cautioned not to mention this to her father, Mims could not prevent herself from chattering about the event and so letting the cat out of the bag.

'But it's Christmas, Probe,' Grace protested softly at his scolding. 'And they've had such a hard time of it during the last five years, I was just giving them a treat.'

'Grace, dearest,' he looked exasperated, 'you're too ill to be doing this to yourself. You only had to say and I would have taken them to the grotto.'

'But I want to be with them.' She gripped his hand, looking him in the eye, trying to convey the depth of her feelings.

'I know, lass,' he said quietly, shutting his eyes and returning her grip. 'I know.'

Keen frosty weather heralded 1919. Vast crowds moved through the city streets and congregated around the Minster to hear Big Peter announce midnight for the first time in years. A fanfare sounded

226

and ten thousand voices united in a cheer, mingling with the sound of brass, the refrain of 'Auld Lang Syne' travelling upon the cold night air and through the Kilmasters' open window, each listener wondering what the year held for them.

What it held for one member of the family was joy, for Kit's son came home unscathed, physically at least.

But for most, victory in Europe was to signal the beginning of a war at home, the year being only days old when strikes and sedition began to erupt from all corners of the kingdom with troops being called out to keep order and tanks rolling into Dublin.

Kit did not mention the latter when she and Toby came to pay a New Year's visit to her nephew, this diplomacy stemming from the trouble caused by Probyn's marriage to an Irish Catholic. Over the years Kit had grown used to Grace, but it was always there niggling in the background and she had no wish to stir bad feeling by raising the Irish troubles. Instead her condemnation was for the industrial sector.

'I'm in total sympathy with the soldiers who are kicking up a stink that they're not being demobilized quickly enough,' said Kit, seated close to her soldier son, her weight sorely testing the dining chair over which spilled reams of fat. 'I wouldn't begrudge those poor lads one gripe after what they've been through. But the rest of these strikers, the miners included, they want horse-whipping, demanding more pay. I know it's a dangerous job but this is just sheer greed. There're pits laying idle. If the miners don't watch their backs the Americans will be sneaking in and outpricing them just like they've done in agriculture and everything else. I remember a time when the unions were just beginning – I was only a little girl, mind, but I can recall the time well – something needed to be done against masters who wanted their workers to sweat blood – but now it's just gone too far the other way. Why, they're holding the country to ransom! You can't have people who don't know what they're doing running the country.'

Probyn quite agreed but, wanting to keep the atmosphere calm, said, 'Still, we've got Toby home, that's the most important thing.' He shared a look with the young man, a look that only another soldier could interpret.

'It certainly is!' Kit beamed lovingly at her son, who was leaning over the table with the children, cutting up a Woodbine packet to make a jigsaw. 'You should have seen my face when he walked through that door!' Her eyes filled with tears at the memory.

'He'll soon have the farm back to order for you,' smiled Grace.

'Eh, don't be finding work for me, Aunt!' scolded Toby with a laugh. 'I'm looking forward to getting me feet up.'

'Getting your feet up? They've never been off the mattress since you got home,' Kit teased her son. 'If you don't want to help your poor mother there's plenty will.' Demobilization had hardly commenced and the figures for out-of-work benefits had soared. 'I feel right sorry for those heroes with no work to come back to. I might take a couple on myself. It's the least I can do.' The brightness of Kit's tone belied her sadness. She thought of dear Worthy striding over those fields. The flu that had killed him was still raging.

They heard the front door open. 'There's somebody in the shop, Joe,' said Probyn.

'Sit there with Toby,' Grace bade her son. 'I'll go.'

'No –' began Probyn.

But his wife went off singing gaily. Probyn let her go, but only because it gave him the opportunity to discuss her health with Kit, the pair of them going into the scullery to whisper.

'I never expected Grace to still be running the shop,' said Kit.

'She shouldn't be, she isn't normally if I'm here to watch her. The children have taken it in turns to help, but they'll be back at school next week. I think I'm going to have to rip that counter out, you know.'

Kit looked sympathetic. Grace could sing and pretend all she liked but it failed to mask her sickness. 'The stay in hospital doesn't seem to have done her much good.'

'She wasn't there long enough. She couldn't bear to be parted from the children.' He shook his head in near desperation. 'But she's going the right way to putting herself back in there.'

His words prophetic, the following week Probyn and his children were once again to witness Grace being conveyed by ambulance to Yearsley Bridge Hospital.

Once more the aunts set up a relay system in order that their sister might get to see her brood, but it was all very trying for everyone.

Probyn seemingly more short-tempered than ever with him these days, Duke took to wandering off even more, not wanting to be in a house that did not have Mother in it and only coming home when it was time to be fed – which seemed to annoy Father all the more. Evenings were the worst, for they had always been such calm and happy times with Mother attending kindly to her children's prattling, hearing their prayers and kissing them good night. Now there was just an empty hour before bed.

The hospital visits upsetting Grace, Mims was not permitted to go at all, in consequence becoming very anxious and confused. Even those who were allowed access found it hard having to leave Mother behind. In the hope of avoiding it altogether, Beata asked if she might go and stay with Aunty Kit until Mother was well again, but Father said that Kit had only just got her son back after all those years at war and they needed time together.

The fact that all these little upsets were kept from Grace had no effect on her mood and she missed her children dreadfully, asking for photographs to be brought in so that she might have some tiny consolation.

It was Augusta who brought these when she and Clem visited one Sunday, laying them on the bed for her mother to examine.

Having spat much crimson this morning, Grace was sucking a lump of ice and trying to look cheerful as she sifted through the photographs of her family, making affectionate comments on each. But coming to the last she made a weak little moan of dismay. 'Aw, we haven't got one of Mims.'

Her mother's distress prompted Augusta to offer quickly, 'Would you like me to take her to the studio?'

Grace performed a grateful nod. 'But don't bother your father for money. There's some in a tin on the mantel.'

So Augusta dressed Mims in her best white lace, tied a ribbon in her hair and went along to a photographic studio, the result being produced on her next visit to the hospital.

There was also an apology for her own appearance in the photo. 'Sorry, Mims refused to stand still so I had to grip her hand. I had me factory overalls on and all.' She wore the boiler suit now and stared down at her trousered leg, twiddling one of her dark auburn plaits. 'I hope I haven't spoilt it.'

'Course not!' Grace reached a weak hand to caress her tenderly. 'It's a lovely one of both of you.' And after smiling upon the boiler-suited figure in the photograph and her little lacy companion, she held it to her scrawny breast, allowing it to lie there whilst chatting to her eldest daughter.

'How are you managing?'

'Nobody's complained at my cooking.' Augusta hoped her smile was convincing.

But Grace read it well. Her lip trembled. 'I do miss you all. I should be there. I'm feeling a lot better now . . .'

'You must stay here till you're fully recovered this time.' Augusta was alarmed that something she had said might induce her mother's premature homecoming. Father had warned them not to say anything that might upset her.

But Grace had made her decision days ago. Looking deeply into Augusta's crystal-clear eyes, she declared, 'I can't stand this, Gussie. I'm coming home.'

'Grace, I despair of you, I really do!' said Probyn when he came home from the office to find her there surrounded by happy children.

Charlotte, too, had much to say after trailing through wind and rain to the hospital and being redirected to her friend's home.

Neither could deny, though, that Grace was much happier in familiar surroundings; radiantly so. Charlotte could not take her eyes off those bright eyes and pink cheeks as she watched Grace move about her kitchen that Saturday morning, displaying happiness in even the smallest pleasures.

'Isn't it wonderful to be able to bake a cake with all the proper stuff,' declared Grace, 'after four years of chickpeas and chitterlings.'

Charlotte heartily agreed, but really wanted to know more about Grace's health and tried to broach the subject.

As ever, though, Grace made light of it and went to call the children in from the street, inviting them in to speak to Aunt Charlotte, knowing that no mention of her illness would be made in their presence.

But Charlotte was equally crafty. Dipping in her purse, she gave a silver coin to the oldest one present, Madeleine. 'Here, I'm sure you'd rather be at the pictures than talking to your stuffy old aunt. Take yourselves off.'

There was an excited putting on of coats and hats and a mass exodus, allowing Charlotte the leeway she sought. 'Now, madam, less of your tricks, tell me how you really are!'

Outside, there was argument as to which picture house the children would attend, the one that Joe prescribed being deemed unsuitable for an infant like Mims. He solved the problem by asking his youngest sister, 'Didn't you hear Mother calling you?'

Mims had not, but went dutifully inside, anyway. When she came out again the street was empty.

Faced with Mims' bawling, Charlotte gave up the interrogation of Grace with a sigh and watched her friend scoop the distraught youngster into her arms.

230

'The mean little devils, they're always running off and leaving her!' Hugging and kissing, Grace took Mims on her knee, first to wipe her tears, then to cut a slice of newly baked gingerbread with which to comfort her, thereafter rocking the child on her lap and singing, 'Wha-at care I for your goose-feather bed? What care I for your thingy-oh! Da-dah-dah-dah-dah-dah-dah-dah-dah-dah, to follow the raggle-taggle gypsies oh!'

Head against her mother's bosom, her own sparrow breast shuddering with emotion, Mims nibbled on the gingerbread, taking comfort in this and in her mother's lovely voice.

It was good that such a little child did not know what comfort the memory of that gingerbread was to provide in years ahead. For the older ones, watching their mother grow ever weaker, the days that followed were most harrowing.

Confined to her bed now, Grace was tended by one after the other, discovering a most compassionate tender side to her eldest son as he helped Probyn and Augusta to nurse her, without being told fetching clean nightgowns to replace ones drenched with sweat, lifting her frail body into another position to deter bedsores.

For the most part it was Augusta who bore the lion's share, for, starting work early she was always home by mid-afternoon, going straight to tend her mother, before cooking the evening meal.

But for Clem there was no shirking either and the moment he came home he would go to his mother with a warmed soft towel, wiping it gently around her face and along her stick-like arms that glistened with perspiration.

Grace beheld him lovingly tonight. 'The woman who gets you will be very lucky.'

He laughed softly but did not reply, sitting on the edge of her bed and tweaking the edges of her woollen bonnet around her cheeks. 'Is there anything else I can do for you, Mother?'

'You can tell Gussie I need to use the chamber.'

'She's up to her armpits in cooking, can't I help?'

'Well, if you don't mind . . .'

'Course I don't.' Showing no embarrassment, Clem pulled a chamber pot from under the bed, then drew aside the blankets and scooped up his mother like a baby. It felt as if he were lifting a skeleton, her bones jutting through the nightgown.

Depositing his mother gently on the china pot, he went to look out of the window until she had finished.

231

Having returned her to bed, he shoved the pot back underneath, then tucked her up snugly, asking, 'Is there anything else I can get you?'

'Just my rosary, love.'

The brown beads rattled as he transferred them from the bedside table to his mother's fingers, then he patted her tenderly and went downstairs.

Grace smiled to herself at his exit, amused that for all his consideration towards her, it had not extended to emptying the chamber pot, leaving such a chore to poor Gussie.

Probyn was the next to come up, bringing her tea on a tray and sitting with her to chat about his day and to make sure she ate everything.

Whilst he was there Grace noticed a small face peep round the door then quickly disappear. 'Duke! You can come in, nobody's going to bite.'

A reluctant Duke reappeared, eyeing his father for a second before coming to Grace's bedside and without speaking, held a piece of paper out to her.

'What's this?'

'I did it at school.' Hands clasped behind his back he awaited his mother's response.

'Is this your writing?' Grace looked proud and held it out to her husband. 'Oh, look, Father, isn't that wonderful for a six-year-old?'

Waiting for his father to pass judgement, Duke hardly dared look at him. Noting this, Probyn felt sorry that he had not tried harder to form a bond with his youngest son and was exceptionally warm in recompense. 'Excellent – worthy of a twelve-year-old!'

Duke hoisted his shoulders in self-conscious manner but was obviously pleased as he grinned at his mother, then galloped from the room. Endowing her husband with an ethereal smile, Grace laid her hand upon his, hoping with all her heart that it was the start of a better relationship between father and son.

Later Duke was to return with the rest of the children to kiss their mother good night and to say their prayers at her bedside. Last in line, acting in nurse-like fashion Beata tucked the blankets around Grace's chin, showing an unusual reluctance to leave the parental bedroom tonight and having to be manually dragged to her own.

Even then something kept her awake: not just the sound of her mother's coughing but some awful nameless fear.

Eventually, though, the coughing stopped and through sheer

exhaustion she drifted off to sleep, deaf to the stealthy procession of feet on the stairs throughout the night.

In the morning she arose to be told that her mother had gone to Jesus.

Whilst Beata and the rest sobbed, even the boys, Mims's first reaction was one of disappointment that Mother had gone without taking her too. But then to her confusion was added alarm, for she was taken in to see her mother lying peacefully in bed and lifted up to kiss her cold cheek, and along with her siblings she burst into tears.

Steeped in his own pain, remembering a morning long ago when he had risen to find that his own mother had died and the rain had cascaded down the walls as he poured out his grief to Aunt Kit, Probyn knew what anguish his children were suffering. But there was nothing he could do to help and in that moment of excruciating loss he wished he could die too.

FOURTEEN

Having always left the running of the household accounts to his wife, Probyn wore a baffled expression as he sifted through the papers in the sideboard drawer, looking for details of the insurance fund he would need in order to pay for her burial. To one who kept meticulous records himself, he found Grace's filing system chaotic. But trying to concentrate on this helped to take his mind off his debilitating grief.

A sombre Clem looked on. Up to now Father had unearthed burial club certificates for most of the children and for himself, but there was none with Mother's name on it.

A brief announcement, 'Ah, this must be it!' Then a sigh. 'No, this is Gussie's – I thought I'd already got one for her.' Mumbling to himself, Probyn put it aside and went on searching. 'The blessed thing must be in here somewhere.'

But when he came to the bottom of the drawer and even lifted the wallpaper liner to see if anything had slipped underneath by accident there was no certificate for Grace to be found.

Clem did not fully interpret the vacuous expression in his father's eyes, regarding it only as a mirror of the grief he himself was feeling.

How could Probyn explain to the lad that because of his mother's failure to put money away for her own burial she had burdened her husband with the ignominy of a pauper's funeral? Either this or throw himself on Aunt Kit's goodness yet again.

No, it could not be the latter. He wasn't a boy any more, he was a man and must face this on his own. There was no question of being able to raise the money. The only item of real value was the piano, but they had tried to sell that during the war and failed, and besides, even if he could sell it, with seven dependants he could not afford to waste money on a coffin. There was also Grace's gold chain, but this had been so dear to her that he could not bring himself to part with it.

Clem had been staring at his father, trying to read his mind, but was now distracted by a shout from outside. 'Mother's coming!'

Clicking his tongue, he went out to chastise Mims but found she was already being taken to task for the mistaken identity by one of her tearful sisters. 'I've told you Mother isn't coming back!'

The woman walking down the street was of similar appearance to their mother, though on closer proximity she was nothing like her at all and Mims started to cry.

Augusta made as if to cuddle her. 'Don't worry, I'll look after you.'

'I don't want you, I want Mother!' Mims jumped up and down in a rage.

For a moment there was acute despair amongst the group, then Augusta saw another figure turn the corner, one they did know, and distressed though she was herself she diverted the crying child with encouraging words. 'Oh look, Aunt Kit's here!'

Hearing the announcement, Probyn wondered whether this was an omen, a sign from God that it was all right to ask for her help in burying his wife. He had not even written to tell her of Grace's death yet. How had she known? But then he saw Kit's face and knew that such extent of grief as was displayed there would never be expended on Grace. It had to be someone much dearer to her heart.

Kit had obviously been crying for a long time; her eyes were red slits in the blotched and swollen face. Scant attention was paid to the children today. Unable to convey her heartbreak she merely held out her arms to Probyn.

'Oh Aunt, not Toby?' When she nodded and collapsed into distraught sobs he could only hold her.

'When? How?'

Between disjointed sentences and tears, he learned that Toby had contracted influenza yesterday. Kit had spent the night at the hospital only to see him die this morning. In a trance, she had come straight here, not knowing what else to do. She seemed totally lost.

The children beheld her tearfully, overwhelmed by this extra bereavement. Racked with grief, Kit was too dazed to notice them for now.

'Gus, fetch Aunt Kit a cup of tea,' ordered Probyn quietly, unable to bring himself to tell her about his own heartache yet.

A lump the size of an orange in her throat that threatened to choke and suffocate her, Kit took a huge juddering sigh, mopped her eyes and blew her nose, then sat there, twisting her handkerchief, saying nothing.

His own anguish put aside for the moment, Probyn wondered how to comfort his aunt. Words were inadequate but one had to say something. 'Eh, I'm right sorry, Aunt, I truly am. Poor Toby, he was a grand lad; you were rightly proud of him. We all liked him. Eh, it seems so cruel for him to go like this after he'd come through the –' He broke off as Kit's face crumpled again. How thoughtless of him to voice this superfluous comment; as if it would not be going through Kit's mind already. He turned instead to practicalities. 'If you want me to help with the funeral arrangements . . .'

'I don't want to be arranging it, Probe!' Kit bleated like a little child. 'I want him and Worthy here with me and things like they used to be. It's not fair!'

'No, no it's not.' He gave quiet agreement and saw little point in making any other offer whilst she was so distressed.

After a while, Kit lifted her tear-stained face and took a deep breath. 'Sorry.'

'No, don't apologize.'

'Thanks, love. I can always rely on you, can't I?' She performed a damp, lacklustre smile, her swollen eyes gazing into space for a good few seconds before blurting, 'Eh, Probe, what harm have I ever done to deserve this?' And she wept again.

'You haven't done anything, Aunt.' Probyn came up to pat the seated figure gently.

A grave Augusta appeared then with a tray and poured two cups of tea, whispering, 'Do you want one, Clem?'

At his nod, she poured another, then left the room.

With only Clem remaining to keep his father and great-aunt company, a period of gloomy silence followed, the trio snatching periodic sips of hot tea, the men smoking, their hollow eyes gazing into midair.

'Where's Grace?' It was not of particular interest to Kit, merely intended to break this awful silence.

Probyn's face altered. Overwhelmed by grief, he squeezed his eyes shut before answering, 'I'm sorry to add to your upset, Aunt, but I'm afraid . . .' a deep breath, 'she died yesterday.'

Kit gasped and looked swiftly at Clem, who was staring at the ground between his knees, drawing furiously on his cigarette so as not to cry.

'I was going to write to you today,' continued an awkward-looking Probyn, rubbing his leg, 'but, well, you know . . .'

'Probe, I'm that sorry!' Kit moaned. 'I thought the children seemed subdued. I don't know what to say.'

Probyn held up his hand. Taking a last drag of his cigarette he threw the butt on the fire. 'You don't need to say anything, you've got enough to concern you.'

Kit broke down again, oppressed not just by recent losses but by old ones too, the awful memory of her dress sprayed with blood as her favourite niece haemorrhaged to death in her arms from the same awful disease that had claimed Grace.

Gripping the bridge of his nose Probyn bent his head for a second. God, how would he cope without his dear wife? He had to keep talking or he would break down as well. 'Anyway, Aunt, as I said I'll help in any way I can.'

Kit blew her nose for the umpteenth time, the handkerchief feeling like sandpaper on her sore flesh, and said pathetically, 'You don't want burdening . . .'

He could tell by the way she said it that she desperately wanted him to lift her burden. 'Honestly, I don't mind.'

'Well . . .' she sniffed, 'I suppose you will have to see the undertaker about Grace, so while you're there . . . if it wouldn't be too much bother, could I come with you?'

He could not allow her to witness his shame, nor could he ask for financial help. 'Actually, Aunt, I've already made arrangements for Grace.'

'Oh, right,' Kit nodded bleakly. 'Aye, I suppose the funerals will have to be on different days so's everyone can attend both, what with us living where we do.'

'Of course,' he reached out to grasp her hand, 'but I shall be more than happy to go with you and help you arrange Toby's.'

Kit lowered her eyelids to emphasize her gratitude. 'Thanks, love. I don't think I'd be able to get my words out without crying.' Even now her eyes brimmed with grief.

'Then I'll be your voice,' he vouched.

Thus it was that Probyn took responsibility for his nephew to receive the finest send-off a man could have with ebony casket and plumed horses, whilst his poor, dear Gobbie was laid to rest in a pauper's grave.

How different was Grace's funeral even to that of her brother with its military honours. Yet, despite the lack of pomp, hundreds of guests were to pay their respects to this much-loved woman, filling up every pew of St George's to take part in Grace's Requiem Mass. Too distraught over the loss of their mother to be moved by this outpouring of affection, it was not until much later in the day that the children questioned the identity of the bunch of strangers who came back to the house along with Charlotte and their father, their mother's relatives taking old Aunt Mary straight home. Alongside the down-at-heel neighbours, the ageing but handsome women stood out with their well-tailored clothes of black silk and astrakhan and genuine jewellery – though even without these they would have been impressive, for they were very tall, taller than Father, with good carriage, lovely wavy hair that still had tinges of auburn amongst the grey, and large noses like beaks. The children were mesmerized, until the spell was broken by an elderly member of the group who spoke with obvious distaste.

'I always said marriage to a Catholic would bring him to this!' Grown even less inhibited with old age, Gwen scarcely bothered to lower her voice these days before applying insult, sounding almost triumphant as she made this declaration. 'This is what you two can look forward to.'

Ethel and Wyn, for whose benefit this had been said, looked most peeved. Having no children and married to wealthy businessmen they were unlikely to find themselves in such a position. But, however sorely goaded by this aged aunt who, for as long as they had known her, had always dressed in varying shades of black that reeked of camphor, one never voiced opposition to Aunt Gwen, kindness rather than fear preventing their objection. Swift to pass criticism on others, this forthright, opinionated old misery could be destroyed with one harsh word. Trying to stay respectful, Ethel and Wyn's only response now was to share a look of affront.

Charlotte too looked offended at this slight upon her friend. She glanced at Probyn but he seemed to be ignoring the remark.

Thanking his neighbours for attending Grace's funeral, he invited them in for a cup of tea but was glad when they refused, knowing that they felt uncomfortable in the presence of such finery. Well, they couldn't feel as uncomfortable as he. What on earth did he have to say to his sisters after almost twenty years? He had been most surprised to see them here, though touched to learn that it had been Kit who had informed them of Grace's death; poor Kit who would have to endure this ordeal yet again when her son was buried tomorrow. It must be enough of a trial to have them all staying under her roof, especially Aunt Gwen. He wondered if Kit had needed to persuade them to come and pay homage to Grace, to whom they had never extended friendship in life, or was it merely because they were here for Toby's funeral and might as well come to this one too, for they would hardly be able to face Probyn tomorrow if they had snubbed this event. But then did it matter? Did anything matter? Grace would still be dead. Oh God, how her loss had devastated him. That he could cook and clean and sew and all those things was not the compensation it had been when she was merely ill; dependent on her spirit, he felt totally helpless.

Feeling a gentle nudge, he looked to his left at Clem and followed his son's gaze to a picture on the wall; it was lopsided. Imagining an impish Grace tilting the frame, he offered a little smile of appreciation, choosing not to put it straight. Positioned on his right, Charlotte moved her hand to lay upon his, momentarily gripping it, until she noticed that his rude old aunt was watching with eagle eyes, and she quickly severed the affectionate gesture.

Probyn's older sisters glanced at each other, not knowing whether to raise the delicate subject – they had been appalled to find that their brother had insufficient money to provide for his wife's funeral – but it was too late now to say he should have come to them. He *had* come to them years ago and they had shunned him.

In the darkness of that February afternoon, teaspoons tinkled, china cups clinked against saucers, but other than polite murmurings there was no real dialogue. On previous awkward meetings Probyn had always relied on Aunt Kit to get everyone chatting but, struggling to cope with her own grief, she could not be relied upon today. However, Meredith was to come to his aid, diverting attention from Aunt Gwen to the children, speaking to them kindly and showing an interest in their lives. The youngsters beamed up at her, having decided she was the nicest, very like Aunt Kit though not half so fat, and appreciated the way she spoke to them as equals.

'Does he work?' Gwen was eyeing Clem, who blushed under her direct stare.

Probyn cleared his throat. 'Yes, Aunt, he works at the Stores, does the accounting.'

'Got more sense than his father then.' Gwen sounded approving. She spoke to Clem directly now. 'How old are you?'

'Eighteen.'

'Same as my grandson,' murmured Rhoda.

Probyn had not seen his sisters for so long it came as a shock to think they were grandmothers. Dear Grace would never have that privilege.

Gwen continued to examine Clem. 'Oh, you'll have been too young for the war, then. My boys were too old and their own sons managed to get out of it, thank the Lord.'

Mind in a daze from her own loss, Kit stared coldly at her oldest sister, now well into her seventies, and wondered why she had been spared the awful calamities of war. Gwen had always been a misery, never did anything for anybody, only ever interested in wealth and status, her sons less than pleasant – thank goodness they hadn't come; she didn't want them at Toby's funeral. What sort of a God would take the lovely Worthy and Toby and leave such people? It was uncharitable, but she couldn't help it.

'Like his great-grandfather in looks, isn't he?' Gwen's eyes still held Clem. 'That's our father, I mean.'

'We always wondered who he took after,' murmured Probyn, raising his cup.

Kit tried to recall what her father had looked like but had been just three years old when he died and had only vague memories. She envied Gwen this too.

Charlotte's big square face smiled fondly at Clem. 'He's a good-looking lad, whoever he favours.'

Used to his elder brother having all the attention, a miserable Duke was looking around for something to do. Having taken a liking to one of his aunt's hats, a creation laden with black cherries, he spotted it now hanging just outside the door and wondered how to lay his hands on it without being noticed. With the adults taking little notice of him he whispered to Augusta for permission to visit the farleymelow and, this granted, he slipped from the room.

Seated in the darkness of the privy, it was quite easy to rip the cherries from their mount and soon he had a handful, popping one of them into his mouth. It took only a second to realize the luscious-looking fruit was inedible, but slightly longer to try and reaffix the rest of them to the hat. Shoving the stalks into the band did not work; they kept falling off. So upon return to the house, the hat behind his back, he quickly hooked it back over its peg, shoved the wax fruit into a convenient pocket and sidled back into the room. No one had missed him.

'You're not married then, Charlotte?' Gwen had noticed the lack of a wedding ring on the woman's hand. 'You've left it a bit late now. What with the shortage of men they'll snap the younger ones up first and you'll be left on the shelf.'

'Charlotte's fiancé was killed in the war.' Even accustomed to the old woman's rudeness as he was, Probyn would not have Grace's friend subjected to it and his face gave warning.

'One of my poor sons-in-law too,' said Alice, tears bulging in her clear blue eyes. 'Eh, dear, nearly every other person you talk to these days seems to be a widow.'

It hit Probyn like a sledgehammer then that this was what he was: a widower.

'How are you going to cope on your own with all these bairns, Probe?' The soft enquiry came from Meredith.

'Yes, where's your Catholic Church now?' carped Gwen. 'I don't notice them offering to help.'

Seeing anger rise to her brother's face, the schoolmarmish Ethel interceded. 'I know we're a bit long in the tooth but Horace and I could take one of your boys. We've plenty of room.'

Meredith, Alice and Rhoda too were quick to volunteer.

But Probyn was still annoyed with them all for the way they had treated Grace. 'I looked after them well enough when my poor wife was unable to cope, I'm sure I can manage now.'

Meredith gently reproved him. 'Aw, Probe, don't let's fall out again. I'm sorry if I was less than charitable to Grace but you know it was the way we were brought up.'

'Don't blame our mother for your actions.' Grief making him act against character, Probyn was unforgiving. 'You're grown women with minds of your own and you made your views clear.'

The middle-aged sisters passed guilty looks at each other, especially those who had gone on to wed Catholics for they now knew what it was to be victims of bigotry. 'I'm sure we're all sorry for what happened in the past, Probe, but we're here now, aren't we? And we genuinely want to help.'

The response was dignified, a hint of the old RSM. 'Thank you, but no. I'm not helpless.' There had been such offers from Grace's sisters but these too had been refused.

Their aid rebuffed, there followed a moment of awkwardness, the sisters not knowing what to do. 'Perhaps we'd better go now,' decided Ethel, gathering the folds of her black skirt and elevating her ramrod-straight figure. 'But I'd hate us to part on bad terms. If you ever need us, Probyn, the offer's still there.'

One by one they rose. Probyn enlisted his children's help in bringing the guests' coats and hats.

Upon finding her mutilated headgear, Wyn gasped. 'What's this?' Probyn looked confused. 'Isn't it yours?'

The response was aghast. 'Where have all the cherries gone?'

Meredith felt something in her pocket, a slow grin spreading over her face. 'I think they're here.' Finding it hard to conceal a look of wry amusement, she pulled out the handful of cherries and tipped them onto the table. One had a bite out of it.

Charlotte sniggered, triggering others, even Gwen rocked with laughter.

But Wyn was examining both the hat and the cherries in horror. 'Someone's maliciously ripped them all off one by one! Who?' She was glaring at the children who rapidly lost their smiles, though the adults remained amused, the incident having momentarily helped to alleviate the grief even for the bereaved. 'Own up! Who was it? Probyn, this hat cost a fortune. I demand that you find the culprit.'

'No need – Duke, come here.' Probyn knew it had to be his youngest son and as much as he would rather have laughed with the others, he had no option but to chastise him in order to placate the outraged Wyn. Of all the days it had to happen. He wanted to laugh, he wanted to cry, he wanted to take the wretched child and throttle him.

But Wyn jumped in first, glaring at the six-year-old. 'Wicked boy! Well, I certainly won't be offering to adopt you! You deserve a good hiding.'

'He shall have one the moment you're gone,' announced Probyn, suddenly growing weary of them all and herding them to the door.

'Who's going to pay for this?' Wyn held up the mutilated hat.

'Come on, Wyn, remember where you are.' The tone of Meredith's voice reminded her sister that they had just attended a funeral.

'Oh . . . yes, right.' Wyn was only slightly less annoyed but managed to make a half-dignified exit in her cherryless hat. 'I'm sorry for your loss, Probyn. I know what it's like to lose a spouse . . . well, we'll see you tomorrow.'

Glancing sympathetically at Aunt Kit, Probyn nodded and leaned over to accept his sisters' kisses as they filed through the front room shop.

On her way, Gwen paused to run her eyes over the poorly stocked shelves and joked at Wyn's expense, 'You don't sell glue, do you?'

Probyn could barely raise a smile.

Last to exit, Rhoda clasped her brother's arm. 'Remember what we said about taking some of the children off your hands.'

He nodded, then, after a final sombre wave, closed the outer door. Suddenly the house was deathly quiet.

With all the visitors except Aunt Charlotte gone, an anxious Madeleine turned to Probyn. 'You're not going to send us away, are you, Father?'

'Most definitely not,' came the firm reply. 'We'll manage between us somehow.'

'And I'll come and help on my days off,' promised Charlotte, curling an arm around the two nearest children and hugging them. 'Don't worry.'

Probyn turned to the errant Duke, his face grim. 'No, there's only one of you has to worry. You blessed nuisance, do you think I enjoy having to give you a beating?'

Duke looked nervous. 'No, Father.'

'No! I don't, but I'm going to give you one just the same. Outside.'

In the days following Grace's demise, Probyn marvelled at how resilient children could be. Unlike Clem and Augusta, who were subdued for much longer, after the initial bouts of tears the younger ones seemed quick to get over their mother's death, going about their lives, playing in the street as though nothing had happened. Of course, he could not know what was in their minds; privately they must be suffering as deeply as he was but were simply getting on with living, which was what he should be doing, but he felt as if he was back in that muddy trench in France, up to his calves in the mire, unable to move one way or another.

Sorting through Grace's few possessions helped to give no sense of finality. He still expected her to come through the door. Every time he saw a crooked picture he thought of her. Perhaps a visit to her grave might have driven it home but out of shame he could not bring himself to go. He would have to go sometime, if only to ascertain the lot number of her final resting place. Until then she was not dead.

Eventually, though, when the sense of grief and anger and injustice had muted to acceptance, he forced himself to visit the cemetery, to be confronted once again by his failure to provide an individual resting place for his wife. He wondered as he stood there solemnly contemplating the snowdrops that peeped through the tangled grass how many others were buried with her, wondering too what Grace would have to say at sharing her eternal sleep with a soldier, for besides a name the temporary wooden cross upon the grave bore a rank and a regimental number.

Far from lending guidance, the visit made him even more helpless as to where he should go from here. For it seemed to Probyn that when his dear gentle Grace had died, the old way of life had died with her. Even those massive losses on the Somme had not borne the same impact, the sense that life had been irredeemably altered. Now as he looked around all he saw were industrial strikes, girls with hems almost up to their knees, a nation obsessed with self-gratification.

Ignorant of any of this, Augusta felt as if she was the only one whose life had changed beyond recognition. Whilst the menfolk went out to work as normal, and the children off to school as they had always done, life for her was very different as she strove to attend both work and home. It was not without irony that, by neglecting her own welfare, Grace had inflicted upon her daughter the very thing she had always tried to avoid: premature motherhood.

The children came down to the breakfast Augusta had set for them before leaving for the factory: a slice of bread and margarine each. Washing this down with a cup of water, they were soon ready to depart for school. There was a row of pennies on the table with which to buy their dinner. Without Mother singing around the kitchen and to wave them off, the heart and soul of the house had died. It was of no hardship to leave this empty place.

At noon, Beata collected Mims from Baby Class and headed back to Layerthorpe, meeting her other siblings en route. Calling in at home for their dinner money and receptacles, they proceeded to the soup kitchen. The rest handing over their pennies for a mug of steaming soup, Beata chose ginger pudding, then all five sat on a low wall to consume it. Lured by the aroma, an emaciated, scabrous white mongrel came to watch, though it gained little attention for the children had more interesting things in their line of vision. Across the road was a tannery, its outer wall partly dilapidated, allowing them a grandstand view of the men at work, slinging hides into the lime pits. During the time it took to consume the soup, two more stray dogs had joined the first; undeterred by its warning growls they sat a little way off, salivating as the cups were raised and lowered.

Staring vacantly into space, thinking about her mother, Beata made a sudden grimace of distaste as she came across a lump of undissolved suet which she hated, and she spat it onto the pavement. In a trice all three dogs leaped on it and a vicious fight ensued, the filthy white mongrel emerging the victor and the others falling back to sit on their haunches, licking their chops and awaiting a fresh opportunity.

Yet another dog, a handsome border collie, appeared on the scene but this one was on a leash, dragged by its owner through the gates of the tannery. When the man emerged he was alone.

'Fancy getting rid of a lovely animal like that,' Joe muttered darkly into his mug.

A horrible image occurred to Beata, who asked what he meant.

'People get fed up of their dogs and cats and take them there to be killed. Look, there's one.'

The rest of the children looked in horrified fascination at the scene across the road. Sure enough, a small ginger pelt was being handled by one of the men.

Thoughtfully, Beata probed her ginger pudding. Coming across another glob of suet she offered it to the white mongrel, who almost took her hand off.

'Poor thing,' she muttered, shaking her throbbing finger. 'Isn't he thin?'

There was murmured agreement, none of them seeming aware that they were almost as underfed as the dog.

It was time to go back to school. The animal started to follow them, then realizing they had nothing for it to eat, took a sniffing detour into the tannery.

'Don't go in there!' Beata caught hold of its filthy coat.

'Why don't we take him home?' suggested Duke.

It seemed such an easy solution to shove the dog through the front door and leave it to its own devices whilst they went on to school.

However, when they came home a horrible stench was to meet them.

'Aw, he's shit all over t'house!' exclaimed Joe, after first laughing, examining the sole of his boot in disgust.

Wagging its tail in greeting, the dog seemed to be proud of its handiwork, having trodden the excrement into every down-stairs room.

'Clean it up, Beat,' ordered Madeleine.

Her sister argued but, naturally, no one else wanted the chore and it was left to Beata who was still scrubbing the carpet with disinfectant when Augusta came home.

After exclaiming over the stench and throwing open the windows, their eldest sister demanded, 'What's that blasted creature doing in the house?'

'We had to fetch him home,' explained Joe. 'The men at the tannery might have got him.'

'That moth-eaten cur? They wouldn't even get a decent pair of gloves out of his pelt. It's probably riddled with flea holes! You can count every bone in his body.' Then Augusta's eyes fell on the plate on the sideboard, which should have contained their tea and now bore only a crescent of pastry at one side. 'Lord save us, it's eaten the rabbit pie!'

Beata spoke optimistically. 'It's left a bit.'

'Only because it couldn't get at it!' An appalled Augusta examined the remnant of pastry which bore the imprint of desperate teethmarks where the dog had struggled for that which was just out of reach to him.

Even as she spoke another outrage came to light, Augusta becoming almost demented by the sight of a bin with its lid knocked off. 'Oh no – he's eaten every bit of bread in the house!'

To cries of dismay the dog was ejected from the end of her foot through the empty shop into the street.

'Stinky old Gusset!' sulked Mims at her sister's cruelty.

'Aw, can't we keep him?' wailed Duke.

Augusta turned on them in tearful fury. 'Are you all daft? We've hardly got enough money to feed ourselves and you let an animal in to eat what little we have got! What am I going to tell Father when he comes in expecting his tea?' Rushing to the larder she cast a frantic eye over the poorly stocked shelves, in her panic grabbing anything that came to hand, dried peas, flour, pepper . . . 'I'll just have to make a soup!'

'We had that for dinner,' grumbled Madeleine.

'Well, you can have it again!'

By the time Probyn got home there was some kind of a meal on the table, though what kind it was hard to tell. Nevertheless he felt sorry for his obviously harassed eldest daughter. 'That smells good, Gus.' He rubbed his hands. 'But isn't it a bit cold to have the windows wide open?'

Face glowing from her efforts, Augusta dashed a lock of hair from her brow and glanced darkly at her siblings. 'You wouldn't be saying it smelled so nice if I hadn't had them open, Father.' And she told him all about the catastrophe with the dog, ending with the explanation, 'That's why it's pot luck for tea. I'm sorry.'

Probyn was stern with the others. 'Don't you think your sister's got enough to cope with, going to work and looking after you, without a blessed dog?'

'It was just so thin, Father,' reasoned Beata.

'And we were worried the men at the tannery were going to kill it,' added Joe.

Probyn only half shared their sentiment. 'Aye well, it's not nice, I know, but might it not be better for it to be disposed of swiftly instead of being kicked out to slowly starve because its owner can't afford the licence? It takes money to look after a dog, that's why there's so many wandering the streets. Their owners can't afford to keep them and neither can we – so don't go bringing any more animals home.'

With Clem coming in at this juncture the meal was dished out.

Mims raised her spoon, then spoke through what felt like a mouthful of pebbles. 'I don't like it.'

Neither did Probyn, nor anyone else judging from the half-hearted manner in which they partook of the meal; the peas were insufficiently cooked and it was like chewing gravel; but he saw the tears of embarrassment in Augusta's eyes and fought to appear as if he himself was enjoying the meal. 'Eat up!' His face was unusually cross. 'Your sister's had to go to a great deal of trouble all because you allowed the dog to eat our tea, so don't let me hear another grumble!'

After making a small effort to chew the mouthful, Mims' face crumpled into tears. At Probyn's sound of despair, Augusta immediately went to hoist Mims from her chair. 'I'll see to her, Father, you get on with our tea.' She tried to lead the youngest child away but, angry with grief over her mother's death, Mims jerked free. 'I don't want you, I want my mother!'

Clem put his face in his hands as the other siblings were infected by Mims' tears. 'For Christ's sake . . .'

Unable to console Mims, Augusta was almost in tears herself, but managed to coax the desolate child into another room so that the others could get on with their meal.

However, when she finally managed to pacify Mims and the pair came back into the kitchen, the table had been cleared and the fire was sizzling suspiciously, leading her to suspect that the meal had been consigned to the flames.

Finding her weeping in the scullery, Clem dealt her a comforting pat, then motioned for his father to assist.

Augusta felt her father's hand on her shoulder. 'That was lovely, Gus. You did a great conjuring job. We just couldn't manage to eat it all.'

This made her feel worse than ever and she broke into shuddering sobs.

Probyn had the feeling it was not just this one meal that had broken her spirit. 'I'm sorry if I've expected too much of you, lass. You're only fifteen, after all . . .'

These too were the wrong words. Augusta had idolized her mother, had tried her utmost to meet Grace's standards of care, had worked herself into the ground striving to look after the family whilst maintaining her job so as not to deplete the household income. Yet it had taken only one small crisis to prove how ill-equipped she was to cope. She felt useless and stupid and unworthy.

'It's just that you're the only one who can hold us all together,' soothed Probyn. 'If it wasn't for your hard work your brothers and sisters would have to leave home and that really would be bad for them.'

Torn between pleasure at this show of faith, and her own feelings of grief and inadequacy, Augusta finally shrugged off her woes with a brisk dab of her handkerchief. 'I'm sorry, Father, I'm just being daft. I was just so livid at that blasted dog for eating your tea.'

Somehow Probyn managed to chuckle. 'I suppose it would have been funny at any other time.'

'Aye,' she chuckled too, though inside she felt only desolation. 'Don't worry about me, I can cope – as long as they don't let any more fleabags in.'

Probyn gave her shoulder a reassuring squeeze. 'Good lass. I've every faith in you.' Even as he said it, after seeing her in such a state he was not at all sure if he was asking too much of Gussie.

Life had just started to fall into some sort of routine when along came the Easter holiday to upset things. Now, on top of Augusta's worry over what she would cook them for tea and what her siblings' faces would be like as they sampled it, there was the added concern over what they would be getting up to whilst she was at work. Of course, household chores kept them out of mischief for much of the morning, but that still left several hours until she could resume her supervision of them. For his own part her father continued to worry too that he had placed too great a burden on one so young, but what alternative was there? He had to earn a living.

Left to their own devices, today the boys had done their chores and were now out scavenging. Madeleine was obviously preparing for a lone outing for she issued last-minute instructions to Beata.

'Can you make sure the spuds are peeled by four?' She donned her bonnet.

Beata objected. 'Gus asked you to do them.'

'I know but I might not be back. I'm off to Buttercrambe Wood to pick daffodils.'

'Who's taking you?'

'Nobody, I'm off on the train.' The Derwent Valley Railway ran along the end of the street.

'How have you got the money?'

'Don't need any. I've made friends with the guard and he says I can travel in his van. I'll have to go now or I'll miss it – don't forget the spuds!' Maddie rushed out.

Beata looked down at Mims. 'It appears I'm looking after you – *as usual*.' Seeing Mims ready to pout she added hurriedly, 'Don't start! We're going to have our outing too.' And off they went on a round tour of their aunts and uncles' houses.

After a day of visiting relatives, the pair made their way home to an empty, uninviting scene. The front room still had its shop counter, but no smiling face shone out from behind it now. With no reason to come home until Augusta returned from work to make their tea, the boys were still out roaming the streets and, as Beata had expected, Madeleine was still out enjoying herself too. Being a conscientious child, Beata set about peeling the potatoes whilst Mims went out to the closet. But, upon her sister's loud screams, she was forced to rush out.

Finding that it was only the ducket lavatory that had turned over by accident when Mims had been seated upon it, she dragged her little sister back into the house and ordered her to be quiet whilst she finished the potatoes. This was a useless instruction. Beata was almost at the end of her tether when the door opened and in walked cousin Wilfred from Bolton Percy, his cheerful face gaining immediate welcome.

The twenty-year-old had the assurance of a much older man. 'All on your own?' He swaggered about the room, picking up objects to examine as if he owned the place. But he had a pleasant way with him and Beata liked her cousin.

'Yes. Would you like me to make you a cup of tea?' She was already on her way to put the kettle on.

Wilf smiled at her, a sudden gleam in his eye. 'That's very kind of you, Beat. Tell you what: while that's boiling, nip over the road and buy yourself some sweets.' He handed over a few coppers.

Beata gave profuse thanks and, grabbing an equally delighted Mims by the hand, left the house.

Their return only a few minutes later with handfuls of sweets coincided with Wilfred's departure. Beata displayed surprise. 'Don't you want your tea?'

'No, no,' Wilfred issued breezily as he loped away. 'I've just remembered I have to go see somebody. Thanks for the offer, though.'

With Mims occupied by the sweets, Beata was able to finish peeling the potatoes before settling down to enjoy her own comfits, both girls managing to eat every one before Madeleine and the boys arrived.

Eventually a tired-looking Augusta came in, her overalls impregnated with the smell of chocolate. 'Oh, what lovely daffs!' Her face brightened at the sight of the vase of flowers that Madeleine had placed on the sideboard. She started cooking tea, having it on the table by the time her father and Clem entered.

Everyone seemingly lifted by the golden addition of spring to their normally dark kitchen, the meal progressed well enough until Mims began to show disdain, shoving the food about her plate.

'Eat up,' warned Probyn, having come to dread meal times.

'I'm full,' said the three-year-old.

'How can you be full?' demanded a tense Augusta.

Mims' lower lip began to jut.

'Oh, not again!' Clem looked sick at the thought of another meal being spoiled.

To prevent further upset Beata quickly explained, 'Cousin Wilf bought us some sweets. Mims ate all hers.'

Probyn was immediately alert, laying down his cutlery to ask, 'Wilf? How long was he here?'

'Only a few minutes while we went to the shop. He said he had to see some –' She broke off as her father jumped up and began to tour the room suspiciously as if looking for something, his eyes running over shelf and mantelpiece.

After a few moments of opening and closing drawers and cupboards, Probyn made the discovery he had dreaded. 'Your mother's gold guard chain!' It had been looped around one of the candlesticks that were attached to the piano. 'Have any of you been playing with it?' At the worried shake of heads he exclaimed, 'Then the little swine's taken it! Damn him!' And he banged his fist so hard on the table that the plates bounced, sending knives and forks up in the air and splattering gravy all over the cloth. 'What did you let

250

him in for? Don't you know he's a ruddy crook?' Red with fury, Probyn's face terrified his children.

Sighing, Clem removed himself from the table and lit up a cigarette.

'I'm sorry, Father, I didn't know!' Beata trembled.

Feeling that he might explode with grief and betrayal, Probyn uplifted his face to the ceiling and roared like a bull, clenching his fists. Seeing him so distraught Augusta broke down and sobbed. 'I'm sorry! I'm sorry!' Having promised she could cope, she felt utterly useless. 'It's all my fault!'

'How can it be your fault? It's my bloody fault!' Probyn's face was still crimson with fury as he banged his chest. But slowly with great effort he began to calm and with a final sigh uttered, 'Oh, Gus, I'm not blaming you, I'm not angry with any of you, you weren't to know, I should have warned you. He's only just been released from a training ship for diddling some other youngster . . . Oh, the bloody wretch. Your mother's chain, how could he stoop so low as to steal off his own?' He could have wept.

Clem was putting his jacket back on, a look of intent upon his face. 'I'm off to sort him out.'

Probyn's arm shot out. 'No! That's my job. Sit down and eat your tea.'

The volatile Clem had to be told twice before obeying, allowing everyone to sit down again.

But after such upset no one could eat, and soon the dishes were cleared away and the younger ones packed off to bed.

'Make sure you say your prayers,' ordered a weary Augusta. 'I'll come and tuck you in in a minute.'

'This isn't fair on any of you.' Seated in emergency council at the table with his eldest son and daughter, Probyn voiced the words he had hoped never to make. 'We need help. I didn't want to split up the family but I've no choice. We just can't cope.'

At Augusta's look of distress he said softly, 'It's not an accusation, love. No one could have done a better job than you. How you've managed at your age to do a full-time job and run a house at the same time for so long is a miracle – most adults would have failed. But it's affecting your health and I can't have you going down the same path as your dear mother. So,' elbows on the table, he laced his fingers and voiced his resolution, 'I'm going to write to my sisters and ask if their offer of help still stands.'

Augusta tried hard not to cry but failed.

He strove to comfort her. 'Now think on, I don't want you to regard it as a reflection on you, or you, Clem. You're fine young people, I don't know what I'd have done without you in the last few weeks and I'm still going to need you here with me, but the little ones will have to go. I can't see anything else for it. It's the only way.'

FIFTEEN

Written in hasty scrawl, the collection of letters was posted early the following morning before Probyn went to work, one being addressed to Grace's sister at Bolton Percy, informing her of her son's crime. The letter of apology was to appear by return of post that same day, its envelope also containing a pawn ticket.

Upon receipt of it Probyn was if anything even angrier with the culprit, for to redeem Grace's chain he must pay its full value and, the article being of solid gold, he found it impossible to raise the funds.

Nevertheless, said Probyn to his family, it wasn't Aunt Nell's fault that she had a criminal for a son. She and Uncle Charlie were lovely people and it was for this reason he was considering their offer to look after Mims. They lived nearer to York than some of his own relatives, making it easier for his family to keep in touch. He had explained to all the children now of the need for this temporary separation and, though the younger ones did not really understand, they seemed to have accepted it.

Shamed by her son's wrongdoing, Aunt Nell was not about to tell Probyn of the problems encountered by Mims' addition to her family. Knowing they were the actions of a bereaved child unable to handle her grief, the kind woman endured the tantrums without anger for several days, before her patience ran out.

But when Mims sank her teeth into a smaller victim, especially as that victim was her own little boy, it was time to act.

Witnessing the assault, Nell grabbed firm hold of Mims and instructed the weeping casualty, 'Now, bite her back!'

Retribution was delivered. Mims gave a yell and pulled away.

253

'Yes! It hurts, doesn't it?' demanded Aunt Nell.

The furious three-year-old stood glowering and rubbing her hand.

'Don't stick your lip out like that, the Devil will come and sit on it!' Aunt Nell levelled a finger at her. 'And if you ever bite anyone again you'll get bitten back. It's a horrible thing to do to people who are trying to be your friends.'

Head downcast, Mims burst into tears.

Aunt Nell was overwhelmingly compassionate then, scooping the little girl into her arms, gently dabbing at her tears and telling her everything was going to be all right. 'You'll feel better in a while, you'll see. Now, come, let's get you both a slice of cake and a glass of milk.'

Snuggling against the matronly breast, Mims shuddered with emotion and nibbled silently on the cake until it was finished.

'Better now?' asked Aunt Nell with a kindly smile.

Mims nodded. Then, her memory stirred by the taste of that ginger cake, she asked, 'When is Mother coming?'

Eyes filled with tears, Nell sighed and set the child on her feet. Unable to think of a suitable reply, she said only, 'I don't know, dear. Best go out and play now.'

With Mims gone there were still another four to re-house – Clem, being an adult and having work nearby, would of course be staying in the family home; Augusta too – but help was on its way.

Within days, eager to make recompense for old hurts, Probyn's sisters rallied to his aid, appearing in person the following Saturday to discuss who should take which child.

Furthermore, 'I think we should get Kit involved too,' proposed Meredith. 'She's always loved children.'

Probyn had not even contemplated including Kit, who was sixty-four. 'I couldn't do that to her, she's too old.'

'She's only five years older than me!' boomed an affronted Ethel.

Probyn apologized, covering his gaff by saying Aunt Kit's enormous rolls of fat made her appear so much older. 'But apart from that, she's still grieving for her own lad. If she'd felt up to taking on the task she would already have offered.'

'One has to have time to grieve, yes, but I think it's more than that with Kit. The last time I saw her it was as if she had nothing to live for.'

Their brother turned reflective. 'Well, she did take a shine to Beat . . .'

'Then don't bother to ask.' Ethel was firm. 'Just send Beata with a note saying you can't cope any more – you know, lay it on thick – and let the pair of them get on with it. You watch, it'll do Kit the world of good to have someone young around; give her somebody to think about other than herself.'

Probyn eventually agreed, though said he would reverse Ethel's suggestion and send the letter first, just to warn Kit what to expect.

Kit's first emotion on receiving the letter was irritation. How could Probyn have inflicted this upon her? She barely had the energy to look after herself, let alone a child. But when Beata turned up alone with her belongings in a small paper parcel, wearing the black-and-white dress that her great-aunt had made the year before, it stirred something in Kit's breast and she set to with good heart, making the little girl feel at home and trying to help her overcome the tragic loss of her mother. Reacquainted with the biddable Beata and her little-old-woman ways, Kit grew deeply fond of the girl and to her surprise found her spirits gradually begin to lift from their deadened state. True, there were times when she would slip back into muddy waters, for no one, not even this sweet child, could make up for the loss of one's own; but, given this lifeline, Kit would eventually haul herself towards the light again.

'Eh, you're a good lass, Beat,' she told her great-niece upon receipt of the cup of tea that Beata had taken to delivering to her fireside bed every morning. 'I shall remember you in my will. I'm sorry it won't be money, that's already bequeathed to . . . well, someone else.' The hesitation was caused by thoughts of Serena, the daughter she had been forced to give away to her sister Amelia. With Toby dead there could be no other recipient of Kit's estate. This might cause speculation, but with everyone over here well aware of Serena's true parentage they could not object. 'Anyway,' she continued with manufactured cheeriness, 'there'll be another legacy coming to you.' She told Beata of the house that she had given to her brother Monty. 'That's your father's father,' explained Kit. 'He's dead now, but when his widow, that's your father's stepmother – I know, complicated isn't it? – when she dies the house will be sold and your father will be one of those to benefit. So you'll be well looked after.'

'Is she that lady in the picture?'

'Why, Good Lord no! That's my niece Beata – well, we were more like sisters really – who you were named after. She was a lovely lass too.' Kit smiled at the living Beata who in looks was nothing like her namesake at all, though there was a similarity of nature. 'And you were well-named because you've got her kindness. Eh, Beat, you've cheered me up no end, you really have. I don't know what I'd have done if you hadn't come to live with me. I wish you could stay for ever.'

Showered with such compliments, what else could Beata do but smile? Yet, much as she liked Aunt Kit, her heart yearned for life to be as it was, with a mother, a father, brothers and sisters, and she mourned its loss.

But with such tragedies heaped upon the family, life could only improve and so it was to do for the Kilmasters, for one of its members in a most surprising way.

A few months after Toby's funeral, Kit received a letter from America. Frowning over the writing, which did not belong to either of her sisters, she ripped it open and read: *Dear Aunt Kit, It is with great sorrow –*

'Oh, my God.' Kit let her head fall to the table, hardly daring to read further. What new sorrow was this? How much could one family bear?

Forcing herself, she read on.

It is with great sorrow that I have to tell you that both my parents died from influenza last month. Please forgive me for not informing you sooner, but as you can imagine . . .

Yes, I can imagine. Having cried so many tears of late, Kit was surprised to find her vision blurred by a fresh batch. But they were not so intense as those shed over her husband and son and, pulling a handkerchief from her pocket, she had soon dashed them away. She and Amelia had been very close in age, though not in character. Amelia had disapproved of what she saw as Kit's exhibitionism. They had not seen each other for over thirty years – since the fourteenth of January 1887, to be more precise. In fact, had anyone asked, Kit could quote the exact moment of their parting right down to the minute. A quarter past three in the afternoon. The time was branded upon on her heart.

It was such a horrible shock and it has taken me some weeks to get used to the fact that they are gone.

Kit envisioned Serena as just a little girl, all alone and heartbroken, unable to picture her as the adult she was.

We have never met . . .
Oh we have, we have!

> *but I feel as if I know you from your letters which my
> mother would read out to Father and me. It is because
> of those letters that I am able to contact you now, you
> being one of the few relatives who wrote on a regular
> basis. Aunt Flora offered to let you know but I forbade
> her from doing so as I wished to do this personally. It is
> what Mother would have wanted. I have postponed doing
> so until now not from thoughtlessness, but because there
> seemed little need for haste as there would have been no
> way you could have come to the funeral and also because
> it was such a hard letter to write. Besides, I know you
> have had your own losses to bear so did not want to
> add to them. I trust you are feeling better now. I hate
> to impose on you, Aunt Kit, but would it be too much
> to ask that you pass on the news of Mother's death to the
> rest of the family? I should be truly grateful.*
>
> *I have been trying to make a decision over what to do
> next but so far have not been able to. So, now that I
> am feeling better, and with no family to speak of here,
> apart from Aunt Flora, I have decided to take a month's
> vacation in England –*

Kit almost fell off her chair. Her heart gave a massive lurch, not
just with shock but with the most terrific excitement. Never in her
wildest dreams could she have hoped to feel such joy again after
losing her beloved husband and son, yet here she was soaring like
a bird. Her daughter was coming home! Oh, Serena, Serena!

She bent over the letter, devouring every word now.

*I have decided to take a month's vacation in England and look
up all my relatives. This I know will be a massive operation! But
I look forward to it very much. I have booked a hotel –*

'Oh no, stay with me!' Finding herself talking out loud, Kit
covered her mouth and, grinning foolishly, read on.

– in London, which is just down the road from you –

'It's miles away, you daft 'a'p'orth!' Kit gasped her exasperation.

'What was that, Aunt?' Beata popped her head around the door
of the scullery where she was washing the breakfast pots.

'Sorry, love. I'm just talking to meself – but don't tell anyone or
they'll come and lock me up.' Grinning at her niece, Kit waited until

Beata's auburn head retreated before bending over the letter again.
– and hope to see you in a month's time.

Kit uttered a silent ecstatic squeal, clenching her fists to her breast. Tears flowed again but this time tears of joy. God had taken pity on her suffering. He was delivering her daughter back into her arms.

Informed of Serena's coming, everyone in the family was keen to meet their American cousin, though none so excited as Kit. There were also reservations.

'What should we do about Aunt Gwen?' was the question raised by Kit's nieces. 'You know what she's like, she might let the cat out of the bag.' All were aware of Kit's colourful past.

'Well, she's managed to keep quiet about it so far.'

'You don't know! She might have told her lads; one of them might inadvertently let it out.'

'Have you told your children?'

'Certainly not!' Illegitimacy was not something to shout from the rooftops; in fact this was one of the few times it had been discussed between the women.

'I'll bet Kit's on tenterhooks.' Meredith bit her lip. 'She must be dreading meeting her.'

Nothing could have been further from the truth. Kit was praying for the days to go faster. The last thought on her mind was what would happen if Serena found out that she was adopted. All she wanted at this moment was to embrace her baby again.

But there were, of course, serious matters to ponder. With Serena thousands of miles away in America and Amelia so deftly maintaining the deception of her parentage, there had been none of this to worry about before, but now things had changed radically. Even if nothing untoward were to occur during this visit, when Serena finally inherited Kit's estate she might want to know why an aunt who was little more than a stranger had left everything to this one 'niece' and to none of the others, a niece who must already be quite well off, having inherited from her supposed parents. Kit had thought about this long and hard but had not come up with any plausible explanation for the girl other than she wanted Serena to have it. Of course, being dead, Kit would not be around to be questioned, it should not worry her, but it did. She could not bear to think of her daughter's heartbreak should the truth inadvertently be leaked – whatever way it emerged it would be accompanied by tremendous shock. So, Kit had decided to leave a letter of explanation in her solicitor's hands to be given to Serena should any question arise after her death, revealing the identity of her real mother and father. Some might view this as cruel – Kit had agonized long and hard over it too – but its details would only be disclosed as a last resort. Serena had the right to learn the truth from the one who had borne her, had adored her and wanted to do the best for her, and not via any other source. It was not cruelty but expedience.

Anyway, this might never come to pass. Why spoil today worrying about tomorrow? Shoving it to the back of her mind, Kit braced herself for the marvellous homecoming, urging the hands of the clock to get a move on.

At last news arrived. Serena was in London! After recovering from the voyage and doing a little sightseeing she planned to visit Aunt Kit in two days' time at the weekend. Would it be possible for her aunt to arrange for some, if not all, of the other family members to gather under the same roof so as to reduce the travelling between them? It seemed silly to waste the precious time she hoped to spend with her relatives. Kit had been hoping to have her daughter to herself and was somewhat crestfallen, but then Serena would be here for a month, her own private time would come. Writing back, she said she would arrange this and also have someone meet Serena at the station. Hence there began a hurried scribbling of letters. Only then did it really sink in. Both excited and terrified, Kit prayed that her heart would not give away her secret.

'She's here! She's here!' Children who had been waiting all morning came tumbling into Kit's farmhouse kitchen to herald the bumpy arrival of a taxi cab.

Confused but happy, Kit bumbled down the path to meet the visitor, others following in her wake, excited children scampering ahead, though they braked upon laying eyes on the young woman who alighted from the cab, a vision of elegance and sophistication – of Amazonian proportions it was true, but with her attire straight out of a fashion magazine she looked magnificent – her copper hair expertly coiffed, her skin like cream and her lips rouged.

Even Kit's smartly dressed nieces were rendered speechless.

Kit could have wept tears of joy at the sight of her daughter, but made do with a cheery greeting. 'I sent a neighbour to fetch you! You must have missed one another.'

'The man in the cart?' The tall, handsome, young woman had been

259

about to open her purse to pay the cabby but now spun round with a beam for her aunt. 'Oh, I saw him but I preferred a less primitive form of travel – hope you don't mind?' She turned back to attend to the cabby.

'Of course not!' Kit wanted desperately to hug her but restrained herself to watch as the taxi made its jarring exit over the rutted track. 'But that must have cost you a fortune.'

'I can afford it.' Serena grinned and extended a gloved hand. 'Aunt Kit, I presume? How do you do?'

Kit had been worried that, in sorting through Amelia's belongings after her death, Serena might have come across damning evidence of her parentage, but locking eyes with the young woman now, she could tell that Serena remained innocent. She beheld the proffered hand only a fraction of a second then used it to haul Serena into an affectionate embrace, squashing her against a massive bosom. 'I'm very well, thank you, dear! Oh, it's so lovely to see you!' Desperate as she was to enfold Serena for ever, she realized how odd this would look and was quick to let her go.

But not quick enough. To Serena such a show of emotion proved an embarrassment and for a moment her air of sophistication was dislodged. Oh dear, were they all going to be like this? To recover her equilibrium she smoothed a copper curl around her ear and turned a rather fixed smile on Kit's entourage. 'Hello there!'

'Oh yes, come and meet everybody!' gushed Kit.

To Serena's relief, the rest of the family seemed not so ebullient, making do with handshakes or the most respectful of kisses.

'Golly, I think my arm's going to drop off!' she exclaimed, laughing, after the final handshake. 'It's really good to meet you all. I've heard so much about you.'

'And us about you,' beamed Probyn. 'Eh, she's got quite a twang on her, hasn't she? You'd never guess she was Yorkshire-born.' There was a barely perceptible falter as he wondered whether he had said the wrong thing; the strain of protecting Kit's secret was like walking on jelly.

But Serena knew all about her emigration as a babe and merely laughed.

The tactile Kit grasped her arm. 'Before we go any further, love, can I just say how sad we were to hear about your mother and father. It must have been an awful shock for you, the speed of –'

'Yes, yes, it was.' A flicker of anguish appeared in Serena's brown eyes. She seemed unwilling to dwell on her parents' deaths. 'But I'm getting over it, slowly.'

'I lost my Worthy and Toby to influenza, you kno –'

'Yes, yes, I know.'

'You can't believe how quickly it strikes, can –'

'No, it was a nightmare.' Desperate for her aunt to shut up, Serena quickly patted the hand that lay on her arm. 'Shall we go in?' She reached for her suitcases but two male relatives got there first.

Hefting a bag in either hand, Probyn and Clem allowed her and the chattering Kit to go ahead, then followed them down the path to the cottage, the rest in tow. Reunited with her family for the day, Beata skipped happily beside her father. Probyn grinned down at her, but soon his mood was abstracted. Always an admirer of the female form, and starved of physical contact since Grace's death, he now found his gaze drawn wistfully to the buttocks that jiggled beneath the soft jersey of Serena's dress; unlike the corseted rears of his sisters, the two perfect globes moved unrestrained. Her up-to-the-minute outfit also revealed a lot of calf.

Glancing at Clem he noted that his son was impressed too, overtly so. Giving a discreet cough of warning, he rebuked the young man with his eyes, whilst secretly envying Clem his youth and the pleasures yet to come.

After they had enjoyed one of Kit's famous luncheons, all the guests announcing themselves to be well and truly stuffed, photographs were passed around of Serena's American home, over which everyone oohed and aahed, and some of her parents and Aunt Flora. Then followed some old ones from Kit's album of Amelia when she was a girl.

'Oh, look there's one of me as a baby!' Serena grinned.

Kit felt a dozen pairs of eyes shoot in her direction. 'Yes, your mother sent it to me,' she answered calmly.

Whilst others were adhered to the interplay between Kit and the daughter who remained ignorant of her origin, Serena leafed through the pages of old snapshots, poring over the ones of her mother, or the woman she thought of as Mother.

With eyes only for her daughter, Kit was the first to notice the tears spill over her blackened lashes. 'Oh, lass, I didn't mean to upset you by bringing them out!'

Serena dashed away the tears, replacing them with the smile that masked everything. 'No, no, I loved seeing them! It's just that I still get upset . . .'

'Well, it's hardly six months since you lost them,' soothed Kit. 'We all understand. Cry if you like.'

But Serena was not about to make herself a spectacle and now put aside the album. 'I haven't come here to make everyone miserable. Where did you put my bags, Cousin Probyn?' Told they were in her bedroom, she hurried up the staircase. 'Won't be a moment.'

In her absence, talk centred on her appearance.

'She's a bonny lass,' opined Probyn.

'She is that,' agreed Meredith, her sisters echoing.

She's got her father's brown eyes, thought the girl's mother. Kit could barely remember anything about Philip, but she remembered those eyes. She glanced up with fondness as Serena came back down with her arms full.

'It's only a few mementoes, just a token, but I hope you like them.' She began to hand out American souvenirs to the senior members and chocolate bars to the children, who received them shyly, still in awe of her.

However, they were soon to be won over for it turned out that Serena had inherited her mother's talent for mimicry. Not self-conscious in the least about being the centre of attention, she entertained them with tales of her voyage here, putting on with great accuracy the many regional accents she had encountered. Kit urged herself to remain dignified but could not help laughing more loudly than the others at Serena's entertaining parody, lauding her clothes and hair, in fact everything about her.

The conversation lulled. Serena gave a jolly pat of her knees. 'Well, do I get to do a tour of this farm of yours, Aunt?'

'That'll take you all of five minutes.' Kit looked deliriously happy. 'It's not really a farm, just a smallholding. We used to have quite a few animals before the war but there's not many to see now.' Noting how shy the youngsters still were of the visitor she put aside her own needs and said, 'Maybe the children would like to show you round. They haven't had a chance to talk to their cousin yet.'

'I'd like that.' Serena hoisted her tall, elegant form and beckoned to the younger ones, two of whom were quick to grab her hands. Normally considering himself above mingling in such company, nineteen-year-old Clem chose to go along too, his aunts nudging each other and winking.

Duke turned to his father. 'Can we eat our chocolate now?'

'I suppose so, gannet.' With Father's permission, the wrappers were torn off, all keen to sample the American confectionery.

But there was to be disappointment. 'It tastes like soap!' Outside now, Joe pulled a face.

Serena laughed, though was slightly offended, retorting, 'Have you ever eaten soap?'

'Our Clem has!' sniggered Maddie. 'It was Mother's cure for a foul mouth and Clem's always swearing.'

Serena laughed with them, her teeth startlingly white against the red lipstick.

Clem thought she looked like a dream. Taking out a packet of cigarettes he put one in his mouth, then faltered, wondering whether or not to offer her one. In the end he did but she refused with a smile.

Then she grew sombre. 'You've lost your mother too, haven't you? It's just awful . . .'

'Even when you're as old as you are?' ventured Beata.

The smile was sad. 'Yes, even as old as me.'

'How old are you?' asked Duke.

'A gentleman doesn't ask a lady's age,' his eldest brother warned him sternly through an exhalation of smoke.

Serena rousted herself from dejection. 'Guess,' she challenged the six-year-old.

He wrinkled his nose. 'About fifty?'

Serena sneaked a grin at Clem. 'Gee, that's quite close.' She was thirty-two.

Joe was puzzled. 'Are you our aunty?'

'No, I'm your second cousin.'

He was no wiser. 'None of our other cousins are as old as you. Did nobody want to marry you?'

Serena feigned outrage. 'Are all Yorkshire people as rude as you? There's plenty have asked me to marry them, thank you very much, but I intend to enjoy the fruits of my inheritance before settling down – if I ever do.' She let out a yelp upon snagging her hosiery on a prickly bush. Bending to rub her leg, she noticed the green fruit it bore and frowned. 'What're these?'

'Goosegogs,' Clem told her.

'Goosegargs?'

The children fell about laughing at the American way she said it and laughed even more heartily when Serena tried a fruit and puckered her mouth at its sourness.

'Well, they seem to be enjoying themselves.' Alice was peering surreptitiously from the kitchen window. In the younger ones' absence, whilst the men talked in another room, Kit's nieces had helped her to wash up and even now this was done they remained in the kitchen to discuss the situation. 'Especially Clem.'

'Aye, he's right smittled by our visitor, isn't he?' Rhoda hung her damp tea towel over a rail near the warm oven. 'And who can blame him?'

Meredith nodded emphatically. 'Serena's a handsome young woman, isn't she?'

Her sisters agreed, only Wyn putting a damper on things. 'She's been spoiled though, being an only child. I notice she didn't offer to wash up.'

Kit sprang to her daughter's defence. 'I wouldn't expect her to, she's a guest!'

'What does that make us?' Wyn laughed at her sisters.

'You know what I meant,' said Kit.

Meredith spoke kindly. 'Yes, we know how much it must mean for you to have her here, Kit.'

'And she's *so* like you,' emphasized Rhoda.

'Eh, don't be going saying things like that!' hissed Kit, rushing to peer through the window to check on her daughter's whereabouts. Secretly, though, she was delighted.

Alice soothed her aunt's fears. 'Don't worry, she's down in the field. Yes, the resemblance is amazing, isn't it? Even down to her lovely clothes. She's got your height, and the same colour hair –'

'Oh, but she's got a much better figure than I ever had! And she's prettier.' There was pride in Kit's voice.

'Nonsense! Everyone always envied you your striking looks, didn't we?' Merry turned to her sisters, who again chorused agreement.

Deeply flattered, Kit thanked them, then looked down at her figure and made a joke at her own expense. 'I don't know about striking looks now – I look as if I've been struck by elephantiasis. Whatever happened? It's not as if I eat that much . . .'

A secret smile passed between the nieces. Kit had made this complaint about her weight for years, and it had become a joke between them.

'Well, none of us is exactly sylph-like.' Ethel patted her own corseted abdomen. 'I can't believe I'll be sixty next year.'

'Oh, don't!' Kit begged her, laughing. 'I can't believe I'll have a sixty-year-old niece.'

Alice groaned. 'Please, don't remind me! I feel the same as I did at sixteen till I look at this decrepit lot.' She indicated her sisters, who gave laughing recognition, giggling as they had not done since childhood.

'Merry, you must be coming up to fifty then?'

'I've got two years to go, if you don't mind!'

'But you're a grandmother! Eh dear, where did the years go?' Kit's huge breast heaved a wistful sigh. 'It seems only yesterday we were all girls. I still feel like a girl till I look in the mirror. We used to have such lovely times, didn't we? Picnics and concerts . . .'

'Well, I've had a lovely time today,' announced Meredith warmly. 'It's been just like the old days.' Then she donned a mischievous smile. 'How thoughtful of you not to invite Aunt Gwen.'

'Perish the thought!' scoffed Kit.

'Still, I suppose it would be uncharitable if we didn't allow Gwen to meet Serena at all,' mooted Alice.

Kit grimaced. 'I suppose it would, though we can't send the poor lass alone and unarmed into enemy territory.'

There was no rush to volunteer, most of them being reluctant to visit Gwen.

Meredith broke the hiatus. 'Well, I don't mind going . . .' She sounded none too sure.

'Oh, I wasn't suggesting any of you should suffer,' replied Kit. 'I'm quite happy to go myself.' To go anywhere with Serena would be a joy. 'But I'd be glad of the back-up, if you mean it.'

Meredith spoke genuinely now. 'Of course. Poor Serena will need all the support she can get.'

'Why would I need support?' Unnoticed, Serena had drifted around the side of the cottage and into the kitchen.

Whilst others blushed and prickled with embarrassment, the guilty laughter was easily explained by Kit who had always been an expert liar. 'We're just discussing whether it's wise to expose you to your Aunt Gwen's bluntness.'

Serena laughed, relieved to hear that they had not been discussing something more intimate. 'You mean she's ruder than those children out there?' And she told them what had occurred.

'You think they're blunt? Wait till you meet Aunt Gwen!' Alice rolled her eyes.

In the event, all the sisters were to accompany Kit and Serena to Gwen's, most of them travelling on the same train and meeting up with Meredith at Leeds station. Inevitably, Kit had to travel in the guard's van, two of her nieces helping to shove her aboard. Greatly embarrassed by this spectacle, Serena stood well out of the way, hoping to dissociate herself whilst onlookers pointed and sniggered.

Worse was to come on arrival. Aunt Gwen was indeed as bad as had been painted, beholding Serena with the dubious greeting, 'You'll get a turned eye with a fringe like that.'

But happily after this the afternoon was more of a success than they could have anticipated, Kit and Serena taking it in turns to keep the gathering amused.

A few hours later, ready to leave, Kit was issuing mental congratulations to her sister for managing to go a full afternoon with only one offensive remark and Serena was wondering what all the fuss had been about.

'Aunt Gwen's not that bad really,' she whispered to her companions as their hostess went to fetch their hats. 'You were just having me on.'

There were muffled guffaws from Kit and her nieces, which were quickly stilled as Gwen came back in carrying a selection of hats.

'Don't need to ask which one belongs to you!' Gwen made great play of examining her American niece's hat before handing it over. 'You'll have a bird nesting in that if you're not careful. I don't know how you dare wear it. You're certainly your mother's daughter, dressed up to the nines, never happy lest she were the centre of attention . . .' Suddenly faced with a collection of penetrating looks from the others, the elderly woman realized what she had said and hurriedly tried to qualify her remark. 'Still, I don't suppose it looks out of place where you live – and you're a pleasant enough lass for all that.'

Knowing how it felt to be the butt of Gwen's ridicule, Kit's heart went out to Serena, who was looking rather hurt and nonplussed. She was about to shepherd her daughter out of harm's way, when Serena murmured, 'Would you please excuse me? I need to make a necessary trip before we catch the train!' And she hurried from the room.

At least her absence gave Kit the chance to remonstrate with the culprit and, at the sound of the back door closing, she wasted no time. 'For pity's sake, Gwen, what are you trying to do?'

'I'm sorry, it just slipped out.' The elderly woman looked unusually repentant. 'She's that much like you with her outlandish clothes and whatnot I just forgot she thinks of Amelia as her mother.'

Kit gave an exasperated tut. 'And apart from nearly letting the cat out of the bag don't you think she might still be a bit upset at losing that mother? She doesn't want Amelia's memory insulting!' Issuing more damning words, she wobbled from the room into the back yard.

266

Ensconced in the lavatory, Serena must have heard her come out for the sound of her weeping stopped and she blew her nose, finally to emerge into the light.

Kit was there to offer comfort. 'Aw, I'm sorry, love! Gwen can't seem to let five minutes pass without insulting somebody. We've all had a taste of her thoughtlessness.'

Serena underestimated Kit's intuition. 'It wasn't the hat.'

'Oh, I realize that. It's going to take longer than six months for you to get over your double loss.'

Lingering in the yard, Serena was close to tears again. 'They were so devoted to each other, Aunt Kit. I never knew anyone with happier parents. I miss Mother especially.'

Faced with that look of torment, empathizing with it, how easy it would have been to announce, no, your mother isn't dead, she's standing right here beside you! How Kit's heart yearned to say it. Would it be so terrible, after all she had suffered in giving this child a better life?

Almost to the brink, she stepped back. Yes, it would be unforgivable, for Serena would then demand to know why Kit had given her away, had not wanted her, and in truth it would alter nothing, would take away not one iota of pain, for Serena would always think of the woman who raised her as Mother. On such short acquaintance, Aunt Kit could be little more than a stranger.

SIXTEEN

Emptiness was to dog the next few weeks whilst Serena went off to visit her father's kin. It should not have been so, for Kit had Beata to keep her company – had once considered herself blessed to have this little girl – but the need to be with her real daughter overwhelmed all other emotions.

Then, as if she were being punished for this ingratitude Kit found herself about to be robbed of Beata's company too as a letter arrived from Probyn. Already in that summer of 1919, flying in the face of industrial strikes and numerous international troubles, hundreds of street parties had been held across the country, the celebration of victory being mainly for the benefit of the children, for there was hardly an adult amongst them who had not lost someone and to whom victory seemed hollow. The inhabitants of Richmond Street were no different and, welcoming the opportunity to have his family around him for the day, Probyn sent out letters to the foster parents saying that a fancy-dress party was to take place the following week and asking that his children be allowed to attend. In order to enjoy the occasion fully they would of course be required to stay overnight.

'I don't have to go.' Noting her aunt's despondency and thinking it was induced by the thought of being alone, Beata offered to remain here, though she prayed not to be taken at her word.

Looking into that earnest face, Kit realized then what a misery she must have seemed to the child lately. The poor little thing, how could she tell Beata that her presence had no bearing one way or the other? Guilt caused her to reach out and tickle her niece under the chin. 'Miss the party? I don't think!'

Beata was secretly delighted, not only by the thought of the party but at being reunited with her father and siblings. Still, she worried about leaving Aunt Kit alone and so, when another letter arrived bearing the information that Serena intended to make a visit to her aunt on the day of the party, it could not have come at a more opportune moment.

Kit could not wait for Beata to be out of the way so that she might be on her own with her daughter, and by the time Serena was due to arrive her excitement was palpable.

Imagine, then, her disappointment at being presented with the middle-aged man who had come to ruin their intimacy. She could have wept.

Sensing that her companion's presence was not wholly welcome – it was hard not to with such a look of devastation on Aunt Kit's face – Serena was quick to say, 'I hope you don't mind Arthur coming with me? We won't stay long. We decided as it's such a lovely day that we'd go to the coast and as your house is on our route –'

'You thought you'd kill two birds with one stone,' Kit supplied the ending.

Serena chuckled uncomfortably and turned to her companion. 'Arthur, this is my Aunt Kit, whom I've told you so much about.'

Kit shook hands with the man, though it was not the usual warm handshake she reserved for those she liked. She was deeply hurt that her daughter had not thought she might enjoy a day at the seaside too, and she held this man responsible for robbing her of precious company. Besides, Arthur was much too old for Serena – why, he must almost be as old as Probyn. Though he had attempted to disguise his age with hair grease, the silver at his temples gave him away. Moreover, she did not like the way he was smirking at her. Even so, she remained polite and bade him go through to the parlour and be seated. He did so, Serena taking her place beside him on the sofa.

Kit responded to the protective urge that had overtaken her. 'Have you and Serena known each other long, Mr . . . ?'

'Hartley,' provided the man, and was about to say more but was interrupted by Serena's laughter.

'Now, Aunt Kit, I can see your little game!' She wagged a finger. 'But we don't have chaperones these days, you know. So don't go interrogating Arthur.'

Kit's smile was cool. 'I'm sorry, I'd no intention of being impolite, it's just that you never mentioned you had a gentleman friend the last time you were here.'

'That's because we only met a few days ago.' Serena now noticed that Beata was in fancy-dress costume and grinned. 'Going to a party?'

Beata projected excitement. 'Yes, I'm off home for the day. Old William's taking me on the cart.'

'Oh, I'm sure we could do better than that,' replied Serena. 'Wouldn't you rather go in a motorcar?'

Beata too agog to respond, Kit jumped in. 'You've got a motorcar?'

'Arthur has, yes.'

Kit was unimpressed. 'I thought you were off to the coast? Going back into York will take you out of your way. Besides, Old William will be here any moment and I'm not about to turn his kind offer down.'

'No, of course not.' Serena appeared contrite, then apologized to Beata, who looked disappointed, not understanding why her aunt had forbidden this pleasure.

'I'll go make a pot of tea. Beat, you stay and keep our guest company. Serena, would you mind?' Kit gestured for her daughter to follow.

With an apologetic look at Arthur, Serena shadowed her aunt to the kitchen.

Here, Kit spoke in a confidential hush. 'Have you any idea of what you could be getting yourself into, love?'

Serena raised an eyebrow for her aunt's audacity. 'I beg your pardon, Aunt Kit, but you don't know anything about –'

'I do!' An earnest-looking Kit grasped the younger woman's arm. 'I wouldn't normally interfere but I'm worried for you. I've met men like him. He won't marry you.'

'For heaven's sake, what is this obsession you people have with marriage?' Serena rebuffed Kit's act of concern, becoming quite annoyed. 'He and I are merely enjoying ourselves.'

'Your idea of enjoyment and his might be two different –' Kit broke off upon remembering that this was the exact phrase that Amelia had used to her in an attempt to stem disaster. Looking deep into Serena's brown eyes, she recognized that same air of defiance that she herself had worn, the attitude that had heralded her downfall. She must prevent her daughter from making the same mistakes. 'He'll use you, then throw you aside like a piece of rubbish,' she said bluntly. 'I won't allow you to waste yourself on him.'

Serena gasped. '*You* won't allow? I beg your pardon, Aunt, but who are you to say what I may and may not do?'

Kit could have told the truth right then, but she resisted the urge. Besides, there was no time to say anything for Serena added angrily: 'You know nothing about me!'

Sadly, this was true. Kit became entreating. 'No, no, you're right, but if you knew how deeply I care for –'

'Treating me as if I'm some, some *innocent*! Well, let me just put you straight, Aunt Kit. I know all about what men want, I learned about it long ago and if it suits me to oblige them then it's nobody's business but my own!' And before a shocked Kit could hand out any more advice she had swivelled on her high heels and minced back to the parlour.

Arthur glanced round in surprise as his companion flopped angrily beside him.

Serena let out a breath and turned to him, murmuring through her teeth. 'Aunt Kit was just giving me the benefit of her experience; seems to think that running a farm in Yorkshire qualifies her to give advice on how the rest of the world should live.'

He winced and proffered a cigarette, which she refused.

A moment of angry silence followed. But Serena was not one to yield to bad moods and now donned a stoical expression. 'Don't worry, I'm not going to allow it to ruin our day out. We'll just have our cup of tea and go.'

He nodded, then nudged her, trying to make her laugh. 'I see now what you meant about your aunt. I've never met anyone quite so huge.' There was awe in his voice.

Almost back to her previous good form, Serena grinned at him.

Then a look of panic crossed his face. 'You're not thinking of inviting her to come with us? My springs –'

'No, silly!' She elbowed him laughingly. 'If she wouldn't fit through the door of a train carriage she sure as heck won't squeeze in your motorcar.'

'And here's me thinking you were exaggerating.' Arthur shook his head in amazement.

'I knew you did! That's why I just had to bring you here and show you. My God, I couldn't believe it when they manhandled her in with the bicycles and baskets of livestock as if it were normal. I nearly died from embarrassment!'

Beata watched and listened as they continued to denigrate her aunt, speaking quite openly as if the child were not even there. Then Serena turned to address her directly, her air conspiratorial. 'I'll bet you kids make all sorts of jokes about her too, don't you, Beata? Come, share some with us. I won't tell.'

271

Beata shrank, not wanting to answer. Though the visitors had their backs to the doorway, she could see Aunt Kit on her way back with a tray of teacups.

'Come on!' A devilish gleam in her brown eyes, Serena prompted the child. 'I'll bet you don't know anyone else so enormously fat.'

'Not outside a zoo, anyway,' chuckled the man.

Serena had warmed to her subject and was shaking in mirth over some new witticism.

Using her eyes, Beata urged the pair to look behind them, but they remained oblivious until it was too late.

All at once aware of Kit's presence, Serena looked uncomfortable and began to twitter excuses.

'Don't bother, I heard every word.' The hurt in Kit's breast was now overtaken by anger. Did they not consider it enough to rob her of what had been meant to be a wonderful afternoon, that they had to callously insult her too? Still smarting over the previous exchange, she was now absolutely furious at what she had overheard, though she controlled it well, sitting down and pouring the tea to all intents and purposes quite calm.

Serena watched her aunt's hand tremble under the weight of the teapot and experienced a twinge of regret for this poor unfortunate woman. 'Aunt Kit, we didn't mean anything it was just – well, you have to admit it was funny, you having to travel in the guard's van.'

Kit spoke quietly, concentrating on filling the cups. 'I hope you'll consider it so hilarious when you're my age and have the same problem.'

To cover her shame, Serena was flippant. 'Oh, come, we meant no harm, I was told you appreciate a joke!'

'Then I trust you'll appreciate my little joke when you find you've been left nothing in my will.' Kit glanced up from her pouring. 'Aye, stopped laughing now, haven't you? First thing tomorrow I'm off to my solicitor's to change it.'

Serena looked only slightly chastened. 'Do as you must, but I repeat, it was merely a joke.'

'It wasn't an amount to be sniffed at, you know! I was leaving you the entire lot. But not now. Oh, no.' Kit enjoyed the look of puzzlement this invoked on her daughter's face. 'I can see you're trying to work out why a fat old aunt whom you've hardly ever met would want to leave you all her money.'

Serena shrugged, then started to rise, announcing casually as she did so, 'It's hardly of interest now you've changed your mind. Come, Arthur, let's not waste any more of the sunshine.'

It was this total lack of concern, the air of boredom on her daughter's face that finally provoked Kit into taking the path she had avoided for so long, one which she would never have taken had she not been so maddened by anger. 'I wonder, would you have made such a joke at your mother's expense? Called her fat and ugly?'

Serena pursed her red lips. 'That's hardly –'

'No, I'd really like to know!' It was not a maternal way to act, but suddenly Kit wanted her daughter to realize the depth of her hurt and the only way for this was by learning the truth. 'Would you have made fun of your mother like that?'

Serena tilted her chin impatiently. 'No, I have to admit –'

'But you thought you'd make me the butt of your humour because I'm just your silly, fat old aunt. Well, I've got news for you, I'm not your aunt, I'm your mother and I *am* hurt!'

Serena went pale and for a second could utter no response. Then – 'That's a pretty low way to get back at me!'

'I'm not getting back at you. I want you to know the truth! I was the one who gave birth to you, who was forced to give you away because –'

'It's a damned lie! Mother told me the dreadful tales you used to make up to get yourself out of trouble.'

Kit was enraged. 'Do you honestly imagine I'd lie about something as important as this? I'll bet you've never seen a copy of your birth certificate, have you?'

No, she had not. Smitten by horror, Serena's mind raced through all her memories, recalling her parents' reluctance to let her handle any official document even into adulthood. It was they who had organized her naturalization papers – had even acquired a passport for her so that if she wished to travel in the future it was all in hand. Even after they died she had never dreamed of examining the private papers in their desk, to question her heritage, had chosen simply to believe what they had told her, assuming it to have been done from the overprotective urge that they had always displayed towards their only daughter.

Aunt Kit was about to disabuse her of this notion.

'Why do you think Amelia never had any other children? It was because she and Albert couldn't have any! So they took mine! Took you away when you were only this big!' With piteous gesture, she held her hands barely apart to show how small her baby had been when ripped from her arms.

'Shut up!' Horrified, Serena covered her ears.

273

'Look in the mirror!' urged Kit, forgetting that she was lined and grey. 'We've got the same hair, the same –'

'I'm nothing like you!' Serena's voice was filled with disgust and loathing at being likened to such a gross spectacle of obesity.

'Like it or lump it, it's the truth!'

'No! I don't want to hear it! Take me away!' Serena screamed almost hysterically at her male companion, whose face showed he was regretting his involvement with her. When she dashed from the house and along the rutted track he moved swiftly afterwards.

Kit's voluptuous breast was still rising and falling when the sound of a car engine ripped through her thoughts, taking Serena out of her life again. Oh, dear God, dear God, what had she done?

During all this Beata had sat there frozen to her chair and was still too shocked to move.

Only now did Kit's devastated gaze fall upon the little girl, glistening with furious tears. 'Eh dear . . . what have I gone and done, Beat?'

Moved by her air of poignancy, Beata came immediately to Kit's side and gripped her hand.

Kit's expression was fast turning from one of anger to despair, her voice hollow. 'I think I can hear Old William coming.'

Beata craned her neck to look anxiously through the window. Sure enough, a farm cart was wending its way up the track.

'Best get yourself off, love.'

'I don't have –'

'Just go to your party, Beat!' A tormented Kit squeezed her eyelids shut. 'Please . . .' Then she opened them again, trying hard to convey sincerity. 'Have a grand time, love.'

Wanting to appear reluctant, though in truth desperate to get away, Beata forced herself to creep towards the door. 'If you're sure. See you tomorrow, then, Aunt.'

Kit performed a weary nod, then called, 'And, Beat!'

The child turned.

'No need to mention any of what's just gone on to your father.'

Beata gave a nod, then finally left, closing the door as quietly as she could.

Alone, Kit was suddenly overwhelmed by pain and nausea. Whether or not it was the argument with her daughter that had caused it she did not know, but it seemed real enough, a bubble of bile forming in her throat. Overtaken by dizziness and grasping items of furniture to aid her passage, she made for the bed by the fireplace. Perhaps if she were to lie down for a moment it

274

would go away ... though the awful scene with her daughter never would.

As Aunt Kit had requested, upon arriving in York Beata made no mention of what had occurred to anyone, and as the thrill of the party took hold it soon left her mind altogether. Her siblings were as delighted to see her again as she was them, and even more pleased with the fancy dress costumes they were wearing. These had been made by various aunts, though obviously some collusion had taken place for the Kilmaster children found themselves representing the League of Nations, each sporting a different national dress and going on to share first prize.

Aunt Charlotte too had made no small contribution, helping their father to string his house with bunting, acting as waitress to the children, ready to dole out jelly and custard, attending to their every whim and thoroughly enjoying herself.

'You look as if you've won a hundred pounds.' Seated next to her in the evening sunshine, the celebrations still going on, this was Probyn's way of paying compliment to her rosy cheeks and sparkling eyes, unable to bring himself to say she looked pretty, for Charlotte would never be that.

'Oh, I haven't had such a good time in ages! And it's lovely for the children to be with their brothers and sisters again.' She smiled at him warmly.

'Aye, if only for the day.' He smiled back. 'I wish it could be permanent.'

Charlotte's voice turned poignant. 'If only Grace could be here too.'

'Yes, she'd no doubt be playing the piano for that lot.' He gestured at the couples dancing along the street to the music of a gramophone. 'Or dragging one of us up for a jig.'

'I haven't danced in ages.' Charlotte sounded wistful. 'In fact the last time was with Grace.'

Both smiled at fond memories.

Then Probyn asked, 'Do you think she'd mind if her husband were to dance with her best friend?'

'I think she'd approve greatly!' Wearing a broad smile, at least as broad as her tiny mouth could deliver, Charlotte allowed him to lead her into the middle of the street to join the revellers.

Unaware of how risky was this bodily contact for a man who had been deprived for months, the children seemed to enjoy the sight of their father and aunt dancing, and went to twirl around them, calling encouragement for them to repeat the episode again and again. It was their attitude which set the idea working in Probyn's head, causing him to become smilingly thoughtful as he danced. Out of breath and his legs aching, after only a couple of sessions he begged to be allowed to return to his seat, and Charlotte sat beside him, remaining there until it was time to go home.

'Aw, do we have to go to bed?' wailed the children as the tables were cleared and carried indoors along with the chairs, the litter-strewn pavement swept. 'It's still daylight.'

'It might be light but it's past ten o'clock,' said Probyn. 'Come on now, don't sulk. You'll be back in your own little beds for the night.'

'Squashed up, you mean,' grumbled Maddie. 'I have a bed of me own at Aunt Rhoda's.'

'Oh, you'll be pleased to go back there tomorrow then, madam?' teased her father.

She sought to placate him. 'No, I'd rather stay here.'

He patted her. 'Well, it might not be long as you think before we can arrange it. Kiss Aunt Charlotte good night and then up to bed.'

Receiving the younger ones' kisses, Charlotte then turned to Probyn. 'Thanks for a wonderful day, Probe.'

'Nay, you've helped in the making of it, I only put up some Union Jacks.'

'You risked your life dancing with my big clod-hopping feet,' replied Charlotte, 'and I truly appreciate it.'

'They're not that big.' It was clearly a lie.

Charlotte planted a kiss on his cheek. 'You'd go well in the diplomatic service, Probe. Good night!'

'Why don't you come next Sunday for your tea?' blurted Probyn, all at once lifted by her affectionate gesture. 'If you've nothing more important to do.'

Noting something different in the way he addressed her, Charlotte turned to look at him, studying his face. 'Thank you ... I'd like that.'

Probyn said he would look forward to it, and suddenly for him next Sunday could not come quickly enough.

The following day, his children went back to their respective foster parents, each with mixed emotions. For Beata, it was a confusing time; still blighted by the tragedy of her mother's death, she was also happy that her father, whom she adored, had given her half a crown for her birthday, with which she had bought a book. Clutched tightly against the jarring of the cart on which she travelled, it was blue with gold lettering and amongst its stories was 'The Little Match Girl', which she intended to read to her aunt this evening.

Thanking the carter who had given her a lift, Beata scampered into Aunt Kit's house, calling, 'I'm back, Aunt!' – full of things to tell Kit about yesterday's street party. 'Ooh, sorry, I didn't mean to wake you.' She stopped abruptly at the sight of Kit still in bed with her eyes half open and her mouth ajar. But then she saw that her aunt was fully clothed and not in the bed at all but merely upon it. The fire was out too, and there was the most awful smell as if the midden men had been.

Butterflies in her stomach, the book clutched under one arm, the nine-year-old wandered up to make closer inspection, performing a nervous darting motion with her fingers to encounter a hand that was only faintly warm. When the hand slipped from the bed to dangle lifelessly the shock of it caused her to back away, heart thudding. She had retreated almost to the door when someone opened it and barged into her, causing her to scream in fright.

'Gee, I'm so sorry!' After a distressful night Serena had come back to interrogate Kit but was now forced to accommodate the child. 'I didn't mean to startle –' She broke off and followed Beata's pointing finger to the one who lay by the inert fire.

Relieved at having someone older to take charge, the anxious child looked to the woman for help, but Serena appeared to have been rendered dumb. She just stood there, glued to the spot, still wearing her summer hat and gloves, her jaw hanging loose. Several moments passed. With no advice forthcoming, Beata knew that something had to be done. Despite her own upset, she laid her book on a chair and moved to the door.

To reach the nearest cluster of buildings meant a lengthy dash across a field and by the time she had arrived and knocked at the door of a cottage it took her a while to catch her breath, allowing the woman who opened it to forestall her.

'Your aunt's sent you to see where Old William is, I suppose? I was going to send word after the doctor's gone.' At this same instant the doctor appeared from another room, adding his voice to hers.

'Your father-in-law's a remarkable man, Edna!'

'So it's nothing serious then, doctor?'

'No! Summat nor nowt, as they say. He'll be back at work in a few days.'

'Eh dear,' sighed Edna, half in admiration, half in sorrow, for the old man's youngest son, her husband, had perished during the war, along with their own boys. 'He'll outlive us all.' She turned to Beata. 'Oh well, there's your answer, my dear. Tell your aunt sorry about the inconvenience.'

Finally allowed to speak, Beata panted, 'She's . . . Could the doctor come to our house, please?' And her fearful gestures at the building across the field prompted swift action.

Alas, upon seeing Kit there was nothing to be done except to certify death and to placate the tearful child.

During all this Serena had remained incapable of speech, merely hovering about in the background as if trying to dissociate herself. But as the eldest, she was the one to whom the doctor spoke now. 'Are you related to Mrs Treasure?' Dressed in hat and gloves, she could just be a visitor.

The other's reply slow in coming, Edna supplied the answer. 'This is Kit's niece, come from America – eh, she was so excited at seeing you! What an awful time for her to go.'

The doctor proceeded in kindly tone. 'I'm sorry. Your aunt appears to have suffered a massive stroke, and not very long ago.'

Still tearful, Beata glanced at Serena for reaction, wondering whether to correct Edna over the relationship. But then the discovery that Aunt Kit was Serena's mother had caused such a furore that she considered it wiser to remain silent. Still looking at the tall young woman she waited for her to cry, but her cousin remained dry-eyed.

Gaining little reaction from her, the doctor turned instead to Edna. 'Could I leave everything in your expert hands?'

At her nod, he left.

Whilst Serena remained mute, Beata tendered a question. 'What do we do now, missus? Should I go fetch Father?'

Edna spoke kindly. 'Yes, my dear, but first I must give your aunt the last offices.' She looked questioningly at Serena. 'No disrespect, but she's a bit on the large side for me to manage.'

For the first time Kit's daughter appeared to understand the situation and what was being asked of her. A look of offence crossed her face. 'I'm not doing it!' And she made for the door, leaving it open so that those behind could witness her haughty departure, which was a shame for they might have been more sympathetic had they seen the tears rolling down her cheeks.

Feeling a wave of disgust for this callous treatment of an aunt she had loved so well, Beata bravely offered to assist, though was unsure what it involved.

Praising her, Edna said the two of them would still not be enough. 'Run across and fetch our Dolly whilst I get started. Tell her to fetch my laying-out bag; she'll know what I mean.'

When Beata returned with the well-built farm girl, Edna had already tied a handkerchief around Kit's jaw to keep it closed and had placed pads of damp cotton wool over her eyes. She had paused to wait for help before removing Kit's soiled clothes. It was a great struggle, brute strength needed even to lift one of Kit's legs, but the three of them managed to do this whilst still maintaining her dignity. Working silently and with reverence, they straightened the large limbs and, under cover of an old sheet, washed the body all over.

'You brush your aunt's hair, dear,' Edna advised Beata who, though her stomach squirmed with nerves, began to unpin Kit's plaited hair, a mixture of grey and auburn.

During the brushing there came a jolt of shock at Edna's deft insertion of clean rags into private orifices. Beata quickly averted her eyes, forcing herself to concentrate on the hair and in seconds the embarrassing moment was over and Kit's body was being bound in strong calico from waist to thigh.

A good deal of sweat later, dressed in a white nightgown and socks, her arms folded over her breast and the eye pads and the handkerchief that had bound her jaw removed, Kit looked as if she were merely sleeping.

The countrywoman laid a gentle hand on Beata's shoulder, uttering softly, 'There you are, now you know the proper way to do it. Never forget that even when a person's gone to her Maker her earthly body still needs to be treated with respect.'

With a pile of soiled linen burning in the yard, Edna invited Beata to stay at her house for the night, saying she and Dolly would tend Kit's stock until Old William was back on his feet.

Beata was unsure. 'I should really go and let my family know.'

'Won't that young woman have informed them?' asked Edna. 'She went haring off quick enough.'

Feeling rather resentful of her cousin, Beata shook her head and made childish supposition. 'She'll be back in America by now.'

But, despite her fury over the disclosure that Kit had been her natural mother, and also with the family who had kept this secret from her,

Serena had gone only as far as London, to the hotel in which she had first stayed upon her arrival. Here she was to fester for the next few days, cursing and crying, livid with Kit for dying and robbing her of answers – for not only had she been duped over her mother but the identity of her father too – whilst in Yorkshire a search was being made for her in order to inform her of the funeral arrangements. It was only right that she be there.

It was mere speculation that caused Probyn to suggest that she might be in the capital and he rummaged through Kit's things in order to find the name of the hotel where she had originally stayed. Armed only with this, Kit's solicitor telephoned the hotel and found, amazingly, that she was indeed there. Uttering profound commiserations, he had further invited her to come to his office after the funeral.

Serena was cool. 'Does there have to be a reading? I already know she left me everything.'

Astounded by her callousness, he insisted she come. 'No, there was no stipulation that there had to be a reading but there is a letter I may need to show –'

'Can't you post it?'

'No, I'm afraid I cannot!' The voice was even angrier now. 'Shall we say tomorrow afternoon directly following the funeral? It would be more convenient than arranging two separate visits for every –'

'Very well, I'll be there.' Serena hung up.

Again the Kilmasters gathered to mourn the demise of yet another of their number, though there were few tears left to shed for poor Kit after so many losses, favourite though she might have been. Relieved that Serena had been found and naturally assuming she would be here, they were disturbed when she did not turn up.

Later, before going back to their homes across the county, a number of them were to visit the solicitor's office for the reading of Kit's will.

There was another shock awaiting.

'Well, you've got a nerve!' First into the room, Gwen was astounded to find her American niece already seated here, her gasp of affront echoed by all who accompanied her. The only one not dressed in black, Serena's bright clothes served as a gross insult to the woman who had borne her. 'If you could manage to drag yourself here, why not Kit's funeral?'

Serena ignored Gwen, in fact ignored all her relatives, directing

280

her brown eyes straight ahead across the huge mahogany desk at the solicitor on the other side of it.

'Mr Shadwell, if everyone's here may we now begin?'

'I asked you a question!' roared Gwen, poking Serena in the shoulder. 'You stuck up little madam!'

'I didn't go because I chose not to,' came the terse reply.

'No, but you're here to see how much she's left you!' retorted Gwen. 'Well, to my mind, anyone who hasn't the decency to attend their own mother's funeral doesn't deserve a penny!'

There was a horrified intake of breath from the others, all eyes upon Serena.

Remarkably, she stayed composed, still not looking at Gwen even now.

'Didn't know that, did you, clever-clogs?' Oblivious to the young woman's indifference and the others' hissed requests for discretion, Gwen could not be silenced. 'Kit wasn't your aunt but your mother!'

Serena's already strained features became even more taut, as did her grip upon the handle of her lizard-skin bag. 'She was *not* my mother.'

'Oh, yes she was!' Gwen formed a knowing sneer.

Her niece heaved. 'If you are referring to the fact that the person in question gave birth to me,' she could not bring herself to utter Kit's name, felt only contempt for the woman who had abandoned her at birth, 'then I have already been made aware of it by the person herself.'

Gwen was flabbergasted, as were the rest of her kin. 'What – *Kit* told you?'

There was a curt nod.

'When?' enquired Probyn, as shocked as anyone.

Serena deigned to glance at him coldly. 'Does it really matter? A couple of days ago, if you must know.'

Things were falling into place now. Kit's neighbour had mentioned that Serena had been there but had inexplicably rushed away. They had assumed this sudden evacuation to be out of grief, but obviously a row had occurred between mother and daughter that had upset Kit so much it had killed her. There were murmurings now between the relatives as the solicitor asked for calm.

Dumbfounded, it took a moment for Gwen to form her words, which emerged as a reproachful hiss. 'You *knew* she was your mother and still you didn't even bother to atten –'

'She was *not* my mother and I'll thank you not to refer to

her as such! A mother is there to cherish her children, not to desert them.'

'She didn't desert you, you daft little twerp!' An angry Gwen bent over the seated figure to spit her reply. 'Kit sacrificed her own needs to give you a better life!'

Wearing a look of distaste, Serena averted her face to escape the smell of the old lady's camphor-ridden apparel.

But Gwen was undeterred. 'Heaven knows I've had to take our Kit to task over the years but all credit to her in this instance!'

For once Gwen's long-suffering victims were forced to praise her defence of Kit. Someone had to represent their much-loved aunt in the face of such disdain.

'She thought the world of you,' scolded Probyn. 'It broke her heart to give you up.'

Others were too emotional to speak, though their angry tears sufficed as condemnation.

With all against her, a red-faced Serena beseeched the solicitor, 'Is it really necessary for me to be here?'

'Well, as you are the major beneficiary –'

'*What?*' It came as a combined screech from Kit's relatives.

'*Please*, may we just get on with it?' begged Serena.

After an interval of embarrassed shuffling the solicitor requested that everyone compose themselves. Whilst they were doing this he handed over Kit's letter to Serena, which she dropped unopened into her bag. Thereafter, the uncomfortable man attempted to read out the will as quickly as he could.

What he had said earlier turned out to be the truth; apart from a few modest bequests to her surviving sisters, nieces and nephew, the bulk of Kit's estate went to Serena. Immediately the reading was over Kit's daughter rose. 'If that's all . . .'

'Isn't it enough?' scoffed Gwen.

Eyes upon Serena's face, knowing that her composed façade must surely conceal a maelstrom of emotion, Probyn sought to put himself in the young woman's place. To learn at such a late stage that the folk you thought of as Mother and Father were impostors must be a dreadful blow. Everyone here had been party to the deception and one of them could at least extend sympathy. 'Serena, we know very little about your real father but if there's any way we can –'

'I've heard all I want to know.' Serena's wrath was not merely at the Kilmasters; her father's kin had been equally deceitful; she would not be seeing them again either. Oh dear God, what was she to do now, this person without identity, this nobody?

But she would not show these people how much they had hurt her. About to make a proud exit, not the slightest crack in her features to betray her agony, she paused only long enough to inform the solicitor, 'I shall, of course, be putting everything up for sale. I want no further contact with this family – and I shall entrust you to make sure that they take nothing more than the items left to them.'

Gwen made a loud interjection and would have hit Serena given half the chance but her nephew held her back.

'You can send the proceeds to me in America,' concluded Serena, then stalked out, leaving a collection of astonished faces behind her.

SEVENTEEN

'Well, I don't reckon we'll see much of her again,' sighed Probyn to Clem and Augusta after relaying the episode when he got home. 'What a to-do.' He looked sadly at Beata who, since Kit's death, had been forced to remain here though this could not continue. 'Aunt Meredith says you can go and live with her for the time being. I'll put you on the train tomorrow. With a bit of luck it won't be for long.' His mind had wandered to Charlotte's impending visit, which it had been wont to do even through all the recent upset. The sooner he proposed his idea, the better for all.

'So did Aunt Kit leave you nowt, Father?' asked Clem.

'Aye, she left me the portrait of my sister Beata. I'd better be quick and collect it or Serena will snaffle that too.'

'But, no money?'

'Oh, I wasn't expecting anything. No . . . no.' Probyn tweaked at his trouser leg. Again his sad blue-grey eyes came up to take in Beata. 'Though I thought she might have left our Beata a bob or two. She was more of a daughter to her than Serena ever was. Eh, if you could have heard the things she said, Clem . . .' He sucked in his breath and shook his head to project disgust. 'Shocking, it was.'

Beata wondered if she should say anything about Kit having been about to change her will, but then decided not to. What good would it do now? There had been no mention of the Villa Garcia thimble that Aunt Kit had promised would be hers. But this did not upset her as much as the loss of her aunt.

She came to stand at her father's knee. 'I'll miss Aunty Kit.'

'So will I, deary,' he answered quietly, pulling her onto his lap in a rare show of tenderness. 'We all will. But Aunt Meredith'll make you welcome, so don't worry.'

After waving Beata off on the train to her new home, Probyn felt rather despondent upon returning to work, though his mood was soon bolstered at the thought of his meeting with Charlotte in a few days' time.

Following his aunt's demise and all the unpleasantness that had followed, it was a rather different atmosphere on Sunday from the gaiety of the Victory celebrations. Nevertheless, Probyn greeted his guest warmly when she arrived.

Charlotte was at first surprised to find everyone else absent, though Probyn hastened to tell her that Gussie and Clem, who were both out with friends, would be home for tea.

At her look of relief, he guessed what was going through her mind; it might appear odd to the neighbours that he had invited a woman to his house, albeit a friend of long-standing.

That it might appear equally suspicious to his son and daughter Probyn had not even considered, and, at the sight of their startled faces when they returned for tea and found Aunt Charlotte sitting next to him on the sofa chatting perfectly naturally, he was driven to blush.

'I did tell you your aunt was coming.' He said it almost defensively, coming to his feet.

Yes, he had, but there was something he had not told them. Something had changed here. Brother and sister glanced at each other.

Then, realizing that he wore a look of disapproval, Clem shook it away. 'Yes, I'd just forgotten, what with the funeral. Hello, Aunt Charlotte.' Augusta too reverted to her normally friendly attitude.

Slightly abashed, Charlotte greeted them both warmly, any further discomfort wiped away by the serving of a lovely tea, which Probyn had prepared himself.

Later, with his son and daughter washing up in the scullery, Charlotte leaned over to whisper to Probyn. 'Why do I feel guilty?'

'Don't worry, you're not on your own.' He too spoke with lowered voice. 'I'm sorry, I should have arranged for them to be here when you arrived. I never thought how it might look. I'm just so used to having you around.'

'Like a battered old piece of furniture,' smiled Charlotte.

'Stop running yourself down,' he scolded.

'Well, as your Aunt Gwen kindly pointed out, they're not exactly queuing up to marry me.'

'You don't want to take any notice of her! Anyway, I thought it was your choice not to marry after losing George.'

'It was.' Charlotte shrugged.

To Probyn this gesture held significance and he pressed the matter. 'So, you might change your mind then?'

Charlotte skimmed over this, 'Oh, who knows? What about you, Probe?'

Pausing over their task, Augusta and Clem strained to listen, but their father's words were delivered in a tone so hushed that they heard only a muffled murmur.

'I miss Grace terribly . . . but if I thought anybody'd take me I'm sure she'd understand if it meant her children could be back together.'

Charlotte had become wary. His words were loaded with meaning, yet afraid of causing embarrassment to both if she had misunderstood, she merely nodded.

'Then, you don't think it's too soon?'

She weighed her words: 'It would depend on what type of person you were asking.'

This line of conversation was abruptly severed as Clem and Augusta re-entered and sat down.

Brightening, Charlotte set off on a new topic. 'I'll bet there aren't many households where the son washes the pots.'

Clem smiled as he held a taper to the fire, then used it to ignite a cigarette. 'Don't have much choice with a sergeant-major for a father.'

Probyn cast a fond eye in his son's direction. 'It'll do him no harm.'

Clem returned the look of warmth, though his eyes flickered suspiciously as he blew out the taper and laid it on the hearth, wondering over his father's intentions.

Charlotte was wondering too, though she was not to be enlightened, for Probyn's son and daughter seemed loath to leave them alone for the rest of the evening. Even when Augusta finally went to bed Clem stayed behind. On purpose?

Probyn was speculating over this too. Whatever the reason, the young man's intrusion forbade him to ask his question of Charlotte and eventually she was compelled to leave.

Eager to be alone with her, Probyn went to fetch her hat, which lay on the counter in the front room. 'I'll walk you home.'

Bidding good night to Clem, Charlotte followed him, then both moved outside into the balmy evening.

The instant they were on the footpath Probyn wasted no time. 'What I was saying before about remarrying . . .'

Immediately they had left, Clem had rushed to the front room to spy from the window. However, seeing them linger, he now put his ear to the door to try to catch what was said. But in the warm breeze the metal sign squeaked overhead, distorting his father's words, much to his fury. Still awake, Gus too was straining to interpret the muffled voices, nibbling her lip in concern.

But their attempts were foiled as their father took Charlotte's arm and moved off before finishing his question. '. . . Could I expect your approval?'

Charlotte felt her emotions torn. 'Well, I do feel a certain responsibility towards Grace. As I said before, Probe, it would depend on the person you had in mind.'

Did she truly not realize what he was getting at? He paused to look her full in the face, making it as clear as he could. 'The person I have in mind is a most upstanding, respectable woman of impeccable morals. I don't have any qualm that Grace would approve. In fact, she thought the world of this certain person.'

Charlotte finally dared to mouth it. 'You mean me?'

'I don't know anyone else Grace thought as much about.'

'She thought the world of you.' Charlotte smiled sadly.

'Aye, well, I can't marry meself, can I?' he joked.

'I'm very flattered by your offer, Probe.'

Turning away, his smile fading, he resumed his leisurely pace. 'I'll take it that means no, then?'

She hooked her arm through his. 'It means nothing of the sort. I *am* very flattered. I do care a lot about you, Probe . . . though it's only fair to tell you I could never feel the same as I did about George.'

'I didn't expect you to for one minute. I appreciate your honesty. I could never feel about anyone the way I felt for my dear wife. I'm not saying it would only be a marriage of convenience – far from it. I have immense admiration for you, Lottie. You were a good, loyal friend to Grace and the children love you. I'm not a man who needs an unpaid housekeeper, I can look after myself perfectly well –'

'I know,' she touched his hand in fondness, 'I saw how you looked after Grace.'

'– I just hate being without a female companion. It sounds daft, I know, me spending all those years away from home whilst I was in the army. I'd think about her all the time, imagining her going about the house singing and what not, and I can't tell you how marvellous it was to come home to her, knowing her cheery face would always be there to greet me . . . but now it isn't. I still expect her to come in the door, you know.' He suddenly noticed that Charlotte's eyes brimmed with tears. 'Sorry, I didn't mean to cast a shadow.' He let go of her arm whilst she blew her nose, then continued as they walked, 'What I'm trying to say is, I might have twenty years ahead of me and I can't stand the thought of spending it alone. It just horrifies me. You do see?'

'Oh, yes.' She gave a last dab with her handkerchief and put it away. 'You're speaking to someone who knows all about loneliness, Probe. It wasn't so bad when Mother was still alive, but now . . .'

He tightened his grip on the arm that linked his. 'I'm really fond of you, Lottie.'

'And I of you.'

'Yet, you still seem hesitant.' Probyn gave a sad smile.

'Not at the thought of marrying you, dear. I'll be quite happy to accept your proposal.' She saw his mouth begin to widen in pleasure. 'But you must ask the children first.'

Probyn was grinning widely now, not least at the thought of soon being able to rectify his sexual deficit. 'It goes without saying that they'll be as pleased as punch. My, I didn't realize what a grand day it was going to be when I got up this morning!'

'Nevertheless, they might consider it to be rushing things. I won't consent without their permission.'

'You can be assured, I'll ask them,' he said as they reached the main road.

With Charlotte's home not too far away the rest of their journey took no longer than fifteen minutes. Prepared to take his leave of her he wore a hint of mischief.

'Do I get a good night kiss?'

She presented her face, accepting his tender peck on her lips.

Smiling into her tiny emerald eyes, he pressed a final kiss on her cheek, waited until she closed the door on him, then retraced his steps with a happy smile, eager to relay her answer to his children.

But what he had considered to be a *fait accompli* turned out to be nothing of the sort, for, when he reached home, Augusta had come down to join Clem and both wore serious expressions that demanded an answer.

Apart from a quick clearance of throat there was little prevarication. 'This might come as a bit of a surprise to you both but a

288

pleasant one, I hope. Your Aunt Charlotte and I are hoping to be married.'

'Told you!' Clem spun to address his sister.

'Oh, been talking about me, have you?' Probyn donned a cryptic smile.

'Yes, and we don't think it's right. Mother hasn't been gone six months yet!'

'You don't have to tell me that, son,' came the pacific reply. 'I miss her too, you know. I'm not talking about marrying some stranger. Your mother loved Charlotte. Of course it won't be the same sort of marriage your mother and I enjoyed – nobody could take her place – but I'm very fond of Charlotte and I thought you were too.'

'We are!' Clem's temper rose. Now a grown man, he was no longer restrained by the threat of a beating. 'We're not angry at Charlotte, we're angry at you. It's too soon, Father!'

'Before you dismiss this out of hand, consider your brothers and sisters. This would mean that we could all be together again.'

Clem's face showed this was a pathetic excuse. 'I'm saying nowt else, Father. You've heard my opinion.'

A dismayed Probyn wanted to retort that his son should think himself privileged to be allowed an opinion on what was essentially his father's business; but instead he turned to his daughter, a note of pathos in his query. 'What about you, Gus? Do you think I should wait?'

She nodded.

Spirits deflated, Probyn studied his son and daughter for a moment, before deciding further persuasion would be futile. Strange how fate had a knack of turning the tables. Now he knew exactly how his father had felt under the hail of accusation he had suffered on wanting to marry Mrs Carr, Probyn one of the worst objectors. His own mother had been dead much longer than six months yet he had condemned what he saw as his father's callous disregard for her. Well, he had got his comeuppance now.

But that was by the by. It was all very well respecting his children's wishes, but where could he turn now for bodily comfort? It had no bearing that he was forty-six years old and his sexual appetite was not as rampant as it once was, he desperately needed someone in his bed at night. He had hoped it could be Charlotte but that was not to be. And the worst thing about it all was that now he would have to go back and tell her.

* * *

289

Charlotte was disappointed to hear of Clem and Augusta's objections, but was quick to understand their point. 'It is rather soon, Probe. They're still hurting.'

'I'm certain the younger ones would back us,' he told her.

'No, don't press the matter.' She did not share his sense of urgency. 'Maybe in another six months' time . . .'

He nodded uneasily, knowing that his sexual frustration would not allow him to wait, and hoping that Charlotte would not hold him to the proposal.

Studying his pose, a look of recognition came into her tiny green eyes. 'Of course, you might have changed your mind by then.'

'Oh, no –'

'I'd understand.'

'Would you?' He held her gaze. 'Really, Lottie?'

Her cheeks turned pink, and she plucked awkwardly at the smocking on her bodice, but dared to broach the delicate subject. 'I don't live in a convent, Probe. I realized what you meant when you said you needed a female companion. You don't just mean a dancing partner, do you?'

He was taken aback by her reference and merely shook his head.

Grace had confided to her friend years ago that Probyn was a man of lusty appetites. Charlotte had been unsure whether she could cope with this but had been willing to try for the sake of the children she held dear. But with the postponement of an engagement such misgivings were now irrelevant, and just to make sure he did not think that her understanding of this matter extended further than words, she made a firm addition. 'If you're hoping for something occurring between us before we're married I must tell you that I couldn't countenance that, so –'

'Oh, I never even entertained the idea!' He had, though. Even whilst not physically attracted to her, he had pictured a naked Charlotte and wondered what it would be like to engage his body with hers. There was no eroticism in the image.

'If in a year you find somebody else you'd rather marry, some-body who Grace would approve of, then I don't mind stepping aside.'

He took her hand and squeezed it. 'No, I shall honour my proposal, Charlotte. But until the children alter their view, I'm happy for us to remain just friends.'

*   *   *

290

Noble gestures were all very well, but they did not solve his immediate frustration. Even in possession of the funds, he had never been one to visit prostitutes.

Unexpectedly, the answer was to come through his work. His organizational skills required at a record office in the north-east, he initially bemoaned the fact of being sent there, anxious that it would keep him away from home for several days. But Clem and Augusta, pleased that it would mean getting him away from Aunt Charlotte, said they could manage. Hence, he finally went off to catch his train.

Always keen to inspect the fairer sex, his current frustration caused his eyes to linger more wistfully over breast and buttock today as he waited on the cold platform, knowing he was merely torturing himself but unable to stop. Even had he been able to tear his eyes away the thoughts would still be with him.

The train chugged in, he got on board and settled back with a newspaper as the engine lurched into motion again.

Once the last page had been read, though, there was still a long way ahead. He wriggled into a more reclining position, eyes half-closed, head lolling with the motion of the train.

'Excuse me, could you just help me get my bag down? I can't quite reach.'

Coming alert, he stood and helped the woman retrieve her bag.

'Thanks, I just need to get something out of it then you can put it straight back, if you'd be so kind.' Her voice held the slightly melodic accent of the north-east. 'There we are! Why, thanks awfully.' She handed back the bag, which he replaced on the luggage rack.

'Don't mention it.' Returning the young woman's smile, Probyn sank back into his seat, thinking what lovely dark eyes she had.

And then it came to him. The journey that a moment ago had seemed so irksome now assumed great portent. His memory jerked by the simple act of doing this woman a favour, he knew exactly where he could get what he needed without having to promise matrimony. Suddenly the rackety-rack of the carriage wheels seemed not so monotonous after all. *Got-to-get-there! Got-to-get-there! Got to get there!*

Having had ample time to plan his strategy during the journey, it was a different matter to put this into action, taking almost as much courage to knock on Eliza Crump's door as to go into battle. With six sisters he had always known how to get on with women, but Eliza was very different from the well-brought-up Kilmaster girls. Such shamelessness would normally repulse him, and yet it was this very thing that lured him to her – at one point during his train journey he had been forced to place a newspaper on his lap to cover his embarrassment as his imaginings became all too vivid. And now here he was standing outside her door.

Even as he prepared to knock he felt it might be a mistake. She could be married again by now. But he would never know unless he asked. He lifted the iron door-knocker and rapped.

She was astonished but pleased to see him, and at first speechless.

'Hello, Mrs Crump. If I've called at an inconvenient moment I can go –'

'No, no, I'm just that surprised!' Without his uniform the RSM did not look so imposing, just another overweight, middle-aged man in a shabby suit, and yet his gaze could still hypnotize. She could not tear her eyes away. 'Why, Probyn Kilmaster, I never thought to see you again.'

Picturing himself running away from her clutches like a terrified virgin, he quickly chased away the image and explained that his work had brought him to the area. 'I arrived this afternoon and once I'd settled into my lodgings I felt at a loose end. It's funny being in a stranger's house, isn't it? You feel a bit awkward. So, I suddenly thought, why, Mrs Crump lives only a short train ride away, I'll go out after tea and pay my respects. It is still Mrs Crump, by the way, isn't it?'

'Aye, it is.' During his explanation a knowing smirk had come over her face. 'So, you've come to see if I've any wardrobes want shifting, have you?'

He gave an awkward laugh.

'You'd best come in then – and "Eliza" will do.'

Inside, she took his hat and showed him into the parlour. 'How's Grace these days?'

He was momentarily sombre. 'She died six months ago.'

'Oh, I'm really sorry.' Eliza's commiseration appeared genuine. 'She was a nice lass.'

'Yes, yes she was.' Don't keep talking about her, he urged Eliza silently, or I'll never be able to go through with this. She detested you. Trying to block Grace from his mind, he injected his tone with brightness. 'But let's not dwell on sad things.'

'No, let's not.' Crooning in sympathetic tone, Eliza came directly to him and bold as brass put her arms around his back and cupped his buttocks. 'Let's just get on with what you really came for.'

He looked startled as she pulled him against her.

'We both know you didn't come here just to pay your respects.' Her black eyes were laughing.

Already aroused by her brazenness, he spoke huskily. 'Your children . . . ?'

'At their aunty's. Don't worry, they're not likely to barge in on us – but just in case they do we'd better go somewhere more discreet.' And she led him upstairs. He could not get there quickly enough, tearing off his clothes as he went.

There was no affection in their union, no spiritual soaring as there had been with Grace, it was just two animals mauling at one another, striving for satisfaction, neither caring about giving pleasure to the other, just raw gratification. The first desperate coupling was brief and explosive, but within minutes he was responding again to her urgent grasping – thrust and writhed and squirmed with her for almost an hour, became glued to her with sweat, fell away from her, laid there only long enough to catch his breath, then seized hold again, each fresh liaison taking more and more effort until both were overcome with exhaustion and, finally sated, they reclaimed their individual forms.

He felt wonderful at first: worn out, depleted, but thoroughly rejuvenated.

Until she purred lasciviously, 'I always knew you'd be a goer. You were wasted on that sick little wife of yours.'

He felt dirty then, disloyal, treacherous. 'I'd better be going. Don't want to miss my train.' Abruptly, he rolled from the bed.

Eliza did not stop him but lay there watching him don each article of clothing, her inspection causing him to self-consciously suck in his paunch. Only when he was fully dressed and waiting to go did she rise and slip into her own clothes.

'When can I expect the pleasure of Mr Kilmaster's company again?'

'I'm not sure I'll be able to –'

'Don't play the hiley-ho with me!' She chuckled knowingly as she fastened the last of her buttons. 'You'll be back for more.'

And, of course, he was, the very next night, and the one after that too, grinding himself into her as if there were no tomorrow – which there was not, at least not for them, for tomorrow he'd be going home. Maybe it was just as well; at his age he wouldn't be able to maintain such virility. It had been wonderful, though –

would serve to keep him going for a month or two, and with a bit of luck the record office might send him up here again in the not-too-distant future.

He was dressed and ready to go. 'Well, I've really –' He broke off, ending his sentence with a rolling hand movement.

'Enjoyed yourself?' Eliza looked amused. 'Yes, I got the impression you had. It's all right, you know; you can say it.'

'I don't want you to think I'm just here for that,' grinned Probyn, for Eliza was an amusing companion too, even if her humour was a little on the bawdy side. And she was a good listener. During intervals between their rabid lovemaking she had coaxed his troubles from him and he had poured them out, telling her of his aim to bring his family back together again. 'You have got other attributes.'

'Pleased to hear it.' She held her head coquettishly.

Funnily enough, he did not feel the least attraction for her, other than sexual, and he experienced no sense of loss in saying, 'It's a nuisance that we live so far apart. Maybe I could call on you again if I'm up this way?'

'Maybe, but of course there's an easier solution. I could move down to York.'

His expression turned to shock as he envisaged his children's faces should Eliza come to call on him. 'Well, yes, that would make it easier but it'd be a huge upheaval for you.'

'What's up, don't you want me to come?'

'I'm not saying that! I was thinking more about the cost.'

'What about the cost of you having to travel up here by train to see me?'

He had not intended such a journey to be at his own expense. 'Well, I just thought I could come if the record office needed me to –'

'You mean you just thought you'd use me as a convenience while you were here,' cognized Eliza.

'No!'

'Yes!' It came as a bark. 'Well, you thought wrong, mister. I'm not here to be used.'

He felt only slight guilt; it had, after all, been her own brazen attitude that had instigated this. 'I'm sorry, Eliza, I thought you felt the same as I do, that you were just enjoying yourself!'

'I was! And I hope to continue doing so on a regular basis.'

He looked totally confused. 'You've stumped me now.'

'You're a widower with seven kiddies, I'm a widow with three, do I have to spell it out?'

'*Marry* you?'

'Well, don't sound so thrilled!'

'Sorry! It's not that . . . I'm just . . .' A puddle of doom had formed in the pit of his stomach.

'Think about it,' Eliza told him. 'Where else are you going to get satisfaction like I give you?'

'Nowhere.' That was a fact. He went hard at the mere thought of what she did to him. But wedlock was a sacred thing. How shallow was the man who promised matrimony purely to receive sexual favour?

'And you said you'd like to see your children back together again.'

He nodded, still in a daze.

'Well then! What's your objection?'

'None really . . .' What the hell had he got himself into? 'It's just, I'm not sure I could afford –'

'You mentioned you got an army pension.'

'Yes, but I doubt it would stretch to –'

'Didn't you tell me you used to work at a colliery?'

'Before the war, aye.'

'Then go back to it!'

He had painted himself into a corner. 'I suppose it would pay more than I'm getting . . .'

She held him in suspense. He looked at her for answer.

'I'm just waiting to hear what your next excuse will be.' It sounded like a challenge.

He didn't really want to marry her, but she made him feel guilty at using her like a whore; that she acted like one was immaterial, it was what he felt that counted and at this moment he felt dishonourable. Weighing up what she had said, he saw that she was right in more than one respect: he would have sex on a regular basis and someone to mother his children. And yet . . . a niggling voice warned him he could be making a dreadful mistake. Realizing that she had not yet blocked every escape route, he made one last stand. 'Eliza, I haven't been completely honest. I've asked someone else to marry me.'

The dark-features pursed in expectation.

'But the children objected, said it was too soon after their mother's death.'

'What happened to her?'

'Charlotte? She's said she'll wait.'

'Ah, I see! *Wait* being the operative word here. You're not getting

295

into her drawers so you've used me as a surrogate wife till you're allowed to wed the better one.'

'It wasn't like that at all!' He hated Eliza's knack of twisting everything. 'Charlotte said if I found someone else I'd rather marry she'd stand aside. I'm just saying that if the children objected to me marrying her whom they know well, they're going to object to you too.'

'Not necessarily.' Her attitude became blasé now. 'They don't have to know about me yet. I never said I minded waiting.' She sashayed up to him, her dark eyes licentious. He felt her warm breath upon his mouth and her fingers sneaking into his trousers. 'Would another six months be long enough, do you think?'

He felt himself weakening. 'I couldn't be sure until the time was right.'

'Well, until it is, you're quite welcome to call whenever you feel the need.' And she stuck her tongue into his mouth.

It was this and the expert movement of her hand that proved his downfall. Vouching to make her his wife as soon as was decently possible, he fell on top of her on the fireside rug, their merger taking him dangerously close to missing his train.

Helping him some minutes later with his panicked buttoning, Eliza finally allowed him to leave, but sought to ensure that she had his full compliance. 'Remember now, Probe, I'm not just here to be used. I'll hold you to your promise.'

Able to fathom the motives of others, he was well aware that Eliza was only marrying him for a better life, but even now he chose to ignore his own judgement; felt unchivalrous for using her. Though he gave firm reply, there was little joy in the notion. 'I'm a man of my word.'

With her kiss on his cheek he left, bearing the dreadful thought that at some point he was going to have to break the news to the lovely Charlotte.

Upon coming back to York he felt overwhelmed with guilt at the way he had allowed Eliza to manipulate him. How on earth was he going to tell poor Lottie he was going to marry someone else? Worst of all was the thought of what Grace would have said at this callous disregard for her friend simply because Charlotte had failed to meet his needs.

Drawn to his wife's grave, he wandered through the large iron gateway of the cemetery and headed up the avenue of lime trees, senses heightened by the quietude of the place, the trilling of a chaffinch, the rustling of a squirrel in the grass. Finally he came almost to the upper boundary of the cemetery.

It took him a moment to find Grace. Since last he had visited, the wooden cross had been replaced by an Imperial War Graves Commission headstone, a whole collection of these gleaming white slabs dotted about the sprawling acres. In today's sunlight the effect was dazzling. Only upon retracing his steps did he find the name Bradley, the name of the soldier with whom his wife was buried.

First ripping a few stray weeds from the plot, he rose and looked down at the earth, strangely enough thinking not of Grace but of all the thousands of soldiers who had fallen.

Eventually, though, he was compelled to explain his actions to her, speaking not out loud but in his mind. Don't think that because I've chosen to remarry it means I've stopped loving you, because it doesn't. I miss you, Gobbie. I'd give anything to have you here. But you're not here, and I need . . . well, you know what I need. That's the only reason I'm doing this, plus the fact that the children need a mother. I can't farm them out for ever – besides I want them back with me. I miss them almost as much as I miss you. I know what you thought of Eliza. I have to agree she is a bit, well, blowsy. But as far as I can see her own children are well cared for and I think she'll look after ours too. If I didn't I'd never even contemplate marrying her. We've talked about the children's religion – he didn't say *our* religion; he had only ever become a Catholic for Grace, and a poor one at that – and I've told her they must continue being brought up in their mother's faith.

He took a short pause for reflection before continuing. I'm sorry for leading Charlotte on. You know I'd never hurt her for the world.

Tell *her* that, he heard Grace accuse him. Well, he would, this very evening. He had always faced up to things and it was unfair to keep her dangling.

But *how* should I tell her, Gobbie? Do I mention Eliza, or do I just say I've decided against marrying full stop? It was not out of cowardice that he prevaricated but out of concern for Charlotte's feelings. How much worse would she feel knowing he had chosen that common creature over her? He hoped he could make up his mind before tonight. Issuing last words of love to his wife, he wandered back along the shady avenue of limes and went home.

*   *   *

Attempting to simplify matters he tested the ground with Clem and Augusta, telling them again of his need to marry. Again, they said it was too soon, this giving him the ammunition to face Charlotte.

'You could be waiting for years, Charlotte,' he explained sadly. 'I think ... well ...' he cocked his head with an expression of discomfort, 'it might be best if we called off our plans, for all our sakes.'

Charlotte showed no sign of the devastation he had feared. 'Oh well, worse things happen in life.'

Gratified that she had taken it so well, he vouched, 'I'll always value your friendship though.'

'And I yours, Probe.' She smiled to show there was no ill feeling.

Probyn wondered if she would have been so charitable had she known about Eliza whom, over the months between then and December, he was to visit only once – though this did not seem to worry Mrs Crump, who entertained him with gusto, confident that she had him.

That Christmas, the younger children were not to come home. Having taken so long to settle in but having now found a niche in their new families it was decided not to disrupt them. Afraid that this could mean they would be unwilling to come back to him when he married, Probyn consulted his eldest son and daughter yet again about his urgent need for matrimony, hoping it might be third time lucky. But no, it turned out to be third light, and whilst not literally shot down he was made well aware of their disapproval.

Becoming slightly vexed by Clem and Augusta's attitude, he decided not to consult them again. He must take hold of his own future, and, after spending the final hours of 1919 in quiet celebration with his son and daughter, Probyn determined to carry out his New Year's resolution that coming weekend.

Looking back, he could not remember causing such astonishment to so many people since marrying a Catholic – astonished himself even. Having rarely acted on impulse since his youth, he now went overboard, first travelling to South Yorkshire where he acquired the more lucrative post of overseer in a colliery yard; next going northwards and announcing to Eliza that he had purchased the licence and they would wed that very day, and informing her three surprised offspring that this stranger was to be their new father; finally, going back to York to hand in his resignation and to tell an astounded Clem and Augusta that their objections had been overruled, he was married and that was that.

'I want no recriminations,' he told them sternly. 'No more

objections about it being too soon. It's almost a year now since your dear mother passed away and she'd be the first to understand why I've had to do this. Now, you might remember Eliza from when we lived up north, or maybe you don't, but, anyway, she's a nice woman and she'll take care of us. I've had to leave her behind for the time being, she'll join us when she's packed up. We're going back to Denaby –'

Clem opened his mouth.

'Shush!' His father pointed a finger, then continued as if uninterrupted. 'There's accommodation waiting and a job – one for you too, Clem, if you want it. All that's left to do is to gather your brothers and sisters back together and we can be a family again.'

EIGHTEEN

Letters were sent out to the foster parents, informing them of the situation and giving instructions for Probyn's children to be sent back to Layerthorpe. There was much reluctance to let them go from aunts who had taken a great shine to them, but Probyn was insistent that all must come. He wanted his children back.

The only one to mar her father's plans, Augusta decided to remain in York, not out of any sense of disapproval – though she did still hold the view that her father had remarried much too soon – but because she had no wish to give up her well-paid job at Rowntrees, there being no equivalent near Denaby Main. Only because her absence would lessen the overcrowding that was bound to occur with the combination of the two families, did Probyn reluctantly agree, though he made her swear to visit them regularly. This she was happy to do, and was there to wave them off when they made their departure from York, a lorryload of belongings having gone ahead. Charlotte had said her goodbyes last night. Relieved that she was still speaking to him after his impromptu marriage, Probyn thought it very forgiving of her and said he would write.

On his way to the station, he turned his head towards the place where the old soldiers normally sat, to issue a last salute. The bench was empty.

After the gracious antiquity of York it was strange returning to the mining village. There were ghosts everywhere: in the memory of family picnics on the Crags; in the polished ebony patches on every street corner, created by generations of miners who had lounged

300

there chatting, now adopting a new poignancy for this old RSM; miners had been dying underground for hundreds of years, but to Probyn this ghostly imprint represented those he had sent to their deaths on the battlefield, he would never be able to walk past it without remembering them.

The removalists were almost done by the time he and his family arrived at the house in Cliff View. With Eliza rattling out orders, telling them exactly where to place the piano et cetera, there was little for her new husband to do but to admire her efficiency.

Traipsing inside, the children inspected their environment. The seven-piece suite was new, their own rather shabby sofa and chairs having been consigned to the tip before leaving. They recognized the piano, the marble clock and one or two of the pictures against the background of flowery wallpaper, but the Staffordshire dogs at each end of the mantel were unfamiliar – in fact most things in the room were unfamiliar, everything meticulously arranged with lace anti-macassars to protect the new armchairs.

Beata had noticed something else too: between two bookends on the sideboard was a collection of leather tomes with gold writing. Closer inspection revealed these to form a set of Shakespeare plays.

'Er! Don't touch, thank you.'

Beata had not been going to touch and felt a sense of injustice as she looked up at the speaker.

Previous to their entry, Eliza had been bustling around with a duster but was now watching Beata with eagle eyes. The rest of Probyn's children weighed her up: her dark hair swept into a bun, the well-built woman wore a smile but it appeared to be one of sufferance for it only went up at one side.

Probyn introduced her. 'Children, I'd like you to meet your new mother.'

Highly excited at learning that she was to have a mother again, Mims had been expecting to see Grace and, presented with this stranger, the innocent four-year-old burst into floods of tears.

'Oh dear, am I that bad?' Eliza chuckled, giving the impression of being quite jolly, but there was also a hint that she would take no nonsense and she made no move to pacify the distressed infant, turning her attention instead to Clem and shaking hands with him.

'Take no notice,' the flame-haired young man advised his stepmother, rather self-consciously for she was bold in her examination. 'She's always like that.'

Probyn sighed and flourished his handkerchief at Mims' sister, motioning for Beata to tend her.

Mims' tears largely ignored, the children were introduced to their stepbrothers and sister. 'Though you probably remember them from when we lived in West Hartlepool,' said Father.

The older ones did, vaguely, though these children had been outside their own circle of friends and the only recognition came from having lived in the same street: Doris, who was the same age as Beata and seemed a nice enough girl, twelve-year-old Edwin, who remained a little aloof, and ten-year-old George, whose tousled hair and askew collar marked him as the harum-scarum type.

After cursory greeting, Eliza said brightly to the children, 'Here, I've made you some sandwiches. Take them out into the yard and get to know each other. I don't want you messing my nice clean house up. Clem, you're old enough to stay, of course.' Her artful comment worked; Clem's resistance already beginning to thaw.

A smiling Probyn watched the younger ones trail outside. 'I don't blame you wanting rid, you must have worked like a Trojan to get it like this so quick.'

She brewed a pot of tea. 'Doris helped – as I shall expect your girls to do.'

'Oh, they're used to it, the lads as well.' He took something from his pocket. 'Have you got a drawing pin?' Given one, he pinned the list to a wall by the fire. 'This is Battalion Orders, tells them what their job of the day is. I've worked it out to include your three.'

Showing approval, Eliza directed him and Clem to the table where plates of sandwiches and pork pie and cake awaited, making forthright comment on the disparity between his lithe frame and Probyn's bulk. 'Eh, you're nothing like your father, Clem, are you? I don't know whether it was wise to lay on all this food. He could do to lose a few inches round his middle.'

Unoffended by her teasing, Probyn delivered a rueful pat to his stomach. 'Aye, that's what happens when you stop marching – Oh, some good news!' He suddenly remembered. 'The army has retained my services as recruiting officer for the area. I shall need to use the front room as an office, if you don't mind?'

Eliza did not mind at all. 'Bit of extra cash won't go amiss. Will you be working at the pit with your father, Clem?'

Probyn replied, 'No, he –'

'He can answer for himself!' scolded Eliza jokingly.

Clem smiled at his stepmother in gratitude, warming towards her even further. All too often had his father done this, seeming to forget that his son was now a man. 'I've got myself an office job in Rotherham. It's not bad money.'

Eliza gave praise, then sat down, beaming. 'Well, my dears, tuck in.'

Outside, taking hungry bites from his paper-thin jam sandwich, Joe said to the boys, 'I suppose we're brothers now.'

'Not real brothers.' Edwin was sullen. 'Our surname's different to yours.'

'What is it, then?' asked Maddie, chomping.

'Crump,' provided Doris.

Joe gave an impish snigger and elbowed Beata. 'Mrs Crump did a trump!'

His own siblings fell about giggling. The others, having been teased many times like this, were unamused. Whilst Edwin merely scowled, George set about the older boy, grasping Joe's neck under one arm and pummelling his head with the other. Though never an instigator of fights, Joe was quick to lash out in his own defence.

Hearing the noise, Probyn marched out, grabbed a boy in each hand and shook them, telling both, 'You haven't been introduced two minutes ago and you're fighting already!'

'It was him!' Dangling by his collar, George indicated Joe. 'He called my mother names!'

Joe glowered at such audacity. One never told tales.

Probyn shook him. 'Did you?'

Joe could not lie. 'I only made a rhyme of Mrs Crump's name!'

'You're old enough to know better!' Releasing George unharmed, Probyn administered three sharp whacks to his son's buttocks, then warned him. 'It's Mrs Kilmaster now, but the only name you'll call her is Mother, do I make myself clear?'

Humiliated at being treated like an infant in front of these strangers, twelve-year-old Joe hung his head and swore to obey, privately instructing himself not to get on the wrong side of this tell-tale again.

However, after a few days the two families began to merge into one, and though the Kilmasters did not like addressing Eliza as Mother, they showed the respect that their father demanded. There was little alternative but to get on in this overcrowded dwelling.

With their father taking up his new position at the colliery yard, and Clem at the office in Rotherham, the children settled down to a routine of education. There being no Catholic school at Denaby, the Kilmasters were obliged to attend the same one as everyone else but were occasionally segregated from the rest of their class and sent to another room where Father Flanagan would come to give them instruction. Saddened to learn of their mother's death he was kindness itself and, though peeved that her widower had remarried a non-Catholic, was nevertheless mollified that his offspring would continue to receive the teachings of the True Church.

This was to have disadvantages in a mainly Protestant school, ones with which they had had to contend before. On Ash Wednesday, the Kilmaster children arrived with sooty crosses smudged on their foreheads and were immediately set upon by the others who taunted them as, 'Mucky devils!' Whereupon the boys launched into a fight that had the whole school involved and which served to get both Joe and Duke a caning and another good hiding when their parents were informed. Then, there was Good Friday, which had nothing good about it for there was Mass in the morning, Easter Vigil between one and four in the afternoon and Mass again in the evening. Belonging to the Church of England, neither Doris, Edwin nor George stuck up for their stepbrothers and sisters. It seemed to Beata that to enjoy the spiritual benefit of the True Church one had to suffer.

There were, however, compensations.

Falling easily into old habits, the nine-year-old would wait until she saw Father Flanagan staggering along to the shop for his mints, then pelted by a different route to be there ahead of him, gazing wistfully into the window.

The ploy working more often than not, she tested her luck again this morning.

'And what will it be today, Beat?' He leaned on the shop window frame to steady himself, pulled a handkerchief from his darned cassock and used it to dab at the dewdrop on his thin nose.

She looked downhearted. 'I haven't any money, Father.'

'Ah dear,' he heaved a theatrical sigh, 'isn't that the very devil?' To tease the child, he made as if to walk on, amused by the look of horror that crossed her face as she thought he was going to let her down. Then he paused. 'Tell me, Beat, what would you buy if ye did have the funds?'

'Maybe some fat ducks, peas and potatoes – no, a lucky stick.'

'Lucky stick, eh? Will it help in picking a winner d'ye think?'

Beata did not understand that he meant horse racing. 'It might do.'

'Let's go see!' And, as she had hoped he would, Father Flanagan piloted her cheerfully into the sweet shop where he asked for, 'A bag of my usual, Molly,' whilst Beata went to a barrel for her purchase.

She took ages, sorting through the sticks of rock, studying each closely as if trying to see through the wrapper.

After a while, the priest turned and frowned, 'Are they not all the same, Beat? I've another Confession to perform in three hours' time.'

Molly whispered in amused tone. 'If there's a black mark inside the wrapper you get a free stick.'

He chuckled and indicated his purse. 'She's getting a free one already.'

Having detected a winning lucky stick, Beata came forward and unwrapped it, announcing in false surprise. 'Oh look, it's got a black mark!'

'Well, I never.' Molly told her to run and claim her free stick, smiling at the priest. 'I think we've both been had, Father – eh, madam, don't be rummaging about looking for another winner!' she warned the child. 'There's only so much luck in this world.'

Laying his hand on Beata's shoulder, a smiling Father Flanagan steered her from the shop. 'I trust you're going to share your good fortune with your brothers and sisters?' Beata supposed she should. Naturally, upon discovering that she had sweets the others were all around her then, not just her siblings but the same children who had taunted her over her religion only days ago, all suddenly wanting to be her friend.

And the generous Beata allowed them to be, even knowing that at the next Catholic ritual these same friends would chafe and mock her for her faith.

The same thought was to occur at Whitsuntide when all the denominations marched together through town – Wesleyans, Anglicans and Salvation Army dressed in their new outfits, come together as one joyful band – and, marching happily alongside, Beata mused over the stupidity of it all: if they could merge today why couldn't they get along the rest of the year?

In such a climate of uncertainty it was comforting to have such a friend as Father Flanagan, plus other familiar faces such as Nurse Gentle, Mrs Rushton and the occasional visit from Augusta, for the children had quickly found their stepmother to be much stricter than their own. Owing to increased numbers there was more reason than ever for the household to be run along military lines and Eliza had quickly extended Probyn's methods to every matter of domestic life. Regimentation was the order of the day, from bowels to bedtime.

Hence, every morning began with a mad rush to be first in the queue for a dose of liquorice powder – not because any of them liked it, but because he who was first in line could also be first to the lavatory, the powder working faster than one could get one's drawers down. Lacking aggression, Beata was always pushed to the back of the queue and would have to stand outside the closet, crossing her legs and begging the one inside to, 'Please hurry!'

With such a bad start, the rest of the day was bound not to get any easier, between mealtimes the children being banished from the house completely unless there were chores to be done, and of these there were many. On Monday they must clean their Sunday shoes and put them away for the rest of the week; Tuesday, mending and darning, the halfpenny card of wool being paid for out of their pocket money; Wednesday they tidied the bedrooms; Thursday, the girls blackleaded the range and the boys polished the fender; Friday, they rose at five cleaned the windows, washed the bricks beneath the sills and stoned the step – all of these tasks before school – yet, having helped around the house from an early age, Probyn's children did not consider themselves unduly hard done by.

In fact, contrary to the austerity brought about by rising prices and unemployment elsewhere, life was rather good for the Kilmasters in those early months of 1920, Father's allotment providing an abundance of food, their fuel supplied by the colliery.

How Beata loved to watch the man who came every quarter to stack this for them, fascinated that he could sculpt such a work of art out of this mundane commodity – though this was no ordinary coal but large, top-quality stuff, clean and bright. Taking these slabs Elijah would erect a black polished wall, forming it in such a way that a space was left for them to get a shovel in. Totally absorbed, Beata would wait to pay him his sixpence, thinking his skill deserved much more.

Yes, coal was one thing they would never be short of, even in summer there would be a fire in the grate, for this was the only way to obtain hot water, the doors and windows being flung wide open to get rid of the heat.

Not that the Kilmaster children had cause to complain about being too hot, for they were rarely indoors and even less so once the summer holidays came, for their stepmother found them additional chores to do. Now, on Mondays, there was washday to contend with. The copper, which normally stood by the fire, would be dragged out into the yard, balanced on two chairs and thence the weekly wash would commence, the possing and rinsing and mangling taking hours. Even at midday they were not permitted to sit down and with only a slice and a half of bread each and a bit of cheese to keep them going, they would have been too tired for play even had they been allowed. Thankfully, Eliza did the ironing, which gave them leave to wander over the Crags or the Ings, staying out all day with a bottle of water and jam sandwiches for lunch. But on Friday evening each had to work on the clipping rug and to complete a square of it before they were allowed out to play and as it was usually seven thirty before they finished they were forced to go straight to bed.

Probyn was a believer in everyone pulling their weight, but upon coming home from early shift one Monday afternoon to witness his children's load, even he deemed this too heavy for such youngsters.

Questioned about it, Eliza looked put out. 'Are you saying I'm treating yours differently from my own?'

'No!' He couldn't accuse her of that.

'Because if you want to run the house like two separate camps it isn't going to work.'

He spoke firmly. 'No, I said at the outset you'd be the one to run the house. But maybe I'll just go give them a hand with the mangling and –'

'You're acting as if I'm using them as slaves!' She was really offended now.

He looked dismayed. 'Nay, I'm just –'

'You were the one who said they were used to it!'

'And so they are, but –'

'You didn't marry me just so's I could run around after them, did you?'

'Of course not!'

'Then come and sit down and stop talking daft!' With a good-natured expression she laid determined hands on his shoulders and guided him to the table. 'You've done your shift for today. It's not as if they've got school to go to, and I'm the one who has to keep them occupied to stop them getting into mischief.'

Seeing that her latter words were true, Probyn nodded thoughtfully, and, everything being rather new between him and Eliza, and not wanting to cause friction so early in this marriage, he decided to go along with her.

Hence, the children's workload was to continue.

*　　*　　*

307

But on Saturday there was to be some light relief with an unexpected visit from Augusta who had cycled almost forty miles from York and arrived pink-cheeked with exertion, auburn hair clinging to her perspiring face.

'My God, you must have set off at sparrowfart!' Eliza brought her a glass of water.

The children giggled, having come to appreciate these small vulgarities.

'About three o'clock.' Puffing and blowing, eyes shining, Augusta fought to catch her breath. The children crowded round her as she propped her bicycle against the wall of the yard, their excitation not just for the arrival of their sister but for the peeping sound that came from the box that was tied behind the seat.

After several gulps of water, Augusta wiped her brow, then removed the lid from the box to reveal several fluffy little heads. 'Brought you some ducklings, thought you could fatten them up. Shall I put them in Father's allotment?'

'No, something might kill them.' Grinning, Eliza joined the children in stroking the fluffy little creatures, who struggled to escape. 'They'd better stay in the yard till they're bigger.' And she tipped them gently out of their container, whereupon they scurried about in panic.

With the novelty of the ducklings wearing off, Eliza invited Augusta in for a cup of tea. 'I suppose you'd better come in as well,' she told the children grudgingly. 'You don't often get to see your sister. But you'll sit quietly, mind.'

This prompted a thought in Joe's mind. 'When will Aunt Charlotte be coming to visit?'

Eliza eyed him, giving a momentary glimpse of flint. Probyn, too, had had the audacity to ask if his ex-sweetheart would be welcome. She had given him the same short shrift as she now gave Joe. 'She won't!'

Accepting the blunt response, though not liking it, all traipsed into the shade of the house.

Despite the presence of her siblings, Augusta still felt like a stranger here, and perched self-consciously on the edge of a chair. She smoothed her hair and clothes. 'Is Father at work?'

'Aye, he's on six to two. He'll be pleased to see you. Clem's gone camping for the weekend with his pal.'

Augusta was disappointed not to see her elder brother but his absence might simplify matters. 'In that case could I have his bed for the night?' Clem was the only one who did not have to share.

Hanging on their stepmother's permission, the children looked delighted when this was granted.

'If you're going to stop you might as well make yourself useful and do the shopping,' said Eliza, reaching for a scrap of paper on which to write a list, and while the tea was being consumed she handed over money with instructions to go to Mexborough market, and also to purchase a joint. 'I think we'll have a bit of Pope's Eye this week.' Gathering her brothers and sisters, and also the three stepsiblings, Augusta set off. To Beata and the others it did not matter that they were off on yet another of Eliza's errands, for here was dear Gussie to take charge and to let them look in the toy shop window and produce butterscotch as if by magic from her pocket.

After visiting the market their last call was to the butcher's shop for sausages, brawn and the Sunday joint, Augusta referring to the piece of beef by its real name.

Rolling a piece of butterscotch between her palms to make it soft, Maddie frowned up at her sister. 'Didn't Mother ask for Pope's Eye?'

Augusta shushed her sternly. True, the cut end of the bone did look like an eye but this devout Catholic was not about to offend the Holy Father by employing Eliza's nickname.

But the butcher was not to know this. 'There you are, my dear,' he cried upon handing it over. 'As grand a piece of Pope's Eye as you'll get anywhere!'

Augusta compressed her lips, but forced them into a smile before leaving the shop.

When they got home Father was eating his dinner. This was good, for his presence might make it easier for Augusta to put her query.

But first came fond conversation with Probyn, who wanted to know all the news from York. Only when this was exhausted did his daughter turn to Eliza. 'Would you mind if I take the children for a picnic?'

'Mind?' Eliza laughed. 'I'd almost pay you. Well, if you're staying out for tea you can take some of that brawn.'

So, armed with sandwiches and a bottle of water, Augusta set off with the children, ostensibly for the enjoyment of the latter but in reality she hoped to benefit too.

'Where we off on our picnic?' Never still, Joe leaped and tumbled beside her.

'Just to Ivanhoe Castle.' She headed for the limestone Crags.

'I want to go to the Pastures,' announced stepbrother Edwin.

'You can't. I've promised to meet somebody at the castle.' Basket over her arm, Augusta strode out.

'Who?' all of them wanted to know.

There was awkward deliberation. If she did not let them into the secret they might inform on her to Father. 'No one you know. He's called Vincent.'

The girls fired questions at her. 'Who is he? How long have you known him?'

She tried to sound casual. 'Just a young man. I met him last time I was here.' In fact she had thought of no one else since that first meeting a month ago, hence her reason for travelling the thirty-seven miles again so soon. Augusta was besotted.

Edwin showed disgust. 'I don't want to hang round while them sloppy devils are spooning.'

Ignoring Augusta's outraged gasp, George decided to be obstructive too. 'Neither do I. Give us our sandwiches and me and Ed will go on our own. I'll tell if you don't let me.'

'He will.' Joe knew this for a fact.

There was a brief argument before Doris sighed, 'Oh, let them go!'

'In that case, can we go an' all?' asked Joe on behalf of his brother Duke.

Augusta sighed, but knowing the males would only be bored and perhaps would spoil her liaison she felt they would be happier in their own company. After a fumbling division of the sandwiches, the two groups parted company.

Arriving at Conisbrough Castle, they saw a lone figure amongst the ruins. He was smoking a cigarette and looking ill at ease, though catching sight of Augusta he waved and came to meet them.

'Is this him?' Doris, Maddie and Beata looked keen.

Augusta nodded with pleasure.

'He's right good-looking!'

Little Mims saw past the dark curly hair and twinkling blue eyes. 'Why has he got crooked legs?' It was an innocent utterance but earned her a ticking off.

Seeing Vincent's cheeks turn pink, and fearing that he had over-heard, Augusta reddened in sympathy. But as they came together any unpleasantness was forgotten.

Seating themselves on the grass amid the ruins, for a short time they just chatted, but it was difficult to have any intimate conversation with all these onlookers, and so Augusta suggested an early tea.

310

Once they had devoured the sandwiches, however, Augusta bade her sisters, 'You stay here, me and Vincent are just going for a walk.'

'I want to go too!' Mims clambered to her feet.

'Then go the other way! We won't be long.' Augusta set off with her beau.

Mims opened her mouth to wail, but Maddie clamped a hand over the maw. 'Shush! You can go in a minute, when it's safe.' And she peered around the ruined wall to spy on Augusta who, thinking she was unobserved, slipped her hand through the arm Vincent offered.

The instant the courting couple had disappeared behind some bushes, Maddie led the sortie, putting her finger to her lips as they crept up to watch.

Vincent was holding Augusta in his arms, her head upon his chest.

The watchers fought to suppress their giggles, Doris clamping a hand over her mouth as Augusta looked around sharply. Then, satisfied that they were alone she lifted her face to that of the young man, who applied his lips to hers.

After watching in awe for a while, Maddie thought it expedient to move away before they exploded with laughter, and at her signal the girls pelted back to the ruins.

'Don't you say owt,' she warned Mims.

'I won't!'

'Good job George isn't here or he would, though,' opined Beata.

'Isn't he lovely?' breathed Maddie.

'Who, George?' Doris made vomiting noises.

'No, you soft 'a'p'orth, Vincent! I love his curly hair. That's the sort I want to marry.'

'Is our Gus going to marry him?' asked Beata.

'Looks like it.'

At this precise moment the couple chose to reappear, Augusta blushing furiously upon overhearing.

Vincent blushed too, but was more forthcoming. 'If she'll have me.'

'Aw, our Gussie's getting wed!' Mims threw herself in the air, landing on her back in a patch of clover.

'Not yet!' But Augusta radiated happiness, her cheeks pink and her eyes sparkling. 'So you're not to say anything at home.'

'That's what I've told them,' said Maddie. 'Your secret's safe with us.' And she whispered, 'We all like your choice.'

How soon the afternoon ended. 'Can we meet tomorrow?' asked Vincent as his sweetheart prepared to set off back over the Crags.

'I can't.' She projected disappointment. 'I'll have to go back to York after Sunday tea. But I'll be at early Mass tomorrow morning.'

Vincent grinned and said in that case he would be there too.

Alas, there was little chance for the lovers to exchange anything more than a moonstruck glance across the pews before Augusta, a punctilious girl, devoted her attention to the Lord. A swift smile upon bumping into Vincent on leaving, and then it was all over until the next time.

Still, there was much to be enjoyed at home, for whilst she had been at church the joint of beef had been sizzling in the oven and, at midday was served to them with Yorkshire pudding, roast potatoes and vegetables.

It had always been Father's habit, when doling out the carved slices, to give everyone a piece of fat to go with it and so he did today. Normally, Beata would cut this unpalatable item into bits and help it down by wrapping it in mashed potato, but on this occasion her happiness at having Gussie here had caused her to daydream and suddenly she found herself with no potato left. Hoping that her parents would not notice, she discreetly placed her knife and fork over the last bit of fat, then sat quietly, hands upon lap. And to her relief, there was no reprimand as the crockery was taken away to be washed.

However, at teatime, when everyone else was given an empty plate off which to eat their bread-and-butter, she was alarmed to see on hers a lump of cold fat.

Casting a dismayed look at her father, she was given the instruction to, 'Eat that first before you start on anything else.' Probyn had no time for trivial moans after what deprivations other youngsters had suffered on the battlefield.

She took a sip from her glass of water. Mother had often given them tea but from the beginning Eliza had announced that tea was too expensive for children. Then she stared at the lump of fat, deciding how to go about this. Cutting it into tiny pieces would make it go down easier but would take far longer. Better to get it over in one go . . . though the very idea made her feel nauseated. She took a deep breath.

It was no good. In a tiny voice, she said, 'I'm sorry, Father, I'd eat it if I could, but I'll be sick if I do.'

'Well, I'm sure we don't want any mess.' Probyn looked enquiringly at Eliza.

His wife pursed her lips. 'Everyone else ate it, why should she be given priority? You'll just make her into a pernickety eater and I've no time for those. Beata, get it down you now.'

Using her most pleading expression, Beata looked at her father, but it did no good. 'Your mother's spoken,' was all he said.

Everyone was observing. Holding her breath, Beata forced herself to swallow the piece of fat in one go, balking as the hard lump filled her throat – and in seconds was on its way up again, along with everything else in her stomach.

Confronted with her vomit-splattered carpet, Eliza jumped up with an angry yell. 'You spiteful little – Father, deal with her! She's done it on purpose.'

Probyn was angry too. 'Beata, you can go get a cloth and wipe that up! What a song and dance over a bit of fat. Good Lord, all I want is a quiet life. Why can't you all just behave?'

Even though Father had not laid a hand on her, his words were just as hurtful. Already on the brink of tears, when Beata was rinsing out the soiled cloth under the tap in the yard and in doing so spotted the ducklings ravaging the patch of seedlings she had so carefully nurtured, it served to push her over the edge.

Hearing her sobs, Augusta was about to go and comfort her, but her stepmother interrupted, 'Leave her! She just wants attention. If you want something to do here's the pots want washing.'

Beata's loud lament was reduced to shuddering sniffles by the time Augusta was free to tend her. Crouching nearby, she handed Beata a handkerchief. 'Your face is all snotty.'

Beata gave a wet laugh, as her sister had intended. Now Augusta put an arm around her shoulders and squeezed. 'Are you feeling better?'

'Your pizzocking ducks have eaten my Virginia stock,' came the sulky accusation.

'Aw, that's a shame.' Then Augusta grinned. 'But never mind, you'll be able to get your own back and eat *them* at Christmas.'

Beata remained miserable, wanting to ask something but unsure if she would like the answer. Tears sprang to her eyes at the thought of it and she dashed them away several times before finally being able to ask, 'Gussie . . .' a strand of cotton dangled from her hem; she twined it round her finger, 'does . . . does Father love Eliza more than us?' Her vision blurred again.

Augusta wanted to cry too. Instead she fought it, saying tenderly, 'No, what makes you ask that?'

Beata shuddered and swallowed. 'He always tells us off when she asks him to.'

'That doesn't mean he loves her more.'

'But he married her so he must do!'

'Yes, but, it's just . . . a different kind of love.' Thinking of Vincent, she blushed. 'He still loves you just the same as he always did.'

Only half reassured, Beata allowed herself to be led back into the house.

NINETEEN

Despite Augusta's soothing words, under the strict regime Beata continued to feel that her father's love was slipping away, that others were in greater receipt of it, not just Eliza but her own siblings.

Recently, in an act that would surely have earned Beata a slap, Mims had lifted the lid of the piano and started to finger the keys, making not an infantile din but a considered attempt to form a tune. Only by reason of it being a Saturday evening, when the restrictive atmosphere was somewhat lightened and Father indulged them in conversation, did Mims escape a rebuke. Under his approving eye Mims was allowed to continue, showing a genuine keenness to play. Even Eliza, unable to perform herself but enjoying listening to music, agreed that this gift should be nurtured with lessons.

'Isn't she a bit young?' grinned Clem. Mims had only just turned five.

'The younger the better, from what I hear,' replied Eliza. 'By the time she's six she should be able to put that thing to good use. What's the point of having a piano if nobody can play it?'

A nostalgic image leaped into Probyn's mind of a laughing Grace tinkling out some joyous melody on the ivory keys; since her death they had lain dormant.

Eliza continued. 'There's a teacher in Conisbrough. Beat can take her.'

Beata jumped in to ask, 'Can I have lessons too?'

Having heard previous experiments, Probyn smiled. 'I don't think you're cut out for it, dear.'

'Neither is our Doris,' agreed Eliza. 'But we might get the lessons

315

cheaper if there are two of them. Let's hear your effort, Madeleine.'

Madeleine lacked enthusiasm. 'Do I have to?'

'Pardon me for thinking I was being generous,' sniped her step-mother. 'Nobody's forcing you. Beata, you can take Millicent over this Saturday.'

And so, denied the pleasure herself, Beata was forced to watch her youngest sister become the talented player that she would have liked to be, taking her every week across the Crags to Conisbrough. Not every moment was enjoyable for Mims. The teacher was highly strung and would rap her pupil over the knuckles with a ruler if she so much as played one wrong note, but it must have been an efficient method for in no time at all it seemed that Mims could perform any exercise that she was given, thus earning praise at home. Whilst the only attention poor Beata attracted was if she inadvertently picked up a pen with her left hand, so invoking Father's denunciation.

What with all the scolding and hard work that went on at home, it was a pleasure to return to school. But Beata had only been back a week when morning lessons were interrupted by an excruciating pain in her leg and by midday it had swollen to twice its size. Hobbling home for lunch, one sock around her ankle, she sought advice from her stepmother.

Chastising Beata for arriving later than everyone else, Eliza hardly glanced at the limb.

'It's probably because you don't get enough exercise. Here, you can eat your dinner on the hoof and take your father's to him at the same time.' She thrust a wad of bread and cheese at the child, along with a basket containing Probyn's lunch. 'And on your way call in at the Picture Palace and book two seats for tonight. I want the best, D2 and D4. Here's two shillings and I expect to see sixpence change so don't be pulling a fast one.'

This hurtful comment adding to the pain of her leg, Beata turned and limped from the house.

By the time she reached the colliery yard she was almost in tears.

Quick to spot her distress, Probyn swung her onto a chair in his office then bent to examine her inflated limb, frowning in concern. 'By that doesn't look too good, Beat. You haven't had the bicycle pump to it, have you?' In kindly fashion he ruffled her hair. Enjoying his attention, Beata smiled despite her pain.

Probyn straightened. 'Tell your mother you're not to go back to school this afternoon.'

Beata knew that if she did this Eliza would find her more work to do. 'I'll be all right, Father.'

'I insist. Tell your mother I've said it needs resting.' He had learned how uncompromising Eliza could be. 'I'll take you to the doctor's when I come home from work. You go ahead and save us a place so we don't have to wait so long.'

'All right. Enjoy your dinner, Father.' Delighting in his solicitude, yet racked by pain, Beata limped home, rehearsing what she would say to Eliza.

In the event, her stepmother was reasonably affable, the cinema tickets seeming to put her in better mood. 'Oh well, if that's what your father's said, you must do as he ordered. Sit in that chair and put your leg up.' And to Beata's amazement she even helped by placing two cushions between the swollen limb and the footstool. But what was even more surprising, Eliza indicated the row of books on the sideboard. 'You can look at one of these if you like.'

Thanking her, Beata said she should love to read one of the Shakespeare plays.

Eliza gave a scoffing chuckle. 'I doubt you'll understand it but here you are.' She was about to place a leather volume on Beata's lap when she drew back. 'Your hands aren't mucky, are they?' At the presentation of clean digits, she looked satisfied and handed over the book, which Beata was to devour for the next few hours, the pleasure it brought helping to take her mind from her discomfort.

Towards mid-afternoon when her father was due home from his shift, she thanked her stepmother for the loan of the precious tome, handed it back and said she should be going along to the doctor's surgery.

Upon her entry here, she was given a number by the receptionist and hobbled into the waiting room. Quite a few people were here already, miners in cloth caps and mufflers, coughing and wheezing and sighing, shoulders hunched by emphysema. Other children might have sat apart, but this little girl chose to sit next to an old man, chatting in friendly manner whilst she waited for her father, enquiring after the other's health in such an old-fashioned manner that it brought a smile of amusement to the wrinkled lips. 'Eh, I feel better already for sitting next to thee,' remarked the oldster.

One by one, the queue was reduced. With only one person ahead of her Beata became concerned that her father was going to be late but then he appeared, and, after another short wait she found herself in Dr Hannah's surgery, surrounded by shelves filled with bottles and enveloped in the sharp smell of ether that she found wonderfully intoxicating.

Dr Hannah, a hunchback, pressed a thumb to the swollen leg and uttered one word. 'Dropsy.'

Beata stared in worried fascination at the deep, thumb-shaped depression in her leg.

'But from what source, heart or kidneys?' Asking himself the question, Dr Hannah inserted the ends of his stethoscope to his ears. 'Unbutton your clothes, child.'

Faced with his own heart condition, Probyn felt an air of doom as he helped his daughter unfasten her many buttons. 'I thought it might be whiteleg like her mother used to suffer, Doctor.'

The physician shook his head and, with his stethoscope to Beata's chest, went on to pose several questions. 'Is her face swollen after lying in bed overnight?'

'Well, a bit – but isn't everybody puffy on a morning?'

'Does the swelling in her leg subside after a night's rest?'

'We don't know, she only got it today.'

Dr Hannah took the stethoscope away from her chest. 'Have you got a headache, Beata?'

'No, Doctor.' She had been studying his deformed spine whilst he examined her, wondering if it was as painful as it looked.

The physician remained grave. 'Well, whether or not it be faulty kidneys or faulty heart, either way there's nothing much to be done, I'm afraid, Mr Kilmaster. Just keep her rested and her bowels regular to get rid of the excess fluid. I'll give her some Blue Buttons for the discomfort.'

Probyn accepted the offering without confidence, for over the years it had been prescribed to him as a cure-all for headache to arseache. Obsessed with the thought that Beata had been condemned to an early grave, he fought to hide his concern as he thanked the doctor and hurried the child along with her dressing, responding to Beata's anxious face with a fatherly smile, which seemed instantly to assure her. There seemed none of the fear he himself was feeling, merely calm inquisition. It was as if she could read his mind.

Told about Beata's affliction, Eliza was unusually kind, allowing her access to the books whilst she rested her leg until it reverted to its normal size.

Once this happened, though, it was back to school and daily

chores, the books being consigned to a rare treat. But despite the fear that she might soon die, and the awful pain she suffered, pain that was to recur many times hence, Beata would remember this as a comforting time, in the fact that it had brought reassurance of her father's love.

From Eliza's standpoint, the fatherly concern that Beata should not be given too many heavy assignments looked more like pandering. 'She's been ill, yes, but she's better now.' Her tone was brusque. 'Spoiling isn't going to make her live any longer, you know. That's half the trouble with your lot, Grace was too soft on them.'

At this slur on one so tender, one so beloved, Probyn felt a surge of annoyance. Eliza was generous with her sexual favours and could also be relied upon for a laugh, but tenderness was not amongst her attributes. But for the sake of expediency he bit his tongue. 'Anything to keep the peace,' he sighed, burying his head in the newspaper.

Peace. Was there any such thing? Every day came fresh reports of soldiers being murdered by Irish savages in the civil war that raged there. He was glad his soldiering days were over, for the way things were going at home the troops could be brought into his own district before very long.

Disputes between colliers and owners were typical in a mining community. If not a full-blown strike or lockout then there was always some threat of industrial action rumbling in the background. Since the war such wrangling over wages had become even more commonplace, but the latest deadlock looked set to obscure anything that had preceded it, for the miners had formed an alliance with the railwaymen and transport workers and the strike debate had naturally extended to them. If they were to support the motion, the whole country could be brought to its knees.

To Probyn, with a family of eleven to support, it was a worrying time, for without union membership there would be no strike pay for him, though his army pension meant it might not be so catastrophic for the Kilmasters as for other non-members. Nevertheless he knew it would mean a difficult period.

When the strike was postponed for another month, Probyn breathed a sigh of relief, maintaining the hope that the Government would come up with some winning package before the deadline. It was but a temporary respite. Despite all attempts to avert it, the agitators were to force events to a disastrous conclusion. On 16 October a state of emergency was declared.

That the railwaymen decided against a sympathetic strike appeared to make little difference. Coal was the crucial element, this being immediately rationed under the Defence of the Realm Act. Their lighting reduced, factories were compelled to close. Within days, thousands of men in iron and steel lay idle. There was rioting in Downing Street. Town centres were almost as dark as they had been in wartime and so was the mood of the people.

Faced with a crisis, Eliza was beginning to reveal her true colours. 'Worst decision I ever made, coming down here.' She shoved a poker in the fire and lifted the coals gingerly so as to produce only sufficient flame to heat the water and not have it burn away too quickly. Her hand might be moderate but her voice was terse.

'It would have been just as bad in West Hartlepool,' pointed out her husband.

His calmness annoyed her. 'Maybe! But I wouldn't have had to make the food stretch so far, and who knows how long it's going to last?'

'It'll last as long as it has to,' murmured Probyn.

Eliza cursed the poor fire, then ordered two of the boys to drag in the zinc bath whilst she herself set towels before the hearth.

Hot water was drawn into a large jug and transferred to the bath.

Joe beheld the few inches of water.

Reading his astonishment, Eliza forestalled his question. 'Before you ask! We've been told to use less.'

'Are the people who make the water on strike?' asked Duke as he stripped.

Father explained to the youngster, 'No, we've got to use less because there's hardly any coal to heat it.'

'But I thought we got our coal free, Father?'

'In a manner of speaking, it's part of my wages, but with the mines closed there's no coal being produced and it's having to be rationed, not just to us, but to the people who run the factories and make the electricity, in fact in every place you can —'

'If you stand talking much longer this bath will be cold as well as shallow,' Eliza interjected.

Probyn eyed her for this interruption, but indicated for his sons to do as they were told, concluding, 'Never underestimate the vital importance of coal, boys. Like water, it's the source of life.'

Throughout the rest of October the peace parley continued, the miners rejecting all Government proposals. But, lacking support from the NUR, their position was weak and when a temporary measure was offered, meeting their demand of two extra shillings per shift if they agreed to increase output, this was put to the members. With the vote producing only a narrow majority for continuation of the strike, there was reluctant acceptance of the Government's wage offer, thus generating a trickle back to work.

Yet again, relief was transitory, for most accepted that it was only a matter of time before the situation resurfaced. It was good, however, to be back at work, and all those involved used the opportunity to build up their coffers before the next crisis, Probyn similarly eager, if only because the restitution of pay would mean an end to Eliza's grumbling.

Marching keenly to an afternoon shift through that wintry November mist he had barely taken two steps beyond his door when he almost collided with Father Flanagan. Since Grace's death the priest no longer held open invitation to the Kilmasters' household; this, added to the fact that the Roman Catholic Church had lost a convert, made for an awkward meeting.

But any grudge Flanagan might hold was hidden well for he stopped to chat.

'Good day to ye, Probyn.' He whipped a dewdrop from his long nose, his moisture-laden finger moving quickly upwards and smoothing the thin strands of silvery hair into place. ''Tis a cold one.' Giving the other only time to nod in agreement he launched into more serious topic. 'What do ye make of this latest outrage by the IRA – fourteen British officers murdered in their beds! Such dastardly cowards. It makes me ashamed to be Irish, I can tell ye.' A grave look on his face, he shook his head several times, before patting the other's arm. 'Ah well, I can see you're off to work I don't want to stop ye –'

'No, that's all right!' Thinking he might have been too unwelcoming of this encounter, Probyn injected his tone with verve. 'I'm early.'

Flanagan rubbed his hands to ward off the cold and explained his presence. 'I'm just going round making sure there's no undue hardship after the strike. Are you all right yourselves?'

Probyn assured him they were fine at this house. 'I don't know how long for, though. It sounds simple enough, the more coal produced the higher the wage, but you and I both know that it rarely works to the miners' advantage. There always seems to be factors outside our control.'

'Indeed.' Father Flanagan nodded thoughtfully. 'And how is young Clem? I haven't seen him at Mass in a long while.'

Probyn looked awkward, knowing the enquiry held a rebuke for him. 'Well, you know what these young people are like, Father . . .'

'And some not so young.' The tall figure cocked his head and tried to force the other into meeting his eye.

Probyn rose to the occasion, but his account was rushed. 'He's got bronchitis, the lad.'

With the onset of the cold damp weather Clem had gone down with his usual debilitating ailment. 'You're welcome to come in and see him.' He gestured at his front door, and, upon Father Flanagan's acceptance, retraced his steps and threw it open.

Eliza's jaw dropped at the entry of the priest. Clem, too, appeared embarrassed for his upper half was stripped bare. Prior to the intrusion his stepmother had been applying balm to his chest and back in order to relieve his wheezing; its pungent aroma filled the room, making everyone's eyes water.

'Sorry, I thought you'd be finished,' Probyn told Eliza, his apology in part for inviting the priest in when he knew her views on Catholicism.

'Carry on, don't mind me,' Father Flanagan told the pair brightly. 'I just came to see how the patient is.'

Clem relaxed a little, and, seated beside a roaring fire, hunched over for his stepmother to continue her ministrations, her hand performing circular motions over his slim white frame.

Somewhat embarrassed by Eliza's rudeness, Probyn displayed manners. 'Please, sit down, Father. Can I make you a cup of tea?'

Flanagan caught Eliza's darting, narrow-eyed look at her husband. 'No, no, you get off to work, Probe. I'll not stop. Hope you're soon recovered, Clem. We'll look forward to seeing you at Mass in a few weeks.' This said, he left along with Probyn.

The pair of them once more alone, Eliza laid a hand on Clem's bare back. 'Eh, I can feel it ruttling away in there. Let's hope that rubbing did the trick.'

Assuring her it had done him good, Clem looked up at her gratefully, trying to hold his cough at bay for he knew what a vexatious sound it was – it even annoyed him.

She patted his ribs in motherly fashion. 'Put your shirt on and I'll get you a mug of hot lemon. We've got to get you right for church.'

And they both laughed.

Though the two men were not to meet in church, there was to be plenty more scope for discussion on Ireland for Probyn and Father Flanagan if ever they met by chance in the street. The new year was to see more desperate battles and appalling bloodshed, the rebels' dastardly acts even extending to the mainland, attempts being made to sabotage oil stores, cotton mills, coke premises, and indeed anywhere that might cause mischief.

With unemployment topping a million, the opening months of 1921 were ridden with disputes over reductions in wages in one industry or another, ranging from all-out strikes to petty squabbles. But none was to compare in magnitude to that which was brewing on the coalfields. Under the terms of the temporary solution mooted last November, the Government had placed joint onus on the coalowners and miners to come to some arrangement on a future scheme for the regulation of wages by the end of March, at which date the Government's wartime control of the industry was set to expire. Both sides were desperately trying to negotiate a permanent scheme before the deadline and agreed about everything except one point: the miners wanted a national wage, whilst the owners insisted that rates must be based on the ability of individual districts to pay.

The Miners' Federation held it to be grossly unfair that their members in poor districts should get less than those in rich areas – the Government had recognized this, why could not the owners see it? Similarly, it was because of such a lack of recognition that the miners were unhappy about decontrol, fearing that it would mean a loss of wages granted to them during the war, and demanded that the Government postponed its plan to hand the industry back to the owners, or at least to continue to subsidize it during this depression. Their fears were not without justification, for, in the last few months, not only had the value of exported coal fallen, but the orders for industrial and domestic consumption had also dwindled, the output figures reflecting these declines.

Abandoned, as they saw it, to the whims of the owners, the miners soon began to see last November's pay rises whittled away by falling output. Faced with a thirty per cent reduction in wages, there was no alternative but to issue strike notices, plunging the country once again into another state of emergency.

Probyn might be laid off work but he was far from idle. As a result of the Government's appeal for loyal citizens to attest for military service during the current crisis, vast numbers of unemployed flocked to respond to the poster in the Kilmasters' front window – 'Your Country Needs You' – and a constant supply of recruits was to keep the old RSM busy throughout the day.

If at home, the children loved to hover outside the curtain that separated the recruiting office from the rest of their house, eavesdropping as Father lectured each man in turn – 'Be warned, the army is no feather bed!' – then weighed him, graded his height against a pencil mark drawn on the parlour wall, asked his religion and measured him for his uniform, then told him to present himself at Pontefract to receive the King's Shilling. Sometimes, they would hear an oath – 'Get those bladdy shoulders straight!' – and unused to hearing such language from their father they would put their hands over their mouths to stifle a giggle. Once, there was even more fun when a woman came down to bombard him with insults over the recruitment of her underage son. But Father remained unfazed, telling her in an unruffled manner, 'Don't concern yourself, madam, the army will make a man of him.' Nothing ever seemed to worry Father.

It was fortunate that the children did not understand how critical the situation was. As the strike progressed, each day brought new crises, the reduction of coal supplies affecting every branch of society, until by the end of the month there was total stoppage, pumpmen included, so pits were at risk of flooding. Volunteers were requested to save the collieries, and, on the brink of starvation, they came in their hundreds to brave the violence of the picket lines in return for a square meal. It was worse than anything Probyn could remember since '93, when he himself as a young soldier had been ordered to control people who were friends and neighbours; control them with bayonet and bullet. It looked as if things were dangerously close to this again, for, along with the enrolment of special constables to protect the volunteers, there was talk of the Reserve being called out

Daily the situation worsened, the entire country hanging on the railwaymen's decision to join the transport workers in voting to support to the miners, every heart sinking as the dreaded announcement was made: the Triple Alliance had decreed that a general strike would begin on Tuesday at midnight.

'Triple Alliance,' growled Probyn, beholding his evening paper in disgust. 'Blasted Bedlamites more like. Since when have they been running the country? I didn't vote them in.' Part of his irritation came from being rushed off his feet, due to the recruitment drive; he had been at it all day, weighing and measuring.

'Mother, I don't think we're going to have enough bread left for pack-up.' Doris was carving a loaf for tea.

'Put it on the list: the one marked "Luxuries".'

Probyn ignored his wife's sarcasm. 'And these journalists don't help, whipping things up.' He quoted: '"Neither winders nor

324

pumpmen will work and pit ponies are in danger of drowning." What rubbish! No miner would let his pony drown. They're running about in the fields having a grand old time – What the devil?' A crash from the front room had him leaping from his chair, Clem too, followed by Eliza and the children.

There was a hole in the front window where the recruitment poster had been, the remnants of it hanging in tatters around the frame, whilst on the floor lay a brick.

To sounds of outrage from Eliza, Probyn bent down to pick it up, his face grim.

'I'll get the bugger!' Clem rushed for the door, no amount of summoning from his father preventing his impulsive dash.

Everyone hurried outside to see a flame-coloured head disappearing down the street in chase of the culprit. There was a scuffle, Clem's head jerked back, then he seemed to go completely berserk, lashing out with fists and boots until the perpetrator crumpled to the floor unconscious, but even then Clem did not seem satisfied for he kept on pummelling the body and only by his father's intervention was a murder prevented.

'Stop it! Stop it, Clem, that's disgraceful!' Whilst children and neighbours looked on in alarm, Probyn struggled to hold back his son, enfolding the much thinner body in his bulk.

'He broke my fucking nose!' Clem was still in a frenzy and had to be manhandled back to the house where his expletive was also to receive condemnation.

'I will not have such filth!'

'He was only sticking up for you!' Eliza rebuked her husband, dabbing gently at Clem's bloody nose with a damp rag.

'Oh, a lot of good foul language is going to do anybody! Not to mention that he almost killed a chap.'

'He deserved it,' said Eliza, apologizing to Clem for causing him to wince. 'Look at the size of the poor lad's nose.' It was beginning to swell, transforming his hawkish beak into a bulb.

'Yes, and how are you going to explain that at work?' demanded Probyn. 'Because you needn't think you're staying off.'

'He never even mentioned staying off,' retorted Eliza. 'He can just say he tripped and fell, can't you?' Having prevented the bleeding, she stood back and looked at Clem, who nodded, silently grateful.

She threw the bloodstained rag on the fire then turned to address Probyn again. 'Hadn't you better get that window fixed?'

*   *   *

There were no more bricks through the window, and in a last-minute decision the general strike, if not that of the miners, was called off, but none of this was to improve the atmosphere that had bubbled up inside the Kilmaster household. Oh, he and Clem had soon made things up, they always did, and one would not have known there had been any bad feeling as father and son relaxed together after tea, discussing the contents of the newspaper, the current subject being dwindling exports. But Probyn's relationship with Eliza was another matter.

'Never mind exports, what about our food?' she demanded, squinting to thread a needle as she made ready to darn a hole in her stocking, the children involved in similar chores.

Probyn explained patiently, 'It's all connected, Liza. Exports provide our food. Those countries which normally buy from us are so impoverished they can't pay for our goods. It's all very well the red dawn brigade demanding and getting higher wages but the bosses simply put up their prices to cover each rise. The country can't go on like that or it'll be bankrupt. And they can't just blame the miners either, it's a collective thing, and it hasn't just suddenly happened – it's been going on for years. We're on the threshold of a calamity here and we're all going to have to make sacrifi –'

'That's easy for a man to say!' snapped Eliza, the harshness in her voice causing the children to duck further into their tasks, everyone hating it when she addressed Father like this, which had been happening more and more during the strike. 'It isn't you who has to eke out the wages.'

To help fight his exasperation, he reached for a cigarette and shoved a taper into the fire. 'Can you not see beyond the end of your own nose, woman? I'm not just referring to our household budget, I'm talking on a much higher level.' Pausing briefly, he drew on the cigarette, producing an angry glow. 'Admittedly, it isn't the bosses who'll do most of the suffering,' smoke emerged with his words. 'Even if their businesses go under they're unlikely to end up in the workhouse, but somebody's got to call a halt, be prepared to exist on less wages, to take less profit, until the country's back on its feet. The Government's got to cut taxes too. You can't expect to have four years of war, producing nothing but weapons and expect your customers to still be there when you go back to producing your normal merchandise. In some ways this depression's a blessing, if it makes people come to their senses.'

'A blessing, is it?' Dark of face, Eliza snapped the thread with her teeth. 'I'll remember that when I'm trying to make half a crown stretch to ten bob.'

With the coal strike prolonged for another two months, there was no chance of Probyn escaping his wife's nagging about money; nagging about everything. And she had no valid reason to complain; it was not as if her children were reduced to taking their daily meal at The Big Drum along with the strikers' children, for Probyn's army pension saw to that.

But whilst they might have scraped by financially, the long period of unemployment took its toll in other ways. Being at home so much with Eliza made their differences more noticeable. He tried to get out as much as he could, hunting for rabbits with the boys, to the allotment or the Old Comrades' Club, but it was impossible for him to stay out as long as she appeared to want. Even when he helped around the house she seemed irritated by his presence – true, any woman would have been, even the gentle Grace had had her moments under pressure, but any altercation with her had been followed by loving amends. There was no such atonement from Eliza.

The more she nagged him the more he resorted to comparison. He and Grace had enjoyed such lovely conversations; all Eliza wanted to do was bicker or carp. Oh, Grace had argued with him, she had been a fiery little thing at times, but there was none of the nastiness that had begun to creep into Eliza's admonishments. She could be really offensive to those who went against her.

In recognition of this, Probyn finally began to empathize with his children, felt sorry and ashamed that he had inflicted such a mother upon them. It had just seemed the right thing to do at the time.

The coal strike pressed on, summer bringing no alleviation of the nationwide depression. Crippled by years of industrial action, factories lay idle, grass sprouting from their roofs, the only sign of industry provided by nesting sparrows, the windows smashed by the bored gangs of unemployed whose number had swelled to two million.

Even when the miners' dispute was finally settled by the introduction of a profit-sharing scheme, there was no sense of triumph, for previous experience had shown that it would be a hard climb back to normality.

Probyn doubted that he would even achieve it, for it seemed to him that since the war the whole world had gone mad. Though a truce had been declared in Ireland it looked as if the rebels were set to acquire independence. His father's words sprang to mind: 'Start breaking Britain into bits and where will it stop? Next thing you know that'd be the end of our Empire.' What on earth had all those thousands of brave men spent four years fighting for? Fighting and dying . . .

'What do you think, Father?'

Joe's voice startled him from his thoughts. Eyes coming back into focus, Probyn saw not a boy but a young man in long trousers, smiling at him expectantly.

'Well now!' He injected his voice with admiration. 'What a dandy. Twizzle round, let me have a good look.'

Affecting a manly gait, Joe swaggered before his audience for all he was worth, flourishing a comb and running it through his slicked-back auburn hair, even being so impudent as to take a Woodbine from a packet on the mantel and insert it between his lips, though not going so far as to light it, taking theatrical puffs as he strutted about, making parents and children laugh.

'Oh, give over,' begged a grinning Clem, 'you're making me puke.'

'Let the lad have his bit of glory!' Eliza was in a good mood at the thought that Joe would soon be adding to the household budget, and had purchased the bargain trousers in an end-of-season sale.

'I had to wait till bang on my fourteenth birthday to get long trousers,' objected Clem, though only jokingly.

Joe looked shocked at the thought that he might be stripped of his new-found manhood, but Eliza was benevolent. 'He's only got a couple of months to go; it'd be daft to put them away. But we shall have to sort you some old ones out for pit wear.'

Probyn was swift to correct this misapprehension. 'The lad won't be going down any pit.'

'What?' Eliza's good mood quickly transmuted to annoyance.

Eyes fixed to her expression, the children saw it as an ebbing wave, placid waters rippling away to reveal the hard pebbled beach beneath, and, at this sudden drop in temperature, they went about their business, leaving the parents to differ.

'Where will he be going then, if you don't mind telling me?'

'I've got him a job behind the counter at the Maypole.'

'Oh, that'll earn rich rewards, I'm sure!'

'You never complained that Clem didn't work at the pit.' The preferential treatment of his eldest son had not gone unnoticed. Had he been a jealous type Probyn might have resented Clem.

'He's got bad lungs; that one's as fit as a lop!' She jabbed a thumb at Joe. 'Anyway, he'll only be on the surface to start with.'

Probyn donned a look of obstinacy. 'No he won't, because I want something better for him.'

'You call shop work better?'

'Soon as he's old enough he'll be joining the army.'

Having come to learn of Probyn's stubborn streak, Eliza knew it was pointless arguing with him and made do with a vexatious retort: 'Good! Then at least we won't have to feed him.'

But of course it would be some years yet before Joe could enlist and the poor boy was to suffer many a grumble about his lack of earning ability, especially when his stepbrother Edwin turned fourteen not long after him. Without consultation of anyone, Eliza despatched her own son to the pit manager's house to seek employment, thereafter Beata and her sisters were to take it in turns to fill his bath, to bash his clothes and clean his boots, to scrub the coal dust from his back, and to listen to his howling complaints that the naphtha soap was taking the skin off along with the grime. With others shouldering the extra work, the money Edwin earned as a pony-driver cheered his mother up no end, though her pleasure still had its barb.

'Look!' she told Joe upon opening their wage packets one pay-day, both boys having laid them unopened on the table alongside their father's. 'See how much more you'd earn if you did a job like Ed's?'

Joe did not respond. What did it matter how much he earned when his stepmother took it all and gave him only sixpence in return?

But his father defended him. 'He makes his contribution, that's good enough for me. It's Joe's wages that have helped us to get back on our feet after the strike.'

Eliza retorted, 'We'd get back on our feet a whole lot faster if –'

'He is not going down the pit.' Probyn remained adamant.

'Oh, it's good enough for my lad but not yours! I'll tell you what, if we are getting back on our feet it's because of the person who juggles the money.' She tapped her chest as if to attach the accolade. 'We're going to have to wait till the end of the year now before the next one leaves school and brings in a wage.' This would be Madeleine. 'You could make it so much easier by –'

329

'No! Be told, woman.' And Probyn's face denied any further argument.

Probyn cast his mind back, trying to recall the moment when he had started to regret marrying Eliza: bitterly regretted it. Oh, there had always been doubts. At heart he had known she was only marrying him to give herself a more comfortable life, but he had ignored his own judgement, for he was an honourable man, and he had managed to get by until recently. Now he saw her for what she was, a lazy money-grubber with ideas above her station, using his children as unpaid servants.

Trapped in his misery, there was no comfort in the church for one who had changed his religion as easily as shedding a dirty pair of socks. Baptized a Wesleyan, he had turned Catholic in order to marry Grace, and now had jettisoned both for . . . what *had* it been for? Not because he was enamoured with the Church of England but for the sake of going to bed with a woman who had metamorphosed to a shrew. He thought of poor Charlotte to whom he had promised to write but never had. How differently things might have turned out had he been allowed to marry her – though he would never blame his elder son and daughter for their opposition; by his own self-centredness he had brought this calamity upon himself. No, alas, not just on himself but upon his dear children. He felt deeply ashamed.

Character traits, long suppressed, began to resurface. Now, whenever she asked him to do things he took his time, wilfully refusing to be hurried. The more she urged him to comply the more obstinate he became, knowing how furious it made her and taking malevolent glee in it. Often, he would ignore her altogether, seemingly oblivious to her presence.

But, whilst it might appear to others that he was utterly calm, below the surface an acid pool of resentment simmered, and, to protect his sanity he began to drift off into his memories. Christmas came, a time when, as a child, he had dreamed of the small treats that might appear in his stocking, or of the feasts and games that Aunt Kit would put on. Now, besides dear Grace, he thought of folk long dead – his mother and father, his first love, Emily, his best pal, Greatrix, lost comrades . . .

Out the latter came, marching in their hundreds from the dark recesses of his mind, decomposing corpses, headless torsos, disembodied faces of soldiers he had trained. He examined each one, trying to look beyond the horrific wounds, forcing his mind to reshape them into the whole human beings they had been before he had packed them onto the trains that had taken them to destruction. Then, unable to mend them, he placed them back in the cupboard and shut the door.

In an attempt to put as much distance as he could between himself and Eliza, on his days off he began to go further afield in quest of succour. Yet it was not his sisters to whom he turned, for the years of estrangement over his marriage to Grace had made him guarded in his dealings with them. Even when attending Aunt Gwen's funeral and being reunited with them for the day, he said nothing. No, it was to his old army pal he went. When first wed, he and Eliza had gone together to visit Bert Dungworth and his wife in the next village; now Probyn went alone, making excuses for his dragon of a wife. Even here he was unable to talk of his marital difficulties, however much he and Bert had shared in war, but at least he felt at home.

Relying on this bolthole, he was devastated to find his knock unanswered one day and, not knowing where else to turn, he caught the train to Pontefract and thenceforth made for the army depot.

Despite none here being familiar, the moment the occupants heard that he was an old RSM, he was drawn into their bosom, shown around every inch of the barracks and plied with questions as to how it had been in his day, fêted throughout the afternoon and long into the evening, copious amounts of ale being imbibed as he regaled them with regimental exploits.

Not for a long time had Probyn felt so exhilarated, admitting this to his eager audience as he noticed the time on the clock and sighing what a shame it was that he would have to leave.

There came an inebriated chorus of dismay and calls for him to have just one more drink with them.

It took little persuasion. He allowed them to refill his glass, not wanting this happy time to end. When they offered him a cot for the night he accepted gladly and drank with them long after tattoo had dimmed the rest of the barracks.

But intoxicated as he was, the depressing reality could not be shaken off and was with him as he closed his eyes: he could not escape her for ever.

For a moment when the bugler called reveille, he was seventeen again, the sound jerking him upright and out of bed in order to escape Corporal Wedlock's wrath. But there was no one else in the room.

Flopping back onto the edge of the bed, he sat there for a while rubbing his face, a cloak of dismay settling upon him as he pictured Eliza's face when he went home. How he hated her.

Trying to force his mind into coherent thought, he remembered that he was on a late shift and hence there was no urgency to leave. But his children might be worried, and, only out of concern for them did he hurry to his ablutions, enjoying a fried breakfast before eventually leaving for the railway station.

His arrival back at Denaby coincided with the procession of children to school and a moment of gladness occurred when he saw his own amongst them and stopped to exchange a few warm words.

But once their cheery little faces had gone on their way, his former dark mood was reinstated as he made his way home, imagining Eliza's greeting.

His prediction was accurate, her angry enquiry spearing him the moment he opened the door. 'And where the hell have you been?'

'I'm sorry if you were worrie –'

'Oh I wasn't worried!'

'No, I didn't think you would be somehow.' He spoke quietly, taking off his jacket and fitting it over the back of a dining chair. 'But just for your information, I spent the night at the depot with some army friends. I had no intention of inconveniencing you and I'm sorry.' The look on his face warned her not to persist.

'I suppose you want feeding.' Her nostrils were flared, as if the very sight of him caused her distaste.

'No, thank you. I had breakfast there. But I'd appreciate a cup of tea if there's one going.' He sat at the table, picturing his nagging wife being hit by a bus and imagining what joy and relief he would feel at her death.

Stiff of limb, Eliza brought him a cup of tea. 'I was just reading the newspaper but you can have it if you like.' She did not seem overly eager to give it up.

When he politely declined, she went back to reading it herself, not another word passing between them.

Waiting for his tea to cool, Probyn shoved his chair back, rolled up his sleeves and went to fetch his boots. Choosing not to employ his usual fireside seat, for this would bring him into closer proximity with her, he put an old newspaper on the table and began to set out his tin, brushes and cloths. Her felt her eyes on him, thought he heard a tut of exasperation, but ignored it and launched into his task.

Throughout his life, in times of worry or anger, Probyn had always found therapy in the cleaning of his boots, failing to recognize that lately he had become obsessive in this task.

Trying her best to read, Eliza was constantly distracted by the scrubbing of bristles upon leather. There would be comparative silence for a few moments whilst he applied more polish and saliva, then the brushing would start up again. On and on it went until she could withhold her irritation no longer and slapped the newspaper on her lap. 'For God's sake, aren't they clean enough? You'll polish the blasted things away.'

He showed not the slightest hint of having heard her, his arm propelling the bristles vigorously back and forth.

Simmering, she went back to reading the newspaper and found something that might distract him. 'I wonder if this woman's related to you. Kilmaster's not a very common name.'

Even now he ignored her, continuing to buff his boots to a mirror-like gloss.

'It's one of these legal things: anyone wishing to contest the last will and testament of Ann Kilmas –'

'Oh, dear God.' Probyn stopped polishing, groaned and closed his eyes, before eventually looking up at her. 'It's my stepmother.' Wearing an expression of guilt, he tried to recall the last time he had contacted Ann. Having received the occasional letter from her, he could not remember at what point the correspondence had dried up.

'Does it say when the funeral is?'

Eliza's tone lacked interest. 'It'll be long past now. She died a while ago.'

Feeling ashamed, he said he would have to write condolences to her offspring.

'Well, whilst you're at it, see if she's left you anything.' Eliza turned the page.

Probyn beheld her with reproach. 'What sort of a person would they think I am?'

'A sensible one! I take it this is the woman you told me about who got the benefit of your aunt's house when your father died?' At his nod, she grew more strenuous. 'Then you're entitled to it!'

'I would have heard by now if I had got a mention. It's my own fault. I didn't treat her very well.'

'She's not the only one! So I'm expected to make ends meet looking after your children while you let others have what's yours?' And she continued to scold him for throwing away this chance when money was so tight.

Under her badgering, he retreated into his impenetrable shell and went back to polishing his boots.

'At least contact a solicitor!'

But he steadfastly ignored her, making her more furious than ever.

'Right!' An angry rustling of paper. 'I'll send for a copy of the will myself then!'

Eliza did send off for a copy of the will, but it was to do her not the slightest good, for there was no mention of Probyn's name, Ann Kilmaster having left everything to her own children.

'And quite right,' approved Probyn, when she told him.

Naturally, it was the wrong thing to have said, but then every word he uttered seemed to annoy her whether intentional or not.

'Oh yes, your own wife's condemned to turning sheets whilst others line their pockets, but that's quite all right!' An old sheet spread upon the table, with a vicious set of mouth Eliza ran her scissors through its threadbare centre, then grasped the two outer edges and began to pin them together in readiness for darning.

He wondered, as he sat trying to read his evening newspaper through yet another haranguing, trying to focus his mind on the print and not the torrent of abuse that was fast inducing a headache, how long it would take for life to reach the point where it was no longer bearable and he would have to walk away or kill her.

The following morning, Probyn was awoken by a splitting headache, the very act of opening his eyes causing him to feel sick. He remained prone for some while, reluctant to move either to right or left, and feeling strangely disorientated, until a tap from the knocker-up told him what time it was.

Feeling Eliza stir beside him, he muttered without looking at her, 'I don't feel like getting up.'

'None of us do,' Eliza was equally sullen, 'but we can't all stay in bed.' After a moment, she herself stretched and rose.

'No, I mean I *really* don't feel like it. I'm badly, Liza.'

Grace would have sympathized, would have crooned soothingly and called him poor thing and insisted he stay there, tucked him up and cosseted him. But Eliza's response was, 'If you don't get up you don't get paid.' And taking it for granted that he would follow, she went downstairs.

It was a great effort to drag himself out of bed and, once on his feet he felt even worse, having to steady himself with the iron bedstead. Feeling as if he might vomit, he closed his eyes. The room began to spin and he sat down on the mattress again.

When he did not come down Eliza yelled up to him, 'Do you want this breakfast or not?'

Taking a few deep breaths, he finally hauled himself to his feet and staggered down the staircase. With every step a knife was plunged into his skull.

Her stepmother's voice having woken her, Beata was the first of the children to come down. Her father was seated in a stiff, unnatural pose at the table, his head bowed. Unusually, he did not lift his face to greet her.

Then, with a hint of decisiveness he pushed aside his plate. 'I'm sorry, I just can't stomach that. I'm off back to bed.'

'You're not, you know!' Eliza warned him. 'I can't afford to lose a day's money. I've just managed to get us back on our feet after the strike.'

'I'm sick, woman.' Probyn spoke through gritted teeth.

'And I'm sick! Sick of trying to make ends meet –'

'For God's sake –'

'Oh, get back to bed then!' she goaded him. 'You're bloody useless. I thought I was getting a man, not an invalid.'

Deeper and deeper and deeper she drove, like a fungus boring into the heart-wood of this fine oak, whilst he held his throbbing head and hoped he would not vomit.

'Look at you!' Her face was twisted in spite. 'You're acting like an old man. Why, you might as well be dead for all the use you –'

'I couldn't care if the Lord took me tomorrow!' So saying, his face blood-red, an enraged Probyn bent and seized the iron fender that surrounded the hearth, raised it above his head and hurled it with such passion through the open doorway that it soared almost to the end of the yard and landed with a terrifying clatter that made Beata cower and tremble.

Eliza was cowering too. Her eyes, robbed of that usual cocksure gleam, were now wide and uncertain and she backed away, fearing that she would be next to feel his madness. But Probyn's anger was quickly spent. Too sick to utter another word, he simply lurched from the room.

For a moment, Eliza remained behind the chair to which she

had clung for protection. Only at the sound of his feet creeping painfully up the staircase followed by the bemused appearance of other members of the family, did she emerge, delivering a rough shove to Beata. 'Get those plates on the table!'

Beata worried all day about her father's health and consequently was first in from school that afternoon. It was a vast relief to see him up and about, though his face was a most irregular colour as he made his way to the lavatory and when he came back it was not to sit down but to head straight for the stairs. Beata noticed that her stepmother did not speak to him, her lips merely pursed in contempt.

About to help with the preparation of tea, Beata heard her father say, 'Ooh, me head,' and she turned to look at him, just as he sank to the carpet in a faint – no, he was not completely unconscious, for Beata saw that his eyes were open and his mouth was twisted as he tried desperately to speak. She gave a little cry and looked at her stepmother.

For a second Eliza remained at her post by the sink, shock spreading over her face, then cautiously she came forth and bent over him.

'Go fetch Nurse Gentle.'

Mirroring her father's paralysis, though her own was incurred by horror, the little girl could not move

'Did you hear me?' Eliza's harsh words and a rough shove jarred Beata into action.

Charging from the house, she rushed to an adjacent street and Fanny's house, but no one answered her knock. After a frantic moment, she pelted to the Rushton household where she knew there would be a friendly face. The window was open and to save time she used it.

Mr Rushton, the colliery policeman, had just come in from work and was enjoying a cup of tea when the voice bellowed through the lace curtain.

'Me father!'

'Eh, Beat, you nearly had me upskelling hot tea on me privetties!' Mr Rushton looked as shocked as his wife, who was clutching her bosom, both peering out of the window at the distraught child.

'Nurse Gentle's not in!' panted Beata. 'Me Father's fallen on the floor and he can't get up.'

Mrs Rushton was instantly calm and went outside. 'Don't fret, honey,' she tried to allay the child's fears as they set off for Cliff View, large breasts thrusting ahead of her under the bib of her pinafore. 'He might not be as bad as you think.'

But when they arrived and she saw Probyn, totally unconscious now upon the floor, her demeanour became grave and, after stooping to examine him, she lifted her face and told Eliza, 'Looks like a stroke.'

A concerned Eliza nodded, plucking at her chin. 'That's what I thought.'

'We need to get him into bed,' said Mrs Rushton, using the edge of the table to pull herself upright.

Eliza gesticulated at a rickety bed-chair by the fire. 'We'll put him on that.' Deftly, she unfolded the wooden frame.

'Ah, good, you're here!' Mrs Rushton looked grateful upon seeing her husband, who had come to investigate. 'We'll need help to shift him; he's a big lad.' She glanced at the knot of children who had just arrived home, bewildered and afraid by what they witnessed. 'Your father'll be all right, don't worry. Beat, be a good lass and run down and fetch the doctor.'

Whilst Beata hurried away the Rushtons and their helpers struggled to convey Probyn's leaden body from the carpet to the makeshift bed that creaked and groaned in protest as his fourteen-stone frame was laid upon it.

Then there was little else to be done except to stand back and await medical help.

Still unconscious, Probyn was to remain upon the bed-chair for three days. On each of these days when Beata and her siblings came home from school they would rush to see if he had recovered, but the answer was invariably the same.

'Don't bother to run, he's no different,' Eliza would warn them with a hint of exasperation the moment they dashed through the door, which to them signified heartlessness, and they paid no heed and gathered round their father, looking for a sign that he might suddenly wake, the stepchildren hovering in the background.

Clem and Joe too made it their first act to examine their father upon coming in from work, both equally anxious.

Though Probyn had allowed his religion to lapse Father Flanagan was amongst those who came to offer his support, this being in the form of prayers. Eliza didn't like him being here, the children could tell from the snide remarks she made after he had gone, but it was a comfort to them and they echoed his appeals to the Lord. So too did Augusta when, informed of her father's affliction by letter, she came on Friday evening, spending her whole time kneeling at his bedside, pressing each rosary bead so fervently in her prayers that her fingers became indented and sore.

If Eliza shared the children's anxiety then she showed it in a curious way, going about her business as if nothing had happened and even berating their desire to linger at his bedside. 'You needn't think you're sitting round him all day. You wouldn't expect to do it if he was like this permanently so what's the point of doing it now? Now, you've seen him and paid your respects, come and make yourselves useful because you're not doing your father a bit of good.'

Had any of them been able to read her mind they would have condemned as even more pitiless the thought that was going through her head as she laid eyes on their father's motionless frame: this is all I need, a helpless invalid to look after besides ten others.

But even going about their various tasks, if in the same room the children's eyes would make constant checks on their father, and it was one such glance from Duke that witnessed Probyn open his eyes. 'He's alive!' His triumphant cry had the others leaping to the bedside.

Their stepmother in the lavatory, there was no one here to curb them except Augusta who, calm and kindly, prevented Duke from jumping on the bed. 'Ssh! Don't crowd him.'

Afraid, Mims' hand sought out Madeleine's. Duke chewed on his knuckle.

Heart lifting, Beata watched as her father's blue-grey eyes struggled to focus, saw the expression in them turn from blurred confusion to terror and then frustration as his lips tried to form speech but could only emit an animal grunt. And the smiles began to fade from the children's faces as saliva dribbled from his flaccid lips, his panic turning to anger, then finally weakening to acceptance, and by the time Eliza returned he had slipped back into unconsciousness.

'Me Father woke up but he's gone back to sleep,' Duke informed his stepmother the moment she was through the door.

Eliza hurried up and peered closely at her husband. Then, 'You're making it up!' she chastised them crossly and sent them back to their chores.

'We're not,' Beata vouched as she went. 'He opened his eyes, we all saw it.'

Eliza responded callously to this show of impertinence. 'Well, he's

338

not awake now, is he? And no amount of romancing from you is going to bring him back to life!'

She was right. Their father was not to recover consciousness again. He died on Sunday.

Once again, dazed with grief the Kilmaster children gathered around a parent's coffin, to kiss his cold cheek. So many cold cheeks. Watching, their stepmother made no move to comfort them, even in her tears being strangely aloof, as if she were blaming Father for dying.

It was left to Augusta and Clem to offer solace to the younger ones, which indeed they did, but for the latter it was a strange time. Bereft though he undoubtedly was, Clem had always felt inferior to his father, and when Eliza announced that she would need his support a shaft of light percolated his grief, he seized his chance to be a man, telling her not to worry, that he would look after her, after them all.

It was Clem, therefore, who made all the funeral arrangements, who wrote to inform their aunts and uncles of Probyn's sudden death, who met them at the station and introduced them to the various neighbours who were to be their hosts, there being not enough room at the Kilmaster house for all these people.

After the interment, though, Eliza did invite them back to her parlour for a tea of ham and fruit cake, even the children being allowed to participate.

'Eh dear.' A crumb-laden plate in her hand, Ethel's unfocused blue eyes were moist as they gazed into space and she shook her head miserably. 'I still can't get over the shock. You don't expect the youngest to go first – well, our Beata was first to go but you imagine there'll be some sort of order to dying, don't you? I fully expected to be next.'

Noting the children's distress, Meredith fought her own anguish and tried to bolster them, tapping Beata's leg affectionately. 'Eh, your father was such a funny bairn! I remember, we once went on a picnic, our Probe wouldn't be more than three – I was only five meself but I remember it as clear as day – he went rummaging about in the grass and fetched Aunt Kit a dead chaffinch for her hat. It stunk to high heaven! But she had to pretend it was just what she wanted.' Succeeding in making them laugh, she chuckled too, but there were tears in her eyes when she turned to Eliza. 'Can we help in any way, dear? Perhaps take the children to stay with us for a while? We've had them before. They're no bother.'

'Oh no, that's very kind but it won't be necessary.' Eliza showed gratitude.

'I don't envy you with ten to care for on your own,' sighed Alice.

'She won't be on her own.' Flattered that Eliza thought him capable of filling the role of man of the house, Clem was determined to repay her confidence in him. 'I'll look after her.'

To his siblings' wonder, Eliza allowed their brother this moment's dominance, beaming upon him gratefully as she added, 'And it's not as if they're all helpless children. Joe and Edwin are young men and Madeleine'll be getting a job.'

This being the first she had heard of it, Madeleine looked at her stepmother sharply. Her own intention had been to stay at school for as long as possible and then go into nursing, but that plan looked destined for failure now.

Finally, paying their respects to the widow and to Probyn's children, the aunts and uncles departed to catch their trains to various parts of the country.

Prohibited from play, the children were forced to sit in respectful silence until bedtime which came much earlier this evening, Eliza irritated by their doleful presence.

As the rest made for bed, a solemn Beata tarried to ask her stepmother, 'Will I still be taking Mims for her lesson tomorrow?'

'Huh! You will not. We'll be lucky if we can afford food now, let alone piano lessons.' Eliza saw Mims' look of dismay and pointed a finger at her. 'And before you start, lady, there are other things you're going to have to get used to. Your father's not here to mollycoddle you now. Mark my words, things are going to change around here.'

Her objection stifled, the disconsolate infant turned and went to bed with the others, Eliza's harsh words invoking not just a sense of loss but one of foreboding.

PART THREE

TWENTY

The changes came thick and fast, allowing the children little time to grieve. Adjacent to the cancellation of Mims' piano lessons on Saturday, Madeleine was packed off to find a job and told not to come back till she had found one; the portrait of Probyn's dead sister, which Eliza had always thought a monstrosity, was taken from the wall and along with other hated items that had once belonged to Grace, was thrown on the cart of a passing rag-and-bone man in exchange for sixpence. The Sabbath brought even more dramatic consequence.

'I'm not pandering to any more whims,' came Eliza's brisk announcement at the time the children normally branched out to separate places of worship. 'Everyone's to go to All Saints.'

'We can't!' This was a rash utterance from fourteen-year-old Joe. 'It's not the real church!' Receiving a hefty smack round the head, he beheld his stepmother with total shock.

She directed a finger of warning, this reflected in her eyes. 'Don't you dare cheek me! You're going.'

Waiting only for Eliza to go into the scullery, Joe bounded upstairs to solicit help from Clem, who was still in bed, Beata following.

'Don't talk bloody daft,' Clem growled from under the blankets when informed of the heinous crime about to be perpetrated upon them. 'Church is church.'

'So you'll be going to All Saints then, Clem?' Beata wanted confirmation that they would not be struck down in flames.

'I'm not going anywhere.' Her eldest brother had decided to take advantage of his elevation to man of the house by lazing in bed.

'But what would Father say?'

'Never mind what Father would say!' Clem hoisted an irritated face. '*I'm* saying do as your mother tells you!' After a brief glare he allowed his head to flop back to the pillow, turning his back on them.

His brother and sister stared at him wonderingly, Beata with tears pricking her eyes. Father had been gone only a week yet Clem seemed already to have settled quite comfortably into the niche he had etched for himself, siding with their stepmother as if now on equal footing with her.

Under the pretext of obedience, the youngsters left the house, but the moment they were outside Joe rammed his cap on defiantly. 'I'm buggered if I'm being relegated to eternal damnation. I'm off to me own church.'

Equally adamant, Madeleine joined her voice to his, the much younger Duke, Beata and Mims merely falling in with them, and, upon reaching All Saints they declined to enter with their stepsister and brothers and went on to St Alban's.

They might have known George would betray them, sitting there gloating whilst Eliza dished out her punishment. Without Father to restrain her she was free to vent her aggression, thrashing each of them with a shoe and telling them, 'You're only getting your dinner because I don't want my hard work wasted! Try disobeying me next week and you'll go hungry!'

It was useless for the brothers to dish out any retribution of their own, for George would simply inform on them for this too. Hence, the following Sunday, Joe put it to his siblings that it was either excommunication or a good hiding from Eliza, and as privately he himself was more afraid of his stepmother than the flames of hell he had decided to go to All Saints.

The others, though dreading the wrath of God that would surely befall them, nevertheless followed his lead, Beata grasping for a comforting thought, 'Perhaps if we don't say any of their prayers Our Lord'll forgive us.'

The rest agreed, though were to find that standing tight-lipped whilst the worshippers made their incantations was bound to draw attention to them, this instilling great discomfort. After what seemed like hours they emerged into the sunlight, swearing they could not go through such an ordeal again and looking tentatively skywards as if expecting to be struck by a bolt of lightning.

But retribution was to come in a more human form. It was the custom on Monday, when the Catholic pupils were summoned from class to attend Father Flanagan's instruction, for the question to be asked, 'Who did not attend Mass yesterday?' The sinners would receive punishment, though the Kilmasters, being raised by such a devout mother, had never had occasion to encounter this.

Today, though, when the question came, Beata, Duke and Mims were compelled to raise their hands.

Father Flanagan looked stern and sad. 'I'm shocked, I really am.' Then, after glaring at them for a moment, he pointed at the contents of a coal bucket by the fire. 'Your souls are now as black as that!'

It was pointless trying to tell him they had been made to do it; one did not answer back. Told to step forward, they meekly held out their hands to receive a stinging rap from a cane across each palm. Then, hands burning with pain, eyes scalded by tears, the Kilmasters moved shamefully back into line.

Faced with the threat of punishment from all quarters, the children did not know which way to turn. Dare they risk Eliza's wrath by worshipping at their own church, or jeopardize their place in Heaven?

As if in answer the Lord sent an angel in the guise of Doris, who, feeling sorry for their plight, told them not to fear betrayal if they wished to continue going to St Alban's. 'I've told our George that if he rats on you I'll do the same to him. He's been pinching Mother's chocolate cracknels and hiding them behind the cistern in the netty.'

Relief flooding their faces, the siblings thanked Doris for this ammunition. Next Sunday, they would return to their own place of worship.

All went well for a couple of weeks, George keeping his promise, under threat from his sister. But in the end it was not George who gave them away, an innocent remark by a neighbour exposing their chicanery.

After doling out another beating, Eliza swore that they *would* bend to her will and, the following Sunday, ensured they went to All Saints by asking Clem to take them.

'I'm relying on you, Clem.'

Their brother wasn't very pleased about being dragged out of bed on a Sabbath, hence his bad temper as he accompanied them right to the door of the church and gave them a shove inside.

Not so easily deterred, they merely pretended to follow Doris, Edwin and George down the aisle, but the instant Clem retreated they scuttled from the heathen temple and on towards the real church.

This pantomime would have continued indefinitely had not Clem turned round by chance one Sunday and caught them in the act. The reprimand he delivered serving to warp their faith both in God and their brother, the Kilmasters decided that a change of religion was inevitable.

This being so, also inevitable on Monday morning, was the penalty served out by Father Flanagan for their non-attendance at Mass. In a much worse position than Joe or Maddie, who no longer attended school and so were spared Father Flanagan's discipline, the younger children despaired that this unjust state of affairs would be repeated week after week if they did not do something about it. But what? The one person they might have expected to help had his feet in the enemy camp.

Taking Augusta's latest visit as their opportunity, they petitioned for support. Whilst appalled that the children were being forced to reject their own religion, she felt helpless to oppose the strong-willed Eliza.

Not wanting to make their predicament worse by speaking to their stepmother she voiced her grievance to their eldest brother, telling him, 'Mother would be horrified by what's going on.'

Clem was unmoved at first. His sister had always been more devout than the rest and he thought her complaint stemmed from this.

But no. 'I do care about them being kept from church,' Augusta admitted, 'but not just that. It's unfair that they're being punished on all fronts for something that's beyond their control, Clem. Don't you realize they're being caned every Monday for not going to Mass?'

'No, I didn't.' Clem's face reddened, his annoyance directed partly at himself. For a young man of only twenty-one the role of surrogate father to nine children was a great responsibility. 'You're right, it is unfair.'

'So will you talk to Eliza?'

'No.' He prevented Augusta's objection by saying quickly, 'She's got enough on her plate without this. You don't live here, so keep your neb out. But I will go and tell Father Flanagan about the change of religion and warn him to leave off.' Leaving his sister only half satisfied, he went to the presbytery there and then to inform Father Flanagan that the children were no longer Catholics.

To their great relief, the name of Kilmaster was not amongst those called out of class on Monday morning, nor during the week that

346

followed. As far as the priest was concerned they might as well be Protestants.

Whilst it was wonderful that the caning had stopped, it went against the grain for those so indoctrinated to change the spiritual habits of a lifetime and Beata felt desperate that Father Flanagan should learn that none of this was of her choosing. Maybe then he would put in a good word with the Lord to spare her from the torments of hell.

Seeing him that Saturday morning on his way down to the shop for his mints, she pelted excitedly after him. Too far ahead of her to be overtaken this time, she could see him entering the shop and she barely had the time to form a wistful pose at the window before he was on his way out again.

'Hello, Father!' Thinking he had not noticed her, for he was so tall, Beata smiled up at him.

But his long thin nose was directed straight ahead.

Taking the preoccupied look in his eye as a sign that he had not heard her, Beata said again, louder this time as she began to skip after him, 'Hello, Father!'

Still no response was given, the stony presentation of his back causing her to falter in bewilderment and watch as he kept on walking.

But any misapprehension that it had all been due to her imagination was to be removed upon their next encounter. Eyes directed elsewhere, Father Flanagan cut her dead.

Too upset to mention the priest's icy treatment to anyone at home, Beata was left to reach the conclusion herself: Father Flanagan looked upon her as a sinner and had abandoned her. That it later transpired her siblings had been given the cold shoulder too had no salving effect. Deeply wounded by the one constant in her life, Beata felt her whole world had crumbled.

Believing that miracles only happened to those of the true religion and now demoted from these chosen ranks herself, she was therefore astounded to be summoned to the front of the class that Friday afternoon and told that she had passed the examination that would entitle her to go to Mexborough Grammar School. Bubbling over with a sense of achievement, she could hardly wait to be let out of class. Upon release, it had become the norm to tarry, for there seemed no reason to get home since Father had died – but not today. She ran like a hare, composing herself only slightly so as not to make Eliza jump as she entered the kitchen.

'Hello, Mother. I've passed my scholarship!'

'Have you indeed?' Stirring a pot, Eliza glanced at her approvingly. 'Well done.'

Hardly able to breathe from excitement, a grinning Beata went to wash her hands then set upon the tasks that Eliza instructed her to do.

Siblings entered one by one and launched into their own chores, each receiving Beata's proud announcement. Finally, the one that she had been awaiting came in, putting his unopened wage packet on the table.

'I've passed my scholarship, Clem!'

'Oh, grand!' Her eldest brother dipped into his pocket. 'Here, I think I've got sixpence somewhere.'

'Eh, you must have money to burn,' Eliza told him, though her mood was even.

Beata swelled with happiness. 'I'll use it to buy pencils for my new school!'

'What new school?' asked Eliza, directing others to lay the table.

'Mexborough Grammar.'

'Oh, we haven't got the means to send you there,' came the mild response.

A look of devastation flooded Beata's face.

'I'm sorry,' said Eliza, shaking her head, 'but school uniforms cost a fortune. No, you'll just have to stay where you are. Anyway, it would be a waste of money. You've only got a couple of years to go before you start work.'

After losing both parents, Beata rarely cried over paltry matters, but the sense of disappointment was so acute that she felt her mouth beginning to crumple and so dashed out into the yard in order not to provoke comment.

But comment was to come. 'I don't know what she thinks I am,' Eliza told Clem, with an irritable shake of her head.

He sympathized. 'They've no idea how much it costs to run a house, have they?'

Joe came in then and laid his wage packet on the table, leaving Mims able to drift out unnoticed to the yard and commiserate with her sister. But Beata felt that nothing would console her. She had been right all along: miracles were not for Protestants.

Inside, Eliza had forgotten all about the previous exchange, her attention focused on Joe's wage packet. 'This has been opened!'

'Aye, I know!' He reflected her annoyance. 'I questioned it meself. They said they'd made a mistake with my money and had to take

348

some out. Eh, I don't know, some people . . .' He rolled his eyes in disgust.

'It's you who's made the mistake if you think I'm falling for that one!'

Joe tried to meet her gaze but it was hard. 'No honestly!'

'Liar!'

Fearing violence, Duke played nervously with the collar of his jersey.

Clem intervened. 'Do I have to go down there myself and see the manager?' His threatening manner caused Joe to give in.

'Oh, all right,' the boy eventually mumbled, 'I bought a watch – but I need one so's I can get to work on time and it were a right bargain!'

'Hand it over!' Clem held out his hand into which Joe reluctantly laid his new timepiece. 'Bloody rubbish! How much did you pay for it?'

'Only five bob.'

'Five –' Clem cuffed his brother round the side of the head, Duke flinching out of impulse. 'Do you think Mother's got that amount of money to waste? We've just had Beata mithering 'cause she can't have her school uniform and now you. But you're old enough to know better. Who sold it to you?'

Joe grimaced and held a hand to his burning ear. 'Mr Watson.'

'Right! You can just go and tell him you want your money back.' Clem thrust the watch at him.

'Shop'll be closed,' protested Joe.

Seeing his stepmother about to protest Clem laid a placating hand on her arm. 'Don't worry, I'll break the door down if I have to.' And, though the smell of boiled onions was tantalizing, he gave Joe an angry push and the two of them exited the kitchen.

The Maypole was indeed closed for business but peering through the glass door Clem could make out two figures still inside and began to thump on the door until one of them answered it.

Let in by Watson, the assistant, he wasted no time in demanding that the culprit return Joe's five shillings.

Watson resisted, going to stand behind the counter as a means of protection. Clem was much younger but had a reputation for uncontrolled violence. 'It was a fair exchange! That's a good watch, that is.'

Ravenous for his tea, Clem was even more furious. 'It's shit! You saw a lad of fourteen and thought you'd take advantage. Now give me the money!'

Watson, though worried, saw that help was coming in the form of an annoyed-looking manager and so refused to budge. Infuriated, Clem seized a pair of scales from the counter and held them aloft, threatening to dash them at the man's head. 'Hand it over!'

'Oy!' The manager had reached them. 'I'll call the police!'

'And so will I if this thief doesn't give me my money back!' The scales still poised, a red-faced Clem told the manager what had transpired.

'Watson, take your blessed watch and give Kilmaster his money back!'

When the hurried transaction had occurred, Clem dumped the scales back onto the counter in such a heavy-handed manner that he broke them.

The manager had had enough. 'Right, that's it, get out and take your brother with you! He's sacked.'

'No he isn't, he quits!' Grabbing a handful of Joe's jacket, Clem ejected him from the shop.

However, knowing that Eliza would be furious at his impetuous behaviour, he decided that he must have a solution for her by the time he got home, and now made a detour to the colliery, saying to Joe, 'We'll get you a job down the pit.'

'But Father always said I could go in the army when –'

'How many times do I have to remind you? Father isn't here any more!'

'I don't need reminding.' Part of Joe's reply stemmed from grief that was still raw, though was mostly uttered from a sense of injustice that Clem had taken the opportunity of their father's death to boss everyone around.

'I think you do!' Cuffing him, his brother headed towards the pit manager's office.

Panicked by the thought of going underground, Joe introduced another obstacle. 'I don't reckon Mr Shaw will grant you favours after you threw that inkwell at him.'

'He won't be granting me favours, you'll be the one doing the persuading, seeing as it was your stupid behaviour that got you the sack!'

Joe would have liked to argue that it was Clem's temper that had caused this, but thought the better of it. With the prospect of being humiliated by Eliza if he did not have a job when he got home, there was no option but to resign himself to working at the colliery until he was big enough to stand up for himself. But he resolved there and then that as soon as that time came he would leave this wretched life and join the army.

Eliza was pleased to have her five shillings back, but her jaw dropped upon hearing the news that Clem had found Joe more lucrative work at the pit.

Faced with her look of astonishment, Clem thought he might have overstepped his responsibilities. 'That is what you wanted, isn't it?'

She came to life, patting him admiringly. 'It is! I was just so amazed by the way you've got everyone organized. Thank heaven I've got one person who puts my needs first.'

Clem smiled as she placed her hands upon his shoulders and steered him to the chair that had once been his father's.

Beata realized then something she had not noticed before. If ever Eliza laid hands on Clem it was to inflict not pain but some gesture of affection. Beata now began to pick up on every one of these tokens as her stepmother moved back and forth around the kitchen, a touch here, a stroke there, a hand draped carelessly across his shoulder as she leaned over the table to deposit his meal. Clem being an adult, his stepmother had always been easy-going with him, but young as Beata was she detected a subtle change between the pair now, a familiarity that normally only passed between husband and wife. It made her uncomfortable.

'Right, you can start.' Eliza took her place at the table, providing a tureen of meatless stew, not out of any sensibility for the children's Catholic upbringing but because there was no money left for meat by Friday.

Lined up with her siblings, most of them standing, Mims was looking with dismay at her plate. There were peas amongst the other vegetables. With great delicacy she used the tip of her knife to flick one after another of them to the side of her plate.

Eliza eyed the small green mound. 'You'd better not be contemplating leaving those.'

Glancing up into her stepmother's threatening face, Mims began to eat her meal as best she could, but very slowly and without relish.

Whilst Probyn had been able to make his youngest daughter eat by sheer mental strength, Eliza had no time for battles of will with a six-year-old. After several minutes of watching this laborious performance and angered by what she saw as ingratitude, she lashed out at Mims, but having no chair and acting on reflex the little girl jumped back, so causing Eliza's hand to come into painful

351

contact with the table. Catching the hint of a smirk on Mims' face, Eliza leaped from her seat and dragged the child to the understairs cupboard, shutting her inside. 'Let's see you laugh your way out of that one!'

Clem's siblings turned to him swiftly, but his only intervention was a sigh before continuing with his dinner.

Panicking, Mims gave a kick at the door. It was immediately hauled open and a leather belt thrust into her face. 'It's either the cupboard or this!'

Before Mims could answer, the door was slammed shut again, but too afraid of the consequences she made no further protest. For a second, defiance lingered and she poked out her tongue at the locked door, stuck her thumbs in her ears, waggled her fingers at Eliza through the wood and pulled all manner of insulting faces.

But she was only a little girl. The darkness began to close in on her. She could feel it pressing against her face, suffocating her. Heart pounding in fright, she dropped to her haunches and began to sob, though quietly so as not to give Eliza any hint of triumph.

Then, as she cowered, trying to overcome her terror, whether real or imagined the scent of ginger came wafting into her prison, curling under her nostrils and settling onto her tongue so that she could actually taste it, imbuing her with a feeling of warmth as if protective arms were wrapped around her. And gradually the panic subsided, her defiant heart adopting a more regular beat. And through those dark, horrible hours that followed she was sustained by the taste of her own lovely mother's gingerbread.

Many another's spirit might have been broken by this treatment, but next morning Mims was her normal self, dawdling over her breakfast as usual.

Always foulest in the morning, Eliza's temper was ready to erupt at the sight of such disregard. 'I'd like you to get to Mexborough before closing time if it's not too much to ask!' This being Saturday there was the shopping to do. 'And if they've sold out of my cakes you'll be for it, madam.'

Not at work today, Clem urged his little sister to do as she was told.

Mims sped up for a time, but soon lapsed and, whilst the others had almost finished, she seemed to be having difficulty with her crusts.

'Anyone'd think you didn't have a tooth in your head, the heavy weather you're making of eating it,' scolded Eliza. 'Look, everyone else is finished and waiting for you! If that's not down you in thirty seconds you can look forward to another spell in the cupboard.'

Protective of her sister, Beata waited until Eliza's attention was diverted, then grabbed Mims' crusts off her, these disappearing under the table. She caught Clem's eye – he had seen her! A suspenseful moment ensued whilst she waited anxiously for him to give her away, but mercifully all he did was to shake his head in exasperation.

When Eliza turned round again Mims' plate was empty. This provoked suspicion. 'You'd better have eaten them.' Making everyone except Clem leave the table, she checked underneath to see if there was anything on the floor, but there was nothing to see. Only half satisfied, Eliza gave the children a list and a purse, armed with which they left for the market, leaving their stepmother and Clem to enjoy a cup of tea in peace.

'It's a good job I've got strong elastic.' Beata hoisted her skirt and delved into the leg of her knickers, withdrawing a crust. 'Are you sure you don't want this?' Glad that the crust was refused, for she herself was always hungry, she devoured it, along with the others that were withdrawn one by one from their hiding place.

On reaching Mexborough, they made their purchase of everything on Eliza's list, ensuring that her favourite cake, walnut with butter icing, was placed safely on top of the basket. After a covetous look in the window of Harry May's toyshop and not overly keen to get home, they decided to call in and visit their sister on the haberdashery counter of Bon Marche, delivering their pretend requirements in lardy-dah tone – 'Horf a yord of rrribbon, pleeese!' – and causing Madeleine great embarrassment before being shooed from the shop by an irate manageress.

Their trepidation at going home turned out to be unwarranted, for Eliza's mood seemed to have taken a turn for the better when they finally arrived, their stepmother engaged in good-humoured banter with Clem whilst he repaired a cupboard door.

In fact she was to remain equable for the rest of the day, even allowing the children a sliver of walnut cake at teatime. Hating butter icing, Beata politely refused, knowing that this was one time she was in no danger of being made to eat something she did not like.

After tea, Eliza announced, 'Millicent, how would you like to play the piano for us?'

Clem looked somewhat shocked. 'Don't you think the neighbours might think it's a bit funny?' His father had barely been dead two months.

'Oh, I don't intend for us to have a knees-up.' Looking conscientious and pressing her hand to his shoulder, Eliza went to sift through the sheets of music in Grace's piano stool, selecting only the most respectful tunes. 'But a quiet sing-song won't do any harm. We've had a lot of bad luck lately, we need cheering up. Your father would have been the first to tell us to get on with our lives and not stay miserable.'

Lifting Mims onto the stool, she placed a sheet of music before her, then went to stand behind Clem's chair, her hands resting on his shoulders. Joining in with everyone else, Beata glanced across the room to see that the hands had set up a gentle caressing. At one point Clem even put up his own hand to cover one of hers, causing Beata to look away quickly as if burned.

Otherwise, it was to be a very enjoyable interlude that lasted until bedtime which, for those under thirteen, was seven thirty.

This being far too early for sleep, Beata, Mims and Doris were still awake when Maddie came up a few hours later and climbed in beside her sisters. Ever-hungry, Beata sniffed Maddie's breath like a dog. 'You've had bread.' Only those with paid work were allowed supper.

'Aye, a whole slice,' marvelled her sister, faintly sarcastic. 'She's in a good mood tonight, what have you done to her?'

Beata could not imagine. 'It wasn't me.'

'Me neither,' chimed Doris.

'She's laughing fit to burst down there with our Clem,' said Maddie.

On the other side of the partition, Joe was climbing into bed beside Edwin, George and the sleeping Marmaduke, grumbling to the speaker, 'Aye, you'd be laughing an' all if you could pocket everybody's wages and give them only a tanner to spend.'

'Is that what you get?' Beata asked her sister.

Maddie nodded. 'I'll bet our Clem gets more than that.'

'You mean golden boy.' Edwin had noticed the favouritism too.

'Aye, Mother likes him, doesn't she?' chipped in Doris.

Beata agreed. 'Still, if he can keep her laughing I'm not bothered how much she gives him.'

'It's all right for you!' came her brother's voice from the other side of the partition. 'You don't have to slave away all week in a bloody mucky pit just for her to rob you of all your earnings.'

Beata wondered how Joe could not recognize that she was equally oppressed. She might not go out to work but having to spend longer in Eliza's company brought a different form of slavery.

'Shush, our Clem's coming!' Maddie's warning plunged everyone into silence, all snuggling under the covers.

Duly, Clem slipped into the single bed that stood only inches away from that of his brothers and everyone settled down to sleep.

Jolted awake in the middle of the night, at first Joe assumed that Clem had got up to use the chamber pot. It was a normal occurrence and, after being briefly disturbed, he himself fell back to sleep. But when he woke again to find the rising sun warming the room and his brother's bed still empty, he became curious, this keeping him from further slumber.

Deciding to investigate, he rolled out of bed leaving only three sleeping figures in it, and crept out on to the small landing – where his tiptoeing figure almost collided with Clem, who was leaving Eliza's room.

There was a stifled cry, a moment of acute embarrassment, then angry muttering from Clem as he gestured for Joseph to get back to bed. 'Can't a man have any bloody privacy?'

'I just wondered where –'

'I got sick of listening to you lot snoring!' Clem hissed aggressively, shoving him backwards. 'Mother said I could come into the double bed for a while and enjoy a bit of peace. That's all, so don't go saying owt to anybody or I'll bloody thump you!'

'I weren't going to!' Joe continued to back away.

'Better not!' Clem poked Joe in the chest, which caused him to fall on top of the bed's occupants, who had been woken by the dispute and who now yelled in complaint as their brother got back in, squashing the smaller ones against the wall.

'And you can shut up an' all!' warned Clem.

'What's going on?' Behind the partition, Beata's muzzy face lifted itself from the pillow.

'Get back to sleep,' growled Clem. 'It's not time to get up yet.'

The house fell silent for another hour, a shocked Joe lying there wide awake, horrified by what he had witnessed. What if his siblings were to ask about the disturbance? How could he share the knowledge that he had seen his brother coming out of their stepmother's bedroom?

It was small relief for Joe that he was not to be the one who broke the shocking story. Unaware that Duke had heard every word,

Clem was plunged into embarrassment when the nine-year-old asked innocently at the breakfast table, 'Mother, can Clem sleep in your bed every night? Then we'd have more room.'

Everyone stopped eating. Ignorant of the facts of life but knowing this could not be right, Beata's heart started to thud.

Blushing furiously, Clem's eyes flew to Eliza. 'I never brea –' But when he saw that her mouth had begun to turn up at the corners, he did not feel quite so bad.

Eliza threw back her head and laughed out loud. She seemed deliriously happy today, the onlookers noticed, her breast jiggling up and down under the white bib of her pinafore as she gave vent to her amusement. 'Why, I think that makes great sense! Don't you, Clem?' She dabbed at her watering eyes. 'After all, you are the man of the house now. You might as well enjoy the privileges.'

Clem ran a self-conscious hand over his angular jaw and glanced at the older children to gauge their opinion. Only Joe and Maddie realized the true significance in all this, their antipathy forbidding them to meet Clem's eye, but the rest seemed unperturbed, obviously grateful for anything that could inject Eliza with such good humour.

With Clem's nod, it was taken for granted by everyone that this was the way things would be.

'But you don't mention a word of it outside this house!' Eliza warned the younger ones, showing them the back of her hand. 'Or else.'

Both Maddie and Joe thought this warning superfluous, could not even bring themselves to voice it to each other as they and the rest made their way to church, though each nursed the private query: how could Clem love a woman who treated his siblings so harshly? But the question remained unspoken, the only reference to the new sleeping arrangement being made later when Maddie snuggled down beside her sisters in bed.

'I can't stand this.'

'What do you mean?' Beata's auburn head turned on the pillow.

'I can't explain,' muttered Maddie. 'You'll know when you're older. There are things going on here that aren't right. I can't stick it. I'm off to ask if I can go into service. It can't be harder work than here and at least I'll get properly fed.'

Next morning, before leaving for work, she put her request to Eliza. Her stepmother was none too pleased at first, objecting that she could not spare her, but when Maddie pointed out that someone else would have the job of feeding her and she would still be sending

356

money home, Eliza gave it serious thought. 'All right,' she said eventually, 'but you mustn't tell a soul – and that goes for you lot,' she warned the others as they prepared for school. 'If anyone should ask, Madeleine's still living at home.'

TWENTY-ONE

Following their sister's departure, her household tasks were divided between the rest of the children. 'Well, you needn't think I'm doing them!' Eliza retorted at the look on their faces when she informed them. 'I do enough running about after you lot.' She was constantly bewailing this, but to Beata and her siblings the only one she seemed to run around after was Clem.

Still, they must be grateful to their brother for diverting her attention from them. Since taking him into her bed she was generally a lot happier.

But happiness was a fragile entity in a mining village, the word 'goodbye' having deeper significance amongst those who earned their living underground, every wife and mother, even the cynical Eliza, spending eight hours of dread until their men were safely home. Even so, with no siren to warn of a disaster, she was not anticipating anything untoward when she answered a knock at her door that same week.

Finding two men bearing her son Edwin on a stretcher, his face contorted by pain, she let out a shriek.

'He's been kicked by a pony, love,' came the swift explanation from one of the men. 'It's his leg.'

Though relieved to hear it was nothing more serious, Eliza moaned in despair. 'God help us, what else could go wrong?'

The strain was beginning to show on the stretcher bearers' faces. 'Well, can you just tell us where to put him?'

Sighing, an anxiety-ridden Eliza ushered them indoors, and watched helplessly as her son, crying in agony, was transferred to the bed-chair where Probyn had recently died.

Having deposited their burden, the men made for the door.

'Well, what am I supposed to do now?' Eliza entreated them.

'I don't reetly know, love. The doctor's seen him, told us to bring him here and he'd be in to talk to thee later.'

With a gloomy nod, Eliza allowed them to leave, then turned to view Edwin. 'Another wage down. Did they say how long you'd be off for?'

In too much pain to answer, her son merely shook his head. The doctor came then, but was also unable to give Eliza an answer. It was just a matter of waiting until the wound healed, he said.

But the wound did not heal. In fact it became even more painful because, as further tests eventually informed them, the bone had become infected. It looked as if Edwin might be a permanent invalid.

Interpreting the word invalid as burden, Eliza fell into a state of aggravation, becoming even more short-tempered with the others to whom she now delegated chores once undertaken by herself, her excuse being that she had a cripple to look after – though to Beata, who took on most of the load, it did not seem that Edwin attracted any more of his mother's attention than he had done previously, Eliza spending much of her time reading and stuffing her face with the chocolate cracknels that she selfishly hid from others.

Yet even without the stress of overwork and a young man in her bed Eliza remained a very unpredictable housemate. She could be in a good mood for weeks, allowing Mims to play the piano or Beata to read a book, then just when they became accustomed to this *entente cordiale* she would fly into a rage for the slightest deviation from her rules. Sometimes there did not appear to be a reason at all. Many a time Beata would feel a hard slap round the head and yet remain totally ignorant of what she had done to deserve it for Eliza would simply glare at her and walk away. Then the next day might find their stepmother as nice as pie. To Beata it was totally beyond comprehension.

One might have hoped that, as the possessor of a kind nature, Clem would direct this towards his siblings and protect them from the blows, but alas no. The surrogate father acted out his role to the full, his sympathy almost entirely for Eliza. As one who found it impossible to control his own temper, Clem knew exactly what she must feel after these unbridled displays, and he empathized with her, guessing that the outbursts were induced by a feeling of helplessness over her situation and knowing how guilty she must feel afterwards. Blinkered by youth and by his sexual obsession with her, he failed to see the difference between the two of them: in him the violent trait was balanced by a compassion totally absent in her. And at twenty-one, he was even less equipped to recognize the deeper, darker reason for his own behaviour: through union with his father's widow he became the man he had always wanted to be.

Beata might have derived some small comfort that the abuse was indiscriminate, meted out to everyone including Eliza's offspring, but some had conjured up a way to avoid it. The minute his mother grabbed hold of him, the wily George would simply hold his breath and go blue in the face until she dropped him like a hot cake out of fear of killing him – then he would laugh behind her back and jab two fingers in the air. Edwin's handicap too went some way to sparing him, and even if Doris might occasionally be the recipient of her mother's volatile temper, she was favoured in material ways.

At Whitsuntide, when their mother had been alive there had always been new outfits in which to attend the procession through town. Now, though, there was insufficient money to reclothe everyone from top to toe. Even the bestowal of new hats was marred by an act of favouritism, for whilst Doris received a proper leghorn straw hat, the top of the range, Beata's looked as if it was made from the material used to thatch roofs, a row of artificial buttercups lending nothing to its lack of daintiness. It did not matter that Mims, being the youngest, only received the usual hand-me-down. To Beata no one was unluckier than herself. Feeling utterly miserable and conspicuous, having to tolerate rude remarks from other children, she hated every moment of the Whitsun parade.

But the humiliation was to continue long after the parade was over, for, too terrified to do otherwise, she was forced to wear the detested hat every Sunday for church.

The thought of running away had never really occurred to Beata before, but now she began seriously to consider it. Born with a wanderlust, her brother Duke had taken to sloping off for longer periods since Father had died, his truancy usually prompted by some upset with his stepmother. Lately he had disappeared again, this absence being the longest of all.

He had been gone for a week now. Maybe he had gone for good, mused Beata, the thought causing an even greater vacuum in her disconsolate heart. Lying in bed that evening after another trying day, she had just made her decision to emulate him when there was a commotion down in the yard that had her and her siblings bounding to the window to investigate.

'You little sod, we've been worried sick about you!' On his way to the lavatory, Clem had heard a scuffling from the coal shed and discovered Duke bedding down for the night. Having been at the receiving end of Eliza's constant grumblings that he should do something about his ungrateful little wretch of a brother, and feeling useless at not being able to prevent Duke's escapades, he was finally able to vent his frustration on the culprit. 'Well, you won't bloody do it again in a hurry!'

Leaning over the windowsill, the others watched in consternation as the offender was dragged into the yard by a furious Clem, who proceeded to deliver upon the small, malnourished frame a hail of unrelenting blows that would have felled a man.

Such was the severity of the thrashing that Mims and Beata began to wail, 'Don't, oh, don't!' – this luring Clem's attention upwards and so allowing a terrified Duke to scramble away from the murderous blows and press himself into a corner, weeping.

Horrified at his own behaviour, Clem hurled a last order – 'Get up them bloody stairs!' – before he himself strode for the lavatory, banging the door after him and thence slumping into an attitude of utter despair, beseeching help from the Almighty. *Please, please, can't You make them all behave? I just want everything to be nice.*

Though having glimpsed what treatment she herself might expect for running away, Beata was only more determined to escape. What had happened to Clem? He had always been fiery, but this odious streak had previously been far outweighed by kindness and she loved her eldest brother. But there had been nothing kind in tonight's actions.

Choosing a totally unsuitable time for her departure, a time when her absence was most noticeable, Beata's escape was to be short-lived. She had only gone five miles before Clem pedalled up behind her on his bicycle and took her back to receive punishment.

The fact that it was not half so severe as the one her brother had received was of little consolation. After being upbraided she was sent to bed and received no food for the rest of the day. Her stomach gripped by pangs of hunger, she was forced to exist on the aroma of onion gravy that drifted up from the kitchen.

Upon retiring later, Joe came in to sympathize, perching on the edge of the bed she shared with Mims and Doris, ready for flight should his stepmother come. 'I wanted to sneak some apricot pie up, but Mrs Trump's stuck pins in it.' This was one of Eliza's evil ploys to deter theft, only she knowing where the pins were hidden. 'But you can have this.' He took from his pocket what looked like a flat dried banana.

Thanking him, Beata seized the locust pod and devoured it.

Joe watched her, casting the occasional nervous eye towards the landing in case he was discovered here. 'Where were you off?'

'Bolton Percy.' This was where Aunt Nelly lived.

'You should have told me. I'd have covered for you.'

'I didn't want anybody else to get into bother,' Beata told him, before donning a look of confusion and lamenting to her brother, 'It's obvious she hates us so why doesn't she just let us go?'

Three years older, Joe had guessed the reason. 'She gets a pension for us till we're sixteen. If we go the money stops.'

On hearing of such mercenary purpose, Beata's expression changed from one of despondency to resolution. 'Well, I don't care how much she clouts me she's not going to stop me running away. I know if I can just get to Aunt Nelly's and tell her what's going on she won't send me back.'

Joe posed a salutary question. 'Our Gussie must have told everyone how mean Eliza is; why have none of them come to rescue us?'

Beata thought about this. 'Gussie doesn't really know how bad it is.' None of them had wanted to spoil their sister's visits by revealing the depth of the cruelty. Besides, it was not something one wished to talk about; if Eliza discovered they had been complaining she might be even worse.

'Why not go to Aunt Ethel's? It's nearer.'

'She frightens me,' admitted Beata. 'Why don't you come too?' It might be easier with an older male to navigate.

Joe turned his blue eyes to the ceiling and shook his auburn head. Unwilling to tell her he was too afraid of the consequences, he pretended that he could cope with the ill treatment better than his sister. 'She doesn't bother me. I'm out at work all day.'

'I'll come,' piped up Mims.

'You're only seven, it's too far for you to walk.'

'Am I seven now?' Mims frowned.

Beata nodded. Her sister's birthday had passed without a card nor even a birthday wish from their stepmother.

'Don't leave me, Beat,' came the little girl's fearful plea.

Beata gave consideration to this. Such a companion would seriously hamper her escape. But then if she went alone and was successful in her bid to reach Bolton Percy Eliza might take it out on the ones who were left behind and Mims, being the smallest, would suffer most. She placated the troubled infant with kind words. 'All right, we'll go tomorrow while the weather's still nice.' And she would put a lot more effort into it this time.

Setting off as if for school, and taking the money that Eliza had given them to buy their lunch, Beata and Mims embarked on the dusty road north.

Unusually compliant today, Mims put every ounce of her determined nature into the hike, uttering not one objection until midday when the hot sun finally wore her down. Praising her sister for lasting so long, Beata led her under the shade of a tree and told her to remove the tight elastic garters that held up her socks. Then, taking off her own socks she rubbed the red imprints on her legs, before unpacking the loaf of bread and bottle of water from the haversack that she had borrowed from Joe and the two sat down at the roadside to slake their hunger and thirst. Too afraid to ask for a lift from passing vehicles in case they were captured, they scrambled behind the tree to hide each time one passed. After half an hour they set off again, black socks sagging round their ankles.

Travelling eleven miles that first day, they finally reached Hatfield where Beata said it would be safer if they bedded down for the night under a hedgerow.

'There might be crawly things!' Thoroughly exhausted, Mims' good behaviour had started to wane.

'I warned you there might be! You said you'd put up with them.' Beata spread her own cardigan at the bottom of the hedge. 'There, lie on that. I shall have to send you back if you don't behave.'

With great reluctance, Mims did as she was told. But as soon as darkness began to fall her imagination ran riot. 'Beat, there's a hearwig crawling in me lug!'

With no chance of being allowed to sleep, Beata sighed and hauled her sister to her feet. 'Away then, nuisance, we'll have to go into that church down the road.'

Picking bits of hawthorn and grass from their clothes and hair, they had just settled themselves on one of the pews when Mims heard a noise and her voice bounced off the stone walls. 'A ghost!'

'Shush!' Beata clamped a hand over the little girl's mouth but it was too late; following the sound of echoing footsteps, a male face peered down at them.

'Who have we got here then?' asked the sidesman.

Jumping to her feet, a dismayed Beata told the church official their names.

'You've run away, haven't you?' He looked stern.

Standing in the shadow of the rood, Beata could not bring herself to lie and merely nodded.

Not bothering to enquire why, asking only where they had come from, the sidesman made a decision. 'Well, it's too late to take you back tonight. You'll have to stay at my house till I can contact your parents.'

It did not matter that they were to be treated with great kindness by the speaker, nor that his wife tucked them into bed after a delicious supper and read them a story along with her own little boy. The runaways' only thought was that they were going to be sent back to Eliza's clutches.

The next morning, informed of his sisters' whereabouts, Clem cycled over to take them home.

Perspiring from his activity, he shook his fiery head at them in exasperation. 'Why do you keep doing this, eh?'

Beata lowered her gaze, wondering how he could remain so blind to their stepmother's cruelty.

Mims was not so reticent. ''Cause she keeps braying us.'

'And no wonder! If you didn't misbehave so much, all of you, she wouldn't have to. Eliza's trying her best to be a mother to you but you're always complaining. If it isn't about your clothes it's about what's on the table! You're both going to have to buck your ideas up. Now come on, let's have you home.' Lifting Mims onto the crossbar of his bicycle, and telling Beata to straddle the luggage rack behind him, he pedalled as best he could towards Denaby.

Their homeward journey taking much less time than when they were on foot, it was still an uncomfortable ride, made worse by the knowledge that there would be retribution at the end of it. Over the miles this dread magnified to such a pitch that, once within sight of home, Mims started to cry.

Sweating, Clem fought to keep his bicycle on an even route, failed and put one foot to the ground to steady him. 'Look! If you promise to behave in future, not to run away again, I'll tell

Mother I've already given you a good hiding. Do you promise?'

Still snivelling, Mims nodded, Beata doing the same.

'Thank you! Now can we just get home without any more ructions?'

True to his word, Clem spoke up the minute he was through the door, telling Eliza they had already been beaten.

Still, she had words of admonishment. 'And what about the money they took with them? That's stealing, that is!'

Beata dared to object. 'But you gave it us to buy our lunch, Mother.'

A wallop was to accompany the rebuke. 'I didn't intend for it to make your running away easier! And the fact that you weren't coming back is another form of stealing. You were robbing me of the pension I get for you living here!'

Fearing there was going to be a scene, Clem ordered the girls into the yard. 'Outside till bedtime!' Thus, for once they were spared harsher punishment.

It was of little comfort.

Resigned to the fact that a successful escape would be impossible with Mims in tow, and not wanting to leave her behind, Beata was hitherto compelled to rely on vicarious means of escaping the awfulness. On Saturdays, after the chores were done, she would pelt up the stairs of Mexborough Library and in this quiet oasis would browse the periodicals that she was forbidden to read at home, devouring lurid stories in last week's *News of the World* whilst simultaneously imbibing the classical music that wafted up from the dance class below.

Once the papers had been read, there were shelves full of lovely books in which to lose herself, books on foreign travel being her favourite, depicting mountains and beaches and rainforests so vivid that, even after the tomes had been replaced and it was time to go home, she was able to fix the contents of the pages in her mind, carry them with her, so that later in her bed she could travel to these distant lands again – China, India, Australia – until dawn brought the reality of another day.

Besides the books there were human friends to take Beata's mind from the abuse at home, wealthier friends whose parents were kind to her and would invite her into their garden to play. It had occurred to Beata that they might help in more useful ways and she had tried dropping hints about her hunger and unhappiness, but these had passed unnoticed, or been misinterpreted as a request for some bread and jam, which was generously handed over. Welcome as this might be, short of condemning Eliza outright – which was unthinkable for one so terrified and helpless – her real dilemma was to remain a secret.

Or so she assumed. In fact, suspicion had arisen amongst Beata's neighbours over the nervous manner in which the Kilmaster children regarded their stepmother, though they restricted their condemnation of Eliza to black looks for now.

'I'm sure she's being cruel to them,' muttered Fanny Gentle to Mr and Mrs Rushton as the trio stood chatting in the evening sunshine. 'I'm all for dishing out a good hiding if it's warranted but those poor little devils look petrified whenever she comes on the scene. You're a policeman, can't you do anything?'

'Have you seen any mark on them?' asked the craggy Mr Rushton.

'Well, no more than the odd bruise – but you don't have to see open wounds as evidence!'

'You do if you want me to arrest her, or at least you have to catch her belting them.'

Fanny sighed defeatedly. 'We'd have to live next door to do that.' Then she made a sudden decision. 'I shall have a word with those on either side of her to let us know the minute they see or hear anything untoward.'

Mr Rushton gave a curt nod. 'In that case I'll happily oblige. All we can do till then is be extra kind ourselves.'

His wife agreed, but thought there might be another way to hit back at Eliza. 'You know, I'm sure she's still claiming a pension for Maddie. The kids crack on she's still living at home but I know damn well she's in service at Wath. Mrs Green knows the woman she works for. I'll bet Eliza's still claiming for her. She seems to spend an awful lot of money on herself.'

'Yes, I noticed she had a new hat and coat,' chipped in Fanny. 'Poor old Probe didn't get mourned for long, did he?'

'I'm going to speak to the Parish about her diddling,' finished Mrs Rushton.

Thus, a few mornings after this conversation had taken place, Eliza was to receive a visit from two people who were quite obviously in positions of authority. 'Mrs Kilmaster, we have a receipt here which you sent to us claiming recompense for clothes allegedly purchased for your daughter Madeleine.'

Eliza blanched. 'What do you mean "allegedly"? They were

bought for her.' This was a lie. Sick of her widow's weeds, she had lately packed up the dress she had bought for Probyn's funeral, along with two petticoats, and dispatched them to Madeleine so that no one could level accusations that the girl wasn't getting the benefit of her pension – but someone obviously had. 'You can see her wearing them if you like.'

'We would like, yes. May we speak to her?'

'She's at work.'

'Then tell us the location of her workplace and we'll go and speak to her there.'

Eliza began to panic. 'Oh, I don't think her employer would be too pleased at you taking her from her chores!'

'Allow us to handle that.' The man's attitude demanded compliance.

For the moment, Eliza was rendered dumb.

'It's been brought to our notice that you are still claiming Parish Relief for Madeleine when in fact she's been in service for some weeks.'

Eliza went on the offensive. 'Who told you that?'

'Never mind who it was. Is it true?'

'Of course it isn't! If you come back this evening you'll be able to see her – about eight o'clock.' That would give Clem time to go and fetch Maddie home.

Her ploy failed, the man being insistent. 'We'd prefer to see her now. I'm sure her employer wouldn't object if we were to call on a genuine mission. Just tell us where she works and we can go there ourselves.' When Eliza was slow to respond he added, 'I must warn you that it's an imprisonable offence to claim for children not under your roof.'

Eliza caved in then, wringing her hands and assuming the air of poor aggrieved widow. 'All right, she is in service and I have been claiming the money but I didn't know I wasn't supposed to and it was all spent on Madeleine!'

'We can check,' said the woman.

'Then do!' Eliza reverted to defiance. 'I've nothing to hide.' Angry now, she gave them the address of Madeleine's workplace. 'The girl will tell you I've sent her all sorts.'

'Nevertheless, it's still not in order. You can expect another visit.' So saying, the man and his companion left.

Subsequently interrogated by the couple, a worried Madeleine brought out the bundle she had lately received from her stepmother.

The woman examined the black crepe dress with a white cross embroidered on its bodice – quite obviously a funeral gown. Informed naively by Madeleine that yes, it had once belonged to her stepmother, the couple were swift to make a return visit to Eliza on the evening of that same day.

'Eh, I think she's been rumbled!' Standing on the corner, chatting to her friend, an alert Mrs Rushton elbowed Fanny and both watched with amusement as the couple on Eliza's doorstep confronted her.

Inside the Kilmaster house, using pegs to insert strips of material into the piece of hessian that would be turned into a rug, the children were listening with baited breath too. They had heard the word 'prison' mentioned!

'I only wore it once!' Eliza was objecting.

'Nevertheless, you maintained that the garment was for your daughter and in doing so acted fraudulently,' replied the man. 'What would your children do if you were locked up?'

'We'd throw a bloody party!' Joe grinned at Duke and his sisters, daring to speak openly, for his stepbrother George was in the lavatory.

Eliza pleaded with her accusers. 'It wasn't done intentionally! What's a widow to do?'

'She'll adhere to the law like everyone else! Now, I'd warn you to think before you answer. Are you claiming for any more that aren't under your roof?'

'No! I swear it.'

'Good, because if we have to come and speak to you again about this deception you'll be in court. Consider yourself very fortunate that you've got away this time. Good day to you!'

Dismayed that their stepmother was not to be incarcerated, the youngsters put their heads down and feigned to be working on the rug as a furious Eliza stormed back into the room. 'Right! Which one of you's been tittle-tattling?'

The children cowered, their sore fingers striving to insert the metal pegs through the tough material.

The only one not working on the rug, a surly Joe dared to mutter, 'It weren't us. We don't know anything about it.'

Eliza launched a punch at him. 'It had better not be! Now get to bloody bed, the lot of you!' And she began to lay about all of them.

Hearing the commotion emanating from the Kilmaster house,

Fanny Gentle and Mrs Rushton beheld each other in dismay at the thought that their good intentions might have brought further hardship on Eliza's victims.

'Ooh, get your Stan,' suggested Fanny.

'He isn't here!' Mrs Rushton chewed her lip for a moment, then, imagining what was happening inside that house, said, 'Oh, I can't stand this.' And she set off across the street to bang angrily on the Kilmasters' door, Fanny in pursuit.

When Eliza's equally irate face appeared, Mrs Rushton warned, 'I'm going to write to Probyn's sisters and let them know what's going on! I'll post it tonight and they'll be on your doorstep tomorrow!'

Eliza curled her lip. 'No, they won't 'cause there's no more Sunday post!' And she slammed the door on them.

'Eh, she's always got a bloody answer!' raged Mrs Rushton. 'Right, well, if she can call my bluff I can call hers. I *am* going to contact Probyn's sisters.'

'Have you got their address?' asked Fanny.

'No, but what's the use of being married to a policeman if you can't find out a simple thing like that? I don't know why I haven't thought of it before.'

Immediately Ethel received Mrs Rushton's letter, she contacted her favourite sister, Meredith, and announced that they must go to Denaby Main without delay. Despite having moved to Lancashire, Merry agreed and travelled over that same day.

Eliza was none too pleased at the knock on her door midway through the afternoon when she was about to tuck into a cake, and was even less pleased on looking from the window to see Probyn's sisters. Having no intention of sharing the delicacy she put it in the larder before inviting the visitors in.

Whilst Ethel remained her usual grim-faced self, Meredith donned a friendly smile. 'Hello, Eliza, I hope you don't mind us dropping in? We've just come to see how our nephews and nieces are.'

'They're fine, why shouldn't they be?' A suspicious Eliza indicated for them to sit down, but refrained from offering a cup of tea just yet.

Meredith gave a chuckle and lowered herself onto the sofa alongside Ethel. 'No reason at all, though I know they must be a handful for you, what with you having three of your own – Hello, Edwin.' She nodded at the invalid who sat by the fire.

Eliza leaned back in her chair. 'The day I allow a bunch of children to get the better of me is the day I turn up my toes.'

This attitude tending to confirm what Mrs Rushton had written, Ethel did not share her sister's diplomacy. 'I'm all for firm handling, but if I hear they've been mistreated –'

'Eh, who do you think you are?' Eliza reared.

'I'm the children's aunt and as such I'm concerned about their welfare. If you can't cope I'd rather you let them come to live with me.'

'Aye, and I'll bet you'd rather have the army pension that comes with each of them and all!' Eliza rose as a signal for them to leave. 'Well, you're not getting it.'

Ethel and Meredith rose too, the latter trying to calm the hostile atmosphere. 'Eliza, our concern isn't monetary –'

'Oh no, you don't have to worry where the next penny's coming from, you're neither of you poor widows like me!' Eliza gave haughty examination of both women's smart clothes. 'How would I exist if I lost all those pensions?'

'But surely the children come fir –'

'They're doing well enough!' A thought struck Eliza and she narrowed her eyes. 'I'll bet one of these busybodies round here has been spreading gossip about me, haven't they?'

'We have heard things we don't like, yes,' admitted Meredith.

'I knew it!' Eliza spat viciously. 'Wait till I get my hands on them.'

Ethel had not been a prison wardress for nothing. Drawing herself up to her full height and using every ounce of her strong character, she warned, 'I hope that attitude doesn't suggest that you're going to take it out on the children because, by jingo, if we get to hear of it you'll be in gaol before you can draw breath!'

Unnerved by Ethel's unyielding face, Eliza was not so free with her own threats now, though she was still very annoyed. 'I treat those children as my own! Ask Clem. Anybody that says otherwise is a liar. Examine them all you like, you won't find a mark on them that wasn't accidental.'

'That's a very shrewd way of putting it,' replied Ethel, planting herself firmly on the sofa again. 'And seeing as how you've offered we'll take you at your word. They'll be coming out of school soon, won't they?'

Taking her sister's lead, Meredith sat down too.

Eliza heaved a sigh. 'I suppose that means I'd better put the kettle on then.'

After what seemed like hours to those waiting in the frosty atmosphere, the children finally came home, first Eliza's own two, followed by Beata and Mims, neither of them spilling excitedly through the door in the manner of old, but each presenting a wary face around the kitchen door, obviously to test what kind of mood their stepmother was in. Probyn's offspring brightened somewhat upon receiving their aunts' warm greeting and answered the summons to come and stand by Aunt Ethel's knee.

'Oh, your hair's grown since I last saw you,' remarked Meredith to Beata.

Touching a shoulder-length auburn lock, Beata merely nodded.

'Where's Marmaduke?' asked Aunt Merry.

None of them dared answer. Eliza would be angry at hearing he had not been at school all day.

It didn't take much for their stepmother to guess. 'Oh, don't tell me, he's gone wandering off again.' She turned to the women with a sarcastic laugh. 'I'd better find him sharp or the gossips will be accusing me of doing away with him.'

'What do you mean "gone wandering"?' enquired Meredith.

Eliza made a disparaging gesture. 'He's always skiving off! Sometimes he's gone for days.'

'There must be a reason for it.'

'There is – he's simple! Doesn't know when he's well off. He'd rather kip in the hedge bottom than in a warm bed.'

During this, Ethel had been looking closely at the children, thinking what a wild, neglected little thing Mims looked, with her long and tousled light-brown hair, and now she pulled up the sleeve of the little girl's shapeless black dress to see if there were any hidden bruises. Eliza gasped at the impudence but made no further comment.

Finding several abrasions, Ethel asked, 'What are these?'

'They're just from playground frolics! Every bairn has bruises.'

Ethel's face was grim as she turned back to her niece. 'How did you get these, Millicent?'

Mims dared not reply, her hands nervously playing with the end of the belt around her middle that made the dress look like a tied potato sack.

Her aunt tried another tack. 'Are you happy living here?'

Mims looked to her elder sister for advice, but Beata felt her stepmother's eyes boring into her and was too afraid to give an honest answer. 'Yes, Aunt.'

Ethel knew the sign of fear and tried to inject more kindness into her voice, unaware that to the children she still appeared stern. 'You're sure? You see, we've heard that you've been treated unkindly by your stepmother.'

Far from instilling confidence, her statement provoked terror. Beata wanted desperately to reply that Eliza was indeed cruel, but what if her aunt didn't take them there and then? Eliza would make their lives a misery.

'Are you happy, Beata?'

Beata tried to smile though her lips quivered. 'Yes, Aunt.'

Faced with this answer, Ethel and Meredith were unable to offer solace. 'Well, if you're sure . . .' Sounding doubtful, Ethel looked into the two pairs of fearful blue eyes and told the girls, 'Then you can stay here for now. But if you ever need us just tell Mrs Rushton and she'll pass it on.'

'Ah! I thought it might be that old bitch,' muttered Eliza. 'She's nothing better to do than spread rumours.'

'Well, rumours or no,' said a grave Ethel, ready to take her leave, 'we'll be here to check up on our nephews and nieces again and if we find so much as one bruise . . .' She allowed her voice to trail away though there was no doubting the threat in it. Reaching into her purse, she doled out coppers to the children. 'This is for you to spend as you like, my dears.' It was issued with another warning glare at Eliza. 'Not for anyone else.'

Lips pressed together in a bloodless line, Eliza let the women out, then closed the door and turned to confront Beata and Mims, pointing a finger at them. There were no words, no smacks or punches, just that ominous finger and a pair of threatening black eyes. It was enough.

Ignorant as to when Ethel and her sister might descend on her out of the blue, Eliza made a concerted effort to curb her violence, and instead began to inflict the cruelty in more subtle ways, sending Beata on messages to the Co-operative Store for a bag of sugar at a quarter to nine, knowing she could not possibly get from the shop to the school by nine, and thus would be punished by her teacher for being late.

Out at work and ignorant of these sly tricks, Clem gave thanks that the corner seemed to have been turned and Eliza was getting along better with the younger ones these days.

Not so the neighbours. It seemed to Mrs Rushton and Fanny Gentle that their efforts to be kind to the Kilmaster children were having an adverse effect, for the kinder they were, the more cruel Eliza seemed to become, her devious methods fooling some, but not them. Watching her like a pair of hawks at every opportunity, the women tried their best to gather the evidence needed in order to bring an end to the children's misery, but up to now Eliza had proved too clever for them.

Had they known what a source of irritation their constant looks and whispers had become to Eliza they might have felt a little less ineffectual.

'They're starting early today,' she muttered to Clem.

'Who?'

'Those old busybodies. They're bloody staring in this direction again!' Pulling aside the net curtain, Eliza glared back at the women, who stood gossiping in a patch of early morning sunshine.

Recognizing that tone in her voice and wanting to maintain the peace, Clem advised her to, 'Take no notice,' as he himself made ready to leave for work.

'I don't!' In turning to answer, Eliza spotted a surreptitious movement at the table; Mims had been about to palm one of her crusts off on Beata. 'Don't you dare!'

Caught out, Beata gave her sister a fearful look that told Mims she would have to eat the crust herself today.

Her attention back on the gossips, anger had begun to bubble in Eliza's breast. 'Look at them, the dirty –'

'I'm going now,' announced Clem cheerfully.

Still fuming, Eliza let the curtain drop, then noticed that Mims was still dawdling over her crusts. In an instant she had flown into a rage, had grabbed the crust out of a terrified Mims' hand and was trying to force it into the little girl's mouth, vicious fingers screwing it all over the wriggling child's face, having no effect other than to inflict a network of crimson scratches.

'Eh! Eh!' Clem strode up to intervene, taking Eliza by the arm and speaking in a gentle voice in an attempt to calm her whilst Mims sobbed and the others stood shocked to the core. 'Simmer down! Don't let a bunch of gossips get you worked up. They're not worth it. Here, come on, sit down. Doris, pour your mother a cup of tea.'

At the sight of the bloody weals on Mims' face Eliza instantly regretted her actions, her anger waning to a desperate moan: 'You'll be late for work!'

'I'm not leaving you like this.' Firm but gentle, Clem made her sit down and handed her the cup of tea that Doris had poured, his siblings wondering how he could show her such charity after she had behaved like a demon to Mims.

Only after making sure that Eliza had recovered did he check on Mims' injuries, telling Beata to wash her sister's face, then dabbing the scratches with ointment. Remaining in the house until he was sure that Eliza was all right, Clem finally went off to work, telling the children to keep out of their mother's way and get on with their jobs until it was time for school.

Both inveterate gossips, Mrs Rushton was still engaged with Fanny Gentle on the corner when two small figures came past an hour later. 'Hello, Beat, on your way to schoo –' She frowned and waylaid the pair. 'Hang on, what are all them scratches around your sister's mouth?'

Smiling, Beata planted a hand between Mims' scrawny shoulders in an attempt to move her on. 'A cat jumped over our back wall and landed on her.'

'Eh dear!' Not believing a word of it, Mrs Rushton held Mims back to examine the angry weals more closely, saying in kind voice, 'There's no need to be frightened of telling me the truth, you know. If a person did this –'

'No, it was a cat!' Terrified that Eliza might see them talking to the neighbours, Beata grabbed Mims' hand.

Fanny was taking an interest in the scratches too, tilting the little girl's chin. 'Must have been a vicious type of cat.'

'It was. A big ginger one.' Following her sister's lead, little Mims smiled and moved on. 'We'll have to go or we'll be late for school.'

'Well, remember where we live. If ever you need help you know where to come.' The concerned women allowed the pair to hurry away, Fanny muttering, 'Aye, it's a vicious cat all right, but one of the human variety.'

Mrs Rushton heartily agreed. 'Aye . . . Oh, talk of the devil!' Spotting Eliza leaving her house and hurrying down the opposite side of the street, both women dealt her a penetrating glare.

Though unsettled by their scrutiny, Eliza paused and made theatrical examination of her clothes, calling to the observers, 'I thought for a minute I'd left me skirt tucked into me drawers the way you two are staring.'

'You're brazen enough to!' retorted Fanny.

Eliza bridled and came across the road. 'Eh, who do think you're talking to?'

'You!' Mrs Rushton joined her friend in projecting annoyance.

374

'We've just witnessed your handiwork on that bairn's face!'

'I don't know what you're on about.'

'You do! And I'm telling you it had better stop.' Fanny took up an aggressive stance, her finger coming close to stabbing Eliza in the chest.

Eliza was defiant. 'Did they say I did it?'

'No, they said what you told them to say because they're that bloomin' frightened of you! Well, I'm warning –'

'And I'm warning you!' Recognizing that the no-nonsense stance was only a front to hide a soft nature, Eliza was not fooled by Fanny's threats and now made her own stabbing motion, actually striking the midwife several times in her bony chest. 'Keep-your-neb-out-of-my-business!' And with barely concealed fury, she stalked off.

'Arrogant cow!' muttered Fanny, rubbing her chest, angry at her own ineffectualness.

'Aye, well, she won't be so cocky with our Stan,' said an equally irate Mrs Rushton. 'I'll tell him to put on his uniform when he goes to see her. Eh, I hope the poor bairns don't get into trouble at school for being late. It's no good, I won't be able to settle till I've had a word with their teacher.' Parting company with Fanny, Mrs Rushton took the same direction as the Kilmaster sisters.

Upon their breathless arrival at school Beata and Mims were indeed quizzed over their lateness by the teacher on the door. Only the fact that this was Miss Carter, the kindest teacher in the school, spared them from punishment. Their explanation about the cat was viewed with the same disbelief as shown by Mrs Rushton, who at that moment appeared.

'They couldn't help being late, Miss Carter!' Mrs Rushton looked anxious as she hurried up to the group.

'Yes, I heard what happened.' Miss Carter showed concern over the scratches on Mims' face, then told them to run along to their desks.

'It wasn't a cat,' said Mrs Rushton. 'It was that stepmother of theirs.'

Miss Carter nodded gravely. 'We've had our suspicions for some time. But there's very little we can do. I've quizzed the children but they seem too afraid to speak up.'

'I know. It makes you feel so helpless, doesn't it?' Her brow furrowed, Mrs Rushton turned to leave. 'Well, I just wanted to inform you the reason they were late so that they don't get punished twice.'

Sadly, Miss Carter replied that not all the teachers were as understanding, but she would try to protect the youngsters as best she could. Saying goodbye to the other she went to her classroom and, before registration, took Beata aside. 'Now, Beata, I'm giving you this opportunity to tell me what really happened to your sister's face. I understand how difficult it must be for you to speak out against an adult, truly I do, but I urge you to tell us what is really going on so that we can help you.'

Gazing into that understanding face, Beata felt sure that Miss Carter must have suffered such abuse herself, but that did not make it any easier to confess. She lowered her eyes and shook her head.

'Very well.' Miss Carter nodded, her eyes and voice extraordinarily kind. 'But if ever you feel able you must come straight to me.'

Going to her desk, Beata gazed upon the teacher with devotion and for the rest of the morning sat nursing her crush.

All her previous efforts to stop the cruelty thwarted, Mrs Rushton's opportunity was finally to come at the weekend. Screams were heard coming from the Kilmaster house, travelling for yards through the open window. 'She's killing me! Oh, she's murdering me!'

Immediately upon hearing this Mrs Rushton bellowed up the stairs, 'Get your uniform on, Stan!'

'It's Sunday for God's sake, woman!'

'Crime doesn't keep normal working hours! Can't you hear what she's doing to those bairns? You wanted chance to catch her in the act – well, come on!'

Grumbling, Mr Rushton nevertheless dragged himself out of bed, pulled his braces over his rumpled shirt, and donned his police tunic.

There were others assembled in the street, all eyes directed at the horrible cries from the Kilmaster house as the policeman strode across the road.

An angry thumping at Eliza's door had her rushing to answer it, upon seeing the official uniform, blurting, 'I'm right sorry for all the din! It's our Edwin, he always kicks up a fuss when I change his dressing.'

'Mind if I come in?' Without awaiting permission a suspicious Mr Rushton elbowed his way past her and into the kitchen, his wife remaining on the doorstep, craning her neck to see inside.

But sure enough, Eliza had spoken the truth; there was the lad, a soiled dressing dangling from his leg, clean bandages and lint awaiting application.

'It's such agony for him,' said Eliza apologetically. 'I try and take it off as gently as I can but the wound weeps and the lint sticks to it.' She went to finish her task as if to illustrate to the policeman the difficulty she had, making soothing sounds in response to Edwin's cries.

Still frowning, Mr Rushton looked around at the other children, who were dressed for church, the girl's shapeless black tunics today embellished with white lace attachments, the boys in starched collars and cuffs. They were obviously in trepidation, but immediately he enquired as to their wellbeing they donned false smiles and said they were fine.

Clem entered then, eyes still bleary from sleep, shoving his crumpled shirt into hastily donned trousers. 'What the hell is going on?'

Mr Rushton answered, 'I came to investigate the din. Folk were worried.'

Clem's annoyed face relaxed and he looked at Edwin. 'I don't blame 'em. It was bloomin' ghoulish.'

'Sorry.' Edwin looked apologetic.

'You can't help it.' Seemingly unperturbed, Clem went outside to the lavatory.

With such an attitude, Mr Rushton had no alternative but to exit, though there was a murmured parting shot for Eliza. 'Don't think you've fooled me. I know what's going on.'

She blustered, 'But you've seen for yoursel –'

'I have seen, yes, and I know frightened children when I see them. Take this as a warning: if it doesn't stop you'll have someone bigger to contend with.' The policeman left.

No longer under surveillance, Eliza dropped her caring façade and threw the lint at Edwin. 'Look what trouble you've caused, you sissy! Do it your bloody self in future.'

Feeling sorry for the one in pain, Beata waited for her stepmother to leave the room, then took up the lint and bandages and quietly applied them herself.

Mr Rushton's wife was highly displeased to learn that her husband's visit had been futile, complaining later to Fanny Gentle, 'Well, it hasn't put me off! I'll still be watching her. Terrified they were, those bairns, terrified! Wouldn't you think Clem would do something?'

'Aye, you would, wouldn't you?' Fanny nodded mistrustfully. 'I reckon there's more to this than meets the eye. Haven't you noticed the way he and madam behave towards each other?'

Mrs Rushton was immediately alert. 'No! You mean . . . ?' She gasped in disgust. 'But he's such a nice lad, is Clem.'

'Oh, I don't blame him! There isn't a man alive who'd turn it down if it's served to him on a plate. But if we couldn't prove she's hitting the bairns we'd have the devil's job of trying to prove *that*, won't we?'

And so with such a lack of evidence, the children's life of misery was to endure, one ghastly month into the next. Armed with Ethel's address, Mrs Rushton promised to notify her should anything be proven, but thus far Eliza remained too clever.

Christmas came but brought no relief, only the memory of better times. Whilst there had never been presents, Christmas had always been an occasion for joy in the Kilmaster household, with plenty of food on the table, a few nuts, an orange and a penny, and fond indulgence by their parents. Eliza's only indulgence was to abstain from her harsh treatment for a couple of hours. Yet, the fear could not be so easily expunged, and the children were to remain tense throughout the Christmas meal.

But there was to be a surprise in the afternoon. Eliza's sister came to visit, armed with parcels for everyone – even Beata and her siblings.

'I've come into a bit of money!' she beamed, handing the parcels to Eliza, who received them with extraordinary merriment and distributed them amongst the family.

Conditioned to receive nothing but unkindness, Beata could hardly believe that such an event was happening. Holding her own little parcel, wanting to prolong the enjoyment of it, she watched as first Edwin opened his to reveal some Meccano, then to further sounds of delight George revealed a mechanical car, which was wound up and set off along the lino, then Doris opened hers – a silver purse with half a crown in it.

Visualizing such a prize for herself, still wanting to savour the moment, Beata pressed and felt the outline of the gift within her own package – yes, it was a silver purse! And there was a hard round object that could only be half a crown! Able to resist no longer she excitedly ripped it open . . . and out fell a packet of liquorice.

Eliza burst out laughing – laughed and laughed with her hand pressed to her side, the sight of Beata's crestfallen face seeming to goad her on to even greater mirth so that in the end tears were streaming down her cheeks and she had to run from the room for fear of wetting herself.

But though she was gone, the sound of her spiteful laughter was to reverberate in Beata's mind. It would stay with her for the rest of her life.

TWENTY-TWO

The misery dragged on into another year, alleviated only by the appearance of Augusta, who visited as often as she could, bringing gifts for Eliza in the hope that it would make her kinder to the children.

Delighted at Augusta's arrival on this Easter Monday, especially as she brought chocolate eggs with her, Mims jumped up and down in glee. 'Our Gussie's come to see us again!'

Eliza smirked. 'Don't flatter yourself. It isn't you she keeps coming to see. Nor me neither.' Having invoked a flush of embarrassment on Augusta's face, her amusement became even more pronounced. 'You think I don't know about Vincent O'Reilly? I've known for ages. You can't keep anything secret round here.'

Seeing Augusta so mortified, Beata was anxious that she should not think any of them had betrayed her.

But Eliza was indifferent. 'Don't look so scared! I'm not bothered who you see so long as you don't bring a bairn back here and expect me to look after it.'

Augusta was even more horrified. 'I wouldn't do *that*!'

Eliza laughed and went in to make a pot of tea.

Looking subdued, Augusta followed her, handing over a bag of Walnut Whips. 'I thought I'd take the children up the Crags to roll their eggs.'

'Be my guest.' Eliza dipped into the bag with a sound of approval.

'We've got painted ones an' all!' Not allowed in, Mims shouted to her sister from the door and indicated the box of hard-boiled eggs on the dresser.

'Aye, they'll serve as your tea,' said Eliza, munching. 'Keep the

380

blessed nuisances out for as long as you like – and gather some sticks for the fire.'

'Sorry you aren't able to come, Edwin,' Augusta apologized to her stepbrother, whose infirmity prevented him from walking, but he did not seem too bothered as he tucked into his own Easter egg.

Madeleine had received the day off, so had Joe, though he had gone fishing. Setting off for the Crags, the brothers and sisters spent a jolly half-hour rolling their eggs, the young ones scampering and screaming after them down the rocky incline. But Madeleine could not help noticing that Augusta was unusually pensive today. Normally there would be an air of eager anticipation as she waited for Vincent to arrive, but today her eyes were clouded as they watched for him.

Seeing a figure appear, Augusta tensed. But it was only the hunched form of Dr Hannah who, accompanied by his sister and her children, watched the egg-rolling from a short distance away, responding to the Kilmaster children's cheery waves.

At the sight of the doctor, Augusta became deep in thought and drifted away into a private world until the person seated beside her on the grass delivered a nudge.

'What's up?' asked Maddie.

Augusta looked startled, before donning a tight smile. 'Oh . . . nothing.'

'I can tell you're lying.' Maddie smoothed the wrinkles out of her black stockings and adjusted the garters on her thick legs.

'That's not a very nice thing to say about anybody.'

The reply was airy. 'I can't help you if you don't tell me what it is.'

'You can't help anyway,' retorted Augusta. 'It's a medical problem.'

'Well, there's a doctor right over there, you clot! I'll shout him.'

Augusta turned to gag her sister. 'No need! I already know the answer.'

'What's wrong with you then?'

A blushing Augusta looked away. 'It's too personal.'

'Oh, something to do with bums, is it?'

Though close to tears, Augusta laughed and shook her head.

'Aw, tell me!'

Turning to look at her sister, Augusta decided she was old enough to hear. 'It's me friend. You know, the one that's supposed to come every month?'

'Ah!' Maddie nodded.

'It doesn't come often enough. I went to see the doctor at work and he said it's tuberculosis.'

The image of their dying mother still vivid, Madeleine was instantly aghast at the thought of losing the most beloved of her sisters. 'But you don't have a cough!'

'I know, but the doctor says that's what it is and he should know.' Augusta looked distraught, but then through her own discomfort she sensed Maddie's anxiety and immediately consoled her. 'He didn't mean I'm going to die, but that I'm carrying it. He says it runs in families and I'll pass it on to any children I have.'

Eyes moist, Maddie looked relieved. 'Are you going to tell Vincent?'

'How can I? He's so nice he'd probably say we won't bother with a family, that it doesn't matter, but I couldn't inflict that on him, on anybody for that matter. He deserves to have children.' Augusta felt as if she had been disembowelled.

Madeleine hugged her knees. 'So what are you going to say?'

Augusta shook her head in pensive despair, then caught a movement. 'Oh Lord, he's here.'

Watching her two sisters deep in conversation, Beata wondered what was being said, for Gussie seemed preoccupied and not her usual self at all. Even now that Vincent appeared on the scene and the children ran to meet him, Gussie seemed reluctant to participate and hardly shared two words with him when he sat down beside her.

After several more rollings the eggs were peeled and eaten, the chocolate ones too. Mims came to sit on Augusta's lap, head on her sister's breast, soaking up the affection denied by her stepmother.

Then, shortly, as was his wont, Vincent took Augusta's hand and led her away.

As usual, the younger ones waited a while, then began to creep after the couple to spy on them.

'I don't think you should today,' warned Madeleine. But when they ignored her she hurriedly pursued them with a grimace.

This time, there was to be more than cuddles and kisses. Vincent brought something out of his pocket, telling Augusta, 'I carved it meself.'

Straining to see what it was, the children were puzzled as to what use could be had from a spoon made of coal, but continued to watch as, with a finger, Vincent traced out the markings. 'That's our initials, and this . . . is the date we'll be married.'

Hearing the combined gasp of glee Augusta spun round and

charged at the children, lashing out at them. 'What are you doing here? Get back over there!'

Spurred by her fury, they scattered across the crags, leaving a tormented Augusta to wander back to her sweetheart.

She bit her lip. 'I have to refuse, Vince.' It was the most painful thing to say, taking her to the brink of tears.

The young man reacted as if pole-axed, the smile wiped from his face. 'But *why?*'

Bereft of an answer, she responded angrily. 'I just have to!'

'What's up with you? Why are you being like this? I thought we –'

'There's nothing wrong. I'm just not cut out for marriage!'

Confused and betrayed, he too portrayed anger. 'And what am I supposed to do now? You've been stringing me along for years –'

'No, I haven't! I didn't mean to anyway.'

'Then *why?*'

'I'm sorry, I just can't!' Tearfully, she fled.

Instead of following her, Vincent gave a harsh snort of frustration and, glowering, he turned on his heel and marched off in the opposite direction.

Unable to prevent herself from crying, Augusta told her worried siblings to leave her alone, speaking through her handkerchief.

'I tried to stop them,' said Madeleine.

Duke looked up at the speaker. 'What's wrong with her?'

'I can't tell you, it's private.'

Beata felt hurt that her sisters could not share the secret with her. 'We're sorry, Gussie, we didn't mean –'

'I'm all right! It's nothing to do with you.'

'If that Vincent hurt you –' began Duke threateningly.

'He didn't! Just shut up, all of you.' Augusta stumbled away to find a private hollow where she could break down and sob without being disturbed.

But they could still hear her.

'Gussie's been roaring,' announced George to his mother the moment they were through the door.

'Oh aye, what for?' Halfway through a book, munching on her third Walnut Whip, Eliza showed scant interest.

Augusta had no wish to tell her stepmother. Eliza had odd views about people with illness and might prevent her from coming here again. 'Nothing.'

'It were that Vincent O'Reilly's fault,' muttered Duke.

Eliza was instantly accusing. 'Eh, you're not expecting, are you?'

'No!' Augusta wished her stepmother would show more under-standing.

'Are you sure?'

With Eliza so unconvinced, Augusta had no option but to tell her. 'I'm . . . The doctor says I've got TB. There, now you all know!' The heated addendum was directed at her siblings, her eyes bright with moisture.

The frown of suspicion dispersed, replaced by a knowing nod. 'Well, I'm not surprised. It's because you're puny like your mother – they say a family never gets rid of it. I suppose Mr Whatsispants took umbrage and chucked you, did he?'

Augusta felt sickened that Vincent could be viewed in such a callous light. 'I couldn't tell him! I don't want to pass it on to any children we might have. I just said, I can't marry him.' Her face finally crumpled.

'Looks like we'd better get you measured for your nun's habit then.' Eliza uttered light laughter. 'Well, you've had enough practice, I've never known anyone have to darn the knees of their stockings as often as you do.'

Listening to the interchange, Beata felt how thoughtless her stepmother was, offering no help, only derogatory quips. She herself pondered over the matter, trying to find a solution to Augusta's predicament. She had seen how angry Vincent had been; it was not fair that he should lay the blame on Gussie when all she had been trying to do was spare him.

Deciding to act upon her feelings, she was given the opportunity when her stepmother sent them all outside until bedtime. With Augusta in the closet, Beata dashed off to Vincent's house.

Mrs O'Reilly answered the door, inviting Beata in. Vincent was seated in an armchair opposite his father on the other side of the hearth, his bleak expression turning dark upon seeing the visitor's identity.

'What's your sister been doing to the lad?' His father teased the little girl. 'He's had a face like cow's bum since he came in.'

Beata didn't laugh, finding it awkward to speak in front of an audience. But when Vincent made as if to bolt she said quickly, 'Gussie's got tuberculosis!' Having commanded an audience, she explained, 'The doctor told her – that's why she said can't marry you, Vince, because she doesn't want to pass it on to your children – but she really wants to.'

His paramour's behaviour explained, the anger quickly began to smooth from Vincent's face. 'She could have told me. I wouldn't have been so hard on her.'

'That's what I thought!' Beata looked keen. 'She'll kill me for telling you but I thought you should know.'

Vincent nodded. 'Aye . . . thanks, Beat.'

She waited for him to say more, studying his face which still wore a look of sadness.

'Gussie'll be off back to York shortly,' she said when he remained silent. 'If you come now you might catch her.'

'No! No, just . . . say Vincent's sorry, and thank her for trying to spare my feelings.'

'And that you still want to marry her?' Beata saw the look that passed between parents and son.

Looking at the floor, Vincent shook his curly head.

His mother showed a crestfallen Beata out, saying kindly, 'He can't risk it, love. Sorry.' With the door closed upon her, Beata's pace lacked enthusiasm on the homewards journey. Dutifully, she relayed Vincent's message to Augusta, watched as fresh tears slid down her sister's cheeks, overcome with guilt that her good intentions had only made things worse.

It was this same feeling of guilt to which she attributed her dullness of spirit that was to continue throughout the Easter break. Even upon returning to school it had not lifted. Indeed, the mood seemed to have transformed itself into a genuine physical illness, manifested in an inability to swallow her meals. The breakfast porridge had been hard enough to get down, but when Beata came home at lunchtime to find jam roly-poly, which she hated, it proved too much.

At the child's distress, Eliza was unusually considerate. 'Aye, you do look as if you're sickening for something.' Frowning, she pressed a hand to Beata's glistening brow. 'Though you're not unduly hot.'

'Me head's throbbing and I'm all achy,' whimpered Beata.

Eliza was still performing her examination. 'Your jaw seems swollen an' all. All right, you don't have to eat that if you don't want to.' She took the pudding away and gave it to Edwin. 'Better get yourself down to the doctor's this afternoon.'

Beata turned to leave the table – and at once everything went black. Through intermittent bouts of consciousness she had the impression of being installed in a motor vehicle, its bumpy passage causing intense pain in her head, before the blackness descended again.

When she awoke, for a few seconds she thought herself amongst the clouds. Everywhere was white and silent and there was the disembodied face of an angel smiling down at her.

'It's all right, my dear,' a soothing voice told her. 'You're going to get well, you're safe in hospital.'

Hospital not heaven. Growing more lucid, Beata realized that she was enveloped in a big white tent, the clouds provided by horrible-smelling steam that was coming in through a corner. The angel had a familiar face. It was the one who had nursed her through scarlet fever all those years ago. Many of the staff, though kind, had been brisk, offering only medical succour. Nurse Kelly was tenderness personified, seemingly unhurried and delivering the kind of support that a child such as Beata needed.

'Just a short while, then we'll have you out of this,' added Nurse Kelly in her gentle brogue. 'You're over the worst.'

Beata's throat was still sore. She tried to speak but could not.

'You've got diphtheria,' explained her carer, brushing a strand of auburn hair from the glistening brow in sympathetic manner. 'I'm afraid you'll be away from your family for quite a little while – but we'll look after you.'

Beata did not care how long she was here. Whilst to others the enforced parting might be traumatic, to one from such an abusive household, being ministered by these tender hands was better than a holiday.

After nine weeks and the required amount of negative swabs, Beata returned home.

But it was not the home she had left. Whilst she had been in hospital, the family had moved to a brand-new house on the other side of the Crags at Conisbrough. Though modern, the dwelling had only one entrance, just inside the door was the bathroom and lavatory, then a long lounge with the kitchen on the left and the stairs on the right.

Duke, who had been giving Beata a guided tour, flicked a switch. 'Look, we've got electric light an' all!'

Beata was still undergoing amazement at having a bathroom.

'Well, we were getting too overcrowded at the old place,' explained Eliza. 'This is much more suitable. We've got an extra bedroom as well.' She noticed then that Beata was frowning at her. 'What's the matter?'

'Nothing!' Beata looked away quickly.

Eliza thought she knew. 'It might stink a bit today but that's only because the wind's in the wrong direction.'

There was indeed a dreadful smell of naphtha coming from Stanley's factory, but that was not what had caused Beata's puzzlement. She had been astounded by how portly Eliza had become in her absence. Her belly protruded like an upturned bowl under the white apron. But who would dare say this?

Beata's attention turned to Edwin, who was up and walking again, though with a pronounced limp.

In fact everyone in the household had changed in her two-month absence, all looking much older and taller. George and Joe seemed like men.

One thing had not changed. Mims still sported the marks of her stepmother's unpredictable moods.

Later, changing into her nightgown for bed, Beata pointed out a bruise on Mims' arm. 'What did you get that one for?'

'Swapped me shoes for a lad's clogs.' Little Mims desperately wanted to make sparks with her own footwear as the boys did, but the only sparks that had flown were from Eliza.

'Right, lights out!' Clem hollered up the stairs.

'She's got fat, hasn't she?' Adjusting her eyes to the dinge, Beata clambered into bed after Mims, Doris sleeping on her own now in this more spacious house, though still in the same room.

The others agreed. 'It's all that chocolate your Gussie brings her,' said Doris.

Snuggling down, Beata then asked them to relate all the family news that had gone on in her absence.

Mims told as much as she could remember. 'We haven't seen anything of Maddie for ages.'

'I wonder why,' said Beata.

Downstairs, Eliza was wondering the same thing, though it was not Madeleine's welfare that concerned her but the non-appearance of her stepdaughter's monetary contributions. This was the second month that a postal order had failed to arrive.

'If there's nothing in the morning post you'd better go over and check what's going on,' Eliza told Clem.

With morning bringing no news, after breakfast that Saturday morning Clem cycled over to Wath upon Dearne to visit his sister at her place of work.

But the door was answered by another maid who told him that Madeleine no longer worked here. Receiving no satisfactory answer as to where she had gone, even after questioning her employer, Clem went home to relay this bad news to Eliza.

Of course she immediately flew off the handle, damning Madeleine with all the foul words in her repertoire – though others were to deem their sister extremely lucky for they were the ones who bore the brunt of this, unable to put a foot right during the rest of the day.

Clem begged her to calm down as she railed at them for one paltry offence after another, lashing out at random. 'This isn't going to do you any good in your condition!'

Though focusing all her energy on avoiding Eliza's wrath, inserting a duster into each and every crevice of the fretwork on the piano, Beata pricked up her ears at this remark. To what condition was Clem referring? Perhaps, glory be to God, Eliza had been afflicted by a heart complaint – Father had suffered from such a 'condition'. It was wicked to wish anyone dead but . . .

'No, you're right.' Eliza fought to compose herself and, taking a deep breath, lowered herself into a chair, hand upon her abdomen. 'Eh dear, just when I thought we were getting on our feet, the little cat leaves us in the lurch.'

'We'll be all right,' Clem comforted her. 'I'll put in some overtime.'

'I wonder where she's gone?' She turned to fix her black glare on the children. 'Do any of you know?'

There was rapid denial, everyone busy about their chores.

'Better not,' snapped Eliza.

A few days later, Beata was on her way to school when a boy approached her, acting as if he were a member of the secret service, his collar turned up, muttering from the side of his mouth as he pressed a letter into her hand, 'Mrs Rushton told me to give you this!' before hurrying away.

Beata made sure she was unobserved before taking the letter from its envelope, a slow smile spreading over her face as she read it. 'I couldn't send this home as Eliza would know where I am,' wrote Maddie. 'But am writing to let you know so you don't worry. I haven't put my address on as she might grab it off you. Destroy it after you read it. I got sick of being in service and am now training to be a nurse. Have saved up quite a bit of my own and also kept the money I was supposed to send home last month, though I don't know how long it will last. See you some time. Love Madeleine.'

Ripping the letter up and casting the pieces to the wind, Beata proceeded to school, mentally wishing her sister good luck. How long would it be before she herself would be free?

Alas, instead of freedom, there were to be more degrading chores, as over the coming months Eliza's ballooning abdomen prevented her from even the most personal of tasks.

'Beat, you'll have to do this for me!' Still damp from her bath, she called up the stairs and, when Beata came down, held out a pair of scissors and indicated her foot. 'I can't bend over.'

Dutiful as usual, Beata hoisted her nightgown, kneeled before Eliza's chair and proceeded to cut her toenails, collecting a little pile as she went. Acting from character, she had taken on the mantle of looking after her ailing stepmother – if Eliza was going to die it seemed only the decent thing to do – yet it did not go unnoticed that she never received one word of thanks for putting cool bandages on the swollen ankles, providing medication for the indigestion, nor for the disgusting task she was undergoing now.

Suddenly, as she was halfway through the other foot the lights went out, causing her to cut too deeply.

Eliza yelled and lashed out. 'I'll bet them little buggers are reading in bed!' If more than three lights were on at once the fuse would blow. 'I'll kill them!'

Luckily at that point Clem came back from the off-licence with a bottle of beer and, having performed this repair many times before, had the illumination rectified in no time.

This did not satisfy Eliza, who barrelled her way upstairs and dealt out a trouncing on the culprits, who were too slow in flicking the light switch, using their library books as a weapon against them.

'Big fat belly,' accused a sobbing Mims as Beata slipped into bed beside her and tried to comfort her. 'I've asked Our Lord to make her burst and all her guts fall out.'

Putting their stepmother's burgeoning weight down to greed, the children's imagination ran amok when, the next morning, they were roused by Joe, who told them Eliza had disappeared.

'I went down for me breakfast and there's no one in the kitchen. Can you lasses come and help?'

They tumbled out of bed and downstairs to investigate.

'Where's she gone?' wondered Beata.

The realization began to dawn on Joe and he glanced at Edwin, who, judging from his expression was hazarding the same guess, but neither wanted to voice it.

'Mebbe she has exploded like you asked for,' laughed Duke to Mims, pretending to look for fragments of flesh upon the wallpaper. With no Clem around either, Eliza's victims could jest to their heart's content.

After the jokes were exhausted, Beata and Doris made everyone breakfast. Edwin did not sit down to eat with the rest. He had not shared the frivolity and seemed preoccupied.

'Wrap mine up, I'll take it with me. I want to get off before Clem comes back.'

'Off where?' Joe looked surprised. Edwin had not worked since his accident.

'Nottingham. There's more chance of a job there for the likes of me.'

The others were astounded. 'Will you be going on the train?' asked George. Edwin fished in his pocket and studied the three coins on his palm. 'Not if it costs more than tuppence ha'penny, no.'

'Then –'

'I'll have to walk, won't I?' He limped towards the door.

Those left behind were alarmed. 'What do we tell Mother?'

'She won't miss me; I don't bring any money in. Besides, she'll have more on her mind.' Without a goodbye, Edwin departed.

'What did he mean?' Beata asked Joe, who blushed.

George too hung his head and muttered, 'Dunno.'

Breakfast over, Beata packed the young colliers up for work and was getting the others ready for school when the door opened, making them start.

Clem was alone. He looked very tired and his siblings beheld him warily, anticipating trouble. But their brother seemed happy that they had acted on their own initiative. 'I'll look forward to seeing this every morning whilst your mother's away.'

Even when Beata dared to tell him that Edwin had left home Clem did not show annoyance, but merely shrugged and said, 'Good luck to him.'

He was in a similarly good mood that evening, and continued to be so throughout their stepmother's absence. He did not say where

Eliza had gone, nor did they ask. With Clem being so nice they had no wish to mention her name and break the spell.

With her oppressor having been gone seemingly for ages and the house a more pleasant place to come home to, Mims had gradually lost her customary wariness upon entering and today, being first home from school, she burst in singing her heart out.

Hence, the gasp of utter shock and disbelief at the sight of Eliza seated by the fire, and for a few seconds she was rooted to the spot by terror.

But her stepmother delivered only a wry smile and an invitation. 'Go and see what I've brought you.' And she jabbed a thumb at the top drawer of the sideboard, which was open.

With tremulous movements, expecting a blow as she tiptoed past, Mims hoisted herself onto the balls of her feet and peeped over the edge of the drawer, what she saw causing her to suck in her breath in surprise. There was a baby looking back at her with grave, navy-blue eyes.

Despite her fear of the woman, Mims could not prevent casting a wide involuntary smile at Eliza, who grinned back in her lopsided manner. 'That's your brother Lionel. Do you want to hold him?'

Mims nodded eagerly.

Eliza pushed herself from the chair and went to lift Lionel from the drawer. 'Sit on the sofa and I'll hand him to you.' She transferred him to Mims' waiting arms. 'Careful! You have to support his head otherwise you'll break his neck.' But apart from this harsh interjection there was no further rebuke, Eliza content to let Mims hold him, even bestowing a smile as the little girl marvelled over his tiny fingers. Falling head over heels in love with her baby brother, Mims did not ever want to relinquish him, but at that point Beata and Doris came in, both bouncing onto the sofa beside her to lay their own claim, and she was forced to give him up to their cooing attentions, all equally besotted. Even the boys, after first washing off their coal dust, came immediately to admire him – like Mims, exclaiming over his tiny digits, their own rough fingers tenderly stroking his fuzzy head. Everyone adored him.

Finally it was Clem's turn.

'Come and look at our baby brother!' Mims summoned him excitedly to the sideboard.

Clem shared a secret smile with Eliza, that was noticed by

the elder more knowledgeable siblings, who hung their heads in embarrassment.

Clem scooped the new arrival from the drawer and cradled him in his arms. 'Aye, we've met before. He's a cracker, isn't he?'

'When did you see him?' frowned Mims, stung that she was not after all the first to learn about Lionel.

'Oh, the other night,' replied Clem, proceeding to rock his son gently, smiling down at him with a paternal gleam in his eye.

'Can I hold him again?' begged Mims but was out-shouted by other eager voices.

Such was to be the case on every day that followed, the younger children rushing home from school, vying to be first to hold the baby, Beata's short legs invariably letting her down though she strove to win.

'Eh, you nearly flattened me, Beat!' Fanny Gentle, in the vicinity to deliver someone else's child, steadied herself against a wall.

'Sorry, Nurse!' panted Beata. 'I'm rushing to get home to see my baby brother.' And she ran on.

'Baby brother,' scoffed Fanny to a passer-by. 'That's what her ladyship's fobbing them off with, is it? Must be the longest pregnancy in history, their poor father's been dead nigh eighteen months.'

Hungry for gossip, the other offered a willing ear. 'So who's fathered it then?'

Her tone disguised, Fanny's mouth formed an exaggerated answer. 'The eldest stepson.'

The listener's jaw dropped in outrage. 'Eh, isn't there a law against that?'

'If there isn't there should be! But how could anybody prove it? She's good at pulling the wool over people's eyes, is that one. Anyway, I've stuck my neb in before, thinking I was helping the kids – she's cruel to them, you know, oh terrible things she does – but it only made her worse. Mindst, I hear she's a bit sweeter since the bairn arrived. Let's hope it keeps her that way.'

Everyone sharing this point of view, it was a vast disappointment to all, not the least her smallest victims, when Eliza's newfound maternity began to wane. Too unstable to be able to control herself for long, Eliza quickly regressed to her old habits.

In fact, nowadays, she seemed positively unhinged. If the bread wasn't cut to the correct thinness so that it was virtually transparent, it would be tossed out of the window and the culprit beaten without mercy.

How could such a monster give birth to such a lovable baby? For Lionel was indeed the bonniest, happiest little fellow, greeting everyone with a smile that was like the flame of a candle in this dark place. Everyone adored him, but perhaps Mims most of all. It did not matter that he had replaced her as youngest in the family, for this had borne no advantage in the house of a tyrant. At least it had not for Mims. Too tiny to offend his mother, Lionel was the only one on whom Eliza never inflicted pain. Not merely for his sake, Mims prayed that he would remain this adorable little doll for ever.

Naturally, this hope could not be met, Lionel seeming to turn overnight from a baby to a toddler. But still, he retained his delightful, obedient nature and there were happy days to be had for Mims, who, given any opportunity, would wheel him in his pushchair over the Crags to parade him before her old neighbours in Denaby.

For a while Beata too had shared in this enjoyment but upon reaching her fourteenth birthday she had gone to work at Kilner's Glass Factory, which left little time for play with her baby brother. It was not of her choosing to stand in one place all day long being deafened by the clinking and rattling of glass. She hated it. Her leg swelled up from being on her feet all day long. Nor was there any sanctuary at home. Oh, the extra money put a smile on her stepmother's face, at least on pay day, but the fact that Beata was earning did not give her any leeway, for, over the weekend, Eliza still had plenty of chores for her to do. It was almost a relief to get back to work on Monday, or would have been had it not been accompanied by the knowledge that she was labouring for virtually no reward – unless one called the sixpence pocket money that Eliza doled out fair recompense. Beata deemed it nothing short of slavery.

It was futile to request a change of workplace, for, wherever she went, Eliza would take all her earnings. Doris had been put into service, but Beata's request to be treated likewise was flatly refused, as she had known it would be.

'Why would I want to send you away?' retorted Eliza. 'I'd not only lose your pension but you'd do a disappearing act like your sister. No, you're staying where you are, at least until you're sixteen.'

Two more years of this awful treatment was impossible to contemplate. Especially when, a few days later, Beata was on her hands and knees washing the floor and felt an excruciating blow to her back. Upon looking up she saw Eliza with a shoe in her hand and a spiteful expression on her face. Then, with no explanation, she blithely replaced the weapon on her foot and walked away, leaving Beata with a shoulder blade so painful that it just had to be broken.

Enough was enough; the time had come to make another bid for freedom.

This time she chose York as her destination. It was further to go but if she could just manage to reach it there was more chance of being able to hide in a city and besides, her sister was there and she desperately needed to see Gussie's dear face. There was no discussion with the boys. Joe had always declined to go with her and Duke was away on one of his rambles, nor did she want to involve Mims. There was no callousness intended – she would travel faster on her own and as soon as she reached safety and told her aunt the truth about what had been going on then someone would come and rescue the others. In the meantime Mims would have Lionel to comfort her.

Two years older and wiser than on her last escape attempt, she was able to put a great deal more planning into this latest bid. By setting off as if for work, it would be a good eight hours before they realized she was gone. There was no money for food and certainly there was no hearty breakfast before leaving, but the strength of Beata's determination would see her through without having to resort to theft.

By late morning, however, this morality had been obscured by the ravenous pains in her belly. As one who was always hungry, she had learned how to trick her stomach into believing it was full by taking in lots of water and this she had done in every village through which she passed, gulping from fountains and standpipes, but there came a time when liquid would not suffice and the sight of a field of vegetables proved irresistible. Only the most ungenerous observer would class the uprooting of one carrot as larceny.

Resting for only ten minutes to consume her paltry lunch, she set off again, her eyes constantly darting over her shoulder at every noise, expecting to see Clem pedalling up behind her . . . and so it was no surprise when several hours later her brother's auburn head bobbed into view, his angry face coming ever closer, an indication of the retribution to come. Totally exhausted and dispirited, Beata flopped down at the roadside to await her nemesis.

But no matter how severe the punishment, she swore to herself that she would never give in. If Eliza wanted to prevent her from running away, she would have to kill her.

Only hours after being dragged back and beaten, Beata set out on the road to work and just kept on going. Although close to tears from the pain in her shoulder blade, this time she stopped for neither food nor rest, pausing only briefly to take in water, then marching determinedly onwards. Out of habit, her head constantly turned to look for Clem, but as yet he had not appeared. Even by late afternoon there was no sign of him. But it was far too early to enjoy any feeling of triumph.

Travelling fourteen miles that first day, she was not about to ruin this achievement by seeking shelter in a church and perhaps being discovered. Hedgerows were to be her only bed. Setting off again as soon as it was light, she made it to Selby before nightfall and could have gone much further had her leg not swollen to twice its normal size. At least it took her mind off her damaged shoulder blade. Getting very little sleep due to the pain, she lay there pondering. They must surely have missed her by now. Why had Clem not come to take her back? Was it too much to ask that she had camouflaged herself so well that he had cycled past her in the dark?

Alas, whilst Beata mulled over a list of possible reasons, Clem was sitting comfortably at home, voicing rational argument to Eliza. 'What's the point of me tearing off after her and losing pay? We know where she's heading. I'll go over to York at the weekend and pick her up.' Gaining agreement, he smiled and disappeared behind his newspaper.

Her leg still badly swollen even after a night's rest, progress was very much slower for Beata on that third day.

Hence, it was such a magnificent feeling after limping eight miles that felt like eighty to come upon a signpost that said York was only three miles away. Now, surely, it was safe to enjoy a moment of self-congratulation.

A farmhouse came into view. Having not passed a standpipe in hours, she felt confident enough now to stop and ask for a drink.

The woman was friendly and answered Beata's request straight-away, watching as the glass of water was downed in seconds. 'By, you are thirsty!' Then her eyes ran up and down the young traveller and she cocked her head suspiciously. 'You aren't running away, are you?'

Realizing how she must look, clothes unkempt, driblets of water turning the dust on her upper lip to a black moustache, Beata donned her most convincing smile. 'No! I've come to see my aunty in York and I've had to walk from Selby as I didn't have the fare.'

'All the way from Selby!' The woman looked amazed.

If only she knew, thought Beata. 'Aye, with nothing to eat since yesterday.' Would she pick up on the hint?

'Oh, sit there on the step, dear, and I'll fetch you a slice of bread!'

Plastered with butter, it was the most wonderful bread Beata had ever tasted. But all too quickly it was gone.

The woman, having brought a second glass of water, had gone back inside. Rested, Beata left the glass on the step, called, 'Thank you!' and limped forth upon the final stage of her journey.

To her utter despair, there was no one in at Aunt Lizzie's back-to-back house in Edwin Street. Beata sat on the step for a good fifteen minutes, but when still no one came she tired of waiting and decided to go to the tenement building where old Aunt Mary lived.

Maddeningly, she found the door locked here too and moaned in despair. Putting her eye to the keyhole, she soon came upright in surprise – then had another look just to make sure. There was a coffin on the table; presumably Aunt Mary was in it. She took a moment to reflect; it had been her mother's opinion that the old lady would outlive them all. She had certainly outlived dozens her junior. Still bending over, Beata screamed in fright when somebody nipped her bottom, jumping around to face them.

Her eldest sister laughed uproariously. 'I was just on my way home from work, saw you come up here. Look at the state of you!' She picked a dried leaf from Beata's hair.

Beata explained quickly. 'I've run away again, Gus. I'm not going back this time.'

Augusta was aware that earlier attempts had ended in failure. 'If Eliza wants you back –'

'I'm not going! Don't tell her I'm here, will you?'

Augusta immediately dealt Beata a reassuring squeeze and was shocked when the other flinched in pain.

'I think she's broken my shoulder,' explained Beata, holding her arm. 'Please, don't send me back, Gus.'

Augusta's voice was rough but her eyes and voice compassionate as she comforted the anxious youngster. ''Course I won't, you daft 'a'p'orth! Away, I'll take you home to Aunt Lizzie's. I've told her all about Eliza so she's bound to take you in.'

Unable to relax, Beata said, 'I won't be a burden. I'm going to get a job in service, then she won't know where to find me.' She grasped her sister's arm, delivering earnest plea. 'But we can't leave the others there, Gus. You don't know the half of it. We have to rescue them.'

Aunt Lizzie and Uncle Matt were very understanding upon coming home from work that evening to find they had an extra lodger, and, hearing the full extent of Eliza's cruelty, paid attention to her shoulder.

'Wiggle it about,' said Aunt Lizzie. Then, 'Oh, if you can do that it can't be broken. It'll just be badly bruised.' Nevertheless, both she and Uncle Matt said Beata must stay as long as she liked whilst efforts were made to rescue her siblings.

Almost asleep from exhaustion, Beata appreciated their mercy, but said, 'I won't be in your hair for long. First thing tomorrow I'm off to find myself a job in service.' She glanced nervously at the door to the street as she had been doing since her arrival. 'That's if Clem doesn't come and get me.'

'Don't worry, lass, I doubt her majesty'll let him come till the weekend.' Uncle Matt did not talk very much but was a kindly man and dealt her a reassuring smile from behind his handlebar moustache, which was powdered with flour from the mill. 'Can't have him losing money by taking a day off work.' He went back to contemplating the fire, playing with the large cyst on his forehead.

Aunty Lizzie refilled her husband's moustache cup with tea from a pot that was decorated with teddy bears, its missing lid replaced by one of tin. 'Yes, don't be rushing off into any old job, Beat. Besides anything else, you're hardly dressed to make an impression. Stay in bed tomorrow, catch up on your sleep and I'll take your clothes to the laundry with me. We'll have you looking respectable again by Friday. Then you can go and see Miss Stroud at the Servants' Register Office. She's a queer sort of woman and her commission's steep but it's worth it 'cause she only caters for gentry.'

Beata nodded. Trying to keep her own eyes open she concentrated on the large eye flanked by buffalo horns at the centre of the diploma that hung over the black-leaded range, which announced her uncle as a member of the Royal Antediluvian Order of Buffaloes. But soon she was failing again.

'You know, I've always thought we were very interesting people,' joked Matt to his wife as Beata jolted herself awake.

About to tilt her pot at Beata's cup, Aunt Lizzie laughed at the youngster's efforts to keep awake.

Augusta took charge of her poor exhausted sister. 'Away, upstairs with you now, Beat. You can have my bed.'

She herself was to sleep on a mattress downstairs that night.

Uncle Matt turned out to be correct in his assumption that Clem would not come during the week. Aunt Lizzie, too, was right about Miss Stroud.

Returned from her interview that Friday, Beata was bursting to tell but only Uncle Matt was in the house, sitting quietly puffing on his pipe when she arrived in the late afternoon and so she withheld her news until she had a better audience.

He explained his wife and Gussie's absence. 'They're on their knees again.'

Knowing this meant they were at church, Beata nodded and said she would get the tea ready. Whilst she was doing this a neighbour entered. Matt's face did not change but Beata knew these visits annoyed her uncle. Mrs Cammidge was forever bringing them gifts as if they were poverty-stricken.

'I just thought I'd bring you a little treat.' She bestowed an obsequious smile.

Matt dealt her a dour nod, lending no encouragement for her to stay. With Lizzie absent, Mrs Cammidge soon left, allowing Beata's disgruntled uncle to peer into the bag at the mixture of cocoa and condensed milk. 'What the hell's she bringing us now – shite?'

Beata was doubled up laughing when her aunt and sister came in directly off the street, allowing her to finally make her announcement. 'I've got a job working for Sir Wilfred Thompson! From tonight I'm going to be living at Nunthorpe Hall.'

There were congratulations all round, though Aunt Lizzie showed concern that Beata had only the clothes she stood up in and, after serving the evening meal, spent some time rifling through her wardrobe, handing her niece a blouse, a skirt and a worn petticoat. 'Here, it's not much but it'll tide you over till you start earning.'

Augusta too donated a nightgown and two pairs of drawers.

Beata gave sincere thanks. 'You're sure you can spare them? I wouldn't like to think you were going without.'

Her sister laughed at the unintended pun. 'As long as we don't get a high wind I'll maintain my decency.'

Armed with these few generously donated items and a tasty meal in her stomach, Beata stood ready to go. 'I'd better make a move.'

'Well, I've nowt useful to offer you, Beat.' Uncle Matt played with the cyst on his head. 'Unless you fancy taking that.' He indicated the bag that Mrs Cammidge had brought.

Beata laughed. 'Not after what you said about it!'

Everyone gathered on the doorstep.

Matt had turned thoughtful, deciding that a girl new to service might be in need of guidance. 'I'm not one for wise words, Beat, but just let me say this. You've only got one friend in this world and that's your pocket. When you've got money in your pocket there's plenty that will call themselves your friend but heed my advice, keep your own counsel, and you won't go far wrong.'

Thanking him for this advice, Beata kissed everyone in turn, then said anxiously to her sister, 'You won't tell Eliza where I've gone?'

'They'll have to pull my fingernails out first,' exclaimed Aunt Lizzie. Augusta agreed.

'Goodbye! Good luck!' chorused everyone as a smiling Beata departed.

She had been gone only two hours when Clem arrived to look for her.

Uncle Matt and Aunt Lizzie had gone out for the evening and Augusta had taken the opportunity to have a bath. She was in her dressing gown, kneeling over the tin receptacle and employing the now lukewarm water to wash her hair when the knock came. Wrapping her long dripping tresses in a towel, she went immediately to answer the door, not even hesitating over her state of disarray for she knew who it would be.

After greeting Clem with a sisterly kiss, she invited him in, but announced, 'You've had a wasted journey, Beat isn't here.'

Sensing conspiracy, he glanced around the room then cocked his head at the ceiling as if suspecting that their sister might be hiding upstairs.

'Go up and check if you like,' came the immediate invitation.

Guessing that this would be pointless, Clem sighed. 'Don't try pulling the wool over my eyes, Gus. I've just cycled forty bloody miles. I know she was heading here.'

Augusta adjusted her turban and replied lightly, 'I'm not trying to pull the wool over anybody's eyes. Beat was here, but now she's gone – and don't ask me where because I'm not going to tell you.'

He groaned. 'So you're going to make me turn round and pedal all the way back?'

'Not right away,' said Augusta brightly. 'You can have a cup of tea first.'

'Oh, too kind!' Clem flopped onto the sofa. 'Eliza's going to kill me if I go back without her.'

'You know that's not true.' Tightening the cord of her plaid dressing gown, Augusta put the kettle on the hob, then crossed her arms to wait and gazed at him with her serene blue eyes.

Defeated, he nodded and stared back at her. 'She won't be best pleased, though.'

Picturing Eliza's displeasure upon hearing he had failed, this was to concern him throughout his long journey home. He prepared himself for a torrent of insults.

But Eliza never failed to surprise him.

True, she was not at all happy, but it was far from the rage he had imagined, only a loud disgruntled sigh.

'I can go around the rest of the family and see if she's with them,' he mollified.

Eliza stared into midair, her voice ripe with disdain for the errant Beata. 'No, let her go, Clem. I'm *sick* of her.'

TWENTY-THREE

Within a week of Beata's escape, all her relatives had been informed of the situation and a council of war ensued, the outcome of which was that a relief expedition must be launched to rescue her siblings. But, well aware that the crafty Eliza would not give up the pensions without a fight, they realized they would have to be equally devious.

Mims knew none of this. The only thing apparent to her was that she had been abandoned to suffer the cruelty alone. Yes, she had two brothers, a stepbrother too, but they were all older and bigger, too big to be stuffed into the dark and frightening cupboard like she was. It might have been said that Mims could have helped herself by eating everything put before her, but this was too simplified an answer. She could not give in and eat the peas she so detested without a fight. And, with no Beata to divest her of the crusts that took so long to eat, these too became a source of conflict at meal times. Hardly a day went by without Mims earning some kind of punishment.

Thank Heaven for dear Lionel, who had become especially dear since Beata had deserted her, though the additional chores caused by her sister's exodus meant that she had not so much time to enjoy him as before.

Saturdays had become exceptionally cherished, for even though there was the shopping to be done, this could nicely be fitted in with taking Lionel for his morning stroll, the pushchair coming in handy for transporting the bags of food.

And afterwards, allowed to spend the rest of the day as she pleased, Mims would wheel Lionel in his pushchair up and away across the Crags, pretending that she was his mother.

In spite of the brutality at home, Mims remained a cheerful, optimistic little soul, this reflected in her jaunty step as she skipped across the Crags this afternoon, shoving the pushchair before her.

'Are you ready, Line?' Calling out to the baby, she gave the vehicle a hefty push, setting the wheels spinning and allowing it to run on its own for as long as she dared, before running to catch up with it. Lionel screamed in delight.

Leaving the pushchair by the road, for it would be difficult to negotiate over the marshy ground, a stroll on the Ings ensued, Mims pointing out all the wildlife to her little charge.

Delving in the wet grass she came across a frog, which was a source of fun for the next few moments. 'Let's find a straw and I'll show you a good trick, Line!' Finding one, she showed him what to do. 'You shove it up its bum, then you go like this.' Putting her lips to the straw she proceeded to blow into it, causing the unfortunate beast to inflate its air sacks like miniature balloons, and making Lionel giggle.

A dozen repetitions later and the frog began to lose its novelty value.

Tossing the poor abused creature back into the grass, Mims led the toddler eventually back to where they had left his pushchair, then it was over the Crags towards home.

To provide more amusement along the way, Mims gave a hefty shove of the handle, allowing the pushchair to free wheel and drawing screeches of excitement from the baby. 'Again!' She dealt the perambulator yet another gleeful thrust, leaving it even longer this time, before rushing to catch up with it. Lionel squealed as his vehicle accelerated over the bumpy grass.

Happy and laughing, Mims ran to grab hold of the handle again – then suddenly tripped over a lump of rock and before she knew it the pushchair was out of her grasp and was hurtling down the limestone Crags, tossing its little occupant up and down and from side to side in a hazardous fashion. Terrified of the consequences, Mims scrambled as fast as she could down the slope after the careering vehicle but too late; upon reaching the bottom its wheels hit a ledge, stopping it abruptly and tipping the baby out face first.

After a moment of shock came the sound of crying. A hand pressed to her mouth, Mims proceeded cautiously, hardly daring to guess at what Lionel's injuries might be. But with the loudness of his wails threatening to reach Eliza's ears she rushed the last few yards, scooped him up into her arms and covered him with kisses, cuddling and shushing him. 'I'm sorry! I'm sorry, Line!'

Under these soothing noises of apology he immediately stopped crying, though this was of no consolation to Mims for she now saw that his face was covered in blood and dirt.

Sucking in her breath, she burst into tears, tears not for Lionel but for herself. What would Eliza do to someone who had harmed her baby?

Startled by this, Lionel made not another sound, merely beheld her with uncomprehending eyes as she spat on a handkerchief and dabbed gently at his face.

Thankfully, much of the blood was deposited on the fabric and with the dirt wiped away his injuries seemed not half so severe – though there was a cut on his mouth that no amount of dabbing would remove.

After this, legs weakened by a state of terror, she slumped to the ground, the baby on her lap. How on earth was she going to explain this to Eliza?

'Doh-doh,' prompted Lionel.

Still dazed, Mims noticed then that his dummy was missing. Searching frantically about her, she spotted the rubber comforter nearby, wiped it on her cardigan, sucked off the residue of dust, then jammed it into Lionel's mouth.

But still she made no move to go home.

A good half an hour passed, during which the fearful little girl racked her brain for some convincing explanation. An idea began to form. Whether or not it would win over her stepmother it was impossible to say, but she would have to test it out some time. Practising the explanation as she went, Mims put Lionel back into his pushchair and made her reluctant way home.

There was to be no last-minute rehearsal, for Eliza was sitting outside the front door with Clem, enjoying the sunshine. Seeing them, Mims immediately broke into a trot, her voice excited as she reached them. 'Lionel nearly swallowed his dummy! I had to hit him to stop him choking! I'm sorry his mouth got cut . . .' She waited apprehensively, expecting Eliza to swoop down on her, but her stepmother's outstretched arms were merely to grab Lionel, whom she swung up into the air with an exclamation.

'Aw, poor baby! Have you been in the wars?' The voice was jovially affectionate, Eliza still holding Lionel at arm's length before gathering him to her breast and jiggling him. 'Silly old dummy, we'll have to get you a new one.'

Mims could hardly trust her ears. Eliza believed her!

At only nine years old, she had no concept of irony, yet this did not

403

prevent a bubbling-up of amusement in the scrawny breast. For the first time in Mims' life she had escaped punishment – for something that really was her fault.

At teatime there was a slice of cake as reward for Mims' quick-thinking. Knowing this glorification would not last for long, Mims enjoyed it whilst she could and she was right to do so, for by Sunday lunchtime Eliza was back to her usual obnoxious self, castigating Mims for dawdling over her meal, before banishing her to the cupboard.

'You know, you could save yourself an awful lot of upset,' sighed Clem, trying to enjoy his own meal amid the chaos.

'Try telling her that!' retorted Eliza. 'If you think I'm giving in to that stubborn, ungrateful little minx –'

'But is it really worth disrupting everyone over a few peas?'

'It's not just a few peas!' Eliza's raised voice pierced her victim's dark prison. 'She wears them like blasted medals!'

Sitting in the dark, hugging herself, Mims frowned over this; she had not realized just how affective her obstinacy had been. Yet there was no triumph to be had. From past experience she knew that the peas would be served cold at teatime and would taste even worse.

Eliza confirmed this, her announcement drilling through the cupboard door. 'Well, if she doesn't eat them tonight they'll be there at breakfast!'

And so they were. The peas that Mims so valiantly avoided – going to bed hungry rather than eat them – reappeared at breakfast on Monday morning, the shrivelled black objects looking more like currants than peas. Pretending that this was what they were, and with nothing else on offer, the famished Mims finally surrendered.

Surrender or no, it did not seem to please her stepmother. Delivering a whack round the little girl's head in passing, Eliza spat, 'Why couldn't you have eaten them in the first place?'

Rubbing her head, Mims awaited permission to leave the table, then went off to school in a state of despondency.

That afternoon, when Mims came out of class she found Aunt Ethel waiting at the gate, accompanied by Joe, still in his pit clothes.

There was no feeling of excitement. Confronted by her elderly stern-faced aunt, the little girl looked apprehensive.

Ethel was not one for preamble. 'Right, Millicent, we know your stepmother's being cruel to you –'

'Oh no!' Mims looked terrified.

'Oh yes! And I'm here to do something about it, so you can stop panicking.'

Mims remained unconvinced. Ethel might have kind intentions, but had no idea how formidable her ram-rod posture, square jaw and emotionally distant personality might seem to a little girl.

'Where's your brother Marmaduke?'

Mims felt her legs trembling. 'He's gone off.' Duke had been roaming the country for days.

Ethel turned sharply to Joe. 'You'll have to find him. We can't leave him to carry the can.'

Joe noted his little sister's bafflement, and explained, 'Aunt Ethel's come to kidnap us.'

Ethel's normally severe expression cracked into a laugh. 'I suppose I have.' But soon she was her businesslike self. 'Now, here's the plan. Millicent, you and Marmaduke – as long as Joseph manages to find him – get up at the normal time as if you're going to school. But you won't go. I'll be waiting on Station Road to take you on the train. Joseph, you'll have to go to work as usual or Eliza might get to hear that you haven't turned up, but take a change of clothing and drop it off at Mrs Gentle's house – don't worry she knows all about it – Aunt Meredith will be waiting at the pit head at the end of your shift and she'll go with you to Mrs Gentle's where you can get bathed and changed.'

Mims plucked up the courage to ask, 'What about Lionel?'

Aunt Ethel looked down at her. 'We can't take him, dear. He belongs to your stepmother.'

Mims was deeply shocked. She loved Lionel – how could she be parted from him?

Watching her face Ethel said, 'If you want to stay here you can, but I don't think you want to, do you?'

Recalling each cruel treatment, Mims knew that there was no other way. Taking Aunt Ethel's outstretched hand, she silently made her choice.

Having made sure they were certain of the plan, Aunt Ethel walked with them for part of the way, then made a detour to Mrs Rushton's, where she would be staying overnight.

Highly excited, yet apprehensive too, Joe and his sister went home.

When they got there, Eliza had already scrubbed the coal dust from George's back and was hanging around the bathroom impatiently. 'You're late,' she commented. 'Water's gone cold.'

'Doesn't matter. Serve me right for standing talking.' Quickly, Joe stripped off and stepped into the scum-laden bath water.

Mims, meanwhile, had brushed silently past and into the sitting room, making a beeline for Lionel.

Assailed by the thought that they would soon be parted, she made an extra fuss of him this afternoon, reluctant to let him go and rushing her tea to reclaim him. In fact, so upset was she at the thought of the two of them being parted she refused to give him up, even when her stepmother instructed her to take him to bed.

'Can't he just stay up a while longer, Mother?'

'What the devil's up with you tonight?' demanded Eliza, hands on hips. 'You've been clinging like a blasted limpet. I said take him to bed right now, and you'll find yourself up there with him if I have any more cheek!'

Whilst Mims hefted Lionel up the staircase, Eliza greeted Clem, who had just come in from work. 'Oh, I thought it might be Duke.'

'He's still not back then?' Weary from a day's mental toil, Clem just wanted to eat his meal in peace. 'If I get my hands on him –'

Worried that Duke might be disabled by Clem's punishment, and therefore unable to take part in the escape, Joe volunteered, 'Would you like me to go and see if I can find him, Mother?'

'Yes and you can tell him to look forward to a good hiding when he comes home!'

Joe rushed out. After scouring the area for an hour, he was beginning to despair, but as a train rattled by and his eyes followed it he eventually saw his brother standing on the embankment and waving furiously to the homebound racegoers from Doncaster, beseeching them to part with their winnings. 'Throw us a penny!'

Clambering over a fence, Joe stumbled down the embankment to a hail of coppers, and rushed to help Duke gather them as the train chugged off along the track.

'Eh, them's mine!'

'I were only helping you!' grumbled Joe, with the addition, 'Tight-arse.'

Looking in no way repentant for the accusation of theft, Duke sat down to count his money. Joe flopped down beside his brother and told him of the plan.

Faced with Duke's silence he added, 'It's up to you whether

you want to come but if you do you'll have to come home with me now.'

Duke was unenthusiastic, clinking the collection of pennies in his fist. His hands were more tanned than his brother's from his habitual outdoor rambles. 'I'll get a hammering when I show my face.'

Joe nodded grimly. 'Aye, but it'll be the last one you have. Tomorrow night you'll be miles away where she can't touch you.'

'I was going to be miles away anyway. That's what I need this for.' He continued to jingle the money.

'Where?'

'Dunno.' Duke stared into midair. His life seemed to consist of one endless search; for what, he did not know.

Joe studied the forlorn face. Burdened with the same aching loss of a mother and the oppression at home, he could understand the desperation that prompted Duke to keep running away, though could not guess what lay beneath: the sense of not belonging, the acute heartache for something he could never have. To Joe, Duke had always been a strange one. 'Wouldn't it be better to have somewhere in mind before you set off?'

Duke underwent serious thought. For most, the prospect of living with caring foster parents would be much preferable to a life on the road, but for one possessed by wanderlust it was a difficult choice to make.

Finally, though, the slender hope that he might eventually find what he sought lured him into making a decision. Even if he did not find it, there would be a warm bed and kind treatment. Hiding his pennies under a stone, Duke accompanied his brother home. Sure enough, a severe beating awaited him, but the thought of Eliza's face when she discovered he had been rescued from her clutches made every blow worthwhile.

Mims had been trying her best not to cry at the thought of leaving her dear Lionel, for Eliza would be suspicious. But now, witnessing Duke's beating she could quite feasibly allow her tears to flow. Packed off to bed, she could hardly sleep.

At five o'clock, along with George, Joe went off to the pit as normal, his younger brother and sister rising some two hours later. After seeing Clem off to work, Eliza followed habit and went back to bed to enjoy a lie-in with baby Lionel, whilst the others ate their bread-and-dripping and got themselves ready for school.

Even in her absence, there was no relaxing of tension for Mims and Duke. The excitement was almost suffocating.

Poised to go, Mims indicated the money that lay on the table; it was to buy bread for their dinner. 'Do we take this?' she whispered.

'Better not,' advised Duke, who had decided to abandon his own cache in the face of expedience, 'or she'll accuse us of stealing.'

Envisioning herself in prison, Mims left the coins on the chenille tablecloth and, without a backwards glance, left the house. Fearing that any moment she would be discovered and hauled back, her heart was thumping and her bottom quivering as she and Duke made their way to Station Road where they could see Aunt Ethel awaiting them.

Then, wasting neither time nor sentiment, their ally took a hand in each of hers and led them briskly to the railway station, and on to freedom.

But for those who had suffered two years of abuse the notion of freedom was hard to credit and even hours later, after being served the most delicious meal at Aunt Ethel's, the pair sat obediently juxtaposed like statues on the horsehair sofa, hardly daring to move. The slightest noise would have their eyes shooting to the door, both expecting Clem to arrive and take them back at any time.

When the door knocker sounded, Mims almost jumped out of her skin, Duke going even further and hiding behind a jardinière that held an aspidistra in a majolica pot.

Shocked by this extreme reaction, Ethel coaxed him out, then sat beside the pair on the brown sofa, bidding them not to worry as husband Horace went to answer the summons. 'It's only Aunt Meredith.'

Sure enough, a beaming Meredith entered, accompanied by Joe. Yet even then Mims and Duke could not allow themselves to believe that life had taken an upwards course.

Exhilarated from their escapades, the elderly sisters shared a laugh at their own audacity. 'Talk about a blooming military operation!' chuckled Merry, tugging at the fingers of her summer gloves. 'I could teach General Haig a thing or two.'

'Yes, Probe would be proud of us,' answered Ethel, feeling ashamed that she had let him down all those years just because he had married a Catholic, and glad of the opportunity to put this right.

Raising her hands to remove her hat, Meredith was horrified that the children misinterpreted her swift movement and cowered as if to avoid being hit. 'Oh, Ethel,' her smile of triumph was doused in woe, 'what has that dreadful woman been doing to them?'

Sharing her sister's anger, though keeping it hidden, Ethel dealt the nearest child a reassuring pat. 'Well, don't worry, she isn't going to do it any more.'

By six o'clock Eliza realized that something was seriously amiss. Had it been just one of the children who had not come home there might be some explanation, but for three to vanish at once she detected skulduggery. Beginning to clear away the pots from their evening meal, she gave bad-tempered instruction to George: 'Get Lionel down then have a look in the street and see if there's any sign of them.'

After removing his little brother from the high chair, George slouched towards the door, leaving it open as he went out to cast his eyes up and down the street.

Clem helped Eliza to clear the table, then settled himself in an armchair, Lionel on his knee.

Hearing voices outside, Eliza immediately went out to investigate, but her son was conversing with Fanny Gentle. 'I thought I told you to go and look for them!'

George looked uneasy. 'Mrs Gentle were just saying –'

'I was just saving George the bother of traipsing up and down looking for his brothers and sister.' Fanny came towards Eliza, carrying the bag that she used for her midwifery. Her mien was smug.

Eliza responded darkly. 'I might've guessed you'd have something to do with it. So where are they?'

'Out of your clutches,' replied Fanny. 'With folk who'll protect them.'

'You can get put in gaol for kidnapping,' retorted Eliza. Clem had come to stand in the doorway behind her, Lionel in his arms.

'How can it be kidnapping?' sneered Fanny. 'They were rescued by members of their own family.'

Eliza glanced over her shoulder at Clem with a meaningful nod. 'Ethel! Well, at least now we know where they are. Two can play at that game. Thank you for telling us, Mrs Gentle.' Summoning George inside, she shut the door in Fanny's face, leaving the midwife feeling that she might have done the wrong thing.

Indoors, Eliza divested Clem of his baby son. 'I'll show her who's in charge! Get over to Leeds and bring them back.'

Clem glanced at the clock. It was only a quarter past six; he could be there easily before dark. 'All right, but if they're already in bed I might have to stay the night and fetch them in the morning.' Tomorrow being Saturday, he would not lose any pay.

'Whatever you like, but don't come back without them. We'll be destitute if we lose their pensions.' Eliza watched him don his bicycle clips, then followed him outside to see him off.

Back indoors, she found a pensive George staring into the fire. Setting Lionel on his feet she slapped her elder son round the head in passing. 'Don't think you're just sitting there doing nowt. There's washing-up to be done!'

At Aunt Ethel's, after enjoying another meal, Mims was being told that she would be travelling on to Lancashire tomorrow, whilst her brothers would stay here. The fact that Ethel obviously preferred boys did not worry Mims, who was glad to be going with the much nicer Aunt Meredith.

There followed an hour of quiet conversation before bedtime and, whilst Aunt Ethel's treatment could never be classed as pampering, and the dark brown Victorian décor was somewhat oppressive, it was wonderful not to feel under constant threat of violence.

'Well, you younger ones had better go to bed now,' came their aunt's brisk announcement.

'Please may I be allowed to go up too?' tendered Joe.

Though admiring the young man's manners, Ethel told him, 'You don't need to ask permission to go to bed in this house, dear.'

Just then the door knocker sounded, setting the children instantly alert again.

When Clem was admitted the younger ones collapsed into paroxysms of fear, Mims almost wetting herself, and when Aunt Meredith reached out a protective hand she flew to her.

After greeting his aunts and uncle in friendly manner and removing his bicycle clips, Clem came straight to the point. 'Well, you know why I'm here.'

'Yes, we do,' nodded Ethel. 'But I'm afraid we can't allow it.'

Clem donned a firm expression. 'You can't stop me taking them, Aunt. You're not their legal guardian.'

'And we've all seen what their legal guardian's done to them!'

'That's not fair, Aunt. Eliza's tried to do her best. You have to understand how hard it was for her to be left a widow with nine of us to look aft –'

'There's not nine of you now, though, is there? And I doubt these poor little mites would still have been there had they been old enough to escape her cruelty.'

'Eliza's not cruel, she just –'

'Yes, she is!' Merry butted in now. 'Stop defending her, Clem. This is your little sister and brother and you're meant to look after them.'

'And until you can be trusted to do that,' said Ethel, 'we're taking over. Now, you'll understand if I ask you to leave.' Like a protective stone sentinel, the children behind her, she indicated the door, which Uncle Horace obligingly opened.

With a sigh, Clem bent to replace his cycle clips, then rammed his cap on and left.

But he had promised Eliza that he would not go home without them and, bearing this in mind, he sallied off to find a lodging house.

Secure in the custody of their aunts and uncle, after a good night's sleep and generous breakfast the brothers said goodbye to Mims, from whom they would soon be parted.

But, 'Our train doesn't go till eleven,' said Aunt Meredith. 'Go outside and get some sunshine whilst I have another cup of tea with Aunt Ethel and Uncle Horace.'

Pedalling up the sloping red-brick terrace, Clem could not believe the luck that had brought his siblings unchaperoned into the small forecourt garden. Applying the brakes, he remained stationary for the moment lest his aunts appear, willing the youngsters to stray outside the gate and make it easier for him to spirit them away. He could hear their voices quite clearly.

'I like Aunt Ethel and everything, even though she's a bit strict,' Joe was saying, kicking his heels back and forth along the strip of path under the bay window, 'but I wished she lived somewhere different. Fancy living in Birdshit Place.'

Mims and Duke convulsed with laughter at this play on words from their brother; the real name was Burchett.

Tensed in readiness, heart thudding in his chest, Clem watched Mims climb up to sit upon the gate, whilst Duke jumped onto the low wall and started to walk along it. It was thus that they were alerted to the danger.

411

The laughter on their faces turned to apprehension. Immediately donning a smile and pushing his bicycle, Clem tried to approach as casually as he could, waving in a brotherly manner. Urging Mims to get down, Joe headed for the lobby, his siblings after him.

To stall any alarm being raised Clem called out in a cheery voice, 'Hang on, Joe! I only want a word.' Having succeeded in delaying him, he propped his bicycle against the kerb and came within grabbing distance of the younger ones.

But Aunt Ethel must have heard his call too, for she emerged and hurried up to bar his entry, followed by her husband and Meredith.

'I told you last night I'm not going back without them, Aunt.' Though his opponent was formidable, Clem stood his ground.

It seemed to work. After holding his determined hooded gaze for a few seconds, Aunt Ethel made sudden capitulation and opened the gate wide. 'You'd better take them then.'

Horrified at this betrayal, Mims and Duke tried to hide behind Aunt Meredith's corseted body, though it did them no good, for their brother soon had them by the hands.

'You and all, Joe,' said Clem grimly.

Wearing a sick expression, Joe turned to beseech the other adults for help, but just as Clem was about to lead the younger ones away their aunt produced her trump card.

'Yes, you take them – and I'll go straight down to the police station and tell them about the carryings-on between you and your stepmother!'

Clem faltered. Neither he nor Eliza were sure if their relationship was incestuous, but both had been made well aware of the immorality of it by their neighbours' opprobrium. He had no wish for it to be broadcast. Still, he held determinedly to the children's hands.

'Oh, I'd be embarrassed, yes,' went on Ethel, to her sister's and husband's admiration. 'But don't think I'm bluffing. I'd suffer any amount of shame if it meant that those poor children were freed from cruelty.' She transfixed him with her steely gaze, one that reminded him of his father. 'Now, you can go back and tell Eliza she can kiss goodbye to her pension.'

Clem looked down at his worried siblings, agonizing between his loyalty to them and to Eliza. 'You want to come home with me, don't you?'

Having suffered at Clem's hands, Duke was too petrified to answer and hung his head, but eventually Mims dared to utter a blunt, 'No.' Immediately, she felt sorry at creating the look of rejection on Clem's face; the way he looked at her made her want to cry. They had shared such happy times together . . . once.

But it was said now. Releasing them, Clem hesitated only briefly, then exited without a further word.

A large man came through the gateway; having almost collided with an angry Clem he turned bemusedly to watch him throw his leg over a bicycle.

'Chris!' Meredith gave a delighted cry at the unexpected arrival of her husband.

'Ted and Wyn turned up last night so I got him to drive me over to fetch you – mindst I had to pay for the petrol, tight bugger.' He waved and smiled at Ted, who was assiduously polishing smears from the bonnet of his Open Tourer. 'Has Clem been giving you trouble?' His eyes followed his nephew as the latter pedalled away.

'Nothing my dear wife couldn't handle,' announced Horace, with a smile for Ethel.

Feeling tremors from the little girl at her side, Meredith bent to put an arm around her. 'Don't worry, dear, you really are safe now.'

Uncle Christmas gazed upon the pretty but neglected child, running his eyes from the black hat she wore – one of Ethel's, a great big thing with a large brim and pink roses on the front – down to the feet, which hung over the backs of her shoes, and murmured, 'The poor little bugger, we must take her out and buy her some new clothes.'

Then after a moment's contemplation, his eyes still on the hat, he suddenly exclaimed, 'Flaming roses – there's a horse of that name running this afternoon. Start the car up again, Ted, I'll have to get a bet on!' And grabbing his wife with one hand and Mims in the other he hurried the little girl towards her new life with the promise, 'If it wins you shall have all the clothes you want!'

Tutting her disapproval, the strait-laced Ethel led her boys indoors. 'We shall have to get you smartened up too.'

Joe and Duke gave one last smiling wave as their sister was driven away in style, though relieved to be saved, both thinking wistfully that Mims had perhaps gone to the jollier household.

It was a very disillusioned Clem who presented himself before Eliza, taking off his cap and explaining wearily that he had done his best, yet to no avail.

But the histrionics he had been expecting never materialized. Eliza

413

just stood there in the middle of the large sitting room, otherwise empty but for Lionel, who played near the hearth, tapping a lead soldier on the tiles. She looked completely lost. 'That's it then, they've all gone.'

Still in his bicycle clips, Clem looked about him, then frowned. 'Do you mean, George . . . ?'

She stilled him with a doleful nod, her eyes dead as coal. 'He walked out this morning. Said he wasn't stopping here to be anybody's slave.'

'The insolent little –' Clem rammed his cap back on preparing to go after him. 'I'll break his neck!'

'It's no use.' Eliza was as he had never seen her before, her mouth turned right down like a crescent moon, her lower lip trembling with emotion. The dark eyes that looked at him swam with tears. 'They've all left me, Clem. Every one of them.'

One less humane might have declared: well, what did you expect, really? But Clem just took off his cap again, sighed and hung his head.

'You're not going to leave me too, are you?'

He came alive then, the emotive query spurring him to rush up to her and take her in his arms, his voice loaded with compassion. 'What, leave you and this little fellow? Never!' Delivering a tight squeeze, he broke off temporarily to pick Lionel up and include him in the tableau, the little boy squashed between them, beholding his parents in wonder as they shared an emotional embrace. 'Bugger them!' Clem proceeded to dab kisses on the tear-stained face. 'If they don't want us we don't want them. We'll get rid of this big place and find somewhere more cosy – and damn the gossips too. We'll move away where nobody knows us, where we can live in truth, just the three of us, you, me and our son. I'm sick of pretending I'm not his father and that you're not my wife.' He looked her directly in the eye and made a last fervent promise. 'As far as I'm concerned, you are. And that's how it's going to be from now on.'

TWENTY-FOUR

Beata had been working at Nunthorpe Hall only a few weeks when a letter came in childish hand to inform her that Mims was now lodged permanently at Aunt Meredith's. It was a huge relief and, in the knowledge that her little sister and brothers had been rescued from further harm and that she herself was in no danger of being sent back to Eliza, despite the badly-bruised shoulder, Beata was able to throw herself wholeheartedly into her job.

Whilst not exactly happy with her lot, it was no more than she was used to doing at home and at least here she would be paid, except that this was a much larger house and the constant running up and downstairs had a bad effect on her leg, which swelled so drastically that it hung over her shoe.

Eyes drawn to the limb, Cook had been watching the kitchenmaid limp about; it was obviously extremely painful, yet not once had Beata complained. 'That leg's giving you gyp, isn't it?'

Still on the move, Beata nodded. 'It feels really taut, as if it's going to explode.'

Cook winced in sympathy and issued a highly unusual invitation. 'Come and sit down a minute.'

'Nay, Mrs Willis, if I sit down I won't want to get up,' joked Beata.

'Do as you're told!' In authoritative manner Mrs Willis stabbed a finger at the chair, then, when the youngster reluctantly sat in it, she bent down to have a closer look at the distended limb. 'My goodness, you'll have to go see the doctor.'

'I haven't got myself a medical card yet.' Owing to the impromptu

415

escape she had no documentation whatsoever. 'He'll want paying and I haven't a bean.'

Mrs Willis saw no obstacle. 'I shall go and ask her ladyship for an advance on your wages.'

Loath to spend hard-earned money only for the doctor to tell her what she already knew, Beata informed the cook, 'I've always had it. It'll go down of its own accord eventually.'

'I'm not hearing any arguments! You can't work with a leg like that.'

'I'm doing my best,' pleaded Beata.

'That wasn't a criticism.' The frown turned to exasperation. 'I meant, it isn't right that you should have to work in such pain. Eh, you never grumble, do you?'

Beata grinned. 'There's not much point, Cook, nobody'd listen. Anyway, I consider myself lucky to have a job at all when some poor chaps who fought for their country are reduced to peddling stuff off trays.' Levering herself from the chair, she said, 'I'd best get on.'

'Well, if you're sure you can manage, but I meant what I said about an advance on your wages and you can get yourself down to the doctor's this evening.'

Thinking it kind of her superior to show such concern, Beata dutifully went off after her day's work, even though she knew the visit would turn out to be a waste of time and money. Added to which, she had no desire to hear confirmation that her life would be a short one; this frightening thought was usually pushed to the back of her mind.

Sure enough, the doctor charged a deposit in lieu of proof that she was insured, then inflicted a series of deep thumbprints in her swollen leg. But there was a different pronouncement than before: 'Lymphatic oedema.'

'Excuse me, Doctor,' she queried this tentatively, 'I was told by someone else that it was dropsy.'

'Dropsy is just a symptom.'

Beata elaborated. 'Caused by a bad heart, that doctor said.'

After further questioning, her examiner put his stethoscope to her chest. 'Your heart appears perfectly normal.'

'So, I'm not a goner?'

'Good Lord, no.' And he repeated his former diagnosis. 'Lymphatic oedema: we don't know how it's caused and there's no cure – though it's certainly not fatal in your case.'

Relief washed over her as the awful burden that she had carried for over four years was instantly lifted.

'Your only recourse is to find a less strenuous job.'

'Some hopes,' said Beata to the cook after a painful walk home. 'I'll just have to think myself lucky I've only got it in one leg.' Reprieved from her sentence of death, she was in jovial mood, despite her pain.

'Eh, you're a good un, Beat!' Mrs Willis shook her head in admiration. 'The fit young lasses I've had through here, moaning about chapped hands, you'd put them to shame.'

'Well, compared to what I've been used to, Cook, I regard it as Heaven.' Beata's small blue eyes twinkled. 'Just as well. I'll be working the next three days for nowt!'

There was little to be done about the pain, but after that initial setback with her wages Beata was eventually able to spend them more enjoyably on her evening off: tuppence for the tram into town, one and sixpence for her tea and ninepence for a seat at the pictures. Yet, it was quite a lonely existence for no one wanted to socialize with a kitchenmaid and, besides, they were all older than she, so, when her sister Madeleine turned up unexpectedly one Sunday afternoon, she was overjoyed to see her, even though the pair had never really got on.

'Oh, *dooo* come in – I'm having an at home!' With the servants' sitting room empty Beata was at liberty to don airs and graces to entertain her sister on this her afternoon off. After the grandiose performance she laughed. 'Eh, it's great to see you! How did you know where I was?'

'I've just been to visit our Gussie.' Wearing a dark blue bucket-like hat that almost obscured her eyes, Madeleine sniffed rather haughtily. 'Just as well, seeing as you never wrote and told me.'

'Well, how did I know where you were?' Beata laughed, though was rather hurt that after all this time apart her sister chose to be so tetchy. 'You never put your address on that letter you sent me.'

Madeleine took off her hat, underneath which her auburn hair had been shingled, as indeed had Beata's the moment she had accrued enough money to visit the hairdresser. Beata took in Maddie's uniform. Her sister had lost weight and looked unusually pale, her skin almost translucent. 'How's the nursing going?'

'It isn't.' Maddie sat down, slung one leg over the other and laced her fingers around a black stockinged knee, displaying a pointed shoe with a large buckle on its instep. 'I can't afford to continue my training, that's why I've come to drum up help. Make us a cup of tea, Beat, I'm gasping.'

Whilst arranging this, Beata mulled over a solution to the problem. Most of their relatives had already done so much for them; all but one. 'Why don't you write to Aunt Wyn? She's supposed to be loaded.'

Maddie brightened. 'Oh, I will then. None of Mother's side has a meg.'

At first delighted to see a member of her family, after being treated like a servant by her sister for the next two hours, fetching one pot of tea after another, along with sandwiches, cake and biscuits, Beata was relieved when the rest of the domestic staff began to trickle in, prompting Madeleine finally to leave.

However, she was to reappear on Beata's next afternoon off.

'So much for your good advice!' The white barn owl face was peeved as its owner thrust a letter at Beata in return for a cup of tea.

Aunt Wyn's reply was short and to the point. Enclosed with it was a three-halfpenny stamp which, said the correspondent, 'is all I have in the world.'

Sighing over their aunt's parsimony, Beata asked what she intended to do.

'Do as I've always done, look after myself!' Maddie swallowed half a cupful of tea in one go. 'That's cold. Make some fresh, will you?'

Whilst, uncomplaining, Beata rinsed the teapot and set out clean cups, Madeleine stated her intentions. 'I shall have to go back into service. I know it's poor wages but at least that way I'll get fed and have a roof over my head and be able to save every penny. You'll put in a good word, won't you?'

'What, here?' Beata pointed at the linoleum.

'Well, I don't mean Buckingham Palace.'

Beata's heart fell. Of all her siblings, it had to be Maddie.

'Of course, if you think your nose'll be put out of joint –'

'No, it's not that!' Beata glanced at the door as Cook entered and, after rising out of respect and hastily introducing her sister, explained the situation. 'I'm just not sure Sir William needs any more staff . . .'

Without embarrassment, Maddie presented her query to one more highly placed. 'I'm sure another pair of hands wouldn't go amiss, would they, Mrs Willis?'

Beata cringed at such forwardness.

After first appearing put out, Cook dropped her officious air and mused, 'Well, we are coming up to Christmas. I could do with the extra help, though it wouldn't be permanent.'

Not mentioning that it would only be temporary on her part too, Madeleine accepted the offer of a trial. 'I can start tomorrow.' And to her sister's dismay, she pulled on her bucket-shaped hat. 'I'll have to go and fetch my things but I'll get back as soon as I can.'

From that day on, for poor Beata life was just as it had been at home with Madeleine bossing her about and expecting her sister to wait on her. Apart from a brief get-together with her family who met at Aunt Lizzie's, Christmas was dreadful. Madeleine had been hired to cover the extra work but somehow managed to delegate the lion's share to Beata, also adding insult to injury.

'No wonder you like working here,' said Maddie, sipping a cup of tea whilst Beata continued to toil, Cook having gone to discuss menus with the mistress. 'I had loads more to do at Mrs Sayner's. You were right, they don't really need two kitchenmaids, though I hope they keep me on a while after Christmas, give me time to save. I don't fancy having to find anywhere else.'

'No, I'll bet you don't,' muttered an angry Beata under her breath, vigorously scrubbing flour and pastry from Cook's work table.

'Come and sit down and have a cup.' Madeleine lifted the teapot.

Surprised by her sister's generosity, Beata heaved a sigh of relief and wiped her perspiring brow. 'Aye, I could do with it.'

But no sooner had she sat down than Maddie clicked her tongue. 'Oh, there's only a dribble left in it.'

Seeing that her sister made only the most half-hearted attempt to rise, Beata found it difficult to hang on to her temper as she pushed herself from the table. 'I suppose I'd better mash another pot then!'

'Well, if you're going to take time off I'll join you. I'm not working whilst you sit and do nowt.' And Madeleine settled herself down again, idling there until Cook's return, whereupon she pretended to have been working hard all along.

Had Beata been contented in her job it would have been a difficult decision to make, but, whoever one's employer, life in service was the same anywhere and she had been Eliza's slave for so long she was not about to be her sister's too. So, after the round of Christmas parties was over, Twelfth Night had passed and Cook made her announcement that one of the kitchen maids would soon have to go, Beata quickly volunteered to be the one.

'You need it more than I do to save up for your nursing exam,' she told a surprised but grateful Madeleine. 'It'll be easier for me to find another position.'

Unaware that Madeleine had been leaving most of the work to her sister, Cook accepted Beata's notice. With an excellent reference and the services of Miss Stroud's Agency, it took no time at all to find another post.

The country manor of Major and Mrs Herron was slightly smaller than Nunthorpe Hall, though Beata was to find out quickly that this did not necessarily mean a reduction in her workload. This being no grand establishment, many of the servants held dual roles, even the butler doubling as the master's valet; she herself had been hired as kitchenmaid, this position normally out-ranking that of a scullerymaid in the downstairs hierarchy, but there being no scullerymaid here, Beata was dismayed to find herself on the bottom rung of the ladder and though she might receive the same wage of five shillings, here it was a lot harder to earn. However, the cook seemed very kind and her employers were equally decent.

The family was of high social standing, commanding respect but also ready to give it. Upon the revelation that owing to there being no convenient bus on a Sunday Beata would have a seven-mile walk to church, Mrs Herron ordered the chauffeur to take her in the Daimler. Beata feared accusations of favouritism from the other staff, but there were none, and when she got back from church it was work as usual, for the servants never had Sunday off but were allowed one half-day and one evening through the week.

The main benefit of moving here came in the form of Lucy Lister, an underhousemaid and six years older than Beata, but this proved no barrier to their instant friendship. Despite the difference in age, Lucy took an instant shine to the new girl and showed keenness to extend their friendship beyond working hours. Beata's first afternoon off coinciding with hers, the underhousemaid said she must come to tea, but first took her on a guided tour of the grounds.

'That's the lodge where we live.' Lucy was what might be termed a strapping lass, with a deep Yorkshire accent and a rolling gait. Snug in her beige cloche hat and coat, she pointed a gloved hand in the direction of the gate. 'Father's the gardener and my brother, Jack's, the chauffeur.'

'Ah, the one who took me to church,' cognized Beata, though made no mention that she found his dark hair and blue eyes most attractive.

Lucy nodded. 'He's a year younger than me. Have you any brothers and sisters?' When Beata listed them, the young woman projected envy. 'Three sisters! By, aren't you lucky? I've always been desperate for a sister.' This was quite evident from the affectionate way she linked arms, and she announced that from this moment on Beata would be hers, though in fact her behaviour was more maternal than sisterly, especially on discovering that Beata was an orphan.

'You poor little thing.' She dealt Beata's arm a compassionate squeeze, then nibbled her lip thoughtfully as they strolled. 'I don't want to pry, but May said she's heard you cry out on a few nights.'

Beata was instantly embarrassed. Ever since running away she had been plagued by a recurring nightmare that involved Eliza chasing her. Even the knowledge that she was safe had not prevented intermittent visitations, the terror being real enough to make her scream. But as nice as Lucy was, Beata was not yet trusting enough to confide in her. 'It was just a silly dream. I hope the noise didn't travel too far.'

'Nobody else has mentioned it. It's only because she's in t'room next door.' With her free hand Lucy tried to tuck a glossy lock of black hair under her hat but it fell out again.

'Tell her I'm sorry for waking her. I'll try not to do it again.'

'She wasn't complaining.' Lucy gave a brisk rub of the youngster's arm to reassure her. 'We were just worried for you.'

Beata hesitated. Then, only because her new friend was so obviously concerned for her, she allowed details of Eliza's cruelty to spill from her lips.

Lucy wanted to cry, but in bluff Yorkshire fashion she threw back her head and made reassuring announcement. 'Oh, I can see we'll have to take you in hand! Starting with your clothes. I mean nowt amiss, but that coat's a bit thin for this weather.'

'It's thin for any weather,' chuckled Beata, displaying the great wear and tear of her navy garment. 'But it's all I've got till I can save enough for another.'

There was immediate generosity. 'You mun wear my old one till you get something better! There's nowt wrong with it, I just can't get into it any more – too hefty.' Besides being taller Lucy was more robust than her friend. 'It's not very fashionable but it's thicker than that.'

Beata smiled and accepted the offer with thanks.

Arm in arm, clinging together not only for warmth against the frost but in fond companionship, they proceeded to stroll through the winter garden, Lucy giving more information about the Herrons. 'I'm sure the mistress will be keen to help. She's a good-hearted soul. Mindst, we don't tend to see much of her, she suffers from chorea. The major handles things, or Mrs Fordham – that's their daughter; she lives here too 'cause her husband's away a lot. She's lovely, a real lady.'

'Yes, I could tell they were proper gentry,' interjected Beata.

'Aye! None of your new money here,' confirmed Lucy. 'And they're very sparing with the bell, don't have us forever running up and down like some establishments.' Then she went on to say that apart from their other married son, the Herrons had two imbecile offspring whom Mrs Herron went to visit every Sunday at a home in the Dales.

'Are those graves over there?' Beata was pointing at the foot of a high wall, in the shadow of which, amongst clumps of snowdrops, were half a dozen small headstones.

Lucy confirmed this and took her to read the names on them. 'Every dog they've had is buried here. Sad, though, isn't it, when some human beings don't get the same?'

Beata nodded, remembering how shocked and shameful she had felt when Augusta had revealed that their dear mother had been buried in a pauper's grave. But it was not something one would confide to an outsider, fond though she was of Lucy.

The latter steered her over the rough, frost-laden grass and back onto the path, gossiping all the while about the other people who worked here – butler, housekeeper, groom, cook, footman, hallboy, housemaids – until they were almost back to the lodge.

'What's that little building over there?'

'Game larder. Oh, and that's Mr Spaven sneaking out of it.' A furtive head with hair like pleated tar and pock-marked jowls looked around quickly upon hearing voices, then, seeing it was no one of consequence, the butler proceeded on his way.

The grinning Lucy spoke conspiratorially now, her head bumping against Beata's as she divulged, 'It must be his day off tomorrow. He's just come to collect his brace of pheasants, ready for market.'

Beata looked scandalized at such underhand behaviour from one of such exalted position. 'You mean he pinches them?'

'Don't let the airs and graces fool you. He'll pinch anything that isn't nailed down, will Bert. Our Jack told me he hides them in his room, then takes them out and sells them on his day off. Robs the master's wine too. Been doing it for years. Don't know how he gets away with it – probably because he used to be the master's batman. Major Herron thinks the world of him. I'm sure he puts something on his hair an' all, it shouldn't be that black at his age. Come on now, let's go have tea.'

And what a wonderful tea it was.

Understanding why Lucy was so very fond of her new friend, Mrs Lister treated Beata in like manner, plying her with all sorts of goodies and dismissing any refusal as mere politeness. Long after she had had enough, Beata continued to acquiesce to her hostess's demands until she could eat not another crumb. It was easy to see from whom Lucy had inherited her bossy streak – though Beata was glad that she was not half so domineering as the mother, who ordered her husband and son about as if she were an army sergeant – just one look at the cut of that square jaw told of her propensity for dominance. Mr Lister was the type who'd do anything for a quiet life and Jack had inherited this trait, both meekly responding to all of Mrs Lister's demands. Beata felt rather sorry for the menfolk of this house and determined that her own husband would not suffer such humiliation. She would treat him like a king.

But for herself she had no complaint. Welcomed so warmly, and returned to the servants' quarters in a thick coat, Beata declared to Lucy that she had never felt so happy since she was a little girl.

Eager to maintain her 'sister's' happiness, Lucy said that she must come for tea again on her next afternoon off. 'Or better still, we can go to the pictures one evening. My treat.'

Beata felt she had been given enough already. 'I couldn't allow you to spend all tha –'

'Be told!' warned Lucy, then gave a wide smile as she waved Beata on her way. 'If I want to treat my sister I will.'

Not really expecting it to materialize, for she could not understand what Lucy saw in someone beneath her, both in age and status, Beata was overwhelmed to find herself whisked off again the following week, first for tea at the lodge, then to the picture theatre to see Rudolph Valentino, of whom Lucy was a devoted follower.

But Lucy was to have even more up her sleeve when next their paths crossed in the stone corridor outside the kitchen, she with her tray of dirty crockery, Beata with a newspaper bundle. 'Eh,

Beat, I've had a grand idea! Have you ever been on holiday? To the seaside, I mean?'

On her way to the dustbin, Beata paused. 'No, only for the odd day out.'

Lucy nudged her excitedly, rattling the pots on her tray. 'Neither have I. Why don't we go?'

Beata's jaw dropped.

'I don't mean this year – there isn't time to save – but if we start putting money away now we could have a week in Scarborough next Whit!'

Infected by the older girl's excitement, Beata agreed.

'Ooh!' Lucy hoisted her fleshy shoulders in glee. 'I can't wait.'

'Can't wait for what?' On her way to the larder, the fat young cook intervened. 'What are you two girls dawdling at?'

'Sorry, Mrs Temple, we're just planning our holiday.' Though her attitude showed due courtesy, Lucy grinned.

But conditioned by years of ill-treatment under her stepmother, Beata made haste. 'I was just taking these mutton bones to the dustbin, Mrs Temple!'

'Eh, we don't have such waste here!' bawled Cook. 'We save them to polish the boots and leather.' Beckoning the kitchenmaid to return she grabbed the newspaper parcel from her. 'Holidays, is it? I wonder you can afford it if you're as extravagant with your own housekeeping as you are with Mrs Herron's.'

'I'm sorry I didn't mean –'

'Eh, I'm kidding, Beat!' The corpulent young woman patted her, shaking her head at such anxiety as was on the other's face. Though unwed her position demanded the title of Mrs, but she was only in her early twenties, fair of skin and blue of eye. 'Haven't you got used to me yet?' She handed back the mutton bones with a firm smile. 'Here, go give these to Percy.'

Only now starting to accept that less ceremony was demanded here than at her last place of work, Beata grinned nervously in response and limped away to seek the footman.

'I think she's had a hard time of it, Mrs Temple,' whispered Lucy sadly, and, lingering in the dingy corridor, briefly told what she knew of Beata's stepmother.

'Poor soul.' Cook shook her pink, dimpled face. 'Well, she's a good little worker. We must do what we can to give her a happier life.'

For Mrs Temple this entailed inaugurating Beata into the ways of the kitchen, her aim that the girl might one day rise to her own exalted position. Finding Beata now cutting up a block of rock salt and pushing it through a fine sieve, she told her that from tomorrow her responsibilities would be increased. 'On my day off, as you know, the housemaids have been taking charge. Well, that's only because you were new and I didn't want to test you too early. From tomorrow you'll be playing a greater part. Don't panic, it won't be anything fancy. I'll leave everything ready and notes to tell you what time to put stuff in the oven. Make a good job of it and I'll teach you all I know.'

It was difficult to make a hash of things with Cook leaving everything so well-prepared, though it was just as well it was, for with all her scrubbing and cleaning to do as well, Beata had not even the time to snatch a mid-morning cup of tea.

Having got the master's meal underway, the harassed girl was about to start on the servants' when Mrs Fordham came into the kitchen.

Adhering to etiquette Beata did not speak until spoken to, but merely acknowledged her superior with a deferential air.

'Beata, isn't it?' A refined-looking woman with skin as flawless as the row of pearls around her throat, Mrs Fordham smiled. 'Shall you be provider of luncheon today?'

'Yes, madam. It's the first time I've done it. I hope it'll be to expected standards.'

'I'm sure it will if that scrumptious aroma is anything to go by. What is on the servants' menu today?'

'Cutlets, madam.'

'Take a joint instead.' Mrs Fordham smiled kindly and backed away. 'I shan't delay you any further. I just came to see how you were coping.'

'Thank you, madam.' Beata smiled respectfully, but after the lady had gone she sighed at the extra work this generosity would cause.

However, with the master's meal pronounced first-rate, it was all worthwhile, and when the hall boy rang the bell, summoning the rest of the servants to dine, there was fun to be had, for she was slowly coming to accept that this was indeed a more relaxed household than the last.

'Eh, Beat!' breathed Lucy, her worried eyes on the joint of roast beef, as were everyone else's. 'Did Mrs Temple say you were allowed to cook us this?'

Beata looked innocent. 'No, I just thought I'd treat you all. You've been so kind to me. Why, nobody'll mind, will they?' She tried to keep a straight face but their shocked expressions were too comical and she started to shake with mirth, chuckling so much that she could hardly divulge the truth.

'Beat, you little tinker, having us on like that!' Lucy nudged her and laughed along with everyone else until the butler came in, at which point the merriment was stilled as the joint was placed before Mr Spaven to be carved, then devoured in silence along with an array of well-cooked vegetables.

But even the butler was to offer his praise before departing to the housekeeper's room for dessert, the hall boy scuttling to open the door for him.

Her superior gone and the others able to speak freely, Beata now found herself showered with congratulations.

'We'll have to give Mrs Temple more days off if this is what Beat serves us!' said Lucy's brother, Jack, tucking heartily into his pudding.

Taking a sip of beer, the recipient of his praise glowed with pleasure, though she knew that Jack's interest did not extend any further than his plate; what would he see in a kitchenmaid who had not yet reached her fifteenth birthday?

Still, there was a great sense of achievement when Beata went to bed that night. Cook too seemed delighted with her performance when she heard about it the next morning. Henceforth, Beata was always to act as her stand-in.

A quick and willing learner, in a matter of weeks the kitchenmaid had acquired sufficient culinary skills to allow her to join in the creation of a dinner party for important guests. But, whilst the great industry of the kitchen did not unnerve her and the straightforward preparation of vegetables caused no hitch, Beata was to find herself overwhelmed by totally unfamiliar victuals.

Presented with a collection of brown speckled birds, she admitted, 'I haven't done snipe before, Mrs Temple. What . . . ?'

'Pluck them gently,' instructed the red-faced cook, preparing a joint whilst minions rushed around her, 'then leave everything on them, the feet, the guts, everything.'

'What even the head?' An incredulous Beata held a long beak between thumb and forefinger. 'What do I do with this?'

'Shove it up its bum,' interjected Percy.

'Don't be so vulgar!' Cook took a swipe at the laughing footman.

'You just tuck it neatly under a wing like this, Beaty,' she demonstrated. 'By the way, did you get those crayfish done?'

Beata looked dubious as she rushed to present the bowl. 'Yes, but there's not much on them, is there?'

Mrs Temple was aghast. 'Eh, there should be more meat than that!'

'Sorry, when I removed what I thought was poisonous there wasn't much left.'

The cook groaned. 'Don't tell me it's in the bin?'

Beata flushed and said it was.

'Clot – I hope it's on top. We might be able to do summat with it.'

This wasn't going at all well. Hurrying away, Beata came back with a damp parcel of newspaper at which Mrs Temple brightened considerably.

'Oh, you wrapped it up! Nothing to worry about then.' Inspecting the contents she showed immediate forgiveness. 'Mix it with a bit of mayonnaise and nobody'll be any the wiser!'

Another bout of furious preparation ensued, over the hours the kitchen becoming a receptacle of wonderful smells.

Transferred to silver tureens, course by course, the meal was sent up, Beata anxiously awaiting any criticism.

Weaving her way around the crowded kitchen with a tray, collecting pots to be washed, Lucy questioned her adopted sister's look of agitation.

'I'm just waiting for the complaints over the dishes I did,' explained Beata, arranging another plateful of delicacies. 'Especially that crayfish.'

'Don't worry, Beat, they're probably all dead from poisoning.' Lucy tittered and rushed past.

Beata showed little appreciation of the joke, muttering as her friend came past again, 'I'm not sure I'm cut out for this. It's too much pressure. I don't know why Mrs Temple's chosen me as her prodigy.'

'Protégée,' corrected Lucy.

'Did you never fancy being a cook?'

'I can't be fagged. I'm only biding my time in service till I get wed.'

'Me and all,' Beata whispered agreement. 'But I daren't tell Mrs Temple she's wasting her time.'

'Oh, it won't be wasted, Beat,' came the sage reply. 'It's your husband who'll get the benefit. What sort do you want?'

'Not too tall – he'd look daft beside me – but dark and handsome.' She gave a self-deprecating chuckle. 'Preferably with bad eyesight.'

'Aw! Stop running yourself down. You've got more chance than me.' A perspiring Lucy paused and sighed, scratching her thick midriff. 'I'd hoped to be married at seventeen and to have four bairns by now, two of each – but I'm still waiting.'

'And so is the master for his dinner!' bellowed Mrs Temple. 'Stop kallin' and get on with it.'

Dealing each other a grimace, the friends threw themselves back into their work, sweating for hour after hour whilst the stack of dirty pots in the scullery grew into a mountain.

For her finale, Cook sliced the top off a full Stilton. 'Right, this cheese is ready to go up. Oh, all the lads are busy. You take it, Beat – but don't show your face in the dining room, just peep round the door and see if you can catch Mr Spaven's eye.'

Forming a look of distaste and holding the cheese away from her as maggots came squirming out, Beata declared, 'If this is high living, you can stick it. I think I'm going to be sick.' And it was with a sense of trepidation she went upstairs.

At the end of the evening, though, her dread was to be replaced by triumph. With characteristic graciousness and an indication of why everyone loved working here, rather than summoning them by bell Major Herron came down to thank his servants personally for their hard work and to say how excellent the meal had been.

Thus, gradually, over the rest of the year, Beata was to gain assuredness, and with the extra responsibility came extra wages, allowing her to put away a sum every month towards the holiday in Scarborough that Lucy had booked for them, as well as improving her wardrobe.

There was a slight hiatus in saving when Christmas came upon them and Beata, knowing that Lucy had bought her a present, was compelled to respond in kind – not that she wouldn't have done anyway. Indeed, wanting everyone to share in her good fortune, she bought gifts for all her family, enjoying the reunion with them, albeit a brief one.

There was also a dress to be purchased, for, in the weeks up to Christmas there was a succession of parties at all the big houses in the area and everyone was to do the rounds, including the staff, who, as reward for waiting all year on their betters, enjoyed their own ball. For Beata all this was like a fairy tale, for it was the first time she had danced – Lucy having taught her all the steps – and especially so as she got to waltz with Jack.

Then it was back to the hard work, but it didn't matter because there was the holiday to look forward to and new summer dresses to buy, for, with fifteen months of good eating Beata had put on a stone and a half. After years of suffering constant hunger there was an urgent need to finish all that was on her plate, just in case it might be snatched away, and with Lucy and Mrs Temple both wanting to nurture the youngster and encouraging her to take second helpings, it was inevitable that on a frame little over five feet, the weight was quick to show.

But Lucy opined she was still too thin, as indeed she was beside her voluptuous friend, and insisted on plying her with cream buns whenever they enjoyed an afternoon in York.

They would be going there again this week to buy Whitsuntide outfits. Imagining what hers would be like as she was driven to church that Sunday, Beata hoped the cold and drizzle would clear up by the time it came to wear them. So immersed was she in her dreams that when a brick thudded against the side of the car she screamed in terror.

'The buggers!' Reflex caused the chauffeur to swerve though he did not stop but drove straight on for he was not about to tackle the crowd of hostile-looking men who lined the roadside.

The incident was over in a flash, but it had completely unnerved Beata and she craned her neck to look out of the rear window as a dark-faced Jack condemned the thugs.

'If they've scratched my paintwork . . .' Still on the outskirts of York, the flustered chauffeur motored on to a safe distance before braking to examine the damage. There was a series of scuff marks on the black chassis. His broad form bent double and he groaned as if in pain and hung his head.

'What was all that about?' gasped Beata, her heart still racing as she bent to look at the damage with him. 'I thought that brick was coming through the window!'

'Blasted pickets!' spat Jack, angry blue eyes glaring from under the peak of his cap. 'I read in the press they've been interfering with the buses . . . Aw, what's the major going to say?' He caressed the Daimler as if trying to make it better.

Quite familiar with Lucy's brother by now, due to the Lister family's embrace of her, Beata projected drollery, her heart rate returning to normal. 'My paintwork's all right, Jack, just in case you were going to ask.'

429

'Oh sorry, Beat!' He turned to deliver a fleeting but sincere pat to the stocky little figure. 'I suppose it frightened the wits out of you, didn't it?'

'I'll live. I still don't understand though. What –'

'The strike, Beat! This blasted general strike, have you not read about it?' His annoyed face was back to examining the Daimler.

'When do I have time to read a paper?' she laughed.

'It's no joking matter!' scolded Jack, and, indicating for her to get back in the car, drove onwards to church, muttering under his breath.

After Mass, as usual, there was her brief weekly meeting with her sister Gussie and a quick exchange of news before an impatient Jack pipped his horn to summon his passenger back to the car.

It was a rather unsettling drive home, knowing that the mob would be waiting at the roadside, but apart from shouted insults as the Daimler went by, there was no further violence.

The moment they were back, whilst Jack went to inform Major Herron of the incident, Beata rushed to tell her friend. 'It was real scary, Luce! I hope they don't attack our bus on Thursday.'

'Well, they're not intimidating me,' vouched the bigger girl, folding piece after piece of linen. 'I'm having my new outfit come hell or high water.'

But the incident had frightened Beata and she remained worried about her coming visit to town.

First however, there was Monday night's dinner party to be got through.

Utterly proficient now, Beata was quite happy to take charge during Mrs Temple's day off, extra staff having been hired to do the washing-up normally done by her. Cook's mother had come in to help too. More obese than her daughter, she moved about the kitchen like a steam engine, huffing and puffing and mowing her way through a stack of carrots as efficiently as a threshing machine, her incessant enquiry punctuating the afternoon: 'Finished! What do you want me to do now, Beat?'

Though thoroughly enjoying the novelty of giving instruction, Beata did not overstep the mark and issued each request politely. 'That broccoli, Mrs T, if you'd be kind enough.'

With such dual respectfulness, each course was sent upstairs without hindrance and at the end of the evening, as was his custom, the master came down to thank them for all their hard work.

Almost caught in the act of transferring a bottle of wine from the major's cellar to his own room, Bert Spaven stood with hands behind his back. Knowing it was a gift to his friends whose wedding he would be attending on Wednesday, Beata bit her lip at his audacity and concentrated on her employer's speech.

'All my guests send their compliments, Beata. You have done a tremendously fine job, thank you – thank you all.' Resplendent in stiff-winged collar and dinner suit, the elderly Major Herron encompassed everyone in a congratulatory smile.

Expecting him to leave, the perspiring servants were obliged to wait there as he tweaked on his silver moustache, mulling over his next announcement. 'It's rather unfortunate that I have to mar the occasion with a warning.'

Concerned that he might finally have been unmasked, the normally self-possessed Mr Spaven blanched, his hands tightening on the bottle of stolen wine.

But the lecture was for everyone. 'Now, you have probably been told of the damage to my car which occurred on Sunday and might be wondering at the cause of it. It comes as a result of this general strike which, if common sense does not prevail, will be thrust upon us from midnight tonight. At the root of all this is, as usual, the Miners' Federation, whose latest demands have, quite rightly in my view, been refused. The matter could all have been so easily solved by the colliers showing some patriotism to work a longer day or the well-paid men reducing wages, but the fact that their leaders have offered no solution leads one to believe that their sole intent is to smash private enterprise. They will not be satisfied until they have brought about nationalization and that, I can assure you, would be the greatest industrial disaster that could befall our country.'

Clasping his hands and looking deeply into each and every face, Major Herron spoke persuasively. 'The British communists and their masters in Moscow see this as an opportunity for creating strife. The TUC has been agitating for a general strike for some time, and in calling out other unions in support of the locked-out miners it has challenged the nation to a fight for its life. Just in case any of you should doubt the seriousness of this, let me tell you that a strike by the transport workers alone would bring about total disruption of the circulation of food, and you might imagine the effect of similar action by the power workers. So you see how very dire this all is. You might commiserate, as indeed I myself do, with certain members of society who have fallen victim to unemployment. But however sympathetic, I sincerely trust that no member of my staff will seek to emulate the Bolshevik example. It would certainly be against their interests to do so. Mr Baldwin is trying his best to get

431

this country back on its feet and we must fully support his actions, however harsh they might appear to some. It will all be worthwhile in the long run.'

'You have our total support, sir,' announced the butler, his pock-marked face assuming a dignified fealty whilst the hands behind his back endured cramp from holding on to the stolen bottle of wine. 'Anything we can do to help . . .' He cast a deep-set brown eye around the gathering, who, as one, nodded in agreement.

'Capital!' The head of fine snowy hair generated pleasure. 'I would not have presumed upon your loyalty but as you have volunteered perhaps some of you might like to respond to the Government's call for help in maintaining vital services if the strike does go ahead.' Rewarded with their affirmation, the old soldier made for the stairs. 'Fine, I shall provide details as and when. Well, that is all, and thank you, once again, for a splendid effort this evening.'

Jack had been commandeered to wait at table for the night. Now that the master had gone he ripped off his white bow tie, grumbling, 'I don't think there was any need to threaten us.'

'Did he?' His sister frowned, as did all the other maids.

'Course! He was warning us if we went out in sympathy for the miners then we might not have a job to come back to. I'd like to know how he thinks we're going to strike without a union behind us.'

'And if you did have, would you be supporting the miners?' asked the butler, putting aside the bottle to flex his cramped digits.

'Not at all, Mr Spaven! I'm just saying –'

'I don't think it's your place to discuss politics, do you?'

'No, Mr Spaven.' Jack showed contrition and his audience went about clearing up the kitchen, but when the butler left in order to secrete his wine the discussion was resumed, Jack denouncing the miners as, 'A bunch of bloomin' rabble-rousers.'

'Eh, do you mind?' Lucy cut in. 'Beat's from a coaling family.'

'Sorry, Beat, I meant no harm,' said Jack. 'I'm sure not all of them are troublemakers. But they're bandying it about that theirs is a starvation wage and it's just a downright lie. I know someone who's a miner and he gets a lot more than I do.'

'But it's a more dangerous job than ours, Jack,' Beata pointed out.

'So you side with them?'

The last thing Beata wanted was to upset him. 'No, I'm just saying that they deserve every penny they get. I wouldn't go underground myself, would you?'

'Well, that's true,' Jack looked somewhat annoyed that she had shamed him into admittance.

'Even so, I don't think it fair that they're holding the country to ransom like this. It might cause inconvenience to the masters but it's the people at the bottom of the pile that'll be the ones to suffer. I mean, what about those in hospitals, old folk and the like?'

'Exactly, Beat!' Jack seemed pleased that she agreed with him on this. 'Great minds think alike.' And he tipped his hat as he went home to bed.

Happy to have resumed accord, a smiling Beata joined in the clearing up of the kitchen, one by one the others going off to bed in order of seniority until there was only herself left behind. With a rabbit to be skinned and her scullery to be cleaned, it was long after midnight before she herself could give vent to her exhaustion, her last thought as she closed her eyes being of Jack's approving face.

With the strike going ahead, that Wednesday Jack was instructed to take Major Herron to York railway station where both would be assisting with the running of the trains.

But, 'What a waste of time,' he reported upon coming home that evening. 'The station was deserted, not one train came in all day until a quarter past four. Must have been a thousand of us volunteers standing around doing nothing. Why on earth the major insists we're going back tomorrow I don't know.' He turned to his sister. 'I told him it's your afternoon off. He says we'll set off a bit later so's you and Beata can have a lift into town if you want, instead of having to rely on the bus.'

'Oh, that's decent of him,' smiled an appreciative Beata.

'I don't know about that. He probably wants to rope you into volunteering an' all.'

'He needn't bother.' Lucy was determined to get her summer outfit.

The butler returned then from his friend's wedding, Cook asking, 'Was it a nice do, Mr Spaven?'

He removed his bowler and smoothed his dark, corrugated thatch. 'Passable, Mrs Temple, passable. A wedding's a wedding, isn't it?' He himself had vouched to remain single. 'Did you get me a newspaper, Jack?'

'Yes, Mr Spaven, but it's only a truncated version so I brought you this as well.' Jack laid a copy of the *British Gazette* on the table.

433

With the printers on strike, the Government had produced their own bulletin. 'It'll help us keep tabs on how the strike's going.'

'I can tell you where it's going.' The butler spoke with confidence as he reached for his newspaper and sat down. 'It's going nowhere. All be over before you know it.'

Heartened by these words, Beata and Lucy shared the hope that it might already be over as, the following afternoon, they were driven towards York.

But it was not to be. The ancient city looked less than attractive on this overcast day, its spires and towers, blackened by the soot of industry, barely forming an outline against the leaden sky, the ambience made further grim by the hordes of unemployed men that cluttered its narrow footpaths.

The absence of trams and trolley-buses was more than made up for by horse-drawn traps and elderly motorcars that had been dusted of cobwebs to play their patriotic role, bearing signs that advised, 'Wave if you want a lift.' From this sector, at least, emanated an air of bank holiday gaiety.

Exchanging good-natured salutes with other volunteers, the major called over his shoulder to the occupants of the back seat, 'All right if we drop you girls at the station? I'd like to get there without delay and it's not far for you to walk back into town.'

Beata and Lucy exchanged glances. Guessing that their master harboured designs on their time, and envisioning themselves being involuntarily trapped into assisting at the railway station, they gave half-hearted affirmative as the car carried them over the River Ouse, meanwhile trying to cook up a suitable response if he were to ask them outright.

In Railway Street, the atmosphere became more bleak, in fact it was downright menacing. Great numbers of strikers were congregating around the red brick Co-operative Society premises that ran the length of the street, either waiting to sign their trade branch registers or loitering after having done so, and a universal look of resentment was to follow the chauffeur-driven car as it passed, making Beata, at least, feel very uncomfortable.

The major used this to his advantage, saying, 'Perhaps it might not be such a good idea for you girls to venture into town today.'

But Lucy made it clear that she and her friend were not to be side-tracked, announcing, the moment they were deposited at the Victorian railway station, 'Oh, they won't bother two girls! Thank you very much for the lift, Major.' And taking Beata's arm she began to retrace the route to the city centre.

'Oh, er, yes, very good.' Their elderly employer seemed disappointed. 'Should you require a lift home after your shopping trip, do feel free to come to the station. Lister and I will be here until late afternoon.'

'Thanks, but we'll be spending the evening at the cinema.' Lucy smiled at Beata.

'I doubt they'll be open!' Major Herron called after them. 'If you find yourselves at a loose end do come and help.'

'We certainly will, sir,' lied Lucy, then dealt Beata a conspiratorial giggle as they proceeded on their way.

The pavements and roads were greasy from drizzle and the girls kept well away from the kerb so as not to be sprayed by the lorries that passed bearing signs that read 'Essential Foodstuff Only'. In the cold, damp atmosphere the strands of hair that protruded from their cloche hats soon began to turn frizzy. Passing under one of the stone archways in the city walls and approaching the offices of the London and North Eastern Railway, Lucy and Beata could see and hear a crowd of pickets jeering at the clerks who were just emerging for lunch. For a moment it looked as if the intimidation might grow to violence as the nervous-looking office workers were jostled and followed by the hecklers down the sloping road towards Lendal Bridge, and it seemed to Beata incongruous that all this took place in the shadow of the war memorial to the railwaymen who had given their lives. Caught up in the unpleasantness, she grasped her older friend's arm, the pair of them with no other option than to go with the torrent of bodies.

But then a sudden deluge of rain drove the strikers for shelter, leaving the relieved girls to hurry onwards like drowned rats over the elaborate iron bridge and into the first shop doorway they encountered. There were others sheltering here, listening to the news on one of the many wireless sets that were for sale within. For a while the girls tarried too, before deciding to risk getting wet, scurrying from one doorway to the next as they made their way about town.

In the main, this miserable state of affairs was to continue throughout the afternoon, one of the few bright intervals being the purchase of their holiday outfits, the other being a surprise meeting with Augusta.

'Sneaking off work?' Beata teased her eldest sister.

'Chance'd be a fine thing.' Hunched into her coat, though still

435

managing to look serene despite her tone of voice, Augusta put a hand up to adjust the hairpins of one of the bedraggled auburn earphones that threatened to unravel. 'Rowntrees has had to shut down due to this strike. We're going to be on a three-day week if it continues. I shall have to try and get myself a little cleaning job to make my money up, otherwise I won't be able to send anything to Aunt Ethel.' She liked to dispatch the occasional postal order towards Joe and Duke's upkeep.

Worried for her sister's poor health, Beata warned that she must not work herself into the ground. 'She's not that badly off.'

'I know, but they're our brothers; it's only right that one of us contribute.' Seeing Beata about to dip into her purse, Augusta stopped her. 'Nay, that wasn't a hint! I'm the eldest, it should be up to me.'

'No you're not. What about Clem?'

'Yes, well, he's got other fish to fry.' Augusta pursed her lips in disapproval of her brother's immorality and, in the presence of a stranger, changed the subject. 'So what are you lasses doing in town?' She smiled at her sister's companion.

Beata displayed her shopping bags. 'Lucy and I have come to buy stuff for our holidays.'

'Ooh, let's see!'

'I don't want to get them wet – tell you what, we're just going for our tea, why don't you come with us? I'll pay,' she added hurriedly, also turning to her friend. 'You don't mind, do you, Luce?'

'No, of course not!' Had Lucy not been informed how good Beata's sister had been to her she would still have read it in the other girl's pacific blue eyes.

Though denouncing it as an extravagant gesture, Augusta nevertheless went with them to the café, but at the rich array of cream buns that were brought out, said, 'Can we move to that table away from the window, I'd hate to cause resentment.' Faced with all the destitution on the streets outside, it felt wrong to sit there blatantly guzzling.

Sharing her view, Beata felt embarrassed that she had not been the one to suggest this, and when they had moved tables she slipped a coin to her sister. 'Here, send that to Aunt Ethel.'

Augusta tried to give it back. 'You'll need it for your holiday.'

'No, I'd put it aside to buy a bathing costume but I couldn't find one suitable. It'll probably be too rainy to wear one anyway. Take it.'

436

'Go on then, bless you. I'm going over to do a spot of cleaning for them this weekend. I'll give it to Ethel then.'

Whilst they dined, Augusta asked the other girls about their coming holiday. 'So are you all set then? I wish I was coming with you.'

Beata eyed a poster that advertised Empire shopping week. 'I'm not turning my nose up at Scarborough but I'd love to go there one day if I could afford it.'

Augusta craned her neck to look at the picture of the kangaroo, remarking drily, 'Australia? There was a time when you could travel there for nowt.'

'We might not be going anywhere with this general strike on.' A worried Lucy licked jam and cream off her thumb.

They went on to talk about how dreadful the situation was and of the many men they knew who were without work. Uncle Matt had been laid off too. Close to retirement age, it looked as though he would not work again.

Augusta said, 'I feel lucky to have been born a woman. There's always somebody needs cleaning or laundry doing.'

Beata gazed at her adored eldest sister, thinking how weary she looked for someone not yet twenty-three. Then Lucy said they must go if they were not to miss the beginning of their film.

After kissing Augusta goodbye, Beata went with her friend to the cinema, but as the major had predicted it was closed, as were all the others. The Theatre Royal was open but they had already seen the play that it had to offer and so Lucy suggested with a sigh that they might as well go and catch a bus home.

Their return to the bus stop took them into the midst of the large crowd of strikers they had witnessed earlier. Suffering many rude comments along the route, occasionally having to step into the gutter in order to pass, Lucy and Beata made their way along Rougier Street. Heads down against the drizzle, they almost tripped over a legless man on a trolley and tried to make a detour but he propelled himself after them, entreating them to buy a pair of the cheap earrings on his tray until they did so and were allowed to proceed.

Flattening themselves against the wall of an old terraced house, trying to glean a little shelter from the narrow overhang of its roof, the girls hugged their acquisitions under their arms, hoping the brown paper parcels would not disintegrate before a bus arrived.

At last a vehicle bearing the destination of Selby turned the corner. But as it approached and they themselves stepped forward to the kerb there was a huge surge forth by the strikers, making it impossible for queuing passengers to get near.

'Excuse me!' Using her elbows, Lucy tried to infiltrate the stale-smelling crowd of men, a worried Beata hanging on to her coat so as not to be separated. Despite both being jostled and shoved in an attempt to prevent them from getting on they eventually managed to fight their way through and scrambled on board.

The volunteer driver revved his engine, warning the strikers that he was about to pull away but they had formed a barrier around the front of the bus making it impossible for it to advance without running them down. They were yelling at him and hammering on the chassis with their fists. 'Blackleg! Scab!'

Lucy was as anxious as Beata now, both girls looking round at the other passengers, who were equally ashen-faced. How swiftly had all this happened. It felt very menacing.

A university student in plus fours, acting as special constable, demanded that the strikers move, incurring a hail of good-natured insults for his lardy-dah manner. But with several regular policemen barging into their midst, flailing their batons, the men at once broke their chain in order to defend themselves against the blows and the driver of the bus took advantage to pull away. Alas the vehicle had got no further than a few yards when it was attacked by a barrage of stones and its windows began to shatter.

Women screamed, Beata and Lucy amongst them, and everyone ducked, banging their heads on the back of the seat in front of them as the bus suddenly jerked to a halt. Outside, the police batons began to swing more viciously, driving the strikers back and forming a defensive circle around the bus but it was of little use, for with the driver's window smashed it could go no further.

One of the policemen jumped aboard to instruct the frightened passengers, some of whom had been cut by flying glass. 'Everyone off the bus!'

Despite her own distress, Beata noticed that the old lady in black bonnet and cape across the aisle was searching her old-fashioned attire for a handkerchief with which to stanch the cut on her right hand, blood dripping everywhere. Whilst Lucy voiced her outrage she slid out of her own seat and in beside the injured woman, taking her handkerchief to the old lady's wound and offering gentle reassurance.

Other passengers were filing off the bus, though were voicing their concern at being exposed to the violence outside.

'You won't get hurt if you stay with me,' vouched the policeman, coaxing them to the front. 'They only want to prevent the bus from moving, come along now, let's have you all off.'

The last to go, Lucy and Beata helped the old woman. 'Would you like me to see you home?' asked Beata, supporting the victim's arm as they went.

The old lady beheld her diminutive Samaritan. 'Thank you, dear, but I'd rather have a policeman.'

Handing her to the care of the officer, Beata and Lucy alighted, once more subjecting themselves to the drizzle and to the threatening attentions of the strikers, who cheered loudly at having stopped the blackleg bus from its route.

'Looks as if we'll have to walk,' sighed Beata.

'And all because of these idiots!' complained Lucy bitterly, then, eyes narrowed against the mizzle, looked down at the swollen ankle that spilled over Beata's shoe. 'Oh, how are you going to manage it with your poor leg?'

A flat-capped striker objected to being called an idiot. 'The walk'll do you good, love, help to get some of that fat off.' His companions jeered.

Seeing her friend blush, and further maddened by what had happened to the elderly woman, Beata sprang to the attack. 'If you had to walk forty miles it wouldn't take *your* fat off – it's all under your hat!'

Yet only under the protection of the law did she dare to issue this retort and after doing so beat a hasty retreat from this dangerous ground, though not towards home. Suddenly remembering another form of transport, she put her arm around her friend, directing her towards the railway station, saying that the major and Jack would probably still be there.

And so they were. The station might be deserted of trains but there was certainly no shortage of volunteers, hundreds of them crowding the platforms, most with nothing to do.

Even so, Major Herron looked delighted to see two more. 'You came!'

'We said we would, sir,' replied Lucy, her bright smile disguising the shock she had just encountered. 'Didn't we, Beat?'

'Yes,' Beata cast her small blue eyes around the station, 'though there doesn't seem much for us to do.'

Lifting his hat to scratch his snowy head, the major assured them that he and Lister had been busy all day. 'I'm reliably informed that another train will be in very shortly. Stow your parcels in the car.' Leaving the servants to their own devices he wandered up the platform to converse with a group of white-collared businessmen.

Whilst waiting, the girls were quizzed by Jack as to the situation in town, giving them the opportunity to relate the exciting episode with the bus.

He was angry that his sister and her friend had been exposed to such danger. 'The louts! They didn't hurt you, did they?'

Lucy assured him. 'No! We just came in for some choice words, but Beat gave them a few home truths.'

His expression was one of reproof for such rashness. 'You shouldn't get involved, Beat.'

This rather annoyed her. 'I wasn't going to stand by and let them insult Lucy.'

Jack quickly changed his attitude. 'Oh, I'm sure that's admirable! I just meant I don't like to think of you in danger.' Out of impulse he curled his arm around the little figure. 'We think a lot about you, don't we, Luce?'

Mollified, Beata smiled up at him, fixing her eyes there for a moment and counting the number of tiny brown moles on his cheeks, the shadow of stubble. Jack returned her smile. Then, there appeared in his blue eyes an expression she had not seen before, as if he were seeing her for the first time. The moment seemed to unnerve him and, before she could enjoy this taste of intimacy with a man who was not related to her, he withdrew his arm quickly. Luckily for him, though disappointingly for Beata, at that point an engine finally came chuffing in and the three of them set to transferring all the parcels and perishable goods to the respective vans and motors.

'Fancy having to do this on our afternoon off,' grumbled Lucy.

Still thoughtful over her contact with Jack, Beata replied, 'Better than having to walk home, though.' Seeing a quantity of fish being put aboard the train now bound for Scarborough, she showed wry amusement. 'Talk about coals to Newcastle. Eh, do you think we should sneak aboard now so we're sure to get our holiday at the seaside?'

Hefting a crate of food onto a trolley nearby, Major Herron overheard. 'Thinking of stowing away, are we, girls?'

Whilst they worked, Lucy explained that she and Beata had booked a holiday. 'Do you think the strike'll be over by Whitsuntide, Major?'

'Without a doubt! At this rate we shall have them beaten within days.'

Beata smiled, though there was more to this display than met the eye, and she hoped that none of her companions would interpret her new-found happiness, nor guess its source.

The major's optimistic prediction looked to be correct. Nine days after it had begun the strike collapsed.

'Well, this calls for a celebration!' In the kitchen, Bert Spaven held up the two bottles of wine he had taken from the major's cellar. 'Set out the glasses, Beata.'

'Yes, Mr Spaven.' Though casting a dubious glance at the others, Beata did as she was told. But when the butler quite blatantly filled each glass and invited her to partake she refused point blank and so did everyone else, thinking he had finally lost his reason.

'Oh well, I'll have to drink it all myself then.' Taking a sip, the butler pronounced it very enjoyable and sat back whilst they watched agog. He turned to Jack with a look of casual disdain on his weathered face. 'I suppose income tax'll go up to pay for all this strike business.'

'Mr Spaven!' hissed Beata at the sight of her employer's shiny shoes padding down the staircase. 'The major's coming!'

'Is he?' Unruffled, Bert made no move but continued to quaff his wine calmly, a look of appreciation on his pocked jowls. He showed no perturbation at all when the major came in, though he did condescend to rise, glass in hand.

'Ah, good man, Spaven, I see you've chosen well!' Major Herron took a glass of wine himself and exhorted his servants cheerfully. 'Come now, everyone, don't hang back.'

Realizing now that it was the major who had authorized this celebratory drink, Beata and the rest of the staff turned smiles of accusation on the butler for his little joke, then were quick to accept the master's invitation, thenceforth to hear his speech.

'Now, everyone, I have the greatest pleasure in announcing that the nation has been victorious against the forces of Bolshevism. After all the bitterness, hatred and uncharitableness of the last nine days – all of it due to Socialism make no mistake about that – the TUC has been forced to capitulate and their members crawl back to work with their tails between their legs. So I would like you please to raise your glasses and toast the nation's victory over the Bolsheviks. To justice!'

Everyone raised their glasses in unison. 'Justice!'

'Beg your pardon, Major sir, but does this mean Beata and Lucy will be able to have their holiday?' Jack thoughtfully asked on their behalf.

Beata smiled at him gratefully.

Major Herron flicked red wine from his silvery moustache. 'The railwaymen are still out, I'm afraid, along with the printers and, of course, the dratted miners – I sincerely hope their employers refuse to take them back.' Then, seeing Beata's woebegone face, he smiled encouragement. 'But I'm certain they'll see sense. Even if they do not, after such a show of patriotism in helping to keep the country moving, especially in your own free time, you can be assured of your holiday. If the railway timetable remains disrupted then Lister shall drive you to Scarborough.'

'Why, that's very kind of you, sir!' Lucy grinned widely at her friend who voiced agreement.

Then, even more pleased at this marvellous announcement, Beata hid her smile in her glass, praising this ill wind that had fanned the spark of romance.

TWENTY-FIVE

Undergoing a complete reversal of attitude, Beata prayed fervently that the strikers might hold out so that Jack would have to drive her all the way to Scarborough, for she had come to want nothing so much as his companionship. Typically, the opposite occurred. Two days after the major's utterance the railway strike ended, bringing with it the prospect of a Whitsun holiday for all, but leaving Beata somewhat downcast as she was forced to wave goodbye to Jack at the station.

'Well, cheer up, Beat, you'd think you were off to a funeral!' teased Lucy at the crestfallen visage.

Instantly brightening, Beata chuckled to correct the impression that she was not looking forward to the holiday. Indeed, she went on to thoroughly enjoy it. But wonderful though it undoubtedly was, in between all the donkey rides and shell-collecting, paddling in the ice-cold waves, the amusements and swingboats, she could not prevent her mind from wandering to the man she hoped soon to call her lover.

It was just plain daft, she told herself on the return train journey. The first proper holiday she had ever enjoyed and the overriding thought was of how glad she was to be going home! All that work, cooking and cleaning . . . but of course it was not the thought of this that made her heart sing.

It was to sing even more joyfully at the sight of Jack waiting on the platform. Struggling from the carriage with her suitcase, Beata turned quickly to her companion, her face a ray of sunshine. 'How did he know what train we'd be getting?'

Lucy instantly detected a change in Beata, understood now the

443

cause of all those faraway looks during the holiday. But though she smiled she made no comment on this, explaining casually, 'I told Mother and Father in that postcard I sent them, but I only mentioned we'd be back around midday.' It was one thirty now. 'He must have been waiting here ages.'

The somewhat irritated look on the chauffeur's face showed that this was correct, though it was rapidly converted to a grin the moment he saw Beata alighting from the train and he rushed to assist. 'Here you are, the pair of you! I thought you'd got ambushed. Give us those cases.'

Lucy explained that they had wanted to eke out the last hours of their holiday, they wouldn't be getting another for a whole year. 'We didn't expect you to be here for us.'

'Nay, I couldn't have you struggling on the bus with all this lot – Good Lord, what have you got in them, the hotel silver?' Jack's address was for both girls but his attention was mainly on Beata, Lucy noticed, as he hefted the cases from the draughty echoing platform to the waiting Daimler.

'Major won't be cross, will he?'

Jack dismissed his sister's worry. 'No, it was his idea.' The luggage stowed and his arms free, he wound one round each young woman. 'By, I haven't half missed my lasses!'

Imagining that the affectionate squeeze was for her alone, Beata's heart swelled with love.

Privy to this touching scene, Lucy smiled fondly as her brother opened the car door for them, wondering how she could help the romance along.

On the way home there were still signs of great distress and unemployment, groups of down-at-heel men at every turn. It was such a depressing sight after their fun-filled week that Lucy urged Beata to tell Jack about their holiday to take her mind off it.

Needing no encouragement, Beata rattled on so much about Scarborough that Jack laughed and said over his shoulder, 'Correct me if I'm wrong, Beat, but I get the impression that this has given you a taste for travel.'

'Ooh, yes, I've always wanted to go to different places. I'd love to go further afield – if I wasn't in service, that is.'

'Aye, you'd certainly need plenty of money to do that – or get yourself a rich husband.'

Beata smiled enigmatically and looked out of the window, wondering whether this was a test. 'If I had a husband I wouldn't care about travel. It wouldn't matter if he were rich or poor either.'

444

'So if you were thinking of asking her, there's your opening, Jack.'

'Lucy!' An embarrassed Beata dealt her friend a sharp nudge.

'Well! I don't believe in beating around the bush. It'd be lovely if you two did marry, then we'd really be sisters, at least sisters-in-law.'

Face burning, hardly daring to look at Jack for fear that everything was spoiled by Lucy's interference, Beata finally chanced a swift peek as the car headed out of the city. To her utter joy he was grinning.

If Beata had hoped that this was the start of a wonderful romance then she was to be disappointed. Obvious though it was that Jack had acquired new interest in her, he was sadly lacking in the ways of the world and his courtship of her was not to extend to anything other than fleeting smiles as they went about their work. Assuming that it was because there was always someone else about, Beata initially expected him to make his move when he took her to church in the car, but no. Though he was assiduous in listening to everything she had to say and his responses were definitely more animated, warmer, they revealed not one hint of intimacy, the discourse between them remaining mundane.

But if this was all that was on offer Beata was content for the moment to survive on fantasy, picturing herself married to this dark good-looking man, perhaps in a cottage down the lane that she so admired, for he would probably want to keep working for Major Herron and consequently would need to live close by. Or if he did not mind changing his place of work they could set up somewhere else, he as chauffeur and she as cook, until children came along. Thus was she happy to make do, for it could be that he was merely biding his time until she reached sixteen. The suspense was almost unbearable.

Awaking to her sixteenth birthday, sunlight flooding the austere room, Beata stretched her arms above her head, raked the sleep from her eyes, then wriggled back into the mattress to spend a few moments in delicious anticipation, envisaging the change that today would bring to her life. Jack was fully aware of this important milestone for she had mentioned it when she had gone for tea at the lodge last week. Also last week had come an invitation from Aunt Ethel; she had arranged, for this afternoon, a reunion of the Kilmaster siblings, who would congregate at her house. That it was also Beata's birthday was merely happy coincidence. Happy? Well, yes, it would be lovely to see them – but she would much rather be spending her time with Jack.

Finally rising, she washed and put on her maid's attire and went down, attending first to the fire and all her cleaning jobs, then taking cups of tea to her superiors still in bed. She returned to the kitchen expectant of Jack's arrival for work, but her state of excitement was rather deflated when he was nowhere to be seen. Moreover, Lucy who would normally be collecting the boots for cleaning at this hour was instead seated at the table weeping over a newspaper.

Beata stared aghast at her friend's tears, envisaging some awful disaster in the Lister household. She looked at one of the other maids for explanation.

Eyes still puffy from sleep, May shrugged. 'She just took one look at that and started blubbing.'

Sniffing, Lucy glanced up, dabbed her eyes and gushed, 'Oh, Beat, haven't you heard? Rudi's died!' She pointed to the article.

Beata leaned over her friend and just had time to read of Valentino's death before Percy grabbed the paper from under Lucy's nose. 'Don't be getting snot all over that before the master's read it!'

'Heartless!' A tearful Lucy berated the footman, then blew into her handkerchief. 'Can I have it back later? I'd like to cut that out.' Crimson of nose and eye, she looked set to burst into tears again. 'Aw, what a shock.'

Vastly relieved that it was so trivial, Beata pressed small comforting hands to her friend's shoulders. 'Eh, and you so keen to marry him.'

Lucy was forced to blurt a tearful laugh.

Beata chuckled and dealt Lucy's shoulders a squeeze to show she understood, before moving away to begin work. 'It is sad, though. He wasn't that old. What happened?'

Going about her own work, Lucy said it had been peritonitis. 'Oh, here's me full of my own woes – happy birthday, Beat!'

Jack came in at that point and, overhearing, announced offhandedly, 'Oh aye, many happy returns, Beat.'

At his entry Beata had spun in anticipation but to her huge disappointment he was not overly attentive, perhaps even less so than usual.

Nevertheless, she thanked everyone for their wishes, then launched herself into the day's tasks.

'I've got a little present for you,' revealed Lucy, 'but I've gone and left it at home. I'll fetch it this afternoon.'

446

Beata reminded her. 'I won't be here.'

The reply was casual. 'Oh, that's right, you're going to your aunty's. Well, have a nice time.'

Cook was last downstairs, she too wishing the kitchenmaid many happy returns. 'When will you be home?'

Beata had started to get the breakfast pots ready. 'I'm not sure, Mrs Temple, not late.'

'Can you be more specific? The major's got dinner guests tonight.'

Beata frowned. 'Oh, I hadn't heard of it. As I'm going over to Leeds I've arranged to take my afternoon and evening together – I did ask permission.'

'I had hoped for a bit of help, but if you don't feel up to it . . .' Mrs Temple looked slightly peeved.

Beata thought it harsh of Cook to accuse her of letting the side down, and also a bit much to expect her to come back early on her evening off, especially as it was her birthday, but as usual she fell into line. 'I'll make sure I'm back by seven-thirty.'

'Good lass.' Mrs Temple dispensed a satisfied nod. 'I knew you wouldn't let me down. Have a good time.'

Aunt Ethel's old-fashioned parlour, with its dark brown paint and oppressive wallpaper, was somewhat overcrowded with Gussie and Mims, Maddie, Joe and Duke all turning up for the reunion, plus the cousins, aunts and uncles who had accompanied them, but Beata enjoyed her afternoon as she passed amongst them, catching up on all their news and receiving birthday wishes.

At the gawky stage between child and woman, eleven-year-old Mims had acquired a more pleasant nature to match her pretty face, telling Beata she enjoyed her education and had lots of friends. The cousin with whom Mims lived confirmed that she was very popular.

'You must be eating your crusts these days,' teased Beata, examining Mims' wavy light brown hair and privately thinking how like Mother's it was. 'I feel rather lost without them up my knicker leg. I sometimes think I might shove a few up there for old times' sake.'

Mims chortled heartily, then divulged in magnanimous tone, 'I eat me peas an' all. Well, Aunt Merry's so kind I don't like to upset her.'

It was Madeleine to whom Beata spoke next. Her coffers replenished by the stint in domestic service, Maddie's ambition to train as a nurse now seemed to be progressing well. Beata dutifully listened, but it was not very long before Maddie was rubbing her up the wrong way and she moved on as soon as she was able.

Hearing that Joe was still employed in the clerical job that his aunt and uncle had acquired for him, she was surprised, for he would soon be nineteen and was quite the man in his tweed jacket and flannels, dwarfing her as he rose to enjoy a smoke by the open window. 'I expected to see you in army uniform by now.'

Alarmed, Joe shushed her but their stern grey-haired aunt overheard as she came past with a tray of tea. 'I didn't adopt Joseph in order for him to waste his life. He's very well thought of where he works. He'll no doubt be manager one day.'

Beata gave him an admiring glance.

Joe smiled for old Aunt Ethel, but the moment she had turned away he bent to whisper despairingly to his sister, 'It's not what I want but I can't go against her after all she's done for me.'

Feigning to be deaf as she moved around with her tray, Ethel enjoyed a feeling of satisfaction that her plan had worked. Remembering how stubborn Probyn had been, she knew it was useless to forbid his son to join the army, he would only have run away; instead she had employed emotional blackmail to keep Joe from error, showering him with opportunity, telling him how dear he was to her and how much store she set on his future. It appeared to have worked.

She paused in front of Duke, who took a cup from her tray. This one, however, had been another matter. What a strange boy he was. For the first year in his new home he had dutifully gone to school, but thenceforth had taken to wandering off for days on end. Unable to fathom his motives, and finding him a bit of a handful, Ethel had approached her sisters for help and when Wyn had volunteered to take him off her hands she had gladly accepted. It had been rather a surprise actually, for Wyn had never been as charitable as her siblings. Now retired to Southport, she and husband Teddy had motored up for the weekend, bringing their adopted son with them.

Feeling awkward under Ethel's scrutiny, Duke thanked her for the tea and, cradling his cup and saucer, wandered over to stand in the bay window alongside Joe, Beata and Mims.

'So, you're living with Aunt Wyn now,' observed Beata.

'Aye, and now I know why she was so keen to have me,' muttered Duke, who at thirteen was able to work for his keep. 'Her and Uncle Ted just want somebody to do all the mucky jobs.' Wyn and her husband had acquired a bungalow with enough land for them to keep geese and hens. 'She doesn't like the geese shitting in the garden, so she has me get up at the crack of dawn and herd them down to the pond, then I have to collect all t'eggs before I go to school and when I come home I have to fetch t'geese back again, not to mention all the other jobs.'

His sisters sympathized, then Beata cocked her ear as she detected murmurings amongst the adults about Clem: 'He's still with *her*; living at Sprotbrough, by all accounts, bold as brass.'

She exchanged looks with her siblings. 'It'd be nice if Clem were here, wouldn't it?'

Duke was non-committal, staring into the distance at bad memories. Joe too remained silent.

Only Mims nodded. 'And Lionel – but not *her*.'

'No, not her,' murmured Beata, and sipped thoughtfully from her cup.

After tea, Mims played the piano for them. Since moving in with Aunt Merry she had been allowed access to the keys again and had improved to such a degree that she could recreate any piece that was put before her. Listening enviously, Beata determined to have tuition herself as soon as her financial circumstances would allow.

Overconfident from the praise, for her next rendition the eleven-year-old launched into a lively jazz tune but was quickly stalled by Aunt Ethel, whose voice rose above the din. 'Thank you, Millicent! I think we'll stick to white man's music, if you please.' And the tempo was deftly altered to fit 'Yes We Have No Bananas', which everyone joined in singing.

The recital ended with a birthday song, then Aunt Merry produced a box Brownie saying they must have a photo to mark the occasion, and everyone teemed out into the late afternoon sunshine, meandering up the sloping street to pose on the bridge that overlooked it. Thankful for Augusta's help with the tea, Aunt Ethel draped her own fox fur around the young woman's neck so that she might be smarter for the portrait.

Several shots were captured, then, noting the lengthening shadows, Beata said reluctantly. 'I'll have to go soon.'

Uncle Christmas gave a teasing nudge. 'Leaving already? She must have a sweetheart hidden away somewhere.'

Feeling a little despondent over Jack's lack of attention this morning, Beata blushed. Her uncle did not know how close he was. But she could quite truthfully attribute her rapid departure to another. 'Cook needs me to help. She's got a dinner party.'

'What, on your birthday?' exclaimed Aunt Merry, sharing a look of incredulity with the others. 'How mean can you get?'

Beata was quick to right this impression. 'Cook's been very kind to me. I don't like to let her down.'

'I'll go too then.' Augusta unwound the fur stole and handed it back to Aunt Ethel as the party made its casual way back to the house.

A short time later, the sisters made ready to catch the bus to York, voicing the hope that all would enjoy another get-together soon, possibly at Christmas.

Whilst Augusta alighted in the city, Beata travelled onwards along the country road. It was a long walk from the bus stop and when she got home she felt not a little despondent, for her leg throbbed unmercifully. The windowless stone passage was dark and the kitchen at the other end of it seemed oddly quiet considering there was meant to be a dinner party being prepared.

Groping her way in, the first thing she saw was an array of tiny flames in the centre of the table – then there was a unified cry of, 'Happy birthday, Beata!' And she saw that they had laid on a little party with sandwiches, sausage rolls, cakes, the master's fine linen and crystal glasses.

It was one of the nicest things anyone had ever done for her and she felt tears spring to her eyes, but managed to blink them away as she was dragged into their happy midst and presented with gifts.

'Sorry for having you on this morning,' chuckled Mrs Temple, 'but we had to make sure what time you'd be home.' With podgy little fingers she handed over a flat parcel which, when opened, revealed a pair of tea towels. 'Put them in your bottom drawer,' whispered the cook, patting the youngster knowingly. 'They're good quality.'

Beata said she could see that they were, passing similar compliment over the gift which Lucy gave her, a monogrammed towel.

'I've never had such nice things,' breathed the recipient, deeply grateful. 'I shan't know what to do with them.'

'You shouldn't be so popular then, Beat,' laughed Lucy.

Even the butler showed his appreciation of her by acquiescing to Percy's cheeky enquiry – 'Can we give her a birthday kiss, Mr Spaven?' – this inspiring other young men to line up and follow suit, and this for Beata was the nicest moment of all for, without giving away any secrets, she got to kiss the one she loved.

450

Was it just her fond imagination or did Jack's lips stray a little closer to her mouth than all the rest?

After that birthday kiss there were few others – one at Christmas when she and Jack had chanced to coincide beneath the mistletoe, another to wish her farewell as she embarked on her second holiday to Scarborough – but these were chaste events, with witnesses abounding, and Beata lived for the moment when Jack might finally pluck up the courage to show his true love.

Still, she remained optimistic, making frequent purchases for her bottom drawer whenever she and Lucy went to town, for money was one thing she did not lack. For all that her lover might be backwards in showing his affection, she was well regarded in general and on her recent seventeenth birthday had been promoted to housemaid, her hard work earning her regular bonuses so that over the two and a half years she had been here her wage had risen to two pounds ten shillings per month – enough to procure the piano lessons she had so long coveted.

Promotion or no, her culinary skills were still required on Mrs Temple's day off, and today she was down in the kitchen taking last-minute instruction on the day's menu.

Having given them, the overweight cook bumbled off to fetch her hat. 'My goodness, I hope it doesn't get much hotter than this.' Already a warm morning, the fire had driven the thermometer towards eighty, promising a rough day for the toilers of the kitchen.

Beata saw that the cook's shoes were unfastened. 'Eh, you'll be tripping over those laces, Mrs Temple!'

The answer was impatient. 'Oh, I'm sick of trying to get down there! I have a job even to get them on and off, let alone fasten them. If I mess about any longer I'll miss my bus.' With perspiring brow and laboured breathing the huge young woman put on her hat and waddled to the door.

'You'll be breaking your neck! Let me do them for you. It'll take ten seconds.' Respectfully pleading for Cook to sit down, Beata kneeled at her feet.

'What's this, worshipping at the Temple?' Percy returned from a trip upstairs and immediately removed his jacket and false dickie to reveal bare arms and a singlet.

'Beaty's saving my neck,' riposted Mrs Temple. 'Which is more than any of you care about.'

This comment was aimed mainly at the butler. Too involved in grating chocolate onto a slice of bread, Mr Spaven completely ignored the riposte, folded the bread over to make a sandwich and disappeared into his room with a newspaper.

'What sort of disgusting person eats chocolate first thing on a morning?' demanded Cook, then: 'Oh, thank you, Beat, you're an angel.'

'You're welcome, Mrs Temple.' Beata stole a glance at Percy's bare muscular arms, then used the edge of the table to haul herself up. 'I've done a double knot so they don't undo. Just give me a shout tonight when you want them taking off. We can make it a regular thing if you like.'

'Why, thank you, dear, I'll take up your kind offer.' Mrs Temple gathered her belongings and directed her sixteen-stone carcass to the door. 'You do them every morning and night and I'll pay you one and six a week, how's that?'

'One and six!' shrieked Percy. 'Eh, I'll do them, Mrs Temple.'

'No, you won't – and get some clothes on. These girls don't want your hairy armpits under their noses all day. That's settled then, Beata.'

'Oh, I don't want pay –'

'I know you'd do them out of the goodness of your heart but while others might take you for granted I shan't.' Cook was adamant. 'You get paid and that's that.' She slammed the door behind her.

Beata was delighted at this bonus and pointed out her own increasing girth to no one in particular. 'It'll come in handy. I shall have to fork out for a new uniform soon. This one's a bit of a squeeze.'

'A woman looks better with some meat on her.' Jack entered to collect a bucket and sponge to wash the car. 'But don't be spending your own money, tell the mistress.'

'But didn't you have to buy yours, Jack?' Both he and the butler had just acquired new suits.

'You must be joking – on my wage?' Jack admired his own smart blue jacket with its shiny metal buttons before hanging it over the back of a chair and rolling up his sleeves. 'It's a shame to keep it just for work. I thought I might wear it for a night out on Saturday. Major's said I can borrow the car.'

'Oh, off anywhere nice?' Lucy came in with a collection of boots and shoes to clean and dropped them at Percy's feet to loud complaint.

'Just for a pint as usual, I suppose.'

'There's a dance on in Fulford,' announced Lucy. 'Me and Beata have got Saturday evening off too. We were talking about going, weren't we?'

Sensing connivance, Beata gave her friend a scolding glare.

It did no good, Lucy asking her brother, 'Why don't you come with us?'

'Give you a lift in the car, you mean,' cognized Jack. 'And pay for you to get in as well, I shouldn't doubt.'

'Aw, isn't he a kind brother, Beat?' Lucy grinned at her friend. 'Thank you, Jack, we accept.'

Beata chuckled, but a few days later when she and Lucy were wandering around town on their afternoon off, looking for suitable attire to wear for the dance, she opined, 'You shouldn't really force him to take us if he'd arranged something else . . .'

'Rubbish! He'll never get round to asking you if left to his own devices.'

'That's what I mean. Maybe he doesn't want to.' Much as she adored him and the rare kisses they had shared, after so many fruitless months Beata was beginning to think his feelings were not as strong as hers.

'A blind man could tell he likes you! He just needs a good push. I know he's chatty but he's not very forward with women.'

Beata knew this from witnessing Jack's subservience to his mother at home. But, 'He wouldn't need pushing if I were pretty enough.'

'You are!' Lucy responded on an impulse of kindness; it was true that Beata was not at all pretty but she was a dear girl and always ready to laugh. 'You just need to make the most of what you've got. Aw, look at those lovely shoes!' She halted and gazed into the shop window. 'Didn't you say you need some?'

Beata dismissed the high heels. 'I'd never be able to wear them with my leg.'

'You don't have to wear them all the time, just for special occasions, and your leg's all right at the moment. Go on, Beat, be a devil.'

Surrendering, Beata went in to try on the lizard-skin shoes, commenting as she tottered, 'It's just as well they've got a strap. I don't know how I'd keep them on otherwise.' But she had to agree they were elegant and, under Lucy's encouragement, finally bought them.

'Well, if you can be a devil so can I,' grinned Lucy, making for the lipstick counter in Boots. 'Don't tell Mother, though. She'd go mad.'

Normally when the pair went out Beata would go to the lodge for tea, but this Saturday evening it was Lucy who came over to the big house, getting ready in her friend's room. Donning flesh-pink stockings instead of the usual working black, Beata stepped into her green dance frock and stood whilst Lucy did up the buttons at the back, she returning the favour. Despite a brassiere to flatten the chest, neither she nor Lucy had the nymphlike proportions required for high fashion, a shelf of bosom marring the dress's straight lines. Overlooking the shelf to admire her scalloped hemline, she spent a moment of doubt over the lizard-skin shoes but Lucy assured her they would be fine. Then, both wearing the forbidden crimson lipstick and a dusting of powder, they scampered quickly to the car and averted their faces as their chauffeur drove past the lodge just in case Mrs Lister might be watching and drag Lucy out to scrub her clean.

Jack was disapproving of their titters. 'I don't know why you want to clart yourself up like a couple of flappers. You'll be attracting the wrong sort of attention.'

Lucy rolled her eyes at Beata, who suffered a moment of misgiving over her application of lipstick.

Then followed a six-mile drive to Fulford.

No attempt had been made to decorate the church hall, which was completely bare apart from a row of chairs down each side, but this feeling of austerity was outweighed by the band on the stage, who played a lively tune. At the opposite end to the stage was a table containing soft drinks, an urn of tea, cups and saucers and glasses.

'Well, fetch us a drink then!' the dominant Lucy prompted her brother.

Frowning, Jack examined the contents of his pocket before asking what she and Beata would like.

'Lemonade,' replied Lucy. 'Come on, Beat, we'll go bag us some chairs.'

Some moments later, weaving a passage gingerly through the dancers, Jack joined them with two glasses, which he handed to the girls. When he sat down Lucy nudged him and cocked her head towards Beata.

'What?' Jack looked blank.

Lucy tutted and turned cheerfully to her friend. 'Yes, I'm sure Beata would love to dance, wouldn't you? Here, I'll hold your pop!'

It was the first time since Christmas that Beata had held his hand. It felt warm and dry and masculine. Brimming with happiness, she placed her other hand on his arm and they set off at a waltz.

That particular dance was soon to end but Jack showed no rush to get back to his chair and asked her for another spin around the room – the lipstick had not put him off after all. He would have engaged her for a third but a happy Beata glanced at Lucy sitting alone with two glasses of lemonade and said, 'It's a bit mean of us. Maybe you should dance with your sister for a while.'

Hence it was Beata's turn to sit holding the lemonade and watch the dancers, but not for long; a young man approached and asked if she would partner him. Startled, she looked him up and down, at a loss what to do, both with the glasses of lemonade and with him. A slight, brown-haired figure with a hesitant smile and kind blue eyes, he was clad in a sports jacket with grey Oxford bags. Finally responding with an apologetic laugh she indicated the tumblers, then glanced at Jack and Lucy. Spotting her friend's predicament Lucy mouthed emphatically, 'Go on!'

Still, Beata hesitated. Would Jack mind? It wasn't as if they were courting. Might she have overestimated his feeling for her? What if she was saving herself for nothing? She could not pass up this opportunity. Making firm decision, she smiled and announced, 'I'll just put these glasses under the chair.' So doing, she was free to take his hand.

The first circuit of the dance floor was fine. The young man introduced himself as Gordon, and, given Beata's name, said, 'I was wanting to ask you to dance before but I didn't want to tread on any toes, so to speak.' He laughed. 'I mean the chap you came in with, I wasn't sure whether you were already walking out with him but when I saw him partnering your friend I thought it safe to come and ask.'

Beata explained quickly that the two were brother and sister and she herself was unattached. Seemingly pleased to hear this, Gordon held her a little closer and nothing more was said as they enjoyed the rest of the dance. He wasn't half as attractive as Jack, nor did she feel any affection for him, but the attentiveness was very flattering. Moreover, as she glanced over his shoulder she saw that Jack was eyeing Gordon's every move with a scowl of jealousy on his face. Why, Lucy had been right about making the most of herself with high heels and make-up. She had never had this effect on men before.

Pleased at having made Jack reveal his true feelings, when the dance ended she intended to go back to sit with him and Lucy, but Gordon held firmly to her small hand. 'Might I have another one?'

Beata nodded happily, though when the band struck up a jazzy number, she looked abashed. 'Oh dear, I'm not very good at this.'

'Me neither,' admitted Gordon, 'but I'm willing to give it a go.' And he launched her into a charleston.

Trying to concentrate on the lively steps whilst also attempting to gauge Jack's mood was difficult, but somehow amid all the gyrating Beata managed to snatch a glimpse of him. So pleased was she to see his jealous response that she put even more gusto into her dancing. It was a huge mistake. Unfamiliar with her high-heeled shoes and the speedy tune, distracted by Jack, drunk on happiness, she missed her footing and speared one of her heels through a turn-up of the Oxford bags.

One foot pinned to the floor, Gordon tottered, tried to take a step backwards but, still skewered by the heel did not, as it were, have a leg to stand on. He toppled over, barging into several other dancers on the way down and pulling Beata on top of him.

Deeply embarrassed but finding it hilarious too, Beata gave in to laughter, trying desperately to free herself. 'Oh dear, I think I've ripped your trousers!' Even as she rolled off, her foot remained entangled in the baggy material.

'If you persist in such behaviour I shall have to ask you to leave!'

She looked up to see the church official who was in charge glaring down at the couple on the floor.

In the determined struggle to remove her heel from the material Beata, still helpless with silent laughter, heard another ripping sound and apologized profusely as she scrambled to her feet. Gordon rose too, with a rueful downcast eye examining his dangling turn-up.

Head down and blushing, Beata excused her way through the crowd of dancers and hurried to retrieve her lemonade from under her seat, not daring to look at her friends but burying her embarrassment in the glass, feeling that every eye was upon her. And the most adverse reaction of all emanated from Jack.

So recently hilarious, the evening now seemed ruined. Not only had she spoiled her opportunity of romance with another but Jack seemed disgusted with her. When he made the cool suggestion that they leave early she did not object.

Lucy tried to cheer her up as they went to reclaim their jackets from the cloakroom, saying it had been awfully comical to watch.

Beata laughed too, making fun of herself, but inside she despaired that she had ruined her chance of matrimony.

However, when they went outside into the summery night to rejoin Jack he seemed to have calmed down a little and even smiled as he opened the car door for them, lending Beata the hope that she might earn his forgiveness. Just before she got in, though, she heard the sound of running footsteps through the dark and turned to see Gordon.

'I just wanted to apologize for embarrassing you in there!' He stood panting and bright-eyed, holding onto the edge of the car door. 'It was my awful dancing that caused it.'

'I think we were on equal footing,' Beata chuckled forgivingly.

With dark expression, Jack snorted and went to crank the car, dealing the starting handle several vicious turns before the engine sputtered into life.

Coming back to where the girls stood with Gordon, he bade the latter tersely, 'Will you take your hands off my car?'

'Sorry.' Gordon complied but soon returned his attention to Beata. 'Could I make it up to you by taking you to the pictures one night next week?'

Seeing that Jack's face had adopted its thunderous look again, Beat faltered. If he wanted her why had he dallied so? But before she could answer he interjected, 'Don't you think you've done enough harm to this young lady's reputation?' He brandished the starting handle at Gordon. 'Anyway, she can't go, she's walking out with me.'

Shocked but pleasurably so, Beata gawped at him.

Instantly contrite, Gordon backed away. 'Oh, I thought . . . Well, you said . . .'

'Sorry,' Beata winced apologetically.

But it was obvious he thought she had been stringing him along and he dealt her the most hateful look as he lurched away.

Lucy chastised her brother. 'What did you say that for? You've just ruined Beat's chances.'

'I said it because it's true!' Jack tossed the starting handle in the car, before turning bashful and glancing at Beata. 'Or rather I want it to be true.'

'Then stop being so blasted long-winded about it!' Lucy dealt him a shove.

Jack threw up his arms at being so pressured and tried to make a joke of it. 'I'm sorry about my bully of a sister, Beat! Will you walk out with me?'

Too delighted to speak, she nodded.

'There!' Lucy grabbed her brother's arm and laced it through that of her friend, holding it in place for a few moments until the trio broke up laughing and, getting into the car, headed for home.

When they pulled into the drive, Jack dropped his sister off at the lodge.

'Now, you're not going to go all coy again the moment I'm gone?' demanded Lucy of her brother. 'When I come to work tomorrow I want the gossip to be that you and Beat are courting.'

Jack laughed. 'It's a promise.' Then he drove off with the intention of depositing Beata right outside the house.

Nursing her desires, Beata prepared to be kissed.

As they approached, though, the headlights picked out a waiting figure, and a most annoyed-looking one at that.

Beata leaned over the back of his seat. 'I thought you said the major gave you permission to take the car, Jack?'

'He did!'

It certainly did not appear to be the case as a curt Major Herron waited for them to get out, then gestured at the open door behind him. 'Come into the hall, Lister. Beata, you may go to your room.'

Taking this unusual route through the square black-and-white tiled hallway, Beata murmured thanks and, head down, rushed upstairs, but once around the bend in the staircase she crouched to eavesdrop through the wrought-iron banisters.

'I don't appreciate having my good nature taken for granted by my staff, Lister, nor do I take kindly to being kept from my bed, so I'll come straight to the point! I did not go to the expense of having that made so that you could go out gallivanting!' He was pointing at Jack's chauffeur's suit. 'It was intended to be reserved for when you are on duty.'

'I'm awfully sorry, sir. You said I could take the car so I didn't think you'd mi –'

'Well, I do mind! You told me that you'd be going only as far as the village pub. I decided to have a stroll down there myself, only to discover Spaven holding court in his new attire as if he were lord of the manor and to be informed that my chauffeur had gone somewhat further afield and was no doubt disporting himself in similar fashion!'

Poor Jack! Beata felt awful at witnessing his dressing-down, but if she moved now she might creak the stairs. What on earth would she do if he were sacked?

'I've given him strict warning that his suit is only to be worn in working hours, and just in case there is any temptation I have also given him a couple of stripes to stitch down the legs of his trousers so that he won't be in a hurry to misuse them again. As for you . . .' The furious major took out a pocket knife and, with several concise movements, removed every metal button from Jack's coat until there was a pile of them on the hall table. 'I intend to have the family crest stamped on these. You can wear your old suit until you get them back.'

Beata sagged in relief that Jack was to be spared expulsion.

'The money for the petrol you used will be deducted from your pay. You can also attach this to your breast pocket.' He thrust an embroidered patch at Jack; it bore the family crest. 'So there will be no mistake in future as to who owns the suit *and* the car! Dismissed.'

Jack slunk out into the night and Beata, seeing the major about to head up the staircase, scampered to her bed.

In the morning, she hardly dared face him. Would he guess she had been privy to his humiliation? If he did then he never said a word on the few occasions he journeyed into the kitchen to collect washing implements for the car, nor was any comment made on the relegation to his old suit. Having spent half the night sewing the stripes on his own trousers, Mr Spaven was in a foul temper and the mood below stairs was dreadful until well after the midday meal when the butler took an afternoon nap, allowing the others some relief.

'What on earth's got into him?' whispered Mrs Temple, pouring herself a cup of tea and collapsing into a chair. 'I made one remark on his trousers and he blew up. I've had to tiptoe round my own blasted kitchen all morning.'

Beata lowered her voice and quickly explained about the previous night.

Lucy breathed a quiet exclamation. 'I wondered what was up with our Jack. I expected him to be all smiles and sunbeams now that he's finally asked you to walk out with him.'

The explosion of noise that followed this remark risked waking the butler but the cook and maids dismissed this completely to offer their congratulations to Beata.

Fearing that Jack had changed his mind she looked most embarrassed and apologetic when, at the height of this boisterous celebration, he entered.

'Why didn't you tell us?' Mrs Temple turned on him.

'Tell you what?' Jack looked wary.

'About you and Beata walking out together?'

'Oh that!' Realizing that they had not been discussing last night's fiasco, Jack broke into a smile, becoming somewhat abashed. 'Well, it's private, isn't it? Between me and Beat.'

'So when are you going to make an honest woman of her?' demanded Mrs Temple, causing Beata to squirm.

'Nay, we've just got together, Mrs T!' A grinning Jack went to replace his bucket under the sink. 'But don't worry, you'll be the first to get a wedding invitation.'

And for Beata this was as good as a proposal.

The announcement that she and Jack would one day be married, whilst wonderful, was to make little difference to Beata's situation. Oh, he took her to the pictures and sometimes held her hand in the dark, but in all the months that followed he had not plucked up the courage to kiss her properly.

'Could it be my breath?' After many a chaste outing Beata finally sought to ask her friend as she and Lucy wandered around town looking for dresses to wear for the Christmas ball.

'Give us a sniff.' Lucy bent nearer. Then, 'No, it's just our Jack being backward – Eh, what do you think of that one?' She pointed at a russet dress on display. 'It's your colour.'

Beata unconsciously twiddled a strand of her auburn hair. 'Yes, but it makes my teeth look too yellow.' She eyed a passing girl whose laughing conversation with her partner revealed a pearly white smile. 'I wish they were like that, so white and even.'

'Don't we all,' said her friend.

Sauntering on, they were assaulted by ether fumes from a dental surgery, causing Lucy to exclaim on a whim, 'Eh, do you fancy some new ones? Then you can buy the dress you really want!'

'I don't know if I could afford it.'

'It costs nowt to ask!' The impulsive Lucy dragged her into the dental reception, whereupon both consulted a price list.

'They're not as dear as I thought,' mused Lucy, then pointed excitedly at a grinning set of dentures. 'Oh, look, those are just the ticket! Such natural pink gums. I wonder what they're made of.'

'Vulcanite,' provided the rather haughty receptionist.

Lucy made her decision. 'Right, I'm having some!'

Beata had to agree that the false ones were much better than their own and the two sat down to wait amongst the ether fumes. 'I love that smell, don't you?' She inhaled long and deep. Her

460

friend beheld her as if she were mad, then was called into the surgery.

Whilst Lucy's request met success, the dentist seemed reluctant to pull out every one of the younger girl's teeth. 'Might you not prefer a half-set to be going on with?' But Beata had made her mind up and insisted she would like the same as her friend, if he would be so kind.

Kind he might be, but the experience was far from pleasant and as she and Lucy stumbled giddily into the street later, dabbing at their bloody aching mouths, Beata felt that her actions might have been somewhat misguided, especially when it was impossible to enjoy their usual tea at the café.

But the discomfort was to be worthwhile when she and her friend went home to show off their brand-new smiles, receiving the admiration of their peers, Jack being most complimentary of all. With most of the work over for the day, the servants were at liberty to gather round and Beata and Lucy were still the centre of attention when their employer came unnoticed upon the scene.

Jack jumped guiltily aside, 'Sorry, sir, I didn't hear you come in! Is the bell not working?'

'Stand easy, Lister.' A benign Major Herron motioned for him to relax. Quick to forgive, things were back to normal between them now and the episode with the suit was long forgotten. 'I've no desire to spoil anyone's fun. I just came for a word with my butler.'

Entering at this juncture, stolen pheasant in hand, Bert Spaven looked aghast and instantly swivelled on his heel to spirit his booty away.

Witnessing this over the major's shoulder, Jack faltered. 'Er, I'll just go and look for him, sir!' And he escaped from the kitchen.

Most of them having spotted the butler's dilemma, no one knew what to say. Percy broke the awkward hiatus, indicating the newspaper that he was forbidden to read and stammering, 'Mr Spaven tells us some general's predicting there might be only another twenty years of peace before there's a new war with Germany. What do you think, sir?'

'I'm afraid I have to agree with that prediction.' Major Herron clasped his hands behind his back, looking momentarily serious. 'It still rankles in the Teutonic mind that we destroyed their empire. They won't be satisfied until they've had another bash. It was a grave error to pull our troops out of the Rhineland – but we shall thrash them again if need be so you must have no worries on that score.' He brought his hands together in a cheerful clap. 'Anyway,

I didn't come here to ruin your evening with discussions of the Hun but the more pleasant matter of Christmas festivities.'

'Oh, that's what we were just talking about before you came in, sir!' Mrs Temple preened under her employer's attention. 'Lucy and Beata were showing off the new teeth they bought to go with their frocks. Aren't they grand?'

'Splendid, splendid!' Major Herron bent forward to examine the girl's manufactured smiles. 'Could do with a pair myself – Ah, Spaven, there you are!' The butler entered without a feather ruffled and was immediately engaged in arrangement of the coming festivities.

Whilst the major was otherwise occupied, Jack and Beata shared a secretive laugh, the former whispering, 'Mr Spaven cut it a bit fine that time!'

Finer than he might suspect.

About to depart, the major said, 'Well, I'll leave you good people to it . . .' Then something prompted him to say, 'Ah, I've been meaning to ask what has happened to the silver mug from the display cabinet in my study.'

There was silence, everyone looking at each other enquiringly. A spirit of unease began to descend.

The major addressed himself to Percy. 'Madden, I seem to recall that you removed the contents for cleaning last week and that particular item has not been replaced.'

The footman looked guilty. 'I did, sir, but I never noticed anything missing when I put the stuff back. Was it the one bearing your regimental insignia?'

'No, the rather ugly one with the twisted handle. I don't care for it but I should like to know where it has gone.' Major Herron became less amiable now, suspicious even.

Even though she knew nothing about it whatsoever, Beata felt culpable under the major's accusing look, as did everyone else.

'Then I'm afraid there's nothing else for it than to search every room and as this was the last place the mug came before its disappearance we must start down here.'

Beata felt sick at coming under suspicion, dreading the thought of her underwear drawer being rifled.

But the thief showed himself to have some vestige of honour. 'No need, sir, it was me.'

'What have you done with it?' Major Herron showed little emotion, not even surprise, merely looking his old batman in the eye.

'Sold it, sir.' Bert's pock-marked face looked hangdog. 'I'm very sorry.'

The major gave a curt nod. 'So am I.' He sounded betrayed. 'And it is only because of your otherwise excellent service that I do not call the police. Lister, would you escort Spaven to collect his belongings, then see him off the premises?'

How quickly it all happened: one moment lord of the roost, the next cast out in front of his minions.

With the major remaining in the kitchen until the culprit had gone, no one could relax, Beata least of all. It was a dreadful five minutes. However, there was to be unexpected compensation.

Major Herron was sombre. 'I very much regret that all of you had to fall under suspicion because of Spaven's treacherous act. We can only be glad that he chose to make his admission before further harm was done. That said, he has left us in a very dire state. It will be impossible to find another butler so near to Christmas.' He looked at Jack. 'Lister, do you think you and Madden could double up as butler until we find someone? It will mean a lot of extra work but I should greatly appreciate it.'

Jack and Percy said they would, of course. Thanking them, the major brought this very distasteful episode to a close and bade his servants good night.

In the excited aftermath, everyone twittering about Spaven's audacity and how on earth he was going to find work after this, Jack turned to Beata. 'Eh, what a turn-up! I never thought to see myself butler.'

'Joint butler,' corrected Percy. 'And it'll probably be me who gets the lion's share, being more used to working in the house than you. You never know, they might not need to get anyone else in after they've seen what I'm capable of.'

After much good-natured jousting between the two young men, Jack gave Beata a quick hug and asked, 'How do you feel about being married to a butler, then?'

Glowing with affection, Beata was too excited to do anything more than shrug with glee. This was more than she could ever have hoped for.

As envisaged, Jack was kept extremely busy with all the extra chores during the weeks up to Christmas, as indeed was everyone else below stairs. Ignorant as to where Bert had secreted the pheasant, they knew very well he had not taken it with him for they were overwhelmed by its awful smell and searched every downstairs room high and low as, under the influence of roaring fires, it went from gamy to putrid and made their lives a misery, permeating not only nostrils but clothing too. Exposed to such stench, there was the danger that the Christmas dance frocks would become contaminated and therefore unwearable. But eventually, following her nose, Beata found the bird at the bottom of an umbrella stand from whence it was quickly removed and disposed of.

The servants' ball was extra special this year. Christmas one of the few occasions when the staff saw their employer's afflicted wife, Beata was pleased to comment that the mistress seemed in much better spirits tonight. That the poor lady was enjoying herself made Beata feel happier too. She looked around the upstairs dining hall that had been transformed for the night to a ballroom, sharing everyone's enjoyment. It was altogether an excellent time, for Maddie had written to say she had passed her exams and was now working at a hospital in Nottingham; moreover, she was arranging to come to The Retreat in York to train in psychiatric nursing. Forgetting all the annoying characteristics, Beata was glad for Maddie's achievement, glad too for the coming reunion and looked forward to delivering her own exciting news whenever her sister did come to York. She had already told Gus but had warned her not to broadcast it for Jack had not yet informed his parents of his marriage plans. Mr and Mrs Lister were obviously aware of the couple's mutual fondness though, treating Beata like a member of their family as they did. They were at the ball tonight, standing beside her. She turned to smile fondly at these surrogate parents, before the band struck up and she found herself in demand.

Following custom, the major started off the dancing with one of the housemaids and this year the honour fell to Beata. Naturally, though, she much preferred to pair up with Jack and, apart from one or two dances with men from other households, was glad to find herself in his arms for most of the evening.

Exhausted but happy, she took a short rest whilst Jack went off to fetch her a cup of punch. Mr and Mrs Lister were still enjoying the dancing, as was Lucy, so leaving Beata temporarily alone to sit and listen to the music and to eye everyone's attire as they waltzed past her chair. Smiling admiringly, her gaze picked out May and Percy, following them for a while. How elegant they looked. No one would guess they were servants. May had on a very modern beaded dress – she must have saved up for ages to afford that, thought Beata – plus silver shoes and a matching purse to complete the outfit.

464

Her eyes became fixed to the little silver purse that dangled from May's arm. Suddenly she was transported to another Christmas, a cruel Christmas, the sound of Eliza's nasty laughter overwhelming all. How dreadful that, even now, she could spoil Beata's life. How could one behave so towards a little child?

'Beat, what on earth's wrong?'

She looked up quickly to find Jack frowning at her in concern, but could not speak for she was as confused as he.

Moved by her tear-filled eyes he quickly put the drinks aside and sat down beside her, putting an arm around her shoulders. 'Is it owt I've done?'

Beata shook her head quickly and took a deep breath. 'No, no, it's . . . just things from a long time ago.'

But though she tried her best to cover it he could see she was distraught and, after a quick glance around him, he took her by the hand and led her from the ballroom to a quieter place.

In an annex that housed the warming cabinets, little more than a cupboard itself, he put up a hand to stroke her hair, projecting gentle concern. 'I don't know what to do to make it better.'

Still she could not voice her torment, but she laid her head against his chest, finding comfort in the regulated beating of his heart.

He held her, trying to think of something to detract from her sadness. 'Major's right pleased with how I'm handling the butler's job. I'm rather chuffed meself, as a matter of fact; think I could manage it permanently. I'd miss driving but, you never know, if I became butler it would improve my status no end. I could get a post with better pay and proper living accommodation. We might even be able to afford a little car of our own.'

He had said 'we'. Beata raised her head from his chest to look up at him.

'By the way, who do I approach to ask for your hand?'

The nasty laughter completely vanished. Joy returned to her fluttering heart. She opened her mouth to stammer that she did not know, but no words emerged, for he quickly stifled them with a kiss. A warm, loving kiss that lasted for long passionate minutes, Beata returning it with such intensity that it seemed to frighten him and he broke away with a gasping laugh. 'I think I heard the announcement of supper! We'd better go before we're caught.'

Reluctantly, she nodded, but clinging to the lovely moment, she answered his question lest there be any misunderstanding. 'I don't think you need to ask anybody. Only me. And I say yes.'

He smiled, then ground her lips with another quick kiss before taking a peek into the ballroom, then discreetly joining the mass departure to the servants' hall.

There was nothing backwards about Jack now. It seemed that, once started, he could not stop kissing her. Furtive kisses in the pantry. Fleeting pecks behind the housekeeper's back. Even on Sunday, stopping the car on the way to church to drag her behind a tree and express his love, stopping on the way home behind that same tree to kiss, kiss and kiss again.

When they arrived home someone had closed the big iron gates. Coming to a halt outside he jumped out to open them, taking the opportunity to poke his head into the car and plant his lips to hers again.

He withdrew with a playful expression. 'I don't know if it's in order to kiss a girl on Sunday, but I'm going to risk it anyway.' And he covered her mouth yet again.

Alerted by the sound of the running motor outside the lodge, Mrs Lister tweaked a lace curtain aside to investigate, saw what was happening and banged on the pane, her frowning gesticulation causing Jack to react quickly. He jumped back behind the wheel and drove Beata up to the big house, his passenger smiling broadly at being caught out, he giving her a rueful smile upon depositing her, whence, both went their separate ways.

A week later, the kiss having been surpassed by many another, Beata had almost forgotten about the incident when she went to the lodge for tea and was taken by surprise when Mrs Lister brought it up towards the end of the meal. 'By the way,' she smiled upon proffering the last slice of cake to Beata, which was politely refused, 'I must apologize for my son's misconduct, dear. He should know better than to treat you like that.'

Puzzled, Beata responded with a smiling frown.

'Last Sunday, when I had to knock on the window to him . . .'

'Oh!' Though still smiling, Beata flushed with guilt and began to wipe crumbs off the table into her palm.

'Most improper, and on the Sabbath too.'

Lucy had heard about the incident. Though respectful of her elders, she smilingly defended Jack. 'They are walking out together, Mother.'

'What nonsense.' Mrs Lister gave a dismissive laugh as she stacked the empty plates.

'But you know he's been going to the pictures with Bea –'

'As a friend, yes, but nothing more. Really, Lucy, after all I've taught you, you of all people should know it's wrong for a man to lead a girl on if he's no intention of marrying her.'

Beata's stomach lurched so violently she thought she might vomit.

Jack looked unwell too. 'I would like –'

'It's hardly relevant what you'd like, Jack, is it?' Mrs Lister was gently domineering, not even bothering to pause in her action of clearing the table. 'The plain fact is that it's impossible for you to marry Beata so you've no right to lead her on.'

He looked perplexed and embarrassed. 'But, why?'

'Why, you soft article?' Mrs Lister's amused exclamation condemned him as a half-wit. 'That should be perfectly obvious to one who drives her to church every Sunday. Beata's a Roman Catholic, isn't she? She'll be marrying one of her own just like you will, isn't that right, dear?' She turned amicably to Beata, who tried to put her view.

'Well, I don't think religion matters if two people –'

'Of course it matters!' Mrs Lister appeared shocked rather than amused now. 'I'm surprised you can even say it. If it doesn't matter to you it matters very much to us.' She was addressing her son again but it was intended for all. 'No one in this family has ever married a Catholic and they're not going to start now, however fond I am of Beata, so you can both put that silly idea right out of mind. Now, anyone want more tea before I take the pot away?'

Immediately Beata shook her head, unable to speak, barely able to breathe, her dreams shattered. Waiting in vain for Jack to stand up to his mother, to fight for his bride, she saw him then for the weakling he was. He said not a word, just sat there tweaking crumbs from the tablecloth, his face a picture of inadequacy.

'I'll have one, dear.' A meek Mr Lister held out his cup which his wife refilled, but the atmosphere was very strained.

Struggling to contain the shards of her broken heart, Beata made a dignified exit, her voice perforating the stunned quietude. 'Thank you for the meal, Mrs Lister. I'd better be getting back to the house now.' Oh Lord, there was an evening's work ahead – how would she ever cope?

Mrs Lister smiled but did not glance up from her pouring. 'You're welcome, dear. It's lovely to have you. See you next week.'

She actually means it, thought Beata, her knees trembling with shock and hardly strong enough to hold her upright. Could the woman not see how deeply she had hurt and insulted her guest?

Without looking at Jack she made for the door. He remained in his seat.

Lucy had the evening off but now she rose, her expression solemn. 'I'll just walk Beat to the house.'

Outside she linked arms with her friend, promising earnestly, 'I'll try and talk her round, dear.'

Beata turned and looked her full in the face, her tone uncharacteristically acerbic. 'Do you really think it'll help?'

After a moment Lucy shook her head and stared at the ground, exhaling her sadness. 'Eh, I'm sorry, Beat. I wouldn't have subjected you to that if I'd known. I can't understand it. Mother never said a word against Catholics before – and she was happy to have you in her house when she always knew what religion you were.'

'That was before I wanted to marry her son.' Beata could not stand to talk about it any longer, wanted to find a quiet corner where she could sob her heart out. Every week for almost three years she had been sitting at that table completely ignorant that the woman who feigned to treat her like a daughter was in fact the worst type of bigot, pretending to like her but in secret despising her. 'You go back now. I'll see you tomorrow.'

Lucy nodded, projecting commiseration with her eyes as the forlorn little figure limped away.

To avoid any questions from the rest of the household, Beata threw herself into the many jobs that needed to be done before bedtime, even jobs that were not hers, donning a mask of cheerfulness whenever she was forced to encounter anyone, and taking out her anger and frustration on a pair of rabbits, which had their guts and skin ripped from them with such ferocity that they were barely fit to eat.

It seemed like a month before she was finally able to escape. Dropping her teeth into a glass on the side table, she perched on the edge of the bed for a moment, trying to contain her sense of injustice and to work out how this had happened, her unfocused eyes staring at the dentures that grinned back at her.

Then, turning off the light she rolled despondently into bed, poured her anger and misery into the pillow, sobbed and sobbed, ridding herself of every tear so that in the morning she might face the world with her usual aplomb. Tomorrow she would hand in her notice, hoping that the major would accept seven days, for she could not bear another month in Jack's presence, knowing she was judged too inferior to be his bride.

*   *   *

Major Herron was upset to learn that this valuable member of staff wished to leave but, believing the lie she had given him, said that her elderly relative's needs must take precedence and she must go to her aunt's aid. 'But if ever you wish to return you'll be made welcome, and if you do not then here is a reference for your further use.'

'That was kind of him, don't you think?' said Beata to her friend upon breaking the news.

'Oh, Beat, don't go 'cause of our Jack!' wailed Lucy, knowing the brave face was just an act. 'I know you'll find somebody else, somebody better. He wouldn't have been good enough for you, anyway. Tell you what, we'll go on the monkey run in York on Saturday night and I'll bet you five bob there are half a dozen chaps wanting to hold your hand.'

'I'm not going because of Jack,' lied Beata cheerfully, then admitted, 'Well, maybe this has just pushed me into it – but I've been meaning to leave for ages. I want to be a cook and I'm never going to get the chance if I stay here. Mrs Temple's still a young woman. How long have I been here, Lucy? Nearly three years and I'm still no more than a glorified skivvy standing in on Mrs Temple's days off. I want to be boss of my own kitchen.' Part of this was true, she did want to be a cook; it was not a towering ambition but better than scrubbing floors. She leaned forward as Lucy began to cry. 'Aw, don't worry. You and I will still be friends!'

Lucy presented a distraught face. 'We're more than friends, Beat, we're sisters.'

'That's right, we are.' Beata petted her. 'And that's how we'll stay. I promise.'

TWENTY-SIX

Sisters or no, Beata chose never to go to the lodge again. Be that as it may, the ordeal of having to work alongside Jack was too painful for words, both of them attempting to make out as if their romantic interlude had never occurred, trying to stay chummy in front of the others. So urgent was her desperation to get away that every night she trawled the situations vacant column of the newspaper, went for three interviews on her afternoon off and accepted the first job that was offered, leaving at the end of the week to floods of tears from Lucy. Jack was nowhere in sight that day.

But the impulsive move soon proved to have been rash. The doctor who engaged her was struggling to maintain himself, let alone a servant, his wife's snootiness and his father-in-law's habit of sitting in his shirtsleeves on a Sunday betraying Beata's new employers as lower class. Handing in her notice within a matter of weeks, she wrote to inform Lucy of her change of address, telling her that she was to work for another military family in Fulford as cook-general, 'Which means dogsbody,' wrote Beata, 'but at least I'll be employed by somebody who knows the correct way to behave.'

Briar House, the home of Lieutenant-Colonel Druce, situated near the cavalry barracks, was a Victorian villa with privet hedging in the forecourt and an enormous garden at the rear. For those who entered through the front door the dining room was off the hallway to the left and the sitting room to the right, but of course Beata was relegated to the side entrance, which led to the kitchen. In here was a big Yorkshire range with an oven on either side and room on top for several pans. It was an unpretentious household. Apart from an old man who came periodically to tend the garden, there was only one other member of staff.

Eve, the parlourmaid, was not half as nice as Lucy, unwilling to defer to the newcomer simply because she held the title Cook. Colonel and Mrs Druce might not be very demanding but with such an uncooperative colleague Beata found herself with much more work to do. Still, hard labour did have its benefits, giving her little time to think about Jack, and even though there was to be painful reminder in her meetings with his sister once a week, the wound eventually began to heal, especially in one so lacking in bitterness, and Beata retained the hope that she would in time meet a more genuine suitor.

One thing was certain, she would not meet him here, for, even though the family owned a car, there was no chauffeur. Gone were the days of being driven to church, but, much nearer now to her place of worship, she could easily get there on foot, even if it did mean a rush to prepare Sunday luncheon.

'I shall have to teach you to drive, Beata,' announced Mrs Druce upon her breathless cook almost tripping in her haste to deliver the meal to the table and explaining why. 'Then, not only can you drive yourself to church but can take me shopping.'

Beata thanked the gentlewoman for her understanding and said she would look forward to it greatly, but her anticipation of this was quickly doused upon reporting to Eve, the parlourmaid saying in her blunt, sullen fashion, 'You needn't think I'm doing all the work while you're carting her round.' And her grumbles must have reached the mistress, for the driving lessons were never to materialize.

Yet, life was not all drudgery. When the parents went away, leaving daughter Alice at home, there would be games of hockey on the tennis court and all kinds of mad antics, for nine-year-old Alice was something of a live wire and Beata, only eight years older, needed little encouragement to join the fun. Thereafter the pair of them would take tea in the kitchen like old friends, sniggering behind Eve's back at the maid's curmudgeonly ways.

Not infrequently, too, Mrs Druce would announce, 'Beata, take Master Reginald to the pictures. He will pay.' And off they would jaunt to the matinée.

And in reward for any extra work when Mrs Druce's elderly mother came to stay Beata would be handed an envelope bearing cash, the dowager handing it over herself and shaking hands with Beata as if they were equals.

Eve treated Beata like an equal too, though in quite a different regard, plonking herself down at the same table without so much as a by-your-leave. Never one to put on airs and graces, Beata chose not to remind this trespasser that it was most inappropriate for a parlourmaid to sit down alongside Cook, though it annoyed her and she was to complain loudly to her friend whenever they met about Eve's lack of decorum.

'I wouldn't mind so much if she were nice, but she isn't! A face on her like a blasted haddock. I've never seen her crack a smile once – probably 'cause it'd take too much effort, I've never known anyone so lazy and catty. I had to follow the rules when I was a maid; I thought when I rose to be cook I'd at least have some respect.'

'It's no good moaning to me.' Lucy was unsympathetic. 'You must put her in her place.'

But this was not Beata's way. Preferring to suffer the lack of deference than all-out warfare, she made the best of life with Eve, though it was very hard to find any rapport, especially as the maid took every petty opportunity to flout the fact that she was five years older than her reputed superior. Spring had just brought the announcement that women were to be given the vote on the same terms as men. 'But, of course, it won't make any difference to you,' said Eve, standing idle whilst the other worked, 'you being only seventeen.'

Leg throbbing, moving from cupboard to oven to table, Beata chose not to rise to the bait but calmly went back to stirring her pudding bowl. 'I doubt I'd have time to vote anyway. I've hardly time to pass water. Have you finished in the sitting room?'

Immediately Eve bristled. 'I'll finish in my own good time!'

The stocky little cook held on to her temper. 'It was a civil question. I thought perhaps if you'd finished you might like to help with –'

'Do your job as well as my own?'

'It's just that you appear lost for something to do.'

Eve put her hands on her wide hips. 'For your information Mrs Druce is eating an orange!'

Beata was totally flummoxed, at which Eve took officious pleasure in telling her. 'I can't get into the parlour. She loves her oranges dipped in sugar and won't allow anyone in whilst she's eating one because she makes such a noise – likes to slurp in private. She'll ring when she's ready.'

Beata gave a curt nod and went back to her work.

As if to irritate, the maid sat down to watch her, offering smugly, 'When you've been here longer you'll get to know all our little quirks.'

Her spoon mixing furiously, Beata wondered if she could bear to remain here much longer with such a lack of friends, and tried to focus instead on her holiday in June.

Upon being hired, she had been told that the Druces always went to Scotland or London for their holidays and that staff were required to take annual leave at the same time. 'But you will be driven to the station and picked up,' Mrs Druce informed her kindly. 'Where might you be going?'

'Scarborough, I should think, madam. That's where we usually go.'

But upon giving Lucy this information so as to enable her to make a booking, she had been surprised.

'I've decided we're going further afield this year,' Lucy had announced. 'Blackpool! Two pounds ten with morning call and shoes cleaned.'

It was less than three months away, but just at that moment, with no one to share a laugh and a joke, it seemed to Beata a very long way off and she wondered bleakly whether she could survive until June.

But survive she did and, her time filled with cleaning and cooking, she was amazed to note that there were now only twenty-four hours to go.

After an even busier day of preparing food for the Druces' travelling hamper, an evening spent packing cases for the entire household and a last breakfast rush, she was on her way.

Due to all the changing of trains it took the best part of a day to reach the other side of the Pennines. There remained just enough light to enjoy a bracing walk along the seafront after tea, then to bed. Sunday was church for Beata and chapel for Lucy, then a lazy stroll across the sands in the afternoon, clad in best attire, imbibing the golden calm that superseded the dark days of unrest. The General Strike but a distant memory, there was a feeling of wellbeing amongst all those who sauntered here, of affluence even. A whole fortnight ahead of her and a full purse with which to enjoy it, Beata felt genuinely uplifted for the first time in ages.

On Monday the holiday began for real, the friends determined to cram as much as possible into the fortnight. With the tide bashing against the sea wall they spent the morning amongst the amusements, laughing hysterically at their reflections in distorted mirrors, tottering along the cake walk, grabbing out for the handrail to save them and screaming when it delivered a small electric shock, though not too engrossed to notice that a pair of young men were following their course around the hall. Beata turned to grin at her admirers, taking in their attire of cream flannels, tweed jackets and open-necked shirts – then the floor opened beneath her feet and she yelled again as her stomach performed a somersault at the unexpected descent. But it was only a drop of inches, just enough to cause a thrill, and with the young men in tow she and Lucy proceeded laughingly to the next stage.

There were moans of disappointment upon coming to a door marked 'Exit' – but just at the last minute a violent draught whooshed up from a vent, fluttering the girls' skirts and invoking a final squeal as they fought to hide their suspenders. Cheeks streaming with tears of mirth, they found themselves out on the promenade with its mingled aromas of rock, fish and chips, candy floss, shrimps and seaweed.

Still there was the need to hold down their rippling skirts as the bracing, salt-laden wind inflated them like parachutes. Whilst still attempting to do so, they found themselves accompanied by the young men from the amusement hall, one on either side of them.

'Hello, girls, enjoying your holiday? I'm Tommy, by the way.' The one who strutted jauntily alongside Beata formed a hook of his arm.

Reflecting his amicable tone, she slipped her own arm through his, using her other to hold down her skirt. 'Pleased to meet you, Tommy Bytheway.'

'Eh, Titch!' He pointed a finger at her laughingly. 'You're too small to be taking the mickey. It's Tommy Lunan.'

Beata echoed his laughter and gave her name. Though lacking most of the attributes she admired, apart from sparkling blue eyes, there was something extremely attractive about this round-faced young man. His light-brown hair had been slicked neatly from its side parting and kept in place with grease, but a lock of it had come free to dance with the wind as he bounced along, one moment pressed flat to his brow, the next standing upright like an antenna. It caused a rush of affection, reminding her of the wayward little lock her father had had, though this was dead straight rather than wavy.

'Where are you from?' His cheeks were pink from the wind.

'York.' To avoid being constantly lashed about the face, she held down the brightly coloured scarf that was knotted at her throat.

'We're from Barrow-in-Furness. I'm a hairdresser, Howard works in the shipyard. What do you do?'

'I'm a cook,' said Beata, Lucy answering for herself.

'Ooh, we've chosen the right ones here!' Tommy grinned at his friend then addressed Beata again. 'How long are you here for?'

'A fortnight.'

'Champion, so are we!' He beamed at her, projecting warm delight. She beamed in return. It was only when he put an investigative hand to his hair and asked, 'Has a seagull bombed me?' that she realized she had been staring, and tore her eyes away with a laugh of embarrassment.

'Oh, sorry – no!' But her admiring gaze was soon lured back. He was just so lovely.

'Would you care for an ice cream?' Howard asked both girls. They said they would.

'You realize you're not going to get rid of us now Howard's opened his purse?' joked Tommy.

'We might not want to,' came Beata's smiling retort.

'I didn't think pretty lasses like you would be so hard up – Hang on, don't move!' Tommy made her stand still and picked something off the shoulder of her cardigan, pretending to cup it gently in his hands. 'It's all right, it's just one of Howard's pet moths. Here, stick him back in your wallet, chum.'

Beata roared with laughter, much longer than was necessary, this encouraging the young man into unleashing more of his humour on her. By the time they had walked from one end of the seafront to the other, with Tommy cracking quips along the way, Beata announced that she had never laughed so much in all her life, her twinkling eyes giving away that which remained unsaid: she had fallen head over heels in love.

With Lucy equally merry in Howard's company, though not half so smitten, the two couples were to spend the entire day together, holding hands, sharing fish and chips and a ball game upon the sand.

So utterly infatuated was she, Beata showed great reluctance to part at teatime, but her friend pointed out that they had ordered their evening meal and it would be ill-mannered not to turn up.

Bouncing the rubber ball off the pavement as he spoke, Tommy chipped in, 'We can meet again later if you like.' The brightness of his face encouraged her; he was obviously as eager as Beata to continue the romance. 'Go to a show or something.'

And so she agreed to go off for tea, wolfing it down in order to get back as quickly as possible to this wonderful young man, her mind conjuring up all sorts of possibilities over what the 'or something' might be.

Her dreams were fulfilled. Following a lovely evening at a variety show, whilst escorting her back to her digs, Tommy pulled her away from the streetlamps into a shop doorway, put his arms around her and applied warm, dry lips. None of Jack's backwardness here. He kissed her long and sensuously, ignoring intrusive footsteps as Lucy and Howard overtook them to stroll past arm in arm, breaking off only to grin and wink at them before lowering his face to Beata's again.

Heartened that he did not seem shocked when she returned his kisses with equal fervour, Beata responded with a passion that had never been granted free rein before, obliterating all trace of Jack. They kissed for twenty minutes or more, until her face had grown sore and her neck ached from craning up to meet him, but her heart overflowed with joy.

He was to kiss her the instant they met again the next morning. Kissed and hugged and held her every day for the next fortnight. They talked and talked of everything, both informative and trivial. By the end of their first week together she knew his religion, his every childhood illness, his shoe size, his inside leg measurement, his mother's maiden name, that he hated suet as much as she did, the name of the first girl who had broken his heart, even his bowel habits. During the second week, with few questions left to ask, there was little else to occupy their lips but kisses, kisses that were to become ever more passionate upon discovering the sand dunes of Lytham St Annes, where lovers could hide from disapproving eyes.

How could she have mistaken what she had felt for Jack as love? It had not been love at all. This was so utterly overwhelming that she could concentrate on nothing else, was barely aware of what day it was – why, it could almost be classed an illness. How devastating, then, to part, especially when Tommy and his friend were compelled to leave a day earlier than she and Lucy. Holidays always passed quickly, but none so swift as this.

Sharing one last embrace at the station that wet Friday morning, Beata's sweetheart seemed equally disconsolate as he passed her a note bearing his place of abode, just in case she had forgotten. 'Promise you'll write to me?'

Grasping it, Beata nodded miserably and stared down at the

scribbled address as if reading, though she knew it off by heart. Fearing that she might weep upon mention of how much she would miss him, she chose something mundane. 'Well, I suppose it's back to cooking for me and cutting hair for you.'

'I won't be cutting hair any longer.'

She looked into his eyes, adoring even the Lancastrian way he pronounced hair as *hur*.

'Won't you?'

'No, I'll be cutting it shorter.'

Whilst the other couple groaned Beata smiled at his attempt to lighten the atmosphere.

He gave a sad laugh. 'Sorry, that was pathetic. I just can't think of anything clever to say. I've never said this before in my life, but I don't want to go home, Beat.'

'Me neither.' Tears burned her eyes, her anguish intensified by the arrival of the train. Sharing a final hug and the bitterest, sweetest of kisses, she watched him board, then waved furiously as his train chugged away. All that remained of him was the scent that clung to her clothes and the crumpled piece of paper in her hand. She stared down at it for a moment, before shoving it in the pocket of her fawn mackintosh. Then, turning, she and Lucy went for one last walk along the seafront.

Added to the ever-present wind was rain. They employed the Chinese painted sunshades they had bought on their first holiday together, hands tight around the stems to prevent them being ripped from their grasp, wandered aimlessly for a while without speaking, rivulets trickling over the oilskin to dapple their mackintoshes. Beata's swollen leg ached, but not as much as her heart.

Knowing how much store the youngster set on her new-found love, and having witnessed her devastation at being let down by Jack, Lucy wondered how to broach her warning, finally explaining gently, 'You shouldn't expect too much to come of it, Beat. I know he's nice but he lives a long way away and men are no good at writing . . .'

Disturbed from her dreams, Beata pondered over this. Lucy was right, of course. Her brothers had rarely put pen to paper. And look how she had taken it for granted that she would marry Jack. She determined then to curb her feelings, putting on a bright face and shoving Tommy to the back of her mind. 'No, you're right there, and they have a nasty habit of coming between friends. You and I came on this holiday together and we've hardly seen anything of each other all fortnight because of those two. What would you like to do for our last day?'

Almost embarrassed at her own childishness, Lucy hoisted her shoulders and confessed with a grin, 'I'd love another go in the Hall of Fun.'

'Me an' all. I look better in those mirrors than I do in the one at home.' Beata chuckled and linked her friend's arm in gay manner. 'Come on then, missus, let's go make the most of it!'

But try as she might not to spoil what remained of the holiday for Lucy, that last day was very depressing and it was something of a relief the next morning to find herself on the train home. During the hours that followed she tried hard to convince herself that Lucy was right and she should forget about Tommy, should consign the last two lovely weeks to a box labelled 'holiday romance'.

Yet however much she might laugh and joke with her friend, secretly she could not quite bring herself to abandon him to oblivion . . . which was why it was such a massive thrill to find Tom's short but affectionate letter waiting for her the moment she arrived home.

Having received not a word from Howard and not expecting to, Lucy was surprised and delighted upon hearing Beata's good news, and was even more heartened that Tommy's missive was to be no aberration, for a week later another arrived, signalling a regular correspondence between the pair. But, though overjoyed to retain contact with her sweetheart, Beata was desperate to hear those words emerge from his own smiling lips and constantly bewailed the fact that it was too far to go over to Barrow-in-Furness in a day.

Tired of having her nights out spoilt by such moaning, Lucy came up with what she saw as a solution: next year they would spend their holiday in the Lake District from where they could have a day trip to Barrow.

'Or maybe Tommy could arrange to spend his holiday there too!' exclaimed Beata, but, gratified as she was by her friend's thoughtfulness, she was to remain tormented by the thought of such a long wait, especially as there was no one in the house to take her mind off things, for Eve was sadly lacking in humour.

Mercifully, her working environment was to be made a little lighter by Sadie, the between maid, who was hired for the shooting season and who proved to be a much happier companion than

Eve. Yet Sadie's optimistic presence only served to make Beata's afternoons off emptier than ever.

She should have been enjoying time off herself that Saturday afternoon in November, but one of Sadie's relatives was getting married and Beata had granted this precedence, 'But try and be back for six if you can, I've promised to meet Lucy at half past.'

The between maid promised she would and went off to her wedding.

Hearing a noise from the direction of the side door somewhat earlier than six, Beata looked up from stuffing a bird and asked Eve. 'Is that Sadie at the door?'

'What would she be knocking for?' Eve was stooped over the local evening press, her bottom in the air. 'I never heard nowt.'

Resisting the urge to deal the protruding rear a hefty kick, Beata went back to her task. But, upon hearing a definite knock she looked up again. With Eve ignoring the summons, she sighed and, withdrawing her hand from the bird's cavity, went to answer it herself.

Expecting to see Sadie, her jaw dropped at the smart young man in suit and tie who poised there, beaming at her. 'Tommy!'

Grinning, he rubbed his hands against the cold, his cheeks almost as red as the poppy in his lapel. 'I thought I'd surprise you.'

'You certainly have. Aw, come in!' Wiping her hands furiously on her apron she exchanging a brief but affectionate kiss on the cheek, shepherded him into the kitchen and bade him sit down by the fire, introducing him to Eve, then fussing over him with an invitation to tea.

'I was hoping to take you out for tea.' His eyes were alight with pleasure at seeing her again. 'Then out to the pictures. It's your evening off if I'm not mistaken.' Her letters kept him informed of her rota.

'Yes! Oh, but I'm meeting Lucy.' She slapped her red hands to her cheeks in consternation.

'You still can, if she doesn't mind me tagging along.'

Beata was still overwhelmed at seeing him and beaming foolishly. 'Of course she won't. Oh, I can't believe you're really here! How –?'

'I heard my aunty and uncle were having a weekend excursion to York so I cadged a lift. The boss very kindly let me have today off.' His round face shared her glee, both seemingly oblivious to Eve's surveillance.

'Where are you staying?'

'The people they're visiting said I could kip on the sofa.' His nose starting to run from the sudden rise in temperature, Tommy pulled out his handkerchief. 'It's only up the road there.'

'Well!' Upon another exclamation of astonishment, Beata shook her head. 'Lucy is going to be surprised, isn't she?'

Indeed, her friend was, and so pleased for Beata that she offered to make herself scarce in order that the reunited couple might spend these precious hours together. But neither of them would hear of it, Tommy thoroughly apologetic for being unable to bring Howard with him and presumably spoiling the girls' night out. Lucy seemed genuinely not to care and went on to enjoy her meal and the consequent trip to the cinema, though afterwards she caught a bus somewhat earlier than usual, leaving the sweethearts to spend the last few hours on their own.

Ignoring the hundreds of other couples who drifted hand in hand along the tree-lined riverside path, who fumbled and kissed in the dark, Beata and her lover enjoyed a leisurely walk home, to all intents and purposes alone.

Tommy apologized for the constant urge to claw at his body. 'Sorry for all this scratting, but I think I've acquired a passenger.'

His action infectious, Beata began to scratch too. 'I wouldn't be surprised. The Picture House is a bit of a flea pit.'

'They're going to be charmed with me at my lodgings, aren't they? Let's see if I can get rid of him onto you before we get home.' Both of them chuckling, he curled a possessive arm around her and sighed, 'Eh dear, I can't believe how it's flown.'

'Me neither.' Her breath visible on the air, she snuggled into his warmth, then, suddenly remembering, she turned to him eagerly. 'Oh, what about the holiday? Did you manage to talk Howard into going to the Lakes?'

'No, he says it's too boring – but don't worry, I've found somebody else to go with.' He noted her look of relief. 'Well, you don't think I was going to pass up the chance of a holiday with you, do you?'

She hugged his arm and laid her head on his shoulder. 'Aw, I wish I was going back over the Pennines with you tomorrow. What time do you have to leave?'

'Not till mid-afternoon.'

'Ah, yes,' she remembered he had come by car. 'I suppose you don't have to hang around for hours changing trains.'

'I was hoping you'd spend tomorrow morning with me.'

Her expression showed she was desperate to oblige. 'I have to get Sunday dinner ready but we can meet for church.' It had been such a relief to discover they shared the same religion; she could not have borne a second rejection by some bigoted parent. 'You'll be glad to hear I go to second Mass.'

His reply was warm. 'I'd get up at the crack of dawn if it was to see you. Shall I come and knock you up – Hang on, I'll rephrase that! I meant give you a knock.'

She laughed heartily and, welcoming any chance to prolong their time together, nodded and told him at what time to call. 'Then you can come back for your dinner.'

'Lovely.' He squeezed her shoulders.

'I'm afraid we won't be on our own – Eve and Sadie'll be there – but it's better than nothing.' She steered him to a flight of steps away from the river, sighing that they were almost home. Equally unwilling for the night to end he delayed her for a while with kisses. But finally, the lateness of the hour made it inevitable that they must part. Escorting Beata to her door, he adorned her lips with one last kiss, then bade her a tender good night.

It seemed as if she had no sooner gone to bed than she was getting up, but with her darling Tommy in mind there was an energetic zip to her elbow as she flitted about the kitchen, getting everything ready for breakfast.

The pots were washed, the kitchen cleared and a joint in the oven by the time his smiling face appeared. That others were present, denying the lovers more than a chaste peck, was something of a let-down, but any time spent with Tommy was a joy to Beata.

Donning her hat and gloves, a poppy upon her breast to match the one on his, Beata took his arm and, asking Sadie to keep an eye on the oven, set off for church.

Cold but bright, it was a pleasant walk, the sun illuminating the crenellated limestone walls that in ancient times had defended the city.

'How's your leg today?' Tommy looked down to examine the limb that had been very swollen last night. 'Am I walking too fast for you?'

'No, it's not too bad.' She smiled, pleased that he was so attentive and that his concern was for her comfort rather than embarrassment at being seen with a girl with an elephant leg.

They passed through Fishergate Bar and into a network of mean narrow lanes, the ambience one of poverty. A wrinkled woman in black shawl squatted on her doorstep, puffing on a clay pipe and enjoying a shaft of sunlight. Responding to her Irish brogue, Beata smiled and wished her a good morning.

Almost to their destination, they crossed a road on the corner of which was a graveyard, Tommy assuming, as it was near her church, 'Is that where your parents are buried?'

'No, Father's at Conisbrough, but Mother's in York Cemetery, just back there.'

Approaching her place of worship, she jabbed her thumb over her shoulder, then found herself prevented from entering with the rest of the congregation, Tommy drawing her aside and lowering his voice to beg impulsively: 'Show me! We've only a few hours together. Let's skip Mass and go for a wander round the cemetery. At least we'll have the excuse of being on hallowed ground.'

Misinterpreting her look of alarm he withdrew his invitation. 'Sorry, if you think I'm sacrilegious –'

'No, no, I don't mind jigging off at all!' It would mean she would not have to introduce him to Gussie, who was waiting inside the church; better for the relationship to be kept a secret until it was on firmer ground after the humiliation of being jilted by Jack. 'But I won't be able to show you where Mother's buried.' She had no intention of admitting to a pauper's grave. 'I was only little when she died, then we left York . . .'

'That's all right.' He took her gloved hand, threaded it through the hook of his arm and tucked it fondly under his elbow. 'I'll come clean. My real reason for wanting to get you in there is because it's the only place we won't have any interruptions from anybody. I like Lucy but, truth be told, I could have throttled her last night for being there.'

'Me and all,' chuckled Beata. 'And we're going to be lumbered with Eve when we get back. You're right, let's skedaddle!'

Scampering away from the church, they laughingly retraced their steps, past the Irish grandmother with her halo of pipe smoke, under the arch in the Bar Walls, skirting through the deserted pens of the Cattle Market and onwards until they came to the cemetery whence they sauntered for a good hour, he pausing occasionally to search for her mother's name on the rows of gravestones, she feeling sad that he would never find it.

After a while the lovers sought a place to sit. With the grass too damp they chose a flat patch of stone, preferring to ignore that it was someone's tomb for its epitaph had been obscured by years of rain and wind and lichen. His arm around her, they sat in silence, listening to the birdsong, the only human intrusion a few distant figures tending graves and oblivious to their presence. Even granted such privacy, it didn't seem right to indulge in passion here, but both agreed that it was wonderful just to share each other's company and to fantasize that this was what it would be like if they could be together all the time.

Inevitably, though, Beata was forced to leave this peaceful oasis, saying the dinner wouldn't cook itself.

But when they got back she found to her surprise that besides Sadie's help Eve had been unusually thoughtful. The pans were full of vegetables that merely awaited heat, the Yorkshire pudding had been mixed and the joint had been regularly basted. However, Beata was quick to detect that it was not for her benefit.

'You just sit down there,' Eve told Tommy, pulling out a chair, the fondness of her smile relaying that she, too, had taken a fancy to him, 'and let us women take care of you.'

Tommy in his innocence welcomed all the female attention, and responded good-naturedly to Eve's rather saucy interrogation throughout the meal. Beata seethed with jealousy. Whilst permitting this familiarity and voicing appreciation for Eve's help, she had no intention of being usurped, utterly determined that Tommy would spend his final hours in York with her alone.

Immediately after dinner, with Sadie about her chores and Eve gone to answer the bell from the dining room, she whispered to Tommy, 'I won't be wanted for a while. Let's go down the garden. I'll tidy up later.'

'Won't your employer mind?' he asked.

'No, madam's very kind.' And she threw on her coat.

Returning with her tray to the kitchen but finding it empty, Eve's expectant smile deserted her, but a look out of the window foiled the others' plans and, grabbing her own coat, she hurried after the couple.

Beata gritted her teeth at the sound of the interloper's voice, but donned a smile as Eve caught up with them. Had the tables been turned Eve would have been blunt enough to tell the intruder she was not wanted but Beata was not so impolite. So, the trio made their way around the garden, one of them attempting to make conversation, the other two wishing she would cease her drivel and go away.

It was a cruel end to what had started out as a wonderful surprise. Beata squeezed Tommy's hand, trying to convey all that was forced to remain unsaid, drawing comfort from his response. They were almost back to the house now. Passing a refuse bin, in a fit of irritation she felt a scrap of paper in her pocket screwed it into a tight pellet and tossed it on top.

'Eh, look at her throwing pound notes away!' The eagle-eyed maid pounced, unravelling the ball of paper and brandishing it at Tommy.

Embarrassed and angry, Beata grabbed it from her. 'I still can't get used to this new paper money.'

'She must have more money than sense!' Eve laughed flirtingly at Tommy.

'You're the one with no blasted sense if you can't see when you're not wanted!'

Eve's smile vanished. Hurt and furious she rushed into the house, leaving the couple alone at last.

But Beata was not rejoicing, ashamed that she might have ruined Tommy's estimation of her. 'I shouldn't have said that but she just got me so mad!'

'No, you were right, she's a pain in the arse.' Uncaring that anyone might be watching from the house, he embraced her, both sharing a rueful chuckle over his apt description. 'I think she was God's retribution for us skiving off church.'

'I'd rather have had ten Hail Marys,' muttered Beata, half laughing, half sad that he would soon be leaving and they had enjoyed so little time together. 'It's all right for you – you can go home. I have to work with the bloomin' fish-face.'

'Nothing would give me greater pleasure than to stay.' He drew her even closer, kissing the top of her auburn head.

'I know.' She moulded herself to him, feeling every warm muscle, inhaling the scent of him, tasting his lips. Drawing breath, she looked wishfully into his face. 'Do you think your aunty and uncle might come to York again?'

'I don't know, but you can be sure they'll have a stowaway.' His tone was softly comforting. 'If not, then at least we'll see each other next summer. Eh, I hope Lucy likes my pal. It was really kind of her to suggest you come over to the Lakes for your holidays, otherwise I don't know when we'd have seen each other again.' He could not seem to satisfy his hunger for kisses, planting yet another on her.

'Yes, she's a good friend.' Beata sighed and enjoyed one last passionate kiss before going with him around the house to the main road.

'Till summer then.' Her voice was wan.

'Till summer.' With a final respectful peck, he was gone.

*　　*　　*

484

It had been a mistake to upset Eve, who was to be even more surly towards her, making the dark months of winter seem longer than normal. Added to everything else, there came an announcement that the King was perilously ill. Genuinely troubled by this, Beata put aside her own discomforts and joined the nation in praying for His Majesty's recovery, such massive invocation appearing to work, for an operation was to bring about a miraculous turn of events.

Miraculous not only in regard to the monarch but for Beata too, for after weeks of being incommunicado Eve finally seemed to decide she had been punished enough, opening her renewed dialogue with an announcement from the newspaper that, 'The dear old boy's on the road to recovery after the operation on his lung. I'm so glad, aren't you?'

Beata nodded smilingly, though, gratified as she was for the King, she could not help but think of her poor mother gasping for breath, without benefit of such an operation, sent early to her pauper's grave. Moreover, she knew it would not be long before Eve was back to her churlish self.

The year turned, but at snail's pace. No longer required, Beata's one ray of sunshine departed, though Sadie voiced hopes that the Druces might hire her again later in the year. Beata hoped so too as she waved goodbye, visualizing the long humourless months ahead.

Arriving at a steady rate, Tommy's letters were the only thing to help maintain her optimism. Yet even these were sullied by the waspish complaints from Eve, whose responsibility it was to fetch in the mail. 'Not another one! I'm paid to take in the master and mistress's letters, not as go-between for you and Romeo.' And she would toss his letters across the table, declaring that she could not imagine what he found to put in them. 'He must be crippled with writer's cramp.'

Attributing it to jealousy, Beata ignored her and, choosing to savour her lover's words in private, slipped the envelopes unopened into her pocket, this her best revenge against Eve, who was obviously desperate to hear what was in them but too proud to ask. Only in the privacy of her room would she open them, reading them three or four times before picking up her own pen, her replies bursting with desire for the time they would meet again.

At last it came. The Lake District with its dramatic, sweeping landscape was hardly the place for someone of Beata's disability, and with all the rambling up hill and down dale her leg was fated to spill over the edges of her shoe, agonizing in its distension, but she would have endured much worse just to be in Tommy's company. His and his only. Fond though she was of Lucy, a stronger urge demanded that she and her lover be alone, and here was all manner of dell and crevice that could serve their purpose.

Having noted the intense looks of desire that passed between Beata and Tommy, and fearful for her friend's chastity, Lucy tried to keep an eye on things, but, without being rude to her own companion, there was a limited amount of time she could devote to this purpose and it was inevitable that Beata would slip away.

Alerted to her long absence, Lucy broke off her conversation with Paul and hauled herself from the grassy hummock where the four had earlier picnicked, shading her eyes to scan the empty country-side. 'Beata!' The call went unanswered. She turned worriedly to Paul. 'I'll have to go find them.'

Still on the ground, he raised a hand to coax her back. 'You're acting like her mother!'

Lucy did not retort that that was what she felt like, but simply flashed him an irritated glare before launching into the search in earnest.

He made a grab for her. 'Let them have a bit of privacy and enjoy ours while we can!'

But she shrugged off his grasp. Paul was a good enough con-versation partner but anything more was out of the question. Sighing, he rose, brushed his knees and followed her, adding his voice to hers.

Lucy's calls became more frantic as she imagined what fate might have befallen her young friend – 'Beata! Beata!' – then all of a sudden a dishevelled couple rose out of the ground at her feet, causing first a yelp of shock then relief. 'There you are!'

Red of face, Beata looked most put out, her hand still locked with Tommy's as she asked accusingly, 'What are you playing at?'

'I'm saving you from yourself!' hissed Lucy and, giving Tommy a reproving glare, she grabbed Beata's arm in possessive manner and led her away, leaving the young men to trail in their wake.

'I don't know what you mean,' pleaded Beata.

'You do!' Lucy glanced pointedly at an undone button on the youngster's blouse. 'I know how you feel about Tommy but I hope you haven't let him take advantage.' With no response forthcoming, she demanded, 'Well?'

Beata fastened the offending button, a humorous glint to her eye and a secretive twitch to her lips. 'You'll just have to keep guessing, nosy neb.'

Lucy dealt her a tut of disapproval. 'Eh, I ought to tip you up and tan your bottom!'

But Beata merely chuckled.

A pause, then an anxious enquiry, 'You really didn't do anything, Beat, did you?'

With an impish smirk, Beata stuck her nose in the air, throwing a backwards look to catch her beloved's eye and twinkling at him. 'Tha'll never know.'

'Right, I'm not letting you loose again for the entire holiday!' threatened Lucy.

And indeed she did her very best to fulfil this threat, right up until it was time to catch the train home. Her stern response to her friend's complaint about the lack of liberty being, 'You'll thank me on your wedding day.'

Beata formed a sad smile as yet another wonderful holiday came to an end and she blew kisses from the train, watching the man she adored fade into the distance. 'Aye,' she sighed, 'but when might that be?'

Existing on letters and with another long grind ahead of her, it could have been a time of deep despondency for Beata but for the fact that something totally unexpected happened to her friend. Within a few weeks of returning home, Lucy reported that she too had fallen in love. He was a valet to one of Major Herron's friends who had come down from Scotland to spend a month here.

'He says he'll write when he goes home but oh, Beat, I'm dreading it!' Lucy was breathless with the swiftness of it all. 'Now I know just how you feel.' She clasped her hands to her matronly bosom, portraying rapture.

Delighted for her friend, Beata sympathized that she had not found someone closer to home. 'And it's going to get harder the longer it goes on. Still, I wouldn't have it any other way. I couldn't imagine being with anyone else but Tom.'

'Me neither – with my Harry, I mean!'

'Well I'm right glad for you, Lucy!' Their arms linked as they set off for town, Beata dealt her friend a congratulatory squeeze with her elbow, happy too for another reason. Since she had promised herself to Tommy it had been difficult for the girls to go out together, Lucy turning admirers away rather than expecting her friend to play gooseberry. Now they were on equal footing.

'Do you think it'll work?' Lucy seemed anxious. 'Existing on letters, I mean?'

'It works for us. You can say so much more in a letter, can't you?'

Lucy nodded enthusiastically, the pair of them enjoying desultory chatter for a while until, eventually reaching the cinema, Lucy drew her companion to a halt. 'So, you're truly happy?'

Beata laughed that anyone could doubt it. 'Yes!'

'Good, then I can tell you something. I've been wanting to tell you for a few weeks but I didn't know how you'd take it. Our Jack's getting wed.'

'Oh . . .' Beata was surprised, though not upset. 'When?'

'Next month. You won't believe it, she's a Catholic. Mother kicked up a stink, of course, but Jack was determined this time. What about that then?'

Even secure in her bond with Tommy, Beata felt hurt. Why could Jack not have stood up to his mother for her? It proved how little he had cared. But she donned a genuine smile. 'Give my regards to both of them. I hope they'll be very happy.'

'You can tell them yourself. You're invited to the wedding. You will come?'

'Oh I don't –'

'For me.'

How could she refuse such a good friend? After slight hesitation she replied, 'Yes, I'd be delighted.'

'Good!'

'There's a nice set of pans in Barnitts –'

'Ooh, don't spend too much!' Lucy sought to curb her friend's generosity.

'They're only seven and six. I don't know whether I'm more careful with my money but things seem to be getting cheaper.' The poverty of her childhood long dispatched, Beata was able to afford almost anything she fancied, within reason.

'I'm sure Jack would appreciate anything.' The delicate subject broached, Lucy steered her into the cinema. 'Eh, I wonder which of us'll be next? Aw, I've just thought! What if I have to go and live in Scotland?'

'I'll come and visit you,' chirped her young friend brightly. 'Eh, does he wear a kilt?'

Lucy dealt her a laughing nudge. 'Nay, you soft 'a'p'orth! Will you go and live in Lancashire or will Tommy come here?'

'I'll probably go there.' In truth they had never discussed it.

'You'll come back and be bridesmaid for me, won't you?'

'If you'll be mine,' Beata smiled.

'Really? Oh thanks! I thought what with you having three sisters . . .'

'I'll need a fourth to balance things up.' Beata chewed her lip guiltily. 'I haven't seen them in ages.' She met Augusta regularly in church but had visited neither Mims nor Maddie for many a month. 'I really should go see how they are and arrange for them to meet Tommy.'

First, though, there was Jack's wedding to be endured.

Following a month of worry over the imagined awkwardness of the occasion, she finally stood before her old sweetheart, shaking his hand and congratulating him, and found that it was not half so awful as she had feared. This was, in part, thanks to Lucy, who had kept the promise to support her throughout the afternoon, the same afternoon as her nineteenth birthday. More gratitude was due to the bride, Mary, who was very sweet and, in contrast to the gushing bout of hypocrisy from Mrs Lister, gave Beata a genuinely warm welcome, even though she was aware of what had occurred between this girl and Jack. But the main reason was that she herself experienced no sense of jealousy or loss. Faced with that good-looking groom she did not imagine what it might have been like to stand at the altar beside him – could have been looking at a stranger – envisioned only her own darling Tommy.

Totally relaxed and happy with Lucy at her side, she went on thoroughly to enjoy the wedding breakfast, even refusing to show how upset she was by an overheard confidence from Mrs Lister to a relative: 'I detest the thought of my grandchildren being raised as Catholics but what can you do? We had to do as we were bidden but this generation has no respect for their elders.'

No, if anyone felt awkward it was Jack. He was quite obviously sorry for letting her down. Though unable to express his guilt it showed in his eyes when, slipping away from his bride, he approached Beata towards the end of the afternoon and drew her away from his sister. 'I'm glad you felt able to come, Beat.'

'Thank you for inviting me. I've had a lovely time. And I like Mary very much.'

Warmth lit the groom's eye. 'Yes, she's a grand lass, isn't she?'

489

'Lucy told me you got to keep your job as butler. Will you still be working for the major now or –'

'Yes, he very kindly found us accommodation nearby so nothing's changed really. He even still lets me borrow the car sometimes too.' Jack grinned.

Smiling and thanking him once again for the invitation, she shook his hand then made as if to return to Lucy.

'I just wanted –'

She turned expectantly.

'I wondered, that is, we both wondered . . . we'd like you to be godmother to our first child if we're fortunate enough to be blessed.'

Beata laughed with sheer surprise.

'I know it's a bit premature, but I wanted to ask you in person rather than via Lucy when it becomes fact, and I know you won't be coming here again after today.'

She agreed that this was probably true.

'I'm sorry about Mother,' he blurted.

'Not to worry.' Beata's face was kind. 'I'm happy.'

'I know, our Lucy told me. I'm right glad, Beat. So will you do it for us? I can't think of anyone I'd rather trust.'

'I'll be honoured,' nodded Beata sincerely, and, as she went to take her leave of Lucy, thought what a lovely day this had turned out to be.

With thoughts as to her own betrothal, she asked if her friend would mind very much if she were to spend her next afternoon off visiting her sisters. It was time she prepared them for the event that she might be moving away. 'Gus has had word that Mims'll be going away to work on a farm soon so I'd better get a letter off and see if she can come over to stay.'

'What about the other one?'

'Madeleine's away in the country looking after a patient. God help the patient.' Beata gave her characteristic chuckle, little sound emerging but her whole body shaking and her eyes screwed up in mirth.

Watching all the other guests, Lucy mused, 'Didn't you ever consider becoming a nurse, Beat?'

The question surprised her. 'Whatever made you ask that?'

'I just thought you might be better suited to it than domestic service.'

Beata gave an adamant shake of head. 'Doesn't appeal to me. I'll leave that to our Maddie. I can't see anyone wanting to marry her!'

TWENTY-SEVEN

Maddie loved her work at The Retreat, its forty acres of beautiful grounds, tranquil wards and progressive methods of nursing far removed from the type of grim madhouse that still unfortunately existed elsewhere. General nursing had been rewarding, yes, but for one who had always been tormented because of her name it was much more deeply satisfying to care for these poor bewildered souls who really were mad, temporarily or otherwise.

Esme was one of the temporary variety, her suicidal leanings induced as a result of parturition. She had given birth twice before and had suffered deep melancholy as a result, but it was her third son who was responsible for triggering this extreme reaction. Unrecognizable from the normally loving wife and mother, within a fortnight of him being born she had tried to drown herself in the ornamental pond of her country estate. Fortunately the gardener had been on hand to save her and steps taken to prevent a recurrence, though her wealthy husband had not deemed it fitting that she should be incarcerated in an asylum, and instead a nurse, Maddie, had been summoned to live in.

Mr Black was some years older than his wife. Surprised by Madeleine's youth, he had initially been dubious about this owlish redhead's ability to handle such responsibility, but within hours was reassured.

Ever watchful, but experienced enough to allow Esme sufficient personal freedom so that she did not feel trapped in her own domain, over the months that Maddie had been administering her care she had seen Esme grow from a terrified, self-destructive wreck who could barely tell the time into something resembling

491

a human being. Now there were signs that her assignment would soon be over.

On the one hand glad that her patient was recovered, she would be sorry to leave. It was a beautiful dwelling, not large but elegant, set in two landscaped acres with rolling countryside beyond and maintained by a troop of servants. At first Maddie had been treated as one of them, but, impressed by her tender ministrations to his wife, Mr Black had soon begun to relax his attitude and to recognize just what this girl had done for him and his boys. Perhaps his feelings towards her were engendered by guilt. He purported to love his wife, yet it had been Maddie, not he, who responded to Esme's anguished yells at any hour of the day or night, who wrestled with her to administer medication, then held and stroked her comfortingly till the devils had been exorcized. Whatever his reason, in honour of this he began to include her in the family circle, even inviting her to sit with them at dinner, and whenever they went on an outing Maddie would come along too, not in the role of nurse but, as Esme termed her, 'my dear companion'.

Maddie had grown close to her patient too. Difficult and exasperating though the mentally deranged could be, she found it hard not to, for, leaving aside the illness, Esme was everything she herself could only ever dream of being: dark and elegant, sweet-natured, graceful, ladylike, altogether lovable. But she envied her also, for her house, her servants, her provider. What Maddie would give for a husband such as this. Yet, hungry as she was for the lifestyle, the craving was not just a mercenary one. At first she had seen Mr Black merely as an employer, a stuffed shirt impervious to his wife's suffering whose only reason for hiring a nurse was to avoid the embarrassment of having the world know that his spouse was in an asylum, who, in response to the poor creature's distress, hid his face behind a newspaper whilst someone else dealt with the problem.

But one day, in a moment when his guard was down, she accidentally glimpsed his true character, saw, beyond the panoply of hauteur, a glint of sheer anguish, and she came to understand that his avoidance was not because he did not care but that he cared too much. He could not bear to see Esme suffer and so he pretended that it was not happening, leaving her to Maddie who coped with it so much better. It was in the knowledge of this that the young nurse began to grow close to her patient's husband too, pitying his dreadful plight, for in the throes of delusion Esme could be very tiresome. And in that same knowledge, at some point, Maddie's allegiance began to shift.

Mr Black felt differently towards her too. She could tell. The private words of gratitude were now laced with a look of devotion. A look that said he felt as much for her as she did for him. Sharing such an ordeal, how could he not?

And tomorrow she would be forced to leave, never to see him again.

But there was still tonight and she must make the most of it, as an excited Esme was doing now, donning her new silk evening gown, applying make-up and jewellery, helped by the young nurse who had also become a friend. It had been decided that Mrs Black was well enough now to receive guests, and a dinner party had been arranged for a few close friends. In appreciation of her services Maddie had been invited as guest of honour.

Fastening the diamond clasp of Esme's necklace, Maddie stepped back to smile at the reflection in the dressing-table mirror. 'You look stunning.'

'Thank you, dear.' Poised at her dressing table, Esme's dark-brown eyes glowed with warmth. Then, taking in Maddie's reflection, she appeared to have a sudden thought for she rotated swiftly and announced, 'You must wear something special too!' And so saying she gave access to her wardrobe.

Maddie looked unsure. She was here in the role of nurse and normally wore her uniform. It might be frowned upon to shed it. But, hungry to play the part, at Esme's insistence, she took little persuading.

Clad in midnight-blue silk, a little too long but otherwise a perfect fit, Maddie gazed wondrously into the mirror, fingering the row of pearls at her freckled throat and pretending for that moment that this was her room, her dress, her necklace, her husband. She would have continued to stare for much longer had not Esme disturbed her dream by saying how charming she looked. Taking the offered arm, she went down to dine in the hope that the husband would be equally influenced.

The atmosphere downstairs was all very genteel, everyone in evening dress. Far from feeling out of place, Maddie adored it and, maintaining the fantasy in her mind that she was lady of the house, fitted in perfectly, until the two little boys and the baby were brought into the drawing room to say good night to their parents. Watching Esme and her husband – yes, *her* husband, Maddie told herself, not yours – watching them fuss over their children her composure

493

slipped and instantly she shrank to her true position, just a nurse who was here to tend a patient, a nurse who would be gone tomorrow and soon forgotten. But then he glanced at her over Esme's head, held her eye with such warmth, such love, that she just knew she had not been mistaken, and hope was rekindled.

The children were put to bed, the adults went in to dine and Maddie was back in control. Disappointed not to be seated next to Mr Black, she soon discovered why he preferred the chair opposite. Throughout the meal there were so many desirous looks exchanged between them that she felt sure one of the other guests must have noticed. It was the most wonderful evening of her life.

Having endured a quiet existence for so many months, Esme was worn out by the excitement and apologized to her guests as first coffee, then brandy was poured in the drawing room. 'Oh, it's been so lovely to see you all! But would anyone mind if I went to bed? I'm utterly exhausted.'

After joking apologies for being so boring, the close family friends said that of course they did not. 'We ought to be going soon ourselves,' added one.

'Oh no, stay and keep Charles company,' begged Esme. 'He's had such a miserable time of it lately and it's been such a magnificent evening.' She began to glide to the door.

Bitterly dissatisfied, Maddie rose from the chintz armchair to accompany her.

But Esme insisted that she did not require help. 'Please, Madeleine, you too must stay and enjoy your last night here. I insist.'

Trying to disguise her joy, Maddie turned enquiringly to Mr Black.

'If that is what my wife commands then that is what you must do.' And with a smile he summoned her back to the circle.

After the door closed on Esme the others stayed for only a short while, but it was worth it just to be granted an extra half an hour in his company. In addition there was the opportunity to keep up her fantasy as the guests finally left, Maddie standing at Black's elbow as he bade everyone good night, nodding genteelly and pretending that she was mistress of the house.

The maid closed the door, the hall fell quiet. A moment of despondency ensued: it was all over, she must go to bed.

Until he said, 'I noticed you didn't finish your brandy, Madeleine. Was it not to your taste?'

She hastened to assure him that it had been very palatable. 'I just didn't have time to drink it.'

'Then you must.' He indicated for her to accompany him back to the drawing room.

Heart pulsating, she hesitated only slightly, then complied.

He picked up her glass of unfinished brandy. 'Would you care for a top-up?'

'Thank you.' She wondered whether he would come to sit on the sofa beside her, but after handing her the crystal he took a separate chair.

However, it was close enough for intimacy. 'I wanted to tell you how greatly I appreciate all that you've done for my wife and for me too.'

Maddie looked modest. 'I've only done the job I'm paid to do.' Then her heart pitched as she realized how this might sound and she added hastily, 'Though, of course, I care greatly for Mrs Black's welfare.'

There was kindness in his smile. 'I can tell you do.'

'I'm so glad she's recovered.'

'So am I. So am I.' Gaze downcast, he stared thoughtfully into his glass, swilling its contents round occasionally. 'But I shall be sorry to see you go.' He looked up then, looked her directly in the eye making her heart beat even faster. 'I'm ashamed that in all the time you've been here I've never taken the time to ask about yourself.'

Her sandy, almost non-existent eyebrows arched in surprise. 'There's nothing much to tell.'

'I know that's not the case. I've watched you. You have remarkable attributes for one so youthful and I'd like to know from whom you inherited them.'

Taking a deep breath, she said, 'Father was an infantry officer. He's dead now, so is Mother.'

'I'm sorry to hear it. And what of the rest of your family?'

'I've three brothers – I don't see much of them; they live elsewhere – and three sisters.'

'And are they nurses like you?' He ran his eyes over her auburn hair.

'No, the youngest one's a scholar and the other two are married. In fact,' she looked around the room, 'this house reminds me very much of my elder sister's.' One after another the lies slipped out.

'Ah, I suppose that's why you appear to be so at home here.' Black smiled and shifted in his chair.

'Yes, I've been very comfortable,' she murmured unblushingly, then lowered her sandy lashes and took a sip of her brandy.

The discourse continued for a while longer. Plied with soft

enquiry, she responded with romance, ashamed of her true background and desperately wanting to remain on a par with her host, not out of any spiteful notion that he would leave his wife for her, but simply for the moment; the last they would have together.

The moment lasted longer than she could have hoped for. He prolonged his intimate quizzing of her long after midnight, showing great reluctance upon finally rising from his chair in order that the servants might be allowed to go to bed. As they made their way up the staircase together and paused on the landing for a second it appeared to Maddie that he was expecting her to go with him, for he took her hand and his green eyes bored into hers for long moments. But just when she felt ready to faint, he dealt her hand a swift kiss and said, 'Thank you for everything, Madeleine. Good night.' And he swivelled on his patent shoes and strode away.

'Good night,' she whispered, then hurried to her own room, pressing her shoulders against the door for a while and listening alertly with breathless anticipation before accepting that he had truly gone.

Thrill mingling with sadness, she too went to bed.

'Dear Madeleine,' said Esme with a little moan in her voice at the breakfast table next morning, 'we *are* going to miss you.'

Back in her nurse's uniform, Maddie felt wretched, both at leaving and for the thoughts that had kept her awake most of the night. 'I shall miss you too. Oh, by the way, I left your dress and necklace on my bed. Thank you very much for the loan of them.'

Esme shared an intimate smile with her husband. 'Mr Black and I should like you to keep them,' she spoke above Maddie's gasp of astonishment, 'as a token of our gratitude and esteem.'

Ignorant over whether such a gift as pearls would be in order, Maddie was not about to refuse, and stuttered her thanks.

Ultimately this lovely interval came to its rightful conclusion. Her case packed, the job done, Nurse Kilmaster stood in the hall waiting for the car to be driven round, in the meantime taking leave of the little boys who had been brought in to shake her hand.

The Blacks insistent on accompanying her to the train, she was chauffeured to a small but busy country railway station where on the platform she finally took her leave of them.

'Thank you once again for everything.' Black removed his hat and engaged her hand in a sincere grip, the intensity of his feelings travelling up Maddie's arm and into her heart. In a panic now that she would never see him again, she gazed into his eyes, imploring silently, *Give me a sign, tell me you want me to stay.*

But his only response was to let go and step aside, allowing his wife to deliver her own gratitude with a fond kiss to Maddie's cheek.

Bereft, she managed to conjure a smile and waved to both of them from the train, pleased with a job well done, happy that Esme was well again, but sorrowful to be leaving the man about whom she would dream all the way home.

Bright of eye, Esme flourished her handkerchief until Maddie's train disappeared into the distance, then, linking her husband's arm, made her way back to where the car awaited. 'The house won't be the same without her, will it?'

He opened his mouth but his response was drowned by an announcement about the next train and instead he merely smiled.

Reaching the car she gave an exclamation. 'Oh, how silly, I left my bag on the bench.'

Black addressed his chauffeur. 'Johnson –'

'No, I'll go. It won't take a sec!' A smiling Esme hurried back into the station.

Ordering the chauffeur to start the car, her husband lit a cigarette and wandered over to a patch of sunshine to wait, holding his thoughtful face to the light.

The cigarette had acquired half an inch of ash before he noticed Esme was very slow to return. He was about to go to find her when screams of horror alerted him. Rushing back to the platform he discovered that his wife had hurled herself under a passing express.

Maddie had only learnt about it when she had gone back to work the following day.

'Don't blame yourself, Nurse,' Matron had said kindly after announcing the awful news. 'There was nothing you could have done. She was obviously determined.'

'But she seemed totally recovered – the doctor thought so too!' Maddie's heart was in her throat, her face distorted by shock and anguish.

Matron remained calm. 'I know. She fooled everyone, even her husband. He has told me I'm not to confer blame on you, nor would I. You could not have done more for your patient. Now, it is all very sad but you must put it from your mind and go and tend those who still need you.'

Though totally numbed, Maddie had thanked her superior and done as instructed.

That had been several weeks ago, since when the shock had lessened, only to be replaced by guilt and shame. Had Esme seen the connection between her husband and this so-called nurse? Interpreted the desire in Madeleine's eyes? Was that what had pushed her onto that track? These thoughts obsessed her as she curled despondently in a chair one evening after work, staring into the fire. Only when the rapping of her door knocker became too loud to ignore did she manage to break away from them.

'Were you in the lav?' Beata's stocky little figure tripped over the threshold of her sister's dingy lodgings, wiping her feet as she went. 'I've been knocking for ages.'

'No, I was just hoping whoever it was would go away if I ignored them long enough.'

Familiar with her sister's sense of humour, Beata made a jocular retort. 'Eh, I could have gone to watch Lon Chaney instead of coming here, you know.' Then, perched on a rickety wooden seat, she spoke more understandingly. 'I suppose the last thing you want is visitors straight after your shift.'

'No, I'll put up with you, as long as you don't stay too long.' Face deadpan, Maddie curled back into her saggy old armchair. 'Mash a pot of tea if you want one.'

'I've not long eaten.' Prior to coming here Beata had made the most of her afternoon off, first a tour of the shops, then egg and chips at a café.

'As long as *you're* all right, then.'

Interpreting satire, Beata withheld the riposte and went to put the kettle on, noticing that the other kept rubbing her knuckles as if in discomfort. 'What's up with your hand?'

'Arthritis,' came the dull response.

'I thought it was only old people got that.'

'Shows what you know then, doesn't it?'

It was not said nastily, just in Maddie's usual tone, but Beata felt her spirits plummet. Was there any wonder it had taken her weeks to carry out her intended visit? She had come here as a dutiful sister to bestow upon Maddie the honour of being attendant at her wedding and this was how she was treated. Spooning tea into the pot, she asked, 'Have you been to the doctor's?'

'Yes. There's nothing they can do. I've got it for life.' Punishment, came Maddie's silent thought, not just her hands afflicted but the rest of her joints too, her whole body seared with pain, right down to her little toe.

'Can I get you some aspirin?'

'I've had some.'

Sympathizing, Beata waited for the tea to brew and looked around the disordered room, wondering whether it was pain or sheer idleness that forbade Maddie to clean up after herself. There was a selection of clean laundry that had been ironed but not put away and was draped over every available bit of furniture. 'Shall I put these in the cupboard for you?'

Still kneading her painful joints, Maddie nodded. 'Aye, I might as well make use of you now you're here.'

Beata went about collecting the linen. Carrying it to a tallboy she found the interior scattered with mouse droppings. 'You've got mice in your drawers.'

'I wondered what was tickling me.'

Beata was forced to chuckle. Laying aside the linen she gathered the black specks, disposed of them, then removed the rest of the contents. 'This sheet'll need washing, they've widdled over it as well – eh, what's this?' A flat velvet box lay at the bottom of the drawer.

Maddie had no need to look. 'Pearls: they were a gift from a patient.' Her tone was even but her heart wept for Esme.

Gaping at the lustrous string of beads, Beata was astonished. 'My God! I think I will be a nurse.'

Maddie responded with sarcasm. 'If you're intending to rummage through the rest of my belongings, I'll save you the trouble, she gave me a silk dress too. It's in the wardrobe.'

Beata clicked her tongue. 'I'm only helping you tidy up!' Any further retort was interrupted by a tap at the door. When Maddie did not move, her sister donned a cynical expression. 'I suppose I'm answering that, am I?'

'You're the nearest, Beat.'

But the disgruntled air vanished upon laying eyes on the box of crimson roses that was delivered by a neighbour, Beata returning all excited. 'Apparently these came while you were at work!'

'Shove them in the bin,' ordered her sister darkly.

Beata was incredulous. 'You don't even know who they're from!'

'I do.' It was not the first bunch she had received from him. 'Now do as you're told and put them in the bloody bin.'

Puzzled and greatly reluctant, sniffing the red roses as she went,

Beata moved towards the back door, but at the last minute refused to carry out such profane command. 'If you want to throw them away then do it yourself, you ungrateful devil! Somebody's spent good money on them. He must think a great deal about you.'

Maddie looked at her then, eyes like slivers of steel. 'I'll tell you what he thinks. He thinks I'm the skivvy that's going to run round after him and his three lads, but he's sadly mistaken!'

There was a tense interval, during which Beata stared at her sister's face, trying to intuit the other's expression. Did it truly depict anger or was that merely to conceal a deeper emotion? She was the one to break the silence, asking tentatively, 'Are they from the same person who gave you the pearls?'

'No! I told you they were from a female patient.' Eventually, with a pained grimace, Maddie relented but, unable to confess what so disturbed her, gave only half the tale. 'All right, if you must know, they are connected in a way. She committed suicide. The roses are from her husband in gratitude for what I did for her when she was alive. Somehow, probably because we were shoved together for so many months, he's got this daft idea that I can give him the sort of tender care that I gave her. It's grief playing tricks on him, that's all it is.' She paused, wondering whether she had said too much, but finally admitted, 'It's not just the roses. He's been sending me letters too, suggesting marriage. I can't give everything up just at the drop of a hat, Beat.'

'Well, if you don't care for him . . .' Beata shrugged.

Maddie hesitated, wrestling with her feelings, then blurted, 'I do like him – but can you honestly see me bringing up three boys, one of them only a baby?'

'No, not really.' Beata's sister had never seemed to share her own affection for children.

'No.' Maddie gave a firm nod of confirmation. 'He'll soon find somebody else, someone more suitable. There's other folk who need me more. No, I've made my decision. My life belongs to my patients.' Her demeanour was resolute.

Feeling frivolous that she had come here to discuss weddings and bridesmaid's frocks, Beata picked at her fingers. 'You mean, you'll never marry?'

Maddie shook her head.

Deciding not to broach the subject of her own wedding now, Beata went to pour the tea and shortly after drinking it went home, seeing her sister through new eyes and thinking how admirable was Madeleine's stance.

The one left behind curled her agonized body into the faded moquette of the chair, once more to brood upon her thoughts, wondering if Beata had seen through the lie, that behind her determined vocation lay the most appalling sense of guilt.

Having gone out before the afternoon post arrived, Beata asked when she got in somewhat earlier than usual on her evening off, 'Was there a letter for me?'

'No.' Eve looked at her expectantly and was about to say more.

But sensing that the parlourmaid was about to delegate some chore, Beata forestalled her. 'Right, well, I think I'll have an early night then.'

In the morning, dallying outside the church after Mass, she told Augusta about her conversation with Madeleine and the noble decision that their sister had made. 'I ended up not saying anything about Tommy. She made me feel quite shallow.'

Gussie absolved her. 'Nay, it's natural for any lass to want marriage. If Madeleine wants to devote herself to other things that shouldn't stop you doing as you choose.' She sighed for Mr Black's cruel bereavement. 'Poor man – but at least he's fortunate enough to be wealthy. I know it can't make up for his loss but he's got it a lot easier than some. Poor Mr Melody's just been left with half a dozen children and he's got no job, you know.'

Watching the man in question trudge gloomily to his home just a short way along the street from the church, his clan in procession, Beata gave a sad nod, recalling her own mother's demise and all the other unhappy memories that went with it.

'I feel desperately sorry for him.' Gussie was still concentrating on the widower's plight. 'I've been thinking of offering help but their grief's still fresh. Anyhow, I've got enough on my hands at the moment, what with Uncle Matt.'

'Is he no better?' asked Beata. Their uncle had been bedridden for some weeks.

Gussie shook her head. 'Aunt Lizzie's none too well either.'

'Can I give you a hand with anything?' Beata should really have been starting on dinner, but family came first.

'No, but they'd love to see you if you've a minute to nip in.'

Beata said that of course she had and went along the terraced street with her sister to visit their elderly relatives.

She was glad that she had, for a few days later Gussie dropped by to tell her Uncle Matt was dead. Whilst hardly shocking, for he had been old and ill, Beata had liked his dry sense of humour and shed a little tear as she poured her sister an early morning cup of tea, the two of them reminiscing about other family members until Eve came in with the newspaper and a pile of letters.

'Oh, am I intruding?' She stopped upon seeing the grave expressions.

'No, you're all right, I've got to go to work.' Gussie rose and, telling Beata she would let her know about the funeral arrangements, subsequently left.

'Our uncle's died,' Beata explained to the maid.

'Suppose you'll be wanting extra time off then.'

'Well, it would be nice to pay my respects to Aunt Lizzie.' Beata spoke through gritted teeth. 'Don't worry, I shan't be long. She only lives in Edwin Street.'

Eve cocked her head as if thinking, then exclaimed, 'Oh, you mean those slums.'

Though insulted, Beata saw that the term was not far from the truth. Prior to working in domestic service she had not truly appreciated the great divide in living conditions. The abodes of her mother's kin, which she accepted as normal, could rightly be termed slum-dwellings. But, knowing it had been Eve's intention to offend, she maintained a dignified silence.

'I hear they're to come down,' added Eve, sorting through the letters. 'And not before time. It's full of disease is Walmgate.'

Beata's nostrils were white as she launched into her morning tasks. 'Well, it won't bother Aunt Lizzie. She's on the list to get one of those nice council houses up Tang Hall. Hadn't you better wake Colonel and Mrs Druce?'

'In a minute.' Eve yawned and put the letters aside, now perusing the headline. 'I wonder if they'll be affected by this Wall Street Crash business. There's one thing for sure, it won't bother me. I've got no money to waste on stocks and shares.'

Recalling the many strikes and lock-outs of her childhood and the political opinions of her father, Beata was spurred by mischief. 'Well, if you think that then you're dafter than you look. It'll affect everybody whether they've any money or not, so if you've any sense at all you won't risk your job by idling there.'

Unable to think of a suitable retort, Eve snorted and minced across the kitchen to make a pot of tea, rattling cups and saucers onto a tray then taking it up to her employers' bedroom, leaving the young cook to reflect on her uncle's death.

*   *   *

502

What with all the upset of the funeral, Beata did not notice that there still had been no letter from Tommy. But once back to her usual routine, she thought to ask Eve, who sifted through the morning post, 'Is there anything for me?'

The answer was negative, and continued to be so right into December, even though Beata had sent several letters of her own. This was so out of character for Tommy, who normally answered all her correspondence promptly, that she began to suspect that Eve was hiding her mail out of spite. The parlourmaid seemed to take such delight in pre-empting Beata – 'Before you ask, there's nowt for you!' – that the young cook was positive her suspicions were correct. She had just plucked up enough courage to take Eve to task when Christmas brought a card, drawing huge relief that she had not acted upon her hasty conclusions.

But then there had been no letter accompanying the card, and nothing else was to come. Three whole months of the new decade were to pass and now it was almost spring. Once again the suspicion began to worm itself through Beata's worried mind. It had to be sabotage. In confirmation of this the parlourmaid had been acting even more strangely of late, rushing to the door the second she heard the letters fall through – and Eve had never been known to rush in her life.

Deciding to creep after her one morning, following the arrival of second post, Beata suffered a jolt as she saw Eve slip an envelope into her apron pocket, and immediately all doubt was erased. Before the culprit could turn round she had pounced on her with an accusation: 'I knew it was you hiding my mail!'

Jumping with shock, Eve whirled round, dealt Beata a furious gasp then rushed along the corridor to the kitchen with Beata after her. 'It's not yours, you stupid twerp!'

'Show me then!' demanded the young cook, hands on hips.

'Keep your voice down!' snarled an angry Eve, then dragged the envelope from her pocket and thrust it under Beata's nose. 'See – it's got my name on it!'

'Oh . . .'

'Yes, oh! How *dare* you accuse me of such an underhand thing?'

Beata was immediately contrite and embarrassed. 'I'm sorry, you were just so secretive . . .'

'Because I didn't want the mistress to know I've gone after another job!' hissed Eve. After glaring for a while she made great play of sifting through the rest of the letters and shoving one of them at Beata. 'There! Is that what you've been gagging for?'

'At last – thanks!' Beata grabbed it, confirmed Tommy's hand-writing and with an expression of relief held it to her breast before unusually ripping it open straight away, she was just so eager to read it. 'I'm very sorry I was –'

'Never mind!' It was not said forgivingly but with a note of impatience as Eve opened her own letter. Immediately she gave an exclamation of triumph. 'Oh blimey, I've got it!'

'Congratulations.' Eager to read Tommy's news, Beata tossed her a brief but genuine smile, feeling dreadful at having voiced such an accusation. 'Will you be better off?'

'I should say so! I'll be housekeeper.'

'Housekeeper?' Beata tried to appear impressed, then quickly lowered her face to her own letter so that Eve might not see the amused twinkle in her eye. There must have been a few lies told for her to be hired in that demanding role.

'I'll have to give notice straightaway.' An excited Eve was already making plans. 'In fact I think I'll do it this minute.' Shuffling the rest of the mail into a neat pile she put it on a silver tray and flounced towards the passage that led to the sitting room.

Left in peace, Beata for once ignored her workpile and made herself comfortable in a fireside chair to savour the letter for which she had had to wait so long.

> *Dear Beata,*
>
> *I'm sorry it's taken me such an age to reply to all your many letters but I've had to think very carefully before putting pen to paper. Things can appear very cold when written in black and white and I don't want it to seem as if I've been trifling with your feelings because that's the last thing I intended. I've thought about this very long and carefully. There's no arguing that you and I get on awfully well and I'm still deeply fond of you but I'm forced to say I don't think anything is going to come of our relationship, us living so far apart as we do.*

Ice began to encrust her heart.

> *We've only seen each other a couple of times in the three years we've known each other and lovely as your letters are you can't form a relationship on paper, can you? You'll want to get married some day and so do I. The fact is, I met someone else a while ago and we've been seeing quite a lot of each other . . .*

It was so unexpected that she was almost tipped from her chair by shock. She stared at the words, unable to believe what she was reading.

> *I'm sorry, I had no intention of hurting you or deceiving you and I'll always regard you with affection but I would beg your understanding on this matter and ask you to release me. I love this girl deeply and with your permission would like to ask her to marry me.*

'Well she wasn't best pleased!' Eve's voice intruded as if through a tunnel, Beata too stunned to react as the parlourmaid returned from her mission. 'What excuse has he got for himself then?'

Face frozen, Beata stared through her. There seemed little point in lies. 'He's asked me to stand aside so he can marry somebody else.' It felt as if another was speaking the words, as if in some nightmare.

It was Eve's turn to be shocked now, though never could it be as acute as the one Beata had suffered. 'Sorry . . .' Hesitant at first, she came to sit down, her tone unusually sympathetic. 'And are you going to?'

'What?' Beata looked and sounded dazed.

'Stand aside?'

The reply was dull. 'Yes.'

Eve reared. 'Well, I know what I'd do if it were me he'd been stringing along!'

Throbbing now with grief and traumatism, an enormous lump in her throat, Beata tried to focus on something else. 'What did Mrs Druce have to say to you leaving?'

'Oh, she gave me a right snotty lecture!' Easily diverted to a more personal topic, Eve launched into a tirade as Beata had hoped she would, allowing the jilted cook to avoid a grilling.

Slipping the unfinished letter into her pocket, with wooden movements Beata went back to her duties. Yet there could be no real escape not even in work, for throughout that day and for many days to come she was to constantly torture herself over what she might possibly have done to forfeit Tommy's love.

TWENTY-EIGHT

Lucy found the news almost as hard to palate as Beata when, a week later, she came to Briar House. Set for an evening in town, she had entered the kitchen full of verve; now she was incensed that her dearest friend had been hurt. After furious denouncement of Tommy, she sat there at the table, deeply pensive.

'Anyway, it's all over and done with now. Don't let it put the kibosh on your good news.' Beata drummed the table, waiting expectantly.

One arm resting on the chenille cloth, the other propping up her chin, Lucy frowned and rolled a cautious eye. 'What do you mean?'

'Well, I could tell by the grin on your face when you came in that you were bursting to tell me summat.' Speaking cheerfully, Beata marvelled that she could hide her pain so effectively.

It did not fool Lucy, who wondered how she was ever going to reveal her own glad tidings to this heartbroken girl. 'Oh, it was summat nor nowt – gone clean out of my head now. Are we going to make tracks? The curtain'll be going up if we're not nippy.'

'Hang on.' Beata narrowed her eyes, pinning Lucy with a shrewd expression. 'You're getting married, aren't you?'

Her friend was amazed. 'How on earth did you know?'

'It didn't take much guessing. Aw, I'm right glad for you!' Smiling fondly, she gripped Lucy's hand across the table and enthused for several seconds about the wedding before announcing, 'Well, that's the second piece of good news I've had today: Eve's leaving tonight and bloody good riddance.' The parlourmaid was upstairs at the moment so it was safe to malign her. 'I've engineered for Sadie to be hired in her place so at least I'll have a friend to go out with when you're up in Scotland.'

An accusing laugh spilled from Lucy's red lips. 'Eh, I haven't gone yet and you've already lined somebody up to take my place!'

'No one could ever take your place, sis. Eh, and I expect to be bridesmaid.' Eyes twinkling, Beata wagged her finger, her devil-may-care attitude encouraging her friend to make excited plans as they set off for the theatre.

Once tagged on to the end of the queue, though, they spoke more discreetly, sparing a thought for the group of unemployed men who chorused to avoid starvation. There had been many such destitute souls along the way, collecting pennies in their greasy, ragged caps, and it was a relief when the queue finally started moving.

Grinning enthusiastically at Lucy to show she was unaffected by the recent rejection, Beata wriggled her bottom into the velvet seat and fixed her eyes on the stage as the lights went down and the curtain up. Once it was dark, however, she allowed her façade to drop.

An air of anticipation settled on the audience. Women had been urged to see this play, *Journey's End*, for it showed what life had really been like at the front. Recalling a distant night when a little girl had sat at the foot of the stairs eavesdropping, Beata was already familiar with what her father and his comrades had endured, but was none the less moved by the poetry of a generation's suffering as depicted here, the skill of the actors making that artificial dugout seem all too convincing. Others too were overcome, the auditorium haunted by tearful sniffing and blowing of noses.

This being so, it seemed safe enough now to allow a tear to slide down her own cheek without fear of exposing the true reason for her misery.

There was no need to keep up the act in front of Gus, who knew all too well what it was like to have her dream snatched away. But the pouring out of her heart after Mass did little to ease Beata's wound and there was the added embarrassment of having to admit she had been jilted a second time.

'Perhaps I'm not cut out for marriage.' The eyes were dry but the voice hopeless.

'What a defeatist!'

'Well, you can talk.'

'You know why I turned Vincent down!' Gussie sounded hurt. 'I couldn't bring children into the world knowing I might infect them with this awful disease I'm carrying.'

'Sorry.' Beata hung her head.

Her sister forgave her. 'But there's no good reason why you can't marry. The right man might be just around the bend.'

Beata forced a chuckle. 'He'd have to be round the bend if he took up with me.'

'Stop running yourself down,' scolded Gussie. 'I'm trying to tell you something. Aunt Kit was jilted twice before she met Uncle Worthy.'

'Really?' Despite her melancholy, Beata showed interest.

'Yes! Aunt Ethel told me. So don't go writing yourself off before you're even twenty-one. In the meantime you can take your mind off it by coming and helping me look after people less fortunate than yourself. I think Aunty Lizzie's losing her marbles and the Melody clan's in a right state. Those poor bairns without a mother . . .'

'Go on then. I've a bit of time to spare before I have to get the veg on.' And, hoping this act of altruism would deaden the pain, though without much confidence, Beata went across the road with her sister to offer her help to the Melodys.

Their knock brought a neglected little boy to the door, his hair overgrown and full of knots, his mouth smeared with dried food. Carrying Gussie's message to his father, he returned to bid the visitors come in.

Mr Melody did not greet their entry, did not even smile, just kept looking into the fire and smoking his pipe. It was left to Mary to offer them a cup of tea, she having recognized Beata from their schooldays. Due to their father's enforced absence for the greater part of the war, there was a large gap in the ages of his children; whilst some were as old as Beata others were still at primary school.

'We just came to say we were very sorry to hear about your loss and to see if there's anything we can do to help,' explained Gussie.

She and Beata eyed the gathering, not daring to look at each other for fear of revealing their horror and insulting their host. The house stank of rotten apples, signifying bugs, and whilst the older offspring had retained some semblance of grooming, the youngsters looked crumpled and rather wild.

'Can ye get me a job?' Mick had been on the dole for months. The young women shook their heads apologetically. 'Then there's nothing ye can do,' he said in his quiet brogue.

Beata wondered how to tell him he was neglecting his children.

Augusta found the necessary diplomacy. 'I remember how hard it was when Mother died. I was younger than Mary, of course, but it was a difficult job. I'm sure you could do with a hand looking after the little ones, couldn't you?' She glanced at the eldest, who consulted her father.

Mick gave a sad shrug, unaware that he addressed Probyn's daughters when he said, 'If you've nothing better to do who am I to stop yese.'

Had Beata known Mick in his youth she would have asked herself what had happened to such a kind and amiable, creative man. But, upon departure from the Melody household some ten minutes later, all she could picture was a human wreck who was going to use her sister as a workhorse, given half the chance.

'It's very sad but don't let them abuse your charity,' she sought to warn Gussie before setting off for Fulford.

'Of course I won't. But Mary's at college. She's really academic, you can't expect –'

'College or no, she's the same age as me.' Beata was firm. 'She's not incapable – and neither is her other sister.'

'Eh, you're so aggressive! Just because we never had a chance doesn't mean they should be denied it. I'll just be giving them a bit of help, that's all.'

'Well, make sure it is.' Beata pointed a finger, but had no further time to tarry for there was the Sunday dinner to cook.

Once on her own again, her thoughts were overwhelmed by images of Tommy.

Not the sort to wallow, over the following months she tried very hard to put him out of her mind, especially on the day of her best friend's wedding. But skilled though she was at conjuring a sunny smile for the photographs, she feared she would never get over such loss. Despite what Gussie said, Beata had the feeling that there would be no more chance of matrimony for her, for she had already met Mr Right; even if someone else were to come along she could not envisage such strength of feeling as she had for that dear man. Besides, there was very little time for meeting anyone, other than on holiday, for she was kept very busy and only had one afternoon off a week, and with Lucy married there would be no one with whom to go on holiday now. An approach to Sadie had been unfruitful, the parlourmaid handing most of her wages to her mother and only able to afford the occasional evening out.

So, life drifted on in the same routine. Another Christmas, another festive meal to cook. Sweating over its preparation, Beata listened to the radio that Mrs Druce had kindly installed for her, an Empire-wide round-up, bringing messages from people in all walks of life from as remote corners of the globe as it was possible to imagine. At one time keen to travel, today the distant, foreign voices only served to emphasize Beata's own sense of isolation.

The next year looked like being much the same too, 1931 getting off to an unpromising start with the death of Uncle Horace. But on a personal front things began to perk up when it turned out that Beata was to get a holiday after all, Lucy inviting her to come to stay with her and Harry in Scotland.

It was marvellous to see her friend again, especially given the news that she would be expected to play godmother later in the year. As ever, the time simply flew by and it was soon back to hard work, but before she left, arrangements were made for Beata's coming-of-age, Lucy promising that she and Harry would come down to York and treat their dear friend to a birthday meal at a posh restaurant and a trip to the theatre. 'Unless you'd rather spend it with family of course,' she added.

Beata laughingly refused, saying that a posh restaurant was preferable to a fish and chip supper, besides which, 'Probably none of them will remember anyway.'

It looked as if she would be right in part, for when, some weeks later, the mail arrived on the day of her twenty-first birthday none of the envelopes was for her. Though slightly hurt, she did not let it affect her work. It didn't really matter anyway for there was this evening's celebration to look forward to, Lucy having confirmed days ago upon arrival in York that the restaurant and theatre tickets were all in hand. In actuality, there had been a nice surprise the night before when Maddie had turned up bearing a card and a tin of shortbread biscuits with nursery rhyme characters depicted on both tin and contents. The fact that none of her other siblings appeared to have remembered this special date made this exceptionally welcome and she smiled now at the brightly coloured tin in passing.

She was still looking happy when Sadie returned from taking breakfast to the dining room, her otherwise empty tray bearing a brown envelope, which she handed to Beata.

'I hope this isn't going to spoil your day. Sorry, I took it up assuming it was for Colonel Druce, but it's got your name on.'

Beata groaned at the thought of what officialdom it might contain, handling the missive with apprehension.

But upon opening it she gave an exclamation of delight. 'Eh, it's a cheque for eight quid!'

'Struth!' Downing her tray, Sadie rushed over, hovering eagerly to find out the contents of the letter that the cook was now reading.

'If I understand this correctly,' frowned Beata, 'it's army pension that accrued after I ran away from home. Apparently if you leave before you're sixteen they stop paying it to your guardian, save it up and give it you when you're twenty-one.' She looked up, excitement written all over her face. 'I must have nearly two years' worth. Flamin' Nora, I've never been so rich!'

'Ooh, what're you going to buy with it?' Sadie appeared as excited as the recipient.

'Well, I've always wanted a piano,' mused Beata. 'But I shan't blow it all on that. They've got some reconditioned ones on easy terms at Jays, no deposit and five bob a week. I doubt Mrs Druce will let me have it here, though, I'll have to store it at Aunt Lizzie's – Oh, I shall have to buy her something, and my sisters of course.'

Whilst she and Sadie were still enthusing a knock came at the side door and the latter went to answer it. 'Here's one of your sisters now, Cook.'

'How do, birthday girl!' A smiling, but rather tired-looking Gussie handed over a card. 'I thought I'd save on a stamp.'

'Aw, thanks, Gus!' Sorry for having doubted her, Beata opened the envelope and, after reading the card, placed it on the mantel next to Maddie's. 'That's lovely. You're early. Have you been at Mass?'

'Nay, I've just finished work.'

Prompted by the smell of ale that emanated from her sister's clothing, Beata remembered then. 'Oh, you got that cleaning job at the Tower Brewery?'

Gussie nodded. 'Anyway, many happy returns.'

Beata thanked her again and invited her to sit down whilst she made a pot of tea. 'Can I get you some toast?'

'I don't want to hold you up . . .'

'It's all right, the family's eating breakfast and they like to take their time.'

'I'll see to things, Cook,' offered Sadie. 'It's your birthday; you have a chat with your sister, tell her about your good luck.'

Beata wasted no time in doing so. Gussie was amazed at such an amount of money. 'Eh, we'll have to start calling her Van Der Bilt,' she joked to Sadie.

Beata grinned and told her about the piano, then, eyeing her sister's shabby garment, said, 'You must come into town with me one day and I'll treat you to a new coat.'

Though grateful, Gussie scolded her. 'Nay, don't be flinging it around. It'll be gone before you know it. I'm sorry I couldn't afford to buy you a present, Beat.'

'A card's quite sufficient.' Toasting bread over the fire, Beata glanced up as the bell in the dining room tinkled.

Sadie went off to answer it.

Gussie pulled something from her coat pocket. 'Anyway, I thought I'd lend you this to wear on your night out.' It was the silver watch she had been given by their father.

Touched, Beata said she would hand it back on Sunday.

After chatting for only a short time Gussie was soon forced to go. 'I daren't leave Aunt Lizzie too long, poor old lass is so forgetful she might have t'house burned down.'

Thanking her sister again, Beata saw her to the door, then stood admiring the watch on her wrist for a while and flourished it at Sadie when the maid returned.

'Oh, that's gorgeous!' Sadie drooled over such an item, holding Beata's wrist to extend her admiration of it.

'She's a heart of gold, has our Gus,' smiled Beata. 'I'm going to wear it tonight.'

Just at this point Mrs Druce came in. The girls broke apart and made as if to return to work but their mistress smiled. 'What was that you were admiring?'

'It's my sister's watch, madam. She very kindly lent me it.' Small blue eyes twinkling, Beata displayed the timepiece on her wrist.

Mrs Druce praised it too, smiling for a good few moments before saying, 'Well, I won't disturb you too long, Beata. I just need to discuss the menu for tonight's dinner party.'

Seeing the shock on Beata's face, she asked, 'Is anything the matter?'

Beata glanced at Sadie, then explained hesitantly, 'Well, you see, madam, I'd arranged to go out tonight for my birthday. I didn't realize you'd have guests.'

'But your evening off was Wednesday,' replied Mrs Druce.

'It should have been but I thought I'd have tonight off instead.' The mistress had never objected to this practice before, so long as there was one servant on duty.

'And it's your birthday, you say?'

512

'Yes, madam, my twenty-first. My friends have come down from Scotland especially.'

The mistress was firm but polite. 'That's most unfortunate indeed, but I was not aware of this and I'm afraid you can't be spared.'

And that was that. No last-minute change of heart, no surprise party as on her sixteenth. She had just time to rush a letter off to Lucy and hope that her friend would receive it in this afternoon's post. After being so elevated by the receipt of the watch and the pension, her spirits had a long way to fall.

Lucy did receive the letter and popped by to offer Beata her condolences later that day, the worst thing of all being that she and Harry must return to Scotland tomorrow so there would be no chance for the friends to celebrate.

Beata was sad, yet not resentful, sighing in her calm, quiet way, 'Ah well, that's just the way of things for those of us in service. You and Harry will have to make sure you enjoy it on my behalf.' And with no further time to spare she went back to the preparation of the dinner party.

At least at the end of a very busy evening she did receive sincere thanks from her mistress, plus seven and sixpence as a birthday gift. Still, it did not make up for her ruined birthday and, laying there at bedtime thinking of Tom, whom even now she missed dreadfully, she would have given every penny away just to have him back.

After Mass on Sunday, she returned the watch to its donor with the explanation that she had not been given the chance to wear it after all.

Gussie displayed compassion, pressing the dainty timepiece back into her sister's hand. 'Keep it then. There'll be lots of other chances to go out for you. Where would I wear it?'

Her attempts to surrender it meeting with refusal, Beata gave up and thanked her sister, who was leaning against a wall as if for support. 'You look right pale, what's wrong?'

'I just feel a bit . . .' Gussie's response tailed away and she suddenly keeled over.

Those still leaving church rushed to help, two men carrying her to a nearby house with an anxious Beata hurrying alongside.

Soon coming round, Gussie was given a cup of sweet tea, then pressed for an explanation by her sister.

'It's summat nor nowt,' said Gussie, her colour slowly returning. 'Probably 'cause I've been fasting before I took communion.'

513

The woman whose house it was exclaimed, 'Oh, now I recognize you. You're the lass who cleans for Mr Melody.'

Seeing Beata's lips purse in disapproval, Gussie tried to make light of her role. 'Well, I've given him a tiny bit of help . . .'

But once recovered and outside she was forced to admit to Beata that she had been going on a regular basis for the past year.

'Right! I'm taking you to the doctor,' insisted Beata.

'Oh, don't make a fuss, Beat.' Gussie looked cross. 'He'll be having a lie-in.'

'Tomorrow then!' retorted Beata. 'And I'm hearing no argument. I'll be round after breakfast to make sure you go.'

And so she was, pouncing on Gussie before she had a chance to go off to her second job.

Once in the surgery, Beata having explained why she had brought her sister here, Gussie apologized for taking up the doctor's precious time. 'I feel such a fraud, passing out like that. I suppose it's only to be expected from time to time with what I'm carrying.'

'And what might that be?' enquired the doctor, stethoscope at the ready.

'Tuberculosis.' Gussie opened her blouse.

A look of cynicism from her examiner. 'Who told you that?'

'Dr Ball-Dodd, about ten years ago.'

After deeper questioning, the physician gave his guarded opinion, 'Well, perhaps that was the general consensus at that time, but medical knowledge has come a long way since then. The only thing wrong with you is a poor diet.'

At first staggered by the news, Gussie tried not to show that she disbelieved him.

'On the basis of what you've told me there are no symptoms of tuberculosis whatsoever. However, you are in dire need of protein.' Intuiting the expression on her face he added, 'It can be arranged for you to receive an allowance to purchase this.'

Hope sparked in Gussie's eye. 'So, it might be possible for me to have healthy children, Doctor?'

'As long as you build yourself up first, I see no reason why not.'

'And I won't pass on TB to them?'

'Not when you don't have it.'

Beata saw a look of absolute rapture pass over her sister's face, her own passions aroused too that poor Gussie had been misled into giving up the man she had loved because of ill-educated assumption, made to feel like a pariah all these years when there had been nothing wrong with her.

But at least the mistake had been discovered in time to prevent Gussie from wasting her life and Beata opined as they left the surgery, 'I bet you're glad I forced you to come now, aren't you?'

Eyes sparkling, Gussie agreed, and was to babble her relief all the way along the street to Aunt Lizzie's, where they had a celebratory pot of tea, nothing able to wipe that look of contentment from her face. It was still firmly fixed when her sister made to leave some half an hour later.

But, Beata noticed, behind that serene expression there was something else too, some secret. On her way down the street, she determined to probe her sister the next time they met.

She was not to discover what the secret might be – in fact, was to forget all about it – for that same day after lunch Mrs Druce made the important announcement that the family would be moving to Chester. She hoped very much that her loyal cook would accompany them. After recovering from the shock, Beata seriously considered this. She had no wish to desert Gussie who, with her overdeveloped sense of Christian charity, might be at risk of overwork and needed someone to curb this. Nor did she wish to leave her other relatives. She would also be going alone, for Sadie had turned the offer down.

But in general the Druce family had been very good to her and with over two and a half million people unemployed it might be unwise to forfeit her job. Things were very unsettled in the outside world. The public having no confidence in any political party, a Coalition Government was now running the show, though it did not appear to matter who was at the helm, none seemed competent to control the unemployment situation. There had been talk of a national disaster and proposals to cut dole money in order to avert it, the unfortunate victims responding with protest marches across the country, all to no avail, for even before Beata had time to make up her mind the crisis came to a head, the pound devalued overnight and Britain was once again hit by strikes. Only a fool would relinquish her job in such a climate.

Knowing the goodbyes would be dreadful, to couch the blow of leaving she organized a shopping trip with her sisters, thinking herself very fortunate to be able to do so when many around her were suffering; new clothes and shoes for her new life and gifts for those left behind, such generosity inflicting alarming cracks in her nest egg. There was also the grand purchase of the piano. Gussie, who had been given the chore of making the payments in its owner's absence, opined it was daft to have it sitting in Aunt Lizzie's parlour whilst Beata was down in Chester. Maybe so, but Beata said she would not be there for ever and if she did not buy it now then she never would, and just to get her money's worth she gave the piano a good old trouncing on her last evening amongst her family.

Even amid such fun the goodbyes were still emotional. But afterwards there was so much hard work that she barely had time to be sad as she helped pack all the Druces' belongings into tea chests, then to unload them at the other end. It was, she decided, rather exciting.

Chester was a very handsome city and not dissimilar to York, with its city walls and historical monuments. Beata tried very hard to adjust. After all, her work was the same wherever she might be, what did it matter what lay beyond the kitchen? But however brief a time she might spend outside the house, she could never quite forget that this place was not home. Risky or no, after only a month she was forced to give in to her heart, hand in her notice and return to her Yorkshire roots.

Colonel and Mrs Druce were sorry to see her go but gave her an excellent reference. Armed with this, Beata travelled first up to Scotland to be godmother to Lucy's baby girl, then back to enjoy Christmas with her family, and, whilst nothing permanent was offered, she was more than able to survive on a number of temporary jobs via the Servants' Registry.

In between engagements, she tended Aunt Lizzie or went over to Leeds to help at Aunt Ethel's, this sparing Gussie, whose protein diet had apparently lasted all of three weeks before the five shilling allowance was withdrawn, some faceless official decreeing that she no longer needed it, though her pallor said otherwise. Deficiency or no, Gus was still paying more than a little attention to the Melody family, so prompting Beata to act in her stead, the expeditions to Leeds also giving her the opportunity to see her brother Joe, who had rarely put himself out to visit her but was pleased to see her all the same.

'Ships that pass in the night,' she joked when, on her latest excursion, they met on the threshold, Joe on his way back to the office after dinner.

'Sorry, I daren't stop, Beat.' Shrugging on his mackintosh, he brushed past her and onwards towards the gate.

'I'll be here when you get back – Eh, have you seen anything of our Duke yet?'

'No, still no sighting,' he called over his shoulder.

'We'll have to get the bloodhounds in.' At the age of seventeen their brother had simply walked out of Aunt Wyn's and no one had seen hide nor hair of him since.

Joe slammed the gate and strode away. 'He always was a queer bugger. Our Mims is here, though.'

Delighted, Beata went in to find Mims perched on the arm of Aunt Ethel's chair, leaning affectionately towards the elderly woman, the pair of them looking at some old photographs.

'By heck, that's a change,' she murmured as her youngest sister came forward to greet her. 'You used to be freetened to death of her.'

'She's less scary nowadays,' smiled Mims. 'I rather like old people.'

Beata raised her voice for the benefit of Ethel, who had grown hard of hearing. 'Hello, Aunt. I've come to clean up for you! Where would you like me to start?'

'Millicent's done most of it,' said Ethel, her grey head turning slowly to look around for jobs that might need attending. 'But my Wandering Jew's looking a bit glum. You can give it a drink, if you like.'

Beata obliged, as she did so commenting on the artificial silk tunic Mims wore. 'That's a nice jumper. I like the colour.'

'Bois de rose.' Mims pronounced it 'boys', not out of ignorance but to make the other laugh, which she did.

'Anyway, what are you doing here? Are you on holiday?'

Mims gave a rueful grin. 'No, I ran away. I detested it.'

Her sister frowned. 'I thought you liked the farm.'

'Oh, that was ages ago, Beat! Yes I did love it but I was homesick so I went back to Aunty Merry's, then I went to Appleton Hall for training in domestic service, then I got a job as a maid but I hated the people I worked for so I climbed out of the window.' She sniggered.

Aunt Ethel tapped her niece's knee. 'Eh, you're just like our Kit. She couldn't keep a job either. Still,' she smiled, 'it's nice to have you young people about. I do miss your uncle.'

Mims dealt her a sympathetic pat and, saying she would go and wash the dinner pots, she went to the scullery.

After tending Ethel's plant and a few other items, Beata asked, 'How's your bunion treating you, Aunt?'

'It feels as if I've got Mount Etna in my shoe,' complained Ethel, with tortoise-like movements lifting her long dress to peer down at the offending foot.

'Let me see if I can make it more comfy.' Gathering bandages and lint, Beata got down on her knees, removed the old-fashioned shoe and, as discreetly as possible, rolled down her aunt's stocking.

Whilst one niece worked on her foot, Ethel called rather croakily to the other, 'Did I tell you I've had a letter from your Aunt Wyn? She thought you might like to go and look after her and Uncle Teddy in exchange for board and lodgings.'

Remembering what Duke had told them about Wyn's slave-driving, Mims muttered under her breath, 'I'm not taking her geese to shite.'

Old Ethel cupped her ear and frowned at Beata, 'What did she say?'

Unable to prevent herself from chuckling at her sister's rude statement, Beata struggled to reply. 'I think she said she might. What exactly does she want doing, Aunt?'

'Oh, just general duties,' answered Ethel. 'She's a bit under the weather and finding it hard to manage the house as well as Uncle Teddy. He's diabetic, you know.'

With the old lady's foot made comfortable, Beata went into the scullery to wash her hands, saying in reproachful voice to Mims, 'One of us should go. She is Father's sister and they all came to our rescue when we needed them.'

Scrubbing at caked-on gravy, Mims was insistent it wasn't going to be her. 'If it was anybody else I might, but I don't like Wyn.'

'You told me only a minute ago that you liked old folk,' teased Beata.

'Wouldn't matter what age she was, she's just one of those people.'

'You've only met her a couple of times.'

'A couple of times too many.' Mims set another dripping crock on the draining board with a gesture of finality. 'Anyway, I've already been promised another job. I'm just waiting for the other girl to work her notice.' Asked where, she added, 'In service again. But beggars can't be choosers.'

'I'll go to Aunt Wyn's then,' decided Beata. 'Just till she gets back on her feet.'

Aunt Wyn lived in a village near Southport where the local inhabitants were mostly fishermen and shrimpers, but she herself dwelled in better style in a modern bungalow with two bedrooms, two living rooms, a large kitchen and a rambling garden. Tantalized by the smell of the sea, Beata was given little time to visit it, being otherwise occupied with driving the geese to the pond, taking a course in home nursing and running around after her elderly relatives. She was not quite alone in her task, for a woman came in to do all the heavy cleaning, but, added to the highly responsible assignment of administering medication and providing a suitable diet for the diabetic, it was rather more than the general duties she had been led to believe. Uncle Teddy was a portly silver-haired teddy bear, quite affable though it was a pity, thought Beata, that he was as tight-fisted as his wife. In illness both were very demanding and it was a mercy they were ensconced in the same bed and that there were no stairs, for she was constantly tramping back and forth between rooms.

Even in her sixties Probyn's sibling was still a handsome woman except for the beakish nose possessed by all her sisters. However, this attractiveness did not extend to her nature. Having had few dealings with Aunt Wyn, Beata had nevertheless long been aware of her miserly streak but was shocked to discover what a snob she was too. Barely had she set foot through the door than Wyn was interrogating her as to the people she had worked for and also her friends.

'There are some better-class people round here but you'll have to pick your mark.' She crooked a finger to summon her niece closer to the bed, then wagged it as she put forth her creed. 'Never make friends with those who are a lower station than you. Always aspire to those who are better.'

Beata replied dutifully that she would, though came to regard Wyn as quite an unpleasant creature, daily evidence emerging of her meanness. The house was crammed with fine furniture and porcelain, her aunt wore good clothes and jewellery too, but when Beata made admiring comment on this Wyn was quick to bemoan the couple's lack of finance. 'I hope you're not expecting payment. Uncle Teddy suffered dreadfully in the Wall Street Crash. We were almost destitute at one point.'

'I wouldn't dream of it, Aunt.' Beata felt offended.

'We already pay Margaret to do the cleaning so it's not as if you've much to do to earn your keep.'

Aunt Wyn affected to be frail, but, so strenuously were these objections delivered that Beata guessed there was little wrong with her constitution; she was simply angling for a little personal cosseting after looking after her husband for so long. Uncle Teddy, already hampered by diabetes and laid further low by a cold, was obviously more deserving of attention and Beata was careful to adhere to his strict diet, although she noticed that his affliction did not prevent him from enjoying a dram with the local clergy who gathered here once a week, not just the Catholic priest but various denominations, this leading her to believe that Teddy might be hedging his bets to secure a place in heaven.

Kind-hearted soul that she was, Beata was willing to give both her care, but it was a lonely life and she was relieved when Aunt Wyn decided she had had enough bed rest and progressed to a chair at her husband's side. However, the fact that she looked much better meant nothing to Wyn, who was none too keen when Beata mentioned leaving.

'I'm not even back on my feet and you expect me to look after Uncle Teddy on my own?' she scolded.

'I didn't mean right this minute, Aunt.'

'It could be weeks before your uncle feels able to leave his bed.'

'Of course I'll stay until you're both fully recuperated.'

Wyn delivered a rather ungracious nod. 'Well, I would hope so. Now, do you think you could bring yourself to making your aunt and uncle a pot of tea?'

'Of course.'

But just when Beata had reached the kitchen door, Wyn called out. 'Before you do that, fetch me those grapes, will you?'

Trailing back, Beata carried the fruit bowl to her aunt and placed it within reach of both invalids on Teddy's bedside table.

'Too sweet for your uncle,' said Wyn, and hugged the bowl to her.

When Beata returned with the tray of tea Wyn was still stuffing her face with grapes, cheeks bulging like a greedy hamster.

'Do you like fruit?'

'Yes, Aunt.' Beata gave an expectant smile.

Juice spurted from Wyn's mouth. 'You should buy yourself some.'

'Why didn't I think of that?' muttered Beata to herself as she went to her other chores, thinking what an extremely odd person her aunt was.

Only days later Wyn was to get all the fruit she could possibly desire when a crate of oranges was delivered to the door. Short arms stretched to capacity, Beata transported it to the recipient.

'This has come from America, Aunt!'

Wyn reached for the docket that protruded from the crate,

exclaiming, 'Oh look, Teddy, it's from old Aunt Flora. She's eighty-six now, you know. The last of her generation.'

Teddy was unimpressed. 'It's coming to something when we have to be sent food parcels from abroad. MacDonald has brought this country to the brink of ruin.'

Wyn was examining the note that accompanied the gift. 'Why, how thoughtful. She wants to give me something to enjoy while she's still alive.' Then a worried thought occurred. 'I hope this isn't all she's going to leave me.'

Struggling under its weight, Beata set the crate down with a grunt, then waited. Surely Wyn would not be so mean as to keep this much fruit to herself?

But this certainly looked to be the case for, after salivating over the oranges for a while, Wyn told her helper to put them in the box room, then spent all afternoon drawing up a chart which she pinned to the wall with an air of satisfaction. 'There!' She made a tick with a pen on the chart, removed one orange from the crate and dropped it into her pocket. 'I'll be able to keep tabs on how many have been eaten.'

Beata was astounded and not a little hurt that her aunt could show such blatant distrust of one who had cared for her every need.

But then Wyn made two more ticks, delved into the crate again, turned to Beata with an orange in each hand and, with a magnanimous gesture, handed them to her niece. 'And these are for you.'

Seeing her pass his room bearing the oranges, Uncle Teddy called genially, 'I see Aunt Olwyn's been spoiling you. Don't scoff them all at once.' Beata murmured that she would try and savour them, privately doubting that there would be any more on offer.

Still she was luckier than Margaret, the cleaning woman, who got nothing at all and remarked upon setting her bulging blue eyes on the chart, 'Does she think I'm going to pinch them?'

Beata corrected this inference. 'Don't forget, there's not just you working here. That chart's for my benefit as much as yours.'

'Well, you might stand for it but I'm not,' retorted Margaret. She could ill afford to lose the wage but it did not prevent her from making the threatening gesture of unfastening her overall.

'Oh, don't leave,' Beata pleaded with the frog-like face. 'They'll have me doing your work as well.' Not to mention that Margaret was the only person here with whom she could share a joke. Thinking quickly, she announced mischievously, 'Let's have a laugh with her instead.' And creeping away for a moment she returned to the box room with pen and ink, making several ticks on the chart.

Margaret thought she got the drift and, grinning, started to remove oranges from the crate, but Beata said, 'No, don't, she might find out and you'll get the sack for pinching. If we leave them there it'll drive the old bugger mad wondering how she's got more ticks than oranges.'

And so it did, the two put-upon helpers sharing secret guffaws as they spied upon the mean old woman trying to work out how it was that her stock of oranges appeared to be expanding.

Gluttony aside, Wyn had also betrayed a greed for gossip, pestering Beata for any titbit she might have overheard during her shopping expeditions. Her niece disdained to feed this because she knew Aunt Wyn would use it to malicious ends. After guzzling only a few of the oranges Wyn was already slandering the donor, telling Beata how Aunt Flora had run off with someone else's husband to America.

'Yes, there's certainly been queer goings on in this family,' laughed Wyn, another skein at the ready. 'And none so queer as Aunt Kit. Dear me, the things I could tell you about her when she was young. I wonder what that painted trollop of a daughter of hers is doing now. Have you heard?'

Beata shook her head as she plumped up Uncle Teddy's pillows whilst his wife sucked and slurped away in her bedside chair, rambling on between mouthfuls of orange. 'I'd love to know what Kit said to her in that letter she left when she died. I wrote to Aunt Flora but she couldn't tell me anything. I don't suppose . . . ?' She looked questioningly at Beata, who shook her head again. 'No, I didn't think you would. Nobody's heard a thing of Serena since Kit's funeral. Still, I can't say I blame her for not wanting anything to do with us. It must have been a shock to find out Kit was her mother.'

'It was,' said Beata quietly, stopping to gather a pile of bedding to be washed.

'Oh, that's right you were there when it happened!' Wyn was instantly alert. 'I only ever got half the story – Come on then stop doing that and give me the details!'

Wishing she had not said anything and not wanting to be disloyal to Kit's memory, Beata made as if to carry the bedding away. 'Oh, it's so long ago, Aunt, I don't recall. I just remember there being this big row and Serena storming out, refusing to believe that Aunt Kit was her mother.' She went towards the laundry.

Guessing that Beata knew more than she was willing to admit, Wyn was peeved. Leaning back in her chair, she spread her fingers, affecting to examine her gold and diamond rings, her tone casually malicious. 'Well, I suppose you of all people must know how she felt, being illegitimate yourself.'

Beata felt her whole body prickle. Still clutching the bundle of dirty linen, she turned. Aunt Wyn affected to be surprised by the look of devastation she had caused. 'Surely one of them must have told you?'

Frozen with shock, Beata shook her head and was forced to listen whilst her aunt divulged the awful family secret.

'Your father committed bigamy by marrying your mother; he was already married to a woman whilst he was on foreign service. She was much older than himself and black as a chimney sweep.' Wyn wore an expression of self-importance. 'He was very young so he could have been forgiven. She must have lured him. Naturally, when he came back to England he left her behind and completely forgot about her till she turned up on his doorstep.' Seeing tears in Beata's eyes, she realized she must have gone too far and brushed at her skirts in discomfort. 'Of course I only heard it third-hand from my sister Amelia. You must ask Augusta if you want the full story. I believe she answered the door to the woman.'

Deeply hurt, Beata could not wait to leave the room. Without another word she went straight to her room where she dumped the laundry on the floor, then flopped onto the bed to ponder long and hard on what she had just been told. How many more people knew about this – was it even true? It could just be Wyn making mischief. She often reacted spitefully if one did not fulfil her request.

There was only one way to find out. Snatching a notepad from her drawer she attempted to write to her eldest sister, but tears got in the way and she threw it aside in temper, her outraged heart thrumming fit to burst. This was not the sort of thing one wanted to commit to paper. If she was to learn the truth about her legitimacy she must go and see Gus face to face.

Without informing Aunt Wyn of the true reason, just telling her not to panic for she would be back soon, Beata used precious shillings from what remained of her army pension and caught a train the following day. It was a long journey and an expensive way to travel, especially to hear such awful news as Gussie was to impart.

'Yes, it's true,' she told Beata softly, the two of them in Aunt Lizzie's scullery, washing up after tea. 'I knew there was something up the minute you stepped through the door. It was wrong of Aunt Wyn to spring it on you like that.'

'So we're all illegitimate?' Beata was shattered at having to utter the word in relation to herself.

'Well, us older ones are, definitely.' Gus played with her work-worn fingernails, her blue eyes downcast. 'After the row when Topsy came, Mother and Father went to church and, well, I think they went through a kind of ceremony, then you were born the next year so I suppose to all intents and purposes they were married then . . .'

'But not if the other woman was still alive,' murmured a devastated Beata.

Gussie shrugged. 'I overheard Mother and Father talking about it once or twice. I don't think they ever knew if his first marriage was legal or not.'

Beata's face creased in bewilderment. 'Why didn't you tell me?'

'I didn't want you being as upset as Clem and I were.' Indeed, Gussie felt that she would never live down the shame. 'I thought Mother and Father had kept it to themselves. If I'd known anyone else was going to tell you . . .' Her hand darted out to grip her sister lovingly. 'I'm sorry, Beat.'

'It's all right.' Beata looked far from all right. 'But one of us'd better tell the others before anybody else does.'

'I'll do it.' Gussie assumed responsibility. 'But just remember, we both know that our parents loved each other, so don't let this affect the way you think about yourself.'

'I won't.' Beata smiled, but her thoughts were dark: Aunt Wyn had already managed to do that.

TWENTY-NINE

Upon Beata's return, guessing why she had gone, Wyn tried to quiz her niece about what she had discovered but, still angry with her, Beata was not about to divulge a thing. 'Gussie couldn't tell me anything more than you did.'

Seated in her usual position by her bedridden husband whilst her niece tended him, Wyn reached out to deliver a beneficent pat to Beata's arm. 'Oh well, it's best forgotten.'

Nostrils flared, Beata remained mute, could not bring herself even to look at her aunt as she underwent various tasks, pouring Teddy a glass of water whilst waiting for him to fill the bottle beneath his bedclothes, anything to keep her hands from Wyn's throat. Receiving his signal, she withdrew the bottle of urine and carried it away, praying for a legitimate means of escape.

She was therefore ecstatic when, a few weeks later, a letter arrived requesting her services elsewhere. Aunt Alice's daughter was having another baby and could not look after her elderly mother as she usually did. Would Beata come in her stead? Aunt Wyn did not like it one bit, but Beata knew that most of her moans and groans were a sham and Uncle Teddy was almost well enough to leave his bed, hence she had no qualms about packing her case. She could not get out of there quickly enough.

Old Alice seemed no burden at all for she appreciated a joke as much as Beata and the time spent looking after her was over in a flash, before it was on to the next relative, then the next.

Finally returning to York, with no permanent abode, she went first to Aunt Lizzie's. Accustomed to being in remote villages for the past year she was shocked that unemployment seemed even worse than when she had left. Of course she had read of the protest marches, the pitched battles between police and unemployed, but it had not truly registered until she was here in the midst of it. Deprived before, the people of Walmgate seemed positively destitute now, hordes of men congregating on street corners, young men who had never had a job since leaving school, whose expressions advertised that their lives had no meaning. There was laughter, yes, but it was hollow, falsely induced by beer they could ill afford but which was the only thing that kept them going.

Against all hope, a hurdy-gurdy man was playing his repertoire. The little monkey extended his mug as Beata passed but all he received was a smile as she turned the corner. Yet another group of young men were to be found outside the Catholic clubroom waiting for a game of billiards. Noting one of the Melody youths, Beata spared him a glance of pity before limping onwards to Aunt Lizzie's.

Gussie wasn't home but a neighbour kept the old lady company. Making a pot of tea for them all, Beat asked if her sister was at work. When Lizzie seemed confused as to Gussie's whereabouts the neighbour replied for her. 'She just nipped out to the Melodys. I said I'd sit with your aunt till she comes back.'

Beata could not resist wandering over to her piano and tinkling a few of its keys. Then, after having a cup of tea and a chat with the old lady, she asked the neighbour if she'd mind staying on a while longer whilst she went to find her sister.

'Oh, if you're going out will you run a message for me?' asked Aunt Lizzie. 'I need some aeroplanes.'

Beata could not help laughing. 'Are you sure you've got the right word, Aunt?'

Lizzie looked cross with herself. 'Those things you put letters in, I can't remember the blasted name –'

'Envelopes.'

'That's the one. I need to write to Uncle Matt and ask when he's coming home, only he hasn't left me any money, you see.'

Beata dealt Lizzie a look of compassion. It was no good reminding her that Matt was dead, she would have forgotten in ten minutes. 'I'll just have a look in this drawer . . . Oh, here I've found one.' She handed over a crumpled envelope and a writing pad and, leaving her aunt happily scribbling and the neighbour in charge, she went out to find Gussie.

On her way to the Melody house, she was to see her sister heading towards Walmgate, a little girl by her side. Hearing the call, Gussie turned, formed a wide smile and waited for Beata to catch up.

After their initial greeting and a discussion of Aunt Lizzie's deteriorating state, Gussie asked, 'Is Mrs Cole still there? I daren't leave her on her own nowadays, I don't know how I'm going to manage when –' Inexplicably she broke off, saying, 'Well, never mind, I've just nipped out to take Elinor to be fitted for a dress. Are you coming with me?' She pre-empted Beata's objection, lowering her voice to a whisper. 'She's only little, it won't cost much, and look at the state of the poor bairn.' Elinor's present dress was little more than a rag.

Beata acquiesced. 'Has Mr Melody had no luck with a job?'

'No, nor his lads neither and it looks like they might have their dole money withdrawn under this means test thing. Still, you have to look on the bright side, we could be living in Germany. Apparently they're going to be paying off their war debts till nineteen eighty-eight.'

'Mm, that's two years before I've finished paying for my piano,' chuckled Beata.

But in the dressmaker's shop Gussie's laughter was exchanged for embarrassment. Whipping off the seven-year-old's attire, she found to her horror that Elinor was completely naked, possessing not a stitch of underwear.

'I didn't know where to put meself!' She hissed to Beata on their way home, the child now equipped with drawers and vest as well as the new dress. 'I wonder if they're all in such a fix? I've never had occasion to see what any of them had underneath.'

'Oh, so you don't go so far as doing their washing for them an' all?' came Beata's wry comment.

Gussie was barely listening. 'The poor souls, it's just as well I'll be there to take them in hand.'

Beata saw her sudden blush and immediately detected that there was something else happening here. 'What do you mean?'

'Oh nothing.' Gus looked shifty. 'Let's just get Nell home first, then I'll tell you.'

Beata was obligingly silent as they returned the child to her bug-ridden dwelling, but the moment Beata had her sister to herself she prompted, 'Come on then, out with it.'

Looking abashed, Gussie slowed to a halt. 'I was going to tell you . . . Mick's asked me to marry him.'

Beata stopped too, for a moment completely thrown. 'Who's Mick?'

'Mr Melody.'

'What! Good God, I know you feel sorry for them but isn't that taking things a bit far?'

Gussie looked most put out. 'I'm not doing it because I feel sorry for them! You don't know hi –'

'I know he's twice your age. I know he's got a large family he wants looking after. Don't you think you've done enough for them? Christ, he must be sixty!'

'He's fifty-seven – and will you stop blaspheming? Age has no bearing how one person feels for another. I care about him.'

Though angry that her sister was allowing herself to be used like this, Beata studied her now. There was a definite bloom of romance to Gussie's cheeks; in fact she had never seen her look so happy since . . . since Vincent. Casting her mind back she compared that young man with this old one. Notwithstanding the gap in years there was a striking resemblance between the two, indeed, Mick could have been Vincent in old age, the curly hair and blue eyes. Ah, so that was why. 'But still, Gus –'

'What?' retorted her sister.

'Are you absolutely sure?'

'Do you think I'm so daft that I haven't even thought about this?'

'No, I just don't like you being taken advantage –'

'I'm not! I think the world of those kids and –'

'But wouldn't you like your own?'

'Of course I would and I intend to have them!'

Beata remembered then the time in the doctor's surgery, the joy on Gussie's face when she had learned that she could have healthy children after all. So this was what had been behind that secretive look. There had been something between her and Melody even then. Yet after all Gussie had been through, how could anyone deny her this basic right.

'I'd better get meself back to that dressmaker's then.' Beata made as if to return up the street, then remarked on the other's look of confusion, 'Well, you'll be needing bridesmaids, won't you?'

Gussie laughed her relief, and linked arms with Beata. 'I'm just concerned about how to look after Aunt Lizzie when I move out. I know I'm only round the corner, but –'

'I'll see to her,' said Beata, privately thinking that Gus should be more worried what the rest of their sisters and brothers were going to say. 'Have you told anybody else about this?'

'No, I thought I'd test you out first,' said Gussie, then, blue eyes shining with merriment, added, 'You being the most aggressive one.'

Beata gave an outraged gasp, then laughed too. 'Do I have to keep quiet about it?'

'No, you can mention it to Madeleine if you see her. I'll write to the others and get everybody together to meet Mick. If we can arrange it, that is.' There had still been no sighting of Duke and it might be difficult for Mims to get over from Lancashire. Even if she had known Clem's address she could hardly invite him to come without asking Eliza too, and that was unthinkable. As they dawdled along she made a confession. 'Eh, Beat, I feel really guilty about the way I treated Father when he wanted to marry Aunt Charlotte. Now I know just how he felt. If only I hadn't been so against the match you and the others wouldn't have been lumbered with that cruel woman.'

Beata was phlegmatic. 'Oh well, it's all water under the bridge. We're still in one piece. Now, about this wedding . . .'

Of the brothers, only Joe answered his sister's call, arranging to come over the next day. Working as a barmaid now after losing yet another job, Mims dared not ask for time off, but replied to Gussie's letter saying she would definitely be there for the wedding and so would be delighted to be bridesmaid.

Knowing Madeleine would take umbrage if she was kept in the dark about the situation, and conversant with her shift pattern, Beata went to the hospital where she worked and invited her out for tea, saying she had something important to tell her.

Maddie was somewhat starchy at this intrusion. Her conscientiousness towards her patients – giving them precedence above the whims of her superiors – had held her back for promotion and the elevation to staff nurse had been a long time coming; she was dismayed that Beata's appearance might endanger this. Commanding her sister to wait outside she finished what she had been doing before donning her nurse's cape and accompanying Beata to a restaurant.

Here she was treated to beans on toast and a pot of Earl Grey.

'By heck, you're pushing the boat out.' Her pain in remission, Maddie was less biting today. 'To what do I owe the honour?'

'I thought I'd best butter you up as we're off to meet our Gussie's intended,' said Beata, then announced his identity.

Maddie was not the sort to fly off the handle but her annoyance was plain to see as she grumbled all the way through the meal about their sister being taken for a mug. 'Pity! That's all it is. You know how Gus adores children. She's only marrying him in order that they'll be taken care of.'

'Well, I thought so at first,' tendered Beata, neatly carving her toast. 'It's worrying that he's out of work too . . .'

'What?'

'But have you noticed how like Vincent he is?'

Fork halfway to her mouth, Maddie curled her lip. 'He's nothing like him!'

'Put aside the grey hair and imagine what he must have looked like as a younger version.'

Maddie chewed furiously and swallowed. 'That's just the point, he isn't young.'

Hardly tasting her meal, Beata fought a rising feeling of despair that her sister was being so obtuse. 'Just clear your mind of any prejudice, put yourself in Gussie's shoes, think what she sees in him instead of what we see.'

'I can't for the life of me . . .' Maddie was about to object yet again. But then, even though she still failed to see what anyone might find attractive in an old buffer like Mick, she suddenly visualized herself on a country station, saying goodbye to the man of her dreams, felt again the loneliness, the guilt, the hurt. Just because she had decided there would be no marriage for her, she had no right to deny her dearest sister this chance of happiness.

Eyes pensive, she scraped the last few beans onto the last triangle of toast, offering grudgingly, 'Oh well, I suppose I see what you mean.' Then she wagged her knife. 'But if he doesn't treat her right, I'll have his whatsits off.'

Pleased to have fulfilled her role as Gussie's emissary, Beata sat back to enjoy her cup of tea. After which she said they had better get moving, and summoned the waitress to fetch the bill. When it came she handed over a florin with the instruction, 'Keep the change.'

'How grand,' teased Maddie as they left the restaurant.

Beata took it in good part. 'Well, you have to be grand if you're going to be a bridesmaid.'

Maddie's face dropped at the thought of being so closely involved in a wedding that she herself would never have, and, to cover her feelings, said, 'Oh, I hope she isn't thinking of asking me. I couldn't face all that nonsense.'

*　　*　　*

She was to repeat this when they arrived at Aunt Lizzie's and her sister did indeed ask if she would accept the role. 'Nay, I'm not bonny enough, I'll only look daft dolled up like a crinoline.'

Gussie laughed. 'I wasn't reckoning on anything so fancy.'

But no amount of cajoling could get Maddie to agree and, after shaking her head adamantly, to change the subject she started chatting to Joe, who had come here after work.

Somewhat bemused, Gussie took a deep breath, smoothed her low-waisted dress into place and checked in the mirror to see that no wisps escaped her auburn bun. 'Right, are we ready then?' There was a sheen of apprehension to the normally calm blue eye. 'I've told Mick we'll meet on neutral territory, so he doesn't feel too intimidated. The poor fellow's really nervous.'

'As he ought to be,' muttered Joe, donning his trilby.

But in a few minutes he was chuckling as they set off, four abreast, along the street to the meeting place. 'It's like one of those stand-offs in a Western where the sheriff and his deputies are off to meet the baddie.' And with a theatrical gesture he drew an imaginary gun from its holster, swivelled it several times then suddenly leaped around a corner to press himself against a wall and unleash a hail of bullets.

'You daft bugger,' smirked Maddie, and to her sisters, 'Pretend you're not with him.'

Mr Melody – or Mick, as they were now instructed to call him, though Beata felt she would never get used to it – looked much healthier than he had on previous occasions. Well, he would if he'd had some silly bugger looking after him, she thought, the others obviously entertaining a similar idea judging by the cut of their faces.

Mick read their expressions too, but, averse to any unpleasantness, forestalled its onset with an animated preamble, reaching out to shake each hand in friendly fashion. 'Ye know, I was totally unaware till Augusta told me that you're the family of my old army pal! Ah yes, dear Pa,' he sighed, 'God rest him, I was most sad to hear he's no longer with us. I never knew or ye can be assured I would've come to pay me respects.'

There were nods and murmurs but then the room fell into an embarrassing silence again, none of them knowing how to begin this. The Irishness in him hating such interludes, Mick began to jabber for a while, about the weather, unemployment, anything. Then realizing that it must come to pass sometime he heaved a sigh and said, 'Look, I can see you disapprove of me marrying your sister, well, I can tell yese, so do my own sons and daughters.'

Maddie showed offence. 'Oh, they don't mind her as the skivvy but not as their mother.'

'Madeleine,' groaned the bride-to-be.

Mick's face crumpled too and he delved into his pocket for his pipe, not lighting it but using its stem to direct his case. 'I'm not going to get embroiled in any argument. Just allow me to put my piece, if you would. No matter what any of you say, I think the world of Augusta and I hope she feels the same.'

Gussie took possession of his hand and gazed up at him.

Faced with such a look of mutual admiration there was nothing any of them could say. Joe stared at his feet; Maddie at the ceiling.

'Well . . .' Beata was the only one to comment. 'I hope you'll be very happy.'

Gussie smiled, then waited anxiously for the response of her other sister and brother. That they both nodded made her smile even wider with relief. 'Right, let's celebrate with a cup of tea!'

But when her back was turned, all three turned their eyes on Mick to deliver an implicit warning. If he made Gus unhappy he would have to deal with them.

This still holding true, upon seeing their sister's face radiant with joy at her wedding no one could dispute that she had found her role in life. Watching the moving ceremony, Beata even felt a touch of envy, wishing it were she who was the bride, marrying not some imaginary man but the one she had loved and lost who would forever visit her dreams, and for a fleeting moment she felt sad and empty, overwhelmed by despair. Oh, Tommy – how she missed him.

But then it was gone, washed away by the happiness she felt for her sister. And there was to be so much more to enjoy in the company of her siblings later that day when, after the wedding party broke up, she and Maddie, Joe and Mims went to a dance to make the most of their time together.

Still in their wedding attire, Joe dubbed them a fine-looking bunch, but singled out Mims for special treatment. Seventeen now, extremely attractive and bubbling over with *joie de vivre*, possessing eyes that could portray both defiance and laughter, she was deluged with requests to dance whilst Beata and Maddie had to make do with their brother for a partner. For a second it looked as if Beata might receive an invitation, but during his approach the young man's eyes dropped to her swollen leg and he veered away to ask someone else. Far from being jealous of their prettier sister, though, she and Maddie gained almost as much enjoyment from watching her whirl around the ballroom as the young men who partnered her. So very like their mother, it was a joy to have Mims around, and at the end of the night Beata voiced the hope that it would not be too long before they got together again.

In fact it was only a matter of months, though this time the assembly was not such a happy one, gathered as they were to mourn Aunt Ethel's death. It was no shock, of course, for she had been quite old, but having lived with her for so many years Joe was understandably more upset than the others.

'You'd have thought our Duke could have showed his face after what she did for him.' He looked round at those gathered in Ethel's parlour after the funeral. 'I mean, look at the ages of some of these old dears, and they've managed to get here to show their respects.'

'Well, he may not have seen the obituary,' said Augusta forgivingly, her arm linked through Mick's. 'And nobody's seen him to let him know. He might not even be in Yorkshire.'

Joe dismissed this. 'Aunt Wyn and Uncle Ted live in Southport but they still came.'

Not wanting to upset her brother further, Beata held the quip to herself but when he moved away to refill glasses with sherry she voiced it to her sisters. 'They've probably just come to do an inventory of Ethel's stuff and stake their claim.' Enjoying a chuckle, she made herself look small. 'I'm keeping out of their way in case they ask me to go and look after them again.'

'Me and all,' smirked Mims. 'I hope they haven't heard I'm between jobs again.'

The others shared a despairing glance, Maddie the one to wail, 'What for this time?'

'Sweeping up too early.'

'You want putting in a bag and shaking up!'

'I thought Clem might have been here,' murmured Gussie, unconsciously stroking her husband's hand. 'I'd love to see him again, you know.'

The rest of her sisters nodded wistfully.

'Mother would be so furious with that woman for driving us all apart,' opined Maddie.

'Eh dear,' Beata looked sad. 'All the old uns are dying off. I wonder who'll be next?'

*   *   *

533

Whilst it was true that the older generation was gradually diminishing, some were still fit enough to enjoy a holiday. A couple of weeks after the funeral, Gussie received word from Aunt Nell and Uncle Charlie to say they were going away for a week. There would be an assistant stationmaster to fill Uncle's role, of course, so there would be no need to worry about trains, but Aunt Nell would be grateful if Gussie and her new husband could come and look after the station house and the pets – with her family of course. This might have been an act of charity, for there was any amount of people who could fill Aunt Nell's request, but whatever it was Augusta was quick to grasp the chance of a holiday for the children, and the following week the Melodys were on their way to Bolton Percy.

Plucked from their bug-infested dwelling and deposited in the countryside, it was tonic enough for Gussie to see such elation on their faces, especially Mick, who had suffered so much during the war and in the lean years afterwards. Why, he was almost like a child himself as he played with the pet rabbits alongside his offspring, groomed and fed and fondled them. How Gussie wished she could provide such a life for her loved ones for ever.

Other loved ones were to have a share in this happiness too, towards the end of the week Beata and Maddie coming over on the train to spend the day with them and to enjoy dinner cooked by their sister.

'This is very tasty, Gus,' Mick complimented his wife.

'It should be, you've fed it often enough.' Her reply was casual.

Aghast, Mick almost dropped his cutlery. 'You're never feeding me pet rabbit, woman!'

The children looking equally shocked, Augusta rolled a dry smile at them. 'Eh, your father's easily fooled.' And everyone breathed again.

Much relieved, Mick shook his head laughingly. 'That poor child doesn't know what sort of a mother he's being born to.'

At which everyone pricked up their ears and looked at Gussie, who had turned pink and said bashfully to her sisters. 'I was going to tell you . . .'

Under murmurs of surprise from Maddie and Beata, Mick asked, 'I haven't spoken out of turn, have I?'

'No, I just didn't know how to begin.' Gussie was chuckling now under a hail of congratulation from her sisters.

But after saying how pleased she was, Maddie added a warning for her aged brother-in-law. 'Well, mind you don't work her too hard.'

Mick frowned and was about to object when there was another interruption to the meal.

'What the hell's that racket?' Maddie craned to look out of the window. The drone grew to a roar as a motorbike came right up to the station house, some of the younger children looking afraid. Only when the rider lifted his goggles did the Kilmaster sisters realize his identity – 'It's our Joe!' – and everyone went out to crowd around him.

'I went to York but they told me you were here!' Still astride the bike, face speckled with dirt, Joe lifted one of the bolder children to straddle it too.

'Isn't that a grand machine?' praised Mick, running envious eyes along the glossy black tank.

Joe pulled off his helmet and smilingly admitted, 'Only borrowed, I'm afraid. No point me buying one seeing as I'm off to sign up.' He handed the helmet to another child who put it on her head.

'What, for the army?' Beata grinned.

'Aye! York and Lancs, same as Father.' Joe looked elated.

Whilst his sisters might congratulate him for realizing this long-held dream, Mick was aghast. 'Give up a good job like yours to be ordered around by some bully of a corporal? You want your bumps feeling.'

Joe smoothed his ruffled auburn hair. 'It's what I've always wanted.' Lifting the child off first, he alighted and set the bike on its stand. 'I'm just waiting for Aunt Ethel's estate to come through probate, then I'll be free to do as I please.'

'You're mad.' Mick shook his grizzled head.

Joe did not give a jot for this incomer's opinion, only that his sisters seemed glad for him.

'Well, just make sure you keep in touch,' warned Gussie, steering him into the house.

'I will,' he promised.

'We'll believe it when we see it,' said Beata, with that character-istic shrewd look in her blue eye. 'You men are all alike. If it wasn't for us lasses making the effort you'd lose contact altogether.'

But true to his word Joe did keep in touch. With his duties as executor fulfilled, before leaving for the barracks he packed up all the things unspecified in Ethel's will, such as crockery and other household items, and dispatched it to his sister Gussie, who was most in need of it. Moreover, he put forth the suggestion that

535

he, Maddie and Beata should club together and make monthly contributions so that Gussie could afford to move to a better house. That bug-ridden dwelling was no place to raise a baby and their sister deserved better after all her own self-sacrifice. Mick's army pension and Brendan's reduced dole being insufficient to keep them, Gus already had several jobs, but these would have to stop once the birth approached. His sisters in agreement, Joe put this to his brother-in-law, who conceded that it made sense, hence the move was made to a newer abode. Once in receipt of his army pay, Joe was to send regular instalments home, along with letters that kept his sisters informed of his progress.

'Eh, he's a good lad,' said Gus, flourishing the postal order that had come with the latest letter, along with a festive card.

'He's only repaying what you've done for him over the years,' Beata reminded her, she and Maddie here on a pre-Christmas visit. 'As we all are.'

Gussie gave a happy shrug. 'Oh well, it's very kind of you all, anyway. Poor Mick, he'd do more but he's got a bad back you know. He's at the doctor's getting it seen to.' She went off to fetch cups from the scullery.

Maddie leaned over to hiss, 'God, I love her but I wish she wasn't so soft! It isn't just her who's married him, she's roped us all in.'

Beata enjoyed a private smile. As much as she might chunter about Mick taking advantage, Maddie had confessed to sitting up all last night with scraps of material and embroidery silks, struggling to finish the dolls' clothes for her sister's stepchildren, determined that they would not miss out, though her arthritic fingers must have been racked with pain.

For herself, well, yes it did annoy her to see her pregnant sister running around after folk who could just as easily help themselves, but then Gussie did seem to glow with happiness. Who was Beata to tell her she was misguided? No, the best way to help was as Joe had said, by financial assistance, and she would continue to do so whilst she had money left from her windfall.

But, of course, there were other ways to help and, now that Gussie was married Beata had shouldered most of the responsibility for looking after Aunt Lizzie. Attuned to their own obligation, Lizzie's offspring were in no way remiss, and indeed one of them was there with her now, but as they had their own families to care for and Beata had no one, it made sense for her to look after the old lady in return for board and lodgings. Though there was more genuine kindness to it than this. After her long spells in hospital as a child, she, more than anyone, knew what it was to feel lonely and isolated, thus resolving to devote her evenings to her old aunt, even though it lessened her chances of meeting anyone else.

Gussie returned with the crockery. But she was not smiling now. Beata noticed that an odd, worried look had taken over her face. She put the cups on the table, though did not set them out. 'Can you pour your own, I'm just off to the lavatory.'

'Oh, not the farleymelow? Aren't we posh today?' commented Maddie, missing the other's look of concern.

But with their eldest sister gone for ages and apprised that something was amiss, she advised, 'Go see what's up, Beat.'

Without objection, Beata went out into the yard, gave a tap at the lavatory door and called softly, 'Are you all right, Gus?'

There came the noise of the latch being lifted and her sister appeared. The ashen cheeks streaked with tears spoke for themselves: Gussie had lost her baby.

. THIRTY

As if losing one child were not tragedy enough, Gussie was to suffer another miscarriage the following summer. It seemed so grossly unfair to Beata that this good and loving young woman should be denied a child of her own. Her heart empathized with Augusta, knew that special kind of ache, for it was a gift that was likely to be denied her too. Alas, that did not stop the wanting. Lately she had grown very broody, but had no one on whom to lavish her maternal feelings, no one save an old lady.

Even this relationship was eventually to be severed as Lizzie became ever more senile, and, a danger to herself, she was regrettably packed off to The Institution. Nobody called it the Union Workhouse any more, though that was what it was and the fact that the name had been changed did not make it any easier for Beata to leave her old aunt here. However, there was to be no liberation, for straightaway there was another relative clamouring for her assistance, a birth here and a death there, and for the next two years she was to find herself drifting between one relation and the next, forever at others' beck and call.

Determined to celebrate the King's Silver Jubilee among her family, Beata arrived back in York in early May. Coming out of the station to catch a tram, she found that they had been put into retirement and was forced to consult a timetable in order to discover which bus would take her to Gussie's. Waiting for an age, listening to all the complaints about how inefficient the new buses were in not stopping or, even worse, not arriving, she began to think that the grumblers were right and instead of waiting any longer she took a cab. It was much more expensive, and with long

538

spells of unemployment her eight pound windfall had been whittled down to mere shillings, but with her swollen leg the walk would be far too painful.

It was good to be back in the old city which, on this sunny day, seemed glad to see her too, for at the foot of the bar walls there were flowerbeds set out with different colours announcing 'Welcome to York'.

There was a more boisterous welcome at the Melody house. At her entry, Gussie's younger stepchildren came running up the passageway to greet her. 'It's Aunty Beaty!' Surrounded, she laughingly acknowledged each child, then dipped into her pocket to hand out pennies.

After all the greetings had been performed, she took a wistful moment to finger the keys of her piano that had been sitting here in her long absence. It had not been lonely, Gussie told her, for the children loved to play upon it. Nevertheless, Beata wondered when she would ever be allowed to put down roots so that the piano might have a permanent abode. It was almost as much of a nomad as she. Still, she was home now and resolved to enjoy her time here.

The Jubilee burst into life with regimental bands that came trumpeting and drumming through the flag-bedecked city to the Minster, a sight and sound that brought a tear to Beata's eye, for it so reminded her of Father marching proudly at the head of his regiment. What would he and Mother think to the lives their children had made for themselves? But it was not a maudlin thought, and Beata was as resolved as anyone to make this a time to remember. The weekend saw a host of street parties, all visited by an overwhelming feeling of affection towards the King and Queen. Even those for whom unemployment had become a way of life seemed keen to take part and, however wretched their situation, however modest the fair, everyone entered into the spirit of the occasion. Not even a heavy and unexpected snowfall could stop them for it just as quickly melted and the Jubilee parties were to continue throughout the month of May, though some of them were perforce to be held indoors.

But that did not apply to the Kilmaster family, upon whom the sun was to shine as if specially arranged, and even if not quite perfect with the lack of one or two of its members it was nevertheless a happy situation, with Joe, on leave from the army, being able to join his four sisters in the street entertainment.

Cheering their brother on as he raced the other men up the decorated terraced street, flourishing Union Jacks, the sisters groaned as he was beaten into fourth place, then commiserated with him as he came to sit amongst them on the variety of dining chairs that accompanied the trestle tables.

'They can't train you very well in that army,' teased Maddie, inserting a last spoonful of jelly into her mouth. 'Even Mr Poulsen beat you and he's got a double hernia.'

Joe explained his deficiency to the children who listened. 'I let him win. I'm saving myself for a better prize.'

Beata studied him fondly. Auburn hair aside, he was nothing like Father in build, nor nearly so imposing. She couldn't imagine this friendly fellow ordering anyone about. Obviously neither could his superiors, for he was still cast as private.

'How long have ye been in the army now, Joe?' asked Mick.

'This is my third year.' Joe put a cigarette in his mouth, then handed the packet to those on either side of him.

Mick refused and lit his pipe instead. 'You're sticking it well.'

'Ah, it's not so bad,' smiled Joe. Almost another four to go. He must have been mad to think he could emulate his father's glorious career. There would be no extension of his stint with the colours. But he was not about to look a fool in admitting this.

Dressed in a flowery frock with puffed sleeves, her hair turned to honey by the sun, a smiling Mims trotted back with the group of children who had been to collect their Jubilee mugs full of sweets. 'Make room for a little bum.'

Another game was in progress. At the children's noisy behest Joe went off to participate, giving up his seat to Mims.

Having had little chance to converse with her youngest sister, Maddie asked, 'How did you get here?'

'Somebody gave me a lift on their lorry,' Mims whipped a red-white-and-blue cap from a ten-year-old's head and put it on her own, then gave it back with a laugh when he objected.

'And how are you going to get back?'

Her sister's expression showed this was not a priority. 'Any way I can. I've nowt to rush for.'

'Oh, don't tell me you got the sack again? What for this time?'

'Spending too much time chatting to the customers. Lend us one of your ciggies, Mad.'

Maddie clicked her tongue but proffered the packet, taking one for herself. She studied the vivacious face with its red lips. 'There's something different about you.'

Mims blew an emission of smoke. 'I shaved me eyebrows off.'

540

'What the hell for?' Whilst Beata shook with silent laughter, Maddie studied the harsh black crescents that replaced them.

'To be like Marlene Dietrich.'

'More like Groucho Marx. They're about two miles higher than they should be.' The artificial eyebrows lent Mims a look of permanent surprise. 'No wonder you can't keep a job if you do daft things like that. So what are you doing about getting another?'

Hurt to have her appearance mocked, though not showing it, Mims shrugged, crossed one leg over the other and wiggled her suede high heel. 'I've tried, but they're gone as soon as they're pinned on the notice board. I'm going to scout round all the pubs when I get back, just on the off chance.'

'Surely you can do better than that?'

'I really like being a barmaid.' Mims tipped back her head in languorous fashion, blowing smoke at the sky. 'You get to meet some lovely people.'

'Blokes, you mean.' Maddie's owlish face looked faintly disapproving.

Beata gave her distinctive throaty chuckle. 'Eh, you looked just like Aunt Wyn then.' She herself could see how the hugely attractive Mims was so popular amongst the men.

This provoked offence. 'I'm not a snob, but I can't see as there's much reward in pulling pints.'

'Oh, I don't know,' Mims gave a cheeky grin and winked at Beata. 'I've never paid for a drink yet.'

Maddie tutted and nipped a strand of tobacco from the tip of her tongue. 'I meant spiritually rewarding. I might be able to get you a training position at The Retreat.'

Mims' expression showed she had never really thought about nursing as a career. 'I'd have to live in York.' Her tone was dubious.

'Unless you want to commute over the Pennines every day,' came Maddie's sarcastic retort. 'Excuse me for thinking you might appreciate the offer.'

'I wasn't being ungrateful.' Jobs being as rare as hen's teeth, Mims knew that she could not afford to refuse it. 'But where am I going to live?'

'Don't worry, I'll sort that out. If worst comes to worst Gus'll put you up, won't you?'

A child on her lap, watching the game in progress, Gussie smiled and nodded obligingly. Hands behind his back, Joe was trying to take bites from a teacake smothered in jam that was dangled from a string. Several failed attempts occurred, his face gradually being smeared with red preserve, until to a triumphant cheer from his relatives he managed to snatch a winning mouthful, and came away laughing to collect his prize, a packet of Capstan.

Mims brightened, slowly coming round to the idea and in the end showing great enthusiasm. 'Nurse Kilmaster – I like it!'

Through a pall of smoke, Maddie gave her a warning nod. 'So do I, and I want to hang on to it so don't you dare let me down.'

Possessed of the same compassion for humanity as her siblings, Mims tried desperately to fill the role, continually reminding herself that at the end of this six-week slog in the classroom being treated like a dim pupil she would at least be equipped to do some good for mankind. She fought to overlook the unflattering thick black stockings and flat lace-up shoes, telling herself that the striped frock and starched apron would one day represent a badge of respect. What she could not disregard, however, was the demand that she must kow-tow, must stand to attention when Sister entered and hold the door open for her when she left the room. She had hoped that this situation would improve once she was on the wards. Now finally arrived there, she found it was even worse.

'Nurse!'

Mims grimaced as a caustic voice smote her between the shoulder blades just as she was about to pass through a doorway with a bedpan. Feigning subservience, she turned to face the starchy figure. 'Yes, Sister?'

'How long have you been here?'

'About two months, Sister.'

'And you have still not learned the rules.' Face haughty, the sister waited expectantly.

Knowing what was required, Mims gritted her teeth and stepped aside, holding the bedpan with one hand and the door open with the other whilst her superior passed through.

'One more warning, and you are out!'

Just at that same instant Maddie's rubber-soled shoes came squeaking along the corridor and in passing Sister she was embarrassed to receive a glare.

'What was all that about?' she hissed to Mims when the danger was past.

The culprit wore a scowl of defiance. 'She's just told me if I don't kiss her gluteus maximus she'll kick me out. Well, I'll save her the bloody bother! Get me an envelope and paper.'

Maddie gasped. 'You haven't even learned how to do hospital corners and you're throwing it in?'

'I'm not putting up with *that*!'

Maddie looked most offended that her sister had shown her up in such an anarchistic fashion, after she had gone to the trouble of getting her this job. 'Aye, you'd rather be saying, "How many pints, gentlemen?".'

'It's better than "Three bags full, Sister!"' retorted Mims, and stalked off to write out her notice.

Amused at the tale of Mims' downfall, though sad to see her go back across the Pennines, there to acquire another job as barmaid, Beata was to remain at Gussie's house for the time being: like an ocean anemone clinging to a rock, washed back and forth by the current, grabbing whatever crumb happened to float past. Happily, amongst all the dross came a rewarding morsel. On her latest visit to town she bumped into Jack's wife and, informed that Major Herron was in need of a temporary cook whilst Mrs Temple was ill, said that she would waste no time in applying.

Her happiness at being instantly hired was rather marred by the discovery that Mrs Temple's illness was serious and it could take some weeks for her to recover. But notwithstanding this the major seemed delighted to have her back, everyone else glad to see her too, though in the seven years she had been away there had been many changes and the arrival of some residents she had not met before.

'Beata, allow me to introduce you to our visitor from Germany.' Major Herron indicated the young woman who had inadvertently entered during Beata's interview and was about to leave until the major called her back. 'Fräulein Froitzhein is staying with us until the climate in her homeland is safer.'

Beata thought this highly unusual after all the uncomplimentary things the major had said about the Germans, but nevertheless shook hands with the young woman, who was some three or four years her junior.

Only later did she think to question the strange acquaintance when chatting to Jack during a lull in their work.

Privy to the upstairs conversations, the butler explained, 'She might be German but she's also a Jew. That new bloke who's in charge doesn't like them, apparently. I think it's getting a bit windy for the likes of her so a lot of them are getting out. I believe Mrs Fordham had much to do with bringing her over. She's a nice young lady, not averse to coming down here and helping out.' He chuckled to his old friend. 'Eh, her name's a bit of a mouthful, though, isn't –' He broke off as he suddenly noticed that the subject of their gossip had quietly come upon them and hovered there in the doorway listening. 'I beg your pardon, Fräulein, I was just explaining –'

'It was me being inquisitive, I'm afraid, miss.' Beata jumped in to spare Jack's embarrassment. 'I do apologize.'

'That is quite all right.' The response was dignified, being delivered in immaculate English with only a trace of a foreign accent. 'I understand your curiosity.'

'But it's not our place, Fräulein.' The butler backed away apologetically as the telephone rang.

The pretty, dark-haired girl directed her reply to Beata. 'Nevertheless, you should be permitted to know why you are expected to serve me and what is going on in my country.' She made as if to get herself some tea but Beata insisted on making it and the young woman sat down to wait. Meanwhile, Jack had put the call through to the major and now returned to listen to the fräulein's explanation. 'I am forced to come here because I cannot continue my studies in Germany. I was to be a teacher but the Nazis are making it very difficult for people such as myself.'

Casting a sympathetic eye, Beata stirred the pot of tea.

'But much, much worse,' Fräulein Froitzhein's brown eyes turned moist, 'I cannot marry the man I love because, as an Aryan, he would have to forfeit all his property. So,' she finished her explanation with a doleful look at the servants who had been discussing her, 'there is the answer to your speculation and now you know the way things are in Germany at the moment with a madman in charge.'

Beata sympathized, and came forward with her tray, proffering too a note of optimism. 'You might see him again when a new government comes in power.'

Fräulein Froitzhein gave a pitying smile, then took the tray, thanked the cook and took it to her room, leaving Beata rather disturbed.

Gauging her mood, Jack felt as sorry for Beata as he did for the fräulein. She had had bad luck with men, himself included, and he now sought to make amends.

'Eh, did I tell you our Lucy's coming down next week, Beat?' Seeing her face instantly brighten, he added, 'I'm going to ask the major if I can borrow the car and take us all out. Let me know when you're free so I can arrange it.'

Dismissing the young woman's problems from her mind, Beata said this would be tremendous fun, then laughed, 'Listen to us talking about time off and I've only just got here! I'd better get on before I get the sack.'

'No chance of that, Beat,' grinned Jack as he went off to perform his own duties. 'You're too well thought of.'

It was no empty compliment. Major and Mrs Herron did seem greatly to appreciate her endeavours and she was very well treated. Instead of just the afternoon off that she had enjoyed as a maid, in her position of cook she was now given a whole day, which was especially useful when her friend eventually arrived from Scotland. It was marvellous to see Lucy and her family again, who seemed to have brought the weather with them for after a cold and unsettled midsummer the temperature suddenly soared to eighty and clear blue skies were to enhance their sojourn. It was exceptionally pleasant for Beata to see two more of her godchildren, even if they did spend their time fighting with Jack's offspring over who was going to sit next to her in the car when he took them all out for a picnic.

Motoring all the way into the West Riding, after lunch Jack proposed a visit to Cragthorpe Hall. Its owners, just as much affected as anyone else by the financial disasters of the last decade, had been forced to open their home to public viewing. The mothers said they could hardly take their children into such a grand residence, dressed as they were in bathing costumes against the intense heat. Beata at once grasped this chance of temporary motherhood, replying that she would stay outside to look after them, totally unaware that she was missing the opportunity of visiting the magnificent house where Aunt Kit had once been housemaid.

Too soon for Beata, Lucy was on her way home again but the glorious weather was to remain, Yorkshire enjoying its driest July for eighty-four years and the drought continuing into August.

It was September before Mrs Temple was finally well enough to return to her post, very grateful to keep it after such a long absence. With mixed feelings Beata prepared to leave, though she was to stay on for a few more days until Mrs Temple got back into the swing of things. At the end of her tenure, Major Herron summoned her to the drawing room to give thanks for

545

all her help and to hope he could call upon her again in such an emergency.

Beata voiced the genuine reply that she had enjoyed being here, then addressed Fräulein Froitzhein, who had gathered with the family in the drawing room. 'Goodbye, miss. I hope it'll soon be safe for you to go home.'

The young woman looked rather taken aback, but did not respond to this except for a sad little nod and to wish Beata luck.

Dispensing with etiquette, Jack carried his former sweetheart's bag to the car. 'I don't think she'll be going back yet, Beat. She certainly won't be marrying her young man that's for sure. The Nazis've totally forbidden it.'

Beata clicked her tongue. 'Makes you glad you live in England, doesn't it?'

'It does indeed!' he said cheerily, handing her to the care of the young chauffeur who had been instructed to drive her back to York. 'It's been grand to work with you again, Beat. Keep in touch, won't you?'

Beata said she would. Indeed, she had remained on good terms with most of those with whom she had worked over the years and was regularly in contact. Next month would see her attending Sadie's wedding.

It was difficult, though, changing jobs all the time and life became a little flat after working with her old pals again. While she could not complain of being idle, the posts she was offered were not of such high calibre and, jumping from one menial job to the next, it was really a case of marking time until something better came along. At least it gave her the chance to save for Christmas.

It looked like it was going to be a white one for, come mid-December, there was an overnight fall of snow and citizens woke to find a fourteen-inch drift blocking their doorways. Seizing on this chance of work, however transitory, ranks of unemployed lined up outside the Corporation offices to be given snow-clearing implements. Whilst two of Mick's sons shivered in the queue, he himself did not, objecting that his back would not cope with such punishment and using this same excuse when the Post Office needed four hundred extra men to meet the Christmas rush.

Braving the harsh conditions to deliver gifts, fighting to keep her feet like the cart horses that skittered over the treacherous granite setts, Beata found him warm and comfortable in his fireside chair whilst his wife underwent the gargantuan task of preparing festivities for her extended family.

'The bag was too heavy for him, Beat,' his loving wife explained why Mick was not out delivering letters. 'The Post Office ask an awful lot of those chaps, you know. I'd hate for him to injure himself permanently.'

'Not much danger of that,' growled Maddie when Beata related the episode. 'I'm beginning to think he must be glued to that bloody chair.'

Beata agreed. 'But our Gus won't have a word said against him.'

The scene was much the same the following week when Beata called to thank her sister for the Christmas gloves, Mick sitting in his usual warm place by the fire reading the newspaper, hardly bothering to acknowledge his sister-in-law as she came in from the cold but holding out his empty tea cup to his wife as a request for a refill.

Having a propensity for doing several tasks at once, Augusta was checking on a cake in the oven, whilst with her free hand stirring the pan that held a stew for dinner, and was obviously in the middle of ironing too, for there was a stack of clothes two foot high on the table. Notwithstanding her sister's talents, seeing her now about to rush to fulfil Mick's request, Beata sought to spare her and grabbed the cup off him. 'I'll mash a pot.'

Whilst she did this, Gussie went back to her ironing, Mick's only contribution being to read extracts of news to the women.

'God rot them, the Italians have used poison gas in Abyssinia.'

Remembering the poor broken men who had been gassed in the war, Gussie paused, iron in hand, to show indignation. 'That's against the Geneva Convention.'

'Not everyone follows the rules, Gus – Pass me that baccy from the mantel, will ye, deary?'

Beata held her tongue as Gussie pandered to his desire.

'Why is the League of Nations not enforcing them then?' She picked up her iron again and dashed it at the linen.

In the act of lighting his pipe, Mick shrugged, then leaned back in his chair to puff contentedly. 'Ye know what they say about rules, they're meant to be broken. Anyway, the League of Nations is a joke, there'll soon be nobody left in it.' Japan and Germany had both resigned their memberships, others were threatening to emulate.

Beata cast her mind back to what Fräulein Froitzhein had said and related this to the listeners. 'The major thinks there'll be another European war. What's your opinion on it, Mick?' Lazy or not he had had much experience of the world.

"'Tisn't impossible.' There was a rasping sound while Mick scratched his white stubbled chin. 'The Corporation isn't preparing air-raid precautions for nothing. If there is another war that's where it'll come from, de air.'

'My God, if it isn't bad enough the miners are threatening another strike over pay we're going to get bombed an' all,' sighed Beata. 'What else could befall us?'

The New Year was blasted in on a ferocious gale, the streets littered with broken slates and twigs. It was as if this was an indication of what kind of year it was going to be, for that same month it was announced that the King was gravely ill and within three days he was dead, the nation plunged into mourning.

Forty-eight hours later, on her afternoon off, Beata stopped to watch a procession of robed aldermen, soldiers, police and magistrates make their way to the steps of the Mansion House where proclamation was made of a new king, Edward VIII.

She happened to be passing through town again on the day that the old king was laid to rest. A single stroke of Big Peter boomed out over the city to command a two-minute silence, dutifully observed by all despite the heavy rain, busy shoppers suddenly frozen in respect, a few of them even sobbing.

Beata could have wept too but for another reason. She had received a letter from Aunt Meredith asking if she would once again go and look after Wyn and Teddy. Wyn certainly knew how to manipulate. She could have written directly but, obviously alert that Beata would think she was malingering, she had used her more popular sister as an ambassador, knowing Beata would not refuse. Whether Wyn was genuinely ill this time, or just wanted a servant, she had yet to find out. But whatever the reason she was compelled to respond. There was nobody else who could go; they all had their own lives to follow. Free of responsibility, Beata had no excuse. Hence, she had been forced to give notice and now stood here with suitcase in hand, waiting for the two minutes to pass.

People came to life again. Continuing through the rain, she made for Gussie's house to inform her sister of her movements.

Encountering a group of nuns on their way out, she showed no surprise, for Gussie's house was as their mother's had been, regularly visited by supplicants of the Church, agents who purveyed a host of religious icons, not to mention neighbours on the cadge. Nodding respectfully to the wimpled brigade, she went

548

indoors to discover that Maddie had chosen the same time to make a visit.

'Oh, I'm glad you're here too. I can kill two birds with one stone.' Beata explained that she had been summoned to Aunt Wyn's.

Puffing on a cigarette, Maddie eyed the little suitcase, a cynical twist to her smile. 'Just as well I was here. It's saved you having to trudge all the way to tell me, I don't think.'

Beata gave a guilty chuckle and offered to make a pot of tea so as not to disturb Gussie in her delicate task of icing a cake. Instead of rotten apples this house had a permanent aroma of baking and vanilla. Putting her talents to good use, as if she did not already have enough to do, Gussie had started to bake and ice wedding cakes for profit.

Always glad to chat with her sisters, today she had something extra to confide. 'I'm having another.' She bit her lip, half excited half afraid. 'Cross your fingers for me.'

'Oh, we will, Gus.' Beata gripped the other's arm, trying to inject confidence.

Maddie donated little more than a grunt. 'Where's the culprit? I see he's managed to extricate himself from his chair today.'

'He's just gone to put a bet on. It's his only bit of enjoyment, you know.'

Beata dared not look at Maddie but sipped her tea, focusing instead on the youngest stepdaughter, who had been kept off school with a cough. Watching Gussie hand the little girl her baking bowl and spoon to lick, smiling upon Elinor with tenderness as she did so, Beata thought how lucky the Melodys were to have her. Her mind inevitably drifted to another stepmother. How could Eliza have been so cruel to little ones when she had had three of her own? For a sane person, it was impossible to imagine that woman's reasoning.

'What are you thinking?' Busy as she was, Gussie had noted her sister's frown of concentration.

Roused, Beata smiled. 'Oh, nowt much, trying to put myself in your shoes. I dreamed I had a baby last night.'

'Ooh, don't say that.' Gussie shivered and crossed herself. 'If you dream of a birth there'll be a death.'

'I suppose it's too much to hope that it'll be Aunt Wyn's,' muttered Beata to Maddie under her breath as their sister went to answer a knock at the door.

The visitor did not disturb them long, having only come to pay for her wedding cake. After she had gone Gussie dropped the money into a tin with a satisfied air. 'Another bit towards the lasses' college fees.'

Maddie huffed in disapproval. 'Shouldn't that be their father's responsibility?'

'Oh, poor Mick – his army pension won't stretch to it. And they're ever so bright. It would be a crime if they weren't given the chance to improve theirselves.'

Silently agreeing with Maddie, Beata gave a sigh and announced, 'Well, it's no good me dawdling here I'll have to go some time.' Reluctantly she rose to put on her hat and coat. 'Look after yourself, Gus, and write and tell me how you're all going on.'

Gussie promised she would.

'Bye, Maddie.'

The reply was delivered on a puff of cigarette smoke. 'Abyssinia.'

Beata did find Aunt Wyn genuinely ill this time and, on viewing the poor frail old patient, immediately felt guilty that she had slandered her.

However, this was not to last long. Once recovered and back in her usual position at her husband's bedside, Wyn thanked her niece in her inimitable stingy manner. Eyeing Beata's tattered footwear, she announced, 'You need new slippers. If you pay a shilling towards them I'll supply the other elevenpence.'

Where would I get a shilling? thought Beata, whose only recompense for looking after her aunt and uncle was to be fed, though out of respect for an elder she did not voice this retort, saying instead, 'That's very kind of you, Aunt, but I can only just scrape together the train fare back to York.' She saw her aunt's dismay. 'Of course I won't go till both you and Uncle are better.'

Instead of her imperious style, Wyn looked pathetic. 'I was hoping you'd stay for good.'

Beata hoped her face did not portray the horror she felt.

'Uncle Teddy seems to be getting worse, tripping over and such –'

He might stay upright if he didn't drink so much, thought Beata, struggling for an excuse not to stay here.

'– and I'm not getting any younger. If he goes down I can't pick him up without help. And I mean if I were to fall too we could be lying there for weeks and nobody would know.'

'But Margaret comes in every few days.'

'It's not enough. We need somebody here permanently.'

'You could hire a nurse.'

'We could if we had the money!' Wyn looked hurt. 'Anyway, we're not invalids, I'm just asking for a bit of family loyalty.'

'Aunt, I'd gladly oblige if I could but I need to earn a living and –'

'Why? You've no children to support, we feed you well, don't we?'

That was debatable, thought Beata. 'Yes, but there are others who need me too, Aunt. Our Gussie's expecting another baby soon. I'd like to be there after she's had such a difficult time of it, and there'll doubtless be somebody else wants me for something once I'm in York.'

'But only on a temporary basis,' pointed out Wyn, 'when one or another of them is giving birth or whatnot. They don't need you like I do. It's not through selfishness I ask, naturally you may go to them if they write, but once you've dealt with whatever it is there's nothing to stop you from coming back here, is there?'

Beata frowned, but could summon no answer. 'All right, I'll stay, but on the understanding that if anyone else should need me –'

'I shall release you of course,' beamed Wyn, suddenly not quite so frail.

With her aunt as stingy as ever and Beata's own funds gradually exhausted over the months that she was here, there was no means of getting up to York – or even away from the house for any length of time, for Wyn and Teddy were always calling for her. Nor was there any entertainment to be had in conversation; if Margaret so much as paused in her dusting Aunt Wyn was on her like a vulture, saying they did not pay her to stand and gossip. The only other people who came here were her aunt and uncle's acquaintances, and Beata was not included in their dialogue, though this did not stop her listening in as she served them tea.

Today's discussion between the local clergy concerned the German Chancellor, whose name seemed to be cropping up more and more in the newspapers.

'When I visited Germany,' the Reverend Mr Love took his cup of tea from Beata without acknowledgement, 'everyone seemed to adore Mr Hitler. He's quite an impressive personality and he's certainly united their nation. It's only the politically motivated ones that bring trouble upon themselves.'

'It's a fact.' Mr Jowett, the minister, agreed. 'It's all very well the League of Nations rattling on about him introducing conscription

551

but he's solved his unemployment problem, hasn't he? And the trade unions. We could do with someone like him here.'

'You wouldn't think we were the ones who won the war,' grumbled Father O'Kelly.

'No indeed.' Teddy leaned towards his guests with a whisky bottle, tipping a dram in each teacup. 'Thank the Lord Mr Baldwin's in charge again. He'll put the country back on its feet. Besides, I don't know why everyone keeps on about the Germans. It's the Russians we should be wary of.'

'True, true,' came an ecclesiastical chorus.

Quietly departing with her tray, Beata was not quite so trustful of these old men's judgement. Confined to the house on an evening she had much time to read the newspapers or listen to the wireless and was acquainted with the great unrest that was going on in Germany, but what worried her more were the reports that the Nazis had started to interfere in the war that was going on in Spain. So too had the Italians, who had a similarly bombastic leader. She had seen both men on the newsreel at the cinema and their military power had frightened her. There was something evil afoot. The politics of it all was beyond her, but, quick to recognize any injustice, she understood all too well that people were being persecuted for their religion, men put out of business simply because they were Jews. She knew how it felt to be discriminated against because of her religion.

She was discussing this some days later with the cleaner, telling her about poor Fräulein Froitzhein, when a bad-tempered Aunt Wyn came upon them.

'Gossiping again! This really won't do, Margaret. I shall have to dock your pay.'

'It was my fault, Aunt,' explained Beata as a grim-faced Margaret plodded away. 'I just think it's disgusting what's being done to the poor Jews, don't you?'

Her attitude having changed somewhat since the news that Herr Hitler and his Nazis had marched in to reoccupy the demilitarized zone of the Rhineland, Wyn was inclined to take more notice of what was happening. 'Well, yes, it is. Uncle Horace would be having a difficult time of it if he was in Germany – if he wasn't already dead, that is. He was once a Jew, you know.'

Beata thought this too fanciful, but the inveterate old gossip insisted it was true. 'He changed his name and converted to Catholicism – like your father had to do when he married your mother.'

'Yes, but Aunt Ethel wasn't a Catholic so there was no need –'

'I didn't say she was!' Wyn looked exasperated. 'Why don't you listen? I just meant he was a convert like your father.'

Beata gave an uncaring nod and sighed. 'Right well, I'd better give Uncle Teddy his pills.'

'Yes he's getting low on water too.' Obviously expecting her niece to provide this, Wyn returned empty-handed to the bedroom. 'I'm not one to complain but I have to say you're getting rather neglectful.'

Beata seethed. She had always been meticulous in providing Teddy's needs. Never had he gone without whilst she had been responsible for his care.

As she went into the hallway with a tray, a letter dropped through the flap. Stooping, she saw it bore Madeleine's handwriting and was for her but she did not stop to open it there and then, just put it on the tray and carried it with her to her aunt and uncle's room.

'Oh, open it,' begged Wyn, after Beata had delivered Teddy's medication. 'We hardly ever get to hear any news.'

Beata would have preferred to read the letter in private but nevertheless sat on the edge of Teddy's bed and ripped open the envelope. The note was short, its content devastating. Gussie had suffered yet another miscarriage. Added to the upset it was more severe than the last and she had lost a dangerous amount of blood. Maddie thought it might be wise for her sister to come home. Gussie's words came rushing back to her: *if you dream of a birth there'll be a death.*

'Well?' prompted Wyn, eyes on her niece's worried face.

Beata told her.

A ringed hand came out to comfort her. 'I'm sure she'll be all right, dear. I know what I'm talking about, I lost one of my own, you know.'

'Did you?' Her mind on her poor sister, Beata sounded vague.

'Yes, in fact it was worse for me, the child was full term.' Wyn tugged a handkerchief from her lace cuff and applied it to her beak, her abstracted gaze misting over. 'I was never fortunate enough to have another. I lost a lot of blood too but I came through it. Augusta will be fine, I promise. Now, isn't it time for my own medication?'

Still in a trance, Beata looked at the clock. 'Yes, I'll get it.' And she went off, returning with a bottle and spoon.

'Speaking of Augusta, I don't suppose she mentioned anything about our Ethel's silver teapot when you last saw her?'

The open bottle of medicine still in one hand, its cork in the other, Beata gave her a dazed frown. 'No, why would she?'

'Oh, I'm just puzzled as to what happened to it. Ethel always promised it to me but I never saw any sign of it when I went to her funeral.'

'I wouldn't know.' Anger beginning to rise, Beata rammed the cork back into the medicine bottle to a petulant squeak. Her favourite subject money, Aunt Wyn was always interrogating her as to who got what in another's will, but how could she raise it at such an awful time?

After exchanging Uncle Teddy's empty water jug for a full one and tidying all the bits of rubbish from the bedside table, she took a damp cloth from the tray and limped around the bed to wipe the sticky circles from the table on the other side, rubbing vigorously.

Wyn watched her for a while, then, after a pause, suggested, 'Maybe Augusta got it. Did you happen to see it when you –'

Beata exploded. 'If our Gussie had inherited anything then she'd have paid for it twenty times over with all she did for Aunt Ethel, cleaning and sending her money for the boys' keep, but she didn't get so much as a farthing! Not one farthing! Does that satisfy you?'

Wyn was most put out, straightening and tugging her husband's blankets into place. 'There's no need to take that tone! Your father would be ashamed of you addressing your elders like that.'

With a gasp of exasperation, Beata left the room, but not before hearing her aunt mutter to her uncle, 'I'd stake my life Augusta got that blessed teapot.'

This was the final straw. Retracing her steps almost at once, Beata announced stiffly, 'I'm afraid I've no choice but to leave you for a while. I'll be going first thing after breakfast tomorrow.'

Wyn opened her mouth to object but was silenced by an upheld palm.

'I'm sorry, Aunt, but my sister needs me.'

'We need you!'

Beata was firm. 'You're not dangerously ill like Gus. I've made sure your cupboards are all stocked, I'll ask Mr Ellis next door to help with the geese and you've got Margaret if you get desperate for anything. I'm sure you can cope till I get back.'

Wyn looked slightly relieved. 'Oh, so you are coming back? When might that –'

'I'll come when I can raise the fare,' retorted Beata, 'unless you'd like to contribute?'

Spidery lines appeared round Wyn's compressed lips. 'Well, if bribery is the only way we can get you back . . .' She reached for her purse, her ringed fingers counting out the exact amount. 'But make sure you don't spend it on anything else.'

Taking the money, Beata went to pack her case. 'Thank you, but don't expect me to come until Gussie's better.'

But would she get better? That was the worrying thought on Beata's mind as the train made its north-easterly journey. *If you dream of a birth there'll be a death.* Over and over with every clackety-clack it haunted her all the way to York.

Normally there would be interest in picking out all the latest alterations to the old city, but today as her bus passed the old castle it barely registered that the grimy curtain wall had been dismantled to reveal the limestone Clifford's Tower in its full beauty.

Alighting from the bus she hurried on to the street where her sister lived, turned the corner and saw a hearse. Her heart almost leaped from her mouth. It was parked outside Gussie's. After temporarily stalling, she took herself in hand and limped on towards the house, her mind filled with the most awful dread. *Please, please, not Gussie.*

No children came rushing down the passage to greet her today. Making her wary way along its brown varnished length, feeling almost ready to vomit from nerves, Beata poked her head into the living room to see Mick hunched in his usual place, smoking his pipe. It did not help; she had hoped that the hearse might have been for him.

The house quiet as death, he could not fail to hear the rustle of her clothes and turned quickly, his blue eyes wide in shock. 'Jesus! Y'almost had me banging me head on the ceiling!' He looked old and drawn.

Beata did not apologize, merely cast her worried glance around the room.

'The kids'll be in from school in a minute.' He arched his back and set aside the book he had been reading. 'Ye can make a cup of tea, if ye like.'

Beata felt slightly less agitated. Her sister could not possibly be dead with the blasé attitude he was displaying. Even so . . . 'There's a hearse outside.'

He stuck his pipe between his teeth. 'Is there? Don't know who that's for. Must be next door.'

Beata almost swooned from relief. 'I thought . . . well, I heard Gussie had lost a lot of blood and –'

'Ach, God love ye, no!' Seeing the tension drain from her body, Mick realized now how worried she must have been. 'She's out of danger now.'

'Thank God.' Beata clutched her chest for a moment, whilst the thudding of her heart began to subside. Then, feeling better, she made to take off her coat. 'Is she upstairs?'

Mick shook his head and jabbed his pipe stem at the door. 'Ye'll find her on the top road at the midwife's house. Mrs Whatsername wanted to keep an eye on her, her being so sick. Er –' he saw Beata about to leave, 'surely ye can have a cup of tea before ye go?'

Beata shook her head, partly in exasperation at his idleness. 'Thanks, I'll have one with Gus.' And she hurried up the street.

Augusta had certainly been perilously ill. So ghastly was her complexion that Beata began to doubt Mick's opinion that she was out of danger. Why, there could hardly be a drop of blood in her. Mims had been summoned here too, but Beata spared her only the most basic greeting, her eyes fixed on Gussie as she rushed to their beloved sister's bedside and scooped up the white hand that lay upon the eiderdown, holding it tightly.

Offering weak greeting, Gussie murmured that she was fine, and, though her teary eyes bespoke her loss, the midwife was able to confirm this. Providing the patient with a cup of beef tea, she said that the haemorrhage had been extensive but Gussie was over the worst.

'Well, you'll jolly well stay here till you're better,' a relieved Beata ordered, Mims agreeing.

'That's what I've told her.' Maddie had let herself in and now came round to the other side of the bed. She had been every day during the crisis, helping the midwife to nurse her sister. 'No going home and running around after that lot. Don't worry, we'll pay.'

Gussie felt too weak to argue.

'Has anybody else been to visit you?' asked Beata, stroking the pale hand.

'Oh, yes, Mick's been with the children.' Gussie accomplished a frail smile. 'I'm very lucky. They've treated me as if I was their real mother. Joe popped in last Sunday, said he was off somewhere to play war games.'

The sisters shared a chuckle.

Later, as the patient dozed and the others watched over her, Beata was enlightened by Maddie that no one from the church had been, at least not specifically.

'I happened to be there when they came round with their begging bowl last week just as Gus lost the bairn, and even when they'd been told that she was at death's door they haven't been near her – but I'll bet you anything they're knocking on Friday for their weekly handout.'

At these sour words, Beata cast her mind back and thought of all the times the Church had let her down. Well, that could be excused, but to treat Gussie like this, she, a stalwart of the Catholic faith, who had braved all weather just to polish the brass on the altar rail, who would give them the clothes off her back if they were to ask, that was unforgivable. She decided there and then not go to church again.

Mims had never been impressed by religion of whatever kind. 'Huh, I wouldn't expect anything else from that lot. I'm still waiting for the half a crown I was promised ten years ago.' Trying to do her best by the defiant child, upon adopting her Meredith had resorted to bribery in order that Mims keep up her mother's religion. It had not worked. Mims hated anybody getting one over on her and had refused to go to church since. She opened a packet of cigarettes and handed it round.

Beata took one, just to be sociable.

Maddie opened the window to let the smoke out. 'So, have they given you time off to come here or have you got the sack again?'

Mims laughed, touching one of her eyebrows self-consciously. Since being shaved off, they had never grown again properly. 'No, Mr and Mrs Tongue let me go straight away when they heard about Gus. I've been with them over a year now and I can't see myself going anywhere else. They're really nice people.'

'That's the landlord and his wife?'

'Yes – they bought me this for my twenty-first.' She displayed the tiny gold watch on her wrist.

Beata admired it, then breathed wondrously, 'Twenty-one! I can still taste those jammy buns the midwife brought us when you were born.'

Gussie awoke then and, remembering her loss, she started to weep.

Their attention was immediately upon her, cigarettes stubbed out, all trying to comfort.

After the tears were over, Gussie sighed and gave a philosophical smile. 'Mebbe next time . . .'

Letting out an exasperated groan, Maddie begged, 'Oh, don't have any more, Gus! It could kill you.' The other two sisters showed they were concerned about this too.

'Tell him to keep it buttoned up,' pressed Maddie. 'He shouldn't be bothered with sex at his age.'

At such graphic comment, her strait-laced sister looked shocked, then withdrew into herself, saying simply, 'We'll see.'

And knowing what that meant, they all sighed.

THIRTY-ONE

After staying a week, assured that her sister was in no further danger and confident she was in good hands, Mims travelled back to Lancashire.

'And you'll be going back to Aunt Wyn's,' assumed Gussie, at home now and the colour returned to her face though she was still in bed.

Beata puffed out her cheeks. 'I suppose I should . . . oh but, Gus, I'm dreading it. She drives me up the wall. I might get a little temporary job first, just so's I have enough money to tide me over – an escape fund, if you like.'

Gussie laughed. 'Well, you know you've always a home here until you find something.'

Beata thanked her and said it would not be for long and, indeed, the time she spent in her sister's crowded household was to be only a matter of days.

But, successful in her quest for temporary work, the autumn found her still in York. There had as yet been only one letter to ask when she would be returning – Aunt Wyn was far too mean to keep wasting money on stamps – though she knew it was inevitable she would have to return some time. Even so, she decided to bide here as long as she could. Wyn would write again if she were really desperate.

In the meantime came a more welcome request from Aunt Meredith, asking if she would help take care of her daughter, who was having another baby, she herself too old for the task nowadays. Jumping at the chance to see her youngest sister, Beata handed in her notice and at her first opportunity caught a train to Morecambe Bay.

The birth straightforward, it was a very happy interlude, at the end of which she was rewarded for her assistance by being asked to play godmother. This would mean her staying on another week until the mother was back on her feet but she did not mind a bit for, owing to her responsibilities, she had not shared as much time as she would have liked with Mims. Now free to rectify this, she went along that Wednesday evening to the pub where the youngest Kilmaster worked, and saw for the first time how truly popular Mims was.

'Right, we're too quiet!' The landlord interrupted his barmaid's conversation with her sister. 'Get on the piano for a while and pull them in.'

Pushing herself from the bar and summoning Beata to follow her, Mims went to seat herself at the piano and immediately launched into a melodious tune, singing along in accompaniment. Her leg aching, Beata slipped into a seat nearby and watched the performance, smiling but feeling rather envious, for already the piano had become a magnet to those young men who had been quietly drinking. Very soon, attracted by the music, others began to drift in from the streets and line the bar, their eyes drawn to the vivacious girl on the piano. Within an hour the landlord found himself rushed off his feet and Mims was regrettably called back to her post, though the men surged with her and the pub retained their custom until closing time.

Treated to several drinks throughout a most agreeable evening, enjoying a laugh and a joke, Beata was left in no uncertainty that she was popular with the men too. As a friend. For though they might jest with her till the cows came home, it was a sad fact that she would never command such looks of desire as were directed towards her sister.

Back in York there was an immediate search for work and within a month Beata was once again entrenched in the type of menial role she had come to expect.

One autumn evening, looking forward to a break from her domestic responsibilities, she had made an arrangement to go to the cinema with Maddie and, after completing all her chores, walked into town. Rather than having tea by herself in a café she bought a couple of sausage rolls, intending to eat them before meeting her sister. The city seemed extra busy for this time of day. There were hordes of jaded men about the streets, seated on the kerbs and every available bench. She commented upon this to the woman in the bakery.

'It's a hunger march come down from Aberdeen,' said the assistant. 'Apparently the Corporation won't let them in anywhere so I suppose they'll be cluttering the place up all night and widdling in people's doorways.'

Beata thanked her and went to find somewhere to sit, watching the comings and goings of the marketplace as she ate. She felt sorry for the exhausted men, one in particular drawing her eyes for he had his boots off and was gingerly pulling bits of loose skin from his heels. Seeing him wince, she responded instinctively and hurried over to warn him, 'Don't do that, you'll tear it right into the flesh.'

He hardly glanced up at her and responded in a thick Scottish accent that she failed to comprehend.

Undeterred, she bent over enquiringly. 'Would you like a sausage roll, love? Sorry, I've eaten half of it . . .'

He shook his weary head, 'Thank ye kindly, dear, I won't take your tea. I've just eaten. Some people have been very good tae us.'

Through concentrating hard she managed to decipher his words and nodded.

'I'll have it, Beat, if it's going spare,' said the man who sat nearby.

Startled to hear her name, she looked at the stranger, whose coat was secured by a piece of twine; a tramp, but a relatively clean one. It was only when the weathered face gave an impish smile that she recognized her brother.

'Duke!' She projected delight and immediately rose to kiss him. 'What are you doing on a hunger march?'

Duke gave his shy laugh. 'I'm not on the march. I was just talking to this chap when you came along.'

'But where've you been? How are you? Have you got a job?'

He chuckled again. 'Which one do you want me to answer first, Beat?'

She uttered a sound of wonder at meeting him in such a coincidental fashion after years of trying to find out where he was, then urged him to say something, anything, so she would know she was not dreaming.

Briefly he told her that he had moved from place to place over the years, sleeping wherever he happened to stop.

She shook her head and looked him up and down, particularly inspecting his clean-shaven jaw and noting his brown hair was tidy. 'You don't look too bad on it.'

561

He realized she had misinterpreted. 'Oh, I've rarely slept in the open, I always get proper lodgings.'

'But how do you afford it?'

'I work, the same as anybody else. The only difference between me and them is that I don't like to stay in one place for too long.'

She was forthright. 'Well, you'd better bloomin' stay long enough to see the rest of your family. They haven't half missed you.'

Duke glanced awkwardly at the man to whom they had both been talking, who had gone back to examining his feet. He leaned close to Beata's ear and mouthed quiet reluctance to walk away. 'I can't just leave him to it.'

Knowing that Gussie would be the first to offer help, Beata turned to the man from Aberdeen. 'I can't promise you a bed for the night but you'd at least be dry and warm – and we could see to those plates of meat.'

He cocked his head and extended a grubby hand. 'Thank you very much, I accept. My name's Andrew, Andy.'

Beata introduced herself, then, suddenly remembering that she was supposed to be meeting Maddie, she clamped a hand over her mouth and bade the men stay here, telling Duke especially not to move a muscle whilst she limped off to fetch her sister.

At first annoyed at being left to stand here so long on painful joints, Maddie was totally converted by the news that Duke was in town and the pair of them hurried back to make sure their brother did not slip away again.

Gussie might show sympathy for the man with sore feet – she was too overwhelmed at the sight of her long-lost brother to complain about the stranger – but Mick was most put out, especially when the answers to his interrogation quickly revealed the other's politics.

'Jesus, Mary 'n' Joseph, what's she doing bringing him into my house? He's a blasted Communist, for pity's sake!' This, when Beata had gone to show Andy where the lavatory was and she herself was in the scullery pouring water into a bowl to bathe his feet.

'How can you tell just from looking at him?' his wife replied mildly, smiling at Duke, who had settled himself unobtrusively into a corner.

'He said he was wid the NUWM – dat's only another name for Commies!' Mick's Irish accent always came to the fore when he was aggravated. 'Chroist, she'll get us put on the black list. He'll have to go!'

Carrying the bowl of water, Beata wove her way through numerous bodies, side-stepping a boisterous child and saying in her calm, quiet manner, 'He has nowhere else to go.'

'That's true.' Andy entered as they were still debating. 'The kindly burghers of York were less than welcoming.'

Everyone had to listen carefully to unravel the accent.

'Can't ye try the workhouse?'

'Mick!' scolded his wife.

Andy gave a bitter laugh. 'I could if I wanted to break stones in the morning.' He strode over a child's prostrate form and returned to his seat.

Mick was impatient, 'Well, is dat so bad if it gives you a bed and a meal? We're all poor. I'm unemployed too.'

'You don't know what poverty is.' The Scotsman gave a contemptuous growl. 'This is a palace compared to the hovels where I come from. I know mothers who dread their children waking up in the morning because they've naught for them to eat – and I mean absolutely nothing – have tae let them sleep as long as they can so they won't start to cry from the hunger pains.'

Gussie intervened, her blue eyes compassionate. 'When is it since you last ate, love?'

'Ach, I'm fine. Folk have been very generous tae us along the way. I'll not take food from those who nae want to give it.' He stared levelly at Mick.

Gussie insisted on him having a cup of tea and a slice of bread and butter at least, providing her brother with the same. Taking discreet bites, Duke remained quietly in his corner, feeling unwelcome under Mick's eye.

Beata placed the bowl of hot water before Andy and advised, 'Soak your tootsies in that while you're having your tea.'

With his wife and two sisters-in-law devoting themselves to the grubby stranger's care, Mick fell silent and lit his pipe.

Later, when Andy had eaten and his feet had had sufficient soaking, Beata tended his blisters, applying salve and bandaging them up so that he could continue the march. Not until the younger children had gone to bed did anyone ask how things had got so bad in his region.

Settling back with one of Maddie's cigarettes, he said, 'It's due to the men who rule us, and it's going to be a hundred times worse if we allow them to get away with cutting our dole money. There's another march not far behind, from Jarrow. What's happened there is a travesty.'

'Ah yes,' nodded a solemn Maddie, rubbing her painful knuckles. 'I've read they've had dreadful unemployment there. Eighty per cent at one time, wasn't it?'

Andy leaned forward. 'I'll bet you didn't know that the fascists are at the heart of it.'

'Here we go,' muttered Mick, but was ignored.

'And that most of the steel you use is produced by Germany?' Seeing their bewilderment, Andy gave a canny nod. 'No, I thought not. Doesn't make sense, does it? Our tonnage is cheaper yet the Government imports millions of tons of the German stuff, at the same time as shutting our steel mills.' At their further bafflement he grew even more animated, 'And let me give ye something even more difficult to palate: not only have British steel makers been pocketing a subsidy from the Government to encourage them to produce more, they've been taking a backhander from the Nazis to produce less.'

The listeners gave a unified gasp. 'But why?'

'I'll give ye three guesses.' For answer Andy patted his pocket, though it did not jingle for it bore not a farthing.

Reared in a conservative household, Beata and her sisters were wary about accepting this extremist's view; could not believe their own appointed ministers would be involved in such a criminal act. It sounded absurd, after crushing the Germans in war then to boost their economy at the expense of British industry.

'Have ye heard of the shipping magnate called Runciman?'

'President of the Board of Trade,' chipped in Mick, puffing morosely on his pipe.

'That's right, *our* Board of Trade, so why has he given Nazi firms preference and prevented the building of a steel plant in Jarrow?'

It was a question no one could answer and there followed an awkward silence.

In the end, Gussie sighed. 'Ah dear, there's things I'll never understand if I live to be a hundred. Would anybody like some cocoa before bed?'

The next day, after a light breakfast and sincere thanks, the Scotsman resumed his march, his host much relieved to be rid of such a bad political influence.

'The tramp'll be going as well, I trust,' growled Mick to his wife when the others had gone to school and work.

'Do you mind!' Clearing the stack of breakfast pots, Gussie rebuked him. 'You're speaking about my brother.'

'Look at the cut of him, woman! We'll be having to fumigate the house after he goes.'

'That's very charitable from someone who used to live in Bug Junction.'

Her husband spluttered at being so abused, but Gussie only laughed and the argument was to end then as Duke materialized as if from nowhere, wearing his greatcoat and hugging his small bag of belongings.

Mick turned away, muttering under his breath about Duke being 'like bloody ectoplasm, creeping through closed doors while you're trying to have a conversation . . .'

'Sorry, I don't want to be in the way.'

'You're not!' said his sister kindly. 'And you can take that coat off right now. I'm going to find a comfier place for you to sleep tonight.' He had previously shared the front room floor with Andy.

Assessing Mick's mood, Duke said he didn't want to outstay his welcome.

But Gussie insisted he remain. 'You're going nowhere till we hear everything you've done in the last six years.'

Persuaded, he untied the string that acted as a belt and shrugged off his heavy coat. Mick turned up his nose at the musty odour and lit his pipe.

'I can only stop a few days.'

Continuing with her baking, Gussie said, 'You can't go until your other sisters have had a better opportunity to speak to you. We couldn't say much with a stranger being in the house. We've all missed you.'

Duke confided that he'd missed them too.

'Have you seen anything of our Clem?'

Immediately he clammed up. Duke had never forgiven his eldest brother, not just for the thrashing, but for the betrayal in merging with Eliza. However, he did not say this to Gussie, but just shook his head.

'Joe?'

He shook his head again but this time asked, 'How is he?'

'He's in the army, Father's old regiment.'

Though he had never got on with his father, who had always made him feel like a failure, Duke was nevertheless glad for Joe and looked impressed. 'Does he ever come to see you?'

'As much as he can. If you stay for a decent while you might see him.' Gussie looked at her husband, who had pulled a face at this suggestion.

Duke saw the grimace too. 'Oh, maybe. I'll certainly hang around to see Beat and Maddie again, though.'

Gussie said, 'Mims'd love to see you too. I'll write to her and see if we can get her to come.'

Mims did indeed show great keenness to come, as did Joe, who was conveniently stationed in York at the moment. With Beata and Maddie returning at their first opportunity to enjoy a deeper conversation with Duke, it was pointed out that this was the first time they had all been together since Father's funeral.

'Well, we're not *all* here,' corrected Maddie, and immediately every mind went to Clem.

The group nodded and murmured, reminiscing for a while about their parents and other dead relatives.

Things in danger of becoming maudlin, Gussie chuckled at Duke. 'Eh, do you remember at Mother's wake when you cut all the cherries off Aunt Wyn's hat and tried to eat them?' Her stepchildren thought this hilarious, both young and old laughing.

Beata groaned at the mention of that particular relative. 'Oh, don't mention Aunt Wyn. This job finishes next week and I haven't been able to find another. If I've nowhere to live I'll be forced to go back there. I was hoping I'd be spared till after Christmas.'

Gussie solved the dilemma. 'If it's a bed you're after you can stay with us.'

'Yes, I'll soon be moving on.' After only a week, Duke seemed restless already.

'I didn't mean you have to go,' Gussie rebuked him. Used to a full house, she was adept at juggling beds and bodies. 'There's room for you both.'

Beata gratefully accepted, and, with no job forthcoming, moved into her sister's house a week later, from then on having to exist on the funds she had put by for Christmas.

Before then, however, an extraordinary event occurred.

No previous hint of the relationship in the press, it was a great surprise to everyone to read on that first day of December that the King had proposed to an American divorcee. Gussie proclaimed this most unsavoury, agreeing with every disapproving word in the newspaper and saying Mrs Simpson was not the sort of woman to be queen. Obviously those in higher authority thought so too, for by the sixth a grave constitutional crisis had arisen and on the night of the eleventh the family was crowding round the wireless to hear the King make his abdication speech.

In the stunned atmosphere that followed the broadcast, pondering over the sensational event, Beata yearned for a man who might sacrifice everything out of love for her. Never far from her thoughts, Tommy's laughing face sprang to life. For a few moments, history was rewritten and she saw him by the fire in the chair opposite hers, a couple of children playing on the rug between them . . .

'I was never right struck on him anyway.' Gussie's censorious voice cut into her daydream as the radio was turned off and household life resumed. 'Always had a sly look about him. And I certainly don't like that hussy he's taken up with.'

Beata smiled at her sister's prudish attitude, but agreed in part. 'I think the Duke of York's more fitted to the bill, not so much of a gadabout. A happy family in Buckingham Palace, that's what we need.' Oh, what she would give to have one.

But she had almost given up hope of that. What chance was there for someone who was plain, plump, with a gimpy leg, and in service – at least she would be if she could find a job. Time and again she had gone into town to scour the notices in the labour exchange and to visit the servants' registry but had found nothing.

Amid blustery showers she limped in again the next day, to the same useless result, the only moment of interest occurring when she passed the Mansion House and witnessed the proclamation of the new monarch – three kings in one year, it was all rather surreal.

What was very real was the lack of money in her purse. Of course she still had the train fare that Aunt Wyn had grudgingly donated but she couldn't spend that. It was ironic really, the shops were reporting their best Christmas ever and the rest of the country beginning to emerge from the Depression, but she herself had not a penny to spare on gifts.

Still it turned out to be as nice a Christmas as she could ever recall, being at Gussie's and watching the youngsters open their presents, her brother Duke being persuaded to stay and see in the New Year with them before he eventually succumbed to his wanderlust and left at the end of January with instructions not to desert them so long in future.

'I suppose I'll have to be making tracks too,' sighed Beata, gossip having reached her ears that Wyn was most put out that she had not yet returned.

But just as she had packed her case a raging blizzard swept into being, leaving roads impassable in Yorkshire and disallowing her to get further than the outside lavatory.

Wearing a miserable expression, Beata looked out at the world of white. 'Oh what a shame. I won't be able to get back to Aunt Wyn's now, will I?' And, grinning widely, she took her suitcase back to her room.

But the stay of execution was brief and within weeks she was on her way back to Southport, the journey taking several hours.

'Where've you been all these months?' said Aunt Wyn by way of greeting at her weary arrival in the mid-afternoon. 'We've had to pay Margaret to come in more often – *and* we've had to sell the geese. We couldn't manage them on our own.'

Well, that was one less chore, thought a tired Beata, disgusted that Wyn had not enquired after Gussie's welfare. 'Sorry, Aunt. I had other people to see to. Anyway, I've brought something to show you.' She fished a document out of her case. Mainly to still her aunt's suspicions but also to gratify her own curiosity she had acquired a copy of Ethel's will, what she found there making her even angrier, for the largest beneficiary turned out to have been Wyn herself, hence the air of mischief as she handed it over now. 'I thought you might be interested.'

Yet even its presentation could not shake her aunt's insistence that she had received less than everyone else. 'It's all legal jargon!' Wyn flicked her hand dismissively and thrust the will back at her niece. 'Anyway, forget that, I've got something important I want to ask you.'

Shaking her head at the old woman's intransigence, Beata folded the document away, then paid attention.

'You know that letter I sent you, asking when you were coming back? Have you still got the envelope?'

Beata frowned. 'That's a long while ago, Aunt. It'll have gone in the bin – Oh, hang on I think I wrote a shopping list on the back. It might be in my coat.' Not the tidiest of women, her pockets were full of such rubbish.

'Can you go look?' urged Aunt Wyn.

Beata went off to rummage in every pocket and returned with the crumpled envelope, at the sight of which Aunt Wyn crowed in delight. 'Wonderful! The stamp's got Edward's head on and it's sure to be worth something in the future, now he's abdicated.'

Her niece felt swamped by despair, but had no time to dwell on it for at this juncture the reverend gentlemen began to arrive for their weekly session and, even before unpacking her case, she was

568

dispatched to make sandwiches and a pot of tea. To her pleasure, though, she found Margaret here, the cleaning woman having been assigned extra work, due to Beata's absence, and the sandwiches already made. All Beata had to do was carry the tray in.

Uncle Teddy was not in bed today, his health quite steady, and everyone was congregated in the living room.

Coming amongst them with a plate, Beata listened to their discussion, first the weather, then the political climate. Their tone had changed somewhat since last she was here.

'Have you heard the latest?' The Reverend Mr Love bit into a ham sandwich, spitting bits of it with his outburst. 'This Hitler chap's demanding back the colonies that he said we stole from him after the war!'

'Oh, he's just getting silly now.' Another erstwhile admirer swiped the air in disgust.

'It is rather worrying, though,' said Father O'Kelly sipping his tea. 'All this rearmament. I get the feeling the Germans aren't too keen on paying off the rest of their war debt.'

Teddy refused to believe it. 'It's just a show. Hitler knows we'd beat him; we've still got the largest navy in the world.'

'They've changed their tune,' said Beata to Margaret, once back in the kitchen. 'They were big fans last time I was here.'

The other had little time to respond for, hearing them talking, Wyn came in. 'Margaret, I forgot to tell you, now that my niece is back we won't require you beyond your usual hours.' She looked at the clock. 'You may go now but I'll pay you to the hour.'

'That's very generous of her,' muttered the cleaner to the niece, 'there must be at least a minute to go.'

Beata chuckled and said goodbye before being summoned to the living room to attend the guests.

If she had thought her uncle and his friends' attitude had undergone a radical change, over the coming months Beata was to hear even more condemnation when Germany's support for General Franco acquired a military role, their planes bombing a Spanish town and killing many people.

It was all very worrying for a young woman isolated from her loved ones, especially with a brother in the army.

'Do you think there'll be a war, Uncle?' Beata had been wanting to ask all afternoon but did not do so until the reverend gentlemen had gone.

Despite his bellicose opinions amongst his male friends, Teddy sought to put her mind at rest. 'In Europe, maybe, but I don't believe it'll involve us this time. Mr Baldwin's too sensible. So don't you go worrying.'

But then a few weeks after this Mr Baldwin resigned as Prime Minister, bringing more speculation amongst the men about war and causing Beata to seek her uncle's assurance again. And again Teddy told her soothingly not to worry, for, 'I believe Mr Chamberlain's a peace-loving man. He won't take us into any unnecessary mess.'

It was good that the Coronation took everyone's mind off the foreign unrest. Whilst Beata herself had little to celebrate, trapped here in this small coastal village, the rest of Britain had much to put the flags out for. They had survived conflict and financial depression, there was ever-increasing prosperity in all but the meanest slums and even these were gradually being razed and replaced in the building boom that had been going on since the war.

With her own brothers and sisters being party to this overall good fortune, each fulfilling his or her desire, Beata told herself not to grumble at her own situation, even when forced to spend Christmas and New Year amongst her miserly aunt and uncle. This stagnation would not last for ever. For now, she must take solace in her siblings' letters, a joy not allocated to Aunt Wyn.

'Well, if she wanted to make me feel as bad as she does then she's succeeded!' At first delighted on that crisp March morning to receive this rare letter from her sister Rhoda, Wyn had soon found it to be a catalogue of illness. 'I feel quite depressed after reading that. I don't know how she managed to write it if she's as crippled with rheumatism as she says. Honestly, she's such a grumbler. I hope she isn't angling after taking Beata away just yet.'

'Beata would never put up with her,' contributed Teddy.

'No indeed.' Wyn looked round as her niece came in with Teddy's medication. 'I'm just saying, I don't know how you're going to manage our Rhoda when the time comes. She's not half as placid as I am.'

Beata frowned to herself. Why did everyone take it for granted that her station in life was to look after them? But, regrettably, this was the design her life was appearing to take. All she seemed to do was wander between relatives, applying bandages, measuring medicine, being godmother to someone else's child . . .

'Turn the wireless on, Beata dear.' Aunt Wyn threw the letter on the fire. 'And we'll listen to some proper news.'

Beata went to click the knob, fetching the broadcaster's voice into the room. '. . . hitherto massed on the Austrian border, are reported to be now entering Vienna –'

'He's done it then,' said Teddy to his wife, both at once attentive.

Alert, Beata saw her aunt and uncle look at each other, their expressions sober as they listened to the rest of the broadcast. There had been grave concern over the past month about the rise of fascism in Europe, not just Franco's success in Spain but also Hitler's underhand manoeuvres to install more Nazis in the Austrian cabinet. There were fears that Czechoslovakia was next on his list. It was all a long way from home, but still . . .

'Go out and enjoy the spring sunshine while you can, Beata.' Aunt Wyn noticed she was standing there doing nothing.

Beata nodded and asked intuitively, 'Might there be anything you'd like me to do while I'm out there, Aunt?'

'Oh, well, you could do a bit of tidying-up if you like.'

Beata smiled grimly to herself as she went to don an old jacket and wellingtons, though in fact it was a release to be out in the fresh air. She enjoyed gardening, wishing only that it could be her own piece of land upon which she was about to labour. Avoiding the spring bulbs whose green shoots pushed their way through the winter debris, first she raked up the leaves, which was quite a lengthy task, for it was a large spread. Then, in between answering her aunt and uncle's demands, she found a piece of old carpet and dropped on all fours on it to tear up the dried brown stalks amongst the new growth.

Immersed in her task, she did not at first notice the little boy who peeped through gaps in the fence and moved with her as she went along the border on her hands and knees. But finally, her back aching, she straightened to relieve it, saw him, a lovely little chap about five years old, and she smiled into his serious face.

'Hello!' she said brightly, but he did not answer, just stood watching her intently for a while.

Then he announced, 'Your eyes are like bluebells.'

She laughed and gave a murmur of pleasure. 'You'll go far, young man.'

He said nothing more, but put his little hand through the fence and began to assist her in pulling up weeds. Seeing those tiny fingers work alongside hers, Beata felt a rush of maternal affection and told him, 'You're very helpful. Do you think your mother would swap you for a quarter of tea?' He said he would ask and, dashing off, was gone for some moments before returning to announce, 'She wants the tea first.'

Beata chuckled and was thoroughly enjoying his company until Aunt Wyn called in that impatient way of hers and she was forced to say goodbye. But, 'Come and see me again, won't you?' she entreated wistfully, knowing that such encounters were the nearest she would get to having children.

Whilst attending Aunt Wyn's demand for tea, remembering what she had said about losing her one and only child, and thinking that perhaps Wyn might share her own deep longing, she said with a question in her voice, 'Aunt, have you read about those Basque refugee children who need homing?'

'Refugees?' Wyn reached for her cup and saucer. 'I think I've done my bit by taking you in. I don't want any more waifs and strays, thank you very much.'

Beata was furious. Though she was not the sort to thrash about and her body remained calm her voice reflected her indignation. 'Right, well if that's the case, I'll go back to York.'

'Oh no!' Realizing she had pushed the placid girl too far, Wyn began to panic and, slopping tea into her saucer, she reached out to grab hold of Beata's arm, 'I didn't mean *you* were a waif, dear. We're very grateful for all the help you've given us, *extremely* grateful, in fact we couldn't do without you – could we, Teddy?'

Her uncle agreed.

'And, of course, you'd be so much safer here.'

Beata still bubbled with anger. 'How is that, Aunt?'

'Well, if there's a war –'

'Uncle Teddy says there isn't going to be one.' Beata looked at him for confirmation.

'Oh and of course he's almost certainly right!' Wyn babbled. 'I don't intend for you to worry, but one never can tell and if there *were* to be hostilities then York will be one of the Germans' first targets, it being a garrison town.'

Beata did not know what to think. One newspaper predicted a war by 1940, yet another was adamant there would be none. She wished her father were alive so that she could ask his opinion.

'Please, please stay,' begged Wyn.

And so pathetically was it issued that Beata decided it would be wrong to abandon this elderly relative, saying resignedly, 'All right, I will – for now.'

THIRTY-TWO

The question of the refugee children was not raised again and, apart from occasional sightings of the little boy when his mother brought him to visit his grandparents, Beata was rarely to see anyone young at all, certainly no one of her own age. Of suitors there were none. Mr Ellis, the widower next door, had made it clear how very fond of her he was and would come charging and stumbling across his garden with strawberries if ever he saw her on the other side of the fence, but he was in his seventies and cross-eyed, and not the type of escort she would choose even if she *had* any choice. Still it was kind of him and, starved for company as she was, she came to value his friendship.

Her only other conversation partner was Margaret, the cleaning lady, though Wyn did not care for their shirking and often aborted their get-togethers. Since the altercation, Wyn had been more easy-going towards her niece for several months, during which Beata had been quite content to help her aged aunt and uncle, who was not a bad old stick really, and if well enough to do the garden would share a joke as they worked alongside each other. Also, to save her legs, he would drive her into town and wait for her whilst she did the weekly shopping. But Wyn had few such niceties and gradually her offensive nature had resurfaced, and only by way of constant threats to leave did it become possible for Beata to maintain her equilibrium.

In the wake of another harsh clearance of air, things were less tense at the moment, at least between Beata and her aunt. The situation in Europe was another matter entirely. Though the radio was in the living room she could hear it as she worked in the kitchen and could not fail to interpret the tension in the news report. As

573

feared, Hitler had indeed set his sights on Czechoslovakia and was threatening war unless his demands were met.

Concerned, she again went to ask her uncle for guidance.

The silver-haired old teddy bear laughed off her worry. 'It's just a small corner of Czechoslovakia he wants, Beata. Sudetenland is a German-speaking region and Herr Hitler thinks his kinsmen should be part of Germany. I suppose it stands to reason – not that I agree with him having it, but I see his point of view.'

Unconvinced, she told him, 'They were demonstrating how to fit gas masks when I went into town the other day.'

But Teddy remained light-spirited. 'I'm telling you, there's no cause to worry. Mr Chamberlain is flying to Munich to sort it all out.'

Beata might have been pacified, had she not, upon departing, overheard Uncle Teddy's furtive response to a similar question from Aunt Wyn.

'It's a very tricky situation, Olwyn, very tricky indeed. I didn't like to frighten the girl but it could go either way. We should be prepared.'

Struggling to get through the next few days, pressure mounting and arguments flaring as she and her aunt and uncle waited for the Prime Minister to return, Beata longed to be amongst her family – *real* family, not just distant relatives who viewed her as little more than a servant but people who loved her – and she teetered on the edge of informing Aunt Wyn that she must go back to York, for if there was to be a war she would feel more vulnerable here than ever.

The waiting became unbearable as, hour after hour, they tuned in for every news bulletin, yet heard nothing of consequence.

Then: 'There will be no war over Czechoslovakia.'

Her ear cocked in the kitchen, at the combined outlet of relief from her aunt and uncle, Beata felt the tension drain from her body and, after offering a little prayer of thanks to the Lord, went into the living room to join its occupants.

Uncle Teddy was smiling. 'You'll be glad to hear Mr Chamberlain's sorted it out, Beata.'

She nodded and, for as long as she was allowed, listened to the rest of the broadcast, which informed her that Hitler had promised to negotiate on future disputes.

'Well, it's all over,' beamed Wyn. 'Let's have some tea.'

The world spared another catastrophe, Beata's own world returned to normal and she set to resume her role as Wyn's factotum.

However, her aunt was to shuffle after her into the kitchen, unusually affable and even helping to set out the tray. 'It's a great release, isn't it?'

'It certainly is, Aunt.' Smiling, she poured boiling water into the china pot and swilled it around.

The ringed fingers set out cups and saucers. 'It's been such a boon to us having you here to keep us company. I was getting rather frightened, to tell the truth.'

Beata nodded judiciously. 'So was I.'

Her aunt's beak of a nose came up to project wonder. 'Were you? Well, you hide it very well. You always seem very calm.'

Beata chuckled to herself: if only Wyn could read her mind.

'And your uncle wouldn't want anybody else looking after him when he's ill. He says you've got such a gentle touch, and you're so quiet about the house; you don't go clomping round like some I could mention. I detest clompers.'

Gratified by this rare compliment, Beata thanked her.

There was a short silence, whilst Wyn pottered about, then slowly she turned to her companion, fingering the string of pearls that graced her silken bosom and said, 'I'd like to ask something of you, dear.'

Stirring the teapot, Beata turned and gave a brief smile. 'Certainly, what can I get you, Aunt?'

'Will you promise me, when I die you won't desert poor Uncle Teddy?'

It was not only the question but the tone in which it was said that took Beata by surprise. Normally there would always be a demand but today Wyn seemed genuinely humble and at her niece's mercy. It was this that led her to reply sympathetically, 'Of course I won't, Aunt. I'll be here as long as you both need me.'

How she would come to regret those words. For it was to transpire that her aunt would be needing her no longer. The next morning there were frightened yells when Uncle Teddy woke to find his wife dead beside him, startling Beata from her own bed and heralding a day of funeral arrangements.

Whilst Aunt Wyn must have had a premonition that she was going to die, the old man she left behind seemed too stunned to realize what had occurred, thenceforth spending the rest of the day drinking himself silly to blot out the shock and leaving his niece to deal with everything.

One good thing to come of the awful affair was that it reunited Beata with her siblings, at least those who were able to take a day off to come to the funeral. One who did was Mims, despite not liking her aunt, nevertheless seizing this opportunity to come and introduce her newly acquired young man to her sister.

'Isn't he lovely?' smiled Beata to Maddie later at the funeral tea, admiring from afar his abundance of dark wavy hair and friendly face, the naval uniform.

'You're slavering all down your front.' Racked with pain, Maddie lit her third cigarette in half an hour.

Having come to associate these waspish comments with a surge in her sister's arthritis, Beata forgave her and asked, 'How've your joints been?'

'Ruddy terrible.' The smoke was expelled in a forceful stream.

'Have you been to Harrogate lately?' She knew Maddie occasionally went there to take the waters.

'For what good it's done, aye.' Another drag. Her face seemed even paler than usual against the black of her mourning attire.

Initially happy at seeing her, Beata knew that spending too long with Maddie would make her depressed and so, after fetching her sister a sherry, she transferred to Mims, who was much warmer company and besides, it gave her the opportunity to chat with that lovely young sailor.

It seemed fatuous to say it in relation to a funeral but Beata thoroughly enjoyed the get-together and the time passed all too quickly. Upon remarking this to Mims she was immediately told, 'Come with us, Beat. You don't have to stay here now.'

But she replied that she could not and sadly waved them off, to resume an even lonelier life with her elderly uncle.

There was nothing in the will for her, which was no surprise at all, so Beata need not have been beholden to Teddy, who was only related by marriage. Nevertheless, she had made a promise to Wyn and, pitying her uncle for she knew how devoted he had been to his wife and must miss her, Beata kept her word and remained to attend his diabetic needs.

But, even accepting that grief emerged in many guises, she had never seen it displayed as bizarrely as was to occur only a few days after her aunt's funeral when Teddy gazed miserably at Wyn's new shoes that were placed neatly under the empty armchair opposite his and said, 'She only bought them a fortnight ago. I wonder if they'll refund the money?'

Beata tried to sound placating. 'I shouldn't think so, Uncle.

They've been worn.' She picked up the shoes and presented the soles for his inspection.

'Only a few times.'

'The shop won't see it like that. Margaret might get some use out of them, though. They're too large for me otherwise I –'

'Give them away?' he almost choked. 'I can't afford to do that. They cost a lot of money. I'm a widower now, you know.'

Beata shrugged. 'I doubt the shop will give you a refund.'

'Couldn't you try for me?' he wheedled forlornly.

Imagining the embarrassment, Beata was loath to do this, but looking into the old man's rheumy eyes, she felt compelled at least to try.

Naturally, the shop refused to take the shoes back, the manager pouring scorn on Beata for even having the temerity to ask. Cheeks burning, she was ejected in no uncertain terms, receiving more defamation from her uncle when he found she had let him down.

This obsession with money was to grow increasingly worse, in widowhood Uncle Teddy becoming even more niggardly than his wife, keeping such a tight hold of the purse strings that Beata had almost to physically fight with him in order to acquire money for food and even then he demanded to know where every farthing had gone.

But only as the enormity of his bereavement set in and Teddy began to rely more heavily on the bottle, did Beata truly realize what she had let herself in for. Never having seen him totally inebriated before, she was to find him extremely nasty in his cups. His drunken insults ringing in her ears, many a night she was to go to bed cursing her decision to stay. Still, she reminded herself of her promise to Aunt Wyn and remained steadfast in her duty.

Whilst Beata managed to hang on to her compassion, others did not. Faced with his incoherent mumblings, the weekly get-togethers with Mr Love and his cohorts began to tail off, and by the end of the year the men of God had deserted this incorrigible old drunkard altogether, not even popping in to wish him the season's greetings.

Apart from the cards from her sisters that arrived on Christmas morning, it was possibly the worst yuletide Beata had ever had – the worst dinner for sure, with only pork ribs and cabbage on the menu. What made her even more furious was that there was always enough money for alcohol. She had tried to outwit him when he gave her cash to buy whisky, spending it on food instead and pretending he had not given the order, but he had reacted in such a vile manner that it did not seem worth it to repeat the episode. It was uncharitable she knew, but in her hungry state she hoped that he would drink himself to death and let her be free.

It began to look as if Teddy shared her view as, over the coming year, he gave in completely to his alcoholism and took to his bed, Aunt Wyn's position at his side replaced by bottles of liquor, whisky on one flank, rum on the other, his days spent taking alternate swigs from each. His only visitor these days was the doctor, and even he was swift to exit.

Beata tried to evade him too as best she could, escaping into the garden or to the shops, though it was impossible for her to stay out too long with her uncle requiring medication and constant jugs of water to flush out his system, and apart from this she knew he would not even bother to get up to go to the lavatory if she was not there to make him. Most galling of all, this sense of duty had compelled her to turn down an invitation to Mims' spring wedding.

In his alcoholic trance, Uncle Teddy cared for none of this. Certainly he was too befuddled now to answer questions about the continuing build-up of military might in Europe. Rarely bothering to consult him on anything, except to persuade him in his more lucid moments to sign for his pension, Beata was to spend most of that summer worrying as Hitler continued his war of nerves, the threat of all-out conflict creeping ever nearer now that he had turned his attention to Poland. Upon the advice of their embassy, German residents began to leave Britain in droves. Small as she had been at the time, Beata retained the violent memory of Mr Kaiser's shop being smashed up in Denaby, and wondered whether it would happen again in this small village.

Yet even now there were posters up in town telling her, 'Don't worry about Hitler, have your holiday'. Educated people, journalists and politicians, who were ignoring all the warnings, who thought the German problem could be solved by a blockade, who did not believe there would be a war, put their opinions into hard print. Beata wanted desperately to believe these rather than the ones which spoke of poison gas and chemical warfare, never more so than upon receiving the news that Mims was expecting her first baby, news that plunged her into a contest of emotions. Would the dear little thing start its life in a world savaged by war?

The weather did not help. Tonight was unusually sultry for September; even with the window open there was no relief. Lying here in bed, she felt like one of the men she had seen through the window of the barber's shop, their heads swathed in hot towels, almost suffocating. She had had a devil of an evening with Teddy, constantly at his drunken beck and call, begging him to cease his obscenities and hoping no one would hear them, trying to prevent him falling out of bed. Exhausted by this and the heat, she was glad finally to be lying in her own, though could not yet settle, expecting him to yell out at any minute, desperate for sleep but at the same time dreading that the morning would bring another bundle of soiled sheets to wash.

It did. Dragging herself out of bed in response to her uncle's childish cries, she winced as she put her leg to the floor, having no need to examine it for it was constantly swollen these days, then limped to Teddy's room that reeked of liquor and urine. He was not quite so difficult on a morning, though there was still a substantial amount of alcohol in his bloodstream and he tottered as she helped him out of bed and into a chair, almost pulling her down with him.

At some time during the night the humidity had gone and in its place was a bright sunny day. That was just as well with these stinking sheets to be washed. Limping back and forth around the bed, stripping the wet linen down to the mackintosh, applying fresh layers and tucking it in, Beata moved to collect her uncle, putting her toes to his and levering him from the chair, finally to reinstate him under the blankets.

After opening the window to let in some fresh air she made to leave.

'Me bottles,' he reminded her.

Knowing there was little point asking if it would be wiser to wait until after he had eaten, without complaint she passed him the bottles of liquor and went on her way, putting the sheets to soak whilst she made breakfast for them both.

Afterwards, her uncle supplied with the Sunday papers, she lit the copper, set to laundering the sheets and finally hung them out, the only one to have washing on her line on the Sabbath.

Once this was out of the way there was the dinner to prepare. At least that was something to look forward to, Beata having managed to get a joint of mutton out of the old skinflint. By this time he had consumed the dregs of his whisky bottle left over from the previous night's binge and was bawling for another, calling her all the names under the sun when she was tardy in supplying it. Only to prevent him disturbing the neighbours did she obey.

Whisking up the Yorkshire pudding mixture, she listened to the wireless as she toiled and sweated, the volume turned high so that both occupants could hear it. Simultaneous to the carriage clock in the living room chiming ten, the broadcaster said, 'Listeners should stand by for an announcement of national importance.' Attending with only one ear, the other pricked for signs of trouble from her uncle, Beata put the mixture aside, dashed a wisp of auburn hair from her brow and set to peeling the potatoes as music returned to the kitchen.

The next moment Teddy was yelling out to her in discomfort and she rushed to answer, fearing he would wet the bed again. Providing him with a different variety of bottle, she waited for him to fill it, then made him comfortable before limping back to the kitchen.

Some minutes later, the broadcaster again cut into the music, his voice so grave as to make her pay full attention now. 'The Prime Minister will make an announcement of national importance at a quarter past eleven,' but this was all he said, and once again the music resumed.

Irked by these interruptions every fifteen minutes and made more annoyed by the blast of heat as she opened the oven door to arrange the potatoes around the joint, Beata urged the faceless voice as it came again, 'Oh, for God's sake get on with it!' And she slammed the door in frustration.

She began to feel quite nervous and, between preparing the rest of the vegetables and going to check on Uncle Teddy, who was as ever being overzealous with the aperitif, her eyes kept moving to the clock.

It was now ten past eleven. Everything prepared, Beata sat down with a glass of water to watch the hands move slower to zero. Someone was giving a talk on how to make the most of tinned foods. Normally she would have gained some use from the recipes given, but not today.

Then suddenly the Prime Minister was speaking. He sounded very old and sad, the enunciation slow and deliberate, its tone setting butterflies fluttering in her stomach.

'I am speaking to you from the Cabinet Room at ten Downing Street . . .'

'Beata! Where's dinner?'

'It's not ready yet, Uncle!' Suddenly filled with dread, Beata rushed into the living room and turned up the volume on the wireless set.

'This morning the British Ambassador in Berlin handed the German Government a final note stating that –'

'I want it *now*!' bawled the drunken voice.

Beata clicked her tongue and leaned towards the speaker, trying to concentrate on the vital message.

'– unless we heard from them by eleven o'clock that they were prepared at once to withdraw their troops from Poland, a state of war would exist between us. I have to tell you now –'

'I'm *dyyying*!'

'– that no such undertaking has been received and that consequently this country is at war with Germany.'

Beata felt that her heart had been plunged into ice, felt again, as she had on the night she had sat on the stairs and overheard her father speak of the horrors suffered by his young soldiers. She thought of her brothers who might suffer the same, of Mims' husband, soon to be a father. She longed to be with her sisters, not this nasty drunken old scrooge whose yelling threatened to lift the roof.

'Now may God bless you all,' came the sorrowful old voice.

'Get in here, you slut! Ssslut, pig . . .'

'May He defend the right. It is the evil things that we shall be fighting against – brute force, bad faith, injustice, oppression and persecution – and against them I am certain that right will prevail.'

Too small to know what was going on the first time, still Beata retained images from her childhood that mirrored what was happening now, the great movements of khaki, the tearful goodbyes, the excited, worried chatter, the fretful looks. Now in addition she was about to be party to the kind of bureaucracy her mother had had to face.

Prior to a national register being compiled, everyone was instructed to carry a luggage label with their name and address on it. Margaret arrived that morning with hers threaded through a buttonhole. 'My husband's always calling me an old bag,' she joked to Beata. 'I might as well fit the bill.'

There was also a gas mask dangling from her handlebars, millions of these having been distributed across the country. Producing her own, Beata put it on, saying in distorted tone, 'Some people say it's an improvement.'

They both laughed, but the sound had a nervous edge to it and afterwards came a moment of sobriety as they discussed the torpedoing of the British liner *Athenia* that had been bound for Canada.

Then it was back to the mundane as they went into the house to set about their work, keeping nerves at bay with conversation.

'I hear we're going to get ration books in the next few days.' In the box room, Beata hauled a stepladder to the window.

'They're not messing about this time, are they?' said Margaret, pulling up a chair and helping her to pin some black paper over the glass, Teddy being unwilling to fork out on curtaining for a room that wasn't used. 'In the last lot they didn't ration until near the end.'

'Maybe this one is near its end already.' This optimistic opinion was as much to cheer Beata herself as Margaret. 'Over before it's begun.'

'Or more likely it's going to go on for a bloody long time,' replied the other grimly, stepping down off the chair and dragging it back into place. 'And they're getting us in practice for pulling our belts in.'

'I'm already expert at doing that, living with that old codger.'

Margaret gave a nod of empathy. 'At least I get paid for putting up with him. Not for much longer, though. I don't need the money now my other lass has started work.'

Beata felt like pleading for the cleaner not to leave her with him, but did not want her to feel beholden.

But the middle-aged woman seemed to sense this, saying kindly, 'There's no reason you have to stay here either, you know. He's got relatives of his own in Southport that could do the job.'

Beata was aware of this, though she had never seen hide nor hair of them. 'But I promised Aunt Wyn I'd do it.'

'Well, I'll stay a bit longer then,' the frog-like face relented. 'But just for you, love, and only for a couple of weeks. I've joined the WVS and I haven't time to squander on the likes of that tight-fisted, ungrateful old bugger. If you ask me there's others more deserving of your care. Let his own kin take the flak.'

Devouring every scrap of news from both radio and newspaper, Beata soon learned that Margaret had been right to be pessimistic, for, after only one week, the Government announced that it was preparing for a three-year war.

Trying to imagine herself cooped up here for so long, she was filled with horror and, desperate for someone more vital with whom to share her life, said to her uncle as she served him breakfast, before the liquor had a chance to take hold, 'I'm told the village is expecting evacuees from Liverpool, Uncle, could we –'

'Riffraff,' growled Teddy over his boiled egg.

'They're children,' corrected Beata, 'some of them really tiny. They'll be missing their mothers and I thought –'

'They're still scum. Full of fleas and scabies.' Before she could prevent it, Teddy flipped his tray to the floor and delved under the blankets for a bottle.

Heart sinking, she stooped to replace the scattered items on the tray, abandoning all hope of fostering an evacuee. How would she cope when she had this overgrown child to deal with? What kind of a home would this be for a child anyway?

Her decision proved to be a blessing, for her uncle's opinion, however prejudiced, was not far off the mark. With their wild, big-city ways the evacuees caused immediate chaos in the village, one of them even being knocked over by a car in the blackout when he sneaked out after dark.

Considering herself to have had a lucky escape, but still wanting to feel that she was doing something for the war effort, Beata joined in the great rush to produce more food, without telling her uncle, digging up his rosebeds and replacing them with seedling vegetables. It was very strenuous work but greatly satisfying as she stood back to admire her efforts.

'Should you be doing that with your bad leg?' Mr Ellis was out in his garden too, a gas mask container slung over his shoulder and a spade in his hand.

She smiled at him but did not dwell too long on his crossed eyes as they made her feel queasy. 'If I don't, nobody else will.'

The gnarled old man gave a nod of understanding and resumed his work. Taking seriously the information on what to do in an air raid given in the pamphlet that had come through his door, he had begun to excavate a trench lined with sandbags in his garden. 'Well, after I've finished this I'll come over and do one for you.'

Viewing his red face and loud breathing, she envisioned him having a heart attack and said hurriedly, 'I don't want to put you to any trouble, Mr Ellis.'

His head bobbed up from the trench as he continued to shovel merrily. 'No trouble, dear – expediency! I'm old enough to remember the Zep raids.'

Beata vaguely remembered them too, at least she remembered the night when Clem had come to sit on her bed and placate her with a white lie that it was only thunder. He had been so kind to her then. Feeling nostalgic, she wondered what he was doing now. At least his bad chest would spare him from having to go and fight like poor Joe.

She was wondering if the authorities would corner Duke when suddenly a distant air raid siren sounded. Even having been expecting this test, it still made her jump and the hairs stood up on the back of her neck as she looked automatically to the sky. 'What are we supposed to do?' she called to Mr Ellis. 'Do I have to get Uncle Teddy out of bed?'

The cross-eyed old face reassured her, its owner clambering out of his trench. 'No, it's just to make sure everybody can hear them.' As the siren was sounded three times, he came up to the fence and leaned on his shovel to explain to her what the different tones meant. First a steady note: 'That's the raiders past signal.' Then an eerie warbling. 'That's the one you have to take notice of. If you hear that you run like billy-o.'

'Where to?'

'My shelter – or whatever one you happen to be close to at the time.'

She looked forlorn. 'I'll never be able to drag Uncle Teddy out of bed.'

Mr Ellis's eyes consulted each other across his nose for a second, before he dealt wise advice. 'Leave him where he is and save yourself.'

However, they were only to hear the air raid siren in practice, never for real and, after weeks of false alarms with nothing happening, the harum-scarum evacuees started to drift back to Liverpool, places that had been closed now re-opening. Along with the rest of her neighbours Beata settled back into her usual routine, albeit a tense one.

After the initial excitement an air of gloom gradually took hold, people beginning to grumble at all the restrictions with which they continued to be bombarded.

November was dreary enough without all this on top, opined Beata to herself, wistfully fingering a late rose that had escaped her dig for victory and bending to inhale its perfume. Overhead, a flock of seagulls was circling, their screams filling the air. It was such an incredibly lonely sound that she hurried to resume what she had come out here to do, which was to give the washing line a quick wipe with a cloth. It was permanently erected these days, there seemed no point in taking it down, Uncle Teddy's bed-wetting having become a regular occurrence. Ironically, he was the only one who didn't grumble, his drunken binges sparing him from knowing what was going on half the time, whilst a lot of other people were cracking up from the strain of wondering when the enemy might strike.

Margaret was one of those ready to blow, thought Beata acknowledging the cleaner's arrival as she hung out the bedding. Her plump cheeks had become empty bags, her mouth permanently turned down, her bulging blue eyes awash with worry that her husband's fishing boat was going to be sunk by a torpedo. But none of these feelings were voiced.

'I see the old pisspot's struck again.' Margaret leaned her bicycle against the wall. 'Oh, Beat, how can you stand it?'

'I amaze meself.' Struggling to prop up the heavy washing line, Beata finally achieved this and turned, panting in triumph.

'Can't you give him less water, love?'

Beata shook her head. 'He needs it for his diabetes.' She chuckled. 'And to dilute the booze.'

'You deserve a medal.'

'I'd rather feel as if I were doing my bit towards the war.'

Margaret tapped her. 'Why don't you come with me to the WVS? It'd get you away from the place.'

'I'd like to but I daren't leave Old Man River. He'll drown in his own piddle or drink himself to death. It seems a bit pointless me trying to keep his blood sugar stable when he's hellbent on pickling himself.'

'Shall I fetch you some wool from the centre then? You can knit a blanket.'

'I could knit Uncle a balaclava with no face hole.'

Margaret laughed. 'Eh, Beata, you always manage to joke.'

Beata did not know how, for she felt as anxious and nervous as her companion, wondering when the bombs were going to fall, concerned for her loved ones in the garrison city of York. But she said with a calm smile, 'Well, you have to, don't you? And being here does have its advantages. If I'm looking after an invalid I don't have to join the Land Army or Munitions.'

'At least you'd get paid, though!'

'I couldn't stand on a production line all day. My leg would explode. At least here I get chance to sit down – sometimes.' She threw up her eyes with a cynical laugh. 'Eh, I haven't been able to get down and register for bacon and butter rationing with the grocer yet. Could you keep an eye on me laddo while I nip out?'

Margaret obliging, Beata went off to enjoy half an hour of freedom. No more rides to town now; the car had long been gathering cobwebs in the garage.

The folk in the outside world were wearing poppies. She bought one too, the remembrance of those who had fallen gaining new solemnity in these dangerous times.

When she returned, Margaret had paused in her chores for a pot of tea and, fixing her bulging eyes upon the poppy, said, 'You're showing me up, I've forgotten to get one.' After pouring another cup, she stared into space, shook her head and gave a despairing exclamation at how many more might die. 'It's just all so ridiculous, Beat,' she complained. 'You've got Russia siding with the Germans when they were our allies last time – the same with the Japs – and Turkey signing a pact with us when they shot us to bits in the Dardanelles! The world's mad, politicians are mad – it's them that gets us into it, you know.'

'I know,' sighed the listener, cradling her cup of tea and remembering her father's response to the invasion of Belgium, 'but what else can you do against a megalomaniac?'

An abusive yell emerged from Uncle Teddy's room.

'Speaking of megalomaniacs . . .' Beata dealt her companion a stoical grin and limped off to tend to her uncle's needs.

When she came back, Margaret had made a decision and was putting on her coat, seemingly in a rush to go. 'I'm sorry, Beat, I can't stand his vile language any more. It's getting me down. I shan't be coming again. Sorry for lumbering you with extra work but . . .'

Despite her heart sinking at the thought, Beata said evenly, 'Not to worry. You do what you have to.'

'Don't forget to put your clock back next Saturday night, will you?' Margaret sought to remind her as she mounted her bicycle and rode away.

'I won't.' Beata waved her off, feeling that it would not matter if she remembered or not. For her, time stood still.

Luckily, hearing that she had been deserted, Mr Ellis was kind enough to step in and sit with Uncle Teddy whilst Beata did the shopping, which had become somewhat of a nightmare in itself with all the shortages.

Having dubbed last Christmas the worst of her life, Beata prepared to eat her words as another December came upon them. It didn't really matter that sugar supplies were very low; with her uncle's diabetes they hardly ate any in this house and the only use she had for it was as currency when bartering with her neighbours

586

for some other rare commodity. Unfortunately that did not apply to bacon, everyone clinging greedily to their ration. Conserving her own rashers as a treat for Sunday morning, she thought of it now as she prepared the evening repast, the imagined smell of it sizzling in the pan helping to get through the rest of the week.

Tonight she and Teddy would be having fish paste sandwiches, the nearest she got to eating the real thing these days, fish being so dear. It probably wouldn't matter to Teddy, whose palate had been numbed by countless bottles of whisky; he hardly knew what he was eating. Buttering the bread, she glanced at the clock, though it was an irrelevant gesture for, it having been a dingy afternoon, the curtains had been already drawn well before blackout time.

Just as she was about to carry her uncle's tray to his room, someone knocked at the door. Greatly aware of the risk of being fined, she turned the light off before answering and groped her way in the darkness.

'Merry Christmas, Beat!' The caller beamed at her.

'Joe!' She gasped in surprise and pleasure. Included in Gussie's latest letter had been the information that all the troops of Northern Command had been granted seven days' leave for Christmas and they would have Joe home, but, 'I never thought you'd trail all the way over here!'

'Well I have, and I come bearing gifts!' The khaki-clad figure swept through the door, kissing his delighted sister in passing, and even before removing his greatcoat began to take parcels from his haversack: a knitted cardigan from Maddie, a cake from Gussie, several tins of food and a lump of ham. 'And the best!' He left the bottle of sherry till last, withdrawing it with a flourish.

Beata could have wept with happiness at the sight of it all, but most of all to have her own flesh and blood here.

Joe saw that she was speechless with emotion and said understandingly, 'Well, it's not much fun you being stuck down here on your own, is it? So I thought I'd have a couple of days with me favourite sister.'

She chuckled. 'You might regret it when you see what's on offer.' And she displayed the meagre plate of sandwiches.

He curled an arm round her and squeezed. 'Nay, it's enough just to see you, Beat.'

'And you,' she told him, hugging him back, then examining the tins he had brought her. 'Though these peaches are even more welcome.' She reached for a tin opener, sharing the contents between two bowls and, with a twinkle in her eye, mimicking her late aunt. 'Too sweet for Teddy.'

'So how's the old bugger been treating you?' Joe took off his cap.

'Abominably,' said Beata. 'Come on, get by the fire and sit down while I take him his tea.'

'You sit down,' he commanded. 'I'll take it, and I'll give him a talking to whilst I'm at it.'

'You'll be lucky if he hears you,' she replied, but did as she was told anyway, relieved to take the weight off her leg.

When Joe came back he was astounded at how bad their uncle's drinking had become. 'My God, it stinks like a distillery in there, and he's out like a light. How much has he had?'

'I've no idea. I don't measure it now,' said Beata lightly. 'I just get the drayman to back his wagon up to the window and tip its contents straight down his throat. It saves on the bottles, what with all the shortages, you know.'

Joe was glad to see that his sister could find amusement in an awful situation. But then a sense of humour was one thing common to all of Probyn's offspring, and, as they tucked into tea, many more jokes were shared at Uncle Teddy's expense.

But on a sterner note Joe warned, 'You mustn't let him take advantage of you, though, Beat. It must be difficult, managing such a big chap on your own.'

She dismissed this. 'Oh, well, others have worse to deal with.' Her allusion to the war brought more serious discussion, Joe lighting a cigarette and telling her as much as he knew about the military goings-on; the seven-day leave must mean they were about to go abroad, though he did not know where.

'Why did the silly old fools do nothing to stop it, Beat?' he demanded, referring to the politicians and sounding very frustrated. 'I was just looking forward to being on reserve and then I find meself back with a gun in me hand.'

'I thought that was what you always wanted?' Beata sipped her sherry.

'To be a soldier, aye – but I didn't know there was going to be another bloody war!'

His theatrically outraged announcement brought more amusement from his sister, but she could tell underneath all the joking he was frightened. So was she. The laughter fading, she said, 'Let's pray it doesn't last too long.'

Joe took a long drag of his cigarette, nodding through the smoke.

It was not so much the thought of dying but the knowledge that he would have to kill people, and at close quarters, that made him feel sick. He did not know if he would even be able to do it.

Wanting to take that look off his face, Beata changed the subject. 'So how's our Mimsy? I'll bet she's getting round.' Their sister was due to give birth next month.

'Round? She's like a bloody house end.' Joe laughed, and this happier note was to continue for the rest of the evening.

Later, glad that Uncle had not disturbed their lovely get-together, Beata made a bed up for the visitor on the sofa before retiring herself.

And in the morning, awoken by Teddy's shouts, Joe helped her strip off the old man's wet sheets and replace them with dry ones, also lighting the boiler for her as she made breakfast, and asking, 'Does he do this all the time?'

Beata lied, not wanting him to worry about her. 'No just now and then.' She limped about the bungalow, making sure all the lights were turned off before opening the curtains to another grim morning.

'You want some tape across that glass, Beat, in case it gets shattered. I'll do it for you before I go.' This Joe did, plus many other helpful things throughout that day before finally having to go for his evening train.

However, during his stay he had been angered to hear all the cursing directed towards his sister and now went to wag a finger at the inebriated old man. 'Now listen, Uncle Ted, stop all this bad language. Our Beata's been good to you and I won't have you upsetting her. Do you hear?'

There were whining promises from Teddy to obey, his uncle slurring as he grasped Joe's finger, 'She's a lovely girl, so good to me, so good . . .'

Shouldering his haversack, Joe shared a last word with his sister. 'I don't know whether I've managed to fettle him or not, Beat, but if he doesn't get any better, you leave. I'm telling you now, don't be taking any truck.'

'Nay, I can manage him no trouble,' she said casually, then kissed her brother goodbye.

It was such a wrench watching him go. She almost regretted that he had been here at all, for after he had gone the house seemed emptier than ever.

*　　*　　*

589

If there were any New Year celebrations then Beata did not hear them, though she was to receive glad tidings from Margaret, who happened to be cycling past when she was putting a bundle of old newspapers out for collection that frosty morning and stopped briefly to chat.

'A bit of good news at last, Beat! Hitler's got cancer, he's only got eighteen months to live.'

Beata had heard such rumours before and looked dubious.

But Margaret assured her. 'It's right! I've just read it in the paper.' Legs planted astride her bike, varicose veins bulging through her stockings, she asked if the other had registered yet for meat rationing, offering to sit with Teddy in order to enable her to do so, but Beata told her it was all in hand. 'I'd better get on with the job then!' She set her foot to the pedal and, with a patriotic gesture, cycled off.

The rest of Beata's day proceeded as normal. Whilst the washing was on the line she kneaded her bread and put it into the oven, then set about baking raisinless scones and other such stuff for the rest of the week. In the afternoon, seeing that the sheets were never going to fully dry in the cold atmosphere, she brought them in to hang over the fire, putting her feet up and listening to a play on the radio before starting her ironing. Providing her uncle's tea to coincide with children's hour, she sat down again to enjoy *Out with Romany*. But then on the six o'clock news she heard that the Allies were expecting a big German offensive in spring and everything came rushing in on her again.

It was one bad thing after another. The Nazis had made their biggest air raid ever on the east coast. No bombs had been dropped and British fighters had driven them off, but still they were getting bolder. And in the same week three British submarines were lost. Encouraged by Hitler's exploits, the IRA had started a terror campaign of its own, causing explosions in the capital, and though that did not affect Beata it was just one more thing to be gloomy about. It felt that everything was against them. Against her.

It was to be the most desperate winter she had ever known. Alongside the rationing of food there was little coal to go round either, certainly not enough to cope with the drastic fall in temperature that occurred at the end of January when the village was encased in icicles, frozen pipes bursting all over the place. Beata was fortunate in that hers had been lagged but it did not make the house any the warmer.

It was so cold that she woke one morning to find her dentures embedded in a glass of ice and had perforce to do without them until she had time to boil a kettle. The idea of getting up to a cold grate set her shivering and the thought of getting Teddy's sheets dry in this arctic climate was almost the last straw, but, being penniless, how could she afford to escape to York unless she walked? And that was just too far. Bracing herself, she rolled out of bed, slipped hurriedly into her clothes, shuddering at the coldness of them, then went to face her responsibilities.

Not until she had lit the fire, boiled a kettle and managed to hack her teeth from the block of ice could she eat breakfast. This by no means the worst of her problems, she then launched into washing the bedding.

Mr Ellis sympathized when he came in later to look after Uncle Teddy and found her trying to thaw the frozen sheets round the fire. 'Maybe if you were to rouse him through the night,' he suggested helpfully.

Beata had already come to this conclusion and though it would mean she would be deprived of her own rest there seemed no other answer. Her fingers bright red and aching from being in contact with the frozen sheets, she breathed on them a few times then went to make Mr Ellis a cup of tea, before gathering all her ration cards and coupons and going shopping.

The meat situation was deplorable. She had gone out for a joint but came home with something completely different. Opening the package she asked with a laugh, 'How do you like our Sunday dinner, Mr Ellis?'

The old man was not surprised by the two pork pies, groaning, 'I know! I went round half a dozen greengrocers yesterday and they hadn't a spud between them.'

Thanking him for his help, Beata was glad when he agreed to while away a lonely hour by partaking in another pot of tea. Mr Ellis was the only friend she had, and even though he was less easy to laughter than before the war he persisted in bringing her little gifts, which she now thought about as she sipped her tea and smiled at him. How sad that it was not enough.

The white world was eventually to thaw and the food situation was alleviated somewhat by the coming of spring when everyone could once again return to planting out their gardens, but there was to be no lessening of the tension as the days crept ever nearer to the expected German offensive. Of course, others had been offensive for months and continued to be so. After another day of extreme nastiness from her uncle, Beata's one recourse was to snuggle up in bed, to dream of her lost love and to think what might have been.

Still thinking about Tommy when she opened her eyes the next morning, it was devastating not to find him there, just another lonely day stretching in front of her. She could have wept. Her leg was like a balloon and incredibly painful. Nevertheless, she was forced to get out of bed and tend her uncle. Thanks to her habit of rousing him through the night there were no wet sheets today, nor had there been any for the past month. Feeling more sympathetically disposed towards him, for, after all, he was old and would soon be dead at the rate he was drinking, she brought him a cup of tea, then set about washing and shaving him before giving him breakfast and leaving him to read the newspaper.

There was not a peep out of him for hours. Worried about this she crept to his room, thinking that he might perhaps have expired but in fact he was only sleeping. The newspaper had slipped from his bed to the floor. Her mind still on Tommy, imagining herself in his arms, she limped in and bent to pick it up, but as she did a hand shot out and grabbed a fistful of her hair. Crying out in pain, she said persuasively, 'Uncle, let go!'

But instead of doing so he gripped her hair even tighter and wrenched it so forcefully that she had to go with it to prevent him tearing it out by the roots. Ignoring her agonized protests he hauled her face down to his and planted a slobbering kiss on her lips.

With a muffled shout of disgust she tried to lash out at him but it seemed to have no effect for the old drunkard just laughed gleefully and held her head with both hands now, pressing her lips to his so that she could hardly breathe. Continuing to struggle and writhe she screwed her mouth up in order to avoid his dribbling whisky-laden lips, but it was of no avail for he was just too strong and in the end it was only by accident that her flailing hand managed to come into contact with the hair at his temples and, giving it a vicious twist, she finally prised herself loose.

Her uncle was yelling like a child and rubbing his temple at the agony she had inflicted but Beata did not care. He had destroyed all her dreams of ever being kissed romantically again. Never would she be able to rid herself of the taste of him. When he cursed and swore and tried to lash out at her she stepped out of his reach and made her escape, hurried from the room, pulling her apron over her mouth as she went, desperately trying to wipe it clean of his foul alcohol-laden spittle, but in vain. Reaching the bathroom sink she cupped her hand beneath the running tap and scooped it into her mouth, gulped it in, swilling it round and round, rinsing it out over and over but feeling that never again would it be clean.

With a final gasp, head hanging over the sink, she leaned there for a while, before unbending to scowl at herself in the mirror, her pink face distorting ever more at the expression of distaste she saw there for that vile old sot. He had tested her compassion to the limit and in that wretched moment of failure she made her decision. Taking a deep breath she pulled her clothes straight, dragged a brush over her pained scalp, and, giving her face one last wipe, she limped to the bureau to seek out the address that Aunt Wyn had once shown her in case of emergency. Well, this *was* an emergency.

Abandoning Uncle Teddy to his abusive tirade she put on her hat and coat and went there now in person, informing his astonished relatives that she would no longer be taken for a mug and they could do their duty by him. Giving them no time for the shock to sink in, she said finally: 'I'll be catching a train around eight tomorrow morning. Don't leave it too long after that before you call on your uncle, he'll be needing his medication.'

Then, turning her back on their flabbergasted faces, she returned to the bungalow to cook dinner.

Her cautious approach towards Uncle Teddy when taking in his meal was unnecessary for he appeared to have forgotten all about the episode. However, Beata had not and she was therefore glad when his relatives turned up the next morning shortly before she was ready to leave.

Handing him into their care, she then picked up her suitcase and went to catch the train to York, her uncle providing the fare, though he was unaware of it.

There was no theft involved. She had earned it.

THIRTY-THREE

So, in her thirtieth year Beata finally came home to York. It should have been a vast relief to be rid of the burden and the loneliness, and so it was in many ways. But, with no money and no job, other worries would soon arise and she determined to find a temporary position in service whilst deciding what more important course to take.

This her first act upon getting off the train, she found it not as easy as anticipated. Her enquiry at the labour exchange revealed that the large mansions where she had once danced at the Christmas ball had now become the headquarters of Bomber Command or military hospitals. She had hoped to be equipped with the promise of a job before asking her sister for a temporary bed, but, too tired to continue tramping around town with her suitcase, she reluctantly went there empty-handed to throw herself on Gussie's mercy.

There was always some slight difference in the old city after each spell away, but now the changes were many. Mingled with the market vendors' shouts of, 'Wrap it up, George!' were to be heard the foreign voices of refugees. Already congested with two-way traffic – bicycles, cars, horses and carts – the narrow medieval thoroughfares were also clogged with soldiers marching to parade. As she travelled through it on the bus it seemed as if even the very foundations of the city itself were being ripped up, great piles of twisted metal forcing a diversion of her vehicle to avoid the workmen who salvaged tramlines for armaments.

Even the most humble abode contributing towards the fight, she turned into Gussie's street to find the railings sawn from garden walls, gone to metamorphose as weapons against the enemy. But not even Hitler could get in the way of spring-cleaning and this was what she found her sister doing upon arrival, her hair protected from the cobwebs by a pair of old knickers. Explaining the reason for being here and apologizing for her impecunious state, Beata promised to assist around the house until able to find a job.

Gussie as usual was unconditionally welcoming and said about the lack of employment, 'Never mind, something'll turn up.' And the only inconvenience Beata's arrival seemed to bring was how to fit her into ablutions. Bath night had already to be staggered, there being so many residents, and one extra tended to throw the schedule into disarray. 'But we'll cope,' smiled Gus.

Whilst the world outside had been thrust into turmoil, the one in here had changed very little. Looking at Mick in his usual place by the range whilst his wife cleaned around him, Beata wondered if he had ever moved in her absence.

'What's that you're reading?' she asked out of politeness.

Pipe in mouth, he held out the book for her to examine. Barely able to understand the title, let alone the content, she nodded and handed it back. He was certainly a man of surprises. Intelligent and obviously well read, he could have made so much more of his life. How sad to waste those talents through idleness.

She herself was certainly not to be idle those next few days. Whilst old Mick alternately read or dozed in his fireside chair, she and her sister threw themselves into the household cleaning, cooked and mended and shopped. This apart, with Easter upon them there was also the task of providing some treat for the children in these austere times. Despite petrol rationing everyone else in the city seemed determined not to miss the holiday fun, and normally so would Beata, but she had not the wherewithal until Maddie came to the rescue, contributing the fare so the youngsters were able to join the trek to the seaside, though, of course, leaving Beata to supervise.

It was certainly a chaotic existence in the Melody household, relatives coming and going through all hours of the day and night, some even having to clamber over her bed in order to get to theirs, but after her lonely life with Uncle Teddy, Beata was not complaining.

She had yet to decide what her own contribution to the war would be. With so much to do and so exhausted that she fell asleep the moment her head hit the pillow, there had been little time to give it much thought. She tried to think about it as she closed her eyes tonight, but, as ever, oblivion descended immediately.

However, this was to be broken in the wee hours by a rap at the front door. Sleeping in a bedroom that fronted the street, she and the other occupants stirred, but, ignoring it, all turned over and tried to go back to sleep.

The knock came again. Beata heard someone on the stairs and knowing it had to be Gussie she reluctantly dragged herself up too and felt her way down the dark staircase to see if there was any trouble. After all, it could be about Joe.

Her sister was just closing the front door again when Beata appeared. Wrapped in her dressing gown and a tousled auburn plait dangling over her shoulder, Gussie explained in low murmur as she bent to put on her shoes, 'It's all right. Mrs Cayley's gone to meet her Maker. Her Tony's just come to ask if I'll lay her out. Go back to bed.'

Glad that it had nothing to do with Joe, Beata made sure that her sister did not need any help before staggering back upstairs. Then, how strange, as she closed her eyes her mind suddenly cleared and she knew exactly what her contribution to the war effort would be.

The next morning after everyone had gone to work and school, she helped with the washing and to get the dinner ready before announcing her decision to Gussie. 'I'm off out this aft to join the WAAF.'

'Good show. Take your gas mask down to the inspection centre at the same time. If you leave it any longer you'll end up being charged for any repairs that need doing – Oh blast, it's pouring down! Help me get the washing in, Beat.' Gussie dashed outside, her sister limping after her, and the laundry was quickly transferred to clothes horses and a pulley over the fire.

Just after this Mick came in from the betting shop, shaking the rain from his trilby and looking with dismay on the washing draped in front of the hearth. 'If there's such a thing as reincarnation I'm coming back as a bloody clothes horse. That's the only thing that can get near the fire on a Monday.'

Helping him out of his wet things, his obliging wife made a passage to his chair and he went to sit in it, letting the women get on with dinner.

After this was eaten, with the rain set in for the day, Beata decided not to go out and join the Women's Auxilliary Air Force that afternoon. 'No good getting drenched. I'll help you with the ironing instead.'

Gussie agreed and, testing the linen on the clothes horses said, 'I don't think this nightie's going to be dry for tonight. Have you one you can lend me, Beat?'

'Aye, but you haven't only got the one, have you?'

'Oh no, but I used my other one for Mrs Cayley. Well, I had to make her look nice, poor old soul.'

Beata was clicking her tongue over such philanthropy, when someone knocked at the door, and the visitor came straight in. It was Mrs Nelson, who owned one of the shops in the street. 'Telephone for you, Mrs Melody.'

Such means of communication only used in an emergency, Beata and Gussie immediately looked at each other in alarm that it might be bad news about Joe.

But, 'It's your sister in Lancashire,' added Mrs Nelson.

Grabbing her mac, Gussie hurried to respond.

When she returned she looked quite pleased. 'They're coming on the afternoon train.'

Delighted that she would get to meet her nephew at last, Beata asked, 'How long for?'

'Indefinitely – little Jimmy's crying got on Uncle Chris's nerves so she didn't want to outstay her welcome.' She looked at Mick, who rolled his eyes at the ceiling. 'Good job you decided not to go out, Beat. You can help me shuffle the beds round.'

Mims was unusually subdued when she arrived, due to feeling unwanted at her previous home, and to some degree through reluctance to insinuate herself into this already overcrowded household, but mainly because she was missing husband, Jim, dreadfully. She was, though, very glad once again to be amongst her sisters. The way Gussie devoted herself to her family reminded Mims so much of her mother. Even more so in the fact that Gussie had used precious rations to bake a ginger cake for her arrival, the taste and smell of it immediately transporting Mims back in time, to herself as a little girl sitting on Mother's knee being hugged and comforted. This, and the sudden news that Jim would be coming on leave in the next few days, soon had her perked up and reverted to her old self.

It was lovely to have her about the house, thought Beata, reminded so much of their mother in the way Mims sang.

Upon her little nephew's arrival, Beata had put aside her intention of joining the WAAF in order to spend more time with him, and she watched fondly now as, waiting for her husband to arrive, Mims changed Jimmy into his best dress and cardigan.

'Wrap him up, George!' Mims bundled him into her arms and transported him about the room, singing and marching like a soldier. 'Umpalara, Umpalara, lost the leg of her drawers! If you find it, if you find it tack it on to yours!' The baby boy chuckled deep in his chest, making the onlookers laugh too. Eyes gleaming from new motherhood, Mims sang and marched until she was out of breath, but when she tried to sit down the baby began to wail and she quickly jumped up again, saying in imitation of an army sergeant, 'Wait for it, *wait for it*!' Then she set off marching again, 'Umpalara, Umpalara . . .'

Finally, pretending to stagger from exhaustion, she passed the baby to another. 'Here, Beat, deal with this article while I have a rest!' And after handing him over she fell into a chair and lit a cigarette.

Beata was happy to claim him.

But in the next second her sister was up again, laughing and crying and flinging herself into the arms of the handsome man in naval uniform who had just been admitted.

Pressing kisses to her face, hugging and squeezing her, Jim finally broke off to greet his baby son, bestowing him with the same affection, whilst others in the room tried to make themselves scarce in order to allow them intimacy.

With this nigh impossible, whilst Jim was on leave Beata volunteered to look after the baby so that Mims could spend precious moments alone with her husband, who could be snatched away at any juncture. And, the gesture not entirely uncalculating, for the next couple of days she got to pretend that the little chap was hers, to revel in the way his tiny head wobbled against her shoulder, the sweetness of his breath, the sheer wonder of him.

All too soon Jim's leave was over. Though desperate at the parting, Mims did not want his last impression of her to be a miserable one and so continued to act the fool right up to his final night. Whilst Beata gave the baby his bottle, she herself put a colander on her head, took a pastry brush from the drawer, flattened its bristles against her upper lip and came marching out of the scullery performing a goose-step and a Nazi salute. 'Attention everyone! Zis is Frau Gertrud Klink, Hitler's perfect voman – Stop laughing!' she yelled as they fell about. 'Zis is serious.

I vill not haf you laughing at my moustache! You will all be shot!'

'Aw, you've made him cry now!' scolded Beata, half laughing, half accusing, as Jimmy's mouth came away from the teat and uttered a distressed wail.

Putting the brush aside, a chuckling Mims immediately plucked him from her sister and comforted him, though still amused as she jiggled him gently, her smiling husband joining in.

Mick had enjoyed the humorous interval too, directing his pipe stem at Jim. 'You'll have to watch that wife of yours. What with all her singing and daft antics they'll be commandeering her to entertain the troops.'

Mims endowed her husband with a look of love. If they could only guess how she felt inside. Meant to protect her son, instead she felt so small and insignificant against a tyranny that threatened the entire world; she could have screamed out loud with the tension of it all. Not to mention that there were only hours left to share with her beloved. She leaned against him now, hugging their son and kissing the top of his downy head until he stopped crying.

'I think we'll give you your bottle, then put you to bobies,' she told him, then held him up for his father to kiss.

Afterwards, seeking peace and quiet, Jim drifted out into the yard and lit a cigarette.

Allowing him a few moments for reflection, Beata could not help herself and went out to stand beside him, both looking up at the stars and listening to the drone of aircraft, and for that moment he belonged to her. He was a lovely man, not just in looks but in nature, and for a second she envied her sister's luck, but then immediately condemned herself, for such luck had many drawbacks, drawbacks she herself would never have to face: the worry that her man might not come home, and that her son might lose his father.

In the morning he was gone, and in his passing came the news they had all been dreading. There had been a big Nazi raid on a French outpost. This was just the start, for within days there was a radio announcement that Scandinavia had been overrun by Hitler's hordes.

'Nothing to worry about at all,' said Mick, tongue in cheek, reading extracts from his newspaper as the women worked around him. 'The German Government has just decided to take over the protection of Denmark and Norway – that's kind of them isn't it?'

The sisters were unamused, having received word from Joe that he was being sent there. But there was nothing to be done: life must go on as normal.

'Can you fetch a lump of pork back with you?' Gussie handed some money to Beata as the latter prepared to exit. This commodity had lately been derationed so at least there would be a nice roast to look forward to for tomorrow's dinner.

Beata nodded. 'I don't know how long I'll be.' She had finally got round to doing something about the WAAF. 'If there's an exam to sit I won't be very long at all.' She gave a self-deprecating grin, then left.

How right she was. Within seconds of the recruiting officer setting eyes on her distended leg, she was back in the street and heading home.

It was such a blow. All she wanted to do was to help win the war but nobody seemed to want her. Feeling very sorry for herself she made her way through town, remembering to collect the joint of pork as promised. But then as she turned a corner she saw a man collapsed on the pavement and all self-pity dispersed as she rushed to help him.

The man had a nasty graze on his forehead, she feared he might have been attacked but as she bent over him, the casualty raised his head and hissed, 'Bugger off, you soft 'a'p'orth! I'm waiting for the ARP.' And she realized then that the blood was artificial and that it was a staged event.

Feeling totally foolish she made quick apology and limped away. At every turn a slap in the face.

Yet however dreadful she felt, she could not be so selfish as to infect her sisters with this mood, and consequently on the way home she rehearsed a more amusing way to relate the incident to Gussie and Mims, and, imagining their laughter, by the time she arrived she was able to laugh about it too.

But such rejection left a nasty wound that, despite her outward cheerfulness, was to fester in her bosom, and her spirits remained low for the rest of the day.

Strangely, comfort was to be administered by, of all people, Maddie, come to visit after her shift, who seemed the only one to detect how significantly the rebuttal had hurt Beata and sought to cheer her up.

Lighting a cigarette, she asked, 'Do you fancy coming over the garden wall with me?'

Beata frowned, then realized her sister referred to a comic character. 'Oh, Norman Evans – I love him!'

'He's on at the Empire next week,' said Maddie, blowing smoke at the ceiling. 'I've got a couple of days off. We could have an afternoon in town, then go see his show.'

'Who's paying?' asked Beata, a gleam in her eye.

Maddie touched her brow as if deep in thought, 'Er, now let me see . . . Well, it won't be thee, that's for sure!' Then to the others, 'Eh, I don't know, I've just had the Chancellor sticking threepence on a packet of fags and now me sister's intent on robbing me as well!'

With no money of her own, the afternoon in town could have been rather unproductive for Beata, though she was to be recompensed by her sister's exceptionally good mood, not one sarcasm passing Maddie's lips apart from that directed against the enemy when, observing from the top deck of their bus, she noted, 'There's not so many men hanging round street corners now, are there? At least we can thank Hitler for getting our unemployment down.'

'Where are we getting off?' asked Beata as their bus trundled through town.

'Rougier Street. I want to go to Muriel Lyons and get a little frock for Jimmy.'

'I could do with a little frock an' all,' teased Beata, hope in her eye.

'Bugger off, yours'd cost more than two and eleven.' As the bus travelled over Ouse Bridge, Maddie pointed to a group of firemen in practice, training their hoses across the river. 'Eh, he can shoot his hose a long way, can't he?'

Beata chuckled and observed, 'Your joints can't be too bad today.'

'On the contrary,' Maddie drew on her cigarette, 'they're bloody murder. But I've seen these magic bandages in a magazine so I'm keeping my hopes up.'

Keeping their hopes up was all they could do. For, on the day following a side-splitting night at the theatre, there came the dreadful news that Norway had surrendered, this, of course, setting them all worrying about Joe and bringing Maddie rushing back to the house.

Pipe in hand, Mick shook his head in condemnatory fashion. 'Well, they've only themselves to blame for being too neutral, encouraging the Nazis to think they can get away with it.'

'And now our lads are going to have to pay for helping get them out of a fix!' Maddie was angry that her brother was expected to risk his life for foreigners.

Mick too was anxious for his own sons, who had just been included in the latest call-up. They had discussed joining up at the outset of war but, remembering his own assignment in hell, their father had forbidden it. Unable even now to get those terrible images out of his mind, he felt sick at the thought of what they might have to suffer.

Maddie still railed, her painful digits fumbling over the lighting of a cigarette. 'It's like the school bully, if you don't stand up to him the first time, you've had it. And mentioning bullies, people are saying this'll bring that posturing prima donna in, whatshisname, Semolina.'

'Mussolini,' Beata chuckled, and, despite her own deep worry, so did Mims.

Mick agreed with a sigh. ''Twon't be long before the Italians come in, for sure.'

Though this was not to happen yet, the news bulletins continued to be grim, the Nazis making hourly progress in their blitzkrieg of Europe.

Having planned a Bank Holiday expedition with the children to Scarborough, Beata was dismayed to be informed just days prior to this by her sister: 'Whit's been cancelled, Beat.'

'What do you mean?' Just out of bed, she was still fuzzy-headed as she came to help prepare breakfast.

Handing her a cup of tea, Gussie looked grave and bit her lip before announcing, 'I've just heard on the wireless . . . he's invaded the Low Countries.'

There was no need to ask who *he* was. Aghast, Beata pondered on the seriousness of this for a moment, before asking her sister to turn the radio back on so that they might listen to the next news bulletin together.

Coming down just in time to hear the tail end of it, which echoed Gussie's statement about the cancellation of Whitsuntide train services, Mick asked lethargically, 'What's up now?'

Handing him a cup of tea, Gussie told him gently, 'Looks like our boys are going to be fighting on Belgian soil again.'

At first shocked, his grizzled head drooped over the table as the magnitude of the news sank in. The women watched and waited for him to raise his face again, which finally he did, his eyes projecting doom.

'It's the end,' he said.

Under threat of the Nazi onslaught whose evil tide crept ever nearer, the atmosphere in the streets was palpable, volunteers rushing to the police station to enrol in the Local Defence Corps, whilst the police themselves swooped to detain aliens who were rounded up and packed off to camps.

Even Mims had ceased to joke now, desperately worried for her husband, who was heaven knew where, and for her baby son. Everyone went about their business like automatons.

Trying to maintain an air of normality in all this for the sake of the children, Beata soothed their disappointment over the trip to Scarborough by taking them for a picnic in the countryside. Though it was possible to be there in ten minutes, nevertheless after the walk her leg was like a balloon. And the war was still there when they got home.

Crowding round the radio at every news bulletin, they listened and waited as, with incredible speed, the Nazi tanks charged across the Low Countries, inflicting one blow after another. First the surrender of Holland, then, despite an epic struggle in which the patriots fought like lions, the fall of Belgium – and then all at once they were into France.

Digesting a tea of cold meat and salad, Beata and her family waited gravely to be told the worst this evening, but heard that, 'The French continue to hold the Somme line . . .' This familiar name prompted Gussie to think of her father and, after a moment's reverie, said, 'Do you remember, we used to call them the Hun, didn't we?' She took a sip of tea. 'When we were young.'

When we were young. Beata studied her sister, who was only thirty-six. Everybody felt and looked so much older in these dark days.

'Nazis or Hun, they're all the bloody same,' commented Mick, puffing reflectively on his pipe. 'How that fool Chamberlain could be taken in I don't know. Thank God for Mr Churchill.'

Mims came in then, having just tucked Jimmy into his cot. Weaving her way around the younger occupants who sat on the rug, some embroidering, another sketching, she said with little animation, 'Oh, have I missed the news? Mind if I nab the press?'

603

Her elderly brother-in-law motioned for her to take it. 'Nothing in it but atrocities anyway.'

'That's nothing new.' Grim-faced, she settled herself down to read, crossing her legs and perusing the evening edition, avoiding the list of casualties. How much lower could the Nazis sink? They had only recently bombed a refugee ship.

But the section of print to which her eyes were drawn now caused her to break down and sob.

Startled, everyone stopped what they were doing. Her sisters projected concern. 'Oh, whatever is it, love?'

Her whole body racked, tears streaming down her face, Mims could not speak, but handed Beata the newspaper and smote the offending section as if wishing she could erase it and bring them back to life.

Beata read it for herself, saying gravely for the others' benefit, 'The Gestapo have rounded up a lot of Polish boy scouts and machine-gunned them.'

After a period of heartrending sobs as she thought of her own baby son being so treated, Mims finally managed to denounce the perpetrators through her tears. 'Little boys, Gus! Ten years old. The cruel, shitten butchers!' And she covered her face with her handkerchief and wept again.

The misery increased. After the Belgian surrender the Allies continued to struggle on in Flanders but were pushed back so brutally that within days they found themselves fighting a desperate rearguard action on the French coast. Totally encircled, they were now to come under intense bombing and shelling, the enemy seemingly intent on obliteration.

A frantic call for volunteers went out, to the owners of any vessel, no matter how small, to put it at the disposal of those in peril. And a rescue mission was launched.

No one they knew was in France – Joe still in Norway, Jim somewhere in the North Sea, Brendan and his brothers not yet departed these shores – but it did not prevent Beata's heart going out to those poor desperate souls trapped on the beach, and though she could not really know how it felt to come under fire she could well imagine their fear as they waited and wondered whether help was going to come in time, or if they were to face the ignominy of defeat, or worse.

For days the evacuation provoked a national feeling of anxiety, knowing that every available boat had gone to help, women stopping in the street to ask each other, had their son or husband or brother arrived in England yet?

Then, oh glorious news! Soldiers began to arrive in droves, hot and tired and smelly, a thousand horrors in their eyes, but alive, and a great wave of relief swept the country, grateful women recounting the magnificent endeavour that had brought their loved ones home.

This evening, reading the account of that valiant armada, myriad small pleasure boats, fishing cobles, yachts and trawlers, that had brought tens of thousands of troops home, Beata marvelled at the ingenuity and doggedness of the human spirit and for that moment felt part of something wonderful and historic as defeat was turned to victory and she silently blessed this nation of heroes, knowing they would fight to the last breath.

With this warm glow of patriotism still in her heart, she finished off the newspaper, then went to help Gussie get the bedtime cocoa, afterwards paying a last visit to the outside lavatory, making sure that no light was showing before slipping into the yard. But there, noting periodic flashes and rumbling in the sky, on her return she urged the others to, 'Come and look at the candelabra.'

And they gathered in the yard to watch the distant firework display, the beam of searchlights, the glow from incendiary bombs and ack-ack guns lighting up the night sky, though, 'It must be thirty miles away,' breathed Mick.

'I suppose we should be grateful we've had none dropped on us yet,' sighed Gussie, her angelic eyes directed heavenwards. The sirens had delivered false alarms so often everyone had begun to ignore them and to sleep through it.

'God help us if they do,' scoffed Mick. 'I doubt we'd be able to get into a shelter.'

'Why?'

'They've had to start locking them up at night 'cause some blighter's forever vandalizing them or stealing the light bulbs.'

Hugging her bare arms, face tilted upwards, Mims uttered a sound of disgust. 'I've never known a place like York for thieving. If it isn't nailed down, they'll pinch it.'

Remembering this phrase directed at Bert Spaven, Beata's mind drifted to her old friends in service whom she had not seen for some time, wondered whether they were contributing towards the war effort, or were they, like her, just keeping things running at home. And in that thought, her former good mood regressed to one of deep inadequacy. Surely there must be something more she could do?

In the middle of June, due to their precarious position, the Allies were forced to evacuate Norway and the Kilmaster women were horrified to learn that one of the ships had been attacked with several casualties. Their first thoughts for Joe, when no telegram came, they began to relax somewhat for they would surely have been informed by now if he had been involved, Gussie being down as his next of kin. Besides, there were more than imaginary things to concern them, for at that same time Mussolini finally declared war on the Allies, and, four days later, the Germans entered Paris.

Their very real worries now were for those who had just gone over, amongst them Mick's son Brendan, who could be imprisoned, or shot.

Still trying to find some more important way to involve herself other than on the home front, Beata went into town on another attempt to get into one of the forces, thinking that at such a critical time they might be willing to take anyone. Despite not a bomb being dropped on York, the war had suddenly become very real since Dunkirk. The surrounding countryside ideally flat for landing strips, squadrons of aeroplanes began to descend like moths on the Vale of York, their Canadian crews inundating the city in their search for billets. Surely someone must need her services.

But once again she was turned down. Going home, feeling despondent and preferring not to encounter any of the neighbours who might engage her in chat, she chose to take the rear entrance. The WVS appeal for old carpets, ropes, rags, rabbit skins, whisky bottles, brass, woollen waste, waste food for pigs, had received a superb response and the back lane looked like a rubbish dump as she turned into it. Spotting something untoward on top of one of the bins, she diverted to inspect it.

At this precise instant, Mims came trundling her pram along the same route, and, despite the feeling that she was going to crack up at any minute, grinned to herself at the sight of her sister grubbing about amongst the rubbish. 'I know things are bad but do you have to go rummaging in other folk's pig bins?'

Looking up, Beata chuckled. 'I'm just getting rid of these rhubarb tops, they'll be poisoning the poor bloody animals.' After brief inspection of other neighbours' receptacles, she transferred the leaves to a refuse bin, then opened the gate to the yard for Mims and the pram to pass through, waited whilst her sister unfastened Jimmy's harness, then followed her indoors.

At the sight of the telegram in Gussie's hand. Mims stopped dead.

Their elder sister was quick to say, 'Don't worry, it's not Jim.' But her eyes were still anguished as they turned to Beata. Too distressed, she let them read the telegram themselves.

Beata's heart stopped. Joe was missing, presumed dead.

THIRTY-FOUR

'I've never really cared for June,' said Maddie in hollow voice, seated amongst the rest of her sisters in Gussie's living room, unable to believe that their brother would never be coming home. 'I like May, when everything's new and fresh, the leaves are just at that perfect stage, but June, well, everything seems a bit too ... overblown somehow, like a blowsy woman, the grass is too long and going to seed.'

'Aren't we all?' murmured Beata, staring into the distance. Shortly after that dreadful telegram, had come the news that the French were on the verge of surrender and their own boys would be fighting on alone. Assailed too by the Government warning that Hitler would attempt to invade this month, the four sisters were braced for a long war.

Sipping her tea, she glanced at Maddie whose magic bandages had not been the dazzling success their maker had boasted. Upon going round to tell her about Joe, Beata had found her like one giant blister. She had recovered somewhat since then, though her skin was still flaking off. Just one more lie from those who promised much but gave little. How could they believe anything they were told? Where now were the ones who said there would be no war?

'I can't believe we won't see him again,' said Maddie.

'We will,' murmured Gussie, secure in her faith. 'He's just gone on ahead.'

On the brink of screaming, Mims abandoned the little boy who played on the mat and hurried out to the back yard, lighting a cigarette.

Staring at her through the window, her sisters projected concern for her wellbeing, though under great strain themselves. 'For once I thank God I'm not married,' said Beata, reaching out to fondle her nephew's little outstretched fingers.

'She needs a diversion,' agreed Maddie. 'Let's take her out for a ducky one evening.'

Beata nodded solemnly. 'If you don't mind looking after this little fella, Gus?'

Cradling a cup of tea, the eldest sister shook her head.

Remaining quiet, feeling left out of all this even though his own son could be dead for all he knew, Mick examined his empty tobacco pouch. With the younger members out at work and college, he contemplated asking one of the women to nip to the shop and buy him some more pipe fuel, but then thought better of it and went himself.

But he was to return quite swiftly with a queer look on his face. 'The boy just delivered this.' And he had in his hand a telegram.

Lips parted. The women turned to look at their sister in the yard.

'It's got your name on it,' a serious Mick told his wife.

It must be confirmation about Joe, then. Gussie squashed her cheeks between her palms, the thought of him being dead too much to bear. 'You read it.'

Mick took a deep breath, his wife and sisters-in-law holding theirs as he opened the envelope.

Then he said immediately, 'He's safe.'

There was a unified gasp. Gussie crossed herself. 'You're sure?'

''Twas himself who's sent it!' Smiling now, he held out the telegram for his wife to read, pointing out the last two words: *Love, Joe.*

Sharing a massive surge of relief with the others, Beata went to call Mims in from the yard but her younger sister had heard their delighted voices and was already on her way in to discover what had caused this, seizing the telegram and poring over it with shining eyes, then joining in the celebration, everyone hugging each other and trying not to condemn those who had caused the painful mix-up, grateful only that their brother was alive, at least for now.

Afterwards, there was the instruction to 'Get the kettle on!' and not a few tears as the strain of the last week took its toll on them. There was also repetition of their plan to take Mims out for the evening, though now there was actually something to celebrate.

'Eh dear, I'm exhausted,' sighed Maddie, looking exactly that, though elated too. 'I'll have to go home and catch forty winks if I'm to last the night.'

Lifting Jimmy from her knee, Mims said she would have to go and find something to wear, whilst Beata and Gussie took the cups into the scullery.

'Before ye go.' Mick took hold of the one about to leave and said in confidential manner, 'You're a nurse –'

'So they tell me.'

Using the edge of the table to steady himself, he kneeled before her. 'Will ye just have a look down me throat and tell me if ye see a lump. I didn't want to bother ye before.'

Maddie peered into his maw, but claimed she could see nothing.

'Right at the back of me tongue – quite a few of them, there are.'

She gave a laugh of derision. 'They're your taste buds, you daft sod!' And, shaking her head at her sisters over this display of hypochondria, she made for the back door. 'I'll just visit the doings before I go.'

Beata smiled at the interchange, then tried to shove her elder sister away from the sink. 'Go sit down, missus, I'll do them.'

'Go on then.' Gussie made as if to go into the living room.

'Eh, I didn't mean you to give in so easily,' joked Beata. But, turning to laugh at her sister she suddenly noticed how thick around the middle Gussie had become and her humour dried. 'Eh, Gus . . . you're not, are you?'

Feeling herself under deep scrutiny, Gussie looked alarmed and put a silencing finger to her lips before rushing back to hiss, 'Ssh! I'm trying to keep it quiet as long as I can – only Mick knows.' She glanced at the door to check that her other sister was still outside. 'Don't say aught to Maddie, will you? I know what she'll say.'

'Well, if I've noticed she's bound to do as well!'

'But promise you won't draw her attention to it!'

Beata shook her head, but groaned and leaned against the cool sink, 'Oh, lass, I'll never stop worrying about you now.'

'Don't.' Gussie clasped her arm. 'There's no need.' With the pressure over Joe lifted, she appeared radiant. 'I know everything's going to be all right this time.'

Hearing returning footsteps in the yard, Beata kept her voice to a whisper. 'But how can you be so certain? I mean, I'd dearly love for it to –'

'I *do*,' insisted Gussie. 'I just do. I can feel it.' And it was said with such conviction that any argument was futile.

Besides which, at this point Maddie came in, forcing the need to talk about something else. Though it did not stop Beata worrying.

Nevertheless, she promised to keep Gussie's secret, and not another word was said about it as she went on to enjoy a very pleasant evening in the downstairs Oak Room of Betty's restaurant where she and her sisters tried to forget about the war, drank and chatted and flirted with a group of airmen, encouraging them to add their names to those already scratched on the large mirror there.

Back at work in the morning and having an early start, Maddie did not stay long, but left enough money to buy her sisters another drink. However, they were not to dally much longer themselves, for, rarely going out these days, both were unaccustomed to alcohol and were soon feeling its effects.

Mims giggled as, upon their arrival home, her high heels misnegotiated the threshold and she tripped. 'Ooh, I think I'm a bit tiddly!'

Thinking how good it was to hear her laughing again, Beata followed her younger sister along the passage.

Mims cocked her head at the sound of a baby's cry from up above. 'Good God, he must have X-ray vision! I've no sooner set foot through the door than he's after me.' And instead of going into the living room she went upstairs to bring him down before he disturbed others.

Beata continued on her way – then stopped dead at the sight of the middle-aged man who sat with Gussie and Mick. It was such a shock to see him after all these years.

'Hello, Beat.' Clem rose from his chair, came forward hesitantly and lowered his auburn head to deliver an awkward kiss. 'I were beginning to think I'd have to leave without seeing you. It's been a long time.'

Though shocked, her reply was warm and genuine. 'It's grand to see you, Clem. You're looking well.' In fact he looked rather drained and worried, as they all did.

'So are you.' He glanced down and winced. 'Apart from your leg. By, it looks painful. Been on your feet all day?'

'No, it's like this all the time now.' Beata glanced at Gussie and Mick as if for explanation as to what he was doing here, but then was distracted by Mims' gasp of surprise as she came in carrying Jimmy.

Clem's youngest sister, too, greeted him warmly and niceties were exchanged. But then there was a pensive interval, during which all that was to be heard was the gurgling of Mims' baby son.

Clem tapped his hands against his thighs, as if trying to find something to say, his attention mainly on Beata. 'Well, Gussie's brought me up to date with her situation and told me about Joe and that. What have you been doing with yourself lately?'

Bidding him to sit down again and doing likewise, Beata listed as much as she could remember. After which there was another long silence. Clem gave her a sad smile, but said nothing. He's expecting me to ask about Eliza, she thought. Well, he would have a long wait.

It was Gussie who explained quietly, 'Clem's come to let us know Eliza's dying.'

Beata looked at her brother, saw beneath the weariness a look of anguish.

'She wants to see you, Beat,' came his soft request.

Beata flinched, all the old hurts rushing in on her. She was ten years old again, vulnerable and afraid, too shocked for the moment to give an answer. Eventually she looked at Mims and opined shrewdly, 'I'll bet you're not going.'

Her youngest sister gave a tight smile, shook her head then looked down at the baby in her arms.

Beata's eyes turned to Gussie. 'What about you?'

'It's not me she's asking for.'

Beata's response was unusually caustic. 'No, it's muggins here she wants to run around after her.'

Clem shook his head. He looked haggard with worry. 'No, Beat, she's beyond that. Me and Doris have been nursing her. She just keeps asking for you.' Hands laced between his knees, he rubbed his thumbs together, his eyes directed at his feet, though not seeing them.

Gussie tendered softly, 'She's dying, Beat. She can't hurt you any more.'

Oh she can! She can, thought Beata, the woman's nasty laughter reverberating through her memory. What could possibly be Eliza's reason for wanting her there? Was it to beg forgiveness? If so, she did not know whether she could genuinely grant it.

'You can't let her go to her Maker alone.'

An argument raged inside Beata's head and heart: why should I go after all she did to me?

Clem waited as long as he could for an answer, but when Beata continued to dally, he became agitated and rose. 'I'll have to go. I've left her longer than I wanted to. If you do decide to come, don't leave it too long.' Kissing each of his sisters and shaking hands with Mick, he made his way to the door.

But there was one last attempt. Beata studied the hawkish face as he took out his last cigarette, grasped it between his lips and scribbled the address on the empty packet, tossing it on the sideboard. 'She really wants to see you, Beat.' He fixed her with those hooded blue eyes for a brief but weighty moment, then left.

It was a measure of Beata's compassion that, sometime during the restless night, she finally overcame her desperate inner struggle and decided to answer the call. Though whether she would be able to face her tormentor once she arrived was yet to be ascertained. Going alone, taking nothing except the borrowed train fare and her gas mask, she made for Doncaster, throughout the journey her stomach constantly churning. She dreaded seeing Eliza again.

When she arrived, hot and dusty, throat dry both with thirst and nerves, it was Doris who admitted her. Her stepsister's face showed signs of intense pressure, though it lit up at the sight of the caller.

'Eh, Beat, how lovely to see you! Come in.'

She had imagined this moment, envisioned herself frozen with nerves, unable to step over that threshold, for once she was in she was trapped. In reality it was not quite so bad. Reacting instinctively to Doris's invitation she was in before she could change her mind.

The house had an air of death. She had smelled it enough times to know.

'Aw, you haven't changed a bit.' Doris spoke in hushed tone, looking up and down the other's stocky frame.

'I don't know about that,' Beata gave a wobbly smile, unable to help herself from glancing up the stairs. Eliza must be up there. 'How are you keeping, Doris?'

'Oh, not so bad.' Her stepsister smiled, then whispered, 'I'll take you straight up.' And with that Beata found herself being escorted towards the woman who had terrorized her.

Her heart fluttered and, with every step, began to race. When they reached the landing the door of the sick room was ajar. Whilst Doris went in to tell Clem his sister was here Beata held back, partly out of a wish not to impose but also out of fear. Able to see everything that went on, she watched Clem administering to her stepmother, with tender motions sponging the waxen brow and stick-like limbs, crooning to her as if to a baby. Such gentleness, for one who had always been easy to violence. At Doris's whisper, he simply nodded and looked towards the door, then, returning his attention to the one in the bed he bent to murmur in Eliza's ear.

Doris came back to the landing. 'You can go in, Beat. I'll go make us some tea.'

Taking a deep breath, Beata steeled herself to do so.

Then Doris added as she went downstairs, 'Mother won't be able to hear you, though, I'm afraid, she slipped into unconsciousness a few hours ago.'

Gaining only slight relief from this, Beata crept in.

Without turning, Clem detected his sister's presence, saying in low murmur, 'I won't be a minute, Beat, I'm just making her comfy. She probably isn't aware of it but I like to feel as if I'm doing something.' He dabbed the thin limbs with a towel, eventually tucking the covers back under Eliza's chin.

Watching Clem's loving skills towards the one he called his wife, Beata pondered on his great suitability for the role, and it was revealed to her then that every one of her siblings had fulfilled his or her destiny: Joe, a soldier like his father; Gus with her big family; Maddie devoted to her patients; Duke free to roam wherever he chose; Mims just by being herself bringing joy to others . . . but which road for Beata?

'Poor lass, I'm glad she's unconscious. She was in agony till the doctor gave her an injection. I'm hoping he's given her enough to see her through.' Gazing at the dying woman, Clem suddenly bent and touched his lips to her cheek. It was such a tender, loving kiss yet it seared Beata's heart like a red-hot brand.

She gulped. What should she say? What should she do?

Then all at once, the unendurable silence was rent by an earthy fart. Startled, she and Clem looked at each other. It was impossible not to laugh. Shaking with mirth, Beata thought, if that's your idea of making amends a simple apology would have sufficed, but she did not say it, for though he chuckled with her Clem had tears in his eyes. And for the first time she saw Eliza not as a monster but as a helpless, naked, little sparrow about to tumble from the nest, and all fear left her.

Then as she stood mesmerized, to the accompaniment of a few crackling breaths, the last slender twig gave way and with a sigh Eliza was gone, bequeathing Clem a look of devastation.

He covered his face with his hands and remained like this for quite a while before raking his fingers down his cheeks, his eyes vacant.

Beata's heart went out to him. 'I'm sorry, Clem.' Sorry for you, not her, she thought privately.

'Never mind,' he gasped through his anguish. 'At least you came.'

She remained there for a few seconds just watching, then said, 'I'll give you some privacy,' and she left the room.

On her way up with a tray of tea, Doris guessed from Beata's expression that her mother was gone and her face crumpled. Poised on the stair, a tear emerged. Then she turned and plodded back down with the tray of tea, pouring three cups to cover her distress.

Not knowing what to say, Beata asked, 'Where's Lionel?'

Doris looked even more anguished and blew into her handkerchief. 'At work. I'm dreading him coming home.'

'Work? Oh yes, he must be sixteen . . .' Beata was still mulling over this amazing fact when her stepsister spoke again.

'Thanks for coming, Beat.' Doris sighed, her eyes glassy as she handed over a cup of tea. 'I know she's my mother but I'm not sure I'd have come if she'd treated me as badly as she did you.'

Beata took possession of the cup, saying quietly, 'Aye well, it's all in the past.' And she genuinely meant it.

Doris nodded and sipped her tea. 'It's nice to see you again anyway. What have you been doing with yourself all these years?'

Beata told her briefly.

'And where are you living?'

'I've been a bit of a gypsy, no fixed abode.' She gave a tight smile and took another sip from her cup, her expression becoming somewhat vague. 'I'm at a loss as to what to do now, though. I've tried to do my bit towards the war effort but I don't seem much use to anybody.'

Doris gave a mirthless laugh. 'It's staring you in the face, Beat.'

Beata frowned at her.

'You're a natural nurse. They're crying out for the likes of you.'

A heavy sigh. 'Oh, I don't know . . . I'm not brainy enough to get the qualifications.'

'Well, I'm not saying you're not brainy, Beat, but you don't need to pass exams. I know somebody who's off to be a nursing auxiliary on these Ambulance Trains they're setting up and all she needed was two references, a certificate in First Aid and Home Nursing, and three years' experience in looking after invalids.'

'Three years?' said Beata, looking amazed and cynical at the same time. 'I've been looking after people all me life!'

'Well, that's what I'm saying, you clot!' Realizing she was sounding disrespectful with her mother expired upstairs, Doris lowered her voice. 'Beat, you don't have to wear a uniform nor work in a big building with beds in it to call yourself a nurse. As I told you before, you're a natural. And God knows, there'll be plenty of poor souls needing you if this war drags on.'

She was quickly gaining enthusiasm. 'And do you think they'd take me?'

'It's a cert, Gert.' Doris's smile was warmly convincing. 'Now, have a cup of tea, pay your last respects to Mother, then get back to York and do something about it.'

Her teacup drained, the time came for Beata to have one last look at the woman who had bedevilled her. Doris came with her, linking her arm as support, but it was not such an ordeal for Beata now; the fear had completely vanished. It was just a dead body, much shrunken in death, and she had seen many of those over the years. Doris stooped to kiss her mother's cheek but Beata was to draw the line at this. It was enough that she had come.

But there was a kiss for her brother, and a last kind word. 'Don't be a stranger, Clem.'

He nodded, before his eyes went back to the woman he had loved.

Then, in the final acceptance that her own love would have to be channelled in much different fashion, Beata left him. And knowing, as surely as Gussie knew that her child would be born alive, that this time there would be no rejection, she went out into the bright day, towards her true vocation, despite the war, full of hope.